The First Day of Spring

Stories and Other Prose

Raymond Knister

Selected and Introduced by Peter Stevens

UNIVERSITY OF TORONTO PRESS
TORONTO AND BUFFALO

Toronto and Buffalo
Reprinted in paperback 2017
ISBN 978-0-8020-2069-7 (cloth)
ISBN 978-0-8020-6198-0 (paper)

Library of Congress Cataloging in Publication Data

Knister, Raymond.
The first day of spring.

(Literature of Canada, poetry and prose in reprint 17)
Bibliography: p.
I. Title.
PR9199.3.K55A15 1976 813'.5'2 76-10475
ISBN 978-0-8020-2069-7 (bound) ISBN 978-0-8020-6198-0 (pbk.)

This book has been published with the assistance of a grant from the McLean Foundation.

Literature of Canada

Poetry and Prose in Reprint

Douglas Lochhead, General Editor

RAYMOND KNISTER (1899-1932) was born and brought up on Ontario farms in Kent and Essex counties and was a graduate of the University of Toronto and of Iowa State University. He was the author of short stories, prose, literary criticism, poetry, and two novels, *White Narcissus* and *My Star Predominant.*

PETER STEVENS, former poetry editor of the *Canadian Forum,* is a member of the Department of English at the University of Windsor and the author of several books of poetry.

Raymond Knister had a strong sense of commitment both to his own career and to literature, particularly Canadian literature. In his ten working years he proved himself a prolific writer with wide-ranging interests.

Although his work has appeared in many anthologies of Canadian literature, there remains a great deal of out of print or unpublished material.

This volume brings together not only his more well-known stories but also all his unpublished stories, a few travel pieces, and several examples of his literary criticism. Knister's stories are often strongly regional, and draw on rural Ontario for their setting and characters. Collected together here for the first time is a group of sketches dealing anecdotally with life in a village in southwestern Ontario. Also included are two stories arising from his experience as a cab driver in Chicago in the 1920s, 'Innocent Man,' and 'Hackman's Night.' His essays focusing on literary matters and the traditions and problems of Canadian literature show a keenly critical mind.

The First Day of Spring is an important rediscovery of one of Canada's best writers of the 1920s.

Preface

Yes, there is a Canadian literature. It does exist. Part of the evidence to support these statements is presented in the form of reprints of the poetry and prose of the authors included in this series. Much of this literature has been long out of print. If the country's culture and traditions are to be sampled and measured, both in terms of past and present-day conditions, then the major works of both our well-known and our lesser-known writers should be available for all to buy and read. The Literature of Canada series aims to meet this need. It shares with its companion series, The Social History of Canada, the purpose of making the documents of the country's heritage accessible to an increasingly large national and international public, a public which is anxious to acquaint itself with Canadian literature – the writing itself – and also to become intimate with the times in which it grew.

DL

Contents

CRITICISM

Raymond Knister 1899-1932

Peter Stevens

Introduction

It is tempting to read the facts of Raymond Knister's life as a legend of the romantic artist, the writer whose blossoming career was cut short by early death. The parallel with someone like John Keats is uneasily apparent, particularly when one remembers that Knister wrote a novel, *My Star Predominant*, based on the life of Keats, and shortly before his death Knister's wife reported in the diary she kept at that time that her husband was full of optimism about his future: he said, 'I feel just as Keats did when he said he was just coming into his powers. I feel as though I am just coming into mine.'

But the facts of Raymond Knister's life need no romantic interpretation. His life is illustrative of the role of the writer in the first decades of the twentieth century in Canada, and Knister himself seemed well aware of the difficulties involved in that role in this new country.

Raymond Knister was born in Ruscom, near Comber, in Essex County, Ontario on 27 May 1899. His father was of German stock, a man who industriously farmed the land in several places in Essex and Kent counties. There is no doubt that such a story as 'Mist Green Oats' is autobiographical, expressing Knister's feelings of entrapment within the farming community, and the emphasis on daily chores had an obvious deadening effect on the sensitivity of the writer. And yet paradoxically much of Knister's success as poet and short story writer derives from his meticulous recording of farm life.

Early in his life he suffered a bad fall in the school playground. From that day he stammered badly and although he was given therapy and in later life practised reading poetry aloud, he never overcame this disability. It is perhaps easier in this light to understand his enthusiasm in the 1920s for the work of Wilson MacDonald, who was not only a great champion of poetry in Canada but also an inveterate public reader of his own work.

Knister's further education was ended by the influenza epidemic which followed World War I, after he had enrolled as a student at Victoria College, Toronto. He returned to live on his father's farm, but the lack of a university degree was no barrier to his own pursuits in literature. From his early days he had been an avid reader. He kept a list of the titles of the books he read from the age of fourteen to his early twenties, and his essays and reviews show a remarkable knowledge of world literature, both of the classics and of new developments in twentieth-century writing.

Early in the 1920s Knister began to concentrate on his own writing both of short stories and poems. His work was accepted and reviewed in the United States, England, and in France, in the magazine *This Quarter*, published in Paris. Eventually he moved to Iowa City, where he took some courses at the State University of Iowa and worked for the magazine *The Midland* which had accepted some of his stories and poems. The early 1920s seem to have been a fruitful period for Knister. His work was being published in reputable magazines, he was writing stories, poems, and novels and reviewing books.

By the end of 1924 he returned to Canada and continued to write in all manner of forms: poems, essays, short stories, novels, and plays. The picture of the writer that emerges here and virtually to the end of his life is of a man confident in his own abilities (although some of his letters reveal that he went through the usual depressing moods that most writers suffer). He was ready to experiment in all forms of literature, looking critically at the past in Canadian literature, trying to assess his own ideas in the light of those past writings, examining recent developments in Canada and other literatures, testing personal ideas against those he was constantly encountering in his own wide reading.

Knister worked as a free-lance writer, publishing principally in the *Toronto Star Weekly* during the years 1925-7. He also reviewed for newspapers and magazines while working on the writing he considered more literary, read widely to prepare the anthology of Canadian short stories he edited, and wrote some scholarly criticism. His first published novel, *White Narcissus*, was written in 1927 and published in 1929. The second novel, *My Star Predominant*, was awarded a prize, some of which he collected, although the publisher went bankrupt. Knister moved to Toronto in September 1926; in the winter of 1931-2 he moved to Montreal, continuing his free-lance work. It was at this time that he became acquainted with some Canadian writers then living in Montreal, most notably F.R. Scott, A.J.M. Smith, and Leo Kennedy.

His life brightened considerably when Lorne Pierce of Ryerson Press accepted his prize novel for publication and also offered Knister a position as an editor. He intended to move to Toronto in the early fall to take up his position with Ryerson. However, in August 1932 the Knisters visited Raymond's aunt and uncle, who showed them a furnished cottage they owned at Stoney Point on Lake St Clair. Knister liked the cottage and when his relatives offered it to him, he accepted gratefully, particularly as it was a short distance from his sister, Marjorie, to whom he was very attached and who was at that time living in Walkerville, a settlement now part of the city of Windsor.

On the day the Knisters were ready to leave the cottage to visit his sister for the week-end before moving to Toronto, Raymond went for a last swim in the lake. He was not a good swimmer and rowed out in a boat without an anchor. His family believe that he was pulled down while swimming by a strong undertow as the boat drifted away from him. Many boats, divers, and a plane searched for his body during the following anxious days. An entry in his wife's diary describes the final discovery: 'The divers themselves were almost pulled down into the holes by the pressure. Finally they found his body wedged in a hole at the bottom of the Lake.'

Although Raymond Knister has never been given the recognition that he deserves as one of the first truly modern writers in Canadian literature, certain portions of his work keep reappearing in standard anthologies of short stories and poetry. His first novel, *White Narcissus,* is still available in paperback and recently a limited selection of his short stories was published. His collection of poetry, first published in 1949, will be reissued in an extended form to include some previously unpublished poems.

This present edition, contains the stories from that recently published selection, but also brings together a wider variety of Knister's prose, both fiction and non-fiction, long buried in magazines, together with several unpublished stories and critical statements. These last make an interesting study, for they reveal Knister's perceptive views about literature, particularly about the position of the artist in Canada and the problems facing a modern writer in relation to the development of his country's literature and the assimilation of new techniques learned from other literatures.

In his early piece about the Canadian short story (published in *The Canadian Bookman,* August 1923), Knister makes a plea for the short story as an acceptable literary genre, not one which becomes bound by commercial demands but one which embodies an author's vision of life. He shows his scepticism about the formulaic approach of the correspondence schools, touching on the inherent Americanization of Canadian stories if would-be Canadian writers follow the standards of the correspondence school which 'has its finger on the market.' Knister is much more interested in the short story as a literary form of artistic merit, stressing that good short stories will arise only out of the study of the best models, although he obviously feels that mere imitation is not enough. The writer in Canada must persevere in his studies, taking what he can from a broad selection of sources, aware that the outlets for his talents are severely limited.

In spite of all this, Knister retains a kind of spirited optimism about Canada and Canadian literature: 'It is hard to be skeptical, not to think that there are infinite spiritual possibilities in a land as huge and undeveloped as this, open to the variety and potency of influences which bear upon it.' He deals with this question with humour and yet reprimands excessive adulation of Canadian products in his 'Canadian Letter,' probably written at the same time as his article for *The Canadian Bookman.* He singles out Canadian authors he admires and shows a surprising capacity to see real merit. Perhaps the two most significant comments he makes are his rejection of a new Charles G.D. Roberts chapbook, even though he generally accepts Roberts' achievement as very good, and his acknowledgment of Arthur Stringer's early attempt in *Open Water* to make a case for free verse.

He developed these ideas later in the introduction to his anthology *Canadian Short Stories,* which ends with a tribute to the short stories of Duncan Campbell Scott. He was not afraid to criticize Scott's poetry. For example, his review of Scott's collected poems complains that one of the poems 'begins with stale afflatus like the copy for a special advertisement to be illustrated in full colour.' This kind of criticism is counterbalanced by some fulsome praise. The impression that this article, and the one devoted to Wilson MacDonald, give is of a critic who wishes to share his enthusiasm for Canadian poets with his readers. Such enthusiasm tended at times to run away with his critical sense and yet the reader is also brought up short by very telling insights and perceptions. Knister was of course writing here for a general audience and perhaps he tempered his criticism in the hope of reaching out in order to encourage a wider readership for Canadian authors.

The same is true of the monthly columns he wrote for *The New Outlook,* in which he reviewed the poems he had read in magazines and newspapers in Canada. There was some uncertainty in his views but that is understandable in a writer who is working month by month with contemporary poems. He was constantly on the look-out for fresh and invigorating material, always aware of the technical facility of a poem, even if it remained only 'pleasant and neat work' as he once summarized a Roberts poem. He emphasized the importance he placed on technique in the letter to a Miss Frankfurth included in this selection: 'Details of craftsmanship scamped or awry spoil any piece of writing for me, and it is only after the mind assents to the technical mastery that the emotion is allowed to reach me.' He labelled one poem as 'windy confusion,' and although he obviously was sympathetic to free verse his standards in that regard were rigorous: 'There is free verse in this ... magazine, but the current notion of free verse appears to be a prose description of a poem, shredded into lines arbitrarily long and short – not a piece of work aiming at qualities of sound, of emotion and image as veritably if more directly, as metrical verse.' He usually picked out some of the better of the minor poets who were beginning to flourish in the 1920s in Canadian magazines: Edward Sapir, Joseph Schull, George Walton among others. He praised the general standard of poetry in *The McGill Fortnightly Review*, quoting with approval poems by A.J.M. Smith and F.R. Scott. He was very careful to suggest to his readers that the individual poems he chose to quote and comment on rose above the dross of much writing published in the magazines: 'Reading the output of verse appearing in Canadian magazines and newspapers is a sadly disappointing business if one is looking for the pure gold of poetry. Perhaps it is too much to expect to find several fine poems each month, but one is struck by the disproportion between our literary pretensions and our achievements.'

There speaks the reasonable voice of a critic who wants to find achievement in the current literature of his own country but who has a well-formulated sense of what is good in writing, a sense we can see at work in the short articles on E.A. Robinson and the poetry of Ireland. It is easy to read into his ideas about Robinson some of his own predilections that appear in his poetry and stories, predilections that recur in the long essay on *The Shropshire Lad.* The tone of stoicism and sadness he sensed in Housman's work applied also to his own writing. Knister suggested that Housman's poetry is the portrayal of a 'soil-loving, life-loving, inarticulate but artlessly downright yeoman' sometimes expressing 'fateful emotion combined with a zest for living.' If Housman did represent for Knister a model for his own writing about the Ontario countryside, then we must examine his work to see whether the same 'zest for living' occurs in it. Certainly these moments appear in some of the stories, even in the dourest ones, 'Mist Green Oats,' for instance. The usual view of Knister's work as being pessimistic and emphasizing the dull routine of farm work and the killing, mind-deadening effects on the sensitive spirit is qualified not only by the epiphanies within some stories and poems, but by the sequence of journalistic sketches written mainly about a specific rural community called Corncob Corners. In this light Knister's comments on *The Shropshire Lad* give a clear indication of a tendency in him which has been overlooked.

His best and most extensive critical works are the two articles on Archibald Lampman and Wilfred Campbell. Campbell for him was a poet trapped by Victorian responses and forms: 'He reacted to the conventional stimuli in the conventional way, supplying a norm of Victorian opinion and taste in verse.' All the values in Campbell's verse were superimposed, not arising from his own vision of the scene or the individual characters he is presenting. Knister found some of the same faults in Lampman. While appreciating the observed detail of nature in Lampman's poetry, he claimed that there is no felt tension between the poet and his environment. Such tension is obviously a major ingredient in Knister's prose and poetry. He argued that Lampman's failure in this regard derives from a kind of colonial mentality: the details in the poems are Canadian, yet the general tone and form come from outside Canada. He recognized that 'to have accepted Canadian experience and written of Canada in terms of nothing else would have been, if not impossible, at least immediately fruitless and unrewarded.' He sensed a change in the later Lampman, a more modern sensibility which would have led to greater poetry for Lampman had he lived.

Again it is possible to see developing in Knister's criticism ideas which inform his own work: the specific Canadian detail with ideas embedded in an integral development of form. Certainly one can feel this process taking place in the poetry contained in the volume published in 1949. In the foreword to that volume, which he intended to be published as a preface to his projected selection of poems, he gathered together some of the notions that underlay his critical essays and reviews. One such notion was that the subject matter of poetry should be

> as real as sweating men and swilling pigs. But the feeling about them is not always so real, any more, when it gets into words. Because of that, it would be good just to place them before the reader, just let the reader picture them with the utmost economy and clearness. In the end we in Canada here might have the courage of our experience and speak according to it only.

That reality is presented in many of the stories. But Knister is not merely a direct realist; he had read too much Anderson, James, and Chekhov to rely on simple realistic detail. His essay on Katherine Mansfield made clear his belief that the realistic surface of a story should contain a symbolic depth: 'Minutiae should matter, should index ineffable inward things.' But he was not totally convinced by Mansfield's method; according to Knister, she falls into sentimental endings, and he missed local colour in some of her stories.

Local colour and surface minutiae are very much apparent in Knister's stories. He describes the atmosphere and appearance of the farm country of southwestern Ontario, and in two factual articles he wrote about Pelee Island and Long Point (not included in this selection) he showed that he was aware of local history.

Much of his feeling about locality and community was expressed in the journalistic sketches about rural life published in the 1920s, mainly in the *Toronto Star Weekly*. For these pieces, set generally in his imaginary settlement of Corncob Corners, he included some of that realistic tone of the rigours of farm life, a tone which is most apparent in his longer stories about farming, but the sketches have a lighter touch. In 'Hitching Bertha to the Sled,' for instance, the farmer's sons certainly have chores to do and the father seems something of a hard-driving taskmaster, but once he is out of the way, the boys have a great deal of fun inveigling the large calf out of the stall and hitching it to the sled. As the calf runs away, ditching the two on the sled into a snowbank, the oldest boy watches. Having been trained to take over the farm, he knows that the calf has been raised to be sold and that allowing it to run free will not put much fat on its ribs. And yet his own yearnings for freedom from the monotonous tasks of the farm are expressed in his closing exhortation to the calf, 'Go it, Bertha.' That sentiment is perhaps not so far removed from that of Len in Knister's most-anthologised story, 'Mist Green Oats,' but the whole tone is different, for Len's thought at the end of that story is 'What's the weary use?' Even though he has experienced one or two bright moments during the depressing farm day, he has also thought about escaping to the city and has interpreted his father's demands on him as unwarranted tyranny. Len and the oldest boy in 'Hitching Bertha to the Sled' have much in common. Len, of course, is a fuller study, and his story is one of muted despair, whereas the sketch, although it is only a simple anecdote, manages to suggest a lighter side to the bone-wearying and 'blind unwitting stupor of life' that Len experiences. This weariness is usually associated with 'Mist Green Oats' in the version printed in anthologies. In this collection a later, slightly different version is used; the addition of two short paragraphs to the end of the story militates against the oppressive ending and indicates that Knister felt there was some hope for Len's life.

Most of the sketches proceed along similar lines. Some deal with other farm animals, most notably in the short pieces in 'A Row of Horse Stalls.' The horses with their slow patience are held up as models for man, although Knister does not use the animals simply as moral examples, for he describes the particular characters of the horses. He makes it plain that man on the farm can retain some sense of himself in the tough battle with the land, just as the horses do. They suffer from the same blind routine as the farmer and they may also harbour thoughts of rebellion:

> If ever they become as experimentally speculative as they are contemplative, if ever a whiff of human restlessness touches them – well, the rest may be left to your imagination. There might be a conspiracy and some fine morning every man who approached a horse might be neatly despatched.

Omens of *Animal Farm!*

Other sketches focus on the eccentrics of the community, and Knister has some good-natured fun with people like Mrs Plethwick, whose obsession with birds leads to the conjecture in the village that she is a cat-killing witch. Blankenhorn, the crusty, miserly farmer, whose shrewdness and cunning are 'as arbitrary as a levelled pistol,' receives his come-uppance as the butt of a practical joke. Knister sees these people as comic characters, although he is never malicious at their expense. He takes a delight in the way in which they get the better of officialdom in government and business, as in the story of the man fooling the customs official, and in Anthony Whicher's tribulations in trying to repair the water jacket for his mill engine. Although Whicher is buffetted, and the repair finally fails, Knister's sympathies are with him. There is something of the old pattern of country yokel caught in the trammels of the city slicker in this sketch, but it is Whicher, the yokel, who is presented as the better man.

It has become almost a cliché to regard Knister's stories as equivalent to those American stories of the mid-west with their themes of entrapment, the sensitive spirit chained in narrow-minded small-town life or fastened to the mindless activity of subsistence farming. Certainly that tone is evident in many of his stories, but the sketches tend to emphasize the irrepressible spirits of these rural people. Knister presents the young sympathetically; they are not all like Len Brinder in 'Mist Green Oats.' Some are like Archie in 'No Gumption,' who is subjected to the tyranny of his widowed mother. By an ironic twist he is able to convert his mother's plan to retain him for herself on the farm into a proposal of marriage to the girl he has been mooning about. Knister ends the sketch at that point: we are not given a glimpse of what might happen to Archie and his wife, for their future plays no part in this story of youth's triumph over petty authority.

A marriage also closes the sketch about Henrietta Gray. She has an impish gaiety of manner that offends the more morose and staid elders of the community, and it is fitting that she marries Hughie, whose motorcycle is a symbol of the carefree recklessness of the 1920s. This same sketch mentions in passing the community enterprises of the young – they are holding a wiener roast on the shore of Lake Erie – and Knister is at his best in these sketches in which he describes group festivities in the rural community. His account of a rural Christmas indicates how it was celebrated both in the family and in the neighbourhood. The neighbours visit for Christmas dinner and then everyone gathers on Christmas evening for a community concert. The farm chores are still to be done on the holiday, and the neighbours still discuss farm matters, and the mailman still calls on Christmas Day. Running through this is the excitement of the children as they prepare for the concert in the evening. The sketch is a simple factual account which catches the festive mood of the family in a small community with charm and without sentimentality.

The best of the sketches about community activities are those devoted to the harvest festival and the community dance. Knister deftly describes the rising excitement and jocular gossip of the farmers' wives as they prepare the harvest home supper in the church hall, which is full of the smell of 'coal-oil, fresh lumber and cooked pumpkin.' All this activity seems haphazard until suddenly the meal is under way. No characters are developed, yet the reader is allowed glimpses of some of the village people, particularly in the jocose banter about the size of some appetites. This feeling of community among the villagers is further emphasized by setting against it brief flashes of outsiders – the minister smiling meekly over his third cup of tea, the schoolteacher keeping her slightly superior attitude to the amateur performances in the concert. Knister makes clear that the performers at the concert are not star material, yet he obviously admires the community's togetherness and camaraderie.

'The Dance at Corncob Corners' best exemplifies Knister's concern with rural values. Although some 1920s dances are included, with the usual square dance, it is only the traditional ones that draw all the people together, young and old. Indeed, a stranger dancing the Charleston too vigorously is curbed by the village constable. The dance is very much a community affair: whole families attend and it is not simply a dance. Supper is served beforehand with the same gossipy tittle-tattle bandied about as at the harvest home supper. Knister stresses the participation of everyone in everything, so that the whole entertainment lasts until the small hours: 'When these people had determined upon making a night of it, a night of it they made.'

Knister also explores change and growth versus the status quo. The two old-time callers in 'The Dance at Corncob Corners' reminisce nostalgically about dances in the past, although the author carefully includes details about the internal feuds that broke out on occasions at those dances. Knister does not sentimentalize the old days, nor does he necessarily side with the modern element. He allows both past and present to be seen in the sketch and the principal effect is one of good-natured tolerance, a tolerance which seems also to be the attitude of the community.

Nearly all Knister's stories deal with such rural communities, but included in this collection are two stories based on his years in the American mid-west and these in particular show his response to the city of Chicago. 'Hackman's Night' conjures up that free-wheeling bootlegging legend of the windy city in the twenties with a clever use of the slang of the period that gives the story a realistic flavour. The story itself does not give much emphasis to the characters, but rather concentrates on abrupt flashes of action, the hackman in question being caught in violent confrontations between rival gangs and between criminals and police. All this action works well for the hackman, who considers himself lucky when the night is over. The story gives some sense of the sordid elements in the city, and the language used charges it with authenticity.

A much better story is 'Innocent Man.' Almost of novella length, it describes the night spent by the protagonist, an innocent man, in the cells of a police department. The telling is determinedly realistic, reminiscent perhaps of some of Stephen Crane's Bowery tales. Ominous threat keeps emerging, sometimes anonymous, sometimes meaningless, sometimes motivated, so that at times the story takes on what amounts to a kind of Kafka-like allegory. Throughout there is an insistence on innocence, even among the others in the cells who are palpably criminal. Jack, the protagonist, is really on the border of innocence. It is established at the beginning that he is somewhat irresponsible, a great tease, and, perhaps technically, evading the legality of his contract for the ownership of his car. The effect of the story is to allow the reader to listen to the excuses and recriminations of the other prisoners. This cross-section of the population forced into cramped cells becomes a symbol of the human condition. All are protesting their innocence but the innocent along with the guilty are subjected to violence and humiliation by one of the guards. Jack in fact feels some sort of brotherhood with the other inmates, so that he can think that 'they were innocent, being men,' until he links them all together in a vision of innocence:

> Yes, they were innocent, these men, even as they had told with their lies. The comradeship, the encouragement, the little gifts they gave one another – their best. The way they strove to some ideal, the best their senses would let them recognize. The effort to win the approval of the people they had learned to admire. Weren't they all good children? Weren't they, these children, these ruffians, these men, all innocent?

The juxtaposition of 'children,' 'ruffians,' and 'men' at the end of that paragraph suggests real innocence, constantly battered by forces both within the characters themselves and also from an external, almost incomprehensible, source.

Early in the story Jack reaches the conclusion that 'when you're innocent, you've got to take what's coming,' subject as men are to 'the weird sneer of Fate.' This vision of innocence is not that of child-like idyllic existence. Indeed, somehow innocence has learned to survive in this place set within a dark and mysterious world, a state of existence that leads also to a recognition of the evil within each man: 'It seemed that right had departed from the world, that the world had departed, leaving this hell of grinning faces that saw nothing but their own evil.'

In some ways the protagonist of 'The Strawstack' is similar to the characters in 'Innocent Man.' He is a man carrying a burden of guilt for a 'crime' against his sister in early adolescence. As he discovers later, he is innocent of injuring his sister, but he nevertheless becomes involved with the world of real crime. Paradoxically, he remains aloof from corruption, in spite of the fact that he has committed crime: 'He had never had great faith in the evil of man.' But on his return to the farm (and the collapsed state of the farm buildings and his memory of his own wayward method of piling the straw in the stack take on symbolic implications vis-à-vis his life) the world of evil crowds in on him. The new moon stares down on him, on the run from the law, and its newness seems to him to offer an escape to a new life. Michael Gnarowski sees the story as one of a double initiation, and there is validity in that reading, although the notion of innocence lost at the strawstack and then strangely regained at the same place under the new moon is consistent with the repeated idea of innocence in Knister's stories.

If the returned man of 'The Strawstack' has 'no great faith in the evil of man,' Mrs Lucier in 'The Fate of Mrs Lucier' has worked herself into a state of acute distress, neurotically terrorized by visions of disasters involving herself. These imaginings could have been used to depict a rather comically pathetic woman, but Knister instead allows them to be etched realistically in Mrs Lucier's mind in order to illustrate her 'plenary terror of the world.' She is forced out into the dark, threatening landscape, and although she is saved from the consequences of her terror, she knows that she has been on the borderline of collapse.

The theme of youthful innocence fading, of the sudden revelation or vague realization of knowledge beyond innocence, runs through many of Knister's stories, whether it is, as in 'Elaine,' a girl's gradual awareness of what kind of woman her mother is, or, as in 'Lilacs for First Love,' a young girl's loss of her romantic notions about men. A more subtle evocation of this kind of experience occurs in 'Peaches, Peaches.' This rather long story seems to wander without focus and yet is cleverly understated. The younger brother, Ed, is somewhat like Len Brinder: he resents the farm chores and wants to be allowed to make up his own mind about his future. He admires the jaunty self-confidence of Murray, the hired man, who is the same age as Ed, yet more at ease with the farm work and with the women hired to pick peaches. Ed agonizes about his own growing attachment to one of the helpers, Florine, and watches with uneasiness as Murray involves himself with Florine's friend, May, although Murray ignores May's apparent seriousness in her friendship with him. Ed has noticed a secret knowingness between Murray and his brother's wife, which grows in his mind without real definition. The hints are all there and by the end of the story Ed has come to a dim awareness about Murray's nature, although he himself still remains uncertain in his dealings with the opposite sex. All this personal confusion is set within the framework of late, hot summer days when there is a surfeit of peaches, giving a background of overblown fruitfulness to Ed's tension, fading away into the fall and Murray's leaving, with no resolution except that Ed is conscious of larger dimensions in human relationships and perhaps of human deceit. What on first reading seems a rather directionless story leaving conflicts unresolved becomes a cleverly oblique narrative on the nature of innocence and the discovery, perhaps inarticulate, of the dilemmas of adulthood.

'Grapes' is a similarly oblique story with a younger boy as the central character who watches an older, reserved man move tentatively towards two adolescent girls. All of them seem caught in a state of unconsciousness about their relations, and in general the unfocussed nature of this story leaves the reader somewhat dissatisfied, although Knister manages one superb scene depicting a time of tense togetherness in a water fight on a very hot day.

The notion of innocence is evoked almost imagistically in 'The First Day of Spring,' as a father tells the story of a local girl's seduction without realizing that his own son has had romantic notions about the girl. The boy is still young and is unconscious of his own romantic admiration. But Knister includes in the story a few details seemingly unrelated to the narrative development. These details add to the realistic framework but, more than that, they point the reader to the boy's growing awareness. His romantic innocence is still strong as he hears a girl's voice (that of the cousin of the girl whose story his father is telling) in the distance. It is almost like the mysterious song of Wordsworth's solitary reaper: 'A girl's voice came from across the fields, a few words of singing, a voice with something wild and strong in it.' At the end of the story the voice returns, 'and then it stopped, as though for an answer.' The warmth of the first day of spring has vanished, the daylight disappears, 'and with the darkness Winter seemed to be returning.' Perhaps after hearing the story the boy's innocence is disappearing too, for the mysterious voice is answered to some extent by the last words of the story, spoken by the boy to the colt: ' "You're going to be broken in," I whispered. He was strangely quiet.'

Innocence is seen in a different context in 'Horace the Haymow,' written in part in an inflated style. This style, incongruous in relation to the subject, is occasionally comic, although the story is closer to the sketches in mood and reworks the conflict between city slicker and country yokel. Again it is the city slicker who is the butt of the story, for he is an innocent in country matters.

Innocence is not the only theme Knister deals with in these stories. As mentioned earlier, Michael Gnarowski tends to see the stories in terms of initiation and maintains that in Knister's writing there are archetypal patterns derived from Frazer and Weston. Although such patterns may be in the stories, it is perhaps easier to recognize that Knister uses a variety of fictional techniques as well as archetypal patterns to develop his stories. I have already mentioned the oblique narrative method of some stories and the use of dialogue as a prime source of narrative. More generally than archetypal patterns, the stories contain symbolic detail, the details mentioned above in 'The First Day of Spring,' for instance, and those in 'The Strawstack.' Sometimes perhaps they are overworked and draw attention to themselves as symbols, but because Knister operates within a realistic framework, the details serve both at the realistic and symbolic levels and on the whole he controls them well.

Most of the stories of innocence focus on young people, but some have older characters as their protagonists. In these cases the theme of loss and apartness surfaces. Billy Dulckington in 'The One Thing' allows his obsession with rearing horses to overwhelm any desire he might have for friendship, although the story indicates early on that he was never considered seriously by the women of the district. His small stature translates into a pusillanimity to such an extent that he withdraws further into himself. His farmhouse deteriorates and his farming becomes minimal, even though he retains a delight in plowing. Incidentally, a paragraph in the story offers an alternate, ironic reading for Knister's poem 'The Plowman':

> He liked above most things, though he did not formulate to himself any reason for the liking, the constant attempt to make each furrow straighter than the last, and, when a good furrow was attained, to keep those following it right, to have each of his 'hands' properly and symetrically shaped.

The poem is usually interpreted as a parable about the search for perfection and man's inadequacy in the face of that search. In the context of Dulckington's life the poem may be saying ironically that such a search for perfection is too obsessive and that such single-mindedness may have a warping effect; in that lies man's inadequacy. Dulckington's alienation is expressed finally by a break-down, although at least there may be in that a self-recognition of the damage his obsession has wrought. At his time of life, however, such recognition may be too late.

Alienation between people takes a different turn in 'Indian Summer.' Knister sets up the withdrawn character of the spinster in describing her furniture and house with its 'narrow windows made narrower by curtains starched stiffly and warped perpendicularly in sentry-like columns at either side.' But, unlike Billy Dulckington, Ida Tenny is keeping hope alive, although the renewal of an old friendship keeps gossips like Mrs Lamb busy speculating and prying. Knister provides the realistic details customary in his stories, details concerned with youth and age such as the kittens and the old tomcat, the young print-clad girls passing Ida's house and the old hens in her yard.

So far the story works well enough, but the melodrama of Gregory's near death as he works in the field opposite Ida's house disturbs the quiet fabric of the story. The thought that the accident was caused because the horse was 'old and lazy' makes a nice point in relation to Ida. She must not be lazy herself, must in fact be more positive unless she wants to grow old alone. So Indian summer dawns at the end as Ida and Gregory talk, but the authorial comment in the last sentence makes the sentimentality of the ending too obvious. Knister himself was obviously dissatisfied with the ending of this story and later reworked it at greater length.

It should be apparent from this brief discussion of some of Raymond Knister's writing that he is a much more varied author than the scanty critical pronouncements maintain. Certainly many of his stories cleave to the same themes but he develops those themes in different ways. The sketches show an obverse side to the view he presents of rural life in the stories that have appeared in anthologies and selections. His criticism shows a man acutely conscious of trends in writing and with an ability to see the valuable both in earlier Canadian writing and in world literature. He is a writer willing to try his hand at many forms of writing. A play based on one of his own short stories demonstrates this flexibility, and it is not his only attempt in drama – a full-length play also remains unpublished.

This selection of his writing should provide sufficient evidence that Knister's place in the development of Canadian literature in the first three decades of the twentieth century needs reassessing. This volume shows that he is not simply the minor writer of a few poems and stories of promise but a more significant figure whose writing would surely have developed fully had he lived.

A Note on the Text

Michael Gnarowski's edition, *Selected Stories of Raymond Knister*, provided the text of the six stories he includes, apart from 'Mist Green Oats,' which has an additional two paragraphs here, a revision of the ending Knister used when the story was reprinted in *Stories from the Midland.* The previously unpublished stories are all in typescript in the Library of Victoria University and, apart from some standardization of punctuation, are printed here unaltered.

All other pieces are given in the versions as printed in the magazines and journals in which they originally appeared, although Knister was an inveterate reviser. Some other versions of his stories exist in typescript, but it was felt that the published versions should be used until all the variant texts can be collated. No changes or omissions have been made in the text.

A wide variety of prose pieces still remain uncollected: some are in the Douglas Library at Queen's University, others are scattered through the pages of many magazines, and the family has much material. It would have been a long task to try to trace all of these writings. This collection has attempted to bring together a significant number of prose pieces by Raymond Knister to illustrate the whole-hearted dedication he gave to literature in the early decades of modern Canadian literature. In the future a full bibliography of Knister will no doubt be compiled and a further collection of his work can then be published. Until that time, this collection, based in large measure on the only existing bibliography, that compiled by Margaret Ray, must suffice.

Acknowledgements

All the material in this volume is reprinted by permission of the Knister estate. I am grateful to Mrs Imogen Givens for her help in seeing this project to completion.

I wish also to acknowledge the help of Miss Lorna D. Fraser, Librarian, Victoria University Library, Toronto, who supplied copies of the previously unpublished stories. The Victoria University Library granted permission to use the following:

'The First Day Of Spring,' 'Peaches, Peaches,' 'Indian Summer,' 'Grapes,' 'Lilacs For First Love,' 'Horace the Haymow,' 'Hackman's Night,' 'Innocent Man,' 'Letter to Miss Frankfurth,' 'The Shropshire Lad,' 'Katherine Mansfield,' 'Canadian Letter.'

Several of these prose pieces appeared previously in magazines and journals and I wish to thank the editors of the following:

Canadian Forum for 'The Strawstack'; *Queen's Quarterly* for 'The Poetical Works of Wilfred Campbell'; *Dalhousie Review* for 'The Poetry of Archibald Lampman'; *Maclean's* for 'The Practical Wife.'

Six of the short stories appeared in *The Selected Stories of Raymond Knister* and I am grateful to Michael Gnarowski, the editor, and the University of Ottawa Press, the publisher, for permission to include these stories:

'The One Thing', 'Mist Green Oats', 'The Strawstack', 'The Loading,' 'Elaine,' 'The Fate of Mrs Lucier.'

The introduction to *Canadian Short Stories* (Toronto: Macmillan 1928) is included by permission of the publisher.

For this volume I have endeavoured to trace the sources of all the pieces included. If I have inadvertently omitted to acknowledge permission, that omission will be rectified in any subsequent editions.

P.S.

Bibliography

The fullest bibliography of Raymond Knister's work compiled by Margaret Ray is contained in *The Collected Poems of Raymond Knister* (Toronto: Ryerson 1949) 39-45. This bibliography gives individual entries about the first appearance in journals and magazines of much of Knister's writings as well as details about the work of Knister which had remained unpublished up to the publication of the bibliography. The reader should consult that source for detailed information about individual pieces by Knister. This present bibliography includes details about Knister's books as well as other material published since 1949, in particular about those stories of Knister's now reprinted in collections and anthologies.

KNISTER'S WORKS

Editor, *Canadian Short Stories* Toronto: Macmillan 1928

The Collected Poems of Raymond Knister Edited and with a memoir by Dorothy Livesay. Toronto: Ryerson 1949

'The Loading' included in Gnarowski (see below) and in Germaine Warkentin, ed., *Stories from Ontario* Toronto: Macmillan 1974

'Mist Green Oats' included in *Stories from The Midland* New York: Knopf 1924, in Ralph Gustafson, ed., *Canadian Accent: A Collection of Stories and Poems by Contemporary Writers from Canada* Harmondsworth: Penguin Books 1944, in Robert Weaver, ed., *Canadian Short Stories* London: Oxford University Press 1960, in Gnarowski (see below), in George Parker, ed., *The Evolution of Canadian Literature in English 1914-1945* Toronto: Holt, Rinehart & Winston 1973

My Star Predominant Toronto: Ryerson 1934. Also published in the same year by Andrew Melrose in England

Selected Stories of Raymond Knister Edited and with an introduction by Michael Gnarowski. Ottawa: University of Ottawa Press 1972. Besides the stories mentioned here as being included, this volume also contains the following stories: 'The One Thing,' 'Elaine' and 'The Fate of Mrs Lucier.'

'The Stawstack,' included in Desmond Pacey, ed., *Canadian Short*

Stories Toronto: Ryerson 1947 (revised edition entitled *A Book of Canadian Stories* 1962) and in Gnarowski (see above)

White Narcissus Toronto: Macmillan 1929. Also published in the same year by Harcourt, Brace & Co in the USA and by Jonathon Cape Ltd in England. Reprinted by McClelland & Stewart, Toronto 1962

BIOGRAPHY AND CRITICISM

Beattie, Munro 'Poetry 1920-1935,' in Carl Klinck, ed.; *Literary History of Canada* Toronto: University of Toronto Press 1965, 728-30

Child, Philip 'Introduction,' in *White Narcissus* Toronto: McClelland & Stewart 1962, 7-16

Gnarowski, Michael 'Introduction,' in *Selected Stories of Raymond Knister* Ottawa: University of Ottawa Press 1972, 11-16

Kennedy, Leo 'Raymond Knister' *Canadian Forum* XII (September 1932) 459-61

Livesay, Dorothy 'Raymond Knister: A Memoir,' in *The Collected Poems of Raymond Knister* Toronto: Ryerson 1949, xi-xli

– 'Knister's Stories' *Canadian Literature* 62 (Autumn 1974) 79-82

Pacey, Desmond 'Fiction 1920-1940,' in Carl Klinck, ed., *Literary History of Canada* Toronto: University of Toronto Press 1965, 685

Stevens, Peter 'The Old Futility of Art: Knister's Poetry' *Canadian Literature* 23 (Winter 1965) 45-52

Stories

THE FIRST DAY OF SPRING

It had been a mild winter, and yet when March came, and days in which wheels threw the snow like mud in stretches of road where snow still lay, the world was changed.

This change was more than seeming. Who misses the first day of spring? Snow may linger on the ground and return, but the new smell is there, more potent perhaps than it is ever to be in lush days of blossoms. The blue of the sky softens, the air lifts, and it is as though the lightness of a life above the earth were being made ready, an entering spirit to pervade the uncoloured and frost-clogged flesh of the world; or perhaps it is as though this flesh had suddenly sighed in its sleep, an exhalation intoxicating to men and beasts. It is as though sunlight on their bare boughs has at last awakened the trees, and the wind through them is now more than a gesture remembered only by the grass.

Perhaps it was the effect of spring on a boy which made me forgetful. Musing in the darkness of the cow-stable after such a day, I allowed Bess, one of the cows, to sip up all the water in a second pail, when her stall mate, Rose, had had only one. I started and pulled the pail away. There was still a very little in the bottom, and this I offered to Rose. She did not want the water, or doubted its existence in the bottom of the pail, so I decided not to get her another. The ground was soft and deep to the narrow hooves of cows, so they were not turned out to find their way to the well at the foot of the hill.

In the other end of the building, where the horses were kept, I could hear my father backing the 'driver' out of her stall, and I knew that he was going to town. As I walked across the barnyard, the straw and loose dirt gave way under my feet with sudden crunches, where the old ice had melted, honeycombed by a few afternoons of warm sun. I ran ahead to open the gate, and Cherry was led through. A long-haired bay mare with trim legs, she held her head high, and trod sedately in the slippery mud of the lane.

This made me smile, for I thought of the chase she had led the colts that morning from 'the other farm' a mile away. After the early chores we had walked to the back of this farm, and captured the more or less unneeded horses which had been wintered there. They had pawed the snow for long grass, and with occasional loads of corn-fodder had kept fat on their ribs. Only in times of storm were they brought into the barn.

They crowded about us, snorting trumpets of fog in the thin spring sunshine – turning, shying, shattering films of ice on the puddles. Father got the halter on Kate, a 'general purpose' mare weighing about fifteen hundred pounds, who, as the senior member of the party, could be expected to lead it safely to the barn. Then he hoisted me on her back, first twisting the halter shank into her mouth; for since the sudden breath of spring had caused the excursion we had set forth without bridles. He came along behind on foot, to see that the others did not linger or stray.

But he needn't have worried about that. The whole herd of horses and colts jumped across the weedy ditch and set up a gallop, strung along the lane, splashing impartially through mud, blue puddles, and dark drifts of snow. The air was like a cool bright tide, and the fresh sound of hens cackling on a neighbouring farm seemed to cry us forward. Old Kate was not to be outdone, in spite of my pulling. I saw that she meant to take me home without stopping at the barn on this place; so I jumped from her back, out far enough to have a purchase on her halter. I got her stopped, tearing the grass at the roadside with my boots. But the colts galloped gaily right on past the gate, never hearing my calls and Kate's rib-shaking whinny – straight to the home place, led in a businesslike trot by this same old driver, Cherry.

She was very mild now, Cherry, as though she meditated on the dusk of the evening and the vicissitude of her fortune. My father pulled the long-unused buggy from the shed, and cautioned me: 'Watch her, she'll be feeling those two feeds of clover hay and oats.' But as we pulled the shafts over her and fastened the traces, she helped by easing back slightly, appearing meanwhile to give heed to a lonely-sounding 'plunk-plash' where another rig was passing along the muddy road. I looked up at her large tilted eyes and high-held head averted while Father went to the house for his overcoat, and told her, with a boy's faith:

'Sure, you'd stand, wouldn't you, Cherry. Not run away.'

Like a dog the driver made a gesture of glancing at me, but retained her statuesque pose, and grinding a stray stem of hay in her mouth, still considered the sound from the road, beyond the hedge.

'Well; now we've forgotten the buggy-cushion,' my father said, interrupting my day-dream, and went into the drive-shed for it. 'Now's no time for automobiles. Wasn't so bad, a mild winter like this, but from now on, until the frost is all out –' He picked up the lines and stepped into the buggy.

Preferring the automobile to the buggy, I pretended to be annoyed.

'Yes, I suppose when the horses are working hard and other people are getting their cars out, we'll begin to use a horse and rig.'

But I really didn't care, and my words seemed to thin away into the chill tranquil evening. I put my hands into my pockets; for – significant of spring – I had mislaid my mitts that afternoon ..... everything was satisfying. This day had been brisk and active, banishing in a stroke the long winter in which the world had seemed so far away and the chores so inevitable and tame. Now we seemed remotely interesting and strange to one another, the quiet horse, my father, and myself.

'I saw Fred Keith and that Merrill girl trying to get through the mud yesterday with their car, and that was a good example of how foolish it is.'

'Muriel?' I asked, in surprise. 'I didn't know either of them was back.'

'And what do you think – You knew he was pretty well gone on her before they moved down east. He must have been, or he wouldn't have up and sold his store and all and moved down there near them. True, he had a good offer, but then, he didn't need to go just *there*. You know, he got the girl in trouble.' He spoke as man to man, as though I was old enough, now, for that. I was seventeen.

'Not Muriel?' I was convinced that he was mistaken. 'I hardly knew they were going together, even, till they had gone.'

'Got her in the family way. Going together! I guess! He was too wise. I knew all along where things were heading. I used to see him hanging around there all kinds of hours. Why, one time last spring, quite late, May maybe, – I was passing along to the other place about four or five in the morning to sow cloverseed, and there was his glass coup' at the road, all the windows covered with fog, and I thought there was nobody in it, but just as I got by I heard a giggle, and you hate to look back – just getting home. Poor girl, I guess if she'd known how it would turn out –'

Father buttoned his overcoat. He sat erect in the buggy, joggling the whip, while Cherry bent an ear alternately to him and to the road. It seemed that his words were a long time reaching me. Then I wanted to be indignant, and could not, in the face of his calm acceptance. He did not gossip until there was something to talk about.

'Why – why, she was just the same age as me. We were in the same class at school.'

'The foolish age. It's all the worse – when some fellow gets them going wrong, I mean. All the more foolish. What I was going to say, I saw them yesterday, stuck in the mud in his coup'. It seemed the thing had caught fire –'

'Caught fire, how?'

But I was scarcely listening, for everything seemed irrelevant beside this strange, half-expected news of Muriel, which yet struck me like a blow. It seemed only a few weeks since I had used to tease her at school, and she had been so pretty that I had wondered secretly if some day I might not be bold enough to try to keep company with her myself. Her auburn hair, and narrow blue eyes, saucy nose, returned to me as I had seen her in the lamplight when she had recited at an entertainment a year ago.

It seemed that I was just getting to know her when the family moved away; and oddly she seemed to me younger then than in the years before. She had been always like a complete, demurely perfect creature in her way, not liable to the imperfections of growth, stages in which most girls are gawky or giggling. I had looked at her as from a distance, and I still remember her somehow as one recalls an early love-affair with a woman older than himself.

'Why, it simply caught fire. They had coal oil in the radiator ... It does seem one trouble just attracts others to it.'

'But how –'

'How did they get it out? Well, I guess it burnt itself out, like. I suppose the oil burnt off the engine, never got to the gasoline or anything. I was surprised to see them a hundred miles from where they belonged. He had a piece of fence-rail and was trying to pry the mud out of the wheels. Had his hat off and his good clothes plastered. I yelled at him. "Hello, Fred, what's the matter with your plug-hat car?" He seemed glad to see me and tell his story. But he didn't feel much like joking, I can tell you. He wanted to get on, as though he was in a hurry, all excited. I seen Muriel in the coup' and started to ask her how the family was. She kind of ducked down, almost, and didn't want to talk to me. He says, all excited, "Congratulate us, congratulate us, we're married!" '

I twisted the heel of my rubber boot in the ground.

'Yes, married. But it's too late. I wouldn't be surprised if they were in jail by this time. By George! I bet they were trying to get to Detroit and the other side. They were in a hurry, all right. They couldn't have been very pleased to see me, though I did stop and get them out of the hole. No, nor they didn't seem to be very pleased with each other. You wouldn't have known them for the same pair, so ... down-in-the-mouth. But that's how it goes.'

I did not have a word to say, or I had more than I could say. It was growing dusk, but a strange new robin called sharply somewhere in the thick jumbled limbs of a crab-apple tree in the garden. A couple of pigeons alighted on the barn ridge, one facing each way, watchfully; we had had a pigeon pie or two lately. Some air over the buildings, a new strange echo of our voices, yet one so old I wondered how I could have forgotten it, filled my heart with a mixture of feelings.

A girl's voice came from across the fields, a few words of singing, a voice with something wild and strong in it.

'Hear her? That's the other one. Pretty much alike, for cousins. Remember how they used to call to each other from one house to the other? Could hear them as plain, when the air was like this! On a Monday morning, when they'd both be putting out washings, they'd try singing a duet, and laugh back and forth. ... Nothing can stop her singing when she gets out.'

But the girl's voice had stopped.

'Well, Cherry,' Father addressed the horse. 'It seems like old times, sitting behind your ornery old hide. Horses are going to want a lot of time to get used to the work. They'll be mighty soft. Got to break in those colts one of these days too, can't get at it too soon. Is there anything you want me to get in town?'

'How about – what you said – he – they might be arrested?'

'Oh. Oh, the way of that, I suppose you should know such things. They was out after her, the police, so I heard when I got to town yesterday. And me just seeing them – When the time came, you see, she had a child.'

'Couldn't he marry her?'

'Course, yes, but then, they hadn't, so ... They might have had a fall-out before that time. Well, what she done, by all accounts, her father went out one morning, and he was stirring the swill-barrel and singing, like you know he used to. The girl got that honest. Quite early it was. He carried a couple of pailsful to the trough at the pig-pen, and he wondered, they didn't squeal like they usually did when he began to feed them. But of course, a lot of fat hogs like that, he couldn't see anything amongst them, until they got lined up at the trough.'

'But what about Muriel?' I asked, and my voice seemed shrill. I had overcome a sense of shame in mentioning her name, a relic of shyness before the girl herself, perhaps.

'Well, she – Muriel I guess had – she'd left just a few minutes before. She, well, what she done – The baby may have been dead before she – She must have gone straight to Fred, and they lit out.'

But almost as soon as he had begun to speak I had turned to walk away. I couldn't bear what loomed over the image of that girl in my mind. Why, she must have gone through things that were incredible ... I turned to face my father.

'Well, of course, you read of these things, but you never think they're going to happen to people you know. But that's how it is when young people start to go wrong. Might have happened right here when they lived here.' He chirped, and tightened the lines.

The old mare swung at once into her long road-stride. 'Don't bother any more with the chores. I'll fix them when I get home.' Father called from the lane, looking back.

From across the fields the light hidden voice came reaching again, and then it stopped, as though for an answer. The air was chill, and with the darkness winter seemed to be returning.

After a few minutes I moved away toward the barn. In the gloom of the stable I stroked the warm nose of a colt. 'You're going to be broken in,' I whispered. He was strangely quiet.

PEACHES, PEACHES

The peach harvest was at its height on the Burkin farm, and everyone was so busy he didn't know what to do next, unless it was to tell someone else what should be done. There were five thousand young peach trees that had just come to growth for bearing the year before, a season of crop-failure on account of winter-killing. This year they were all bearing, and heavily. The early peaches made up nearly half of the orchards, and nearly all of these were ripening at the same time. The Yellow Saint John, a large, delicious red-cheeked peach almost the earliest freestone, was ready; and at the same time the Prolific, a smaller, redder peach, was starting and had to be gone over by the pickers at the beginning and end of that week. A score of things had to be looked after promptly and properly before the fruit was in packed, lidded, and stamped baskets. Then the marketing in itself was enough to drive a man wild in this year of heavy crops in the Niagara District and all along the western end of Lake Erie. The Burkins were eating, drinking, dreaming peaches, riding to town with baskets in the back seat, finding rotten peaches loose in the car on the way to church, thinking of peaches while the minister prayed, cursing peaches when, overwearied, they tried to sleep at night. Peaches!

There were sixteen girls with baskets and ladders straggling down the endless rows of trees. Some could hardly carry the light six-foot step ladders from one tree to the next, yet kept nimbly climbing and filling baskets, which they carried to a centre row down which a light dray came now and again to collect a load. Others, big middle-aged women, easily capable of pulling an eight-foot ladder about, were discouraged when it came to getting up on one to pick from the top limbs, and sat down on the first rung to talk or think. Then the younger girls offered them the shorter ladders, and climbed after the higher peaches. The trees had to be picked carefully of all that were ripe, or by the time they came to them again these would be spoiled. You couldn't put a too ripe peach into the basket; if some householder found several peaches brown and fuzzily spoiled because of contact with a soft one, it would be as bad as stealing. And then, there were other uses for the ripest ones. They were usually perfect for eating out of the hand, or if too ripe, anyway there was one delicious bite, which you took and quickly, without getting the juice over you, threw the rest on the ground.

Oh, picking peaches was all right, when the weather wasn't too hot, and there was a breeze from the lake, and someone in the bunch to laugh or spring a joke once in a while. You came out on the seven-thirty car in the morning, that meant getting up pretty early, and went back on the five car; a long day by the time you got back to town and in your own house again. But it was a change to get out in the country for a few days and earn some money for yourself and carry home a basket of peaches or two every night. Nothing said about that, as long as you brought back the baskets in the morning. They were supposed to be the over-ripe ones, and that meant you had a small canning-bee on your hands nearly every night. But having peaches steady on the table took well with the men and the kids at home all right. And the canned ones would taste good in the winter, though it was hard to think of winter, and even all these advantages made you tired to think of it when it was August and you had to climb up and down the ladders in the sun, and pile basket after basket of peaches in the row for the democrat to come along and collect.

Every half hour or so there would be a rattle on the hard gravel path, and the little blood team would come storming along with the light wagon, to pick up a load. Fifty-six eleven-quart baskets it would take. But when the picking was good and the gang felt right they could keep ahead easily. A tall, fair young fellow with a large roll-brimmed straw hat wrapped the lines around the ladder of the rack, leaped to the ground, and began swinging the baskets aboard. The mischievous little horses pulled from side to side to nip at the leaves of the peach trees. The leaves were bitter, and the horses didn't really like them, but kept on from nervousness. They would pull limbs and the ripe peaches would fall. The man would swear and slap them with the lines, but it did no good. He was alone, and he had to get the load on as quickly as he could. But the little low trees spread so that the horses could reach the outer limbs easily. You just had to let the horses do as they pleased. If they were so wrought up with the hectic speed of the farm that they couldn't keep still, tossed their heads and grabbed for bitter peach leaves, it was no good kicking them in the ribs; they'd try to run away, you wouldn't be able to trust them while you walked two rods for a bunch of baskets. They liked to come tearing down the slope, wheels rattling, while you tumbled off brand new empty baskets in fours stuck into one another's handles. Turning at the end of the orchard, the hired man picked up a load of full baskets on the way back. He was a student at the agricultural college, paying part of his expenses by working on a farm from the middle of April, when school closed, to the middle of September; and gaining experience at the same time. He was raised in the north, a different kind of country, where peaches were always dear and scarce in season. He was making up his mind for good that farming was no cinch, and that it would be as well to arrange for some white-collar job when he should have graduated. If a fellow could make a living without all this running his legs off, and packing peaches until midnight before market days, with no time off except to catch a little sleep or bolt enough feed to hold you up for another six hours, he would be silly not to try to do it. One season of this was plenty, and then some.

Up on the barn floor were six or eight women around a couple of large tables. One end of the floor was filled with the heaped baskets brought from the field, and they picked these up and poured them out and repacked them, and nailed the lids on. One of the women seemed to be an expert with the hammer; she fastened the lids with little metal clasps that you had to strike just right or they turned and didn't hold. These baskets, with the flat lids, were piled two on top of two more, crosswise always, until it wasn't safe to go higher, then another tier was started. There would be one hundred and fifty, two hundred, two hundred and fifty of these packed baskets started. Young Burkin would come in and shout: 'How many baskets ready to go, girls? The woman who nailed would reply, 'About two hundred.' – 'No!' Ed Burkin would answer. 'The truck only took a load away an hour ago. You girls are sure out-doing yourselves.'

'They send 'em in to us, and we've got to pack 'em.' a little married woman with yellow hair and sallow skin would chirp. 'Blame the pickers out there, if you blame anybody.'

'All stamped now?' Ed asked anxiously. 'Every basket has got to be stamped, to pass the Inspector, you know.'

'Sure, I stamped 'em, as fast as they was piled,' said the little woman whose head moved like a bird's.

'All right, then. I wish Amos would get back with that truck. He's only gone to Wyndham too. Must have trouble selling them.'

'He better get home in time to take us to the station for the five car,' sang one woman.

'Won't have time for that,' teased Ed. 'Got to get another load out of here as soon as he gets back. He'll take you all the way to the city with the truck if he's not back in time to take you to the seven car.'

'Seven car! Listen! Oh, Lord,' groaned the big woman who nailed the lids. 'We go home on the five, Mister, or we don't come back tomorrow.'

'Well, I hope he gets back in time,' said Ed dubiously. 'But it don't look like he's going to.'

The light wagon came rattling up the hard lane, rounded the curve to the barn grade, turned, and began to back toward the barn door, the team shaking impatient heads. As soon as the rear wheels had jumped over the doorsill, Ed was seizing the full-heaped baskets, two in each hand, and carrying them to the back of the barn floor, where the packers could get them. The space at the front had to be kept for the lidded baskets when the truck came for them.

Murray March jumped down from the front of the wagon, warned the horses, and came around to the side, where he began pulling the baskets off and carrying them in, winking meaninglessly at Ed Burkin as he passed him among the women.

'How many more you got out in the orchard?' Ed asked him.

'How many what?' Murray returned with his slow grin. 'Girls?'

'No, baskets of peaches full,' said Ed particularly. Some of the girls and women here were giggling.

'Oh, couple more jags, hundred baskets by the time they're all rounded up.'

'Heavens! I don't know what Amos is going to do with these peaches. It's beyond me. There's more than two truck loads right here on the barn floor. And if he goes to market tomorrow he spends till noon, or maybe all day, getting rid of one load.'

'Looks bad,' agreed Murray, leaning his arms on the back of the wagon rack. They were speaking in lower tones of a matter in which the pickers, as strangers and temporary hirelings, were not concerned. 'Is he advertising for people to come after their peaches to the farm?'

'Yeah, going to have another ad. in the city paper tomorrow, and the Wyndham weekly too. But there's orchards all along the road. People come with their own cars and want to do their own picking and argue about the price. For all they take, you lose a lot of time monkeying with them.'

'Well, the peaches ain't getting ahead of the pickers, as long as you got this gang. They're sure clawing 'em off. As fast as I can haul 'em into the barn.'

'No, that's right,' said Ed despondently. Their conversations turned in circles like this. 'But the peaches is getting ahead of *us* just the same. Looks like we won't be able to sell 'em when they do get picked.'

They pulled off the rest of the baskets, resting their bellies on the edges of the rack to reach those in the centre of the load, rather than take the trouble of climbing up.

'I guess I'll go with you to the orchard for the load,' said Ed, looking at his watch. 'If Amos ain't back in time to take the girls to the car, you'll have to make a dash with the light team. Got empties enough out?'

'Just as well to have plenty.' Murray dived into the granary and brought out eight under each arm. Ed did the same, then the two youths jumped on the rack, and the wagon whirled round the corner. Murray was supported by the taut lines but Ed, who was not quite as tall, had to reach for the other's shoulder to keep from reeling.

He did not think of Murray as the hired man, for they were of an age, and they had been companions since spring. There was an impulsive veracity about Ed, and a more cautious, tacit acceptance, sympathetic or cynical, about Murray, which made them interesting to one another. They showed almost equal solicitude over the fortunes of the peach crop on the farm.

'If Amos'd had gumption not to set the whole place out to one or two varieties, it wouldn't be like this,' Ed muttered, aggrieved.

'Well,' agreed Murray, 'if he had a taste for peaches in large gobs he sure has got what he wanted this year, all right.'

The spring wagon was bounding down a slope, dust rising behind it. This particular lane between two rows of trees was used for distributing the empty baskets, and the girls brought the full ones here from two or three rows on either side. Eight rows of trees, with two girls on each, were being carried through the orchard. They came to some of the pickers, behind the others.

'You should make them keep even if you can, Murray. When some of them hang behind it makes it kind of bad.' He began to tear the baskets apart and distribute them along the row, the horses slowing to a walk.

'It's the other way around. The trouble is there are two or three ahead and the rest get discouraged. Those two girls that came at noon are putting it all over the city girls for picking peaches.'

'We'll see if they stay good all day, tomorrow. These have got so all they think about is getting a basket or two fixed up for themselves when it comes about four o'clock. They can't work after that.'

'Yeah, they do kind of slow down. Gee around here!' The wagon started back, and met the first of the pickers, a large stout fair girl of eighteen, and a dark, slighter one a little older. Murray jumped down and hoisted the full baskets up, while Ed laid them in tiers across the rack.

'You're making them town girls look slow,' said Ed, not caring whether he were overheard. The girls shyly did not answer, until the dark one finally laughed.

'Aw, shucks, this is just play,' said the big one. Murray chirped to the team, and they went on a few yards until they came to more full baskets. There were glimpses of the girls, working on ladders or on the ground. In a few minutes the load was collected, and at a more sober pace the team started for the barn. Ed gave a shout. 'Come up to the barn girls, in about fifteen minutes. Time to quit!' he bawled.

'Let 'em go,' he added. 'Time we get these unloaded, it'll be time to take the girls to the station, if Amos ain't back.' The little horses spurted, the neckyoke and tongue jostling as the front wheels jerked.

'Some rusher you are,' Murray said goodnaturedly. 'Amos'll be back, all right.'

'There's got to be some rushing if they're going to be sold,' Ed said gloomily, wondering fleetingly whether he should have spoken so when Murray was the actual driver of the team.

They backed to the door, slid the baskets off the wagon and ran with them to the end of the barn. The women were packing, rapidly, silently, knowing that the last few minutes of work were at hand. 'Well, that brother of yours ain't here yet with his truck,' said the woman with the tack hammer.

'I guess you'll have to ride to the station on the wagon,' said Ed. 'Murray, you go to the house and tell Eleanor to give you fifty or sixty dollars and we'll pay the bunch.'

'All right. You goin' to take the team and gather up the pickers? They got baskets to carry and they might be a long time.'

'That's up to them,' declared Ed. 'I haven't any call to cart their peaches. If they want to miss the five car, all right.' He went outside to the end of the barn and yelled down the orchard for the pickers, proud of the volume of his voice, then went back and started figuring wages with the packers. 'You all paid yesterday?' he asked.

'No,' said one, jocularly.

'Nor the day before,' said another.

'I hadn't ought to pay anybody when Amos is away, then I'd be sure you were coming tomorrow.'

'Yeah, that's what H.H. Slash tried on us, and we left him. Whenever I don't want to come, not having my money won't stop me from staying away. I can always tell somebody else to get my money for me.'

Ed had turned away and was not listening. By the time he had made change and paid all the girls in the barn, the others began to straggle in from the orchard. Wearily they swung their baskets of peaches onto the wagon. Others set them down and waited for orders. Ed got a box and began to hand the girls and women up. Some squealed and giggled, others were quiet and careful. The last ones were paid. 'Ten to five,' said Murray with a grin.

'Now, everybody here? It's ten to five, and we got to go.' Ed motioned to Murray to take the lines and drive the team. Murray's long legs took him from the doubletree to the folding seat which he bent back over the front ladder and sat down. 'All set?' he asked, chirping. The team swung into a swift trot down the lane.

'Sure Mike,' yelled one. 'Don't let us miss that car!'

Ed grinned after the load, his thumbs hitched in his suspenders at the top of his khaki trousers. He turned back to the barn floor when he saw two girls coming around the corner, empty-handed.

'Oh, hello! Think you was lost out there alone?' It was the two farm girls who had called up at noon and offered to pick and been brought over by a dark French youth.

'We didn't know what time it was, and the others left the orchard quite long ago,' said the slim one. Though she was dark, Ed saw, her eyes were blue. She was French. The fat one snickered. The sun was still high, and she knew when a farmer's day ended.

'I guess you got lonesome,' said Ed. 'You knew that long fellow with the team was going away and you got lonesome.'

The dark one laughed merrily, and the other said as a matter of interesting information, 'I was getting hungry, the more peaches I ate.'

'Well, I guess we won't bother to go back to the orchard, although it ain't six yet. There's lots to do in the barn. Let's go in and take a whirl at it.' They followed him in silence to the barn floor. The packing table was covered with baskets half empty and half packed. He explained how the peaches had to be as good at the bottom as at the top, and that real ripe ones were to be left out – the ones likely to spoil in a day or two. These weren't going to be shipped, or they'd all have to be pretty firm, almost green. He felt that it was more or less a waste of time, for the fat girl, May Webster, took fifteen minutes to get a basket packed level. Florine Gravel, the older girl, was quick and expert at once. Ed thought he'd have to have her with the packers. Her hands were pretty as they flew about and she seemed fresh and dainty after her afternoon in the hot orchard.

Murray returned with the wagon and went on to the orchard to pick up the last load. He looked into the barn as he passed, but Ed did not offer to accompany him. By the time the girls were getting on to packing and he returned, it was a quarter-of-six.

'You don't mind working a little late, do you? Sometimes we turn to and pack till midnight. Anyway, your brother hasn't come after you.'

'But no; Mr Burkin, you would take us home tonight, if he brings us in the morning.'

'I didn't know that, or I'd have gone before. It's too late to go before supper, so I guess you'd better have supper with us eh?'

'It is too far to walk,' said Florine. May laughed.

'I'll drive you home right after. Come on in and have supper with us. Your folks won't worry, will they?'

'Not as long as we get home by dark,' said May Webster. The other smiled. As they strolled toward the house Murray came striding up behind them from the stable.

'Say, those girls were scared they were going to miss the car,' he remarked. They laughed, feeling companionable and apart from the larger group as they crossed the back yard. At the door, preceding, the girls hesitated a little, as it occurred to them that besides these friendly young men there would be a housewife to face. But Mrs Burkin, a tall woman of thirty with blue eyes and auburn hair, dressed for afternoon, was polite. She put on one extra plate and since Amos was not there, Murray sat in his place. The kitchen was large and dark, with a veranda over one window and a vine over the other. They had plenty of sliced tomatoes and peaches.

'Funny thing about peaches,' said Ed. 'You can eat them in the orchard all day, and then they taste just as good as ever sliced with cream.'

Mrs Burkin made sociable queries of the girls, but they were not talkative, and rose as soon as they had finished their tea and cake. Ed followed them outside, and Murray came after with the milk pails in his hands and bareheaded, his hair still smooth from its supper combing. The haze of dusk was coming, and between distant trees an expanse of Lake Erie lay flat and slate-blue, shading to yellow at the horizon. Ed told the girls to get themselves a basket or two of peaches to take home. He went to back the car out of the garage.

'I thought maybe you were going to wait till I got done milking and take me along,' said Murray.

'Naw, I don't want you along till I decide which I like the best,' said Ed loudly. The girls, on the way to the barn, giggled.

May got into the tonneau of the touring car with the baskets, and Ed quashed an impulse to tease her about her size. They went along the gravelled town line for a distance, then east, to reach the Webster farm, then back south to take Florine Gravel home. 'So this is the Gravel homestead,' he said when she told him to turn in. 'Funny name, to a stranger at least.'

'It's like Brown or Jones in French.'

'You can come in the morning then, can you, and your brother will bring you? Doesn't matter if you're not so terribly early. By eight eh?'

'Shore. Thank you for the peaches.'

He would have liked to linger a minute in the dusk to talk to her, but it wouldn't look good. A couple of half-grown brothers in overalls grinned at him as he crossed the yard carrying her basket of peaches. Smoking a cigarette, he drove home leisurely, digesting peaceably the huge supper he had eaten.

As he turned into the lane his lights showed up the dusty green truck, standing in the yard as Amos had left it. Ed got up on the rack and felt about among the loose empty baskets. He half expected to find a few full baskets, but Amos had sold them all every time up to now. He got down and started the powerful motor, wishing there had been some excuse for taking it out on the road, and backed up to the still-open barn-doors and unloaded the baskets, then turned to let the headlights show up the packing tables. He heard the steps grating across the gravel lane, coming from the house.

'Amos just got home,' Murray said, 'as I was finishing putting the milk through the separator. Having supper now. How did you get along with your two girl friends?'

'Fine. I'll be taking them out again tomorrow night,' laughed Ed. 'Unless you want the job.'

'They wouldn't wait till after milking.' said Murray dryly.

'Oh, hell,' sighed Ed, sitting down on the running board of the truck. 'You couldn't sell me all the peaches in Ontario for a nickel on time, right now. Ain't that the way they appear to you?'

'I don't see 'em at all. Meanwhile we got to. Are we going to pack again tonight?'

'Might as well unless Amos says different. What's he say?'

'I guess he had some fun getting rid of his load this afternoon; had to go clear to Wallacetown with it and peddle from house to house at the last, he told Mrs Burkin.'

'He'll have to give the baskets a year's subscription to the *Farmer's Advocate* with every order, pretty soon.'

'Say that big girl was funny, out in the orchard. She pretended to be terribly afraid of getting up the ladders, you know. I told her no one was looking.'

'I bet you did. Suppose she climbs the strawstack every night for bedding for the cattle. They worked pretty good though, eh?'

'Yes, and I think they're more careful what they put into the baskets than the others. She says, "If I fall will you catch me?" '

'What did you say to that?'

'Oh, I kidded her along. I says, "I'll catch it if I'm underneath when you fall." '

'Ha, ho, ho. Did that hold her?'

'Yep, she went on picking. The other one's a cute kid, but quiet. Those black eyes, eh? I don't think she's as slow as May. I should think she'd interest you.'

'Her eyes are dark blue, not black, you goof. Those baskets all stamped? Say, the heavens would fall if I was to go out with a girl one night now. Amos would never let me hear the last of it.'

'Well, he can't very well stop you from taking them home, can he?'

'I tell you what, I'll let you drive them home every other night, only we got to agree not to do any poaching.'

'Hell, your ideas of going courting, as the old farmers call it, are queer. Nobody could make any head way with another one along. And as for poaching...'

'You talk like a lady's man; I suppose they give a course in that at the agricultural college.'

'It's about the only thing they don't give us a course in. There are about twenty-four brands of ignorance we're supposed to overcome.'

The truck headlights lit up their faces and the wrinkles in their clothes. Murray was a fair youth, with yellow hair. Ed was shorter, dark, with a stubble of dark beard and a straw hat which shaded his face. You couldn't see too well for packing, because the lights were not high enough and you had to face them.

The steps of Amos sounded on the plank floor, and raising their heads they saw his lantern but could not see him for the glare in their eyes. He seemed to take a long time to come the length of the truck, and they looked up again, rather self-consciously.

'I see the ameter discharges considerable with the lights on full and the motor not going,' observed Amos, in a comfortable after-supper voice. He had stayed in quite a while talking with his wife. 'But I reckon I put her over enough miles in the daytime to make up,' he chuckled, as he came to the table, a young fellow of twenty nine or so, more stooped and not so sturdy looking as Ed, his junior. 'Say,' he continued, 'you boys don't need to pack tonight. They've got quite a pile ahead of us, haven't they? Must be two loads there, eh?'

'About that,' said Ed, throwing his hat aside with a stubborn air.

'Let's just load the truck up for morning and call it a day. I got to get to market in the morning, leave about four.'

'O.K. by me,' said Ed. Murray looked up. Amos got into the cab and pressed the starter, backed out, turned around, and backed in again. Ed got up with him, and moved the baskets from the back to the front. In another half hour the load was ready. The outer baskets were tied to inner ones with twine. When you hit the bumps at thirty-five or so, things jump; then there's the slant of the road, and occasional hills. When everything else was done a large rubber tarpaulin was tied over the whole load to protect it against dust or rain. The truck was driven into the long driveshed beside the touring car, and they were ready to go to the house.

'Everything fed, watered and milked, eh? I guess I'll just take the lantern and have a look around.'

On the way to the house in the warm darkness, Ed pretended to stagger and walk knock-kneed with weariness. The grandfather's clock in the sitting-room was striking ten as they washed their hands and Murray March combed his hair.

II

In the next few days the fruit farmers did not find much encouragement. The local markets would not absorb the early peaches without great efforts in salesmanship and cutting of prices below the cost of production. And as for late ones, the crop was going to be even heavier. Amos Burkin had an advantage with his young trees, well-tended and sprayed. The peaches were perfect quality, and he sold constantly to the better grocery stores in the city. He took two truck loads to the Wednesday and Saturday markets, unloading one early in the morning and leaving Ed to sell then going back for the second. It became harder and harder to get the people to buy, especially since the other growers, with fruit of poorer quality, undersold him. Some Saturday nights he stayed on the market until eleven.

As for the boys, left on the farm, Saturday night was a night off. They might have gone to town, but they decided to take the weekly bath in the lake, though it meant a walk of nearly a mile through a neighbour's farm. On the way they called for Dave Blain, and the three pursued their way laxly, tired from the week's work and full of supper. Dave Blain was another agricultural college man, ready to start his third year like Murray, and they got discussing the life, the meals, the work, girls, and collecting of specimens in this subject and that. Ed now and then chimed in with a comparison with the college he had attended a year. The meals had been vile, he said, but he had read a book a day.

There was a considerable height to the bank where they climbed down to the beach, and a group of cottages was only about an eighth of a mile away, so they had to be careful to wear bathing suits, even after dark. Farther on the beach was stony and muddy; here it was perfect sand, maybe even better than in front of the cottages. Some night they might come on some of the cottagers bathing there, maybe a bunch of girls – three, for preference. Dave had to go down, feel the water, yell, 'Warm as milk!' and dance up again. The young men swifly doffed shirts, pants, and underwear in the shelter of some bushes halfway up the bank. Dave Blain was into his suit first and hopped with wildly circling legs down the bank and across the beach and into the water. Then he gave a yell as the surprising cold rose about him, and threw himself headlong, reaching his arm out smoothly and leisurely in a crawl stroke. Murray followed, but stalked into the water until it was about his calves, then lowered his hands and wrists into it. 'Get used to the cold that way,' he called, and Ed followed his example.

Ed, who had lived within a mile of the lake all his life, had just last winter learned to swim in a pool in Hart House Gymnasium. It seemed hard to put into practice what you knew, when the water was cold and though apparently calm rolled over your head with a simple abruptness you could not avoid. He stood up and spluttered, snorted the water out of his nostrils, and spit.

'Look, this is the way,' said Dave when he and Murray had laughed. 'Just lay in the water and roll from side to side, easy. Only keep your legs stiff, and beat them up and down.'

'Yeah, I know. Just wait till I get my breath.' He threw himself down, and started, his head out of water to the neck, his arms thrashing. His face became dark from breathlessness, but he kept on, until suddenly his leg was pulled from behind.

'Come back, don't try to go to Erie Pennsylvania, you'll get stuck halfway. There might be a hole here.' But Murray's head was well above the surface, and he was standing on a sandbar.

'Whoosh! I must have made a hundred yards, didn't I?'

'In ten flat,' said Dave. 'Come on, Murray, I'll race you.'

'You would, you little runt?' Murray threw every effort into the race, and after a long struggle Dave gave up, seeing that he was being passed.

They sat on a half-imbedded bleached log and rested their aching limbs which had seemed heavy as they came out of the water.

'Old man Cairns lives in one of these cottages,' said Dave. 'He gets his milk at the boss's. Sends his girl over every morning about eight with the Dodge sedan.'

'*Cherchez la femme!*' said Ed.

'What? Yeah, *cherchez!* If I could find her I wouldn't have to *chercher*. Lord, I've forgotten the French I learned in the army.'

'I bet I know how you learnt it,' said Murray, who was a year or two younger and hadn't gone to war. 'Why don't you marry the girl, since you got her on the brain?' He had an awkward air of badinage.

Dave sighed. 'No, you don't know the half of it. Some of the dames in this country wouldn't sleep nights either if they knew.'

'Would they be scared?' asked Ed. Murray burst into laughter.

'They might, at that,' said Dave. 'If they knew what the men they're sleeping with now knew. ... Come on, let's take one more dip, then get dressed.'

'Too cold,' Ed said. 'The air may be colder than the water, but you can't tell my hide that.'

'Yeah, we stayed out too long, let's get dressed,' said Murray.

'Gee whinniger, I stubbed my toe! If it wasn't for the dames in those cottages we wouldn't have to climb this bank in our bare feet, and sit on benches and burrs while we got into our clothes.'

'If it wasn't for their menfolks, you mean,' said Murray. 'I guess they wouldn't mind watching, themselves.'

'Here, didn't you fellows bring any towel? You can have mine, – after I'm finished!' Murray said nothing, and Ed, silent too, knew that he didn't want to cast reflection upon his employer's wife, who had given them none. It was hard to dress sitting down, but you couldn't stand up because the cottages were near, and anyway people might be strolling along the beach. They laced their shoes and climbed the bank, leisurely, following fissures and slopes and clinging when opportunity offered to projecting roots and rocks.

'Well, two weeks from today,' said Dave, 'we'll be back at the old school, and dating up the old girls. This thing of never seeing a woman all summer is all right maybe. There's just the old folks where I am, you know.'

'Never trouble trouble and trouble'll never trouble you,' said Ed, aimlessly laughing. Murray seemed silent, and they glanced at him in the dark, following in the narrow path overhung with peach boughs. Ed laughed.

'That's the way to talk, and then you go back and date up about one woman a semester. By the time you're graduated you're on speaking terms with most of the women of your year.'

'Yeah, if it ain't money it's work puts the brakes on,' Ed said. 'But there ain't many good-looking women in my school, I can tell you.'

'Better be an Aggie,' Dave suggested. 'Murray and I would help the sophomores at the initiation, just as a personal favour.'

Through the soft gravel of the cultivated orchards they trudged, the sand filtering into their shoes. They were almost too weary to tease one another, even to talk. Work from daylight to dark for months, and the consciousness of another environment to which they were to return kept them from caring about local dances and going to town more than once a week or so. Unless of course one should have met a special girl, which might happen anytime, anywhere. The sky was dark and cloudy, yet they could discern, half with the eye of habit, the peaches on the trees at either side. It was too dark to pick one fit to eat.

'I seem to be stepping on a lot of peaches,' said Ed.

'The old man don't care shucks for the peach crops,' said Dave. 'If somebody drives in with a car, he says, take all you can pick, dollar a bushel. Claims there's nothing in 'em this year.'

'Not at a dollar a bushel,' said Ed dryly. 'But then he's only got a small orchard. Don't bother to spray, or work the land, does he?'

'Sure, I was discing in the orchard up to a month ago. He just thinks there ain't the market, and rather than lose money, he puts the time on his tobacco. Forty cents a pound last year.'

'Maybe then this year,' grunted Murray. 'You can't get Ed and me to trade jobs with you.'

'Well,' laughed Ed, 'peaches may not make a fortune, the price they are, but when you take out a load you bring back a pocketful of the cold hard mazume, anyhow.

He thought of the hundreds of dollars Amos kept in his bedroom for days until he had time to take it to the bank.

III

For a week there was a lull, between the early and the later varieties. The Yellow St John peaches were finished, vanished, as though their fair large roundness had never existed. The little Prolifics were coming to an end too. They did not bulk up like the others, though the trees had been 'loaded.' The gang of pickers dwindled to four or five from the city, and May Webster. Nowadays Murray could take time to pick a tree or two himself beside the team, when he went out for a load. Ed stayed in the barn and packed, and Florine helped him. A truck-load or two a day was all they put up. Everyone was more free and easy, now that the gang was smaller and they knew one another better. There was enough to keep you busy, but you did not have to kill yourself. Amos was mowing the second cutting of alfalfa which meant that in a few days the boys would have to turn to haying, hard work and no let-off in excitement. Instead of bolting meals and rushing out again to chivvy the packers and get Murray to take the pickers back to the orchard on the instant, Ed and Amos lolled in their chairs and looked at the Toronto morning paper for five minutes and let the girls talk together while they fed the stock and did the noon chores. When they had all left the barn but Florine and Ed, and the breeze blew from the Lake through the open doors across the barn, and Ed could catch the fresh starched smell of Florine's clothes, he felt pleased and at the same time pleasurably excited.

They talked intermittently while they packed. Ed had never known a girl so ready with sly quaint replies or one who at the same time stimulated him to teasing remarks himself. Her blue eyes, hair so dark it was almost blue too, her slightly thick retroussé nose and laughing lips, her laugh that was always rather throaty and excited even when it expressed only amusement, all began to have a particular allure for him.

The truth was that he could not remember spending hour after hour with a girl in this way before. It was a lucky chance, brought about because they couldn't take Murray from his job nor leave May or one of the other girls in the barn because someone responsible had to be there to take care of the occasional party who came to buy. So there the two of them were, and Florine's fingers flew briskly and skilfully, and Ed's too, when he was not nailing the lids down and piling the baskets and loading the truck. Yet they had plenty of opportunity of getting acquainted.

His sister-in-law was a very grown-up sort of person, with whom he wouldn't have thought of being familiar, and in truth, she was as old as Amos. Ed had never kept company with any girl steadily. He stopped going to church and had no interest in dances, so that he did not meet any; then when he had come home from a year of college he had been less inclined than ever to seek out a local girl. Now, when one was forced upon him as it were, by circumstances, he found her surprisingly interesting. A sort of restraint made him still more eager. It would be a bad business to start 'going with her' at least until after the peach season was over. Aside from the lack of time, you couldn't expect to have discipline that way; and besides, no matter when, people would gossip, he thought. It was necessary to talk to her very circumspectly, not to get into deep water. It might already look as though he had been 'going with' her, when he had been taking her home from work nearly every night.

'Don't you get tired stooping over that packing table all day?' he asked her. Looking at her slender waist he was reminded of some intimation that she was delicate. Why should she want to work, then? A few extra dollars, he supposed, without being tied to a position. 'Would you like a chair or a box to sit on?'

'No, I have to get up to move the baskets away, and I like the change. I'm all right. I wouldn't trade jobs with May or them.' She smiled. This candour was engaging, and even, if you wanted to look at it that way, flattering.

'Aw, you're trying to kid me now!'

'Sure, I know which – what is it? – which side my bread is buttered.'

A car glided softly across the barn door, coming to a stop. A short thick man and two boys of ten or twelve got out of it. Leisurely, the man entered the barn, pausing to look about.

'Plenty peaches, eh?' he asked whimsically, looking from the girl to Ed.

'All you can eat,' returned Ed. 'Help yourselves. When these are gone, there's more out in the orchard.'

'Hear that, boys?' The boys advanced to a basket piled with bruised fruit and took a couple.

Florine and Ed continued to pack.

'Only got the one kind, eh?' asked the man, breaking a peach knowingly. 'Freestone, eh?'

'Yes, these are good for canning and eating both. But the Elbertas will be on next week. Some wouldn't have anything else to can. They're not so nice raw. Little bit bitter, or tart at least.'

'They'd take a lot of sugar to can, then. I guess we'll have two bushels of these. We can decide about the Elbertas later. How much?'

'Two and a quarter by the bushel. Eighty cents a 'leven-quart basket.'

The man took a five dollar bill from his pocket, and Ed made change. 'Might bring the baskets back if you come around again. They cost about thirty cents apiece.'

'Sure, if I get another lot I'll bring these baskets back,' the man laughed. 'But I'll still be ahead of you.'

'That's all right. You can have twenty bushels, if you bring all the baskets back but the last two.' Ed looked around to see if Florine was listening. She was packing carefully, fitting a large last peach into the middle of a basket. He enjoyed joshing with customers like this. Some of them were odd fish. He emptied three eleven-quart baskets into a bushel measure, and the two boys carried it by the handles to the car. Their father called to them to wait till he came before they tried to put it inside.

When they had gone, Ed and Florine had a laugh together at the transaction.

'I like dealing with people one at a time like that,' Ed said. 'I don't like it on the market, where a dozen are asking you questions all the time. They won't buy unless your stuff is the lowest price and you tell them it is the best and a whole line like that. But I got quite bold when I was at it a while,' he added reflectively. She laughed, but not in such a way as to make a stranger of herself. She seemed to take the whole business as a matter of course. Ed had the odd feeling that they were like man and wife, tending a shop, perhaps. The man was the real head and made bargains, but the woman knew what to do too, and she was one with him in the business as in everything else. He brushed the notion aside quickly. He had no right to it. The farm was Amos's. If anyone was to feel that way in the barn tending customers, it should be Amos and Eleanor. And somehow Eleanor seemed too much of a lady to be seen packing peaches. Amos had been lucky when he married her: she had some money coming when her old man died, and there was a widower uncle too, leaving her property. She was the kind who had been brought up carefully, and her place was the house. She dressed up carefully every afternoon, whether she went out or not. You wouldn't see her out in the orchard or packing peaches, or standing on the market. Ed wondered how Amos had got up enough nerve to ask her. It seemed to him now that she was as old-acting as a fellow's aunt might be. You never wondered about her as you might about some young women; such thoughts never came into your head. Now if he were to, say, marry this girl, he would feel that his wife was no match for Amos's. But then, he might be better matched. After all, they would be a good deal younger than Amos and Eleanor. But it was silly just to think of. He wanted someone to go with, not marry. And she would have to be smarter and more fashionable, more sophisticated, than Eleanor, besides being a good deal younger. He had glimpsed one such girl in college, but even she had been two years farther on than he, and must have been his own age. No, this flurry about girls because one happened to cross your path was silly.

'Why are you not talking?' said Florine as she picked up an empty basket and prepared to pack it.

'Not thinking!' exclaimed Ed jocularly. 'What would a fellow do with thinking when he's with a pretty girl?'

'Hmm. When he's with a pretty girl. That's different.'

'Now you're fishing for compliments.'

She laughed her gurgling and excited laugh. 'Now why should I be expecting compliments?'

'Because you deserve them I suppose,' remarked Ed with elaborate casualness, which made her laugh anew. He wondered why. If she thought him funny or strange, it was up to him to become more so, to burlesque himself and make her aware that he was conscious of it; that she had made a mistake.

'Say, if a fellow was to start thinking around a pretty girl, he'd be lost, that's what he'd be. If anyone asks my advice, I always say, don't think when you're around a pretty girl. And they don't.'

'They just kid 'em along, like you!'

'Me kid 'em along?' said Ed with a reluctant grin. 'Not much. I speak my mind, that's why I'm so popular.' He was flattered; perhaps he could; sometime, just to see what she would do, he would steal a kiss. She was so neat and slight, he would just put his arms around her. She'd fight, probably, or give in with pretended resentment.

In the orchard the pickers were a jolly bunch as long as Murray was among them. He was what they called 'quiet' but so good-natured, easy-going. If anything was done wrong, he assumed it was a mistake.

and explained to you. Sometime he would stay quite a while in the orchard, picking with a high ladder in the tops of the trees, so that the girls wouldn't have to, until there were enough to make a load. The little sallow fair woman was picking now, and said she liked it better than packing; it wasn't so hard on the back, though sometimes your neck got kind of tired, looking up so much. She had her sister with her out here, a girl of about eighteen, with hair the color of buckwheat honey, and complexion so smoky you wondered whether her skin was dirty or not; a girl not lively or enthusiastic but rather impersonal and sensible acting. The others seemed to be married women, young enough to be able to do some work, and old enough to be sensible. Amos was pretty careful, hiring them. Of course they were dressed in cotton dresses and aprons, and some had strew hats or bonnets, or nothing on their heads. May Webster had an old-fashioned sunbonnet, and the sister of the pale one wore a dark ribbon to keep her hair up. After a few hours of work they didn't look too tidy. May Webster was better acquainted with the city crowd now, and it wasn't so large that she felt a stranger. Since all the women and girls made a point of talking to Murray and making a fuss over him, asking him to take a tall ladder to get peaches in the high limbs, and to bring a bunch of baskets to where they needed them, and even left full baskets about where he would see them and carry them over to the row along which he drove collecting his load – since the others had this right, why shouldn't she? But she was so shy about it, acting as though it was some kind of trick, that Murray's attention was attracted, and he joked and kidded her. The big girl would be covered with blushes; but when he was not paying her any attention, she would keep her eyes upon him as though he were the Prince of Wales.

IV

Sunday morning everyone rose late. Murray was the first out, but the horses were whinneying at the stable for their breakfast before he was out of the house. Ed roused and dressed when he heard them. In their working clothes the two young fellows watered and fed the teams. It had been the little ones, the blood horses used to gather up the peaches, that had done the whinneying. Then Murray walked back the lane to meet the cattle. The cows were coming up of their own accord to be milked, it was so late. While he was gone, Ed took up a dungfork and started to clean out the horse-stable. When he had the cement floor clean and smooth Murray was nearly finished milking, so he started for the house. On the way, hens and turkeys ran across his path, so he pulled back a tall barn door on its squeaking pulleys, and closed it behind him again. A fine havoc the fowl would make with the peaches if they got a chance! In the granary he got a pail of wheat and broadcast it about the bare yard. Leaving the empty pail at the barn door he resumed his walk to the house. It might look better to wait for Murray but he couldn't wait all day. If breakfast was ready he would sit down and eat it, no matter who was there or absent.

Eleanor was stirring the porridge over the natural-gas. She was wearing a kimono which she pulled together when she saw him. 'I thought it was Murray,' she said. 'Have you been up long?' Her hair seemed disarranged, and she seemed sleepy.

'I guess the horses thought we weren't going to come to the barn at all today,' said Ed. 'Amos ain't up yet, eh?'

'No, he didn't get home from the city till eleven or after, I guess.' She hurried into the pantry to take dishes from the shelves. 'He was coming when I left,' she laughed. 'You'd better wake him.'

'Let him sleep,' said Ed soberly, drying his hands. He sat down behind the table at the wall, and reaching into the corner picked up a magazine from the stand. It was in a tight roll of brown paper, unopened. He had subscribed to *The Century*, having seen it on the reading table of the college library. He was reading an entertaining article on life in the South Seas. It seemed that nothing could be more enjoyable nor untrammelled. But civilization was coming to ruin the integrity of the people and their manners, leading them to add new and dangerous vices to those traditional with them. It was a hell of a world. He looked up and growled, 'What's keeping Murray, anyway, want to act as though he's got all the chores to do? You and I better eat and let him and Amos eat when they're ready.'

'Sh – he's coming,' said Eleanor. She began to take up the porridge.

'Well, it's a wonder.' What did it matter to her what he said about Murray? You'd think he was company instead of hired help.

Murray came in and washed and combed his hair. He had been in the milk-house outside, where he had been putting the new milk through the separator. It could be heard still humming.

'Come on, Murray, I'm waiting like the pigs. Thought you'd never come. Eleanor didn't like it when I said I wondered whether you'd ever come. She seems to think you're company, instead of one of the family.'

Murray glanced at her before replying, as he pulled out his chair. 'I'll have to put on company manners, then, eh?' He seemed pleased with himself, as though he had been witty.

'Hey, you fellows, what's your hurry?' asked Amos, coming down the stairs and into the kitchen. 'It can't be more than nine o'clock, can it?' he asked ironically. Sitting down he pulled his heavy shoes from beside the stove, and yawning, laced them. Ed saw that Murray glanced at Eleanor, but he needn't think she was different clay altogether. She had been raised on a farm, though her old man had retired when she was old enough to go to high-school. When Amos was ready for breakfast and sat down, she started to eat hers. She had been sitting at the foot of the table pouring tea and attending to the wants of the young men. Everyone was eating oatmeal with the indifference of habit, in silence. Ed was thinking that if he spoke, it would be about wishing they could have a prepared cereal now and then. But it was just as well to keep it to himself. This was her house, now.

His father and mother had retired to town a couple of years ago before Amos had got married. The old man had done well. There were a hundred and seventy-five acres, which would make a good farm for the younger brother too when he came to marry. Only, a house would have to be built. Then, most of the orchard was on the part that Amos was to have, with the old brick house. He'd get the big end of the deal, being the older. Some little frame shack would be put up for Ed, no doubt, and besides, he would have the smaller part of the farm. Meanwhile the old man charged Amos a low rent for the whole thing while he was getting on his feet; and he was supposed to pay Ed wages. There didn't seem to be any arrangement for an education. The money for his year at university had come from his father but now it couldn't be expected of him when he was retired and not making money. And you couldn't expect Amos to pay enough during the few months he was home to keep him during the college year. As for marrying and settling in a house of his own, the others probably thought he was years away from that. Well, he might, he just might surprise them if he wasn't permitted to have an education. It would be fun to see how taken aback they would all be if he were to announce that he wanted to get married right away – this fall.

As it was, they thought he was going back to college, though he had told them he wasn't. Amos was going to be generous and give him the money. Like hell he was, Ed thought savagely. He had been working on the farm like a man since he had been knee-high to a grasshopper, and if his father couldn't afford to send him, he wasn't going to let Amos do it. They could go to blazes.

Amos was the first to speak. 'Well,' he said, while he put his spoon into his porridge plate for the last time and set them aside. 'Do you suppose you fellows could take care of the customers while the boss goes to church?' He glanced teasingly at his wife, knowing that she did not like to have it said that they sold peaches on Sunday. That was one of the chief demarcations of virtue and vice in the community; some sold peaches on Sunday; others, when the hard cash was offered them and the peaches ready on the tree or maybe even in the baskets, turned it down. But these latter could not go to church with an easy conscience and look the preacher in the eye when he shook hands with everyone at the door.

Eleanor was not without a sense of humour; she put her head on one side and said, 'I think I'll stay home today, and take care of the place, and let all you men go, for a change.'

'Oh, we wouldn't think of asking you,' said Amos.

'It would be no task at all, I'm sure. I'd just have to tell the people who came they couldn't buy anything here on Sunday. Not a bit of trouble, I could listen to the sermon on the radio.'

Ed laughed, and Murray smiled. 'They'd be climbing the fences and carrying away their cars full, while you were listening,' Ed said.

After breakfast the men went directly to the barn. There was always enough to be done that had been neglected in the rush of the week to keep them busy until noon, if they wanted to take the time. Amos unlocked the drive-shed as they went toward the barn, and stopped to look over his truck. He had had a puncture in one of the tires the day before, and wanted to see how it was standing up. Again, it was just as well to see how the oil and gasoline and water stood, for the start Monday morning. There wasn't much time to fool around cars and trucks in the week-time. As long as the thing ran you were satisfied.

Ed and Murray went through the horse-stable into the barn. The cattle were hanging about the doors, though the milch-cows had been unchained as soon as milked. 'It looks as if,' said Murray, 'they have nothing to drink. I guess we forgot to let the engine run last night.'

'Oh, hell, the tank's empty,' said Ed. When they had tried to start the gasoline engine beside the well they found that it did not contain gasoline. Murray picked up a dungfork and began to clean the cow-stable, and Ed went to the drive-shed with a gallon can and a funnel. Amos was there, pouring water out of a topless sprinkling can into the radiator of his truck. Ed unscrewed the openings in a drum of gasoline and the liquid gurgled and shot over his funnel.

'Be careful, you're wasting it,' said Amos.

'Wasting, hell,' said Ed. 'The barrel's too full, that's all. There ain't enough air getting into the top to let it run straight.'

'Better siphon it out. I guess you could do that.'

'Ain't no hose around.'

Amos pulled a dusty and cobwebbed piece of rubber hose from a rafter, and extended it to Ed, who looked at him. 'Oh, all right,' he said and inserting one end into the gasoline drum, wiping the other end on his clean shirt sleeve, he put it into his mouth and began to draw, his rather full eyes looking at Ed. If he was angry, the feeling had to take expression in what he said or did. The gasoline came, he dived the end of the hose into the gallon can, and spat vigorously.

'What does Murray say about going back to college? Is he going when it opens, or is he going to stay with us till the peaches are done?'

'Doesn't say anything about it,' Ed returned.

'That's funny. You and him are pretty chummy, you two college boys, ain't you?'

'Still water runs deep,' said Ed with a grin, waiting.

'It's too bad his school opens so dang early. I expect the peaches will be pretty well cleared when it's time for you to go. But you'd think an agricultural college could stay closed a little longer in the fall.'

'It closes earlier in the spring,' Ed reminded him.

'It's the end of September, isn't it, or the first of October, your college opens?'

'Darned if I remember, and darned if I'd care if I did.'

'You must have some literature about it. ... No sense acting silly about it. The old man asks me every time he sees me, and I've agreed you're to go back to college. If I need help in the fall I can hire a man.'

'Well, that's awful noble of you both, but I don't intend to go, thanks all the same. I guess there's plenty here for me to do.' Ed held the gallon can stiffly out from him as though it would soil his clothes. He turned to go to the barn.

'All right if that's the way you look at it,' Amos called after him, but though he let his temper slip to that extent, he amended by adding, 'There's lots of time to think it over before the time comes.'

Ed went on as though he had not heard.

The cows were bawling as though they had been without water for a week. Murray had disconnected the pump from the jack and was pumping by hand, but the water had only spread over half the surface of the broad tank. Ed ran the gasoline into the engine, primed her, cranked, and had her going. Murray promptly hitched the jack to the pump while it jiggled up and down. He might not have been so anxious to start pumping if he had known he had to fill that tank, Ed thought, disgruntled, he hardly knew why.

'Let 'er rip,' Murray called. They walked around to the other end of the barn.

'It seems late,' Ed said. 'I'll go up and put down enough hay for the day, and you get straw in to bed the horses and cows, eh?'

By the time they had the chores done and were leaving the barn, Amos was backing the touring car out of the driveshed, with Eleanor already beside him.

'There's matrimony for you,' said Ed. 'Got to go to church whether you want to or not.'

'Sure, it's as good a way of getting out of the chores as any other,' said Murray with a lazy laugh. 'He wouldn't trade places. ... If you and I could just tell somebody to do the chores we wanted to go to church, eh?'

'Yeah, he thinks he's the boss, all right. Hasn't got a brain cell working. Talking to me about going back to college; he'd pay my way. If the money's all his, I don't want any of it. I told him where to stick it.'

'Say, why don't you take that little French girl out and give him a scare? He'd think you wanted to get married.'

'Same reason you don't take out that fat Webster girl, I suppose. I ain't interested enough.'

'Now, you're interested, Ed, only you don't like to say. You're scairt you might have to marry her.'

Ed laughed. 'It ain't likely to go as far as that. She don't give a darn for me. We just been kidding each other along.'

'Sure, that sounds all right too. That's the way these grand passions start.'

'Tell, it's the truth, anyway.' Ed was rather annoyed to think that it was the truth, that he seemed to have made no progress toward an interesting relation with Florine. She was a cute kid alright, and she could keep him off the track so well that he hadn't kissed her yet.

'But say, May Webster is completely gone over you.' Ed laughed uncontrollably.

'Why, that's a good one, all right.'

'But she is. It makes me laugh to think of it. Every night when I drive them home May has something to say about Murray, what a nice boy he is. And say, the other night what kind of hint do you suppose she gave me?'

'Pretty strong one, the way you're stringing it now.'

'No, but honest ... She says, "Can't Murray drive a car, Ed?" she says. I says, "Say, I never thought of that." '

'Silly. She's simple, all right. She didn't want it to mean that.'

'I tell you, she's completely wild about you.'

'Yes, ain't it too bad? Now if I had a real nice-looker eating out of my hand like you got – '

'Aw, talk sense,' said Ed impatiently. 'She's not, and you know she's not. But May – she sure is a goner.'

'I suppose – the fond thing,' said Murray in a resigned tone.

'Fond – that's a funny word,' said Ed. 'I didn't know you went in for old English or Middle English, or whatever it is.'

'That's a word we have up in the north, meaning kind of soft and silly and harmless.'

'No woman is harmless,' said Ed sagely.

'Don't you wish you knew it?' said Murray. Ed laughed.

'Sure I do. I ain't got the technique. I would have a job stealing a kiss. Where does a guy get the nerve?'

Murray shrugged. 'Maybe he don't need any, it just happens.'

'That,' declared Ed, 'is beyond me. Unless it would be a different kind of girl from any I've ever known.'

'Well, no, I don't think that follows. Oh, a lot depends on the girl, of course, but the time and the place are more important than you might think, too.'

'Well, you wouldn't want to be making indecent proposals, as they call them, in church, I can understand.' Ed laughed; 'We're strong on theory all right, but as for cutting loose with the wine women and song like the college magazines talk about – we must have gone to the wrong colleges.'

Murray had a frown like puzzlement on his brow. 'As far as making proposals in church or any other place goes, from what've seen of ladies' men, I doubt if they bother to make 'em anywhere. Things just happen.'

'Now that,' said Ed, striking his fist on the table with enthusiasm, 'is probably the root of the matter. That's the way with most things in this world – they just happen. It must be just the same with a fellow when he – when he starts an affair with a woman. But the question is, how in thunder do they happen?'

'That's what a lot of us would like to know,' said Murray, wagging his head. 'I'm not any ladies' man myself, and I believe in heading away from trouble. But all the same I think I can see how the boys get into it.'

'Just let Nature take its course, eh? Hurray for Nature, says me. I'd like to sow a few wild oats, in a fence corner where they wouldn't get tromped on like.' His jocular tone was not meant to indicate a lack of serious intent. He really hoped that Murray would be able to give him some words that would enable him to pursue a course likely to make life more interesting. In college he had been a sort of lone wolf, living in a boarding house away from the college, and meeting other students only in classes and on the skating rink. 'It's too bad, really, that it's so late in the season and you have to go so soon. We might have started something with those two girls if we had had more time.'

'Yeah. But there's nothing to stop you now. What help do you expect me to be? Think I should throw a sling-rope around the two of you and tie you together?'

'Well, there's courage in numbers.'

'Maybe up to a certain point. If you put me in the front seat with one girl, I would promise not to look around.' Murray was rubbing his chin.

'Say, you want to shave, don't you? Should have reminded me.' Ed lit the gas burner and filled the tap at the sink, which brought water from the pressure tank in the barn. 'Amos and Eleanor'll be home soon, I suppose.' Murray got out his razor and soap and brush. 'So the conclusion of our conference is that we are a pair of impractical theorizers.'

'Oh, I don't know. Maybe not so impractical after all,' said Murray as it were indulgently.

'Sure we are,' Ed insisted. 'That's all it ever amounts to, talk.'

By the time they had shaved and Ed had changed into a white shirt and collar and the trousers of a suit, and Murray had gone out to throw the horses some hay, Eleanor and Amos had returned. Eleanor came straight to the house, and Amos stopped to talk to Murray on his way in.

'Should have been there, Edward. He was preaching about reconciling religion to the intellectual life. Old Mr Blodgett slept as usual.'

Ed looked up from his magazine politely. 'That's all right, but where's the intellectual life?' He was surprised to see that her face really seemed to glow as though the sermon had made her happier. She came back to the kitchen in a minute, in an old dress, and started getting dinner. Murray went up and dressed. After dinner, of which they all ate heartily by habit, there did not seem to be much to do. The boys went out on the veranda, and Amos took a nap in the sitting-room. After a while he went out and took a walk through the orchard which during the week he scarcely had time to go through. The young fellows talked and read and smoked. There was silence in the house. Presently Amos returned and gave each of the boys a long oblong large peach, yellow, but for a deep red cheek on one side.

'What do you think of that, you fellows? There's going to be three or four thousand baskets of those. When I went down the hill I could see them, and I could hardly believe my eyes, when I saw them red as doors. We'll have to start on them tomorrow. Round up all the pickers we can find.'

V

It was hard getting started Monday morning. Amos, of course, went early with a truck load that should have been sold Saturday. Ed spent an hour calling all their old pickers in the city, and adjuring them to come out on the nine car if they couldn't make the seven, or on the eleven. Or even promise to come tomorrow. May Webster and Florine Gravel and other local girls came on time, brought by their folks. Murray went to the orchard with them, distributed empty baskets in the new rows of Elbertas, and got them started to pick. In a little while the loads of full baskets began to come up to the barn; but there was no one there to pack. Ed cursed, packing by himself, and selling two or three bushels to motorists. He went to meet the nine car, and only three girls were there, and not the best ones at that. He set them at packing.

In the orchard the gang seemed full of spirits as though glad to get back at the job. Sunday had been as dull for them as for him, Murray thought. The peaches were about twice as large, and the trees for some reason not so tall as the earlier varieties. They certainly were raking them off. Florine and May Webster were working down one row, sharing a ladder between them, and four other girls were taking two other rows. This section of the orchard lay along a stream which was screened by trees and thick bushes of sumach. As Murray drove to the end to turn around and collect a load, he saw May coming out of these bushes. She had disappeared some time ago and he had thought nothing of it. But it seemed a little strange that she should have gone so far. Probably wanted to avoid him, he thought, until she stopped and said something as he passed. He didn't know why he pulled the horses up; perhaps because he didn't know what it was she had said.

'I said you seemed to be in a hurry, for Monday morning.'

'You're pretty industrious yourself, May. I see you and Florine keep ahead of the others most of the time.'

'Oh, me, I'd rather go lie down alongside the brook and have a snooze. Don't you feel lazy a day like this?'

'I feel lazy any day,' said Murray with a laugh. 'But we got to keep going.'

'Aw, I guess nobody'd say anything if you was to stop a minute to talk to a person.'

'Oh, I suppose not, but when there's so much to be done, you feel like keeping at it.'

'Anybody'd think you didn't like me,' said May, with a curious boldness.

'Sure, I like girls,' said Murray quickly.

'All kinds but my kind,' said May sadly. 'Is that what you mean?' He saw that a tear was starting from her eye, and the way she held her head averted from him and downcast, it was going to run right off the top of her not-so-badly shaped nose. He should have slashed the horses ahead in the first place. It was too late now. He stood on the wagon, trying not to look at her, and she was not looking at him. Why in thunder should she feel sentimental about him? He had merely treated her like the rest, goodnatured and decent, like a foreman over them. He might as well take a couple of jumps at once, since apparently he held kings.

'I tell you, May, we been working so hard here, I never have the time to get out and get acquainted with girls I might like. And now it's got so it's too late. Next week I've got to be back at college, so I'll have to – to give up all hopes. But maybe I'll be back next summer.'

'I – I'm sorry you're going, Murray,' sniffled May.

Murray's pity was converted to a disgust based on some kind of fear. He couldn't turn it into amusement. He twitched the lines unobtrusively, hoping that the spirited little horses would bolt; but they stood rooted. 'So'm I in a way,' he said, with an awkward lightness.

'You're just saying that, Murray. You don't care.'

'Say!' he exclaimed. 'You're not feeling well, are you? Suppose you just go over to the stream there and sit down for a while till you feel better. You can bathe your face, and I'll tell one of the other girls to come over if you like.'

'No, you won't.' She lifted her head and trudged off, her old-fashioned blue print sunbonnet high. Murray grinned as he walked his team along the row to pick up the baskets. She was really not worth bothering about, in any case. Though she was not so homely when you got a good look at her, even though she was crying. It would certainly be foolish to say anything of this to Ed. He was silly enough.

In the afternoon reinforcements came from the city, and the barn floor was soon piled high with lidded baskets. Amos had returned after dinner, and Ed had loaded the truck while he was eating. He was going to take this load into the north country twenty miles beyond the market town. No doubt the storekeepers there would have been canvassed before by other growers, but some of them might take a few baskets. He might dump them on commission to a jobber, on the way back, ship them from the station in town. They had tried that with small lots to a Collingwood firm and a Toronto firm before; the returns were not back yet. Some of the packers agreed to stay until the seven car, since they had come so late, but that meant two trips with the horses. They went at the usual time. May and Florine said they had to be home a little earlier for supper, so Ed set out with them in the car at a quarter to six, and drove forty miles an hour.

After their own supper there were the chores, and they were sitting wearily in the barn door talking when Amos drove into the yard, put on his brakes smartly, turned off lights and motor, and stepped down as jocundly as though he had been out for a little pleasure spin.

'The wanderer returns,' sang out Ed sombrely.

'Hello, you kids,' said Amos, coming over to them. 'How's tricks?'

'Not so hot,' said Murray. 'Take a look at what's here.' Both ends of the barn were still open. Amos peeped.

'Gee whizz, you got some peaches, eh?'

'They was clawing them off,' Murray explained.

'Must have picked five hundred baskets today,' said Ed.

'And they're just getting steam up in them Elbertas.'

Amos threw up his hands and went into supper, less jocund.

Ed rose with a groan and brought the truck over to cast its lights upon the packing tables. Wearily the two began to sort the fruit and place it in tiers.

'These are harder to pack than the others,' said Murray.

'Makes the girls cuss. The top row has to be on its flat side, and of course it doesn't look worse if the red side is up.'

'I get you,' said Murray ironically.

'Honest, I'm so tired I'm nearly drunk. The notion of a few more hours packing in those headlights does not appeal to me a bit.'

'It looks as though it's got to be done. Peaches are perishable.'

'That's a fact too. There, I put a rotten one in the basket I was packing, and threw a good one into the soft basket.'

Amos came out with the lantern in a few minutes. 'Boys, we've got to solve the problem. And I think I've found the solution. Anyway, I'm going to take the car and run over to the Junction.'

'Did you have much trouble getting rid of them today?' Ed asked.

Amos shook his head, but they knew what he meant. 'My plan is this, what do you think of it? I'm going over to the express agent's house and get rates for a refrigerator car to Winnipeg. They'll get there a couple of days after they leave here. And they should bring about twice as much as here where the market's glutted. I was reading in the *Farmer's Sun* yesterday that Toronto is flooded with Niagara fruit. There seems to be a glut on the market all over. The highest grade is eighty-five cents an eleven-quart basket, and you can bet it's going to get worse from now to the end of the season. What do you think of the idea, fellows?'

'Well, it should be better than to leave them rot on the ground.'

'It'll provide work for a bunch of worthy people,' said Murray.

'No, jokes aside, doesn't it seem that it should be better than taking a chance on selling them here? We'd have to ship to Toronto or Montreal anyway, and everybody's going to do that, doing it now.'

'Doing what, Turkey trot?'

'Why, it should be all right,' said Murray soberly. 'And if it means handling the whole crop in one transaction, it should save a lot of worry and running.'

'Then I'll do it. I'll just hop into the car now.' They noticed as he left the light that he was wearing his dark blue coat over his working clothes, and wondered why he had asked their advice. In a little over an hour he returned. The agent said he could get them a car for tomorrow noon. He had unlocked the station and wired for it in his presence, a full-size refrigerator car, which would hold eighty thousand pounds. They were to figure out how many baskets that would be, so as not to overload it. Arrived at this solution of the problem, they felt better, and closed the barn up and put the truck away without loading it. The express car would not be ready until noon anyway.

In the morning there seemed to be a hundred things to do. The seven car was met by the truck, the country girls arrived, and the pickers were instructed to pick only peaches firm enough to stay fresh a week at least. The packers were questioned about their packing of yesterday. Had there been any large proportion of over-ripe peaches in the baskets packed? After tearing the lids off twenty-five or so, Amos decided that there had not and that they might all go in the express car. But in packing the rest they were to be more careful than ever. Then he had to take the car and try to round up a few more pickers. It was not so easy. Boys were no good, except to pelt one another as soon as your back was turned and eat what they didn't use in battle. Men were unobtainable, and wages too high anyway. And most of the local women who were willing to go out were working in other orchards. He came back at noon with a huge woman of about fifty and massively melancholy mien, accompanied by a boy of eight or ten, from whom she had refused to be parted. Ed, looking out of the window from the dinner table, remarked to Murray that there would doubtless be no difficulty in disposing of their crop now. The woman could eat the sour and the kid the ripe ones. Amos, coming in hungry at the moment, said, rather aggrievedly, that that was the best he could do. He would put an advertisement in the city paper for tomorrow. Don't let him forget to phone it in after dinner.

Murray informed him that the stock of eleven-quart baskets with handles nailed to them was near depletion. Amos raised his arms, and swore. He would have to get some boys in the village to nail handles on the rest. They had spent weeks nailing handles on baskets of all sizes, expecting to sell a lot of small sizes on the market and elsewhere. But fruit had been so cheap that everyone wanted eleven-quart baskets. And they had only nailed the handles on about two thousand of them. There was only one more thousand to be nailed. He would have to get in touch with the basket factory and order another three thousand, or if possible exchange some of the small sizes for elevens. He tore from the house, and Eleanor was left to call the paper and give the advertisement. Two hours later he returned with three small boys, their mouths pursed sober, their eyes inscrutable. Stacks of nested baskets were brought out, and bunches of handles and cartons of tiny nails. They were soon driving the nails with a blow apiece and racing. Murray came and found some of the handles not sticking very well, and reprimanded them.

Ed meanwhile had got the truck loaded and started with it after dinner for the station. The trip was only about six miles each way, so that he counted on taking quite a few loads in a day. When he got there the local that brought the car had just arrived, and after unloading some miscellaneous goods at the depot, began shunting. When the agent seemed to have a moment to spare he informed Ed that he might as well take his truck to the other side of the track, as the car was going to be switched over there. Ed backed and turned and went out to the highway and in along the switch, and sat over the wheel a few minutes until the car was placed. Then the engine shunted back to the main track, the brakeman coupled her, the conductor confided a few farewell remarks to the station agent as he gave the last signals and stepped aboard the caboose as it swept by at a respectable clip. Then the agent went in to report to the dispatcher, came out, and wandered across the track and took the seals off the car and opened the doors. It was a swell car, a real refrigerator car, the kind that went in an express train and looked like the pullmans so far as shape went. Ed walked from one end to the other inside it, and it echoed to his voice. There was even ice in the bunkers at the end, as he found when he climbed up outside. The agent said something about leaving the ventilators open as long as they were loading, because there wasn't enough ice to do any good. The car would be iced at Detroit.

On an express car that was to cost over twelve hundred, the agent came in for considerable commission, so he was very obliging, and came over from the depot whenever the truck hove in sight, unless he was meeting a train, and helped place the baskets, puffing and sweating the while. They figured that a proper load would be nine tiers deep, and that would make over fifteen hundred baskets. Ed kept hauling from noon till ten o'clock the first night, taking Murray along to help as the agent had long ago quit. Over five hundred baskets were packed away, and he was beginning to catch up with the packers.

Next day it seemed late again before the gang could be got started. The boys were not doing a very good job nailing handles, and Ed was sure that he or Murray could have nailed as many as all of them together, but there was nothing to be done. They didn't try to drive every nail with one stroke while he was about, or Amos. Amos stayed at the barn and watched the packers and parlayed with customers – Ed was sure he spent too much time on them and even went down into the orchard with old friends of their father. Ed drove off in a huff to get a load of new baskets and handles which had come to the depot at Wyndham, and reflected on the way that if it had been a matter of selling peaches Amos would have wanted to go himself. He didn't seem to trust his brother to that extent. But if it was unloading peaches with furious haste in a sweltering dark night, or going after a load of baskets, that was good enough for Ed. No, Ed reasoned with himself, perhaps it had just occurred to Amos that Ed enjoyed driving the truck and that he might now be given his share of it. Such a thought naturally wouldn't occur to him when there was a prospect of selling a load for a few dollars more than Ed might have got for it.

In spite of his urgency, it was late dinner by the time he drove into the farmyard, with a load of baskets nestled in tall piles above the ladders of the truck – a topheavy load. The boys and Amos unloaded them while he ate his dinner. Eleanor had finished the dishes and after pouring his tea went to fix up for the afternoon. He was later than yesterday with his first load for the express car at the Junction, and again he and Murray took a load over in the evening. Amos came along this time, to see what kind of car they had given him, and how the load was shaping up. Ed drove home at savage speed over the gravelled roads which were like a washboard from the summer traffic – clinging to the wheel while the others bounced to the jolts of the unloaded springs. As he lay in bed and from some vague determination to make a full day of it read a magazine by an oil lamp, he remembered that he hadn't seen Florine for a long time. Was Murray driving the girls home these nights, or Amos? Amos, he supposed. Murray would have the chores and the cows. And then, he wasn't interested in May. But he might have been in Florine, 'my little girl,' thought Ed sleepily, waking himself up enough to blow the light out.

VI

The car was loaded by Thursday noon. Amos went along to the Junction and watched the agent make a shipping bill as casually as though it represented the expressing of a box of hot-house flowers. At last the doors were sealed, a discussion of the ventilators was over, and they drove away. Amos looked back at the car standing lonely at the switch. He was worried about the icing of it en route, and wondered whether his consignee would wire on its safe arrival. Ed told him that he should have stowed away aboard it and gone with the peaches to see that they kept. They had caught up temporarily. The huge gang had cleared off every Elberta reasonably ripe, and the car had taken all but a hundred or so baskets. But the back orchard, which seemed later, was going to come on them like an avalanche next week.

With a small gang they went over the orchard for the ripest, Friday and Saturday. Amos took the truck on the road again. Ed and Florine were packing. She was a cute kid all right, and he was annoyed that there were so many interruptions to their conversations. The boys were still hammering away at baskets in the driveshed, and more and more motorist customers were coming. When she looked at him she laughed, for some reason. She went into the granary to set aside a basket for herself. Ed followed, and put his arms around her. For the rest of the day she laughed at him more and he was uneasy and excited about his failure and a determination to better it at the next opportunity. He drove her and May Webster home as in the old days, morose and solemn, and did not cheer up when he was bidding her good-bye. He couldn't make up his mind to tell her he would come and see her tomorrow. He didn't see how it would help matters, and said nothing.

When he got home he found a shiny new sedan drawn up in the yard, and Amos talking to the man in it. Nothing surprising about that. He found a devil of a lot of time to visit with people; there was even nothing strange about the identity of the man, a garage owner, who liked the taste of peaches as well as anyone else, no doubt. But when they strolled over and began eying the old touring car as he was getting out of it he got nervous.

'Missed all the gate posts and stray hogs,' he said, 'and didn't even take off a buggy wheel. If you inspect the tires you take all responsibility for any punctures occurring while you are driving her.'

Amos replied as though he had not heard this thrust. 'I'm thinking of making a deal for the sedan over yonder.' The other man was circling the touring car perfunctorily. He nodded when they told him she ran all right. He had seen her on the road for four years. Ed went away to the barn and told Murray that his college year had gone up in gasoline smoke. When the chores were done the car-dealer was gone and Amos was leaving. They asked him to wait while they climbed into their clothes. On the way to town he told them that the deal had been made and he was going in to sign the papers and bring back the new car. In the barber shop they met Dave and some other fellows, and they all went out to see the new sedan, the City Ann, as one called it. Amos had to give them a ride from one end of Main Street to the other and back. Traffic was thick and the road unpaved and dusty save in front of the biggest stores, where it was oiled. Amos drove about ten miles an hour, and led a procession of honkers.

They got home at midnight and tumbled into bed. Not even Murray was up before eight the next morning. It was Sunday, for which they thanked Heaven. After breakfast Amos strolled at ease about the yard admiring his newly dusted car, which sat in the middle of it, where passers-by could see and surmise that it was not an early visitor's. When Murray went to the house with the milk he did not come back to the barn, and Ed, continuing with the stable cleaning, which had been neglected two days, wondered where he had gone. Having finished the chores with a fine feeling of martyrdom, he found Murray talking to Amos, quite confidentially, apparently. They were sitting in the chair seats of the car. Ed came up to talk to them through the window.

'Murray says he'll stay and see us through,' Amos said. 'Can't blame him for not wanting to miss school, but by jingo we're in such a box, we're buried in peaches, that's all. We got to keep shovellin' ourselves free!'

Murray laughed, and there was emotion in his voice. Ed glanced at him. He often marvelled at Amos's ability to 'get around' people and drive difficult bargains obviously to his own advantage. He supposed that Amos had put it up to Murray that loyalty demanded that he stick, now that they had got so far. Now Amos quickly turned the conversation to the car, and they found after microscopic investigation that there was a scratch near the tire carrier, and almost no gasoline in the tank. Nor was there any in the galvanized drum in the driveshed. Ed insisted that they should run down to the village at once and get gasoline, or someone would be stranded with the thing. Amos didn't like the idea of running the car up and down the roads at once. The neighbours might think he was showing off. He was going to church and he'd get it then. As though the words had been a signal, Eleanor stuck her head out of the window, calling musically and not querulously. Amos went to fix up for church.

'Too bad gasoline costs money,' said Ed, 'or I'd drive the thing down and get her filled myself. Should take the drum down and get it filled.'

'Nice car to take her out in,' agreed Murray.

'Say,' Ed looked around toward the house. 'I've got an inspiration. We'll bone him to let us take the car this afternoon. We haven't been out with the other one, Lord knows. He can't refuse. But when we get away and she's full of gas, maybe we won't travel, eh?'

Eleanor came out and smilingly admired the mirror-like finish and the upholstery. 'Now you boys will be wishing you came to church,' she said. 'Maybe you'll get ready and come next Sunday.'

'I guess I should go once more before I leave,' said Murray. Eleanor got into the car. Ed wondered at her not saying anything about his agreeing to stay a couple of weeks longer, though Amos must have told her in the house. He came out now, in his dark suit and good felt hat. The young fellows stood and saw them off. The new car slid away smoothly, and once out of the lane she got away quickly.

'They'll knock an eye out of the people waiting for church to start.'

'I tell you,' said Ed with gleeful solemnity, 'if we don't get that car for this afternoon we're fools.'

They leaned against the fence of the yard and were starting one of their conversations when a Ford drove into the lane from the direction in which Amos had gone. 'Somebody for peaches.' said Murray.

'Oh, hell, what'll I do?' Ed asked. 'If Amos hears of it – '

'Is this Mr Burkin's farm?' asked a nasal voice. A large sunburnt face stooped out beneath the car top. Ed nodded. The other got out. 'Got some peaches picked, or are they all down in the orchard?' There were two women in the back seat, with a clothes basket between them. Here was a certain market for a couple of bushels at least. Ed reflected that it would make Amos mad, but when he was about to sell on that account, he thought that it might come to his father's ears that peaches were being sold on Sunday on his farm.

'I tell you; we've got them all right, good ones, priced right, but I can't let you have them today. We never sold peaches on Sunday. It's a rule my dad made. Sorry, but you know how it is.'

The man was silent an instant, unable to take offense at this smooth representation of the case. 'Won't sell, well, what you know about that? I couldn't get away in week time, you see.'

'Well, we'll have them all next week and the week after, if you can make it then. Or if you came a long distance you can get them today, from the neighbours. You won't have to go far.

'Well, say, that's right obliging of you. I guess I'll get 'em today, I come a long ways, all right.' The car ground ahead. 'Much obliged.'

'Seems to me I've seen our friend before,' said Murray with a gesture of the head toward the departing ones. 'These dialogues they have at the church entertainments: Uncle Hiram.'

'Stage type,' said Ed, strolling toward the house. 'I'm going to put on my Sunday best for this afternoon. You with me?'

'Sure, only I know where we'll land.'

Ed could not contain his grin. 'You know more than I do, then. Where do you want to go?' Preceding, he held the screen door open for his friend.

'Well there are one or two girls who might be interested in seeing a feller's new car.'

'You mean May Webster and what's her name? You wouldn't want to get near them, would you, with only a couple more weeks to go?' Murray did not reply to this reference to his agreement to prolong his stay. 'Still, you can go quite a ways in two weeks.'

'Too far, maybe.'

'If a fellow's slow he'll never go too far.'

'I tell you. You think I'm not game, I'll take you up on it. We'll go and call on those girls this afternoon.' Murray sat at the kitchen table reading yesterday's paper.

Amos and Eleanor were surprised to find them both dressed up. Ed wore an iron-gray light-weight suit he had had for several seasons, and Murray his good navy blue, with an expensive dark tie, which Ed jocularly tried to barter away from him. At dinner it was as though they too had attended church. But it seemed that their unanimity and good spirits were owing to something else hard to explain, unless it were the fact that Murray was to be with them longer than they had expected. When Eleanor insisted on his having a second piece of her fig pie with rich whipped cream top, it was with a girlish pretty air, almost a blush – or was it the heat of the stove? Ed had never thought of Eleanor as pretty. You might call her noble-looking, statuesque, a fine woman, with her pink and white features, large but not coarse, and her heavy crown of amber hair. But there was an air about her now. ...

'I suppose everyone admired your new vehicle of expression,' he told Amos. Eleanor laughed.

'They weren't much more surprised than us. When I came out of church and started to get into another old car without looking, Amos gave my arm such a jerk!

'That's something I can't understand,' Amos said. 'When you catch me mistaking anything of mine for someone else's, let me know.'

'Always pick the best one, that's my motto when I make a mistake,' Murray said. Eleanor glanced at him.

'Sure.' Amos's voice almost echoed Murray's. Ed, his eyes on his plate, pondered. What ailed Amos? He had no reason, surely, to be jealous of Murray. Yet, there seemed to have been something strange in the atmosphere between them at times. Then little incidents returned to Ed's mind, pictures of Murray and Eleanor laughing together when he came into the house, Murray's generally almost pointed silence in respect to his employer's wife. ... Of course Amos was an idiot to think such a thing, but well, you could hardly blame him. Perhaps that was why Amos had put off so long asking Murray to stay and help finish the crop. And then, perhaps that was the cause of the emotion the young man had shown in making the decision to stay. Ed passed his cup for a third cup of tea in silence. Amos was telling how easy on gasoline the new car was supposed to be, and how fast it would go after you had driven it slowly the first thousand miles. But the moment was not yet.

Ed waited until after dinner and got Amos alone when he was starting for the back pasture with some salt for the cattle. Amos was not too keen about it, but Ed had his arguments ready. The matter of college was still between them. He didn't need to ask if it was because he was mad at Murray. They were to take a little spin in the car, yes.

No sooner had Amos disappeared than they put their hats on, and started. Eleanor was listening to some service given by radio. The motor had a stiff intensity about it as though it would just automatically bore up hills or through tree trunks. They droned along, thrilled with importance. Murray gazed from his window with head held at an aristocratic angle. He was a good-looking youth. It occurred to Ed that he had no idea of the other's family. They were probably very good farm people, and well-to-do. The car turned north on the town-line, the road that led to the market town, but it turned off after a few miles. Then they turned into a yard neat and bare as most French farms are, and turned about before the little gate to the house lawn. Florine came running out, her eyes gleaming with candid pleasure.

'How did you find your way?' she asked with a gurgle of laughter.

'We had to try out the new car,' Murray said; she was nearest him.

'Say, I didn't know who it was at first. Is it yours?' she asked Ed.

'It's mine for this afternoon. It's in the family, I guess.'

'He means,' explained Murray genially, 'that Amos bought it last night.'

'Well, it's a beauty, yes. How it is pretty! Did you buy it for take your girl for joyriding?'

'Sure,' said Ed, 'jump in.'

'Won't you come in please to the house?' said Florine as though not understanding.

'We thought maybe you'd like to go for a drive,' explained Ed. 'We'll call around for May too. I think Murray is very anxious to see her.'

Florine laughed her gurgling laughter. 'Shore, I will like it. Wait one minute, I will get my hat.' She walked sedately back to the house.

'Wonder what her people are like?' Ed speculated. 'The boy that drives her over sometimes is long and skinny and wears homemade overalls and jackets. I didn't think there were any more in Ontario. Mamma is big and fat and counting her beads, I suppose, and papa is smoking his corncob with homegrown hump. Eh?'

'Maybe they're human just the same,' suggested Murray.

'Here she comes.' Ed laughed good-naturedly as Murray got out and held the front door open for Florine to sit beside him. She was wearing a stiff brown changeable silk dress, and a light-coloured straw hat with tiny daisies in it. She was amused and pleased, and anything but ill at ease. But there was astoundingly little to say, after the endless repartee to which they were accustomed as they packed peaches in the barn. That was probably the presence of Murray. Things should limber up a little when they got May in the back with him.

The Webster house was far back from the road, beside a long lane. A dog ran out barking at them. Ed had a momentary fright lest he should scratch the finish of the car, which would give Amos something to talk about.

Sure enough, when May came bouncing out to the car, her face wreathed in smiles and looking as though she had been taking a nap, everyone began talking and laughing at once. She insisted that they come in while she fixed up to go with them, but they remained in the car, until May burst forth again. Murray said 'Permit me, Moddam,' as he held the car door for her.

Once on the road, she and Murray were never still. Ed found himself listening with a superior air, which he thought was shared by Florine. She certainly appeared more ladylike than May. But that Murray was an accomplished kidder, all right. The funny part was the way May seemed to be gone on him, to adore him, positively. There was no doubt as to whether she would let him kiss her. It would be fun to have them in the back seat after dark and suddenly switch on the ceiling light. Right now Murray probably had his arm around her, but it was not worth while glancing around. Florine was not bothering with them, but maintaining a ladylike pose, her knees crossed.

'Any particular place you'd like to go?' Ed tossed back.

'Wherever the car goes,' sang May.

'There's no dancing places open on Sunday,' said Murray.

'That leaves it to us, Florine. Where do you want to go?'

'Just a nice drive, not too long. Say along the lake.'

'All right. We're going along the lake, folks. Too bad you haven't got your bathing suits. I'll tell you when we get there,' he added.

'Maybe we could hire them,' suggested May. Ed was silent. He did not want to spoil such an occasion, when they were immaculately dressed, in an immaculate car, by driving down sandy roads to some crowded resort and cavorting on the beach and in the water, with the publicity which May would inevitably draw upon them. That would be just a trifle too much.

'May says she wants to go wherever there are no peaches,' he called. They all laughed. 'And the faster the better.' Ed stepped on the gas, the car swept up a low hill at thirty-five, and he stepped harder. Amos would have plenty of opportunity to treat it carefully.

'Now we're going,' said Florine with her gurgling laughter.

'Woops m'dear,' screeched May from behind.

They were crossing a broad ridge which carried the main Detroit-Buffalo highway. A roadster with two men and a girl in it appeared before them as if by magic. Ed was going forty at least, and what spared them a crash was the fact that the east and west highway here curved, and the intersection was unusually broad. The roadster had expected the curve, and was under control. Ed's car swayed dangerously on the side of the ditch, righted itself and swept on evenly.

'Made to order,' remarked Murray.

'If you want to scare us out of ten years' growth it was just right, Ed Burkin,' said May Webster. 'Better not do that again!'

Ed snorted with amusement. Florine looked at him enquiringly.

'I guess I better let Amos break her in for speed. It's his car anyhow.'

'There were two killed at that corner last summer,' said Florine. It was strange that she was aware of things going on here, living hidden on a back road as she did, Ed thought. He was touched somehow.

They went on through a low-lying country of dark rich soil, different from the gravel of the peach orchards. Here were vast fields of beans. Large old brick houses and fine barns marked the farms. These were successful farmers, consistent, growing beans every year. If a fellow worked hard and didn't give up in bad years, or spend too much in good ones, or have a mortgage to pay on, it was possible to be comfortably fixed after twenty-five years. Maybe it wasn't such a bad life after all. It came to Ed that he too could take over a sizeable farm, work it to suit himself, even marry and have a house of his own. Or if he was in no hurry about settling down he could make Amos toe the mark, give him more money and shorter hours, and sow some wild oats. Where was the sense of yearnings for some imagined larger sphere? He didn't even know what he could be. If he could imagine himself asking his father to mortgage the farm to put him through seven or eight years to make a doctor or lawyer, what then? Would he like it, especially when he would have to slave for years to pay back his borrowing? There must be other occupations, more interesting, and just as dignified and paying, but he was blessed if he could think what they were. Florine was asking him something. To blazes with the whole question. It would solve itself, when he did not turn up to register for his second year at college.

'What?'

'May was telling me to poke you in the ribs and wake you up.'

'I like that. Why, I'm the life of the party. Wouldn't have any excitement if anyone else was driving.'

'I don't like excitement. Do you?' Her dark blue eyes were looking out of the corners of their lids at him.

'Not a bit. But I like people who like excitement, even when they say they don't.'

She turned to her window, then said. 'Now you're keeding.'

'Say,' Murray called. 'May wants to go in swimming. She says she'll race Ed for the cones.'

'Oh, Murray Karch! I never said any such thing.'

They had come to lower country again, and a sight of the blue lake above young cedars. They turned to the right, on an oiled highway, passed various gasoline stations and confectionery booths, and came to a row of cottages and a pier. There were people in bathing suits here and there along the shore, but it was marshy, being on an inlet called Rond Eau. They left the car and walked out on the pier. A score of people were looking absorbedly into the water, and what they saw was a man swimming on his back under water. It was less than six feet to the sandy bottom. He was moving his joints like a frog's, and his eyes were open. May turned away and clung to Murray's arm. It made her feel like heartburn, she said, trying to adjust her vocabulary to the select company.

From a word dropped here and there, it was evident that the primary attraction for these people was a large launch which could be heard thrumming half a dozen miles down the Eau. 'Air-plane engine ... Liberty motor,' a young boy was saying. They decided not to wait. By the time they should have got back it would be getting late in the afternoon. They were fifteen miles from where the girls lived.

They drove back along the ridge, through the peach country. The land was dry, and weeds grew among the rows in the older orchards. In some orchards the ground was yellow with ripe peaches fallen. Ed exclaimed triumphantly. They at least had not let the peaches swamp them. He felt like a conqueror. The powerful surge of the car beneath him confirmed it; they had struggled and won, and they would win more through struggle that would become a value in itself. As martyrs came to like their hair-shirts, Ed felt that he would always look back to these days of furious unending endeavour. But you should be able to relax too, to accept pleasures like a man of the world. A year before, and at the time of his entrance to college, he had been a boy, he felt. Now, he was about to enter the stage of manhood. Yet, somehow, he was sure that that would be disappointing.

He was to be excused from conversation as the driver and the employer and host; but the two in the back seat became more pensive also, apparently. Perhaps Murray had reached his limit. They were silent as they drove into the long lane of the Webster farm. May's father came out of the house to the little gate.

'Come on, get out,' he said, 'you can't go home right away now.'

'Oh, we had a grand drive, Pa. We went clear to the Eau.'

They sat talking half among themselves. It wouldn't do to ignore the old man. He would think the Burkins uppish. Ed opened his door, and Florine got out too, as though accustomed to visiting here. May and Murray got out, Ed began asking Mr Webster about his second cutting of alfalfa, but the other didn't grow any, and his clover was not ready yet, as he was letting it go for seed. He was at fall-plowing, and corn-cutting was done. May gave a yell. 'Now, Pa, you can do something for us. I'm going in and get the camera, and you can take a picture of us.' Ed glanced at Murray, who had a smug smile, as though there was a joke on somebody. 'That's right,' he exclaimed, 'bring on your camera if you want a chance to take two goodlooking couples at once.

When the old man pointed the camera at them, May was beaming brightly enough to ruin the negative; Murray had adopted an easy hands-in-pocket pose of a well-dressed-young-man-with-his-hat-on. Ed held his hands down stiffly at his sides, and tried to outstare the low sun, while Florine was smiling with pursed lips, leaning forward a little, her head bent a little with an intimate look. They all started talking at once when the father looked up. Then somehow the two girls disappeared, and the fellows were left talking to Mr Webster. Time was passing, but they were surprised when May appeared at the back door in an apron, and told them that supper was nearly ready, and to go into the front room and sit down. Ed started to object; they should get home. Amos would wonder what had become of his new car; but Murray was silent, and he seemed to be in the minority, and didn't want to be a kill-joy. The old man held open the screen door of the front steps – there was no veranda – and told them to make themselves at home. He went away to the barn.

The two young men sat on a horsehair lounge and eyed each other accusingly, then laughed aloud. The girls were laughing and talking in the kitchen. Finally Murray's eye lit upon a stereopticon, and they viewed Niagara Falls and the royal palace at Brussels. Ed adjusted his neck-tie, stretched out his legs upon the heels, and surrendered himself to gloom. 'Amos will sure give us hell,' he muttered.

The girls came into the room. 'The things are on the stove,' said May, 'and will be ready in a few minutes, soon as the tea kettle boils. Now we might have some music while we wait. Don't you play, Florine?'

The French girl shook her head. May sat down before the upright piano and played. Really it was quite charming to one with an empty stomach, and an uncertain mind. Ed asked her the name of the piece. 'Beethoven's Minuet in G,' she tossed back as she went to the kitchen. The tune haunted him, unrecallable.

The table was set for four only. There was corn on the cob, of the garden, not the field variety, fried potatoes, cold meat, and preserved plums, and a plate of cookies large and deep as saucers. They did not need to talk much while there was food before them. When the meal was finished they went into the front room again, and May played for them. Ed wanted the Minuet in G. There was an ordered harmony about it strangely moving to him. Now that supper was past he would have willingly stayed the evening. It was Murray who suggested that they must get back. Florine got her hat, and she and Ed sat in the rear seat, while Murray had the privilege of driving the new car.

'We had a good time at May's, yes? She plays music good?' They had dropped into the middle of the deep seat, and her arm and elbow brushed against him. It would be quite easy now to reach out and grasp her fingers, but it was just as well not to start anything. 'I'm glad you came around – with your new car.'

'Good time was right, only there wasn't enough of it. You and I don't need any one to help us talk together.'

'They don't help much, eh?' she whispered, laughing. She glanced at Murray. Ed had counted on his sympathy and had not bothered to lower his voice. Suddenly he felt that she was not adverse, that if they were to be alone something, anything, might happen. Desire began to stir in him, strangely conscious, for it had not been so in her presence before, even when he tried to kiss her in the barn. He felt that he could pursue her for ever. Murray was driving absorbedly, saying nothing, though he must have wondered at the silence. Ed slipped his arm behind Florine, but they were meeting a buggy and another car. Then they were turning into her home yard. Still there seemed to be no-one about, until a couple of boys came to the open stable door and watched.

'I had a good time. It was nice of you boys to come. Would you come in my house now?'

'Can't,' Ed said. 'Got to go home to do the chores.' It was Murray upon whom this was imperative. He had an impulse to say he would come back in the evening.

'Well, good-bye, Florine,' said Murray. Ed climbed into the front seat with him. She stood, flatteringly, in the yard until they had turned on the road, and waved at them. Ed lifted his hat.

'Good-time had by all?' Murray asked.

'Sure. Only I was wishing at the last we had taken the car in the evening.'

'You are getting reckless. May's a good cook, and musical too. She had the chance to shine this time. There may be better-looking girls...' Murray wagged his head.

'It's just possible,' Ed laughed. 'Why should she be so cow-like? Her face is actually twice as long as Florine's. And her old man seems to be a good head, or at least a good farmer.'

'Did you see the boy in the back yard as we were coming away? Her brother, I guess. He was goofy-looking.'

'No, I was busy getting you to do the driving.'

'Sure. Give the young fellows a chance.'

'Just what do you mean by that?' Ed laughed excitedly. 'Say, her arm was moving against me a little, or else it was the motion of the car. Her hand is prettier than her face,' he added.

'Just a slight inclination, eh? Enough to show you which way the wind was blowing.'

'Oh, hell, my imagination, probably. But you know, we could have some fun with those girls if there was more time. You better stop this college business, like me.'

'No, I got to keep on, I guess.'

'What you going to teach, Animal Husbandry?'

'Peach-marketing,' said Murray. 'I see our neighbours don't bother to take down their "Peaches For Sale" sign on Sunday.'

'Yeah, and don't they have a lot of company? Four cars in the lane.'

When they drove into their own lane, Amos was making his way to the house with two milk pails. 'Wow!' said Murray under his breath. 'And me driving.' Amos nodded at them coolly as though he didn't notice, and kept on toward the house. They followed him toward the milk-house.

'Well, I got to go change my clothes,' Murray said.

'So you found your way back all right,' Amos said. 'Run out of gas or scenery?'

'Neither,' said Ed cheerfully. 'We went and took a couple of girls for a spin, then we discovered the afternoon was getting on and they wanted us to stay for supper. Thought it wouldn't take any longer there than here and we got away right after.'

'Where's Murray?'

'Gone to change his clothes.'

'Tell him he don't need to. I've done the milking, and the horses are turned out. If you want to walk back and bring up the little team for morning, all right. Don't have to.'

'You didn't want the car for anything, did you?'

'Oh, no – well, Eleanor wanted to go to the church in the city to-night. There's special services, Harvest Home.'

'Should have said so,' Ed turned away to the house. Eleanor's voice was exclaiming over something, laughing musically, and her eyes were beaming at Murray. 'It must have been funny,' she said. Ed went to his own room and changed into his old clothes.

VII

It rained during the night, but the gang of pickers and packers were at the station in full force. By the time they were distributed, with baskets and ladders, in the back orchard, the leaves were dry; but though there were no tall weeds or grass in the cultivated orchard, to spoil skirts, the ground was a little muddy. The pickers were rather disgruntled when Murray brought them up to the barn for lunch. The temporary lark had turned into something surprisingly like work, which one resumed after a rest with a decidedly Mondayish feeling.

After half past two it began to rain heavily. The wagon was at the barn unloading, though the team galloped back, and the pickers were drenched by the time they were under cover. It was a warm rain, and no-one seemed to mind much. The drops were drumming upon the tin roof of the barn above their heads. The packers kept on working, and the other girls talked and laughed and took off and put on clothes, indulging in tricks and horseplay. Ed grinned and teased them. He suggested that they see who could climb the ladders up the haymow as far as the beam, but they declined that kind of race. Amos was out on the road with the truck, and Murray was putting the horses into the stable. Florine seemed to have her nose out of joint in this exuberant group. She was dressed in an afternoon frock; and kept on packing sedately. The other girls seemed to think that she was some kind of favourite. Or did Ed imagine it? He did not enjoy being the only male in this cavorting crowd of females. There was something tense, expectant, in the air. The smell of the damp wind, the damp clothes, the dry hay in the mow, the peaches, and the warm wet clothes mingled in a semi-aphrodisiac effect. He made room for two or three more girls to help with the packing, and began to stick the empty baskets together in fours. Those which had been brought in were wet and warped. He hoped that Murray had not left any behind because of anxiety to bring the girls in. It didn't take much to ruin baskets.

Why didn't Murray come up from the basement and do something? But there were chores down in the stable of course. Ed thought he might let this show run itself for a few minutes and go down himself. He opened the trap door and began to climb down the ladder. The stable doors were closed and it was dark. He knocked his foot against a manger as he stepped down. He heard the outside door in the other part open, and going through the alley found Murray looking out into the yard.

'Rain's hardly over yet,' Ed observed, thinking that the other would close the door, but after a moment Murray took up a fork and began to clean the stable, pitching the straw and manure out the door. They talked a few minutes, then walked around outside to the driveway, to enter the upper barn where the packers were. May came running from the direction of the house.

'Why, where you been?' asked Murray in a surprised voice.

'To the house for a drink,' said May softly. Ed remembered that he hadn't seen anything of May from the time the load of pickers had come to the barn. Funny.

The sun came out as they stood talking, but it was too late to go to the orchard again. Murray went to hitch up and they got the bunch on the democrat to take to the car. Only Florine and May and another woman who lived up the lake remained. They were nailing lids on and stamping. Besides the name of the grower, the name of the consignee had to appear. Ed arranged the rubber letters to form the name of the Winnipeg firm to which they had shipped the carload, for as soon as another express car arrived they would begin loading it. Amos phoned to the station agent at noon to order one. The devil of it was this rain might ripen them faster, and the delay in picking would not help any. If the pickers were any good, Ed fumed, they would be willing to stay later. Florine laughed at him, still deftly packing. She herself would not have liked to be asked to go out to the wet orchard at a quarter to five and work till dark, she hinted.

'Can't you two find something better to quarrel about?' laughed the neighbour woman. May was sitting glumly on a table, making no effort to pack.

'I guess Murray'll take you girls home on the wagon,' said Ed. 'Won't that be nice? May would like him to see her home.' Florine laughed. 'Amos wouldn't like me to get his new sedan spotted up.'

However, Amos was back with the truck shortly after Murray returned with the wagon, and as it was not time for chores, let Murray take them home in the truck. The husband of the woman from up the lake arrived, and they packed away the peaches she had earned by picking.

In the evening of comparative leisure, Murray went through his trunk, sorting things, and wrote a couple of letters. Ed read a magazine, and even returned to Carlyle's *French Revolution*, which he had been trying to read since spring. Less than two short chapters put him in a doze in which words of ferocious import had autonomous vigour danced among themselves in his brain, and he blew out the light.

By Thursday night the second express car for Winnipeg was filled and gone. The flood of peaches stopped as though at the turning of a tap. There weren't fifty baskets of Elbertas left on the trees, and there were no later varieties. There was a general clearing-up, packing baskets together and putting ladders away, and it was all over. The alfalfa had been left in cocks for two weeks, and was yellow. Friday afternoon they hauled six loads to the barn, and Saturday morning continued. Then at noon Murray shaved and dressed and Amos, having business in town, took his trunk and him to the depot. Ed felt rather disconsolate as he trudged behind the plow alone in the field at the road. He felt that there had been some confidence withheld in their relations toward the last. Just about the time of the beginning of the peach season, when their extraordinary efforts should have made them more companionable, a reserve had seemed to spring up between them which they had belied with jocularity and manifestations of good-will. It was strange. It must have been those girls. Had Murray taken a notion to Florine, and become resentful because he was relegated to May? Then, Amos had seemed rather churlish with Murray sometimes – silly ass, jealous, probably of their friendship. There never had been a better hired man than Murray, even Amos would admit that. There was nothing on the farm he didn't know how to do and, more important, when to do. What he was going to do with an agricultural degree if he got one, Ed didn't know, but probably that easy-going exterior hid an ambition which would make him a cabinet minister or some other kind of great man.

About four o'clock Ed wrapped the lines about the plow-handle and walked toward the house. The trees on the high land swayed vigorously. It was fall now, summer had gone with that day of rain the first of the week. A long, long fall until the end of November, there by the southern tip of Lake Erie. Well, he would go and see Florine sometimes, and in the winter go to town and skate on the rink. He went into the kitchen and turned the tap. As he drank, the stillness of the house seemed broken by sobs shrill and abandoned, a tempest of grief. He tiptoed out as quickly as he could. Thunder! he thought, as he walked toward his team, Eleanor. What did that mean? She didn't like it because she couldn't go to town with the men? They couldn't take Murray's trunk in the new car. But she had said nothing to indicate such a wish. It must be that she was sorry that Murray had gone. Well, he was a pleasant quiet fellow to have around, with his upright tallness, his blond head – but where was the farmer's wife who regretted having one less man to cook for? The cause of her grief was obvious, and it filled Ed with something like awe.

Although he wrote at once it was more than a month before he got a letter from Murray. Their days had nothing in common now, and the letter had an awkward sound, a tone of reluctant duty in the writing. He referred to constant letters from May Webster. Poor girl! He had written one to her which he supposed was a mistake, as it would make her keep on with her foolishness. Ed tore the letter up and did not answer it. What a hell of a life life was anyway. Somehow he had kept away from Florine, seeming to have lost interest in her. He felt like going to see May, just to cheer her up. Poor honest, homely, good-hearted May was going through endless dreary days in a lonely farmhouse stuck in the middle of fields, with nothing but that worthless heartbreaker to think about; cooped up with dreams of summer delights through a winter of loneliness and longing.

At any rate he would not make any pretences or raise any expectations in Florine, he thought.

MIST GREEN OATS

It was not until after he arrived home from taking his mother to the railway station that he began to realize how tired he had become. 'Now don't work too hard while I'm away, Len,' had been her last words on kissing him, and before he left the train. While he was riding slowly homeward his thoughts had been busy hopping from one detail to another of the morning's activities: of his coming up from the field at eleven o'clock and stabling the horses, of the bustlings of last-minute preparations, carrying the grips out and expostulating with his mother as she stood before the mirror straight and young-looking in her travelling-dress, of the stirring numbers of people about the station and the platform waiting and staring, who made him conscious of his Sunday coat, overalls and heavy shoes. And his mind had leaped on ahead of her to his cousins whom she would see, and what he thought to be their life in the remote city, as he pictured it from the two or three holidays he had passed there in the course of his childhood.

In the lane at the end of the barn when he arrived home his father was hitching his three-horse team together, square-framed and alike in size; and throwing a word now and then to Syd Allrow who was sitting hunched on the handles of his plow which lay on the ground behind his team of blacks. The boy nodded to Syd, and his father, seeing his look of surprise, said hurriedly, 'Syd's helping us a day or two. Thought I'd get an early start. Go right on in now, and have dinner. We'll be back in the apple orchard when you come.'

The boy began to notice as he had not before that his father's face had become a little thin and bitten of apparently new wrinkles. The acute stridor of haste and the spring work, the heavy anxiety, the lack of help – he turned away when his father hastily came around to that side of the team. Walking toward the house he heard Syd make some inertly voiced remark or query.

The victuals were cold, but his dinner was awaiting him on the table in the kitchen. When a few minutes later he began to take the dishes away he left off abruptly, remembering that he should have time for such tasks in the evening, when the work outside was done. Then he recommenced and finished clearing the table, for Syd would be there, they would be hungry and wish to have supper as soon as possible after coming from the field.

As he moved about he was not oppressed now by a sense of haste, by a fear, almost, of something unknown threatening their determination which yet chivied and lured the men of farms through those ontreading days of late spring. The season had been retarded by late frosts and heavy rains at seeding time, and the later work, corn-planting and plowing, must be done quickly before the soil became intractable. Such conjunctures, with their own necessity, were at the source of what might in certain types of men evolve as a race against time as much for the sake of the race as for the prefigured prize. He mused.

This released sense must have come from the variation in the plan of the day. At this hour of the afternoon he was used to be in the field, or choring about the barn. Alone in the house Len Brinder's movements became slower as he made the turn from kitchen to pantry and back again. His mind went to the city toward which his mother was now speeding, where the streets and buildings and the spirit of them, which every one of the crowds about him seemed in a way to share, were wonderful from a distance of two years. It was impossible that the spirit and the crowds could mean anything but life rendered into different terms, understandable and entrancing. Everyone appeared to be full of active keenness, a beauty, and, for all it was deceptive, no one appeared to work. Automatically he continued moving the dishes about.

His father and Syd were both finishing a round when he arrived at the end of the apple-orchard. The horses of their teams were already beginning to show wet about their flanks, despite their hardened condition. As they came toward him the heads of his father's three horses, which were pulling a two-furrow plow, bobbed unevenly, and their loud breaths produced a further and audible discord. The noses of Syd's black team were drawn in to their breasts, for they were pulling a walking-plow and the reins passed around their driver's back. There was little wind among the big mushroom-shaped apple-trees.

'Well,' said Sam Brinder from his seat, 'Syd's finishing the lands for me. Do you want to strike them out? It will be pretty hard around those old trunks, though.'

The boy did want to. – 'Not much difference, is there?' – and at once turned his team into line. The absence of his father's accustomed brusque unconsciousness struck him readily enough as a blandness affected for the benefit of the neighbour.

The hardness of the ground astonished him. He wondered how he could have thought of anything else since leaving his plow in the morning. He was obliged to hold the handle at a wearying angle in going around the trunks of the big trees, and to twist it back to a normal position in the spaces between. White dust like a smoke burst forth from between the ground and the fresh soil falling heavy upon it. All along the orchard the spurting dust preceded him, thin portions rising with a little wisp of breeze about his face. When he reached the end of the long furrow he was almost panting from the wrestle. 'This is going to be hard on horses,' he said to himself. 'The hottest day yet.' The ground seemed to have become petrified since the day before. 'I'll have to rest them oftener now, just after dinner. Later on we can go,' he thought, as he turned again for the return on the other side of the trees.

It was necessary to plow two furrows around each row of trees before the big plow could be used. As the end of the orchard was reached each time the ground seemed harder and the boy's arms more stretched and tired. As the time passed the horses began to give signs of the strain. One of them would put his head down and make a forward rush, straightening the doubletree, while his mate seemed to hang back – then the other in turn dashed ahead, leaving his mate behind.

'Straighten 'em up there. Make 'em behave!' his father called from the riding-plow, and banished Len's own vexation with the team. He tried but languidly to bring it under control, while he thought, 'It's the ground. The horses are all right. They're willing enough.' Nothing could be more willing than a horse. He'd go until he dropped if the driver hadn't sense enough to pull him up, to keep him from foundering himself. It was the cursed soil. The plowing shouldn't have been put off so long. It needn't have been. Why couldn't they have left some of the manure-hauling, some of the pruning, and done this first? And other people were able to get men on some terms, why couldn't his father? Then, why must he take such a busy time as last week had been to go to the city to see about the mortgage? These questions were like arrows pointing a center in his thoughts: the feeling of being ill-used. Bad management was to blame, but he could not, yet, hold his father responsible, whom circumstances seemed to have rendered powerless. The boy's hat was sticking to his brow as though clamped there with some iron band driven down like hoops on a barrel.

Sam Brinder and Syd were talking at the end of the field. What did they have so important to talk about? They had been at the same spot when he started back from the other end. He didn't rest his horses that much. He was too interested in getting the work done to be so determined to take part in a confab. He would show them what he thought. He'd not give his horses half as much rest as they had theirs. That would shame them, maybe, the lazy – 'Ned! Dick! Get up here, you old – '

Tight-throated in the dust, wrestling bitterly with the stony soil, he went up and down the rows. These thoughts lasted him a long time and he forgot everything about him except the wrenching heavy plow and the rhythmic swinging single-trees and the creaking harness. Time and the sun seemed to stand still, breathless.

They started on again with a jerk when an hour later he heard his father hailing him through the trees.

'Go up and get us a pail of water,' Sam Brinder called. 'Your horses can stand the rest anyway, I guess.'

'Well, I'm not thirsty, but if you are, of course – '

'We've been back here longer than you have, remember,' his father added.

The boy looked at him, wrapped the lines about the plow-handles and went up the lane toward the well. Walking was queer alone now; easier, perhaps? It almost seemed to be done automatically, his body leaning slightly forward.

He went to the house, and brought the pail back to the well, drank slowly and gratefully of the cold water. ...

He was walking down the lane at a moderate, stooped shouldered pace. The light summer clothes hung about his gaunt form. Well, the afternoon was going. Four o'clock when he had left the house. It might be nearly half-past four by the time he got back to work. Well, no. Five, ten minutes had gone now. Not more than ten more would pass, before he should have taken Syd and his father their drinks. Even at that; twenty minutes after four; the afternoon was going pretty well. ... Syd would be for supper, of course. Kind of nice, they had been alone so much since his older sister had left them and gone into an office in the city. Could it be as hot as this in the city, where one might go into the ice-cream parlors and the movie theatres? Different it would be, anyway.

In the orchard the sunlight seemed to pack the heat down below the boughs and above the earth. The boughs seemed to hold it there, and to make room in some way for more heat, which the sun still packed down. His feet in the heavy shoes seemed to be broiling; the socks hung loose about his thin ankles and over the hard unbendable uppers. The horses needed a rest, his father had said, eh? It was they who needed the rest! He'd give them rest enough, all right, from now on. At each end of the field. If his father didn't mind, why should he try to do more than his share?

'Well,' said Syd as he reached for the dipper, standing in the furrow and looking up at him, 'how you standing it?' At the unevadable reply, 'Oh, all right,' he added:

'Getting about enough of farming? I was that way myself for a while. Seems kinda hard work after going to high-school, I s'pose.'

That was like him! When it was almost a year since Len had left high-school. 'Oh, I'm used to it by now,' the boy replied coldly.

Syd mopped his face with a patterned handkerchief, spat, swung a line, and said, 'Well, I guess I'll have to be getting along. Boss'll be makin' the fur fly, if I don't.' He smiled at the joke, as a farmer's son himself, and independent of the whims of bosses. 'So you're keeping batch now? I better not bother you for supper.'

'Yes, you're to stay for supper. There's no trouble about that. Yes, mother thought she'd take a rest before the canning came on. ... ' He added, 'Gone to the city,' with a smile he suddenly felt was meant to appear brave.

'Tchka! Bill! Sam! Get outa here!'

His father said: 'You'll have to go up a little earlier than us and get supper ready.'

Len made no reply. Assent he felt was too miserably unnecessary, and he stood looking in silence back of the plow.

'Not making much of a job,' said Brinder. 'I got to stand on it most of the time. You got to be quick and keep shifting the levers. You got to have 'er just so. Some job, all right!'

As he walked across the scarred and lumpy headland the boy made an effort to feel at odds with his father, and to conjure an image proper to the aim. He saw him, a clipped-moustached and almost spruce figure, going away from the house to attend perhaps a meeting of school trustees, to raise his voice among the other men. Trying to find in his memory cue for a critical attitude, Len began to wonder how he himself appeared to those about him, going through the gestures of daily living.

What were people made of anyway, he reflected, bitterly deprecatory – but extravagances, ludicrous to everyone but themselves?

The sweat was caked in salt upon the flanks of his horses when he got back to them. One horse's head was held in a natural position; the other's back and head were level, and its weight slouched on a hind leg.

Stiffly the three plodded on again. As one long round after another was made, night almost seemed to be getting farther away, rather than nearing them. To lean back in the lines as he found himself wanting to do and allow the plowtails to pull him along was impossible. The point would shoot up and the plow slide along the ground until he could get the horses stopped. In spite of him sometimes it did this, when it struck a stone or when it came to a packed area of ground, and then the boy had to drag its weight back several feet into its former position; shouting at the horses and pulling them back at the same time.

But at each end of the field he gave the team a long rest, sitting on the plow-handles as the clumsy implement lay on its side. He dangled his legs and moved his feet about in the heavy shoes. The soles were burning. Looking at the wrinkled tough leather, which seemed to form impenetrable bumps, he noticed that the toe of the right shoe was turned up on the outside with a seemingly immanent bend, given it by the slope of the furrow which he had for days been following. Every day the same! With the impressionableness of youth he could not believe that there had ever been a time at which he had not been tired out. Every day the same. The weariness of last night and of the night before, the same. But this day was far from spent yet. Tonight as well as the usual chores there would be work in the house.

He looked for a long time across the wide pasture at the end of the orchard. Several cattle were on its gently raised surface. Their feet seemed to be above the fence on the lower ground beyond them, which could be seen at either side of the rise. The sky was clear and high, and it seemed to give the cattle a lightness which should make possible for them any feat. It looked as though they might with one fabulous jump easily clear the fence in the distance and be free. For what – free? They would break into the green oats or wet alfalfa and kill themselves. The boy sighed and raised the plow-handles again. Over in the midst of the trees sharp sweet notes of birdsong began to come, giving the place in his present mood a chilled look. The grass became pale before his eyes and the sunlight a little milder broke among the branches as among windy streaming snowflakes.

The horses pulled evenly now. They were going with a seemingly terrible swiftness. The boy staggered and strode along behind them, wrenching the plow as it threatened to jump to the surface. They found it easier, charging through so rapidly, or else they wanted to get each stint over as quickly as possible for the rest at the end of it. Stumbling and striding along behind, Len hated them. Boy and horses began to sweat more profusely. 'They always get that way about this time. It must be getting late.' The sun was shining in his eyes.

As he reached the end his father shouted across to him, and he stooped to undo the tugs.

It was when he reached the house that the desire came to him to take off his shoes. He seemed to have walked on lumpy plates of hot greasy iron for innumerable ages. He sat down and untied them slowly, and the mere loosening of the leathern laces made the feet ache relief. He walked about the cool kitchen oilcloth in his socks. Then a fancy struck him. He opened the screen-door and went out on the lawn. He shoved his feet along in the short grass and rubbed them against each other. Such immeasurable sweet pain he had never known. At first he could scarcely bear to raise his weary feet from the depth of the grass. Presently he would lift one at a time in a strange and heavy dance, for the pleasure it was of putting it down again among the cool soft blades. The lowering sun variegated the green of the different kinds of evergreen trees back of the house, of which he always confused the names. Something of beauty which, it seemed, must have been left out of it or which he had forgotten, appeared in the closing day. Something was changed, perhaps. He did not know how long he had been there, scrubbing his soles about like brushes in the grass, and regretfully hopping, until he remembered that the men would be coming in for their supper at any minute. Beginning to wonder whether anyone had witnessed his movements, he went into the house and relaced his shoes.

The men were eating their supper. After they had washed their hands and faces outside of the back door, throwing each dirty basinful away with a dripping hiss into the light breeze, they entered the house. Syd sat very straight on a chair by the wall, with his arms folded, and looked at nothing in particular. His black shirt was still open at the neck. Sam Brinder bustled about helping Len to complete the preparations. 'Now, the eggs. How'll ye have the eggs – Syd?'

'Doesn't make any difference to me,' Syd gravely replied.

'Come now, you've got to say.'

'No, sir. Have 'em how you like. You're the doctor.'

'Well, suppose we have them fried.'

Now, as they ate heartily, they said little, except to urge upon each other and accept or refuse more food. The room became warm and filled with the soft sounds of their eating and the steaming kettle on the stove. There was the humming of one or two flies about and between them recurrently. Presently a prolonged lowing was heard from back of the barn. 'Cows are coming up the lane of themselves,' said Brinder. 'We won't have to go after them. Pretty good, eh, Len?'

Then the two men began to speak of the crops and the comparative state of the work on neighbouring farms.

'We're pretty well forward with our work,' said Syd, 'but there's more of us for the amount of land.' He referred to his two brothers who were at home. 'Still, you fellows are getting along pretty well. You're getting over the ground lately, all right.'

The significance came to Len of 'you fellows,' making him angry and sad. A great partnership it was, he told himself, wherein his share consisted of unrequited work. Then he thought that Syd had meant to be flattering or condoling, and though he imagined that he should be vexed with him for that, he could not. The conversation was sliding on over well-worn topics, with the slight necessary variations. The sun's rays were horizontal now, the raised window blind let them strike on the lower part of Syd's clean-shaven tan face. It was not every night that they had company, even in this fashion. The boy liked Syd, after all. It reminded him how, many years ago as it now seemed, Syd had known of a Hallowe'en prank which he with some of the high-school boys had played on one of the farmers thereabout. And he had never told. ... The Hallowe'en joke had been to him, as much as anything else in his boy's world, a social due.

The three sat in the room which the flat rays from the window made to seem dusk-filled, and the two elder continued talking. Len moved his fork with the ends of his fingers, tilted his tea-cup, and thought, when he thought, and did not merely fill himself vaguely with a pleasant sense of Syd's identity, of the work to be done yet.

Presently they rose, and the boy remained in the house to do the washing-up while his father did the chores.

Slowly the dishes were assembled and slowly and thoroughly wiped. Unused to the work he took a long time to finish it. Besides, he thought, there is only more work waiting outside. 'There's always work waiting outside on a farm,' he reflected. 'There'll be plenty of it right here when we're all dead. Wherever it's all getting us to – ' But he saw some of the older farmers about him, and those who were not to that extent in neediness, still working as hard and during longer hours than anyone. They had come to like it. He envied and condemned them for that. There was so much of the world to see, so much of life to discover, to compare with what one might find in oneself! Suddenly Len was confident of this.

He went out into the dusk. Innumerable crickets joined voices to produce a trill. A wind was blowing and he sniffed it gratefully. 'As fresh – as fresh, as on the sea,' he muttered, slouching toward the barn. The cattle were in the yard, spotting the gloom. He could hear their windy coughing sigh, which was at once contrasted with the loud drumming snort of a horse as he burrowed about in the hay of his manger. The closed stable was loud with the grinding of jaws on the tough dried stems.

There was no sign of his father about, though he gave a shout. He wished to know which of the chores remained not done. There was no answer. The milk-pails upside down showed that the milking was not yet begun. 'Likely gone home with Syd for a visit,' he grunted at once, without taking any thought of the matter. He fumbled about the harnesses in the dark. 'Thinks he'll lay the chores on me, I s'pose. I'll only unharness the horses and water them. If he doesn't like that he can do the other.'

When he returned to the house he glanced at the alarm-clock on the shelf. A quarter past nine. He picked up a magazine and took it with a lamp into the next room. Frequently when the family went to town a magazine was brought home. Before that his reading had been restricted and this began only after Len had quit high-school. He for some time found the change grateful from his dry studies. He was drowsing with his elbows on one of the magazines when the screen-door slammed and Brinder entered the house, coming on into the room where his son was sitting. The boy, fully awake, pretended to continue his reading.

'I saw you weren't out at the barn, so I came in. You didn't get the chores all finished, did you?'

'No, I just worked 'til a little after nine, and then quit and called it a day.'

'Is that so! You could have quit when you liked, if you'd asked me. I didn't order you to do the chores, remember, I asked you how many of them had been done.'

'As many as I had time to do after doing the work in here.'

'Well, you didn't have many hours work in here, did you? How much did you do?'

'I gave the horses water and unharnessed them.'

'Oh!'

'Why, did the time seem so long over at Allrows'?'

'Over at Allrows'?'

'Yes. Didn't you go home with Syd?'

'Well, that's a joke, that is,' said Brinder, turning away. 'I went back to the pasture after old Belle. She wouldn't bring her calf up with the other cattle.'

Len was nonplussed for an instant. His father went on, 'It'll pay not to pay so much attention to the clock when a busy time's on, you'll find.' He entered the kitchen, shutting the door behind him.

The boy did not try to check his anger at this. It was increased by his knowledge that his father's was controlled.

'I'll find, will I?' he shouted at the closed door. 'I'll find where there's an eight-hour day to be had, you can bet on that!'

He heard his father grunting in the next room, and the creak of his lantern as he jerked it shut. Then the outside door slammed behind him.

Len was painfully awake now, but he could not keep his mind on the printing before him. His imagination ran amuck through possibilities. But he did not see them as possibilities. The actuality stood before him of every movement from now until the time he should have reached the city and entered on some transcendently congenial and remunerative occupation. The vision, with its minutiae, lasted a considerable time; then another came of his going to sea. When he judged that his father would soon be coming into the house again he took up his lamp and retired to his own room.

The next morning he came downstairs bearing the blackened lamp in his hand, to find that his father had gone out, leaving a fire for cooking the breakfast. It was half-past five by the clock on the shelf, and the boy at once began preparations for the morning meal. Before the table was set his father came in with the milk-pail. They greeted each other somewhat shamefacedly and busied themselves with straining the milk and taking the dishes from the shelves.

As they were sitting down to the table Mr Brinder looked at the clock: 'It's later than it seems; that clock's away slow.' He appeared to be in a hurry, and the meal was consumed in silence. When they had finished the father said, 'You clear up here. I'll not water the driver nor your team. If I'm gone to the field when you come out, you water them.' He went away apparently without hearing Len's monosyllabic assent.

The morning was not yet more than faintly warm. White clouds were loitering about the sky, and dew hung in the grass beside the path worn to the barn. The boy slipped the halter from the head of Lass, the driver, pride of the farm, or at any rate very much that of himself. He drove her out into the yard, where she might go for a drink. Meanwhile he began to harness the team with which he intended to plow.

In a moment Lass entered the end of the stable in which he was working, instead of the other, containing her box-stall. For months one of the rollers on the door leading out of that end of the barn had been broken, so that it had been necessary to lead her forth from the part in which the other horses were quartered. Now, as she came in by the old way, long after the door had been repaired, there was something about the whole matter, about the inertia and preoccupation which had so long made them neglect it, more than about this unnecessary use of the old mode of entry, which enraged Len immeasurably. He could not have explained his rage with its sudden choking of his throat. He leaped at the little mare shouting, 'Get out of here, you! Before I – ' He reached her side and struck a blow at her muzzle. She jerked her head up, turning around, and slipping and sprawling on the cement went out. He at once became ashamed of himself, and when he had got her into the stall gave her an extra handful of oats. They watched each other while she, ears pricked, ate it. Lass did not object, as most horses did, to the impertinence of being watched while she consumed feed.

Throughout that morning the boy was nearly as tired and even more languidly bitter than the evening before. The soil seemed as hard as ever, the horses plunged, the orchard was still longer.

Wonderful high steep and billowing clouds were in the sky. They were like vast mounds and towers of tarnished well-lit silver. He sat on the side of the plow and looked over toward the part of the orchard at which he would finish his plowing. The green of an oats field beyond was visible under the apple-boughs. It was even now beginning to take on a gray misty tinge. Soon the oats field would seem an unbelievable blue-gray cloud, glimpsed from beneath the apple trees. In those days the granite of oats would call the eye throughout all the country. The heads would seem to dance in the high sunlight, and fields of wheat would bow and surge in amber-lit crests. The rows of young corn would be arching to either side and touching, black-green and healthy. The smell of it, as he cultivated and the horses nipped off pieces of the heavy leaves, would be more sweet than that of flowers, and more bland. The year would pass on, the harvesting of wheat, of barley and oats, fall-plowing again, threshings, the cutting and husking of corn, the picking of apples in this same orchard. Yes, one could see the beauty of it distantly, but when the time came he would be numbed to all with toil.

That is, this round would take place, the years pass on, if he remained on the farm. Would he, or, rather he asked himself, could he do that? Nothing very alluring was to be seen ahead in the lives of anyone about him. What was his father getting out of it?

His plow could scarcely be held in the ground at all now. The point had become worn off and rounded, and he at last went over to his father for a heavy wrench with which to break it off squarely, which would for a time postpone the necessity of replacing it with a new one. Syd was starting back to the other end of the orchard, and waved a heavy arm at him. Len pretended to be busy disengaging the wrench from his father's plow, but looked up an instant later to watch the steady progress down the field of the team of blacks; and Syd held the plow handles with an appearance of firmness and ease.

'You needn't bother going for the water this morning, I'll go after it,' his father was saying.

'Plows nice, finishing the lands up, don't it?' Len asked significantly, ignoring the remark.

'Well, if you wanted to do that, why didn't you say so in the first place?'

'Oh, don't bother changing us around now! I'm getting used to the hard part.' He still looked after Syd.

'No, I won't ask him to change now.'

Len walked on, more uninterruptedly now, but shouting shrilly at the horses as they jerked ahead. Stopping midway of the field he set the clevis to make the plow go deeper. It saved him some of the effort to hold it in the ground. But the horses found it still heavier going. At the hard spots at each end big blocks of cement-like earth were turned up.

He was calculating the length of the orchard and there-from the distance walked in a day, when his father came with the drink. Pulling his watch out Sam Brinder said, 'It's not as late as it seems. I've set the clock on, by my watch. It's five minutes to eleven, while the right time is twenty-five minutes to eleven. I'll holler when it's time to quit. Your team is doing all right, not sweating.'

Later as he came to the end of the field he heard his father and Syd, who happened to finish at the same time, talking together.

'Yes, and she can go, all right; nice roader,' his father was saying.

'Well, I think this other one would just suit you.'

Were they speaking of Lass? Once or twice Brinder had considered disposing of her, and Len's dread of such a possibility was such that he would never discuss it. But she might be sold now. Anything, it came to him, might happen now. His father would just like to sell her to spite him, he knew. The ache of his anger was redoubled by the memory of what had happened that morning. He recalled now his deep-founded liking for the little horse. One evening he let her out in the field with the others. How she trotted! Proudly, with arched neck and tail streaming behind, she moved about among the other horses with great high free strides. 'She can trot circles around the others,' he thought. Presently she stopped, standing poised and throbbing with life, snorting, ears forward, looking at him in the doorway. And he clapped his hands and she trotted off once more. Then she became still more frolicsome. Her heels shot up again and again, and he could hear the swish of her long heavy tail as she kicked. ... Yes, it would be just like him to sell her.

Time passed, as if in despite of itself. The boy plodded on, his mind enfolded in these thoughts, and consciously aware of only the flopping aside of the earth before him, of the dust and the hard gravel slope of the furrow-bottom. The fatal impressibility of youth was lapping chains about him. It seemed that he had never known anything else than this dolorous wrestle in the dust. The hard clamping of his hat-brim pained his forehead. He wiped it and the grime came off on his handkerchief. The ache in his legs was not to be forgotten, but his mind swung from the certainty of the loss of one of the few things – the only one it now seemed for which he could care. He began to wonder about the time. His shadow slanted a little to the east as he faced north: surely it was after noon. He could not remember whether the shadow slanted more in the spring or in the autumn: it was surely more than twelve o'clock.

Automatically he continued work after the accustomed respite. What was the meaning of this clock business? The clock had seemed accurate enough yesterday to catch the train by. But it had been slow this morning, and now, his father said, it was fast, and fast so much. There was something strange about all this.

But as it became later there ceased to be anything strange in the matter to Len. It was part of a plan, that couldn't be doubted. To pretend that they had begun later than usual and at the same stroke keep him at work later – it was sharp, all right. Indignation and a respect for his own penetration filled him. This, he reflected in bitterness, was what he must expect from his father henceforth. And the latter would regard it as no more than just discipline, probably. But he'd be shown. 'He'll only try that once,' the boy muttered, his face fixing and his fingers tightening on the plow-handles.

Standing at the end of the field he looked about him. Through the trees he could see his father's three square-boned horses straining onward amid the shouts of their driver. 'Sitting down, having a nap,' he thought, relishing the fact of taking this as a matter of course. Farther over Syd was going in the opposite direction, holding his plow as steadily it appeared as though the ground had been softened by days of rain.

'I'll not make another round,' he reflected. 'Or it will be a good while before I do, anyway. If he thinks he can do that sort of thing he's going to get left.'

Whistling a shred of an old tune he sat down on his plow. 'Have a good rest, Ned,' he addressed the nigh horse, 'you started early enough, anyway.'

He was aware of the long barred stretch of blue-green oats now still nearer. The high sun instead of making it more vivid seemed to give its surface a hazy quality. A dragon-fly hung motionless against the mild breeze and seeming to battle with it, wings alight with a sparkle of swift motion.

'About noon when you see them things,' the boy thought.

From three-quarters of a mile away came the sound of the Allrows' dinner-bell. Old-fashioned people. It was dinner-time, then, all right. Sometimes, though, they had dinner earlier, or later. He pictured the Allrow boys and their father, quitting work in various parts of the farm, and Mrs Allrow, plump, easily pleased woman, with her grownup daughters preparing the meal. How long was it since he had been over to their place? That, he reflected, was the trouble; one didn't see anyone new for weeks at a stretch. The desire for various contacts had made him impatient of the people he might have known better, had he cared. He got through the day's work, but curiosity demanded leisure and energy. People on a farm like the men on ship-board in the old days, saw too much of each other. That was it. But that could be remedied in his case, Len reflected with a quickening of the pulses. ... Not an inch would he drive further. His father must learn that his little trick wouldn't work. As he sat, waiting for the call, he decided that if he discovered that the clock really had been advanced, he must leave. He pictured all the details of this, his father's queries and expostulations and his own determined silence. He would pack his suitcase, take his few dollars out of hiding and walk down the road. ... He kicked at the side of the furrow, gazing downward. ... How sore his feet had been last night! ... But he wouldn't walk very far, only to the railway station. For he was going to the city. No, he would ask to be driven there in the buggy, drive Lass himself. If only one could keep himself unbound! But there'd be that one friend he'd always miss! ... He would ask politely, unemotionally, and his father would not be able to refuse. ... He'd just step to the house and 'phone central and enquire the correct time.

His father's call struck a surprise in him, and he rose stiffly and unhitched the horses. He noticed that both the others were unhitching also. They didn't intend to let him go up and prepare the dinner alone. But he'd never let that hinder him. He'd step to the 'phone in their presence and find out the truth about this matter. Robbing him from both pockets at once!

He hurried toward the barn, determined to arrive there first. He came to the watering trough; and when, after waiting for the horses to drink, he had stabled them, he was so agitated that he was struck with a weak surprise to hear Syd and his father talking quietly outside while they separated their horses. He intended to go out of the building and directly to the house, having fed the team which he had been driving; but he changed his mind and went back and began to put hay in the other mangers, then made for the house and washed before them.

He heard their voices; their heavy feet scrub the grass of the yard. ... knock against the step.

'It's a seven-foot cut, they tell me,' Brinder was saying. 'Now wouldn't you have thought a six-foot cut would be big enough, on a farm like that?'

'Old Dunc says he may as well get a big one now. Alfred'll be getting a tractor soon as he's gone, he says.'

'Great old joker. He don't mind having big things around, himself.'

'Then I guess he's sure he'll have the job of driving it now he's getting old.' Syd laughed. 'It'll make the boys hump, to shock behind it, though.'

'Yes, they raise pretty good crops, just the same.' Mr Brinder was putting water in the kettle, while Syd combed his hair. 'How'll we have the eggs, boys?' The voice sounded absent from the pantry, whence the regular sweep of the bread-knife could be heard.

'Well, they were pretty fair like they were last night. ...'

Len moved from shelves to table with clean dishes. Syd sat with his arms folded on a chair tilted against the wall. He intercepted one of the rounds by asking, 'Well, how you coming? Ground soft where you are, I s'pose!'

The boy grunted in reply and managed a half-smile.

Soon the meal was ready, and as they sat down to it he remembered that he had not gone to the 'phone as he had promised himself. He would do it as soon as the other two were gone, and he would be left alone to wash the dishes.

The two voices went on, with a calm interest, business-like inevitability, and the meal was almost over before Len realized that there was something in his mind being worn down and smoothed away, as old ice is worn away by spring rain. They talked as though they had been travellers in a desert who had become parted by accident and now met to recount all they had been through. But what they told was nothing, they meant simply to demonstrate to themselves that they were together again. Then what he thought of as the unreality of it oppressed him. A change of circumstances, the presence of strangers seemed to compel one to make little changes in one's words, in one's actions. Elements of the frank, humorous, the straight-forward, of eagerness in the gallantries of conversation were there. Perhaps Syd's family would smile to recognize him. His father was different too. But weren't they both after all as much themselves in any guise as they could be?

It occurred to him that his father was seeking something in the commonplace exchange. His father had been young too, once. He tried to imagine that youth, his aims and desires and ways. The thought unaccustomed held him for a moment, but he could not imagine them as different from his own, and the idea came that his father had betrayed them. Then as he looked at the lines in the face, scars of weather, toil and the scarifications of experience, he began to descry the blind unwitting stupor of life, reaching for what it wanted, an ox setting foot on a kitten before its manger.

He wanted to rise and rush from the room. The sound of the two with their talking kept him from his own thoughts.

They continued to discuss the fallibilities and oddities of neighbours until the table began to look emptier, and then he noticed his father say, 'So you think you'll not be able to help us any more, Syd?'

'Well, not just for the present,' replied Syd pleasantly, as though correcting Mr Brinder in an important inexactitude of statement. 'Maybe sometime after a while.' ... So Syd was going; going too. They were both going, his conscious mind repeated, though something that had been fierce and silently stridulous began to shrink within him, and he began to wonder how much he meant that.

He rose and left the house. He went down the lane and along the road which led toward the corner where, on the main highway, their mailbox stood.

There was nothing but yesterday's paper, and a post-card from his sister. The latter contained only the most banal message, documenting the fact that its sender was alive and, it added, in good spirits; and that the boss said her vacation would come in the next month.

The relationship of the brother and sister was not known to any especial tenderness, and yet, as he thought of the sense of her presence in the first few days after her return, of the feeling while at work of somebody new waiting for him at mealtimes, he couldn't but look forward to it, and he realized and now admitted to himself that his struggle had found an issue. A dull quietude came upon his mind. He tramped back home, his heavy feet upon the hard rounded road.

He found that the men had gone to the barn when he reached the kitchen. Syd would be hitching his horses and going away.

His mother – she would be beginning her holiday among the impossible wonders of the city. He thought of the endless confidential chats she would have with her sister, his aunt Charlotte, as they would rock together in the first afternoons, and the family would be out at work or at play. Already he began to miss her. Nearly two days were gone. But he should have, though only until realization, for expectance the last one of her absence.

Then he was struck by the triviality of what he allowed to pass as excuses for abandoning the determination he had so highly taken.

Once, clearing the table, he looked at the clock, but he did not let the reminder stay with him. As he wiped the dishes slowly, he looked at it again, and said aloud and consciously:

'What's the use? What's the weary use?'

Then, at the coming of an impulse as he was going out, his brow knitted, and he stopped a moment and went back up the stairs to his room. When he returned it was with a laden suitcase in his hand. He set it plainly on the floor before the table, and then thought, 'No, that's too plain. He'll see it anyway – ' and put it to one side.

With a beating heart he went out of the house, whistling.

THE LOADING

Jesse Culworth's air that morning announced that he did not even wish to seem tranquil. His wife, sensitive, as always, to his temper, felt that. So did Garland, his son. When he came in at half-past six from the before-breakfast chores he glowered silently half-sitting, half-leaning with folded arms against the sewing machine, toward the boy, who was washing at the kitchen sink. 'Come, Ma,' he said to his wife, 'dish the porridge up! We're just ready.'

When he had washed they sat down. The room was dimly lit by vine-covered windows. Sunbeams made numerous rays through the leaves of virginia creeper, targetting at bright spots on the fading dark paper of the opposite wall. The table at which they sat seemed to half-fill the kitchen. Jesse, strong-looking and unbent of shoulders at forty, ate his oatmeal with melancholy gusto, at times heavily regarding his wife at the other end of the table. He held out his cup and saucer in silence for more tea. As Nettie filled the cup he said, 'Whoa!,' his use of the accustomed word so abrupt and morose that, startled, his wife passed the cup back. He drank the tea slowly. On his regular thick features a slight moisture could be seen in the dim light of the warm kitchen.

'Going to take them hogs in to town this morning,' he announced to his son as he leaned back in his chair after finishing the tea. 'Old Gus told me last night he guessed he'd take 'em.'

The good humours of Jesse rather preceded than followed his visits to town. He would see Charlie Alten, or some others of his early friends driving about the village in their motors after the closing of their stores. Always after greeting one of them he would bite his lip and mutter to himself, drawing back his shoulders, 'What a fool I was, what a fool! They didn't have any more schooling than I did. To go out on that blasted unearthly farm!' His mother who was living in the village after the death of her husband persuaded him into taking a farm as soon as he had finished high-school. She was intolerably afraid that he would not 'settle down,' for until his death her husband had not. Jesse stuck to the farm during good years because they might continue, and he wouldn't quit in a poor year because then it and the stock could not be sold for what they were worth. Of late the years seemed mostly alike. The details of his ill-luck became to him of less and less interest except as a subject for objurgation. To heavy rains and droughts he resigned himself almost with enjoyment. If anyone's clover failed to 'catch,' it was his; if anyone's wheat winter-killed, his did. Hoof and mouth disease broke out miles away to head straight to his stable.

'I should guess he would take 'em, the price he's paying now!' Culworth grunted, looking to his wife for approval of the wit.

There was silence. Like most men he had made a phrase of his own, which he liked to use. His was, 'the devilishness of things in general.' He took pleasure in using it in the presence of his wife. Aside from her feeling of a discomfortable approach to blasphemy Nettie Culworth did not like such words to be said before her son. Now Jesse eschewed it in a feeling of deprivation. Yet he came down hard on the boy if inadvertently he used any of such gross terms as naturally he would pick up. Jesse seemed to think that no one else was justified in such behaviour.

Without speaking Garland finished his glass of milk and rose. Lifting his chair back from the table he set it against the wall.

'Load 'em in the wagon, eh?' he asked.

'Yes, but the darn horses haven't come up from the bush yet. You'll have to go after them. They'll stay all day.'

'It's too bad they can't learn to come up in the mornings,' said Nettie, looking at her fifteen-year-old son. 'It's a long walk back there.'

The boy had taken his broad curling hat from the nail. 'Oh, I don't mind it,' he mumbled as he let the screen-door swing to behind him.

II

It was the beginning of a June day, warm yet fresh. The young boy walked down the rail-fenced lane to the back of the farm; and the surrounding grass and corn, the weeds in the fence-corners, the inadvertent sounding of insects, a bird alighting on a top rail, the mist hanging in the middle distance and opening a horizon about him as he went, made a whole which was more to him than the vague thoughts which came to his mind. He was at peace. He kept steadily on his way toward the bush, still a wide hidden shape before him in the morning.

The bush was beautiful in its attempted negation of colour, its fragrance and a kind of reserve of warmth. The trees stood dozing, or whispering a little softly so as not to rouse the others. Near the front of the lot, where they were fewer, some of them had always had each a character of its own for Garland. One, he could not tell why, reminded him of an old calm church elder as he stood outside the church after service and greeted the people, his long beard moving. Another one was like a statue of a lion. It was strong-rooted and gnarled. Another was some slender fleet animal, he knew not what, and he wondered, before pausing in the wake of phantasies of his earlier childhood, why it had not sprung away and left the bush since he had been there last.

The boy began calling through the thin woods as he walked. He was at a loss in what direction to go that he might find the horses. He began to walk around the edge of the bush within a few rods of the line fence. The echo of his voice seemed muffled distantly, and to come back about him through the trees and the mist. The near trees became columns upholding clouds as he moved toward them. He had made almost a complete circuit when he decided to strike in to the centre of the wood and to finish examination of the outskirts if necessary afterward.

Now uneasiness came to him, as he thought of his father's waiting, and he walked more quickly.

III

Jesse was growing more and more impatient as the time passed. When he had fed the hogs generously he greased the wagon and put the sides on the rack which was used to haul livestock to market. He could have found plenty of odd jobs for an hour yet, but he did not think of them in his increasing disquiet. He would go to the head of the lane and look down it for the string of horses which should be coming. 'Blame the boy, what's ailin' him?' he muttered. The sun was beginning to shine out warmly, and to Jesse as he came forth from pitching down hay for noon from the loft to the stable below it seemed as though the morning were half gone. His annoyance was not lessened when he considered that probably he might not with a show of justice reproach the boy.

He went to the house. After he had taken a drink of water, he breathed heavily, glanced at himself in the mirror above the sink, and stood over the bare cleared wooden table a moment, his hands on each side of yesterday's paper.

Nettie Culworth came from the pantry to look into the oven.

'I wonder what on earth can be keeping that boy! There's no get-up about him. He's been gone for hours. Lot of help he is!' The back of his hand bristled across his mouth.

'He's likely doing the best he can, Jesse,' his wife replied, not pausing in her work. 'Don't scold him when he comes up. It's a long way back there.'

He grunted as he started up from the table and the screen-door cracked to behind him, but made no answer in words. A little relieved by this passage he strode to the corner of the barn. The horses were coming up the lane, old Dan leading them, and Garland behind. Impatiently the father waited.

'Well, you've been long enough!' he called as they came nearer. 'You had to run them all over the bush before you could get hold of them, eh?' He was smiling.

'No. ... I couldn't find them, father.'

'Oh! – Well, round 'em up there, hurry up, don't be all day.' He slid the door open and stood back at one side of it.

But the other horses were not inclined to follow old Dan into the stable. They swerved away from Jesse and around the small strawstack in the middle of the barn-yard.

'Git after them!' he called to his son. 'Be quick! Bring them around the stack and I'll watch here.'

The boy was already gone, and there was a moment of rustling through the straw and a dry musty smell, then the horses came tearing and plunging from around the stack. Jesse shouted and waved his arms, but he had nothing in his hands to frighten them back. They passed him and went down the lane. Garland leaped the fence and headed them off there, while Jesse strode to the stable door. 'Show 'em next time,' he muttered, gripping a fork-handle firmly. His impatience, or whatever it was, was augmented by the failure to stay the horses in the presence of his son.

This time one of the horses, head and tail up, came alone from behind the stack. The man ran forward to steer it into the door, but it darted away, leaving him beside the wall when a second one came toward him. He ran swiftly to the gate, growling between his clenched teeth, 'Who-oah, *you*!' He thought for an instant he had it, but it was passing him. He unconsciously swerved a little when he saw that they were going through the gate together and did not see protruding at an angle from the post a stiff wire, which grazed his cheek. He stopped and held one hand to his face intently a moment, not looking around, then with set jaw and without a word twisted the wire violently until it was broken off.

Garland looked on at this a moment, then remembered the horses, and went to drive them up a third time. The animals appeared to realize that their mischief had gone far enough for that morning, and came around quietly.

Jesse and his son entered the stable in silence. The boy was making for the box containing the curry-combs and brushes, when he saw that his father took down a collar from the peg. He also lifted down a collar and began to unbuckle its top. Jesse went to a stall.

'Get over here!' he said.

The animal seemed to hesitate, and did not move, so he quietly laid the collar down and bracing his powerful frame against the planks pushed the back part of the horse violently against the opposite wall. Then he seized and held it by the halter and began to kick its stomach. 'Show – you!' he grunted between the blows. After that he put on the collar.

Garland stood looking on, pale, for a few seconds, then he entered the stall of the other horse. When he had buckled the collar about its neck his father was waiting with its harness, instead of that of the horse which he had just been abusing. The animal started, knocking its knees in a tattoo against the manger, as he flung upon it the heavy harness which hung down over it behind. Jesse lifted the harness again, and came farther forward in the stall before again flinging it on the horse's back.

'What's the matter with *you*?' he asked tensely, seizing its halter and backing it in order to get at the hames. 'You won't eh?' he continued as the horse made a convulsive movement forward, and struck it on the side of the muzzle.

'Father!' cried Garland.

'What's ailin' you?' asked Jesse, looking at his son for a second.

The latter said nothing, but looked shamefacedly away toward the strong glare of sunlight on the rhomboid of dirty stained cement within the door, which made the rest of the interior of the stable still more dim. Outside the sun shone fiercely on the ragged edge of the tarnished strawstack and made each straw where a forkful had been freshly taken look like a precious bit of gold. A dry stifling smell came from the hot barnyard.

'What d'you have to start them running around the stack for then? You knew too well! Or else you'll never learn.' The unshaven face was yellow-black in the dim light as the man wrenched the straps into place. 'What are you standing there for?' he exclaimed, raising his voice. 'Haven't you lost enough time yet, eh?'

The boy reached up the pegs, standing on his toes, and with an effort swung a heavy harness down from them. It was dankly coated with greasy sweat. Holding the front of it in his hands he moved toward the stall. Jesse came and seizing the rear of the harness swung it to the horse's back. The animal pranced and nearly trampled the boy's feet.

'What d'you got to drag it over the floor for? If you can't pick it up, leave it alone.'

They went out into the heat of the sun a short distance along the dry lane to the pig yard. The enclosure was meant for a paddock but was long since beaten to a dust by the little hoofs, and only straggling unpalatable weeds stood yet, gray with dust. It was necessary to get the hogs into the pen in order to load them. Finally after a protracted hot struggle this end was accomplished. Each one demanded individual cornering and persuasion, but the last one of all required them after a few minutes' chasing to capture him. Seizing his short hind legs they dragged him raucously complaining to the pen.

When the door was closed on him and his comrades rallying around to welcome with excited gruntings his escape, Jesse had begun to accede to a grim good-humour. He had shown them! And Garland had employed quickness and a good deal of wiry strength.

'You'll make a farmer yet,' he said, as though unbendingly. He took off his hat and rubbed his brow with a colored handkerchief. Then he thought of the scratch from the wire which unaccountably he had forgotten. 'I'll go put something on my face,' he added, glancing at Garland. 'You hitch up on the wagon and we'll go over to Crampton's for their chute.' He went to the house hastily.

IV

Coming home the boy remarked, referring to the neighbour whom they had just left, 'So Andrew is going to retire?' though Crampton had just been informing them of his intention.

'Yes, the old sucker. After being as stingy as sin all his life and drudging night and day all his life like a slave he can go to town to die of bein' afraid he'll last longer than his money will, and wanting to work out on some farm, even somebody's else, since he's left his own; and being ashamed to.'

Without enthusiasm the old man had made his announcement, but he had thought the consummation worthy of a pride which he did not care to show, it was clear. His son, who was to have the running of the farm thenceforth, was not so well able to conceal his feeling. Turning aside from them talking together in the stable to hide his uncontrollable grin, he had shouted gruffly at a horse, putting back into its manger some hay which it had turned out.

Garland was silent as he looked absently at the surrounding fields, ashen and green rectangles in the violent sunlight. He sat on the low rear ladder of the wagon, and the irregular cackling rattle of the wheels lulled him. A lazy bit of dust hung alongside the wagon as they drove. The long road was empty, and seemed to hold, more than the farmyard they had just left, the hush and warmth of noon.

'Never be a farmer,' said Jesse, brooding. 'It's one thing or another. Either you have a heavy crop and everybody else has the same, and you take what they give you for it, or else, if the price is decent you've got but little or none. And it's always work, work – more work than if you did have a good crop. We'll have to go into business, you and I. Hardware business out West, eh? If I'm ever able to get shut of this farm,' he added with an intonation of bitterness. He brought this out as though it had long since been formed in his mind.

'Maybe we'll find a buyer,' said Garland. Lolling against the rear ladder he was again in the green woods of the morning, peering through the soft air cobwebbed with mist for the shapes of the horses showing through it vaguely in the depths. His calls rang on the thick air, but farther in the wood echoes were muffled, somehow. The horses made no movement or sound in answer, but did not try to escape when he came up to them. Dan raised a sleepy eye as he heard him coming. 'You old rascal!' Garland said when he had caught hold of his forelock. 'You brought them here, you know you did.' The wise old boy shook the end of his long nose from side to side and snored. They all blinked at him lazy-eyed, enjoying their truancy, but not then interested enough to attempt to make a get-away. Slowly they twined out of the bush and up the long lane. For a distance he held Dan by the damp forelock of his lowered head, old Mack and the others following. But when they came to the foot of the lane Garland slipped back behind them all, so that his father might not scold him for taking the risk of their getting away from him; and followed whistling in the sun and the light rolling waves of fog past large maples and oaks that overhung the lane. Broad circles of ground beneath the trees were beaten to a finer dust by the hoofs of the horses and cattle. Even then the mist was spreading and thinning. There was promise of a very warm day. ...

'I want you to be something better than a farmer,' his father was saying impressively.

'Oh, I don't know,' Garland answered uncertainly.

'Get along, Dan!' shouted Jesse, slashing with the lines.

They rattled on a few hundred yards and came to the home gate. They swung out widely to enter it. Garland suddenly cried out, and his father turning saw the heavy chute which protruded from the rack about to strike the gate-post and slide back, crushing the boy's legs. He pulled and shouted at the horses, and at that instant gate post and chute caught, but slightly, and the structure was moved only a few inches back from its place.

The boy's face was pink and sheepish, but his father was pale. 'Well, what *are* you thinking of this morning?' he shouted as the wagon went down the lane. 'Will you never learn? How often have I told you to look out for things like that? You could see blame well what was coming. But I've got to watch you like a baby. Ever *see* such a boy! *I* haven't enough to do, I must always be turning around and watching him. I'll have to have his mother out to help me take care of him. A great lot of good – ! Whoa!'

They drove into the bare yard and reached the pig pen. Jesse jumped down indignant. Garland continued to stand shamefaced by the back ladder of the wagon. How had he come to make such a blunder? It was true that his father had frequently warned him about such things. He must have been asleep. Still, he might have been able to jump off the back of the wagon if the chute had come any farther toward him, if the wagon were not going too rapidly. Well, another time –

He was roused by hearing his father say, 'Well, are you going to help me take this thing off, or aren't you?'

At that he stepped quickly forward and began lifting the heavy bulk. Slowly it was twisted back and forth and eased to the ground. Then he jumped down and helped to drag it into place inside the door of the pen.

'Go get some chunks to block the wheels – the damn horses won't stand, I know – while I back the wagon into position.

Garland went away to a pile of rubbish outside the barnyard fence. He was in a sort of daze of which he was scarcely half aware. He kept thinking of his first whiff of the sweet and gauzy-aired day from the little open window of his bedroom; of his mother's cheerful greeting, and the strange sadness he had felt at his father's early ill-temper; again, of the beauty of the morning bush, and sense of myriad mist-thralled birds when one of them broke silence for an instant, for a note. Inappositely he began thinking of evenings when he rode down the lane home on the disks musically tinkling, grating or clanging over the stones as the hungry and tired horses made for the barn; of the wonderful pleasure it now seemed to come in at dusk to the warm supper in the little bright-windowed house. The wind would rustle the vine dryly against the clapboards and the panes, but he would be warm and replete and in the light. ... Poor Mother! Poor Dan, the old slave! Unaccountable pity for everyone and everything enwrapped him.

In that instant he was fumbling about among old sticks and rubbish and pieces of rusty fence-wire for the blocks of wood. A call from his father roused him and he started up to come bringing them. He saw over in the green wheat field a horse with its head down. 'It's old Mack,' he thought. 'We couldn't have tied him up with the others. ... But how did he get there, how will we catch him?'

The rear of the wagon was about three feet from the building. 'I haven't got it just in position,' said Jesse. 'I thought it was no use until you brought the blocks, they fidget.so.'

He went forward, and Garland, taking no account of his movements, went in behind the wagon and looked down the slope of the chute at the pigs. He leaned over the straight lip of the frame. They were peaceful about the trough eating another meal before they died. The boy considered them with a strange pain at his heart. He could not understand his sorrow, and he was turning away silently when he heard a shout.

V

His father had gone to one side to consider the way in which the wagon would have to be maneuvred in order to bring it to just the right position in relation with the chute. He saw that it must be moved forward to get it in line for backing. He stepped quickly to the heads of the horses to lead them up by the bridles. With straining eyes and forward-sloping ears they both shied back from him, their powerful braced legs pushing the wagon back with a terrible inexorable swiftness, like the piston-swing of a great engine, it seemed. Yet it was a long moment. ...

Jesse found himself on his knees, his arm reaching up to a horse's rein. If there had been a sound he had not heard it. In silence the sun was beating down on the dirty yard about him, on the scattered grimy weeds which had withstood the browsing hogs. A little cloud of dust lazily wandered away, twisting slowly across the ground. Then he heard the guzzling of the hogs at the feed he had given them – how long? – five minutes ago. And somewhere a bob-white was calling, portent of a day of rain.

Trying to hold his eyes shut, on his hands and knees he crept around to the back of the wagon.

INDIAN SUMMER

Ida Tenny could not deny to herself the feeling of a certain pleasurable, or at least anticipatory, confusion. The days went on, passed in a rhythmic swiftness it began to seem, and something of their interest unconsciously attached itself in her mind to the freshening if still spinsterly relation to Gregory. She went through the accustomed tasks in the house until the middle of the week.

In the perfection of weather farm work was advancing on every hand. Earlier in the season it had been a little cold, and the warmth now was scarcely past luxuriousness. She and Cam Dougal, her farmer, conferred more earnestly about the farm operations now that they were doing than when plans for them were being made. The delayed corn had been planted nearly a week before, and showed long thin rows of the tiny green plants against the brown soil, where a few weeks later would be tall stalks arching and shading the earth. The field opposite Ida Tenny's house was of alfalfa, and already cut and drying in the June sunlight. Today a man was raking there with an old-fashioned one-horse rake, moving about with what could have seemed an unpleasant assiduity in the white heat of afternoon. Ida, with her lifetime's habit of work, did not think of that.

Yet this day somehow had come to be a time for musing. After last Saturday night she could not tell what he'd do, but surely it would be something; and it might transpire any evening. She had thought of this as she brought the green porch chair and the faded sofa out on the veranda – continuous summer weather appeared to have arrived – and was sitting there, reading the mail brought by the route-carrier when Thyra Lamb walked in, with short, quick, and yet erratic steps, clicking the iron gate giving on the lawn.

'Thought I'd bring that spool of A. silk thread back, I kept it so long.' She peered up with a sidelong glance of humour, before stepping onto the veranda.

'Oh, no hurry about that at all,' Ida made reply, turning the paper inside out, long arms wide-stretched.

'I bought a new one, and now more of it's used than was of yours, but then only a little, and Alma says, just take it along, 'taint likely Miss Tenny'll be wanting it to make any gay dresses with, like's if she was a young thing – that wears these short skirts!' This, Ida Tenny realized automatically, was meant as a string by which to drag a halter of conjectural gossip about her neck – or had she become unduly sensitive since the half-final parting (if he construed it in that way) from Gregory?

'No, I'm not doing much sewing lately. I didn't have any spring sewing, really, what you might call spring sewing. I bought me a ready-made dress the other day, of silk poplin.' Thyra Lamb could not know (thank Heaven for that!) of that other dress she had bought and could not wear, could not bear even to have tailored – orange-glinting tricolette, after throes of desperate choice in which she felt in another element. She had laid it away. But though as often as she looked at it she asked herself, 'I wonder what'd got into me, that day, I was so reckless,' she didn't really feel chagrin at the wasted money.

'You did! Bought a new one! Has it got these knife-pleats on the skirt?' asked Mrs Lamb.

'No, it's plain, with an over-skirt. Won't you come in and see it?'

'Course I will.' The chirping tone swooped up, and the small features became animated. She seldom, Ida Tenny felt sure, found pleasure in other people's houses or clothes, but was always impelled even to make excuses for inspecting them.

They went along the side veranda to the kitchen, where Mrs Lamb looked furtively, and as though from habit, behind the door to see the rotary washing machine. Notwithstanding broad waves of light from the windows the room seemed dim. There was a high paper-scalloped shelf bearing two lamps, one large, one small, of glimmering chimneys; and the linoleum from which in broad strips the colour was worn, long rug neatly woven of rags, the silent stove.

'Your kitchen's just like it always is,' she assured Miss Tenny, breaking the silence and looking back as they went into the sitting-room. 'I declare I could have come in three years ago and 'twould have been no different. Four!' she added indignantly.

The tall woman laughed. It was what Mrs Lamb had said frequently enough before, and in the light of her new preoccupation Ida felt that she had minded more than she knew her eternal spinster sameness, the pausing days of her quiet round in the lingering years. Now, suddenly she felt sure, things might not be changed, perhaps, but they could not surely be the same.

It was in the spare room, off the sitting-room, that she kept her good clothes, few, and of astonishing age for the greater part, in an old chest of worn surfaces. She took down the brown silk dress and they looked at and fingered it. They spoke in low tones, as though, it seemed to Ida's freshened consciousness, repressed suddenly by the dulled furnishings and the slightly musty odour. Thyra Lamb had not commented on this room, and there was after all something perfunctory in her interest in the dress, though she followed the old course of invidiously admiring comment unthinkingly, as if uncertain how to bring out what was on her mind. Finally:

'Yes, you're getting all fixed up, all right! I don't blame you! Course you would, all right, seein' all that's going on, these days.'

Miss Tenny was looking at the brown folds. 'Yes,' she agreed in rather absent tones.

'Yes indeed, from what I hear tell around, about you and Gregory Hackling.'

'That's kind of funny. About Mr Hackling and I.' The tone now was of inquiry and expectation.

Mrs Lamb allowed her to wait a moment, then went on, 'They say you'n him's taken to keepin' company again.'

Slowly and vaguely Ida Tenny answered, as she began instantaneously to recall that other day, in April, when the same woman had come to speak of Gregory's helping her get his hogs out of her field, Cam Dougal being away. 'Now if you had a man of your own, now. ...' Why should she remember the words of a gossip whose primitive notion of humour had so long, one now realized, made her exasperating? But wasn't it that day those same speeches had made her really aware of Gregory after these years apart; or had it been himself coming, had she begun to – think, before? 'Now if you had a –' Her mind flashed back to the present as she spoke:

'A report like that might easily get abroad, the way people are always willing to afford themselves time to look into other people's affairs.' This careful sarcasm would only make Mrs Lamb smile.

'Then it's true, ah, it's true,' Mrs Lamb replied to a fluttered calm.

'They'd learn we'd been keeping company by seeing Miss Hackling and I going to town together, I suppose!' Suddenly the spinster wanted to laugh. It was becoming an inquisition. One looking on, she thought, would wonder what the man was like that they should quarrel about him. Well, it wasn't quarrelling – Gregory hadn't risen to quite that value. She reassured herself half-incredulously.

'Yes, and him along too, I heard.'

'Well, that's true, he went with us to town one Saturday night. Has it got about maybe what particular articles each of us bought?' But she thought it unnecessary to mention their last trip alone, without his sister. Though Mrs Lamb would have heard.

'There *was* mention of an automobile,' said the latter unabashed by satire. 'It looks bad,' she went on with a wise laugh. 'It looks as though he's going to pop the question, or something's come over him, to think of him parting with money enough to buy a car, after the way he's always said he'd never have one of them on the place.'

Miss Tenny folded the dress at this, and took it to the chest. She could not even feel astonishment at this bold assignment of her motives. They would not have paused in the sitting-room, but passed the golden-oak sideboard laden with multi-coloured dishes, the veteran unused chairs, and the round table in the centre with maiden-hair fern and the patterned chenille cloth hanging to the floor. It was cool there and the day looked bright from the narrow window made narrower by curtains starched stiffly and warped perpendicularly in sentry-like columns at either side.

Mrs Lamb stopped at the door, looked around, and announced, 'It seems like you don't want to stay inside on a day like this. We'll soon get enough of the heat, if this weather keeps up!' She moved on after her hostess.

The latter stood a moment looking out across the field of alfalfa opposite, above which heat-waves, the first she had observed that year, played in the light spring-like air.

At their feet rosebushes spread thin laden branches abroad on either side of the steps, and made the large white house less bare and unadorned than most of the year it seemed.

'My, aren't those pritty? They *are* pritty! There's nothing I like better than roses. They don't stay long, 'less o' course you have different kinds.' Her deepening smile seemed to Ida Tenny reminiscent of well-tended bushes at home, which had long been her pride, so that no one about there possessed such roses. All kinds, they made the prim house almost winsome. Bridal garments –

'I'll have to have Cam Dougal's young-ones come over tomorrow and mow that lawn.' She looked practically at the long grass of the lawn to the road. 'It's just beginning to grow well, now the last rains are having their effect.'

'Yes, I always like to keep mine – ours – short too, especially when the almanac says like this year, it's going to be a dry-time. The grass'll dry up, and if there's anything I hate it's long yellow grass. If it's short it doesn't look quite so bad. A rain has some chance to have some effect, anyway, if it comes then. I tell you what. Let me tell my boys to come over and do a real good job on that lawn. They're bigger than

Cam's boys, Stephen is anyway, and they'll do it right, not cost you any more, though they have farther to walk.'

'Less maybe you *promised* them they could do it.' she went on, since Miss Tenny did not answer. 'But even if you did, they don't deserve nothing more than'll just happen to come their way. I could tell you lots of things about that hired man of yours you don't know, *I'll* bet. But there, I never did want to be one to go 'bout making people trouble.'

'Cam Dougal has always been quite satisfactory in his work, I don't know of any other man I could trust so well to look after a farm that wasn't his own. Do you know of anybody?' But that wouldn't corner Mrs Lamb.

'Well – maybe you're right now, I don't want to be one to go and say.' They had sat down by this time in faded green porch chairs, looking across the disputed lawn to the neat white-painted wire-fencing which enclosed it. 'What's he doing now? My man's getting along with the spring work.'

She might have been referring, instead of to her husband, to a hireling, Ida thought. In a pause the visitor went on: 'Do I know of anybody, you said? Anybody who could work your farm better?' She seemed undecided to continue, adding, 'I'll tell you what I heard! If it's not true it'll set my mind at rest anyway, that's one thing! I heard that Gregory Hackling has asked you to marry him. Some says you rejected him, and some says you're thinking of accepting him.'

Even her heart must have failed her, and she obviously did not know what to say in the shocked silence. She went on half-defiantly, 'Well, I did hear he was getting the car to please you. If he did that he's certainly making up for lost time.'

Miss Tenny aggravatingly refrained from saying more than, 'Who's been telling all this?'

It was the kittens which saved them, or Miss Tenny, from deeper embarrassment. Two little bunched grey creatures leaped around the corner of the house, and came toward the veranda steps until they saw the women there.

'Those the ones you had the day I was over a while ago? Yes? They seem grown some, but then you'd see they got good care, all right, wouldn't you?' Her smile with this seemed all at once disagreeable to the spinster with her knowledge of the other's dislike for cats of any kind.

'Topsy and Cinderella. Yes. ...'

'Troubled with rats, I s'pose. They're pretty good, when they *are* good. Better than having rats around, I s'pose. *I* always use traps.'

'You should have seen them the day Miss Hackling came over, a while ago, to go to town with me. It was a day like this, only not so warm. I had left the window in the kitchen open, with a telescopic screen under it. I guess I must have neglected some cooking or something.' She shouldn't have confessed that; it seemed shiftless. She hurried on. 'It was only partly telescoped, so that there was a little space open – there were no flies then, of course. Well, the little ones were in the house, and Tom, the old one, jumped to the sill of the window and saw them. The hole was just big enough that he couldn't get his head in. He mewed and mewed, but he couldn't quite get his head into the room. Then the kittens got up and scurried over to the sill and began to tease him. He stretched his paw around the corner and tried to reach them and made a terrible noise, but they just kept on, till his miawlings got to frighten them and so they scampered away.'

She had come to a subject which, while it really interested her, with her perversity carried herself as well as her caller away from the perilous topic of a minute before. She did not fear Mrs Lamb's smiling in recognition of this.

'But ain't they too much of a nuisance?' This tone was a call for absolute candour. 'Now I know a lot of folks that wouldn't have a cat in the house. I wouldn't myself, and there's a fact. Sneaky, and getting into the pantry and everything.'

At that instant they heard a scratching at the screen door, half ajar, and then it was opened, and the huge striped grey cat stepped out on the veranda, and administered dignified buffets to the little ones when they fawned about its feet. They seemed determined to dispel its mood with teasing, but the large animal took to a dismally sharp screech, and bare-toothed spittings. They shrank. Miss Tenny was roused.

'Here, you big brute, do you want to *kill* those poor little things?' she asked excitedly and as it were unconsciously. She reached around the door into the room and seized a limber switch. With a yowl of different tone, the old cat made a low swift shape for the corner of the house.

As she replaced the switch and turned again to her visitor there was a little flush about the rather thin brown face, with its slight hollow back of and below the mouth. Momentarily silence came. Then Thyra Lamb smiled a little and said:

'Well, you do keep order, anyway!'

'I had to keep Topsy and Cinderella in nearly all the time before it got warm enough to have the window open.'

'Why don't you kill off that big overgrown brute? What I'd do, if I had it.'

'Well, I've had him so long.'

'You've had it so long!' Mrs Lamb mocked her tone humorously. 'Well, what did Christina Hackling say – you was talking about her. I bet she told you just what I do.'

'She laughed at them. ... Yes, the same, just about.'

'Then you and her went shopping to town, eh? She and you's getting real sporty, ain't you now? I never thought I'd see the time when you and her would be going around together so much,' specially after you giving Gregory the mitten that time.'

'But,' objected Miss Tenny, 'that was a good many – quite a while ago.'

'I know, but the Hacklings don't forget anything like that. I bet she holds it against you yet. Her aunt Jemima I remember – '

'Why – Christina Hackling is a real lady, always been one to me, and I wouldn't like to say anything against any of her people. ... I doubt if she ever thought of anything of the kind.'

'I see where we're getting to now. They say you can tell how far they've gone, by the way they stick up for the relatives.' Her ridged face laughed long at her perspicacity.

Miss Tenny bit her lips.

'Oh, you don't want to think people don't see all that goes on. Especially when it comes to Gregory and you keeping company. Ha, ha!'

The spinster was frank to herself in wishing her visitor gone.

'Then him getting that automobile. Do you know what make it is?'

'No, I do not.' She bit back the 'yet' which nearly followed.

'After him getting it for you? That's no way to appreciate it!' The woman's boring eye discovered the man raking hay across the road, who was coming to the end of the field. 'I see you have him right opposite here.'

'Oh! – Who?' Ida was perplexed.

'Why Gregory, of course. Didn't you see him working there?'

'But what's he doing over in Camp's field?'

'I suppose you mean to tell me you didn't know he's taken that field on shares. Old man Camp don't want to work it himself – '

'Oh, that's it!' Ida smiled at the portentous manner of the intimation.

'Seems to me you don't keep track what's doing around very well. Yes, I guess he got a good bargain for that field.'

But Ida feared the approach of the rake to the road, for there was no telling what demonstration the Lamb woman would make, and rose. 'Come around back and see how my chickens are getting along. I have hens setting already.'

'You and your hens! I'll bet they're not doing as well as mine! Well, we'd better see.' She rose and followed the straight figure of the spinster around the corner of the house, on the lawn where no path was worn, just as the man with the hay-rake came to the road.

With a freshened sight as that of a stranger Ida Tenny passed the large flat stone buried to its surface in the scantly-greened earth about the back door. 'I've been having a lot of trouble with keeping them off the door-yard.' A few heavy Plymouth Rock fowl moved about the spot.

'Why don't you sell those old birds of yours, if they bother?' Thyra's tone was that of one humoringly proffering counsel to a child. 'My lands, if I had no more that I really had to do than you, I'd do different, seems to me.'

'Well, I did make up my mind to call Hochenmeyer up and ask him to come in when he was going past some time and look at them. But you know what those Jews are like when once they think you want to get rid of a thing. He'd think I was dying to sell them, if I asked him to make me a bid on them. Then I was going to have Cam Dougal take them to market Saturday, but he had some other work on foot, he always has, so I don't know what I'll do now; wait a bit, I guess.' Her voice, energetic and calm, not sharp, in this long speech, told that she was interested. Only herself knew that she was banishing pre-occupation, talking, at least, against it.

'Why – do you really want to sell them?' Perhaps the mocking tone was only partly simulated, and she really thought that in settled Ida Tenny such a decision appeared revolutionary. 'You'll be turning everything upside down, yet.'

Her companion smiled resolutely, looking about the bald and tufted dooryard, at the garden-rakes and hoes standing against the end of the wood-shed, a long prop leaning at a great angle to the wire clothesline with a languid disdain of peril suggestive of a toper leaning over the parapet of a bridge. Farther back loomed the barn, a huge and vaguely grey shape, with an old-fashioned windmill rising out of it amidships. The wheel above the single heavy pole uprearing it looked at a distance like a pie-faced caricature of a clown with a scrawny neck. The boards nailed across the pole for steps made you think of climbing them, and wonder why you never had, so that it wasn't so much like a neck at all. She reminded herself that these were childhood comparisons, though one identified them as truly now as when they first had suggested themselves.

Mrs Lamb was speaking. 'Uh-huh! agreed Ida, and then tried to recall the words to which she had agreed. It was said that Mrs Lamb did not get along well with her husband. ... Inconsequently she thought of the tremendous vigour of Mrs Lamb's church-working. The woman felt herself responsible for the success or failure of most of the entertainments. An appeal for church funds aroused her. She saw that each one baked or sewed what was assigned, and ran things with militant rigour. She was everywhere, a thin little important figure. Nothing escaped her eye.

She was peering a little curiously, leaning forward as she talked and watched Cam Dougal's tow-headed eldest coming into the barn with the cows. 'I bet that young-one's up to something. What's he so early about, I wonder? He gets out of school early, and then he goes straight for the cows. It ain't natural for a boy to be so industrious. If Cam was around I'd give him a hint about it. It ain't like it was winter. He's got something up his sleeve.'

Not as if it were winter. Ida Tenny figured the early dark, the hurrying chores in the late snowy afternoon, herself with shawl about her head feeding the chickens; and a sense of the swift-following seasons and a sadness the product of change which was no change. She turned away.

'Well, come over and see me again some time, Thyra,' she called as the small figure tripped hurriedly across the lawn to the little gate. Yet it was in her heart to have said, 'And I'll learn all the news that's not true.'

Her insistent desire for the visitor's departure, which half-consciously puzzled her, was relieved at last. Luckily the man had just begun his return to the far end of the field or, she was prepared to feel, that woman would have stopped him, told or asked him Heaven knew what.

She went into the house, the kitchen, and sat down, thinking. She endeavoured to reach her real impression about this gossip. What had come over Thyra Lamb? Had she really heard the things she was so determined to tell? It was of course possible, but the locality boasted no more incorrigible gossip than that woman herself. And was not her thirst for novelty pathetic, trifling, in the long view of it?

It was minutes before she began to think of the implacable nature of the report, and how it would swath her in itself until she was as fatally enwound as a mummy in cerements. Fatally, yes. To think of people actually talking about her relations with Gregory Hackling, which didn't exist, she thought vexedly – but she would be honest – didn't they? wouldn't they? – It was more than she could bear. It would not be so bad to marry a man as that, quite. When you were married there'd be no more gossip. Consciously she told herself that one didn't want to think of these things, they might cause a decision either way to be regretted. ... 'The attempt and not the deed confounds us!' She thought smilingly of a memorized Shakespearian soliloquy of her school-days. 'But – silly! that was about a crime of course.' Gregory hadn't even been in that part of the country then.

She was roused from her study. She became conscious of the kittens dancing about the suspended thread tied to the arm of her rocking chair. She considered them as though for the first time in days, in their oblivious toyings and leapings athwart each other.

Everything was neatly in order. The linoleum was scrubbed clean, the stove was of a shiny blackness, except for one lid burnt a light pink, which, never polished, was used for toasting bread. The neatness of the whole house could scarcely be excelled.

She went through the rooms to the front porch, taking from a drawer a lace collar for her new dress, on which a little work had still to be done. The middle of the afternoon had come, though the sunlight seemed as direct as before. The man working in the field opposite her had nearly finished his raking. The long windrows of hay lay across the field, a blent series of dark waves in the distance; with, nearer, a wash of yellow-green stubble between.

She had looked across at that field and watched the growth of crops and the work in it, for nearly ten years, since her brother, dying, had left her the farm and its cares. Why she did not become tired of the view she did not know. Perhaps it had been because she had not really looked at it. Yet she foresaw the activities which the remainder of the season would bring, before snow smothered the grass. At the next cutting of hay the ground would be dry and dust would follow the rake as it came toward her, Gregory perhaps driving it. Now the man was too far away for his face to be seen, but she thought that she recognized the long-backed figure as his. The flies must have been troublesome, for she noticed that the horse continually switched and swung its head.

The sewing rested unheeded in her lap while she leaned forward and gazed toward the man, as though to find in the sight of him an answer to the question she was putting to herself. Now they passed under the shade of a tree, and she realized that they had come to the end of the field. Gregory Hackling – she saw that it was Gregory – stopped the horse to rest it after the long pull; and she at once became engrossed in her sewing.

Presently she heard the rake rattling and squeaking as it was turned around and they started back toward the other end again. Musingly she considered the man as he drove on down the field, the swing and jerk of his arm as he pulled the lever up which released the bunch of hay, and the jerk of his other arm as the horse swung its head about for flies, drawing the lines with its motions.

She had seen men at work haymaking a hundred times before, probably, and it was not quite interestedly that she looked on now. Her thoughts were of what she would do if the presupposed rumour really became current. Still more she thought of what was to be done if the dictum of Mrs Grundy were to assume the mien of prophecy instead of only anticipation. If he really did ask her, what on earth would she do? It was not just the decision itself. The very idea of the possibility of his asking her was unnerving to think about, since, she told herself, it was so long since she had thought of it.

She noticed two or three print-clad school-girls of various sizes loitering down the road, their books under their arms or hanging in leathern schoolbags from their shoulders. It must be getting late: she took up her sewing again. By this time Gregory was nearing the end of the field once more.

In a moment the girls had passed, and the ramshackle creak again became audible as the rake turned about. Suddenly there came a loud 'Whoa!' and Ida looked up to see, for an instant, the figure of Gregory standing alongside the horse and in front of the rake, apparently engaged with mending a part of the harness. Then with an impatient shake of the head the animal went on. Just what happened could not be known, but Gregory must have caught his foot in the lines and been thrown down on the ground. He shouted at the horse again. But the animal knew that no one held the lines, and that sent it on all the faster. Gregory seemed to be under the rake now, dragged along the sod by its teeth.

Miss Tenny leaped to her feet and was across the road and beside the fence in an instant. She stood there, tranced and breathless, seeing all this. Then: 'Girls!' she screamed. 'Girls! Mr Hackling! He's going to be killed!' The school-girls looked around in astonishment at the apparition, and from her gesturing arm over to the man and the horse.

But then, unbelievably, as the trot was increasing in speed the man seemed to twist about and grip the bottom of the shaft and draw himself up to sit upon it, whence he could reach the tied lines and bring the animal to a stop. He dismounted from the rake, and having looked around in uncertainty waved his hat vigorously. Ida waved her arms in reply, and the girls waved. Both she and they were unconscious for the moment of other spectators. Then, finding herself leaning over the fence of the field, the woman returned to the house, as Gregory looked to his harness again.

She was still warm and shaking as she entered the door. It had all taken but a moment. If the horse hadn't been so old and lazy! If it had been really frightened!

She moved restlessly about the rooms, her embroidering forgotten. She had so nearly climbed over the fence. What then? It had been so near, she saw his swift movements, the beauty of relief in his face when he waved his hat. Something else, intangibly, had been near. It in some way brought back the months of their courtship. She could not remember now what had broken them off.

Did she think that it was his stinginess? He had followed his calling with a doggedness coupled with an intelligence she considered unusual, so he was now in a position which among farmers was held as enviable. She recalled his pride in his fields, his herds of swine, of cattle; of small, and as she had thought niggardly consummated dealings. ... How short the years were, in reality: five years, ten years, nothing. She thought of girlhood imaginings, unforgotten after all. ...

Should she go out to the lawn – to the porch, Gregory would see her – . 'Like as not he's scared to death by now, to have anything to do with me for fear of being forced into a false position.' Still, he had not been so introspective when she had known him. She refused a flashed fancy-blighting image of him, plain, prosaic enough, after these years in the wake of the main chance. Time had passed; time was still to pass. ...

It must be late! How long had she been wandering about the rooms like that? She drew her hand back from the tips of the sword-fern. The leaf would drop off.

But the sun was still high. 'He'll expect me to be different, I know,' she was saying as she passed out to the lawn. 'I know he'll expect that, somehow.'

Then Gregory was coming out of the gate and rattling along the road past her house. Terror seized her. 'It must be early, I thought it was earlier,' she thought. 'What is he going home now for?'

She saw his sheepishly boyish grin as he pulled up his horse – and as she advanced to the fence.

'Quite an escape you had, that was – !'

Yes, there was something to be said. The rake had stopped now. Gregory had begun to talk. At his words, through a blur, of happiness perhaps, a certainty came that impossibly she had cheated the years, silenced their importunity forever.

GRAPES

The first thing which drew my attention to the new hired man was his pronunciation of his name. 'James Cu-cu-Culihan,' he told me it was, when with childish bluntness I asked him. He had been standing about on the back veranda in an embarrassed manner, but now he walked away to the barn, although Father wasn't home yet from the field for supper and nobody had given James anything to do, since he had just come.

I stared after his angular, stilted form, and then rushed in to the house and told my mother. She was slicing part of the noon boiled potatoes in a frying-pan, making vigorous motions with a clacking baking-powder can from which most of the red paper had been worn, and she scarcely looked up.

'Yes, he stutters,' she said; and that seemed to be all there was to the matter. But in my eyes it gave rise to a way of looking at James as a rare creature from whom nothing would be unforeseen. Strangers came seldom to the farm.

His appearance was not so strange, when one considered it, though probably I stared a good deal during that first supper. He was, as I should judge, about thirty-one years old, and he had a large long face with tow hair and pale-irised blue eyes, and a long nose of no shape. My sister Lucy and I sat at one side of the table and James, at the other side, could easily look over our heads at the bright calendar picture of a barefoot girl carrying two puppies across a stony ford. Most hired men would have directed some word of jocularity at me at least; but on the other hand, most would have addressed my mother just as he did, 'No, m'am, thank you, m'am.' James seemed always very inoffensive and shy about the house, and a good worker outside. He always wore overalling. On cool days he could be seen in the fields or about the barn wearing a blue jacket to match the long bibbed light pants over it. The lines of this garment made his gaunt form yet more tall. On hot days, amid the crops, when the jacket was discarded, there would be a blue shirt. And he changed complete sets of them every week. This made him conspicuously tidy and spruce at such gatherings as threshings or bees, where other hired men were in evidence.

Those were busy days though I do not seem to have been impressed by the fact. My father was a young man, not yet forty, and not well off, and the land which he had set himself to cultivate did not give him much opportunity for impractical reflection. Like most farmers in that part of Ontario, his parents had come to it at a time when nothing was there but bush. They had hewn, plowed, and ditched two large, well-equipped farms from the raw bush, but my father, one of the younger members of the family, was given a cash amount as his inheritance. He 'worked out' for a few seasons, then bought a farm by means of mortgages – two hundred acres for which he was now trying to pay. Help seemed disproportionately dear, and as yet I was able to lend a hand only to the extent of carrying water to the field, or putting down hay from the mow for meals, or splitting kindling. While the hired men were not expected to do more than their bosses, they were not allowed to lag too far behind.

When Sunday came, we children had a surprise. Mother was clearing the breakfast table, and there was no sign of Father or of James Culihan. But on my plate and Lucy's lay large packages of chewing gum, wrapped in fringed tinfoil. As I jumped at mine, shouting to Lucy who followed down the stairs, my mother explained. James had left them for us. She had never approved of gum, saying that there was no nourishment in it, and when she did buy us candy it was the most we could do to get her to compromise with gum-drops.

'Where is James?' we wanted to know. It seemed natural to be concerned about the whereabouts of one who could do a thing like that

'He's gone to church – to mass,' our mother told us. 'All dressed up, and never a chore done, for all of him.'

'Why does he go so early? I thought he was English,' said Lucy.

'Of course not. He's Irish,' I proclaimed. 'Lucy thinks nobody but Frenchmen go to mass.'

But we were not encouraged to talk about James, even after a certain tension had become apparent between my parents and him. One night at dusk, which is not early in the summer on that flat farming land, Father came from outside pail in hand to strain the milk in the pantry. I swung the hammock on the veranda at the end of the open kitchen. Mother was wiping the last of the dishes, and as she came out for the kettle to scald the milk pail, he raised his voice to say to her,

'Speak to him about it? That does no good. Al Wondron told me that. "Ed Binter," he says to me, "if you can keep him from robbing the cream-cans, he'll make you a good man. That's all there is to it." I didn't think much about it at the time. ...'

'Well, it's not any joke,' my mother answered. 'It's got so there's no use hiding the milk-pans anymore. He knows right where they are. I've got so I just leave some out, and let him skim them. We ought to get a lock, that's what we should do, lock everything up.'

'No,' my father declared, 'when it come to that, a man has to lock up things in his own house, that's no good. ... I'd sooner see him leave, first.'

So it was real, this oddity which I found in James, and which my parents had seemed in a conspiracy to ignore. I ran to the stable as though to assure myself of his continued existence. He was there, bedding the teams with straw brought from the stack outside in the barnyard; and I must have looked at him very seriously, for he smiled with his sallow features, not straightening his long back above the fork, and asked me:

'W-well – You didn't think the stable had m-m-moved away, d-d-did you?'

As quickly as I had come, I turned and ran. 'No, I just thought of something,' I called back, leaping from the beam of the stable door, into the dusty yard.

I slept in a little room which stood at the head of the back stairs, and which opened into that of my parents. That night I woke up and heard excited whispering. My mother stirred, and her words bristled with anger.

'There's that man going downstairs again to steal the cream. I can hear the stairs squeak. Wake up!' She shook Father. 'I tell you, it's got to stop. If you're not man enough to go down there and tell him, I'm going! *I'll* tell him a thing or two. If you think he's going to rob us like that, and the children – '

She made a motion to rise, and Father, grunting, turned over. When she told him again, I knew that he sat up, and muttered and rubbed his eyes. 'Well, we can't let him go now, there's the second crop of clover not even – Yes, yes, I'm going!'

I was creeping quickly and stealthily down the cool wooden stairs at the back of the house before I knew it, and opening the stair door a crack to see across the kitchen, into the pantry. There was James Culihan before the shelf, and a large spoon moved quickly from his mouth to the crock, never spilling. In a moment Father came from the front of the house, waddling sleepily. He stood at the door, a short thick shape in his hanging night-gown, elbows uplifted as he rubbed his eyes. James must have known that he was there, but he didn't turn around. Father rocked with sleepiness and yawned audibly. 'Cr-cre-eam!' he drawled, just like James. 'You won't be able to look at cream for a mule's age, if you keep on.'

James turned his long head at this, so that a lamp showed up behind him, and mumbled, gripping the big spoon in his hand, 'I've g-got to have it, y'-y' know.' He seemed to look at my father in a puzzled kind of way.

Father squirmed, as though blinking at the light, hunching his shoulders, and rubbed his chest with a large fist that gathered his shirt. He turned away, yawning, into the darkness of the house.

When morning came I thought it might have been a dream, as I dressed hurriedly and went downstairs. My parents and James were at breakfast.

'No cream for your porridge this morning,' my mother murmured indignantly, as she put the bowl before me. It was perhaps the first word which had been spoken.

James himself appeared unaware, until his face became a trifle ruddy.

'Well, James, I'm thinking it'll be you for the job of going to town this morning,' Father said bluffly.

'Very well,' muttered the man. 'Did ye mean soon?'

'No, to meet the 'leven-fifteen. Couple young ladies coming out from the city today. It's today, ain't it?'

My mother nodded, but looked no better pleased than before. She did not intend that James should meet the train. I recalled that a week or two before she had received a letter from two daughters of her older sister, which said that they expected to come out for a visit to the farm during the last half of the summer holidays.

When they arrived it became clear that if I had known them before I should never have forgotten any announcement of their coming.

Beretta, or as she was called, Prettie, was only sixteen, and when she alighted from the buggy which Father had driven to the depot for them, she seemed to bounce into my mother's arms; then Doris in turn presented herself. 'Here!' said my Father, while he swung their grips from the buggy, at the same time holding the lines. 'Here, am I left out of this? 'Sposed to give the driver something, ain't you?'

Prettie took him at his word, giggled and rattled with the utmost nimbleness, 'I'm shocked, mortified, flabbergasted, and disgusted.' We children danced about the group, and it was the first time we had heard such a string of long words, but we were to hear them frequently enough to memorize them ourselves.

Her sister Doris was half-a-dozen years older, a brown-haired girl with grey eyes and a slightly tilted nose; more serious, or more conscious in her enjoyment of life: sometimes she would attempt to check the exuberance of Prettie.

The whole place seemed enlivened by their coming. Mother forgot to look worried, but inspected with admiring comment some of the clothes which they unpacked before dinner, and asked them how long they might stay.

'I want you to stay as long as you – can stand it,' she added, looking about the little 'spare room,' then smiling.

Lucy was examining a toilet set, and paid no attention, but I fancied that the girls glanced at each other.

'Oh, we'll stay as long as the country'll stand *us*,' said Prettie readily.

It was nearly noon, and while Mother hurried about the kitchen the girls and Lucy and I stayed in the sitting room.

'We got a hired man, he gives us gum,' Lucy told them.

'Yes, I forgot to mention it,' my mother said as she passed the door. 'You girls'll find him most interesting, a beau for you! Only I'm afraid he won't be staying with us long.'

'How would he know which one to take?' I asked practically. They all laughed.

At dinner when the men had washed, the girls came into the kitchen and were introduced to James. I noticed this as a most genteel ceremony; the girls bowed and did not shake hands, and both said, 'Pleased to meet you,' which Lucy, afterward, seemed to consider one word.

Before these two city-bred young ladies James was more nearly silent than ever. But they laughed and talked obliviously, and he too became absorbed in their anecdotes and clever 'cute' sayings. 'Doris is all right, except her left side,' Prettie said, and James became red with smothered laughter.

After supper that night grapes were passed around. There were a couple of rows of vines along a ditch back in the middle of the farm, which no one had investigated until that afternoon when the girls proposed taking a walk. Mother had given me a basket, and I had gone with them.

When the loaded platter came round to James, he raised a bony-wristed hand and said in his nasal voice,

'Grapes! Gr-apes? My la-ands, grapes! I never want to look at a grape again. I ate a six-quart basket once, and I never want to see a grape again. It was at a f-fair,' he added abruptly.

Our consternation, amusement, and that of the grown-ups, I suppose, was as strong as the feeling of James. We all enjoyed grapes more as a by-word, after that.

Only rarely did he speak at the table, and not much more frequently outside, working. But there he was nearly irreproachable. He never had to be called in the mornings, and he was as silent in his exertions at dark, if necessary. He was best to feed pigs, and he was nothing great with horses, but my father laid this to his ancestry; some new Irishmen, he said, could not back a wagon out of a barn door. Occasionally James became excited and abused the horses, when he was pitching sheaves to the wagon toward sunset.

Still, my mother had made up her mind. 'No other woman around here would stand for his depredations,' she told Doris, who was wiping the dishes in the pantry. Doris seemed to take this unconcernedly; as for Prettie, she declared that James was too funny to live. I no longer paid much heed to James, and it was with hints of duress that I was constrained to cut wood for the house and to do the other chores which were normally my lot. Those moments were gained which I could steal to be with the girls. But they too liked the open air, the unregarding carelessness with which they could pass the days on the farm, lolling in the hammock on the veranda, helping in the house, or rambling, in any kind of clothes, at large.

The wheat and barley had been cut, shocked, and mostly hauled into the barn, and the oats were waiting, as high as my head – one of the heaviest crops I can remember – that year. It was so rank that a storm lodged it, and I found a spot near the lane where the twisted stalks formed something like the framework for a miniature hut. I made the most of this encouragement, and soon showed my little house to Lucy and to Prettie, planning that we should hide in it when the load of barley came up the lane and I was supposed to be on hand to drive the horses for the slings. This appeared a scheme of most seductive ingenuity, but it did not work out just as I had planned. To mark the spot for myself I had stuck the branch of a tree into the ground nearby. But when the load passed up the lane, and my father called me, he saw the branch and knew that I was hiding. When the next load passed, he did not call, and I made off behind the wagon, so that he did not see me until I was at my post again, untying my team; but my father gave me such a tanning as I had never received for years. I was forced to realize his practical view, but I was surprised that he didn't see anything novel or interesting in my idea. Crusoe's immunity to human irruption was not for me!

I do not remember where the girls were during this episode, probably they were in the improvised house. But Doris as well as Prettie never tired of seeing the ropes pull the solid stratum of grain-sheaves together into a great bundle, vastly and deliberately twisting as it was drawn swiftly to the peak of the barn, where it shot down the track and, at the pull of the trip-rope, the slingful dropped with a swish. The mow quivered. Outside, while this was taking place, I would be pulled along in great stamping strides by the lines on the hard-mouthed team; and the muscles would wrinkle on the horses' hips – until, as the load struck the track, the heavy rope which had throbbed level with my head would fall, and the doubletrees would drop with a clap on the ground. Then I had to drive back to the barn and pull up the slack rope.

Even when they were in the house the girls were on the look-out to see whether the wagon-load was nearing the barn, and one or other of them might run out with a little pail of water for the men. I do not know how it began, perhaps through some accidental dropping of water on Prettie as she handed the little pail up to my father on the load, or perhaps the girl herself threw the remainder of a pailful at him, but it seemed to become customary for some of the water to be used in such laughing warfare. Even James clutched the dipper in a belligerent attitude when he had finished drinking, and there would be a thrilling threat in Prettie's voice, as she squealed imploringly and ran behind the load. But that tone took too much for granted, and she would be cool with him afterward. James never actually threw the water.

Another Sunday came, James Culihan appeared downstairs dressed in his best before breakfast, and laid the gum beside my plate and Lucy's. Then, as we thanked him, counting the much-wrapped sticks, he put his hand in his coat and laid out two more packages [for the girls]. They were not at the table yet.

Mother glanced around from the stove, where increased untidiness of attire foretold her Sunday dressing-up; she was stirring porridge and turning eggs. Her lips tightened.

Father came in with the strainer-pail, wearing a clean shirt, but still unshaven. He did not want to let appear his annoyance with a man who did no chores on a Sunday morning.

'Yous kids, now, is going to get sick, with that gum,' he observed as he wiped his hands on the roller towel which hung alongside the wash-basin.

'We won't!' We grinned at him, waiting.

'I chew mine one piece every day,' Lucy told him. Such childishness disgusted me.

'Not for mine,' I amended decisively. 'All at once.'

As soon as Father and Mother had sat down, Doris and Prettie came into the room. Prettie stared as she pulled out her chair. 'Somebody's being good to us?' she cried.

'That's James' treat,' said Mother primly.

'Really?' Doris made this an urgent question, but without appealing to James. 'Thanks very much!' She did not appear conscious of her quick flush. She shook her head at me across the table.

'Do you really think gum's good for little boys?' she asked. 'What are you going to do with yours?'

James became really red. As it were unconsciously he said:

'I w-was giving the children some.'

My father grinned teasingly at the girls.

'That's the stuff!'

James was very spruce that morning as he started away on his long walk to Brangton wearing a light vest, a silk handkerchief in his black coat, and grey trousers down to the heels of his shoes. He looked young, if yellowed in weather, even for thirty, but if you knew him, still exceptional.

Only the two girls were left at the table. Prettie stretched her bare arms.

'I nearly went through the floor,' she said, yawning.

'What in the world made him think of giving us gum?' Doris wondered.

'Oh, I know, I guess.'

'Does he go to church every Sunday?' Doris asked my mother as she came into the room. 'And dress up?'

'Every Sunday. He never asks for a horse. It doesn't make any difference how far away from church he is, from what I hear, he always goes to mass.'

'Maybe he promised his mother, in Ireland,' Prettie speculated.

'Was he born in Ireland?' said Doris idly.

'No. I don't think so. Don't ask *me*.'

Doris jumped up and began to clear away their dishes. 'What do you think about it?' she asked Father, who was shaving in the kitchen.

'Him? Oh, he's a good man, make a good man for one of you girls, I should think! The way I got it figured out though, better wait till he gets over his cream fever, like he got over his grape fever, and he won't want any at all. Only trouble, you might have to milk the cows, then.'

Doris laughed, and told him that she would give him plenty of warning before she decided to take such a step.

'You send me an invitation, and I'll put on my Sunday clothes.'

Everyone seemed to be talking for something to say, but I listened because they had scarcely spoken about James before. Prettie, however, was thoughtful.

'It must have been some girl,' she mused, still at the table. 'He's been at the county fair – you have county fairs in Canada, don't you? – and bought that nine-quart basket of grapes, and then his girl declined to eat them, and he had to save the money, so he ate them.'

'Maybe,' said my mother. 'But more likely you've been reading too many story-books.'

Things went on as before during that week, at least to my impercipient eyes. The following Sunday, at the little red-brick church by the road, the girls went into the choir, having been invited by the choir leader to help her weak covey of songsters. I felt a thrill of surprise and pride as they tripped up the aisle in the line, followed by the three beautifully groomed young men, and with preoccupation took their places in the choir chairs. But no sooner had the first hymn been sung, and the congregation and the choir around them settled down, than they looked at each other as though surprised and amused, and Prettie's lips moved in a whisper. It was plain that the disturbing sight must be at the rear of the building. I glanced at my father, his knees crossed, his large hands folded over his yellow watch chain, looking expectantly at the minister. I glanced at my mother, not even the trimmings of whose hat were moving; and Lucy beyond, gazing wide-eyed before her. Then I determinedly turned my head. In the back seat, near the door, was James. 'James Cuckoo-Culihan,' was what Prettie had whispered.

The service was infinitely long to me, despite vivid anecdotes of the minister, describing squalor he had witnessed, owing to intemperance. The girls became more remote all the time, until I wondered whether those exquisite creatures could be our Doris and Prettie. They had ceased to look interested, after that recognition of amused glances, but were not self-conscious. – I seem to have felt that they appeared distrait.

Finally I could stand it no longer, and turned my head again. James was almost directly behind me. He was not looking at the girls, but at the three spruce young men of the choir. A man stately and grim from some far city, he was – in the glimpse I had caught – with his long face, sympathetic, disillusioned, obscurely strange.

Possibly the grown-ups influenced my half-conscious reflections, or my uneasiness required romantic invention. I was glad of the stirring about in the crowd when the benediction had been pronounced, of the fresh air coming in at the door as I approached it. Outside, the steps were filled, and the bare ground about them, with women and children talking while they waited for their men to bring the horses and buggies. Prettie and Doris came up to Mother, all smiles. I was a distance away, and didn't hear what they said, but my mother seemed dubious, then agreed, 'Yes, it does make it kind of cramped.' They made their way out of the group, and began walking along the road.

Father was a long time bringing the horse around, probably taking the opportunity to talk with some neighbour in the church shed; Mother and Lucy were engrossed with neighbour-women, and as I was about to go around to the shed myself, I noticed James, stalking to the road at a deliberate pace. The girls were not out of sight.

We drove home slowly through the August afternoon, Lucy and I facing backward on a little seat before the dashboard of the buggy. Not much was said until my father chuckled and, looking ahead, remarked that James was going to overtake the girls, if he didn't watch out. I turned, and there they were, light dresses showing up as they loitered along between the rows of weeds which lined the ditches. James was just coming abreast of them when we trotted past. I looked back through our little swirl of dust on the empty road, quiet like the land on all sides with its Sunday quiet. They seemed to be talking amiably, and I caught a gesture of Doris to a farm yard. Probably they were asking 'Mr Culihan' about some of the country things which they saw in the farm yards as they went along.

The sun was still high when we got home, and supper usually was earlier Sunday evenings. Things seemed strange though, since it was not customary for James to be with us at that time; nobody knew just where he did spend Sundays after church.

I searched for eggs in the barn, and when I came out into the yard, what should I see down the lane but James and Prettie, like a couple in a picture-book, going for the cows. But I could get nothing out of anybody about it. Possibly James had volunteered to get the cows, and invited the girls to go along. Somebody might have dared Prettie to go. When they came back, the girl went directly to the veranda, with her short lithe steps, her colour high when I teased her: 'Prettie and her beau, Prettie and her beau!' At supper, the girls giggled, and James was grave and seemed foreign and formal; my father had his old clothes on for the chores.

It was the blue overalls and shirt again in the morning for James. The men were hauling in the last of the oats; it was getting toward the end of August, and the second crop of red clover was waiting. The weather continued hot, extraordinarily. I dare say that up to that time, summer had seemed to me more or less an indivisible season, but in the hammock one afternoon Doris stretched her arms above her head, and yawned, 'August is always *so* hot!' From that time August was identified in my mind as the Hot Month.

About the last day of the oats hauling, the man and the horses nearly gave way under the heat. The mows were nearly full by this time, and working up under the roof was almost stifling. Added to this, the slat slings began to break more or less regularly. Before, the heavy rope had broken and James had spliced it; the wheels of the car had sprung so that it had nearly fallen from the track with its load, and my father had taken a wooden mallet and climbed to the peak of the roof to hammer and bend them into shape again. But now for some days we never knew when the slingful might spill or even drop in its entirety on the wagon beneath. Then the rope beside me outside would flop slack, the horses I was driving would plunge forward, and for the men there would be nothing but to pitch each separate sheaf over the beam.

The afternoon seemed to be going well enough, except that the air was even more close. But during the third load when I drove back to the barn and began dragging the slack of the rope, I learned that a slat had broken when the slingful had reached its goal above the mow. This saved the work of pitching, but it seemed likely that part of the ropes would be lost in the tangled mass. My father had gone up to the mow, and I could hear him and James grunting. It was the first time I had heard either of them swear. I crept up the ladder and sat on a wide beam, watching them tug and strain, while rivulets ran through dust and chaff on their faces. This variation in the course of mishaps seemed to provoke my father unusually, and presently he told me somewhat impatiently to go down from there and get them a drink.

When I reached the foot of the ladder I called to Doris and Prettie who in the hope of finding a breeze were moving the hammock from the veranda to two maple trees beside the lane. 'Water! Water!' They must have thought, as I lazily hoped, that a fire impended, until I raised my arm in a gesture of drinking. I sat down until one of them should have come, and heard Father's voice resound dully against the roof. 'This heat's pretty near got me bushed, James. Let's go down until he brings us a drink. It's enough to make a preacher swear, this.'

They stood in the barn door fanning themselves with their large straw hats, their foreheads red, when Prettie came with the dipper in one hand and a pail of water in the other.

'Here, let's have that pail. Dipper's all right if you're not really thirsty, maybe. Give James the dipper.'

Prettie took a dipperful for James and handed it to him, and the pail to Father. She held out her hand for the dipper with a mischievous demure mouth, and James gave it to her, not quite empty. Father wiped his lips, and sighed windily.

'A-ah! Now if it was just as handy as that to take a bath!' He made a gesture with the pail toward Prettie. Without ado she threw what remained in the dipper in his face.

'Oh, you would, would you, little – ' He had meant to miss her, perhaps, but she was away in an instant, and he hurled the water with full force; a good deal of it fell on her head. She screamed in surprise and mock agony and kept on running toward the house. Father laughed loud and long, the water streaming from his own face.

'Thought she was going to get away! That'll teach her!' He pulled out a red handkerchief.

After a moment or two, James seeming uneasy, he said, 'Well, this isn't mowing them oats back. Feel some better, anyway. There's a trifle breeze here, but none at all up there.'

But just as they were entering the barn, they received an impartial dash of more cold water. Prettie had crept in at the other end of the driveway, with another pailful. Father was not at all disconcerted. 'Get me some water, quick, horse-stable pail.' He turned to me, and I, willing conscript to the side of my sex, sped away, returning with two pails half full, while he was chasing Prettie around the wagon on the barn floor, his heavy boots resounding on the planks to frighten her, and finally out into the yard, she dousing water at him with her hands from the pail whenever he came near. When she saw me coming, she screamed to Doris, and Doris dashed into the house, to reappear with another pailful.

'No fair!' he shouted, dodging about, when the two of them got after him. 'Help, James, are you going to let them drown me?'

James had looked on with a slow grin, unmoved again after his first wetting.

'James better not!' they panted, one trying to hold my father's hands while another splashed him liberally.

But I went to his assistance, and getting between them and James, dodged a dipperful, which struck James' already damp yellow locks. 'Now you got to help, James!' I yelled, and at the same instant he beckoned me to hand him the pail, and I ran for another.

When I came back everybody had become in earnest, puffing, dodging, holding, giggling hysterically, a fantastic group in the white hot dazzling yard. Lucy came out with another pailful, for her side, and it looked as though we would not be enough for the agile girls.

'If ever I get hold of you – !'

But they were too wise, until I came up behind Prettie and threw water down her neck. She screamed and jumped – toward James. A sudden determination brightened his eyes, and he had her in his long arms. She screamed and struggled, but he bore her kicking across the yard to the stable trough, and there, with some difficulty, he managed to dip her at full length in it, repeatedly.

'That's the stuff, James!' Father applauded, laughing, and giving up the fight with Doris. Doris laughed too, but it was plain she didn't know whether she should or not. We all stood around puffing, while Prettie, still panting too, made off to the house, water gleaming in the sunlight as it dripped from her tightened clothes. She didn't know whether to laugh or to cry.

'Don't go away mad.' But she only gave a wave of the hand, and her sister followed her to the house.

'Whew! Worse than working, a day like this!' Father wiped his streaming, clean-shaven face, wrinkled with grinning, and looked at James and me. 'Didn't think you had it in you, James. You're quite a ladies' man!'

James didn't answer this good-natured sarcasm.

'Well, they were kind of asking for it, you know,' he declared. He didn't stutter now, and seemed more freely disposed.

'That'll do us good, cool us off, anyway, on a day like this. Some baptizing! Do they baptize like that in your church? Oh, I forgot, you're not a Baptist!'

James giggled, almost. 'My – they wanted me to be a priest, but I, I didn't want to go to school.'

'Now, James, you know that's not the reason!' I could hear my father teasing him as I went away to the house to investigate the girls after their battle. But they weren't to be seen, and my mother seemed to take a grim pleasure in telling me so, and in asking me to gather up the pails and dishes which had been taken away.

At supper it seemed that the atmosphere had been changed; everyone talked more freely, and James almost considered himself one of the family. Prettie made a face and mischievously referred to her liking for grapes, but Father would laugh, and said:

'Now, you can't tease James, can she James? He's too shy.'

'Might tease me t-too often,' was the return.

The two men seemed to be more comradely and confidential with each other from that day, and I think that once or twice I interrupted stories not meant for any but adult ears.

Sometimes now, the girls were not quite so vivacious at meals, and Mother would smile without particular reason. James rose before the others, placing his chair up to the table, and went out to lie down under a tree near the stable while the horses ate their grain, but not to sleep; or he worked at those chores usually apportioned to the boss.

Only once more do I recall that James Culihan crept down the stairs for the cream. I heard a tinkling in the pantry but, though I waited, my parents apparently had not heard it. I stole down the back stairs. But he was gone, and I heard the girls laughing in their room. I stood at the foot of the stairs and listened. Prettie seemed almost exhausted with laughter, then Doris joined in with a subdued peal, and both recommenced. I scarcely could distinguish the words, but was sure I heard something like:

'I guess he's human, after all!'

It was some fascination in the fresh voices and their merriment which made me linger, wondering. I turned away in the darkness, and as I did so I heard a creak above, as though a door were shutting. James had listened too.

The time came when the girls had to return home to the city, Prettie to high school, Doris to a stenographer's job. They enjoyed the early days of September, spending many hours out of doors. The last afternoon, Doris and I went back the lane through the middle of the farm for the cows.

As we came up, we saw James near the fence of the corn field. He had been cutting corn, and paused in his slashing, wiped his sickle, and took off the wide and soft-brimmed felt hat which men wore to keep the sharp dry leaves of the corn from scratching their faces. As he pulled out a blue handkerchief, he saw us; the cows had passed on a distance ahead. He made a step forward and leaned over the fence. 'Good-afternoon!' he muttered, as if perfectly unaware what he said. 'How, how do you do? ... ' Plainly he wanted to enter into conversation with us. Doris smiled and went on. She smiled absently, as we walked down the lane toward the barn, not listening to what I was saying. Farther on Prettie and Lucy, who was barefoot, came hippetty-hopping to meet us, and frightened the cattle, so that one got away and headed toward the bush. I went after it.

James Culihan was standing, blue and tall, looking after the girls in the heavy fine September light. I don't think that he saw me, or was conscious of his surroundings, tarnished corn behind him, of the half-plowed field of pale stubble across the lane where Father was working, or of the creeping cows and the sallow-growing trees which edged the fields, so steadfast and afraid. But I remember them, and I see him as part of that picture – the sickle in his hand, his straight figure, yellow head up as he gazed. Then he turned to his work, smiled reflectively, and said in a meaningless tone:

'We'll see. *We'll* see.' Turning, he saw me.

'Heifer got away on me,' I explained. I climbed over the fence and watched him cut armfuls of heavy-eared stalks.

'That's right. Don't make the girls run after them. B-best to be a gentleman about it. ... Will you be glad when the y-young ladies go?'

'Naw.' But it occurred to me that it would be different when they were gone.

I stayed awhile, hunting for sand-cherries, and feeling that something should happen or be said. Once, with his arms about a shock of corn which he was tying with a bent stalk, I heard him exclaim suddenly. 'That's the worst of it. ... But you hear of it happening.' When he started and looked about, I had turned to go on my way.

After supper, James sat in the house a moment listening to my father talking about getting his seed wheat. Doris jumped up promptly with the rest of us children, and declared that we must play a game of ball. Mystified but willing, I produced a bat made from an extra long piece of stove-wood. We soon had the bases fixed, with chips from the wood-pile to mark them, and a hole knocked into the earth beside the home plate by tentative blows of the bat in the hands of the 'man' up who awaited my curves.

James came outside and stood awkwardly buttoning his jacket which flapped about his angular form. Everyone was calling to everyone, it seemed, and Doris to nobody in particular, standing beside the home chip:

'This is a game, all right. Got to please the – kids.'

She struck the ball, and scurried with swift short steps and upheld long skirts to the base. My father came out and shouted.

'Look at the kids, eh! Look at her, would you!'

'They wanted to have a game of ball to see how fast we could run, I guess,' gasped Doris. I wondered why she should find it necessary to avoid complicity. Her cheeks and eyes were bright, as she came running back.

He went to the stable, a pail of swill in one hand; and James, after hesitating in the failing light, followed.

'Come on and play!' I called. 'Not now,' James replied as curtly. Doris and Prettie glanced after him at this tone. The raciness of our cries echoed from the buildings. Pigs had begun to squeal with intermittent shrillness through the board fence as the feed approached them.

In the morning, it was decided that the seed wheat might as well be got from the mill, in trade for some of ours which was not yet threshed. So the girls' trunk was put into the wagon-box, and James and I started on the slow journey to the village.

It had rained the night before, and the roads, so long dry, were flaky with half-wet mud which the buggies tossed up. Large flakes stuck to the wheels of the wagon, and slipped off at times. The trees beside the road flapped desultory wet leaves in the morning air which was heavy and close in despite of a faint motion. Across the fields came a rumbling of freight cars as they entered the siding to clear the way for the early mail-train.

We drove to the station and James took the trunk off and had it checked and saw that it was placed on the baggage truck. Then he turned to the grist mill on the opposite side of the street. I stayed on the platform of the station.

In a few minutes a horse and buggy trotted around the corner, and stopped beside me. Mother dismounted first, and I tied up the horse while the girls pulled a suitcase from the box behind the seat.

We looked up to see James Culihan waving a red-handed arm at us. 'Well – G-good-bye, girls! Good-bye!' He shouted, smiling almost ecstatically.

Prettie and Doris giggled as they waved back at him, the blue faded figure lifting sacks of wheat, and Mother said, 'Isn't that funny! He never spoke to you before, I do declare, until now you're going away.'

'He's glad to see us go, I suppose,' said Doris as we turned the corner of the building. 'Such rattle-brains as we are.'

'He's not going to find everyone will put up with him like we have,' her aunt returned. 'He's going himself one of these fine days, I know that much. Still, I dare say he might be worse. ... '

Tickets were bought and the train pulled in.

'Give James Cuckoo-Culihan our love,' called Prettie from the train platform.

'Prettie!' said Doris automatically, raising fingers to her hair.

'What do I care for the people?' asked that young lady in the hush of the stopped train. But it was not stopped long, for nobody else got on. There was a flash of their handkerchiefs at the window, the click, passing faster and faster, of wheels over a joint in the track just before me.

'Well!' My mother was a little impatient. 'I've got to do some shopping, and go to the post-office.'

'I'll go home with James,' I declared, sullen suddenly for no particular reason.

Passing out of the village, James and I looked from the crossing at the steel level to a blue point at the horizon.

'Well, they couldn't always fool with me. I guess they'd see. ... "Come again." ' He muttered so that I could scarcely hear the rest. ' "Good-bye! Come again!" I told 'em, all right."

LILACS FOR FIRST LOVE

Two young women were talking together in Laura's apartment – Laura herself and Molly Bronx. Talking with the abandon of girlhood chums who were still girls enough to communicate the raptures of an old friendship in dear half-forgotten days. Talking with the tolerance of matrons of this generation who after all knew their world.

'To think you're married now, Laura!' said Molly. 'I've never got over being surprised at you. All girls say they never will. But you were different.'

'Was I?' asked Laura dryly, with a twisted smile. She became thoughtful a moment, then she spoke:

'Let's look at some of those old snapshots we took. They must look funny now.' She disappeared into a bedroom, and came back with an old box full of trinkets and snapshots. At one end lay a bundle of letters tied with a ribbon.

'Why Laura, you shouldn't keep old love-letters lying around like this, now you've settled down! I stuffed a cushion with mine, and Phil found it out, and thereby hung our first quarrel!' Molly spoke lightly.

'I know it. I burned all but these, and they're not love letters. They're from Angus Walsh.'

'Angus? I'd forgotten all about him. He's the one who went to war, wasn't he? And didn't he come back to see you afterward?'

Laura smiled. 'Probably as I fancied him he never existed. But I keep his letters – just an odd fancy, I suppose, or to remind me of a lesson I learned.'

'Oh, I *thought*, you know – something told me then – that you were in love – '

'No – not in love. We might have been, but I didn't understand things then – '

'Understanding – why, my dear, that's just what you have! Didn't everybody use to tell you everything – Oh, this is Angus here, is it, wearing his Highland uniform?' She was looking at the snapshots. Laura was looking away to the window.

'No, I was very romantic then, very shy, and very ignorant in the way only a young girl can be – when she reads a lot, and knows a great many things and some of them are not so. But I didn't know *that* then.'

'Tell me about it.' said Molly.

'Needless to say he was my first beau.' Laura did not look at the snapshot in her friend's hand. 'A handsome dark youth in the kiltie uniform, when I met him. Very tanned from the training camp; his jaunty little cap sat at a ridiculous angle on his curly black hair. He had the whitest and evenest teeth I ever saw a boy have, and his eyes were black or dark blue, and they glittered like those of a Japanese doll I used to own. I had scarcely outgrown dolls, but I was one of those big girls, and tall as I am now.

'It was Edith, my sister, who trapped me into meeting him. I was playing catch with Marie in the lane one evening, when Edith came to the door and asked me if I wanted to go to a movie.

'At that age I regarded Edith as an arch-tyrant always telling Mother about me and finding housework for me to do. And she thought me a healthy young lazy-bones who was always getting out of doing something. So it was quite a surprise to be asked politely to go out with her. Naturally I grinned sarcastically and asked what was wrong now. She was annoyed. Her young man was in town, with a friend, another soldier. And Lily, the girl who was supposed to go with the second boy, had got word that her steady was back in town that day. Would I take her place?

'Of course I didn't want to go out with a man. I never had. But Edith insisted he was merely a boy, and got me ready, and away we went, leaving Marie on the veranda. The boys did not come into the house. They had got as far as the gate when we sallied out. In our town the boys and girls were not much for formalities.

'Edith introduced me to the two soldiers. One, a rather slight English-looking fellow in khaki smiled at me and turned to Edith, and they walked along together, Edith fussing with her hair buns at intervals.'

'Weren't the styles funny then!' Both young women smiled.

'The other one,' Laura went on, 'the dark kiltie, started talking to me as we followed the others. If he was put out at Edith's bringing such a kid, in middy and skirt, he didn't show it, but was very polite. I wasn't impressed by any obligation. I remembering wondering whether I might not have a chance to get away and let them hunt someone else. I was feeling shaky, especially as some of the high school kids were on the street.

'But I felt I had to talk a little, so I made rather ingenuous queries: when was he going over, did he like the army, did he feel strange in his kilt at first. It was rather fun walking with him. His pleated skirt flew out around just like my blue serge one did; only his knees looked so big and bumpy I couldn't help laughing. So we both laughed.

'We all stopped at a confectionery store and the boys bought us chocolates. Then we went into the show. The picture was quite good though rather mournful; but I couldn't feel bad with Angus offering chocolates all the time.'

They both laughed, and Laura added, 'And once he played with my signet ring.

'All this is quite simple,' she went on soberly. 'I don't suppose I can make the point clear. Why should I have had any feeling at all about such an episode? I know that I didn't know I had any at the time.'

Molly shrugged.

'It was quite dark when we came out of the show, and we took a walk through the park and along the beach of the Lake, following Edith and Fred. When we came to some broken stone steps he asked me if I wouldn't like to stop and look at the moon. We let Edith and Fred go on by themselves, and sat talking and asking questions as though we had known each other for years.

'I had developed a sort of aversion to boys during my school days, because they wanted to tease you or pretend you were dumb. But this boy was different. So natural, and good-looking, going off to a strange country to fight; about to see all sorts of adventures. Somehow I only saw him marching along behind the band with the other kilties, their feet tramping in time, their skirts swaying in rhythm. He was only two years older than I was. He had wanted to go over with Fred, and lied about his age, to get in. When I told him I wished I was a boy, he shook his head quite seriously and said I should be glad I was not. Somehow he stroked my hair as he talked, and it did not seem strange that he should, or that I should be sitting on the beach in the dark. We agreed that it was a beaut of a night. He wished his camp test was down by the lake like this. Then we heard a clock strike and started for home.

'Edith eyed me rather queerly as we came up to the veranda, I thought. I suppose Mother had put me in her charge. We sat talking for a while, but everything I said got twisted, and everybody laughed. I would have been the life of the party, but they reminded me that I was only a kid, out for the first time. I remember I said my hands had got cold down by the water, and Angus said he would have to see about that. Then when he let my hands go I said my nose was cold!'

'Kids are funny when they're that age! I – '

'It seemed whatever I said they laughed, so I lapsed into silence. Fred tried to get me talking again, but I knew Edith would tease me, so I kept still.

'Finally they showed signs of going. Angus walked out to the sidewalk and said he was sorry this was his last leave, but he would remember it over there. He said he would write in a few days, and wanted me to promise to write to him.

'I ran upstairs quickly for fear Edith would want to talk to me, and locked the door. I threw my clothes off quickly and turned the light off, but did not feel sleepy, so I sat by the window watching the moon over the house tops, hearing frogs croaking somewhere back of the house. But I was thinking mostly of the way his voice changed as he talked, the rhythm of walking with him down the street, the way his even white teeth had bitten into the chocolates. And that reminded me we had left the box on the steps. I would tell Marie she could have some if she went down for it early tomorrow morning. At last I tumbled into bed beside her, and slept.

'Next day Mother seemed very nice to me, but Edith couldn't leave me alone. She tried to get me talking about boys – the subject interested her – but she always repeated things I told her at awkward times, and I didn't want to talk anyway. Nothing could be so real – not to mention so brave and comradely as the way he had squeezed my hand and said, "I like you a lot, Laura. Here's hoping we meet again." That was what I kept seeing and hearing.

'When his letter came in a few days – a very short friendly one – I read it repeatedly and wanted to reply to it right away. But I found that quite a task. My letters seemed to be too intimate and too kiddish. So I would tear them up. Soon he was in France, and I could let myself go a little. They sent us trinkets and cards from wherever they were stationed, and the letters came gay or sad depending on his mood. I used to spend whole evenings answering them.

'It still worried Edith that I would not tell her any of the contents of his letters. She kept Freddie's picture on the dresser in her room, and she and the girls would have a great time reading letters and telling secrets. But I kept his – Angus's – picture hidden between the leaves of an old picture book in a box with his letters. I had to keep hiding the box in new places for fear Edith would find it. At night I always sat by the window a few minutes before turning in. I liked to think of him sitting in the doorway of his camp singing with other boys. Or maybe off in a corner of the dug-out thinking of me – thinking hard, perhaps, so he wouldn't hear the stories the boys would be telling about cheap girls.

'I knew he would not like to hear such things any more than I wanted to hear the whispers – terrible stories, they were – about the way the boys carried on while on leave. I knew Angus was far above all that. I was not so sure about Fred, because I remembered him as laughing too much to suit me! So the war went on, and I waited for letters to answer, and dreamed a great deal, and read, and planned things to do or to send over. Mother helped me pack boxes for him.'

'Yes, it was a strange time,' sighed Molly. 'No wonder our generation is different. Our mothers didn't have their eyes opened so suddenly.'

'And it was a different world they saw when they did wake up, too. Well, suddenly the Armistice came, and Fred was home on nearly the first boat. But Angus's battalion was transferred and had gone on into Germany, and I did not get any more letters for a while.

'Edith and Freddie seemed to do a lot of quarrelling when they were together. He was very jealous, and found out she was getting letters from a fellow out West. One day he went to the post-office and getting a letter for Edith, in a fit of jealousy he opened it. Edith was awfully cross and sent him away. A few days after he left a letter came for him in her care. She opened it and read it, to get even.

'It was from Angus, written during a trip through England and Scotland. I guess it was an awful letter. ... Or perhaps it was just a gossipy account of his trip, and he mentioned incidentally things which would amuse Fred. I didn't know then that boys sometimes boast about things. ... Edith was bound I should read the letter, or at least two or three lines of it for my own good. After much arguing I scanned them hastily, nodded, and rushed up to my room.

'It was evening again, the same lovely sky welcomed me, but I could not look at it. The darkest, farthest corner of the room was where I wanted to hide my face. My eyes smarted, but no tears came. Feet of clay! All the bitterness of life seemed suddenly revealed to me. If he only had been dead, I could have cried my heart out and made an ideal of him for the rest of my life. But this was different. Just a dull, icy ache, and a realization that there never had been any boy who dreamed of me while others cheapened themselves. He went along and took his good time – common clay like the rest.

'Marie came up and pretended not to notice anything, so we went to bed without speaking. But I could not sleep for many nights after.

'Next day I went about laughing, and Edith was deceived into thinking I didn't remember the letter or didn't know what it meant.

'Those were terrible days, but they were nothing to the time when I got a telegram, saying that he had landed at Montreal and that after he had seen the folks at home he would look me up. All week I steeled myself against his sudden appearance. Every car that seemed about to stop made me shiver. But as he didn't come I felt better. Sunday afternoon Marie and I went driving through the country with Mother and Dad. The country seemed so lovely and brooding, as it does when you're young and unhappy. Coming back Dad stopped the car and let us pick a big bunch of purple lilac from a bush at the roadside. We got home after dark, and I came running into the house with my arms full of the lilac.

'I heard Edith's laughing voice on the veranda: "Here is the good soldier at last," and I was gazing into the questioning eyes of a stranger.

He was in civilian clothes now, but handsomer than ever. He came forward with his hands out, and asked me if I did not know him. I said Oh yes, and hurried into the house to put the flowers in water. I stayed away as long as I dared, while Mother and Dad tried to make up for my lack of welcome. I picked off a spray of lilac for myself when I should have to go back. Mother came out and putting her arm around me began to say something, but I hurried into the front room. I sat sideways from him, so as not to have to meet his eyes. But I knew they were on me, and that my face was burning.

'To make it worse, Edith was there. Mother and Dad left the room, and she went too, after making a few teasing remarks about my spending a lot of time reading his letters.

'If we had gone out for a walk it might not have seemed so bad, and I might have kept up some sort of conversation. But I could scarcely hear my own voice or his. He was talking eagerly about the war and about England, but he must have seen that something was amiss. Under the influence of his voice, some of the things we used to write about in our letters came back, and I must have talked a little.

'The only real thing in the room seemed to be the bit of lilac I was toying with in my hand. Perhaps he felt that too, for he asked me to put it on his coat. As I was putting it into the buttonhole of the lapel, he carelessly dropped his arm about my shoulders. His warm hand seemed to sear me, and I thought of those two lines in his letter to Fred.

'I started and turned, saying I wanted some fresh air, and he followed me out on the lawn. It was a cool windy night of early summer. I wondered whether the wind would not blow away this horrible spell.

'But in a few minutes the car he had come in called for him. I remember his taking a last wistful look at me, puzzled – and saying that I was the loveliest and saddest little girl he ever knew. He did not make a joke of my queerness, and seemed reluctant to leave me without finding some trace of the girl he remembered. Perhaps he suspected the trouble. He didn't ask to see me again, you know.'

Mollie nodded.

'So he was gone in the darkness, out of my life forever, and I was free to go up to my room, where Marie, who understood my moods, pretended to be asleep.

'I slept too, for I dreamed. The smell of the lilacs may have come drifting up the stairs and through the open doorway. I gathered large bunches of it, Marie helping me, and then we flew with them to a lonely grave in a strange torn country. Then the grave turned into my box where I kept my letters hidden. And the box, with the lilacs in it, rested on my heart, a heavy weight.'

HORACE THE HAYMOW

'Here, you? Hope that'll hold you!'

Llewellyn Lewel swung a well-loaded hay fork over the high boarding of the box-stall, and the alfalfa fell with a swish on the straw within. The towering black horse laid his ears back, arching his neck, and tore out a bunch of it, twisting it savagely with lengthy lips.

There was a giggle behind him, and Llewellyn turned. Albert Hoon, the youngest son of his employer, peeked through the cracks at the black horse, who was now pawing the hay into the similitude of a bed.

'Horace the haymow!' He giggled again.

'What's the joke?' Llewellyn asked irritably as he turned away. It seemed dusky in the poor light of the stable, and it must be getting late, even for chores. 'If you had to grow hay for him, like your dad, you wouldn't be laughing, maybe.'

'That's what you called him, "Horace the Haymow," ' said Albert, injured, trotting along behind past the stalls. Clearly, to Albert a joke was as much a joke at the hundredth telling. He ran forward and threw himself on the closed door, swinging out on it to relieve his feelings in a joyous arc. Then he overtook Llewellyn, who was proceeding toward the house, and turning, walked backward before him.

'Llewellyn, I wasn't laughing at Horace, Llewellyn, not exactly. Paw says you got to drive Horace to see your girl tonight.'

Llewellyn stopped in his tracks and pushed back his hat from the brow which three weeks of spring work on the farm had not yet tanned.

'The – the dickens you say! I'm not going to drive that lummox.' He walked on again. Ridiculous! Pure surprise had taken him aback. But the Hoon boy persisted.

'Yes, he did. The car don't work,' he said.

'I'll make it work.' Llewellyn turned toward the garage, cursing mentally. He had to call at Hymer's to get Conrad, his new friend of the next farm and then they would get the girls. ... 'He said the car wouldn't work, eh?'

'Yes he said you got to drive Horace.'

'Bunk,' said Llewellyn, thoughtfully. 'You tell your pa "Bunkum" for me. Will you do that?' He took off a glove and laid a white finger on his slightly amplified and peeling nose, and considered. 'My God!' he invoked, muttering, as the full force of the stipulation struck him.

'Drive *that!* I'd have to build him a straitjacket or whatever they put on horses. I guess I better go see the old man.' He turned away from the implement shed where 'the car' was stored.

'Come on!' yelled Albert Hoon to Orval, his older brother, who was shelling corn on the ground before the chicken coop. "Llewellyn's going to see Paw!'

'Chook! Chee-hook!' Orval called shrilly.

A groggy miscellany of hens staggered out from the roost, and languidly nailed and gulped the kernels, stretching.

'He wants a rooster for dinner tomorrow. It's Sunday,' he explained with eleven-year-old abstraction. 'Can't go.'

'How you goin' to catch him that way?' asked Albert, a more practical youth. 'Come on to the field. I'll help you afterwards. Paw's going to give Llewellyn the bounce. Bounce!' He picked up a stone and sighting with one eye dropped it to his toe, which dodged.

'Can't,' repeated Orval. 'Chook! Cheeyook, yookyook! Anyway, he ain't. You don't know nothing about it. Didn't I hear what Coon Hymer told my paw. Paw ain't mad. He *laughed*. But wait till Llewellyn begins to hitch up. I'll be there then.'

'What'd'e laugh about?'

But Orval shook his head.

'Cheeyook! Cheehook! Conrad and him was both laughing.'

Albert turned and trotted after the lean form of the city hired man.

'Kick old Homer's seat for'm,' Llewellyn muttered. He was nineteen, and Homer Hoon thirty-five, stockily built, so the figure pleased his imagination. The little boy trotted up beside him.

'Yer dad's in the back field, I s'pose,' he growled.

The sun was still high, though clouds were gathered about it. The two passed among straggling apple trees, dry and withered, but blossoming in what had been an orchard once, and came to the end of the field which Homer Hoon was planting to corn.

It extended interminably before them, grey clods of the dried loam. A wire cable stretching from a stake at their feet to the other end of the field, clicked vibrantly. This was caused by the planter, coming toward them at a vast distance. Alongside the cable in a general way, ran the tracks of the planter, as sinuous as snakes. They could hear the stentorian voice of the driver:

'Come on here, Jason, Blue!' The team marched briskly to the click, click of the machine. Nearer, it could be seen that the wheels of the planter wobbled crazily with a sedate regularity.

'Ho, boys!' sang out Homer, hoisting the marker and holding the attached rope in the crook of his elbow. One of the wheels clicked independently of the mechanism, for the steel rim was broken; and both reeled dizzily at the slow turn.

'What's the matter with those wheels?' asked Llewellyn, gruffly preparatory. He figured that any admissions would count in his favour.

'She don't just balance,' explained Homer Hoon genially. 'The right wheel has took more beverage than the left.'

'Paw, Llewellyn says, "Bunk!" ' Albert hovered about the planter.

'I thought you said I could have the car tonight,' began Llewellyn.

'Yeh, I did.' Homer had descended from his seat, pulled the iron stake from the ground and, braced against the tugging of the attached cable, drove it in the ground again a yard to one side. He grunted. 'But the car ain't in shape. You'll have to drive Horace.'

'You had it out yesterday. Can't I fix it myself?' ventured Llewellyn.

'No, I'd rather fix it *my*self,' his employer returned blandly. 'You'n Horace'll get along like a, like a cowbird in a owl's nest. Never mind, Llewellyn,' he added, and shook his yellow head with its flopping felt hat. 'I been a young fellow myself. I know how it goes. But she won't give you the mitten just because you drive Horace. Come on here, Jason, you old hound. Got to git this field done, goin' to come a storm, 'fore mornin' '.

This was small comfort to Llewellyn. The corn planter gave four clicks, and he looked after it like one stranded on a weary shore.

'Can't I take Tom?' he bleated.

'Not the way you been workin' him all day. Get up!' The team was about to accept the excuse to stop.

'Tim?'

'You take Horace, and be satisfied.'

'Oh – ' Llewellyn turned away to the house. It wasn't so simple after all. And after assuring both Altea and Conrad that he would provide the ways and means –

'Llewellyn, where you goin' to die when you go to, Llewellyn? Say it again! Where you goin' to die when you – '

'Drive that old fossil,' muttered the youth. 'Couldn't get him between the shafts. Why, the buggy wouldn't hold the four of us anyway. Might as well not go.'

Just the same he spent more than half an hour in making his toilet, though he had shaved at noon. Altea wasn't going to see him dressed like a rube, anyway. He rubbed his jaw ruminatively before the mirror. He had been lucky, coming to the country to work on a farm because his mother and the doctor insisted that his eyes needed rest, and because he himself privately had determined to 'make the line' at Queen's where he was not yet enrolled, and wanted to be hardened by scrimmages with wheat-sheaves – in view of this exile from bright lights he had been lucky to find such a girl as Altea Hodge. He had told her so himself, and she had seemed deeply interested in his well-documented telling. In the city she would have been surrounded with goofs wanting to take her places. But here – he hadn't heard, though he had not asked, of a single rival. Unless – but of course Conrad Hymer wasn't one. Conrad, a neighbour of both farms, was a good fellow. He had looked a little queer when Llewellyn proposed taking Altea, while Conrad was to take her younger sister, Doris; but he had accepted, finally, and had been keen on it ever since, called him up by phone that very noon. They would make a good foursome for the drive and the movies. Later, of course, the time would come when it wouldn't be a question of foursomes. Llewellyn felt more like his town-bred self as he came out of the kitchen door in his tight-fitting suit.

'Goin' out for the evening,' remarked Mrs Hoon, following him to the door with the dishwater.

'Yes ma'am,' said Llewellyn kindly, then glancing apprehensively behind him and at the progress of the dishwater across the yard.

Albert pounced on him from around the corner of the house.

'Llewellyn, your toes don't come to there.'

'Albert, come here,' called his mother.

'They don't, eh?' Llewellyn smiled reluctantly in the pride of his new long flat-toed brown shoes.

At the stable a problem confronted him. The harness was to be got on Horace. He should have dressed later.

But first Horace must be caught. The two Hoon boys rallied, and stood wherever he wanted to turn. He saw Orval nudge Albert largely.

'What's the matter with you boys, didn't you never see a fellow hitch up a horse before? Where's his halter?'

'Not Horace,' said Orval truthfully.

'Not Horace, eh, well you're goin' to see Horace come out of there meek as a lamb.' Llewellyn spoke as though abstractedly, but his heart misgave him. He chose the largest halter in sight, and strode past the newly cleaned stalls into the alleyway, and through the door into the box stall.

'Keep that door shut!' he adjured the boys, unnecessarily. 'This horse likes to pick little boys up by the scruff of the neck and carry them – ' He paused and looked at Horace; and Horace with a snake-like twist of his long neck probably meant for a nod, and a slight salutary snore, looked at him. 'Away off, away...'

Llewellyn's voice trailed, and clearly wishing himself there too, he was backing to the door, when he heard the kids snicker, and extending the halter limply advanced a step.

'Look,' said Orval impersonally. 'Horace has long shoes too, like Llewellyn.'

It was true. The brute's hoofs had not been trimmed for years apparently, and, long and black, they shuffled the straw as Horace lounged forward.

'Hoo boy, hoo boy!' soothed Llewellyn, reaching for the head of his steed. 'Come here, what you want to be built with such a high head for? Come here!'

He was breathless and foiled in spite of his height, because Horace was higher, and by a gentle swing of his head evaded the halter.

'I'll *stand* on them old dooks of yours, and then see how you like it. Hold still!' he exclaimed, becoming angry and dodging about, grasping the animal by the foot-long ropy forelock which hung over both eyes. With vision unobscured Horace allowed himself to be haltered, probably reassured by the aspect of his assailant.

'*Now*, we got you!' said Llewellyn, recovering his breath, and drawing the shank of the halter through a crack in the board wall. 'Just got to get the harness on you now.'

'Ain't you going to clean him?' asked Albert. The boys were still peeking through at the proceedings. 'Paw does.' A gray dust lay over the blue-black fur.

'*Me* clean 'im? Not while I got a lucid interval. Your pa can, if he wants to. Yer pa ain't never hitched him in a buggy, either. I'll bet a case on that.' Llewellyn found it more seemly to continue his monologue than to do this himself.

'Pa never tried,' said Orval, jealously defensive.

'You ain't put it on him yet either,' Albert, with his flair for the essential, told him.

'My, it's hot!' The youth sighed, wiped his brow, and came out of the box stall to hunt a buggy harness. 'Clean 'im!' he muttered indignantly. 'Clean the pelt of that old black bear, when Altea won't know whether he's a giraffe or a stack of black cats.'

But he slung his arms from his coat.

'A shirt,' he reasoned, 'is easier to clean than a coat; and he is some dirty.'

'Keep that door open!' he snarled at the boys. 'How'm I to see in here? Goin't to be too late to go anyplace anyway,' he added disconsolately. But never mind, she would think all the more of him, for venturing forth with such a daunting equipage.

The buggy harness would be too small of course, in its present shape. He lengthened the backband and all the straps, straining at long unused buckles.

Horace, standing serenely and cocking an eye at what impended, chewed seriously once or twice on a relic of hay in his throat. Nor was he impressed by the feel of the spiderweb weight of the flimsy harness on his back as the boys were by the sight of it. They howled.

'Tie some strings on and make it big enough!'

Llewellyn pretended not to hear them, and jerked the harness down. Samples of the long hair of Horace adhered to it. 'If they'd washed your wool when you was little, it mighta shrunk and kept you a respectable size.'

Horace switched lazily with a five-foot tail and knocked his hat ajar as he was going away.

'You dirty old lummox,' cried Llewellyn, annoyance and rage causing him to lose his fear. 'As a reasoning quadruped you got the gumption of a stove. If I did what I'd ought to, I'd cave in your old ribs for you, you old – Well.' It was late. He wiped his brow and hat-brim with a handkerchief. 'Nothing for it but the work harness, I guess.'

But when the work harness belonging to one of the other horses was hoisted heavily upon Horace's back, it too had to be lengthened in places.

'We'll get the bridle,' volunteered the boys, becoming impatient of the slowness of the proceeding. They handed it through the door and slammed that after Llewellyn had turned away. He jumped sideways.

'Ain't you got no sense, you want to scare him?'

Albert sank weakly against the wall, and jolted Orval in the ribs, giggling.

Though bits were sometimes attached to his halter, Horace was not used to bridles. He tossed his head out of reach gently but deftly and decisively, until in desperation Llewellyn threw his whole weight on it, and Horace gulped the bit, rolling his eyes in an edified manner as he assumed the headgear.

'You old cow!' said Llewellyn with contempt. 'You're simple. No trick to harness you up. Some bossin' around's what a horse of your temperament needs. You're pretty tame after all.'

Horace simply but enigmatically looked at him.

'Well, boys, I got him now. Open the doors, and we'll take him out and hitch up.' Llewellyn made no attempt to conceal his pride of accomplishment.

The door opened, and the hulking Horace squeezed through, the harness brushing on both sides. Save for the undignified haste which this noise caused in him, he gave the effect of an elephant accoutred with a palanquin.

A tall form in black clothes jumped aside in exaggerated surprise as they came forth, and Conrad Hymer lifted his twanging voice in imitation of the crier at a county fair:

'Bring on your three-year old entire – Where'd you get it anyhow? Going to try to drive that thing? You must think them girls is filled out some since Sunday night, if they got to have a four-legged tractor like that to pull 'em.'

Llewellyn received this jocosity without warmth.

'Pull that buggy out of the shed, why don't you, and not stand gawpin'. Never see a heavy draft animal before?'

This, to one who had been born and raised on a farm, was too much. Conrad Hymer stood gazing with mouth open, as though undecided what that aperture should properly emit. Finally he spat and said, walking to the shed for the buggy,

'Heavy draft is right. Some outfit, you got to let me tell 'em. Won't the boss let you have the car?'

'No, he won't,' snapped Llewellyn. 'I been spending a pleasant evening here getting this brute togged up, and now you come around belly-achin' –'

'Now that's too bad,' soothed Conrad. 'Me, I been entertaining myself waiting, and worryin' maybe perhaps you'd got blew up in the gas tank or something, or eloped or something, and finally I walks over to see ... Whooh, heavy draft! Whooh, animal!'

One on each side they raised the shafts and pulled the buggy over Horace's sketchily clothed rear portions.

'Anyway, this ain't goin' to do for four of us. What we going to do with the girls?'

'Oh, you and me'll go for a lil drive ourselves. Won't that be nice, Coonie? All by our lonesomes.' Llewellyn simpered, as though to a child.

'I guess we won't,' returned Conrad. 'Come to think of it, we got a democrat to home. We ain't going to give up now, after going through all this nervous strain.' He winked in the direction of the boys. They started to chase each other around the equipage.

'*Boys!* Go 'way, keep still!' Llewellyn was grasping the bridle as though a circus ring had sprung up around him. Horace looked down along his nose at him wonderingly, sighed windily, and opened his mouth, yawning.

Llewellyn unflinchingly retained his hold of the bit, notwithstanding. It was wiser, if dangerous. He could see a vast expanse of tongue, and a huge array of teeth. If his hand left the bit, or Horace made a grab – It would feel like rivets.

'Don't be funny,' he chided, coolly. 'He who laughs last, you know – Say, is it right, Coon, what they say when a horse grabs hold of anything with his teeth he's got to close them, sort of automatic?'

'Sure is,' said Conrad, tugging at the traces. 'They like to grab a fellow by the arm, right by the muscle, when he ain't looking. ... Well, I guess we got him ready for the parade, all right. Leggo. I'll hold him while you get your coat.'

'You was long enough about it,' grumbled Llewellyn, feeling injured now that nothing had happened to justify his courage while he held the bridle. 'Gosh, I'm sweating yet,' he said as he stepped into the buggy.

'Shoulda left off your collar and hames. Me, I ain't hot. Nothin' to get wrought up about. Though they do tell me that Horace put one man in the hospital.'

They were passing the house, and the boys rushed out and followed them down the lane. Orval hurled a disheveled rubber after them, gravely, as though considering it the ceremonial thing to do.

'Good luck!'

'And – and-whenyougeter, hugger!' yelled Albert excitedly.

Beyond a ponderous stumble, this irruption did not move Horace. The harness jingled rhythmically and loudly, the chains on the tugs of the work harness swung and occasionally struck the varnished spokes of the front wheels. From his tranquility Horace might have roaded it singly in buggies all his life. Conrad retained the lines and drove.

'Come on here, get a jersey on!' Llewellyn felt bold. 'We've did the deed! Who'd a thunk it!' He seized a line and slapped a portion of the reaches of back extending like a tableland level with their faces.

The long tail uncoiled itself from between the shafts and whisked Llewellyn's hat neatly away. When he returned to the buggy wiping his hat, the appendage was still hanging over the dashboard, half covering Conrad's feet. Conrad pointed to it.

'Hang on to that, you better,' he recommended. 'And let me guide him after this.'

'That's right,' rejoined Llewellyn cheerfully. 'I wondered what was the matter. You didn't have no man at the helum. That's me, from now on. But,' he added hopefully, 'we won't need anybody in the democrat, will we?' If they could only reach the home of the girls safely, a pleasant evening might be spent after all.

By the time they had hitched to the democrat at the Hymer place it was dusk.

'Them girls is going to be sore on us, no question about that,' said Conrad equably. Llewellyn's heart registered 'Going down!' After going to all this tumultuous trouble – . He never should have done it if he hadn't thought a great deal – and very seriously – of Altea Hodge, with her blue eyes and whisking bob.

But obligingly Horace clumped into a trot going out of the Hymer lane, his ears bent for home; and since they were going in that direction anyway, all was well for the present.

'He'll go all right even when we have gone by your place,' calculated Conrad; 'because he'll get all warmed up; and when these light horses gets warmed up, they never know the racin' sulky's behind 'em at all.'

'He won't know this one's behind him at all,' observed Llewellyn, looking down from his eminence at the rattling and swaying wheels of the democrat, 'if it falls to pieces as soon as it looks to be wanting to.'

'Don't you say nothing against this democrat. My grandfather built this himself.' But Conrad became serious. 'Wonder whether the girls'll want to go to the show in this outfit. That's what I'm thinking about. What do you think?' he asked anxiously.

Foreboding was not foreign to Llewellyn, either; but they did not have to wonder long, for soon they were in the environs of the Hodge demesne.

They steamed grandly up the lane, Horace ploughed the dust and grass with his great long hoofs, until they reached the side lawn. Then, apparently catching sound or sight of one of his kind, he released a long-drawn and bellowing neigh.

Promptly the two girls appeared at the door, fully dressed and gloved.

'Loud at the portals sounded the clarion,' said the one preceding. Altea was witty, and one cute kid, Llewellyn reflected, looking down at the tufts of hair which protruded from her toque. He had been shivering after the wild noise of Horace, but he said brightly, for he too had read Scott, in high school:

'And as at the magic of a charm, the fair ladies appeared at the casement.'

'We wondered whether you was going to forget to come,' said Doris. 'How do you get that way?' She pouted, looking up at Conrad, and though he too was paying attention to Altea, he replied, gruffly:

'Us, oh, we been thinking up something. Thought we'd have a float or something, like at a First of July parade. But then we figured maybe this ud do.'

'Won't you jump up and join us?' asked Llewellyn formally, to clinch the engagement made before by phone.

'Well,' said Altea doubtfully, ' "The Sainted Sinner in Sackcloth" will be half over when we get there.'

'Come on Altea,' adjured Conrad familiarly (as though she were *his* girl!). 'We'll go to the other theatre. They got a second show, and we'll get there just on time, if Horace can stand the clip like he was here a while back.'

Llewellyn saw his chance, and leaped to the ground. He would leave Conrad to drive as he had been doing, and at the same time do the correct thing himself.

'Here, Miss Hodge, allow me to help you into the curricle,' He gestured toward the rear step of the carriage, and handed her up over the wheel before Conrad took notice.

'No you don't,' said that gentleman, and jumped down. 'Hang on to your cords.' He handed the lines to Llewellyn, and climbed to the back seat beside Altea. She screamed and Llewellyn shouted:

'He's kidnapping me away, Mr Lewel!'

'Hey, you're stealin' my girl!'

General laughter and unscrambling.

'Bet you can't climb over the front seat, Altea.'

'How'm I going to get up!' wailed Doris.

'Here, I'll put you up.'

Somehow they were sorted out until only Llewellyn remained on the ground. But Horace had begun to reconnoitre his position. He whinnied loudly again to his invisible affinity, while the democrat trembled in unison, and took a step forward, pawing the earth. A few scoops of soil the size of saucers whizzed among their ears.

'My Godfrey!' gasped Llewellyn, clutching the lines. 'He's going to – Horace!' He commanded gaspingly. 'Whoa!'

'Hold 'er, Newt, she's a-rearin',' quoted the Hymer young man. The girls merely giggled uncertainly. Conrad winked permissibly at Doris, and nudged Altea ahead.

'Say, Llewellyn Lewel, *you're* goin' to get it, if your old horse spoils Mama's lawn. Anyway, come on, us folks in the gallery's rarin' to go ourself.' Doris beat on the floor of the conveyance with her slippers.

'We in the tonneau, if you want to be classy,' Altea smiled graciously.

To make things something less than classy for poor Llewellyn, the Hodge dog, a large benevolent looking collie, trotted toward them, investigatively.

'So that's what's the matter. He's afraid of Rex!' said the girls.

'Whooh, Horace! Whooh itty boy! What, what's who scairt of?' Then Llewellyn saw the dog. Dogs were one of the pet aversions of Llewellyn's life. How often, since he had grown to his present lank and burly estate, had he not fled from them, colliding with lamp posts as he looked back, throwing sticks, stones, even his own headgear, to keep away some poodle directed at him by mischievous small boys of the block.

But here there were no sticks or stones handy, and pride forbade the use of his hat. The big collie advanced, friendly but decisive, dead for him.

'Get out, get outa here!' gabbled Llewellyn excitedly. He backed against the wheel of the democrat, and nearly dropped the lines, but instinctively grasped them again and made a cut in the air at Rex. Rex was perplexed. Obviously here was a strange-acting man, and one whose trouser-cuffs must be sniffed at all costs. Nothing dismayed, he dived for the said appendages, and Llewellyn launched a kick at him, which with a doleful yelp Rex neatly dodged. He sat down a few yards away, and scratched behind one pricked ear with an otherwise inscrutable expression, while Llewellyn scrambled into the seat beside Altea.

'Wanta keep dawgs away from me,' he remarked with casual bravado, albeit rather breathless. 'Get up, Horace!'

'I'll say so.'

'Poor Rexie darling, was him hurty?' Doris wanted to get out of the rig to comfort him, but Conrad grinned at her and pinched her arm. They were on an old footing, for they had gone to school together, though she had been in the Primary Class – she was now attending High School – while he was in the Entrance Class.

'Why do you let her go with such a dumb-bell?' she whispered fiercely, accenting the last word to make it audible.

'Can't be helped,' returned Conrad cheerfully, but hopefully. Funny of Llewellyn to have chosen these two for chum and best girl – but maybe Llewellyn wouldn't think it so funny if he knew.

Altea reservedly said nothing about the dog episode, though she smiled politely in identifying the current meteorological phenomena.

'Yes, looks like rain. But – ' He brightened. 'We're on our way, anyway, Miss Hodge. – Oh, that reminds me. Back there I heard you call me Mr Lewel. That won't go, now, I want to warn you.'

He felt reinstated in his own importance. Instead, he should have felt a diminution of confidence in noting the demure glance she gave him.

Clop-clop! Horace waded horsefully onward, his huge limbs like paddle-wheels in the swirls of dust. He seemed so purposeful that Llewellyn began to wonder whether he could get him stopped, in case – An occasional snort was his only relaxation, which caused the passengers to stop talking, and the girls to employ handkerchiefs.

Though the evening was advancing, rigs on the road were few. An automobile passed them, containing a group of young people who laughed at the sight of the equipage.

'That's Syd Howard, from town. I know him,' remarked Llewellyn complacently.

'Oh, we're aristocrats, we are!' piped Doris. She soon became more good-humoured, however, in the unaccustomed circumstances. They rivalled the vanished automobile load in hilarity.

'Talk about your market load of chickens,' could be heard from Conrad.

'Why, what a nice horse he is,' said Altea. 'He's not a bit slow, if he is so big.'

'Oh, no,' cheerfully mocked Doris from behind. 'We'll run over some poor Ford one of these minutes.'

'What's his name, Mr Lewel?' asked Altea, hoping that Mr Lewel had not heard her irrepressible sister.

'Horse, just Horse,' said Llewellyn magisterially.

'Why – how fun-ny!'

'Well, that's all they called him when I got there. So I nicknamed him Horace. And he et so mucho hay, I called him Horace the Haymow.'

'And when he cuts up, he's hit one mit the head over, by Llewellyn the Lammer,' rejoined Conrad who had been listening, 'and goes back into his hole.'

Just at that instant Horace repudiated his niceness, for a dog ran out to the road, and streaked after them. Horace seemed to lift as on a wave.

'Go 'way dog!' bellowed Llewellyn in a tone which mingled horror, detestation, and panic.

The harness jingled, and Horace lumbering took up a gallop for a jump or two, and then subsided when the dog took himself off, his eyes glowing with quiet satisfaction in the dusk.

'Narrow escape,' said Doris. 'I won't sleep a wink tonight, I know.'

'I should say it was,' agreed Llewellyn anxiously, leaning over the dashboard and looking at the axle, to judge its distance from the hocks of Horace. 'If he was to hit his hind shins on the front part of this craft, he'd just naturally toss her over his head frontwards.'

'Oh, I hope he isn't wiggly,' said Altea tranquilly. 'You know the kind. Lift their feet up in the air and wiggle them a couple of times before they put them down; and put them down in pretty near the same place.'

'Horace? I guess not. Nothing highfalutin about him. He wiggles right along, he does.'

Nevertheless it began to seem that perhaps Horace was not adapted to precipitate locomotion. For it had grown dark apparently with great suddenness, and they were still about two miles from town. Moreover, automobiles became more numerous as they approached town, and the headlights more disturbing. The girls began to see in imagination their triumphal entry in the metropolis, prefiguring the weirdness of their own appearance under the white lights. Both were glad when Altea gave tongue to this motivation:

'Don't you think it might be better to not try to go to the movies now, it's so late?'

The occupants of the rear seat held views:

'Wouldn't take much trying, now,' said Conrad.

'Why, but what in the world would we do?' demanded Doris.

'Yes, there's that; where would we go?' amended Altea.

'Say, that's some pretty keen idea,' hastily rejoined Llewellyn. He had begun also to use his imagination, to the premonitory tune of seeing Horace running amuck among who knew what density of Saturday night traffic.

'Here's a road right here. What about takin' little drive down this one?'

It was a dark road, save for an occasional lighted window. Comparatively speaking, dark, that is. The roadway glimmered whitely and the little puffs of dust could be seen when Horace placed his leisurely feet. Occasionally a great tree or a group of trees overhung them, and the noise of their passage echoed among the boughs. An ideal place. They did not talk so much.

'Gosh, I'm glad we came around here. Some scenery, eh? beautiful, just matches!' Llewellyn considered this the subtle equivalent, so far as words went, to a passionate declaration. When it went beyond words – He slung his arm over the back of the democrat seat.

'You folks lost your tongues?' enquired Conrad, as though it were any of his affair!

'Looks like a storm coming,' remarked Llewellyn coldly.

The others looked up, and burst into exclamations. Behind and at one side of them a tall black rampart of cloud, bright-edged, could be seen advancing upon them.

'And me with my new spring coat,' blubbered Doris in half-mock agony. 'Drive up, Llewellyn, so's we can beat it home.'

Llewellyn endeavoured to comply as well as he might in the position of his arms.

'Pretty mean of her, ain't it?' he asked fatuously, 'to want us to hurry up like this, when we're – '

'It does look as though the storm's coming this way,' said Altea apprehensively, ignorning this complimentary innuendo. A sweet kid, Llewellyn reflected, and not so stuck up after all. Next time the others wouldn't be with them.

But the storm, as a matter of fact, showed no inclination to badinage. The black cloud seemed to advance on them more rapidly at every minute. A wind roared out of nowhere, and all clutched their hats. Horace's heavy mane rose and stood out from his neck as though he were moving at breath-taking speed.

In actuality, however, he was jogging along contentedly, little better than before.

'Really, he doesn't seem to be going very fast, does he?' Altea murmured.

Who so pleased as her knight to obey his lady fair. He chucked the lines, clucked with his lips, slapped Horace upon the rear quarters, and even removed his arm from the back of the seat to do these things.

Horace finally was shocked as well as hurt by the unseemly evidences of an interest personal in nature. With a deft flick he reached Llewellyn's hat and at the same time knocked one of the lines from his driver's hand.

'Whoah! Whoa there!' Clinging to the one remaining line Llewellyn pulled him short about.

'Why don't you jump down and get around to his gable end?' enquired Conrad coolly, as though quite prepared for this. 'He's going to tip this outfit into the ditch if you don't.'

'Holy hellcats!' Llewellyn had already leaped to the road.

'Gable end!' giggled Doris.

'Horace is all right. He just feels hurt because we think it's funny he weighs nineteen hundred pounds and doesn't want to go like Man o' War.'

Conrad appeared even to be enjoying himself. He would get wet, of course, but the blame would not be upon his shoulders.

'Oh, *why* did you bring us out in this kind of rig?' asked Altea finally turning to her old beau, tears in her voice. She saw the gray wall of rain a hundred yards away, and heard Conrad:

'Not my doings, you know.'

And Llewellyn:

'Why, he's gone and got the shaft loose on this side.'

And then a bark and an agonized human howl, and the rain burst in a torrent upon the party. They cowered in the democrat, helpless, and the scream came again, full of agony. It was Llewellyn.

'Go 'way, get away! Get away!' At the abject fascinated terror in his voice one would have thought that some beast of the jungle confronted him. 'Oh, my Lord, can't you come – help me? Help! Conrad!'

'Hector, Hector my dog has fleas,' said Doris in an hysterical parrot-like voice, as though quoting.

'Why, what's the matter?' asked Conrad, looking out from between the lapels of his coat. 'Why don't you get in and drive on?'

They peered out and could see the form of Llewellyn writhing in agony at the front of Horace, with the dog hovering near, as though in curiosity. Llewellyn was feebly motioning it away.

'Get out! Go home! I'll kill you – ' The minatory adjurations he further employed were such that the girls were glad to avail themselves of the noise of the storm.

'What's that?' asked Conrad.

'You darn dumb-bell, come and let me go. You can see well enough what it is. I'm caught.'

The fact was that just as the rain struck them, a dog ran out, and the too startled Horace, so that he placed his long-grown talon upon one of Llewellyn's long-toed new shoes, and confidingly let it rest.

'Well,' said Conrad callously, when he had reached him and driven the dog away and backed Horace from his position, 'Why didn't you straighten up and jerk him back by the bit? What'd you done if I wasn't here?'

'It's all right for you to talk,' complained Llewellyn. 'What did you leave the shaft on that side unbuckled for?' Dripping they crawled back into their seats.

By this time the first gusts had departed, and a businesslike rain had started.

'What was the trouble?' asked Altea coldly.

'Well, it's funny somebody would be a little bit interested about it?' grunted Llewellyn, injured.

'Horace stepped on his toe,' explained Conrad.

Instead of sympathy, Llewellyn got the surprise of his life.

'Llewellyn Lewel, you're a fool!' exclaimed Altea, her voice indignant to the point of tearfulness.

'Same to you and many of them,' returned Llewellyn punctiliously.

'Don't kick a man when he's down,' said Conrad, who could afford to be generous.

'You'd let Horace do it though, if he wanted to,' snarled Llewellyn.

All the way home Doris and he bickered, with pacificatory eggings-on from Conrad. But Altea after her blanketing description was silent.

When they reached the Hodge farm Conrad jumped down promptly and assisted the girls to alight.

'Well, we got you here, anyway!' Part of Llewellyn's assurance had returned with the going of the rain, and since they were not asking him to stay, he ventured,

'Next time there won't be no Horace, and we'll –'

'There won't be any next time, either,' retorted Altea with decision.

Automatically Llewellyn slapped the lines on the broad back before him. Nor did Conrad make an attempt to board the homefaring craft.

'Leave the democrat where you got it,' he directed. 'And you can tell the boss to take the day tomorrow to fix his car. Tell him I said it would be all right to do that now. I got to stay and talk to Altea here.

On the road the youth wondered – and wondered – how he had been so blind.

THE RETURN OF THE NANCES

The air of the spring evening was cooler, but sweeter, than the chill newly occupied house. Hector Nance's home now was just beyond the end of the village pavement, and he tramped firmly and with rather long strides, over a walk of narrow wooden slats. He was a heavily-brisk, stocky, rather flat-bodied man of middle height or less, with large aquiline blunt features and a pale dark complexion. The hair beneath his derby hat was a deep strong black, only faintly peppered with gray.

Since his return that afternoon, with a freight car of furniture unloaded into hayracks, the village had seemed strange. Now King Street was empty for the supper hour, and even urchinhood was at home. Yet the look of the place was little different from the two years since he and his wife had left it, followed their sons to the city, and established a job-printing business. Here was a huge new garage with show-windows, reception-room, entrance and exit driveways, where once had been a venerable harness shop, a millinery and a barber shop. Yes, there must have been changes recorded week by week in the Ruston *Echo*; he had not been there to record them nor to solicit the augmented advertising accounts. A stranger edited the *Echo*.

A green-and-white clapboarded building protruded to the sidewalk, leaving the little houses at either side as though they lingered back shyly. In the dusk, its front was dimly alight: great panes of thin glass at either side of the door. Hector Nance remembered that he had been sent by Mrs Nance to 'Wilton's' for something she could prepare quickly in the midst of the upheaval.

Henry Wilton himself was in the shop, bent over the cash register, a tall, dry-faced young man who looked as though he had been powdered with the flour used in his baking. He straightened at the jingle of the bell against the door-top, and nodded.

'Ho! Mr Nance! Back for good, Mr Nance? I saw the loads of furniture going by from the freight shed.'

'Yes, couldn't leave the old town for good. Put me up a loaf of bread and a can of salmon, Henry, will you?'

'Were you going to start up in opposition to the old *Echo*, Mr Nance?' Wilton looked up blandly as he tore a sheet of paper from the roll at the end of the counter. He had been a birth-announcement and a name in the school reports, and an overgrown lout, in Hector's time. There was something annoying about this conversation, though Hector could not say what it was.

'You've sold the business you had in Walkerville. Or was it Windsor?'

'Windsor. I turned it over to the boys. They like job-printing better than running a newspaper. For me, since I'm quitting, I'd rather be in a place where I know the people. So here we are,' he added, with what he felt to be inept heartiness.

'Very glad to have you back, I'm sure.' This was in the polite tone of a suddenly-occurring afterthought, while Henry looked blandly again at another entering customer – a stranger. It was mingled with the sound of the bell and the door closing, which shook the front of the building. Hector turned away brusquely. 'Tinkling cymbal,' he thought, annoyed with himself and Henry. Was it because he had lived in the city where people veiled their curiosity? Yet Henry's had been no more marked than his own would have been in the interests of news, once on a time.

He was walking home in the direction opposite to that which formerly had taken him home. It occurred to him that one thing was fortunate; he would not have to pass, every time he came uptown, the house he had built five years ago. That was at the other end of the village, among its aristocracy.

The street lamps of the village shed dim circles of light on the edge of the roadway and the last remnants of last year's grass along the sidewalk as he walked home, hungry and tired from the day of bustle. He met Dave McKellar carrying a spade over his shoulder, as he came within the edge of one of the circles. He'd known Dave years out of count. Funny old fellow, like the rest of us, more or less, when we're getting along in years.

'Good night, Dave!'

Dave looked at him sharply, and without pausing returned his greeting. 'He doesn't recognize me,' thought Hector Nance, chagrined. He would have turned to look after the man, but it was Dave all right, who himself probably would be turning around to look. 'I suppose it hasn't got noised about much that I'm back.'

The wooden slat sidewalk, when he had passed the village and its lights, was a little shaky. 'We'll have to get after the town fathers about this,' he thought, remembering with pleasure some of the reforms he had consummated as editor and councilman himself.

He was reassured by this almost automatic thought, then depressed, with the sense of strangeness and unease which surely could not belong to the simple meetings of this last half-hour. Merely tired and hungry, he decided he was, at the mercy of foolish thoughts. The gate to his yard swung slackly aside under his hand, but he pulled it back and latched it carefully. No, Hector Nance had not lost hope, or been forced out of his place. He had wanted his boys to have their chance, as he had had his with no father to interfere.

Mrs Nance was reading before the stove in the closed, warm kitchen, which was cluttered yet bare. The table was set, well-filled, for two.

'The *Echo* isn't much like it used to be. You ought to see – '

Hector Nance smiled but did not look at the paper when she got up to make tea and slice the bread, nor ask her in what corner she had found it. He carried his coat and hat away to hang in the hall.

'That supper looks good,' he remarked. 'What do you say to not going to that prayer meeting? If we feel industrious there's plenty of settling to be done. But we're better to rest and be comfortable as we can.'

'Well, I was just going to suggest not going.' Mrs Nance looked at him. 'Only it was nice of Anne Craven to ask us on sight.'

'Yes, it was Anne,' assented Hector dryly. Mrs Nance knew what he meant. The gushing spinster who had rushed up and exclaimed over her old neighbours had carried no official weight in her invitation. Mr Crawford, the venerable deacon, was the one to have asked them. They had always smiled at the deacon and his oddness. Yet it was a little surprising that he had stalked right past when their furniture was being unloaded from the wagons, without seeming to see them.

'It would have been fun, of course, to see the deacon perform. Remember the time he stumbled, and read from the Bible, "And the Lord sprang unto Moses"?' Hector's laugh was deep and mellow.

'Oh, yes! – you weren't there, were you?' She was wondering at his apparent willingness to attend now.

'Oh, but I heard about it,' Hector said literally.

There was something almost of a honeymoon flavor about these days. For two weeks he stayed about the house, discussing, arranging, rearranging things as his wife directed. He started to dig the garden which extended from behind the house, alongside it and the lawn, to the street fence. Old weeds of last year and long neglected sods occupied him. Occasionally farmers coming into town with wagonloads of grist or swaying buggies or Fords, hailed him: 'Working up your farm, eh? Does you town fellows good to sweat. Glad to see you back,' they would call over their shoulders, and certainly without thinking whether their subscriptions had been paid up when Nance had gone.

They didn't seem to realize that he'd been away, or that the place could be different for him. Perhaps it was the same with town fellows. A couple of them talking with him would soon get to something of which he'd never heard. 'That was when – You wasn't here when that happened, was you, Hector?' Art Sterling the shoemaker said, glancing at Andy Applemeyer, the drugstore man. 'Well, the way it happened. ...'

There were plenty of such incidents. You might think people did so purposely, to make him feel out of things, he thought bitterly, plunging the spade into the black earth.

He had never been one to loaf in barber shops or before livery stables, or on the veranda of the hotel, even in search of news. And now there was no need to fear being out of things. Yet one had to observe that the village seemed to have new people, new interests – and a new indifference. For all the notice it took of him, he might have been any stranger moving into the commonplace frame house on the back street.

He was sure that such thoughts did not bother his wife. She bustled about happily, intent on getting the rooms of her house neatly arranged. She did not complain that her furniture was too large or fine for this house, or that the house was not so good as the one they had built and left. She was well-pleased to be away from the city, and among people she knew or understood.

Two weeks after they had returned, Hector said, briskly, as he wiped the dinner dishes:

'Well, I see that I can't live on my money. I guess I'll go see Bannister at the Planing Mill about a job in his office.'

Mrs Nance did not reply, but brushed crumbs from the table-cloth to a tray. She had expected him to announce a job any day when he returned from 'downtown.'

John Bannister was in his office when Hector reached it – a tall, upright-headed, thin man, gray-moustached, in workingman's clothes. He stood behind the high counter leafing an account book, as though he had no time for the high stool beside him. Yet there was nothing impetuous about him.

They shook hands, and spoke casually.

'You haven't come to see us, Hector. I was glad to hear you were back. Our town cannot afford to lose a good citizen, you know.'

'So I – so they say,' Hector spoke abruptly, and began talking of business conditions in the city.

They were old friends. It seemed to Hector as they talked that he'd forgotten what John Bannister was like, how sterling and ungrudging. Presently Bannister said:

'I've been thinking, Hector, that I'd like to have a man who knows something about business in my office. I thought perhaps I could get you to take care of things, except the typing – . Grace has been doing that, but her mother wants her to have more time for her music; besides she can't see to things when I'm not here, and know just what lumber people need for their purposes, and maybe go out to the yard with them to show them, like a man. Had you thought of doing anything now, or were you just retiring?'

It was to see him about that, Hector Nance assured him, that he had called. 'He seemed to remember that we had been friends once,' Nance said to his wife that night. He laughed with thoroughness. 'Lots of people seem to have forgotten that I ever lived here before. I suppose if they thought about it at all they just thought they had settled my case. They didn't need to think of me again; but here I'm back to upset things.'

Mrs Nance looked thoughtful.

'I suppose ... I suppose that's it. Or maybe,' she added brightly, 'they didn't notice we'd gone.'

'They might have,' said Hector laconically.

He attended church services regularly now, a custom he had got in the city. Before, he had let his wife go alone. The matter-of-courseness of the people was breathtaking. Perhaps it was the new minister who made things strange. Old Mr Bowring used to hold people in bunches after church, ducking, shaking hands, questioning, clapping backs, holding a reception.

He became used to living, incognito, as it were, in the village where he had been a person of consequence. In the mornings on the way to work he passed the old shop from which he used to issue weekly his *Echo*, and the low-ceilinged rooms above it where in earlier times he had lived with his wife and little boys. The new house he had built he occasionally saw, and its owner, who had bought the business. They gravely saluted and passed on.

Once in a while some customer in the office of the planing mill told him how much better the paper had been when he had been running it; and it was plain that there had been a decline. The fellow depended on boilerplate, and did not ever write editorials, but slightly amplified news notes for the front page, reports of baseball games, or hockey games, or descriptions of somebody's new house. Hector Nance was cheered by belated praise and the payment of an occasional overdue subscription. He had given up a good many of these as 'bad debts.'

The boys seldom came home, though Windsor was not far away, and they did not seem to feel that he was interested in their business. Yet it was expanding, and each had bought himself a car. He told them that they need not make further payments to him for the present. His job at the planing mill, he expected, was a steady one. And since they were incurring high expenses ... 'The money's not much good to me anyway,' he thought, 'and may never be. If I do need it I can get it. They're good boys.'

He settled into the familiar life of Ruston, an accustomed sight, walking along, a solid, intelligent figure, his whole body bent slightly forward, wearing a light black overcoat with the velvet collar turned up about his throat, and a derby hat. He no longer stopped and was stopped by half the people he met.

He got on very well with his work in the mill. In a thorough way he soon made himself familiar with the details of the business, and would instruct whiskered farmers putting up fence, or experimental townsmen building their own garages, taking them out to the piles of lumber in the yard, passing through the screaming mill which trembled with the whirl of machines and the vibration of the powerplant and the roll of heavy belts.

Since Hector Nance had never learned typewriting, and John Bannister's daughter did that work, there were hours in which he found little to occupy him. He got in the way of going out and piling lumber in the yard, or helping to unload a freight car at the spur. He took the overalls which he wore from behind the office door with relief, for he felt that the heavy work, not too continuous, was doing him good. When he came home at night he rather proudly told Mrs Nance of his 'manual labour.'

Though he was almost humorless himself, it was fun to listen to the talk of the labourers as they unloaded the cars. But the jokes known as practical, to him were tricks they played upon one another, and he would pause to tip back his derby hat and wipe the sweat from his brow, rather puzzled.

Once a week Toots Bellman used to come to the yard for a load of free shavings, and hang around between times. Practical jokes were the specialty of Toots, but the men did not become annoyed with him.

Toots Bellman was a youth of seventeen or eighteen, short, always wearing shinily dirty pants too long and bulky for him, which made his legs seem still shorter than they were, and a shaggy felt hat on his grimy tow-head above his narrow pale jaundice-coloured face. He laughed with a sinister involuntary 'He! He!' showing narrow dirty teeth with dark spaces between them. When his words began with certain consonants, it was as though he spat them out.

He had been a famous personage in the village since he had become old enough to walk, and good little boys obtained a horrid pleasure in any intercourse with him which they could snatch. He 'played hookey' a good deal and openly refused to go to school. When he was about twelve years old he stole half a dozen neckties from a store. He was sent to a reformatory, and still had to go to school when he had returned, until he was fourteen. Then, undersized, shrewd, and strong, he began to make a sort of living trading horses, buying wild western colts, breaking and selling them.

His father also traded horses or anything else, with those who still thought they could get ahead of him; but his chief business was the keeping of a butcher shop. Mr Bellman was a middle-sized man with good features, red-yellow tan, and a tawny moustache which he sometimes clipped straight to bristle along his upper lip. He always wore a soiled dark heavy suit, which made him feel well-dressed beside the overalled and motley-clothed farmers to whom he went to bargain for a head of cattle or sheep. He drove about in what was called a light road-wagon – a one-seated buggy without a top, having a small runged open box behind. Everyone knew he was a sharp one, but he always found a farmer ready to do business with him. He seldom was to be found in his butcher-shop, for it was tended by one or other of his frowsy daughters, who rushed in bare armed from the house alongside. They appeared up-town in the afternoon in marvelous handmade clothes and complexions.

Toots rode about the country on a horse which someone had trusted him to break, or on a rickety or vicious one temporarily his own. He shouldered a place, bargained as shrewdly, with as much winning horse-play, as an old-timer. 'What a' you got to deal today?' he would ask, and jump down, a bowlegged small figure, to look through the stables.

Respectable people were not bothered by his known dishonesty. He was Toots.

At Bannister's mill, getting loads of shavings to bed down his own and his father's horses, he lounged about the yard, sitting on a pile of lumber, tearing a furry strip of bark from a plant edge, chewing tobacco, laughing, until moved by one of the rough-voiced mill hands. He would stare fixedly at the middle-aged man in overalls and light shirt and gloves handling the planks.

'Some come-down for old Nance, all right,' he sneered to one of the men. 'He used to think he was pretty smart, all right, going aroun' town all dressed up, and living in his big house. He just thought his socks never stank.'

Hector Nance passed from a vague impression that the boy was sneering behind his hand and making the men laugh, to a realization that Toots for some reason intended to make a practice of ridiculing him, and insulting him with the position he had once held in the town. He ignored such smallness as long as he could.

One afternoon when it had become hot piling lumber in the yards, he laid off his hat. He paid no attention when Toots came over and began an exchange of genial insult with the men. Soon, a customer called Nance to the office to 'settle up.' Toots, with a grimace which almost made the others split, picked up the hat and hid it in a hollow of shorter boards at the end of a lumber-pile. Then he drove off with his load of shavings.

It was nearly six when Mr Nance came back to the lumber-piles, without the overalls and gloves. He was looking for his hat. One of the men finally told him where the hat might be. They were unwilling to spoil the joke, they would have said, but in truth they did not know why they went on working without paying heed to his search.

After that Toots and Hector Nance avoided one another, and in the presence of others always had a sneer or an innuendo ready. It was as though he wanted to say: 'You thought I was nobody in those days. Now we can see who's nobody.'

Hector Nance came home from work a little late one evening, to find his wife taking off her hat and gloves.

'You've been out, Elvira?' he asked.

'Yes, you remember, don't you, I said the WCTU meeting was to be this afternoon?' She seemed flustered.

'Why, yes. I suppose you didn't get everybody's characteristics classified until late, eh?' They smiled at one of his three or four jokes.

She broke in eagerly. 'Oh, you can't think what happened! They held the election of officers, and whom do you suppose is president for next year?' She stood there in the hall as though she had to tell him the story before starting to get the supper.

'Let me see,' he murmured growlingly, not wishing to make a mistake. 'Would it be Mrs Beith? Or – '

'It was me!' Mrs. Nance bent her head forward, taking out and putting a comb in the back of her hair. She moved off to the kitchen with a lively step.

'Ah, ha! – Fine, Elvira!'

He sat in an easy chair and watched her movements in silence. She was a small, rather slender woman of sallow complexion, wrinkles beginning to show, and a triangular straight, or now slightly aquiline nose. She appeared at least as old as her husband. He began to think of what she had had to put up with in coming back like this. The house really might be fixed up, if he decided to buy it. A new veranda would help. Some people had frame houses veneered with cement blocks or brick. To remodel the house though, might mean that the boys would have to be called upon. At least he would talk about it with her, soon.

In the morning as he walked along the wooden sidewalk, thoughts came to him which he did not recognize as having their origin in the news his wife had brought home. Usually alone in the pleasant early morning, for the school children from the country did not come for nearly an hour yet, he enjoyed walking to work.

'This town's slow,' he declared, as he tramped along on the trembling slats. 'Sure, too. In another year things will be just the same as before we went. I could run for any office I might like, better than when I had the paper. I guess character is what counts. If the boys get along well in the next five years they can pay me back with a lump sum, perhaps. I could buy the paper again. What's five years? I'd make it go, again. I'm going to tell the Council some improvements that have got to be made in this town, anyway. I'll wake 'em up a bit, no matter what happens.' There was an enlivening coolness in the morning air, and a shower had laid the dust upon the road.

It was very warm by one o'clock, and the walk from home back to work was noticeably long. He went forward doggedly, his dark coat on his arm. Maple trees shaded the sidewalk most of the way, but they did not seem to alleviate the heat. The mud of the street was being made to dust again, and lay in flakes upon the wheel-tracks. The whole village seemed to drowse, hating to awaken to the reality of the day and only an occasional man was about, going to work. Later in the afternoon, and in the evening, boys and men would begin to mow the grass on the lawns, and buggies and cars would line the street, for it was Saturday.

Flies stood on the sidewalk as Mr Nance tramped toward them, bent slightly forward, his head in line with his spine, and hoped with boyish truculence that they would rest there until his foot reached them.

Bannister's daughter had finished her letters at noon, and the mill owner himself had gone into the country to make collection for some barns he had built. Hector Nance was alone in the office. In a couple of hours he had finished his work, and stood looking out of the window over the platform scales on which loads of coal and gypsum were weighed. Beyond the drive leading to the back of the mill yard stood a big maple casting the edge of its shade upon the window. When the limbs swayed a little in the breeze, spots of light and shadow moved evenly across the sill and floor. Loud, regular, and echoing blows began to come from somewhere behind the building. They were hammering thick hoops down on the staves of a tank.

Somehow he was oppressed by a sense of the phantomlike uselessness of all this endeavour, and, what was worse, a sense of its precarious existence. In an hour, surely, the feeling would be a mere absurdity.

Squeaks approached, and Toots Bellman drove past the window with his rickety 'democrat,' its wheels slanted inward at an absurd angle. He did not look in, but stared ahead as though unconscious of the man watching there.

Hector Nance turned away. A farmer had driven up with a bag of flour on a straw-covered wagon-box, and appeared in the door.

'You ain't got any lumber here,' he drawled, grinning, 'that would do for a partition?'

'What kind of a partition? In a house?'

'No, in a barn. I could do with a few clapboards too, though.'

'You'll want undressed stuff, then, for the partition. Just drive around that way, I'll go ahead.'

But on the way to the piles they stopped and Hector went into the rear of the mill building, through the sliding door, wide open, in which Toots Bellman's rig was standing. The man to whom Nance spoke about the clapboards said they were right there. So they began carrying them out to the wagon. There was no sign of Toots about, but the large bransacks full of shavings were in his democrat.

The loudness of the mill was like a showerbath out of which they stepped on turning the corner. At the second trip the farmer got talking with one of the workmen inside. Returning, Hector Nance measured out two more armfuls and took up one of them, looking back to shout:

'This makes up your lot! I'm going for your undressed stuff.' The farmer went on talking.

Hector stepped out of the mill again, and the whirlpool of the storm of sound. He walked along the row of raised lumber piles to the back of the yard, the noise growing thinner behind him.

Toots Bellman was coming out from behind a half-used pile at the end of the yard with two long boards under his arms. As they drew together, Hector Nance saw that there was something of impudent bravado about him. He held his lower lip in with his narrow separated teeth, and limped along with the heavy burden. He was watching Mr Nance persistently, and plainly intended to brazen it out. 'He'd just leave it around at the end of the mill until he drove past – but I'm here,' thought the man. Toots was proceeding with gaze averted until something made him speak.

'Hot day for this job,' he said.

Nance stopped beside him.

'Look here, boy, this won't do,' He spoke shortly, but not harshly.

'What won't do, you old – warhorse?' asked Toots flippantly, spitting.

'You know what – well enough.'

'Guess I do know, all right. I mind my own business, and I know how to keep from going bankrupt.' He started on again, sneering, his strong shoulders sloping with the weight.

Hector Nance looked after him, not knowing how to retaliate, with an immense rage swelling within him. Did the young tough expect to get by with theft on such a pretext?

Toots turned his head when he was twenty yards away, and shifted his load so that one hand was free. With it he made an insulting gesture. 'You old stinker!' he brought out with the same spitting motion.

For a second, two, Mr Nance stood rooted, then ran heavily after him over the cinders. Breathlessly he shouted:

'Damn! Damn you to *Hell!*'

Toots Bellman dropped the boards and turned. He brandished his fists frightenedly, as the heavy, white-shirted figure lurched toward him. 'I'll tramp – you!' he heard between the swinging blows. 'Down!' They were jumping about on the clattering boards for a long time, it seemed, back and forth, and away. Toots warding off desperately – a grotesque pair behind the great brown boxlike building.

'Tramp him! Tramp him!' The words crowded the mind of Hector Nance. He had felled Toots when shouts penetrated to him, and the farmer and a mill hand had seized him.

The following Friday the *Echo* carried an account which stated that Hector Nance, a bookkeeper in the local Planing Mill, had been fined $25 and costs by the magistrate presiding at the Division Court on that day, for assault. The plaintiff, James Bellman, and two witnesses gave evidence sufficient for conviction. Nance, however, it was stated, pleaded guilty without making a defence.

Bannister, taking the matter gravely and tranquilly, had come to see Hector Nance the day after the fight, and suggested an apology to Toots. Hector Nance sent him away discomfited, for he was still warm about the affair. Knowing that people would laugh about 'the fight' oppressed both of the two grave men.

But as the days passed, and he fancied that people looked at him curiously, noncommittally, Hector Nance would have gone to the Bellman's save for his own obstinacy. He knew it was the chance they wanted. There were two defined classes in the town, and theirs the least considered. Now he had both classes against him. He felt braced when children, unconsciously voicing the opinion of their elders, jeered at him when he passed. For the absurd wrongheadedness of the whole town – the town he had once loved – had become plain to him, and made him positive of his own righteousness.

Mrs Nance did not go out at all now. She was sure that her husband would not have printed such an item about a respectable citizen.

It was about a month after the trial, on a rainy day, that Mr Bannister, having an hour clear of interruptions and customers, to go over the accounts with his bookkeeper, pulled a grimed paper from his vestpocket:

'Better enter this on the books. The lumber Toots Bellman got that day – '

'Why?' Nance looked up dumbfounded. 'Did he order lumber?' He stammered. 'Did you tell him – '

'He called me up at the house at noon, and asked me whether he could get a few planks to mend a stall with when he came for the shavings. I told him where to find them if no-one was around.'

'He might have told me about it,' said Hector with a rueful smile. 'But I thought you were overlooking the faults of both of us, or rather, my temper and his theft.'

'No, he wasn't stealing it. Did you – you didn't think he was taking it without telling me? Was *that* what made the trouble!' There was scarcely a smile to be discerned beneath John Bannister's moustache, but there was a deep joyousness in his tone. Hector Nance felt strangely easy.

'No,' he admitted. 'I don't suppose that was the cause of the trouble. There *were* other things before. And he used somewhat rude language then. But I did think that.'

Bannister was a man of few words, and his triangular eyes were again on a ledger. Hector Nance stared out of the window.

'Well, I'll go now and do what you suggested. I'll apologize. It would have been better before. But you can understand.' It seemed to him that the important thing in this episode was not the innocence of Toots, nor his own steadfastness, but the tolerance of John Bannister.

'Yes. It's half-past eleven. You might call on your way home now.'

Outside was a windy day of streaming rain that drenched the ragged leaves and slapped them to the boughs. The very air was filled with prophecy of autumn as he walked along, looking from beneath his umbrella mostly at the washed and flowing sidewalk.

The little one-roomed butcher-shop seemed to be empty. He went to the house, next door. The remains of a rotting wooden sidewalk from the street to the front door, was strewn like debris of a flood; and instead of walking in the little ditch where it had been, he went to the house on the sodden grass. He knocked at the door and looked about him. As he stood thus on the veranda, the portions of the house within sight appeared still more dilapidated. Creamy flakes were loose on the formerly white clapboards, and pink flakes on the perpendicular corner boards that had once been red. One of the veranda steps was missing.

Realizing that he had had no answer to his knock he went around to the back door, keeping outside of the streaming eaves.

Mrs Bellman appeared in a damp-looking, dragging dress. Her yellow hair which was not yet gray hung in her eyes, her shoes seemed unlaced, and two or three small children supported themselves by her skirts as they leaned out from behind her.

'Is Mr Bellman in?' asked Hector Nance. 'Or his son?'

'No, they're away.' She looked at him out of suspicious eyes.

'Well,' he began hesitatingly, lowering his deep voice, 'I wish you would tell James that I am sorry about what happened between us, and for the way it happened.'

'You want to apologize, you mean,' said the woman sharply. She had been listening gloatingly to his words.

'Yes, I wish to apologize.'

Mrs Bellman looked in his strong face with the iron-gray hair rimming it, silently, wondering at his gentle tone. And then, nobody had compelled him to come like this, when it was all over.

'I'll tell him.' She nodded the frowsy head emphatically. 'It's too bad – '

'It's too bad it happened,' agreed Mr Nance roundly. 'I'm sorry, even if we were both to blame.'

She nodded silently again, gulped as though she meant to say something, and closed the door in his face.

A glimpse of their life vanished behind the scarred door, in untidy bits of wornout furniture, dirty stove, half-swept kitchen floor with dust pile.

When he had finished dinner he told his wife. She patted his shoulder and gave for the tenth time her opinion of the Bellman family.

He smiled, learning a wise acceptance to balance his loss of self-righteousness. And things so imperceptibly became what they had been in old days, that it was with surprise that he recalled a year and a half later the time at which he might have regarded as irony his proposed appointment as magistrate and town clerk. But not only was he nominated, he secured the election.

THE ONE THING

As it puffed down the road that cloud-tapestried October day, the team found the wagon-load of sugar-beets behind it increasingly heavy. The road was clay, and deeply rutted, notwithstanding the wide and deep ditches draining it on either side. Presently the driver pulled up his horses. As their wet flanks heaved, their breath showing in the dank and heavy air, he looked about him. The land was perfectly flat. From the slight elevation of the road he could see long bleached after-harvest grainfields, varied with dull tracts of beets, and rows of soiled-appearing corn-shocks, stretching sombrely, wire-fenced, to the backs of the farms, where stood thin forests, which did not shut out streaks of gray sky. Though these distant forests did not noticeably obtrude on the vision, they hid the horizon on all sides, and his gaze might travel in certain directions so far as two miles, but always it brought up against trees. Across the ditch at his left, beyond the wire fence, was a solid-looking block of corn, still uncut. A rustling came from this, but a few yards in, and a voice, not loud, but high-pitched and monotonous, which seemed to give forth curses.

As the voice came nearer to the end of the field, a very short man, of scarcely more than half the height of the corn, but of ordinary thickness of body, was disclosed. He looked up the road scarcely ceasing his shrill muttering, and, bringing his gaze back to look down it, caught sight of the teamster.

'Eh! *Hello!*' he shouted loudly, his voice much lower in pitch now.

'Hello!' replied the man, just about to drive on. 'Pretty muddy, ain't it!'

The little man did not answer, but looked after the teamster in silence.

The latter, on reaching the railway spur where the beets were unloaded, was not long in imparting his bit of news.

'Say, I heard that little fellow, Billy Dulckington, swearin' like the divvle as I come past his place. I kinda stopped to give the team their wind, and first thing I hears him cussin' away like four of a kind, kinda thin and weepy-like.'

'You don't say!' His colleague straightened for a moment to loosen a crick in his spine, then bent to the job again. 'Oh, he's queer, always queer. Funny thing, though, I never knew him to be so much for cussin'. Kind of satisfied, always seemed. The one thing he cares about is his horses.'

Hitherto Billy Dulckington's queerness was a matter which had not at all preoccupied the community, and it was only in referring to him in the presence of strangers that one was reminded of it. He was a bachelor, an old bachelor now, but he was still saluted with the familiar diminutive. There was something pathetic in a man of fifty-three years, who carried at most times a bristle of beard speckled with white, being greeted always as 'Billy.'

No one, practically, had ever taken him in the slightest degree into account. When he had been young, his small stature and the amusedly tolerant attitude of the buxom and well-grown young women of the district had kept him from the manifestation of any serious intentions in regard to courtship; and excepting this, a certain amalgam of pride and stubbornness should have made him avoid seeking it. For, aside from his shortness, he was not handsome. His chin was narrow, but came well forward; his nose was long, and almost perpendicularly overhung his upper lip. His little eyes were fishlike below a sloping forehead which was perpetually wrinkling with the rising of his eyebrows in apparent astonishment at the simplest remark made by anyone with whom he happened to be conversing. One seeing him now would find it difficult to visualize him as a child.

Still, it was not at all apparent to a neighbour, speaking with him, that he had ever concerned himself much with whatever in himself or in his life had been peculiar. Almost it was possible to believe him to have been unaware of it.

As a young man he had enjoyed his first vacation by going to the Canadian National Exhibition at Toronto in one of its early years. He found much to interest him there, but what pleased him more than anything else was the string of imported Clydesdales. He became enamoured of one filly, which had won first prize in the two-year-old class, and haunted the stables where she was continually waited upon, until the day he was obliged to come home. There was something impressive in the size and strength and beauty of these magnificent beasts, something which enchanted him and called forth his longing.

Before he left he secured the address of the importer who owned the filly of his choice, and when, two years later, his father died, he went to see this dealer. The horse he had wished to own had been disposed of, he was told, but he was able, after a long and solemnly beatified process of choice, to pick out one which he liked almost as well. Later, he came to like this mare even better in some ways, for she was heavier-bodied and more squarely built than his first love. He paid for her by putting a mortgage on the farm, which was, until then, free from incumbrance.

That was a main day in his life on which he unloaded Lowry Lass from the freight car, and brought her to his farm. It was Saturday. There were neighbours in the village, in the stores, in the blacksmith shop, everywhere, it seemed. On each the serious task of appraisal and of commendation was, in his presence, incumbent. More people were met on the road, and though with many of them Billy had scarcely exchanged a word for months, to all the circumstances of the quest were imparted with unaccustomed and composed absence of reticence.

His purchase caused a seven-days' sensation, and proved a gratefully fresh topic and source of difference, for no one in that part of the country had paid so much for a single horse. When the discussion had simmered down, it was, in the main, settled that he was foolhardy; there, beyond a covert jealousy on the part of a few neighbours, the matter dropped. From one of these latter Billy purchased a team-mate for his mare, a great rawboned animal, nearly as large as his own, lacking quality, but which was, with characteristic equity, equally well-tended.

In the following years he worked hard. Illness had always been unknown to him, and since coming to manhood he had usually found himself capable of working advantageously beside men much larger than himself. With his stubby legs and puckered brow he was capable of leading any man he had ever hired at hoeing corn; and when sugarbeets came to be grown in that district, with his short and tireless back he could have held his own at beet-thinning with most of the Belgians, who were held as a rule to be far superior, at such back-breaking work, to the natives. With puffing and straining he shovelled his own beets from his wagon up into the high box of the railway car.

He did not hire much help in those years. His farm was one hundred acres, but he preferred to plant no more hoe-crop than he was able to manage himself, with one helper at the busiest part of the season.

He was dumb in his obsession with his horses, except on the rare occasions when strangers chanced to come to his farm who he imagined should know a horse when they saw one. The conversations on these occasions tended to become somewhat recondite, involving discussion of this or that greatly pedigreed individual; for, having attended one or two of the greater exhibitions, Billy was the local authority on this subject. He was emphatic in his deprecation of the new style of Clydesdales, just beginning to 'come in'; the upstanding, light-feathered, bright-gaited kind he held to be like hackneys, carriage-horses, and that was for him the lowest depth of condemnation. The almost uniform lack of enthusiasm attested in regard to his own stock he explained in various ways; as he recalled their conversation, this man must have owned Clydes himself, that one was too frightened of ministering to his pride; the other knew nothing of that whereof he spoke. He had tried to interest some of the big horsemen of the East and Quebec in his stock. His herd had increased steadily with the lapse of years, but he could not assure even himself that it increased likewise in quality. Meanwhile he continued to keep the other branches of livestock represented, but not proportionately, nor in like quality, on the farm – pigs, milch cows, and a herd of steers which roamed in his 'bush' in summer and were tied in one end of his barn in winter.

After about fifteen years of this he was gradually becoming more prosperous; not very rapidly, for many of his acres went to supply pasturage and hay for his growing herd of horses. Still, the mortgage was paid off, and there was a gradually increasing balance to his credit in the bank.

It was at about this time, in the late autumn, that the father of his brother Tom's wife died in the next township. Billy was going to be present at the funeral. He curried and harnessed his horse, hitched it to the buggy, blanketed it, and left it tied at the tie-post beside his back door while he went in the house to dress. By the time these preparations were made he was a little late. He had not made enough allowance for the unaccustomed drive by quitting work earlier than usual for dinner. He was just reaching up hastily to pull the blanket from the back of the 'driver' to go away, when he heard a squeal at the horse-stable. He ran, jolting over the rough clay ground, and found three of his big colts loose in the building. In the corner beside the door two long hayforks were knocked down. He had left the colts outside in the barnyard, but somehow they had opened the door. On getting inside they must have found the quarters cramped, behind the other horses, and trying to turn around, and jostling each other, perhaps kicking, the forks were knocked down with the sharp tines sticking up. He watched their limbs narrowly as he drove them out again, and fancied that one of them limped slightly. Following it, he noticed that a little blood appeared on its left hind pastern.

At once he scrambled over the barn-yard fence and ran to his buggy. As he came near the village, which was three miles from his home, he met the funeral procession emerging from it. First came the minister, alone, with a cream-coloured silk scarf wrapped about his little gray beard, for it was a dun fall day, full of a raw wind; then a democrat full of pall-bearers, then the hearse, then the mourners. In the second carriage of these was the tall brother, with his wife and children. Billy had stopped his horse beside the ditch, and taken off his hat. Squeezed in the right corner of the buggy seat, his little thinly-haired head seemed almost hidden in his huge turned-up overcoat collar, as he looked askance over it at the passing procession from his fish-like little eyes below the astonished, unconsciously raised eyebrows. His brother eyed him redly, without gesture, and his sister-in-law seemed, whether from grief or pique, not to see him. He waited in the raw fall wind which was streaming over the flat land, until the long procession of fifty or sixty 'rigs' had passed. Then he went on, belabouring his horse with blows and with hoarse words.

The veterinarian was not at home. No. He had gone to the funeral. Billy turned away. He must have been too preoccupied to notice the doctor among the passing procession. He drove back leisurely, trusting to meet him returning from the funeral, for the cemetery was only three-quarters of a mile from the village. He did meet many people returning home, some of whom looked at him queerly, but not the man he sought. He hated to go into the cemetery now. It was only a short distance back; and the doctor would hear his message as soon as he returned home, and would at all events find it necessary to return there for his instruments.

Billy did not see him until the next morning at half-past ten o'clock. One of the farmers present at the funeral, Doctor Hickson explained, had asked him to come home with him to look at a sick steer. He had not returned – the drive was long – until after midnight, and he had slept late in the morning, not being aware of Billy's message. Hickson was a large men, with a sandy moustache, a certain dignity. When Billy's voice, hoarse with anger and the cold he had caught the day before, burst out at him, he was wrathful in a discomfited manner, his customary pugnacity of tone ineffectual before what he sensed of absurdity in such an altercation.

He announced blood-poisoning. It seemed that the fork-tines had pierced into the ankle-joint, and that the swelling would not go down in the future, but would remain much as it then was.

He was somewhat calmed when he had finished his diagnosis and recommendations for treatment.

'I hear this morning,' he said to Billy, 'I hear that your brother doesn't think much of your not coming out to the funeral.'

'No? It wasn't my fault. I was all ready to go.'

That was seven years ago. Tom had soon learned the real reason for his brother's defection, and begun to find excuses for him in his heart. But the breach, slight as it seemed, could not easily be closed, and he was unable to obviate a change in his conduct. They nodded, spoke when they met, and never ceased to 'change threshing'; but their neighbouring ceased. There were three, four farms between those of the two brothers. Billy seldom left his except to get the necessities at the store, and when he had a hired man he frequently sent him on such errands. He seldom met any of the family. Still, there seemed to be a notable amelioration in the manner of Gertie, Tom's wife, as time went on; and the children were really friendly when they saw him – taller now than 'Uncle Billy,' all of them. As for Tom, constraint had always been a main ingredient in whatever coldness he had exhibited. Though trouble-makers had given Billy a few bad hours by telling him that Tom had said that he, Billy, 'cared more for his old horses than for his family,' he had by and by come to disbelieve the tale.

Billy had been becoming less sociable as time went on. Until he was almost forty he had occasionally gone to church; sometimes in the winter he had attended one or two socials or concerts. At the former, he usually, by the lottery method, managed to get a partner with whom to eat the customary lunch – and some young fellow accompanied her home. Now this had long ceased, and he was fast coming into the category, always, in the country, seeking for itself new recruits, of the queer. On some winter nights the light from his lantern could be seen gleaming from the windows of his stable at ten or eleven o'clock. He was currying the favourite ones of his numerous horses. It was to him a joy familiar and recurrently consummate to slick the colts down with rags, to rub their pasterns, brush out their manes and their 'feather,' to admire the round spring of rib on their well-turned bodies. Summer nights he worked always until dark. Often after that, in the dusk, he might be seen trotting a little colt up the lane. He broke them to halter very young; they were then more tractable, and proved so later. For years he had always driven two teams, making one 'round' of his long fields with one, and leaving it to rest while he made the next 'round' with the other. He needed no rest himself. Still, he was not making as much money now as he had been making. He could not part with any but the most inferior of his horses, and, to his mind, each even of those embodied the culmination of quality. His herd continued to become larger, yearly requiring a little more pasturage and the use of more land for hay and grain, and even encroaching on the space in his barn before devoted wholly to cattle.

With all this he became more generous in his outlay for them. Every one of them must have a blanket to keep its hair short in winter, though he told himself that it was because he had from year to year been obliged to postpone putting up the fine new bank barn which he constantly visualized for his horses. They must have stockfood by the barrel, bran by the ton.

As for his life in the house, nothing could be more narrowly avaricious, in the matter both of time and expense. Food and clothes he bought in bulk, comforts only when they had promoted themselves to the rank of necessities. His rooms were neat, not only because of his care of them, but because of the paucity of effects which might have given them a cluttered appearance. The roof of the room in which he slept developed a leak. He moved into the next one, and when it rained caught the water in his old room in a tin pan.

At the beginning of the eighth year of his estrangement from his brother, his favourite horse began to give evidence of ill-health. It was one of the offspring of the original Lowry Lass whom he had brought home from the East, the only one which he now owned. Lena was the name he had given her. For some time she had attracted Billy's observation as being spiritless and failing in appetite: on this day her condition appeared to be sufficient cause for anxiety. Her uneasiness alarmed him the more for seeming inexplicable. He did not cease his work of husking corn in the barn, and continued until nightfall to persuade himself that it was of no account, that the next day would see her chasing the young colts about the barn-yard. But he had no sooner finished his brief supper than he began to prepare for the drive to town, and to recollect the things which he needed and must buy there.

It was January. The night was already quite dark. A thaw had broken up the road, which was now a mass of hummocked and holey clay, with a pair of deep, narrow channels jaggedly traversing it longitudinally. In these the wheels revolved, bringing up watery mud, and making a continuous rolling splash. The wind was not strong, but seemed high, and the telephone poles on the other side of the deep ditch rang forth for him dully with deep resonance. The poles seemed miles apart, as the horse plodded and wallowed onward, while he nursed an anxiety which half consciously he hoped so to make baseless. ... They became the thrumming years, as he puddled along and past them. Again their sound reminded him of music he had heard at Flossie Tintern's recital some years before. It was not often that he was reminded of music. He began to whistle, but ceased, his deviations from the tune formed such a travesty of the remembered impression.

He occupied himself with recollecting the years which his love of his horses had given him, certain things an infinitesimally different life might have brought him, certain hours of his youth, certain episodes in the childhood of himself and of his brother Tom. 'Tommy and Willy!' What differences between them then? He had forgotten, but not forgotten their round of chumming and wrangling, to which his memory now lent a sadness immeasurably pleasing. He appeared a most matter-of-fact little man, unaware of any stunting of his own life, of any lack in his happiness; and now he thought suddenly to see that life and that lack with eyes other than his own. Every few moments he lifted the fixed regard bent on the swift dripping spokes revolving muddy-yellow in the light of the dangling lantern, imagining that he had traversed miles, and cried in his thin voice, which, rising, always seemed on the point of breaking: 'Gidyap! Gidyap!'

Doctor Hinkson was at home, and as soon as Billy had done his bit of buying at one of the general stores they set forth for the farm. Now the moon occasionally showed her face tauntingly among the predacious and headlong clouds, and the wind still drew droning music from the telephone wires, as they drove over the shadows of the poles upon the track, but Billy's thoughts wandered back no longer from the frozen headland of the present. The two said little beyond questions and replies relevant to the condition of the mare, Lena. In due time the house and barn came to view. Far back from the road, they looked peculiarly isolated and unkempt, almost abandoned. The little house especially appeared to Billy, somehow, in a manner new to it, pathetic, as they thumped softly down the lane from the road.

Billy tied his 'driver' up, unchecking it first, that he might be able to reach its head; blanketed it; and followed Dr Hinkson to the horse-stable. Lena was in one of the box-stalls. She had been uneasy, for the straw was bunched unevenly about the floor. She came forward to meet them, lowering her large and intelligent-looking head, with its narrow white stripe down between the eyes. There was a moisture at the nostrils. Hinkson felt her ears.

'Fever.'

He continued for a moment to look her over.

'Well?'

'Hh-m! It's a case of distemper, with influenza involved.'

' 'Tain't serious, though? It won't be serious?'

'Well, no; not if we're careful. Give her plenty of bran mash, and whatever water she will take. I'll drop around in a couple of days. Did I leave my mitts in the buggy? I suppose we can mosey back to town now.'

It was more than a week later. A lantern, upheld by its wire handle stuck horizontally in a crack in the plank partition, lighted the box-stall dimly, except for the huge shadow cast by Lena, and by the three men at one side of it.

'Well, she's a valuable mare,' Tom was saying, his breath making a slight fog before him. 'She'd be quite a little loss.'

'The worst of your good horses, though, something's bound to happen to them, and then their value's cut in two,' noted Hinkson after a leisured instant.

The two big men did not smile; they spoke quietly. They failed in Billy's eyes to express a sense of what this danger to Lena really entailed. He went back, in a moment, over the week of nights he had watched and cared for the horse, and the mazes of thoughts. Perhaps if they had urgently expressed concern or sympathy he should have been only the more suspicious of them. At best he was not able to dispel a latent impression that the two larger men were somehow siding against him in a concealed amusement.

'But – doesn't she seem to be picking up a little better now than she was a day or two ago?' he had to ask diffidently. 'What do you think, Doctor?'

'Well,' rejoined Hinckson, gravely considerate, 'I guess she is. That was about the crisis, one week after the case opened. But I see now that I'll have to lance that throat.' It was the second time he had made the latter announcement in the course of the vacillant conversation.

'You've had to drench her with gruel, I'd say,' remarked Tom, shifting his position. 'She couldn't eat or drink anything with her throat like that.'

'Oh, yes.'

'Well; too bad: if you had sent one of the neighbour boys over to my place I could have come over just as well as not. You'd have to have a barrel to stand on, I suppose?'

'Lena's quiet. I tie her head up high, and I can reach her easy with the bottle.' Billy did not mention the necessity of standing in the manger to administer the dose.

'Well, gentlemen,' said Hinkson officially, who had gone to his satchel for the lancet. 'Here we are! Got her tied strong there?'

Billy went to one side of the mare, and Tom to the other, as much as possible to keep her from moving while the lancing was being done.

'Tim Sheen, he had a mare down with this once, you know,' began Tom, after a moment, when the horse jerked slightly and the veterinarian stepped down weightily from the box on which he had been standing.

'There, she's done!' he asserted.

'Tim was drenchin' the gruel to her just like you, Billy,' continued Tom, 'and all the time feelin' her throat, to see if she was gittin' the lump. He kinda thought she had one all right, but old Doc Kearn didn't think she had – didn't want to lance. Well, he *kept* givin' her the gruel, and urgin' Kearn to lance her throat, but he wouldn't, for more'n a week, and then first thing *they* knew, the lump burst in her throat.'

'Good-bye mare, then, eh?' said the veterinarian, smiling.

'Yuh! There was the time Tim realized on her hide. Haw!'

Billy was silent.

'Well, now,' said Hinkson, turning, and speaking in a new tone, 'I'm pretty sure you'll find this fixes it, Dulckington. You'll have to keep giving her the gruel for a few days, of course, and giving her every care. I'll drop around day after tomorrow.'

The two brothers went out with him into the keen-aired and austerely starred brown night, and Tom talked with him, while the veterinarian took the halter from his horse's head and put it in the rear of the buggy, then unstrapped the blanket, and tucked it in around his knees outside of the buffalo-robe, and for yet a few minutes after that. Then, when he had rattled away over the rocky roads, the two brothers talked, of crops, of neighbours, of the taxes for a new drain, of Tom's children. After that Tom walked home, head bent to keep the biting air from his throat, in what seemed a ghost of summer moonlight, from a moon far-slid and waning over the distant forest.

Billy went in to have a last look at Lena and the other horses. A few minutes later he trudged wearily to the house; and after holding his hands, crooked with the cold, over the cook-stove for a time, abstractedly shaking his head in the darkness and gazing at the red cracks of firelight, he climbed to the cold bedroom, and slept soundly.

It was more than two months later. Billy was busy with his spring plowing. Plowing was one of his favourite jobs about the farm; he liked above most things, though he did not formulate to himself any reason for the liking, the constant attempt to make each furrow straighter than the last, and when a good furrow was attained, to keep those following it right, to have each of his 'hands' properly and symmetrically shaped. And he was proud of the straight and steady gait of his teams, perhaps a source of his skill and his pleasure in it. An odd figure he appeared to anyone passing who saw him, with the two huge drafters, forging so far ahead of him, and making more evident than ever his disproportionate littleness. His faded overalls were turned up two or three inches above his shoes, and he stepped along with brisk, brief strides. His second team was waiting at the end of the field as usual.

He had been thinking much more, since the conversation of the night on which Lena had begun her recovery, about Tom and Tom's family. The second boy, now, Bill, named after himself, was a bright lad, already well-grown, much taller than himself. Until recently the idea of 'getting on in years' had never occurred to him; now he was beginning to accustom himself to the thought of, sometime, willing his property to someone.

But he was a tough little knot yet, he felt. The passing years had meant nothing of change in his strength as yet. The zest of the spring wind, brushing the trees and the manes of his horses, the various and wholly relevant notes of the new birds, the inconceivable freshness of colour on distant foliage, the smell of upturning soil, seemed strangely to banish any sombre implication from a new disposition toward his namesake.

His horses had a new-old dearness for him. He would go to their heads and tighten more snugly the hame-straps, loosened slightly with the heavy pulling, in order that the load might not rest on the points of their shoulders. Now he bethought himself and took time to stop and eat an apple and give the core to Lena, working today for the first time since her sickness.

As he came to the head of the field, at the road, he saw his brother coming along with a load of 'chop.' Undecided at first, he finally waited for him.

'Hello! Hello!' called Tom, somewhat vociferously. It seemed to Billy, as he answered him, glanced at him with those unconscious raised eyebrows, that he was making a too obvious effort to prolong a truce, that in his effusiveness he was confessing too plainly to past bitterness. Billy half unconsciously became more constrained. Had Tom begun to think of his son?

'I see the old mare's around again,' Tom was continuing easily, now resting accumbent, his elbow on a bag of grain.

'Yes. ... Yes, she's coming fast now.'

'Well, the old girl wouldn't last much longer anyhow, I suppose, but still, you hate to lose her.'

'Won't last much longer!' cried Billy in sudden ire. 'She's got enough life in her to – Won't last much longer!'

'Why, you know, a horse can't last forever, no more'n a man. You don't want to get too set on those horses of yourn, you know. There's nothing perfect in this world. I guess you sold off the best ones anyway, and got money out of them.'

Billy hopped. 'Set on those horses of mine, eh? They're the best horses in this part of the country, and don't you forgit it!' he stormed in his high voice. 'Can't last – ' he caught his breath – 'Can't last forever, eh? We'll see who lasts longer, you or me – or my horses!'

'Get around here, Kate! Crazy fool!' So he described his brother to the team.

But Tom had driven on by this time.

Billy continued his plowing, perfectly careless now as to the manner in which it was done, rehearsing to himself the conversation again and again. He left the field earlier than was his wont, finished his chores earlier, and busied himself fondly for hours with his horses. Then he tramped up the uncarpeted wooden stairs to bed.

He was unable to sleep.

Had Tom really said what the gossips had told him he had, those seven – eight years ago, that he, Billy, cared more for his horses than for his family? Than for his own soul, one had said. Perhaps those folks had not invented it. It was not probable that they had made it up out of nothing. He had never sold any of his best horses! Never had he meant to, he was sure. So far as concerned his own judgment, he was convinced that he was lucky to get rid of the poorer ones at low prices. Still, had not some of the purchasers, one or two anyway, taken his own horses and won with them in the show-rings? And done better still with the second and third generations? Did that really mean that those he had kept were still better, notwithstanding his disinclination to spare the time and expense necessary to fit them for exhibition? These many years! His trust in his own judgment could not prove baseless, after these many years! Tom had got hold of some of his stock, too, through another buyer. Tom must imagine that his two or three head were better than anything Billy had. ... 'Jealous ... jealous,' he thought, as he dozed, between sleeping and waking. 'Too set on those horses. ...'

The thing began to obsess, to gain occupancy of his mind as the weeks passed and he worked on alone, preparing his land and putting his crops into the ground. Though he had not time for anything else, besides eating and the minimum care of his stock, he had plenty of time to think of it as he rode on the discs, as he trudged stubbily across the lumpy fields behind the drag. It began to tell on him, though he would never have admitted it, scarcely would have realized it himself, and would have been astonished had he been told what a large proportion of his time and thoughts the old fester occupied.

He decided to hire a man a few weeks earlier than usual this summer. Somehow he did not feel capable of all and every sort of work alone. In due course he got a lank boy from the next township. The dull and varying round of days went on. The lad was glad enough, of an evening, to quit work before Billy did, and to go down to the village on his wheel. Billy, he said, was certainly queer. No joke could make him crack a grin, and on the other hand, he didn't have go enough to get mad and swear, not even at the horses; a terror to work, though. It is to be supposed that the boy found the life somewhat sombre.

One night as he was snoring heartily in his little room beneath the sloping roof, he was aroused suddenly. Moonlight in a slanting strip lay before the window. There was a sense for an instant of a silence dead, inanimate, broken; then he awoke to a chilling voice from the next room, thin, almost evil, yet almost tearful.

'Nothing but a damn fool You're nothing but a damn fool!' it whined, quite rapidly. 'Some man ought to knock your head in, they should! Knock your old head in! Nothing but a damn fool! I *told* you you're nothing but a damn fool.' Billy seemed to stir a little. 'Ever know me to run down another man's horse?' the voice went on, high pitched but not loud. 'Only a damn fool!'

An interval of silence was a reanimated corpse. The lank youth shivered. Was Billy mad? Did he mean to affront him? What had he ever said to Billy about horses? He racked his brain. Should he throw the little old runt out of the window, he asked himself with one portion of his mind, in an attempt to bring home to himself a sense of his own bravado. He'd wait –

The thin voice, always on the point of breaking, went on, in a repetition of the same words over and over. He was sure he heard a sniffing, was almost sure of a sob.

'Ever know me to run down another man's horse? That's no way for a decent man to do? Only a damn fool! Some good man ought to knock your old head in! I *told* you you're nothing but a damn fool!'

THE PRACTICAL WIFE

For a few months after marrying, Chris Calcut was very happy; perhaps as happy as he was destined to be. The thought of Estella waiting for him in the kitchen, as he walked through the supper odours, the yard silenced of fowl and stock for the night, was more than pleasant, more still, than daily food of contentment. It seemed to him that he should hasten his steps, run to the door to make sure of the incredible thing; that he should tarry and close the chicken-coop, savouring the complacent certainty.

Not that any of these delicious qualms appeared to the inadvertent eye. His father might smile beneath his moustache sometimes, or even ask him if he could leave his wife long enough to take the team as far as the blacksmith shop; his mother might complain that she saw almost nothing of him – that was, not more often than, perhaps, three times a week, when he might bring her a supply of feed for her hens, or bring her the horse and buggy to go to some women's meeting of an afternoon, when Estella did not care to drive the car.

But Chris didn't look over-impressionable – an active, lean, long-faced, vivacious fellow, always laughing, able to get on with nearly everyone and to get ahead of most people in a deal. Not too selfish to do well, either. He was practical. When Estella told him that the cook-stove leaked gas so badly that it gave her a headache, he did not tell her that it had been good enough for his mother. He grinned and promised to fix it.

They lived, Estella and Chris, on the home-place. The plan had been that 'the old people,' his parents, should settle to a more or less retired way in the new bungalow built on the adjoining hundred, unattended by barns or other buildings. The young pair after a trip up the St Lawrence took over the homestead, and its life so familiar to both. But the old man – a burly, red-moustached figure not really old, used to come to the barns in the mornings early, continued to work in the fields, and returned promptly after dinner and supper to do the chores, often before Chris had come out of the house.

Remonstrance did no good. 'Why, you'd forget all about there being any such thing as chores!' Mr Calcut would say half-jokingly. 'Well, when they get a new wife – I know how it is – !' And Chris told him it was no use his retiring, if that was the way he went about it. Now they were talking about hauling timber from their bush, and gravel and sand from the lake, to build a new set of buildings about the bungalow. Then each would have a farm to himself, though father and son would continue to give a hand now and then when one or the other needed it specially.

Co-operation was a favourite word with young Christian Calcut; and from its functioning he expected much to come for the farmers generally. In his own life he counted on it from Estella. She was inexperienced, true, and for the rest of this first season his mother was boarding the hired man. But she knew what it meant to be a practical farmer's wife, he was sure.

There were bound to be misunderstandings between them, Chris had told himself. He had taken that for granted almost unthinkingly. Automatically. The differences would be merely by way of enhancing their regard: on the surface only; and no such thing would come until their relation otherwise, would seem almost – if it were possible – dulled and torpid.

He did not announce this certitude to Estella, but Chris was not conscious of anxiety about the outcome. Getting things straightened out the first few weeks meant a deal of trouble, but how could he know anxiety at that time? He was twenty-nine when he married, and knew himself and her too well. Estella Symons had been the school teacher who boarded with the family for three terms. She was a sensible girl, forehanded; 'with a mind of her own,' his father allowed, if a little young for Chris. And she came of good people, down East.

For one meal, or two, after his promise to fix the gas stove, there seemed a slight coldness between them – not even that: taciturnity. But it was afterward, only, that he remembered to notice it; which should have proven how small the matter was.

Then one day there was no pie for dinner, and the biscuits Estella had made were ruined.

'It's that stove,' she told him, patiently wiping a strand of hair from her forehead, almost like any ordinary housewife.

Chris rather smiled at this, and promised once more: 'You leave that stove to me. I'll tend to it one of these days; then there'll be no reason why we can't have everything tip-top right up to snuff. Get your recipe-book out ready. Eh?'

Estella was about to speak, but judiciously stopped, then smiled.

'I can't see what could be wrong with the blamed thing, though,' he went on, frowning impartially.

'Neither can I,' Estella murmured.

Chris laughed suddenly and largely and seized her hand. 'The bride explains her cooking!'

Estella started. 'Not at all.' She withdrew her hand, indignant. 'So that's what you think! Well, I'd just like to see anyone try to cook on that old thing. The gas smells so I can't stand it, and I can't have the door open this windy weather, and if I do go out of the room ...'

'Things burn, of course,' he said, laughing again.

She bit her lip, then agreed: 'Well, since you're going to fix it ... But I almost wonder whether you realize what it's like. Don't you smell the gas, when you come in?'

'Yeh. Pretty rank when you first come in. Get used to it after a while.'

'Are you so sure? If you were in it all the time, perhaps you wouldn't.'

But Estella rose and put on water for the dishes, afraid that already she might have said too much.

'Well,' yawned Chris, 'I feel different than a little bit ago. Not so hungry, somehow. I guess I'll go and see what those horses think about getting a few loads of corn-fodder up.' He had certain ideas about the joviality proper to the man of the house.

He meant to be a practical farmer. For Chris there was only one degree to the adjective in that connection, the positive. He would have told you that a farmer was practical or he did not remain one at all. He might possess money, and continue to own land and have it tilled, but that wouldn't make him a farmer. A farmer was a man who worked his own land, did his own planning and who knew how and could, and usually did, do everything about his place, from planting potatoes to shovelling sugar-beets. That is, a real farmer, not a back-to-the-lander, or an experimenting crank, with a lot of book-learning. Yet, not just unadorned 'farmer.' You knew about new theories, variant points of view, yet chose deliberately and usually to stick to 'sensible' handed-down methods, making use of innovations when they were not so new but that they had proven themselves. Not to lose your head was the main thing, but be long-headed in a quiet way, and use plenty of elbow-grease. Thus: 'practical farmer.'

When Allan and Dick chose to be, one a civil engineer, the other a doctor, and Chris, the eldest, stayed at home, a neighbour might ask Mr Calcut what he was going to make of him. 'Going to make a practical farmer of Chris,' his father had said, watching the tall, ruddy-faced young man read the minutes of the local Farmers' Club.

Chris Calcut was not one to neglect his duty to the community, which, to be just, he regarded as part of his duty to himself. He belonged to all the farmers' organizations in his district, and in some of them made his voice heard, held office. 'A progressive young farmer,' the older men would say, publicly referring to his adoption of their own principles with the resilience natural to youth. The community needed such young men, men with opinions, who could do things.

In the job of hauling corn-fodder into the capacious barn for the winter a few days slipped by. The autumn, as usual in south-western Ontario, had been prolonged and allowed the men to get the corn husked and the fodder removed, so that winter wheat could be sown in the same fields. Taking things on the swing in this way appealed to Chris, and he liked to schedule his work mentally as he went about it. The warmth in the middle of the day, which was changed to exhilarating coolness just when it would have become tiresome, the consciousness of much work done efficiently, meant a great deal to him. But the day's summit was reached when he walked from the stable, leaving the horses eating contentedly, crossed the yard in the slanting sunlight to the weathered house, old but renewed in interest by the presiding grace of Estella.

How good to be content with everything at the end of the day, and to have her waiting for him now. In these months it seemed that they had become acquainted all over again. Women, to be sure, were queer creatures, but not so much so if you were sensible with them, practical. Right at first when she kept it up about the stove, on a rainy day he thoroughly cleaned out the stovepipe and the chimney. Another time he had tightened up the pipe above the floor, and the chamber where the gas and air were mixed. One had to be reasonable....

Chris was interrupted in his thoughts as he entered the house. There had been no supper smell to greet his hungry expectation. In the kitchen, the old stove, even, was still and cold.

'Estella!' he called; he did not know what to make of it.

There was no answer. He started for the stair door, but came back, stirred the stove-lids, and put on the kettle for tea. Possibly she had been to some women's meeting in the village, if one of the neighbours had called for her, and had just returned. Or perhaps she had not returned yet at all. When the gas roared beneath the lids he went to the stair door and called up the stairs:

'Estella!'

At first she did not reply. Then: 'Well! What is it?' The voice was impatient, as of one unwilling to be disturbed, and in it there was something else which he had not heard before, stealthy, as though she did not want to answer at all. But he paid no heed and asked:

'Who housed the jury this afternoon; and whose reputation did they settle?'

'I wasn't at any meeting, if that's what you mean.'

'But – what – what's the matter?' He was striding largely up the stairs and to their room. Estella was lying there, her eyes directed to the window.

'Are you sick, dear?' Her hair, though, was done, and as she sat up he noticed that she was dressed as if for going out; pretty, he told himself once more. She did not speak for a moment, but the usual detachment, almost languorous, with which she received him changed as she spoke, in a way which seemed to get beyond control spring to the borders of vehemence like a sudden fire in autumn grass.

'I've told you and told you, that stove is not fit to use!'

'Th – that – stove?' His mind groped. '*Oh*! The stove!'

'Yes, that stove.' She smiled almost pityingly, as she never had smiled at him before. 'The smell of the gas, I think I told you, would asphyxiate anybody. You know you promised to fix it.' Her tone regained coldness as she spoke until Chris wondered if he knew her at all. Nevertheless, with the foundations of everything shaking under him, he was determinedly off-hand.

'Why – sure. Next time we go to town, I'll have to see about getting a man to come out and see about it.' This promise came almost automatically. 'Seems as though I can't get it done myself. Of course, though, I might – '

'Please don't use that phrase again,' she began with chilly precision. 'I'm sick of it. And surely even you should see that you're not taking anybody in. "Fix it myself!" I'll fix it myself. Oh – ' Her voice broke, almost hysterically. 'Such absurd – '

Chris tried to comfort her, not knowing that it had got beyond that stage. 'But, Honey, why didn't you tell me the old stove was so bad as all this – as bad as it is.'

To his further bewilderment she twitched away and then began to weep.

'*Why* wouldn't I? Why, Chris Calcut, you know very well you've talked about it and talked about it, and I've told you the smell of gas was unhealthy, and makes my head ache, and you always said we'd have to get it fixed ... I'm not going to stand it any more. Now you can cook your own supper – cook your own meals till you do. I'm not going to stand – you'll have to either see to it or get a new one.'

To Chris, there was something in his reaction as though a trusted head of stock had suddenly kicked at him. Astonishment was followed as a shadow by indignant and just rage. The proposal to spend money unnecessarily, as it seemed to him, lent a conviction.

'A new one,' he commented dryly, and stiffly turned to the door as though to close the discussion. 'I guess if it was good enough for mother and she never said a word about it – ' Without touching the door he went along the hall to the stairs. 'Maybe we can get along.'

'Good enough for your mother!' she screamed. His words seemed to release a flood. He had never heard that tone, as though he were some culprit schoolboy walking away from punishment. 'Oh, oh, oh! For his mother. It's the last straw. That's all he cares. Just because his mother was easy enough to let it go on, ruining her health – *I'm* not to say a word. And anybody knows the headaches I have...'

Chris stood at the head of the stairs, scarcely knowing what he heard. Married life was full of surprises! He had thought that she 'had a mind of her own,' but that she ever could go on in this fashion – it seemed incredible. Perhaps he had said something without knowing. He scarcely understood until a last sentence struck upon his consciousness paralyzing as a revolver shot:

'I won't, won't stand it – . I'll go home.'

... Now, as he stared about the kitchen in which he found himself, anything seemed possible. He couldn't, he couldn't let her go away. Unthinkable. Still, if she did insist – keep her by force? What had got into her? He strained his thoughts to a frenzy of desperation. What could he do? If he could think of some way of pacifying her, even of making her laugh – But everything was surely designed to aggravate her further.

The gas roared and sang from the burners, and the tea-kettle, which must have been empty, crackled. He paid no attention, but there was a spreading smell of fumes, catching the throat. ... It was unheard-of. She had never cried before in his memory, like that, nor spoken an impatient word. It became more exasperatingly mysterious every minute. He rose and turned the gas lower, and held a lighted match to the joints of the pipe which rose from the floor. No flame, not even in the chamber where the air and gas were mixed. He had fixed that, long ago. What more could she ask? Up to now Chris had thought that Estella was satisfied with his efforts. He sniffed, sniffed again. True, there it was! He'd have to put up the stove in the sitting-room right-away – it was getting to be fall-like anyhow; and then she wouldn't have to be so much in the kitchen. Of course though, there were the meals.

If she stayed. His heart stirred chilly again at her forgotten threat. What could he do, what in the world, to keep her – ?

Automatically he walked to the pantry, and looked over the shelves. How often the boy had come in from school or the field when his mother wasn't looking – not that she cared – and got a lunch. The shelves were no longer full as once they had been. It was true that Estella had blamed the stove, particularizing the smell when the oven burner was turned on. No, she had not baked so much lately. Why, looking the place over now, it seemed there was scarcely enough for their supper. He felt injured, as though Estella might have cooked up a good lot of food before she took it into her head to fly off in this style.

But he had been struck, vitally, like an animal which does not know it has been wounded. Chris Calcut turned to go outside, but there was no refuge there. He sat down in a chair unconsideringly, and tried to think. Something must be done!

How suddenly life had become a desert! Why it was absurd. Surprise was vaster than sorrow, tugging at him. He wasn't angry, remembering now that she had kept it up, nagging some fellows would call it, these last few days. The old saying was wrong; it didn't take two to make a quarrel. He rose abruptly, went to the stair door and listened.

Yes, there were movements. He could hear her pull some things over the floor of the closet in which were kept the trunks and suitcases. Before he knew, he had bounded up the stairs and into the room, his stiff shoes clattering.

She did not look up. With set face she was packing one of the suitcases on the bed; a club bag gaped open on the floor. Chris stood in the door stupefied.

'Estella. What are you doing, Estella?'

She searched one of the drawers of the bureau, jumbling the contents. Her dark hair seemed darker against her paled profile. How could she be angry when she was so pretty?

'I didn't mean anything. How did I know it was so bad? You needn't go away. ... Silly, that would be, and then think how ... I take it all back.'

He felt helpless as a kid. And she looked like some little girl who had been playing house and, disappointed, was going home to tell her mother about the big nasty boy. Her mouth pursed as though she were going to speak, and all at once tears came from her eyes. She tried to work an instant as though he were not there, and then turned away; but she could not hide the shaking of her shoulders.

Chris went up to her and put his arms around her, looking into her face. Without their having said anything he found that she had her head on his shoulder, sobbing without respite.

'You know – you – oh, you...'

She wanted to reproach him, and yet did not want to, and weeping made it physically impossible to say or think of anything except his nearness. All afternoon she had thought of the growing strangeness between them; and it seemed that the time lay in a distant and happy past when she had said jokingly that that old stove would be yet the cause of a lot of trouble. It was petty, and after tinkering with it once or twice Chris nearly always grinned when he soothed her. 'The little things that matter!' she smiled bitterly. And each day was coming nearer to winter, when the doors would be closed, and the gas would be downright unhealthful; perhaps she would be asphyxiated, even, and Chris would come in and find her – Then he'd know – The problem altogether was too much for her. She did not know whether there was a plumber in town, and when it came actually to getting one, she thought that she was afraid of hurting Chris. She went to her room that afternoon resolving not to have anything more to say about it. She would try to act reasonably and avoid hard feelings; then she went over it all in her mind, and this was the result.

'Why didn't you tell me...' he was saying. 'Why didn't you tell me if you were bothered that way?' Then he essayed a lightening of tone as he saw the two interpretations which might be given to his question. 'Eh? Why didn't you?'

She turned her head away from him, weeping unrestrainedly now.

'That's right, *laugh* about it. I dare say it's very funny. Just because your mother stood it all the time, *I've* got to: for five months now, without saying a thing. You don't care, you just promise, and then go away and forget, all you care about is your old cattle, and farm. Your wife doesn't matter.'

'It's true I – well, I didn't know it was so bad,' he muttered, not knowing what to say. 'That's all.'

'Oh!' breathed Estella. 'That's what it is. You thought I was fibbing all the time when I told you the stove ... Well, I thank you for your kind opinion. Now, will you please leave this room? I have packing to do.'

Confounded by her readiness, he backed automatically. 'Aw, Stella, have a heart. You don't mean that.' He tried to grin in his old way; a burlesquing of his own uncouthness. But it was blank tragedy he saw in the cold hallway as her hand turned the door against him. He seized her hand, and her words were muffled against him.

'Buffoon! ... and get the car ready...'

An inspiration struck him. 'Say, Stella, what do you think of this. Let's take the old car and go to Dealborough, *eat at a restaurant!* What do you think of that? And go to a show afterward if you like.' A real inspiration. He couldn't recall when he had been inside one of the local restaurants. Farmers avoided them pretty well, unless detained, and a long way from home. But he felt like being reckless once.

'All right.' She dabbed at her cheeks. 'G-get the car...' She looked at him, remembering that he might now have had the car ready to take her to the train, and then smiled uncontrollably, reluctant tears still trickling down her cheeks.

Chris kissed them away. 'Maybe you'll want to drive this time.' This, too, was a treat, for Chris had barely allowed her to learn. It made him uneasy to ride in a car driven by anyone else.

The smooth autumn roads were suddenly strange, and insecurity lurked in the thinning forests. It was as though the shadow of change, of more than one departure lay muffling the spirits of the two, and not until they had reached Dealborough, parked the car in a church shed, and sought King Street, that they were themselves.

'Which one'll we start on?' asked Chris. 'Both of 'em are run by the dirty Chinks. Unless – how about going to the Universal Plaza House? They could maybe give us all we'd want.'

'The hotel!' Estella was taken aback. 'No, that would be too – '

'All right.' After all, money was money, even on a celebration.

In the restaurant they found one of the unoccupied wooden cubicles along the wall, and took off their hats and coats with a care for conventional gesture.

'Might pull the curtains,' suggested Chris, with delightful sobriety.

'Better wait until the waiter's gone.'

'First thing, better look these over, across and unpendicular.' He handed her a menu card, while she perused another. 'Takes a woman so long to make up her mind, anyhow...'

'Mmm. There are so many things ... '

By this time a small Chinese boy had come to the entrance of the cubicle, bringing tumblers of water.

'Well,' declared Chris. 'I know what I want – if you got it,' he added to the boy. 'Got any fly-ee oystees?'

'Don't, Chris,' murmured Estella, smiling in spite of herself, and relinquishing the attempt to choose something. Like her husband she had been reared on the farm, and such an episode as this was a delectable novelty. She stuck the menu-card between the salt-cellar and the sugar-bowl.

'I'll have the same, please,' she told the boy.

'Flesh, nace,' said the boy.

'A-all right. We'll see about the fixings later.'

They spent a long time over the meal; Estella told him all that they ate at the wedding-breakfast of one of her schoolmates; of some trick of those days; of her father's tastes in cookery. It was eight o'clock when they rose, beginning to become acquainted again.

It seemed almost a shame to leave the cozy little place, with its red-shaded electric lights just the right height on the wall. They had coal-oil lamps at home, but Chris mistook her expression.

'Don't be anxious,' he said, lifting the shoulders of her coat from her chair. 'We got lots of time. Just across the block. Not as if we were just getting up from the table at home.'

In the show he was jolly and satirical at first.

'That's "*Long Ago*",' Estella told him when the orchestra began the prelude to a picture whose theme mingled risk of limb with imminent moral disaster.

'Sounds more like "*Never Was*".'

They sat silent for a long time, moved, if not exalted, and were rather quiet on the road home. The story of the film concerned a married pair, not unlike themselves, they thought – except for the trappings of automat-civilization. Misunderstandings arose, and then only a mistaken telephone message was necessary to precipitate penultimate dole. Of course it turned out all right, but think of the unhappiness! And when it need never have begun.

They drank in air which seemed the bouquet of amber moonlight. This time Chris drove, with one hand, and it seemed that these last five months had never been, that he was taking her home from church once more. Except that now there was not the same need for conversation. Oh, they were moved again by each other, and it was perceptibly a glide to another plane when Chris said conversationally:

'Wouldn't have thought so many people got out to the show, week night like this – not as if it was Saturday or some holiday or other. But then, the harvest being over, and so on – '

She smiled at his reasoning tone.

'Well, we'll have to go out ourselves more,' he declared. 'That's all there is to it.'

Estella did not reply, save to press a little nearer his shoulder.

'Yes, dear,' she said, and something in her hand struck Chris with a pang. It was as though she did not believe him, not quite literally. He gave the car more gasoline. Nonsense! He was just getting sensitive, goodness knew why. But he meant it. They were going to get out more, if the farm went to rack and ruin; she'd see. But he did not repeat it aloud.

When they drove into the unpainted frame garage, before she got out he kissed her, as in the old time. But, walking to the house, it came to them that everything was changed; they had seen the country through which they moved with the cherishing eyes of people pulled from an abyss; and now the sight of the old place itself did not make return reassuring. A tenseness came into their silence as they lit the lamps in the kitchen. It looked bleak. The stove was cold and grimy, with lids displaced. Estella choked a sob and turned away to her room silently. The lamp lighted the turn of her quivering cheek.

If Chris did not seem to notice, it was because he was too dumbfounded. Decidedly things were not simplified by their evening away. What could he do? Of course, any place would seem squalid, after the movies. He heard the scrape of her suitcases over the floor. He stopped – and then sighed. She was moving them back into the clothes closet. It was lucky he had not followed to the room. Setting his jaw, he took off his coat, his collar and tie, and put on a smock and overalls.

Things would work around; a lucky escape after all, he felt, as he tried all the joints of the pipes again with a lighted match. Why, things like that were going on all over, wives picking up and leaving their husbands for any little thing! Of course when the men were unreasonable goofs – And still, he could not make out what ailed that stove. Yes, with the burners going it did smell, no question about it. Estelle was right.

He went on to the garage and collected several wrenches, determined to find out what was wrong and fix it if it took all night. Womenfolk had a good deal to put up with!

At half-past one he heard a stirring behind him, a murmur, and turned to see Estella on the back stairs with a lamp in her hand. He moved uneasily, with a sudden sense of not knowing what to expect. But she did not scold him; her voice was low and quiet.

'Why don't you go to bed?' she asked. 'I thought – you had gone to the barn, about chores or something.' Solicitously she watched him work, her chin on her hand, while she sat sleepily on the stairs. She had lain, intent on her own fears, not hearing...

'You go back to bed,' he commanded, in a preoccupied voice. 'And don't worry. I'll get it fixed, temporarily, until we get a new one.'

She giggled, almost hysterically. 'As if that were so terribly important! You seem to forget that you're not getting any rest. How can you work to-morrow that way?'

But she went, moved, as he was, by the few abrupt words exchanged. It was as though the memory of how they had nearly allowed their happiness to be wrecked was a dream they shared.

Yet Chris was not sure that he would not have to give in to the stove. In his desperation he went to the length of taking the oven door off its hinges, and at intervals, as Estella dozed, she could hear the lids rattling and a general clashing of old iron. But when in daylight she came downstairs, the fire was going and he was putting water in the tea-kettle.

'Noise wake you up?' he asked blithely beaming at her with streaked countenance. 'Guess what it was.'

'I don't want to know, as long as you've got it fixed. What was it you said you wanted for breakfast?' She bent over the table and blew out the unneeded lamp.

Chris gathered his tools, looked beneath the lids at the two top burners which hummed and crackled merrily with a sniff of satisfaction, and hesitated as he was going outside.

'I've a notion not to tell you. You'd die laughing.'

'What was it?' She humoured him, yet she was afraid that the trouble had been owing to some inexpertness of her own.

He put down his tools carefully and moved toward her. She held up the paper bag of oatmeal she was bringing from the pantry.

'Don't!' said Estella. 'You're all black.'

'Well,' said Chris. 'It's blacking in a good cause! But this is what happened. Can't you guess? Well, do you see that little damper at the back of the stove? Right almost behind the stovepipe. You never did before, and neither did I. But mother did. I turned that, and presto-change. All right. Don't smell any gas now, do you?

'N-no. Is that all that was the matter, though? But it was away out of sight.'

'I *wondered* why mother never mentioned anything particular being wrong; and you never told her.'

'Of course,' she murmured.

'Now what do you say? Eh?' He put on what she called his 'growly' voice.

She was half laughing, half sobbing into his shoulder. 'I don't say anything ... Thank you. But, oh, weren't we silly!'

Then they were both sober, reflecting that they would never be so foolish again. They would be at least on their guard. For a moment they really believed that.

THE FATE OF MRS LUCIER

She rocked in her living-room, an arm uplifted, holding a curling iron to her hair. She talked with great calmness to Mrs Slagwin, the only neighbour to whom she could tell her story. With careful fingers she separated each string of hair, and wound it about the iron which she withdrew from the gas heater beside her. Her even plaintive drawl moved on, on, her features were as pastelike as ever throughout, her wide milky eyes as slow. Yet there was something dogged about her attitude; she actually burned her clay-coloured hair by her deliberation with the tongs. ... Her face was grey, as twisted leaves beside a frosty road are grey.

'I felt,' she said lingeringly, 'that I might lose control of myself any minute.' And such an event as the visit of her middle-aged cousin from the West with a son and nephew she did not know, was scarcely more than mentioned.

She had been back to Huntville to see Ruby on the farm. Since she and Lyniol had rented it to the son-in-law and retired, she had felt out of place. The ways of even the church people and women's societies in the city misgave her. But at Ruby's she was at home; she went about noting changes in the house and farm yard, more absorbed, almost, than when she stayed there month after month. The worst thing was leaving Lyniol, who was not likely to take care of himself in her absence; his neck looked thinner than ever, each time she returned home. And when he was working at the mill that way, he would eat one meal at least in restaurants; and that was so expensive.

On these visits to Ruby Mrs Lucier was apt to forget that she was the visitor, and not a rabbit-like woman never leaving the farm save for church; strange to any other countryside, and never conceiving the city. Before she knew December had turned, and it would look odd to be back again at Christmas, if she stayed longer. Ruby, driving her to the station in the buggy, insisted again that the parents should come to 'her' home, this first Christmas. Perhaps that would be nicer, Mrs Lucier reflected in the train. Ruby had not left her horse, and Fred Langton, the agent, had seen that she got on safely. 'Thank you. I'll – I'll be all right now,' she told his back as he hurried to the baggage end of the train.

Though it did not stop more than a minute, she had a chance from the plush seat to see the village, dirty and amorphous as though behind a grimed pane, – its murky lights starting in the mist from hunchback dwellings, its cinder-veneered mud fleetly changed through a bell's clanging to fields with narrow bright pools, reeling jagged forests – to see these with something of a stranger's objectiveness. They stayed with her.

Limply uninterested, but not aware of dejection, she did not see the other passengers, humanly. She scarcely dared to look about her. This was a situation, and the vague potentialities of travel made her uncomfortable. She smoothed her black skirt, looking directly ahead; regularly she looked at individuals and to the pane, her mind marking time thirty-five miles to Blenden, where she was to take the inter-urban car to the city.

Here it was foggier still, shouts and the slow blasts of the engine echoed lonely, and the fence wires were wet before all that space of bare country about the two-roomed station squatted in the light of stretched wires and rails. Night was coming too soon. She hurried inside.

The waiting-room, with its dusty floor, blue-gray wainscotting and plaster, long brown bench, was spacious and echoing after her habitude of tiny cluttered farmhouse rooms. She pushed her suitcase half under the middle of the bench, and sat looking into the red-seamed bed of coal in the open tall portly coal stove on its sheet iron platform, and the huge iron spittoon containing sawdust. The single lamp, above the wicket, cast shadows, and by a dusty reflector, a ray that seemed made of motes.

Just when she had got herself settled men entered one after another: three – and then the stout, dull-eyed station agent, wearing an unofficial cap with the earflaps down, dispatches and lantern in his hands. 'Looks like pretty raw night out,' he said generally, in a tenor, and crowding into his office closed the door. The train hooted back lonely.

Two of the three men stared after him. The oldest made some reply, disposing a miscellany of luggage. He was a short, jagged-whiskered, hard-bitten man, respectable enough, Mrs Lucier thought, in dress; he did not have much to say to the others. They were younger: one of stocky-slender build, determined-looking, wide-shouldered; perhaps thirty-seven years old, yellow-faced with high cheek bones and heavy, straight-hanging lips and sloping flat forehead. He too sat down, and then rose as though conscious of a long wait, to walk about with the other, perhaps younger, very tall with a short blue overcoat beneath which light trousers showed and long shoes. Jauntily rode his cylindrical head a cloth hat, over his long seamed dark countenance with its curly lips and slanting chin.

The words tossed among the three were random, abrupt, and casual, as though they were impatient, or tired of each other's company. Mrs Lucier couldn't tell what they said. She was given up to the sensation of being thus alone. Truly, since their retirement, she had seen more than in all the years before! What would Lyniol say to see her now? The young men, first one, then the other, sat down moodily.

How long before the street car would come? She had forgotten whether it were due at seventeen minutes after seven or seventeen minutes to eight. At least the wait was always endless, each time she had to remind herself that it really would come to an end. What if the car should be late reaching the city – a night like this? Lyniol would be worried. ... Perhaps he would go away and leave her to get home alone. The streets were so misleading at night, and where could she inquire the way? If he could, if he could! She shivered and held her body erect leaning forward with mourner's mien.

Less than a week ago she had read of a wreck, and there were plenty of others of which she wouldn't hear. She began to prefigure details. Just what would she do in a wreck? One would be thrown headlong, of course, backward or forward, depending upon the direction of the oncoming train. The windows in pieces would fly to slash faces. Probably the whole train would be thrown into the ditch, but the car in which she rode would not get the greatest shock. Unless it were full she always was careful to choose a car as near the middle of the train as possible. ... Hadn't she made some mistake and got into the last one? Which car – ? She came back with a start to the waiting room. ... But even in the middle of the train you wouldn't be safe, if it were 'telescoped.'

The men were looking at her. If only someone would say something. The two younger ones crossed in their walks as they stopped at a red-veined map of Canada, and muttered something to each other. Instantly all her senses were alert, she was watching. ... Yes, when one of them, the tall sinister one, came to the older man on the bench he half-whispered, 'Like her ... ' wasn't it? And both of them looked at her, a cold calculation. If something didn't happen she would scream – and if it did.

...No, it was not a train she was to take, of course. But even street cars might have accidents. There was the great ditch, or the electricity might run amuck and kill people, somehow. She always thought of how a car looked from outside, clanging briskly along in the night, while at a burst of light, a flash from overhead, her heart leaped to her mouth. Bowling recklessly along, the people exasperatingly oblivious and – it seemed, since the windows were so bright – gay. Like Lyniol. She recalled her annoyance with his sitting blandly unconscious in front of the telephone, not six feet from it, in a thunderstorm, really paying no attention to her warnings. In a buggy, when the wheels slipped into a rut, she might scream, she couldn't help it. ... And that time she had gone with Lyniol to London Fair, when Ruby was small. She had no purse, and Lyniol had gone away 'for a minute.' He came back with some neighbours he had found, and joked, really joked at her agony: 'I thought you'd gone and left me.' With the only asperity she knew she recalled almost the chief misunderstanding with Lyniol. He had refused to shoot a cat which had scratched her. The cat might very well go mad, and then. ... She lay awake nights thinking about it.

Yet sitting there it seemed to her that only in the last three months had she come to know the plenary terror of the world. In the city you could not forget, ever, all the desperate things, men and machines ready always to maim or rob, kill, and disfigure. How was any one to know when she was beside a thug, a hold-up man? (Would the car never come?) Only afterward, robbed, or never, if the revolver or chisel were brought out...

When she looked again the older man glanced again at her. It was feigned recognition, that was what it was! She did not know where to turn. They began to speak very casually about something ... trying to allay her suspicions, but they only made them more painful. She was not so easily fooled.

Looking about the room like a caged bird, it appeared vast, and her death-screams would be lost in a corner. ... Perhaps the agent had gone home, out a back way. There was silence. ... What was more deceptive than time, going on, and on, even when it seemed to stand still? Fast or slow. She might have been there only a few minutes. Perhaps the car wasn't coming at all that night. There was no traffic now at the Lake, since the exodus from the summer resort; and perhaps the company had become so careless that they wouldn't mind missing a train now and then. Or a strike. What was the last she had read in the paper of the municipal dissention? After all she had been at the farm for two weeks, and she couldn't tell what was going on. Perhaps Lyniol would arrive at the door any minute with a hired car, jitney. If it were not he, but someone else, who pretended ... that Lyniol was sick, wanted her at once. Then these three men would appear, would demand passage. The driver couldn't refuse ... or perhaps it was all made up, the driver hired, bribed.

By refusing to look at the men she had recreated them hideously in her mind's eye, and she was surprised that they were not so gruesome after all, but like three ordinary travellers of a not too successful class. The tall youth lounged to a seat near the door. Why *must* he sit near the door? The yellow-faced one began a discussion of motor tires with the old man, which he joined. Perhaps they were thinking of that, of a car they had waiting outside. They thought that she was wealthy, had smuggled goods over the river at Detroit. ... Anyway, imagine three men travelling together! A long man and a short looked sinister enough, too chummy ('thick as thieves'). But when there were three, and they looked as travel-worn as these, as tired of each other and as familiar. ... The youth laughed suddenly at some saying, and the yellow-faced man smiled, showing strong dark teeth. The man with the jagged beard hid his merriment grimly beneath it, and became the most terrible of all.

For moments at a time she could not hear or know what went on. Her mind raced like an unloaded engine. With an effort of the neck she stared all about. There was no place. In the ceiling was a trapdoor the colour of the plaster. Could she be sure the shadow did not swerve? If it opened suddenly and a rope descended. All kinds of ways, all kinds of places for putting victims' bodies. The stove door yawning before her hot eyes!

The talk had stopped for a long time now, but again one of the men was walking about, yawning loudly, hands clasped behind him. 'And this is the East!' he muttered passing her. The East, the East; wasn't that some sort of password? She searched her memory for shreds of an old newspaper serial. She looked up timidly as a rabbit from brush watches a passing hunter. The smell of coal had gone, the blue gas no longer twined upward from the middle of the stove; the hollow vast of the room was desperately cold. ... The windows deep with blackness gathered from the immense night, the dreary hum of telegraph wires to immeasurably distant bright cities, like paradises.

The telegraph clacked and twittered, prickling along her nerves like red-hot pins in memory. A vast insufferable quiet held the little station between forefinger and thumb, in gingerly patience. No breath. The stout agent appeared, drawing a bunch of keys from the door. Was he going to lock the office for the night? He put them in his pocket.

'Car's kind of late tonight,' he said cheerfully. Perhaps he was in the plot. 'Makes it kind of bad for you people. Oh, well, she'll be here any time now.'

Swinging the coal scuttle up, he threw its contents into the stove. He slammed the door to, opened the bottom damper, shook the grate. He was going home, he was leaving her –

The bearded man was answering him, benevolently. 'Quite a little wait for you too? Do you have to stay until it gets here?' He was going to offer to wait instead, and then, then – !

'Oh, no, I go home, as soon as the express pulls out.' The clear full tones drew the woman back to reality.

Mrs Lucier rose after a futile movement abruptly, and walked shaking half across the room. The motion roused her to another self, but she was watching if They made a suspicious move. The wicket was closed, the door closed – Perhaps all –

'Did you want something, lady?' the agent asked her wild look.

'A – a return ticket to Huntville. The train, there is a train goes, isn't there, soon now?' her voice did reach him.

'Why, yes, due in about six minutes. On time too.' He would think she had forgotten something at home. Warmer air came through the wicket. They would think she had – remembered something – that she was being pursued – and follow her. And in the village, all dark, they could – They weren't buying tickets, to be sure. But even that meant nothing.

But the great light of the train shone into the station windows as the ticket was stamped and shoved through to her hand. The lamp was dimmed. Her heart leaped. With trepidation and quivering foretaste of triumph Mrs Lucier marched to her suitcase.

The tremor of the platform, emerging from blackness like a raft out of depths thrilled her as always on taking a journey. But she climbed into the train with such a feeling of refuge as home could never give. (She saw a living-room at home – Ruby's home – in all its dear monotony.) The world was shut out and she saw the victims of its innumerable crimes, their torturings, last writhings. ... Warm, light, the gliding, soporifically swinging train was like heaven, in which sprawled tired bored gods. They didn't even notice her. Everything glided forward with a non-deceptive illusion of soundlessness, past that same bushland, glittering water, sodden fields blotted now. Only the blackness of void, effectively held at bay, lay behind those windows. She needn't look. The trip was less than an hour, but it was passing. ... The night would face her again.

A uniformed boy entered with a tray slung from his neck, and announced with a perfunctory but clearly audible monotone, 'Apples, oranges, chocolates, peanuts...' Just loudly enough to waken the men dozing under newspapers, or an occasional woman, head nodding on a hand propped to the windowsill. Mrs Lucier had an impulse to buy. Unheard-of action, it would express in a way her triumph, her thanksgiving at escape. The boy clairvoyantly half-paused, but went on, 'Apples, chewing-gum, oranges, chocolates, peanuts!' The door opened and slammed against a sound of rushing wheels and rushing wind.

The brakeman called 'Huntville, Huntville!' at each end of the aisle, and before she knew it she was walking with accelerated steps to the door, receiving the final jolt outside at the platform railing. She glimpsed the station in large squares of light emanating from the train windows.

Mrs Lucier shied from the cars, glancing beneath, and hurried down the cinder path to the road. Fred Langton coming from the head of the train, greeted her, surprised. She hesitated. 'Yes,' she answered, turning half around, her suitcase swinging. 'Yes,' she added nervously. Then she went on again in the fog toward the street remembering that his way home led in a different direction, and she could scarcely ask him...

She went forward past the little houses. Their lights in back rooms were dimmed by fog. Dark moisture stood on the narrow cement sidewalk under a light, and heavy beads hung on an intricate front lawn wire fence. Heavy drops spattered her hat and the pavement as she hurried forward, a dark half-bent figure, long-skirted, dragging the suitcase.

The sidewalk went past the last house, on to the muffled brick church at the corner. Then there was the cinder path to the graveyard, and after that she walked more hurriedly, stumbling, along the road by the deep mist-filled ditch. She swerved and held to the middle way, because of the ditch. But there might be buggies, or an unlighted car. Along the edge again, her shoes squelched neatly in the seeping limp grass. She gripped the handle of her suitcase for a leap either way. At last, after long struggle and seeming escape that things happened. At last, after half a mile in wet clay she came to a wide frame house set back from the road.

She crossed the ditch over a shaky plank bridge and stood, savouring triumph and dread, panting, her hands on the iron damp gate. All about was the fog covering the fields. The branches of a large maple curved down and let fall irregular drops in a pattern of sound upon the grass and the rustling water of the ditch. Yet it was almost bright. There should have been a moon, she realized. Buildings and trees stood out clouded, in a lifting haze. Her gloves had become wet through on the iron. The light remained in this house, and she opened the gate and gathering herself together went boldly to the front door.

'Well, Agatha Lucier! You *did* come in to see me before you left! I was wondering – Come right in.' The large woman seized and kissed her, still talking, her head held at the kissing angle. 'Here's Mrs Lucier, Andy, Alice.' Children were entering from the kitchen where they had been hindering homework. 'But have you had supper?'

'No. I mean, I – My, isn't Alice growing!' Mrs Lucier exclaimed with mild fervour. 'And Andy! Why he's as big as his father, nearly.' She felt bold, and backed by the gods of circumstance.

'And walking were you, alone? Isn't it raining?'

'Oh, you know I'm never afraid of the dark.'

An hour later, after a substantial meal, Mrs Lucier peered from the window, fancying a light through the fog-waves. Ruby's light? But she would not call up and have Ruby's man come for her. It was too terrible a night. Besides, it was more than half-past nine o'clock.

She wouldn't tell Ruby, not right away. Yet ... 'I made up my mind I'd just have to come back. One minute, and I'd lost control of myself.' Sometime she would have to tell.

THE STRAWSTACK

He had walked ten hours before he came to it. Usually he did not walk so many hours in one stretch. He was able to wander far enough, he had found, walking three or four of a day, when he went at all. In the years since he had left the place, far enough.

He could not understand fully yet what brought him back now. All the years which might have done so had failed. His first homesickness had been a sandbar only from which he soon floated away not free, and distantly.

The place was the same, with the sorrowful sameness he found in the chances of life, in its monotonous recurrence, unescapable; the horrible rise and sinking of the sun, moons. And tiny beyond his toughened expectation. Only a few minutes' walking, the passing of a few sombre reflections which did not save themselves from the monotony, was the meaning of that lane to the back of the farm which had appeared so unending to the boy going back in the dark for the cattle after the day in the harvest-field.

The trees were shrunken, grizzled, and unkempt, stood vagabonds, in an air of desperately-attempted sturdy carelessness. The fields, worse; tiny closed places, which his unthinking toil had made into sky-seeking deserts of plowed land or unfathomable mazes of corn.

As he looked, the wind shook dirty stubble that was a great brush waiting for the fur of some monstrous wallowing animal; shook weeds by the fence-corner, which, brittle, he marvelled did not shatter – who had broken them with difficulty in childish hands and, stripping leaves and branches, used them for goads to drive the beasts.

The tinyness of everything large in his memory drew a terror about him which, too searching, he could not try to understand. He had not known his memory demanded so much from the place, had created so much of it.

Through the fields he came from the road caved with woods at the back of the farm, seeing little and experiencing a sadness which crushed him closer and closer and made him wonder, when if the pain had been physical he should have cried out, why he could have thought to find surcease here, and why his mind had not shied back from the contemplation of return, knowing its own danger.

The sun had set when he came forth from the woods, and the incomparable quiet was there which comes before the moon rises or the greater dark begins. He found himself asking, 'I wonder if there will be a moon tonight,' before his memory told him of last night's dark as he tramped the endless bald road.

Dark splotches in one little field were peacefully still, and the cool munching of cows had something obscene about it, like the ravening of wolves at the finding of a dead hunter: the field, dead, was not the less silently complaining, he saw.

He came nearer, and they woofed and scampered leadenly away, turning about to face him at a distance. He went on without seeing them.

The wind lifted again, and he stopped with a jerk which drew his head back, stiffened as before a brink. His face was compressed in a colour of terror which made his unshaven features frightful. Then he stepped on again after an instant, with limp strides as before. It was only a few days, one day ago, that he began to hear a soft crackling, a tearing in one side of his brain answering to the tenseness of his moods. And still it was hard to forget, to remember the tiny flapping of the ripped silk band about his felt hat.

It was the house which shocked his numbness most, which filled him with a sorrowful terror of all new revelations he should have learned before, if this was yet the place of all his furbished memories. It was so ugly, with its tatter of clapboards and peeled paint, two boards torn off at the ground, showing black underneath. Verandah posts hung baseless, steps were not there. One ridge of the roof as he looked at it against the red sky was bent, the spine of some old animal worn down with burdens.

He had gone nearly all the way around before he became conscious that no life was in it, and realized that he had not expected any, though someone must be caring for the farm. Years since his mother and father had died – while he was serving his first term.

He stepped back from the house to the barn, desperately recalling that the yard had seemed as wide as a field when he ran out in the night for an armful of wood to put in the stove.

The tiny stable which had seemed so long when you stood behind the row of stalls and looked across the hips of horses between them! The roof which it had seemed such an Alpine labour to mount and affix a little wooden windmill. He turned away quickly, fearing that someone might be within, passed the corn-crib, the pig-pen, and came back of the barn.

A strawstack was there, sprawling dark-brown over a great area of soil, unbuilt, but taking what shape it might as it was spewed forth from the thresher. It must have lain there three or four years. Hummocks and holes were about its edges, made by time and the burrowing of animals.

He crept among these for a place which would shelter him for the night, recalling how his father had disapproved the sprawled carelessness of such stacks, and the prudence with which his own were built, before the boy's eyes, looking on with a child's curiosity which made all things pertinent.

He searched out a place, a hole in the side, pulled handfuls of straw and enlarged it, and at last leaned back looking out from where he sat beneath the edge of the cupola roof toward the back of the farm.

He sat, burrowing and making the most of the warmth and trying to refuse his thoughts. Many a farmer's barn or strawstack had made his bed for the night in the course of his wanderings without his dreaming of coming so to the old place.

He took out of a package some cheese and bread with bologna and hard cakes. The dark had come on, and a musty smell from the old straw he had moved spread around him. It brought back in a whelming wave the nights on which he had gone to sparrow hunts. The parties made up, they took different ways and went loudly talking by dark roads to neighbours' barns and stacks, carrying lanterns. Reaching their hands into holes about the eaves of the stack, they seized the birds, or held a net before it and beat upon the straw beside the hole. The birds flew out with squeaking chirps. They twisted off the heads to take for proof when the bodies became too bulky. The greatest number won the catchers an oyster-supper, which the losing side bought and helped to eat. The oblivion!

But sometimes stepping up to the stack, a bird would fly out, blindly in the dark, wind of its wings velvet against his cheek, and be free. ... The smell was about him yet, making more keen a sense of the years since those times.

They had not seemed such unforgiven years as they went. It was when he looked at them all from one point that he loathed them suddenly, their whirling inconsequence swinging to crime that lent nothing to hope, until he could blot them away with diversions to give memory worse stings for the future.

The years muffled him as he went through them, persuaded him that they were brief, that they would change, deliver to his hands chance. But, waiting, the wanderings, the wanderings they had led him.

Because of the witless inanity of a moment.

He was only a boy when it happened, fifteen years old. His parents had gone to the village that afternoon, and left him to do the chores about the house and barn when he returned from school. His sister, younger than himself, came home together with him, running after when she had left the other girls at their gates. They set about their tasks.

Presently he came to that of filling the woodbox, empty from the day's burning. A huge woodpile stood in the back yard, the outcome of a day and a half of buzzing. At the bottom, where he had been pulling out the wood, the sticks had become bound in, for the pile had been thrown together into whatever shape it might take as the cutting went on, and was not yet piled in tiers. So he climbed to the top and began pulling the sticks out and tossing them down below.

The little sister came out of the house to help him, for she was lonely in the house; and stooped down to the ground to pick up the sticks as they tumbled and dropped to the bottom.

Faster and faster the sticks twirled down to one side of him, the boy stooping over all the time and not looking where they fell.

Then he did look around, under a sudden impulsion, and seemed to hear a low moan broken. One of the sticks had been lighter than most and flew to strike the little girl on the forehead.

He jumped down the pile without consciousness of doing so until he stumbled on a projecting piece and nearly fell headlong on the thickset stubs.

She was lying on the ground, with a bruise above her temple. He could not waken her. He pulled at her shoulder, called her name in tones that fought with fear and could not rise to loudness.

He lifted her and carried her into the house, with unwitting dragging steps, such a breaking heart as he had never known before. Dusk was closing about the flat country. In the vivid wind the leafless trees howled madly in sorrow, and from the barnyard came cattle's lowing.

Inside it was darker, as he moved to a couch and placed his burden upon it. He looked at the little form for a moment, unable to think. Then he called her name again, and went to get cold water.

There was no sign. The child was still as before. Still he looked at the glimmering form in the dark, the furniture crowding about him, with such a heart within as he thought must at any moment bring his death. He called her name and with fear-sped legs fled from the house.

The dark was there, holding back like an ambush of armed ruffians. The boy ran the gauntlet of it to the road, and stood waiting, listening and peering. There was not a sound, and as he watched, the thought came on the wings of a different terror that perhaps it was better so. He made a movement to set off in the direction opposite that from which he expected his father's and his mother's coming. The world was suddenly so big. ... He must stay a little yet. He must return to the house and get his overcoat and mittens.

He entered again and secured them and went to the side of his sister. With a great effort he again shaped her name with his lips, but he dared not feel her wrist or her forehead.

As he left the place he felt that he could not go far. He himself would die under the weight.

In the darkness of early morning he got aboard a freight train. Six months later he heard that his sister had recovered and come to no further harm, but those ten or fifteen minutes never were to be less in his memory than the years which they had become.

There was no need for his continued wanderings, except in himself. He might have returned at any time after he had learned, but those few months, few instants, had shaped the rest of his life. From town to city he went, falling in with groups ever more questionable. He was surprised mightily after his first serious crime and began then to wonder whither he was tending. After prison he thought that he would make another start, and all would be well. But he had merely a steeper slope down which to glide.

Prison meant little to him. The change in the routine of his days hid no other change. Life was the same and left him with the same feeling after a few weeks behind the high iron fences and walls as it had outside. In spite of his conviction that he should think of nothing else. Some perversity in him kept his thoughts from wandering there. People were outside, people were there, inside. He was able to find as much and little in one place as in another.

It was not altogether indifference. Other men who seemed to be of his calibre knew him from meagre intercourse to be a pal. Without more than a few words, or probably, he felt, the capability to any extent of understanding him. That was his defence in all his wanderings, the reason for his escape from many a dubious situation, and it was his bane. People of the class he came sometimes to frequent in the way of affairs couldn't think badly of him, and they could not understand him. When they began to trust him he could not resist showing them in error, and he constantly thrust himself back beyond beginnings.

While imprisonment meant little, freedom for a time did live with him. He was surprised with his own pleasure in all the manifestations of a trivial life around him. His record at the prison had been good, and with the encouragement of that he went to a ranch far off in the hills and got a job which in time was changed to a responsible one. But it was the same there. He began to realize that he was trusted, even to things beyond his normal activities. The upshot was prison again, and came near being lynched, but he left the stolen horses in time and managed to be caught by a brace of police.

Prison again, and he could not mind it this time either. It occurred to him one day that it was wrong, that he should be ashamed and repentant. The idea clung with him and bothered him the remainder of his term. He fancied that if he could not come to care there could be no hope for him. He wondered why something within him refused to care, and he asked the chaplain. The worthy man, puzzled, in ten minutes gave him enough reasons to make him more uncertainly dumbfounded than ever.

Freedom never came to him afterward. He rustled now in the straw. How could it after those years. ... Yes, they were years; the old place made him realize. Drifting about from city to country he could not try to find himself again. And now he had made the final break with, pitiful to call it, his destiny. – With himself, which could not spare him again. The crime he had committed he had always looked on as the last in the world for him. He would have, in its revelation, prepared for the last. Now it was done. At once, when he had hidden the traces, he had made for the old place, passing through that part of the country to another city, begging and tramping, callous of discovery, splitting a pile of wood now and then for a bowl of bread and milk. He walked all the first night, rested, and came on again through the day, desperately certain that if he could be once more there, all would be well.

Now he had come. He looked out of the hole in the straw at the long fence which stretched from alongside the stack and shot, long and arrowy, to the back of the farm. When he had been a boy the fence was a rail one, crawling snakily, in the corners of which the cattle nibbled the ground bare of grass, and where may-apples sometimes grew. Despair burst through his soul at the thought that he even now refused to care, that his crime, his crimes, refused to present themselves to his mind in the colours in which they existed in the daylight of other men's sight.

His sight was never daylit. His trouble. Something dark and all-shrouding must be holding the light within him. If he might only search even over the world and find something, some sharp beauty he had never known, which would tear apart the curtain that stood, elastically resisting prisoners' blows, between himself and life! The search alone would steady him, set him again upon his feet.

He was leaning backward, the brim of his felt hat resting against the solid straw. He rolled his head from side to side wearily as he lay staring at the old pictures from his life which filled the entrance of the hole, against the bare dusty sky.

The nights he had lain so, or in the dark of a barn, his eyes seeking slits to light night skies. Or in the filtering dusk rose and went on as the stars thinned. A November morning, when crows had cawed with constricted throats, susurrant and shrill. The roads, though; they were what he remembered, not one by one, but as a great stretch before him containing all the different sorts he had come upon, waves of dust or of mire. But rarely he really saw other things. The limp crows flopping by. ...

He had never had great faith in the evil of men. In spite of his farings among them he had still somehow blinded himself to much of the worst in them. And now he began to see the worst, and at once to know that the worst was in all. The faces came before him, in animal-like roundness or animal-like sharpness of feature, half a dozen, more, of the men he had thought to know, until they had shown themselves. Now he looked at them and knew that *they* knew, they understood, and defied or conciliated remorse. Theirs was not his numbness to conscience.

Something pricking was against his neck and he sat up, and half turning round, felt in the straw until his fingers came on the end of a piece of string. He drew it forth, the stiff-fibred binder-twine, used to bind the sheaves, and blown out with the straw. He probed about in the straw again, to get any others that might irritate; and pulled out three or four, which he threw down beside him.

He leaned forward and looked out. It seemed to have become a little lighter. Fields, fences, and trees stood and lay in a pale and black dust. Then at one side he saw the moon, slight, sabre-thin, with the round penumbra. Below stood trees, short thin branches reaching up like baby fingers toward a mother's face.

A new moon! Why new? How could one call anything new? People must have thought sometime that when they became gross and replete with light the moons died. Or their souls appeared again on the other side of death. Then it could be right to call it new.

He drew back into the straw cave on his hands and knees, and felt the bunch of twine. (The dread moon, and the frost!) The coarseness of it beneath his hands brought back a vision of an old rope swing dangling in the wind, seatless, from a maple bough opposite the back door as he left the house forever. He had taken the rope long before from about a bag of binder-twine and climbed with twisting, stubby, bare toes, to tie it to the limb. Many an afternoon the two children had swung on it, while the leaves of the maple limb shivered with the shock. One day he sat on the seat idly after twisting the ropes together and then letting them whirl him around, and looked up along it to see that it was only twine after all like the twine in the balls, that was used in the binder. Some day he would twist some together and make a rope of his own.

His fingers still held the bits of twine in the straw. Then he took them up and tied them together. He stopped. Why was he doing that? He threw them aside as though in sudden fright.

Yet why should he be afraid – of himself? His weakness had been not being afraid, perhaps. He could not pick on that part of him which should be blamed. He leaned back again and a straw brushed the band of his hat. His heart leaped before he could remember once more the cause of that half-noise, half-feeling. It reminded him that he was in a strange condition when he could imagine the crackling within his head. Yet not when the knife fell did his heart feel, and he was quiet as he put away the corpse. A strange condition, truly, he scoffed, having committed that crime, not to care to think about it, about punishment or danger.

He shivered.

Then the old despair filled him once more. He could never care. Were all these years an effort, a seeking to care about life, about sin? His mind pictured the shrinking and remorse which he ought to experience at the very thought of his deed, and strangely for an instant it began to come, in something of the way which another must feel it. Then he groaned. It would only be the same years over again, the same walkings, cold alley-brawls, debauch, the years alike and he limping over them as a dog on a treadmill; to learn and discover nothing but death and sorrow. The strange things men made of themselves in the course of years, and the terrible part of it: that they never knew, until moments such as this. All; if it were only such as he!

He found himself on his hands and knees tearing the straw out in handfuls, sifting it, searching out the lengths of binder-twine. Then he stopped in sudden fright and made to leave the place. He tried to think: the posse; they knew his record, might seek him here. But it was not that. ... He looked about the dark ground and sleeping trees that held so much of his real life. Then he came within again. His movements stirring up the sharp musty smell of mouldy straw.

He tied the strings together, sought more and more of them, frenziedly began braiding them. 'I can't think,' his mind warned him, 'I must not think.' Soon he could be heard saying it aloud, rhythmically 'I can't think, I'll not think. ... I'll not think, I can't think.'

And soon the thin moon would come and peer in short-sightedly, and see nothing there.

ELAINE

She stood at the door of the little coop-like waiting-room on the tracks of the electric line which led to the city. She was embarrassed in the strange long leather overcoat Miss Chathern, whose father had been so good to the family, had given her before going back to town for the winter.

On the bench inside the coop, with school books and patent lunch-basket beside her, sat Addie Weyburn, the storekeeper's daughter. She was never particular about what she wore, and yet Elaine fidgetted; it seemed like a favour in Addie not to notice, but, glancing up, to call promptly, in a brightly-inflected, careless voice, as though to someone speeding away in the distance:

'Oh, Elaine starting back to school, eh?'

'My, yes!' Elaine plumped on the bench, not very jauntily, without saying anything more, for her mother was just behind. That would take Addie by surprise.

Yes, her mother was standing in the doorway, a figure of energy. She had told Elaine how before marrying, and even after, she had worked on the fields, and the jokes of some of the hired men. ... Her face and brown hands, not noticeable at home, matched her worn clothes, so that they seemed to have weathered together – save for a startling pink butterfly bow which she had pinned to her hat that very morning.

She looked Addie Weyburn up and down, who was not abashed, but said:

'So you're the ruling power!'

'What do you mean, I'm the ruling power?'

'You're the one that's making Elaine start back to school again.'

'I'm sure I never meant for her to stop at all. But sick three days, and then. ... That's the reason – *Of course* I'm sending her again. Elaine, darling,' said Mrs Wilks settling beside her daughter on the bench and pursing her mouth with prim sweetness, 'What time is it?'

Elaine spoke apologetically, glancing twice at her wristwatch, 'It's – Oh, it's twenty minutes after seven.'

She could not help looking to see whether Addie Weyburn smiled at the bare red hands and the gold wristwatch. And her hat was brown straw and a lace veil, her pumps were flimsy with wear. But her mother put a good face on everything.

'Where are your gloves, Elaine?' she asked, and then hastily added, 'Oh, you've forgotten them. Well!'

No one else was in the waiting room but thin Fred Jameson, another high school student, who seemed to pore over the expression of Mrs Wilks. There were heavy voices outside, for men did not use the coop unless the weather were bad and the wait long. Presently in an interval of silence one of the men put his eyes to a hole in the box where a clapboard had been torn off. Mrs Wilks bridled and smiled so quickly and the face was gone so quickly, that Elaine wondered whether or not she should believe her eyes, until two, three separate guffaws were heard, and as suddenly silenced, and the voices began again.

There was a step on the shivery platform, the starting of a car outside, and Mrs Irwin, the new neighbour-woman, came in at the door. 'Good morning, Mrs Irwin.' – 'Rather chilly this morning, Mrs Wilks.'

Tossing her head and pursing her lips, Mrs Wilks began to talk rapidly. Elaine was surprised: her mother had seemed to hold aloof from nearly all of the neighbourwomen, even the ladies in the village. 'Jealous old mustangs!' she called them. But whenever a man came to the farm he got on splendidly with her, laughed and joked....

'Seven-thirty, Elaine tells me. The car should be back from the Lake. I heard it go down, and then there was a sweet picnic. I was just scouring the milk pails. "A lick and a promise is all for you," I says, "this time!" And I do like to keep things clean...' She laughed. 'Don't it stay *dawk* late these mornings? But it's really not so bad, I say, when you've managed to tear yourself loose from bed!'

'You seem to have fine Novembers here, Mrs Wilks. It's so nice, I wish I could drive the car myself, when I go out.'

'Was that your husband drove you here? Oh ... I didn't think I recognized him. Fine Novembers, I should think we did, Mizz – Did you know Mr Chathern?' She smiled, showing a gap in her teeth, and considered. 'He was here in the summer, one of the summer cottagers. If he was here, we wouldn't have to wait, Elaine and me, he'd be driving – motoring in to town every day.'

Addie Weyburn gave a snort, surprising Elaine, while Mrs Irwin looked attentively at her neighbour, who went on:

'What can be the matter with that car this morning? I'm sure Elaine's watch is right. Just as soon as Elaine passed her Entrance I says, "Now you've got to have a watch. You deserve it for passing, and you're not going to high school; you're going to be sensible – " ' Mrs Wilks laughed – ' "and stay home and help me." But I changed my mind. ... It's a lot of bother, though. I thought we'd be late. I made up my mind I'd not have Henry drive me. "You're not a-going to do it, Henry Wilks," I says, "You don't hitch up your horse for your daughter other days," I says, "and you're not a-going to for me!" That's how I am. He said it was different, and it is, kind of, but – Oh, shoot, if you show a man you've got some independence...' She tossed her head.

Elaine shivered. She had barely spoken to her schoolmate, and seemed incapable of anything but to listen with a miserable fascination, though her eyes stared straight out of the door. The fence wires on the opposite side of the track were white with frost, and perhaps she was thinking of some impossible 'dare' which would cause her mother to put her tongue to the wire, so that the frost would clutch it, wrapping and twisting....

Almost before the grinding squeal of the car reached them, she had jumped up.

'My, how did you know?' asked Addie, rising then too, and preceding her outside to the car steps. The two girls sat on one of the lengthwise seats at the rear, and Mrs Wilks and Mrs Irwin, following the men and the boy aboard, sat in the first cross-seat ahead. Two of the men were opposite.

The conductor came and shifting his cap on his forehead punched Addie's Season Ticket, and while Elaine hesitated Addie said to him, 'I'm bringing her back – to Toonerville.'

'I see you are. Coming regular now?' He was short. 'Where's your ticket?'

'Yes,' said Elaine timidly. 'Mine's run out. Mother will settle. This is her right here. N-no, the other one!' Addie laughed at the mistake, and then whispered:

'This is one of his grunty mornings,' adding aloud, 'Oh, Elaine, you can't imagine how awful it's got since you stopped. Old Pinchott he just gives us homework *all the time*.' She lengthened the vowels deprecatingly. 'That's all he does in class is take up homework and give us more homework for the next night.'

'Poor old Pinch – ! It's the same as ever, I suppose!' Elaine laughed haltingly.

'Of course it won't make any difference to you,' her companion mocked. 'You'd even stay in the stuffy old school at noon and read books from the library – when they left the key in the lock! Remember that time Old Pinch caught you reading Shelley? I read it myself after that!'

They grew silent. Elaine was thinking of the warm classroom, and herself eating sandwiches as she read. Yes, it all would be the same, though perhaps nice and strange at first. She could think of nothing to say, and wondered whether Addie could distinguish the words of her mother, ahead:

'Oh, yes, Mr Chathern, when he heard Elaine wanted to go to high school, he says, "Well, put me down for one of them Commutor's Tickets, is that what they call'em. Can't let anybody stay out that has ambitions to go to school." ' She laughed. 'Those are the very words he used. He's so funny, you've no idea. And talks away to us as though we were – For the milk, he used to come to our place. Well, a lot of the cottagers used to get their milk from us, come to that. They said – they said it was so much richer than they could get in the city. But that was only to September, and they're gone back to the city long ago now. I don't know whether Mr Chathern would notice me at all now if I *did* meet him in the city. But he told me he'd be back – The book of tickets is run out now, you understand, and I'm going in to see about another one myself. The manager ... Oh! Mizz Whasname, I wonder if you could tell me, is it the manager I should go to see?'

'My, don't those Fords dance up and down when they try to pass the Street Car?' Addie exclaimed. The two girls laughed at the little car on the high road rutty from the many loads of sugar-beets which had passed over it. 'Next year I'm going to drive our car in every day; you'll see. Or maybe Father will get me a runabout.'

Before they knew it they had reached Millbrook, the junction with the steam railway half-way to the city. A group of girls got on at the other end of the car, laughing and seeming with their books and parcels to fly to pieces as the car with a resonant throbbing abruptly got under way again.

'Say, ain't you going to speak to me at all this morning, Addie Weyburn? Sitting 'way at the other end.' It was the blonde Marie Shafer screaming, and Addie said to Elaine:

'There's Carrie Minhurst, I've got to see her, and Marie.' She was taking her books and lunch. 'Come along, join the merry throng.'

But she was already halfway down the aisle, and Elaine shook her head, smiling, and turned away.

It must have grown colder outside. Flakes of snow struck the shaky windows of the car. But perhaps they would turn to rain. No, the sun was coming out, and the frosty pastures would be flooded yellow again. The bright-tipped grass made the girl think of walking barefoot in it: it seemed only a week since Bruce and Preston, her younger brothers, had put on their shoes for the winter. The bush at the horizon was smoky and sparse. A few cattle moved against it, where a windmill whirled. Smoke came from farmhouses, and yet they seemed so much colder than the big red barns. ... She felt as she did sometimes in school, thinking, or listening to old Pinchott read poetry, when her eyes went strange and everything seemed small and far, and Pinch only an inch high, and the windows bright tiny pictures. Only it was somewhere deeper, in her mind – all over, not just her eyes, now.

'And Preston and George, they always have colds all winter, but Bruce goes around without mitts; little imps, you can't...'

The girls ahead shrieked with laughter, as though in answer to her mother. The men, with shapeless overcoats and hats, with neckties askew against dark shirt collars, looked at the girls, and one was smiling. 'Consolidated schools...' She could hear an occasional word because they raised their voices, allowing for the noise of the car. They were sober farmers, one with hollow dark cheeks one with drooping grey-yellow moustache. 'Second mortgage...' Like her father, who would take her on his knee, and who believed everything, all the charming and diverting things she told him about, that she had found in books. How glad he'd been when her mother had decided that they could send Elaine to high school. Yet she never could have gone, but for that good-natured Mr Chathern.

She took up a book which had been assigned her class for Supplementary Reading, and turned the pages. '*The Little White Bird*, by J.M. Barrie.'

'...hundreds of lovely fairies, hastening to the ball, the married ones wearing their wedding rings around their waists, the gentlemen, all in uniform, holding up the ladies' trains, and linkmen running in front carrying winter cherries, which are the fairy lanterns ... The tablecloth varies according to the seasons, and in May it is made of cherry blossoms.'

And there was Minnie Mannering, who never revisited the shore of the Serpentine nor Peter with his good boat the *Thrush's Nest*, because she couldn't bear to say goodbye forever to Mother.

What was it she had heard from across the aisle? 'Old Chathern's carryings-on this summer; going in now to see him ... girl must know; feel sorry for her.' *What* was it? She tried to remake the words, but those were the ones which came back to her ear, the only ones.

And her mother was struck silent, queer; didn't she glance, didn't she smile at the men opposite? 'If he won't give me credit for it a few days, I don't know ... He'll maybe do that.' Her voice jerked on. She always made up to strangers. ... Mrs Irwin was listening politely to her, but what did she think?

Surely – what could it mean? But he was such a nice, comfortable man, and friendly, and his daughter – So clever and funny, her mother used to say, and send the kids off to play, and Elaine to watch the boys – so that she could talk to him. ... If only she had imagined them. But no. 'Feel sorry for the girl. Going in to see him now. Old Chathern's carryings-on.' Those were the words her mind kept repeating.

The fields had given way to dusty houses, cold pavements, shivering maples. ... It would be warm in school. The girls laughed still, seeming to come back from a distance, The red brick school came in sight, and they got off, and Fred Jameson, then the men, Mrs Irwin, and other men who had appeared from nowhere. Most people had entered the car and looked surprised when Mrs Wilks called to the conductor:

'We're going to the end of the line with you. Come, Elaine, we'll be getting off. Wake up, we've got to hurry, you don't want to be late. And I've got a lot to do, shopping.'

Elaine sprang up, closing her book.

'All right, Mother.'

'Pull you sleeve over your wristwatch, child. This is something else again.' Mrs Wilks smiled knowingly. 'And don't for all sakes look so bewildered, like you had lost your last friend.'

HACKMAN'S NIGHT

Berwind knew when he went into the restaurant that something was astir. Though he had his own fish to fry, seeing things generally was part of the frying.

Another part, at present, was feeding himself. You don't push a hack around the streets of the widest-spread city in the world – and one of the hardest-boiled of towns – without getting hungry at times.

About two-thirty to three o'clock every morning, Berwind started to bethink himself of a likely place to have a lunch. Of course if he chanced to pick up a load before he had decided where to eat, he did not refuse it. Loads were too scarce, and it might prove something more than a jerk – a real trip across the city, with a fifty-cent tip. You never knew. And when you got to the destination, you might pick up another load within a block or two, or while you were dead-heading toward eats. Still you kept on, if you were a case-hardened taxi pilot. Such runs of luck were rare enough you didn't want to break them to eat.

It was just such a run of luck that Berwind had completed tonight. Conscientiously he had kept cruising, but when he saw it was three o'clock on leaving one load, he determined to go into the first all-night restaurant.

The neighbourhood was not too ritzy. It was on the West Side of Chicago, on a diagonal street, Blue Island Avenue, well toward Cicero, that haven of big-time gangsters.

The first restaurant turned out to be an ordinary-looking frame two-storey building on a corner, with a sign, EAT, in large illuminated letters with a smaller one, also illuminated, DANCING, beneath. Wondering who would care to dance in this far from palatial hall, Berwind stuck his hack at the curb, and advanced to the entrance. His leather-legginged legs felt cramped after the night of driving.

The modest architecture of the place was embellished by no awning over the sidewalk, much less a carpet. No glare of lights to take the bare cheap character of the building away and make it one of the 'Nite Clubs' sown freely about the city.

'Not a load out of here in a week,' Berwind muttered. There was a Packard touring car near the door, and around the corner a bulky Lincoln.

Just as he put his hand upon the screen door he was smitten with doubts of the place. A strange instinctive hesitancy almost made him drop his hand and turn away.

No one was in sight but a black-faced Greek behind the cash-register. But instead of looking out to the street as an idle man would do, the Greek seemed to have been giving his attention to the back of the room. There was a partition, and alcoves with seats back there, but perfect quiet.

'Bowl of oatmeal and bacon and eggs,' ordered Berwind.

'No oatmeal yet,' said the Greek. 'Too early.'

Berwind grunted. He should have waited until he struck one of the white-fronted kind.

'Stack of wheats and maple syrup, then. And the bacon and eggs.'

The Greek went to the back and called the order through the wicket. 'And coffee, driver? ' he asked.

'Coffee,' said Berwind.

'Coffee,' said the Greek. But a burst of conversation had buzzed out in the back part. It seemed to have begun when they heard the Greek say 'driver.'

Berwind glanced back hastily. The voices were low, but filled the room ominously. They spoke in the esperanto of the streets. What nationality they were he did not bother to guess.

It was none of his business if they wanted to lay low until they learned who had come into the front part. But he grinned at himself in the mirror while he waited for the wheats, to think how perfectly silent they had kept for a minute or two after his entrance. What would have happened if he had been a plain clothes dick, or had spoken with a certain accent?

The grin in the mirror vanished, and Berwind was looking at a regular-featured youth with yellow hair in pompadour, and white forehead above the red mark left by his cap. The lower part of his face was darkened by the soot and grime of Chicago's streets, and his blue-gray eyes were evilly shadowed. He had to grin once more.

The cap lay upside down on a stool beside him, and his feet were alertly on the rail. He beat a tattoo briskly upon the counter while he waited, and occasionally whistled. He was not trying to hear any of the talk in the back room. It was easy for a guy to know too much, and pay for it.

Suddenly the Greek spoke up from the cash-register.

'Cut the noise, driver. There's people back there.'

'I get you,' agreed Berwind. 'I'm people too.'

The wheats arrived, and he attacked them. The conversation was buzzing lower in the back room. He could hear a word now and then.

'Say, if you guys think you get everything that shakes down from the racket without a split, you got another guess,' came clearly in a dead calm voice. There was silence. Berwind fancied he could hear breathing. If there had been movement it would have been followed by violent action, he guessed. Shots, maybe. He was sorry he had ordered bacon and eggs to follow this. He should take it on the lam as soon as he had eaten the wheats. Yet he hated to do that, aside from the fact that it would look funny. He sloshed the maple syrup – it was the real stuff – on his cakes, and made time.

'Hike the price, then,' someone was advising back there.

'I don't care how you do it,' the first grim voice went on. 'I'm declaring myself pardners, that's all. Pardners, see. And I'm asking you to shake on it friendly. When I heard of this get-together you wanted to have, I knew you guys wanted to do the right thing. I knew you wasn't thinking of double-crossing me, or trying to take me for a ride, unless you wanted to be hi-jacked different than you ever been high-jacked.'

Another voice chuckled. It belonged to one of the last speaker's henchmen, Berwind guessed.

'Take you for a ride, nawthin,' said another plaintively, placatingly. The murmurs went on, punctuated frequently by uneasy laughs.

Berwind was calculating the tips he had had that night. He had been in restaurants where he did not mind counting the cash in his pockets. Not this time. What he had would be chickenfeed, probably, for those fellows in the back, but all the same he didn't want to be doing anything which would hinder a getaway.

When the tips were more than enough to buy his gasoline, he figured how near they came to buying his meals. They were good enough tonight to justify something special – a banana split, or a drink – in some other place.

Just as he had finished this calculation, he heard a sound which caused him to seize his cap with his left hand, while ostensibly eating tranquilly as ever with his right.

The sound was that of a plain old-fashioned sock on the jaw, a thud and a heavy breath released. Talk in the back part seemed to have died suddenly. Now immediately following the sound of the blow, and the clattering of a chair, came a revolver shot.

Instantly three men appeared, headed for the door, brandishing revolvers, every one.

Berwind saw it was too late to run out ahead of them. He stood beside his stool, cap on head.

'Get out, Yellow,' growled one. He waved his rod in a way which made unnecessary the qualifying, 'Quick!'

Berwind made time to the door, and ran to his cab. When he bent to crank it, he was surprised to see the man who had threatened him pulling open the door of the cab.

Before the motor started to hit, he saw that the gun man had climbed into the cab and slumped into the corner of the seat. It was not so surprising after all. The others had not left yet. They were hovering about the Packard, watching doors, and doubtless allowing him time to make a getaway. So that anyone who happened to hear the shot and looked out would see them making off in the Packard, and not suspect the man in the cab – who was doubtless the man who had fired the shot. Well-trained.

There was nothing for it. He climbed to his high seat, and slid back the wire-reinforced window between himself and the tonneau.

'Where to?'

'Get the hell outa here,' grated the other, slumping lower than ever 'And don't pull that flag.'

The gun was still in his hand, Berwind saw from the tail of his eye, obediently getting his cab into high about as quickly as he ever had done. There was no come-back. What was next? Would he be held up? Not likely, except to supply an alibi. These birds were big-time.

It was more likely that he would run into a yellow runabout, and a hardboiled official of the cab company would enquire into his carrying a passenger without having pulled the meter flag.

'Next time I'll go hungry,' he muttered morosely.

They had shot southward to Western Boulevard, and the proximity of the Canal was not reassuring, somehow. Every little while you heard of bodies being recovered from it. And some, most likely, were never recovered.

'All right, brother,' grated the man in the back, sitting up. 'Pull your flag now if you want to, and charge me plenty. I didn't want anyone to know I was in the cab, that's all. Turn north up here at Marshall Boulevard, and head for the Park. Nice morning for a drive in the Park, ain't it?'

'Sure is,' agreed Berwind. 'Any particular spot in the Park?'

The other laughed.

'Any particular spot? he repeated, as though asking the question on his own part. It made Berwind's blood run cold. 'Not just for me, driver. If you know any nice drives, take me to 'em.'

'We'll go near one of our taxi-stands, then,' Berwind promised himself, silently.

'I'll tell you,' said the other suddenly. 'Take me to Cicero when you get through giving the Park the o.o.'

At this moment Berwind became aware of something which caused his heart to jump fishily, and his arms to go cold. The Packard with the other two men was following his cab!

The first thing which occurred to him was that they meant to take him for a ride, or to let him take himself for one. Once in a while a cab was found deserted, usually off in the sticks, and the driver's corpse was discovered later, riddled or strangled. That, perhaps, was what he was slated for. He knew too much. The Packard would overtake him; it would be easy for this fellow to keep him covered, and then they would take him for a ride in the nice suave Packard. His first and last ride in that famed vehicle.

Still, as likely as not, they merely wanted to pick up their confederate when they came to a convenient spot in the park. They'd tip him as nobody but drunks had tipped him yet, and tell him to forget everything.

That seemed to him much the best and most convenient solution, and he would gladly forget these fellows and all their concerns.

However, it was a question whether they would see the reasonableness of such a plan.

Still another plan they might have: to get into his cab, all three, and leave their Packard, which was probably someone else's Packard, in some secluded byway of the park.

'Step on it a little,' advised the passenger.

Berwind's toe prodded the accelerator button.

Already they were approaching the red lights at Jackson Boulevard. How simple and easy it would be just to slip down Jackson to the Loop, and the familiar streets and crowds. Still, one place was no safer than another with these bimbos trailing you.

'Don't worry about the red lights, unless there's a bull around, or some traffic crossing you. It's safe enough at night,' adjured the passenger again.

'Okay,' agreed Berwind, keeping the hopefulness from his tone. He knew that if he did such a thing on his own account, he would scarcely go a block before a squad car or motorcycle would overhaul him and threaten him with assault, summons, and summary loss of his operator's license. Surely he deserved a break, and they would run him down this time too, incidentally taking this hard egg off his hands.

Not a bit of it. He had plunged over the line before the light had changed from yellow to green, and the Packard, slowing, passed just as it was about to change back again from yellow to red. If anyone were watching they might agree that the two cars were shaving seconds pretty close. On they plunged again.

Or, Berwind's mind calculated swiftly, the Lincoln might be following the Packard, and he might have a ringside seat on another shooting-up. No doubt these birds had bullet-proof glass in their cars. For himself, he would doubtless be the goat. That was usually the way things turned out. He'd just have to hold himself ready for whatever was to happen.

To his surprise they kept on until they were in the midst of Humboldt Park. And there, with casual talk of the birds and flowers of the place, the strange passenger demanded to be put down.

Berwind looked curiously at the short, well-built man in dark suit and hat, with serene face, but his hand in his right coat pocket. In his left, to be sure, he held a ten dollar bill, which he tendered to the driver.

'I don't want any change, kid,' he said. 'Never mind the slip.' when Berwind began to pull it out of the meter. The wave of his hand was emphatic dismissal. 'Thanks,' said Berwind, and shot away.

Without looking back he knew that the Packard had been idling along behind at the moment the man had alighted from the cab. The other would be picked up instantly.

'Good-bye to this park,' swore Berwind. 'Me for the Loop and giving the depots a play.'

Anything, he felt, was better than such a jolt as he had just escaped from. He might hit the nearest stand, and put his cab in line until an order by telephone came to his turn. And meanwhile he would have something to tell the other cab-drivers. Their ears were appreciative of such stories, he knew. Wherever two or three were gathered together and a query was made, 'How are the breaks?' such stories were listened to with mirthful appreciation. What would the fellows make of this one? Some of the wise ones would be sure to tell him he had not played the gang right to get the real jack. He should have been taken in cahoots, or the devil knew what. No, he guessed, he wouldn't go to a stand, unless he failed to pick up something.

What route would he take to deadhead for the Loop? North and Division were likely to be slow at this hour. Might almost as well keep on to Fullerton or Diversey and the Lake Shore route.

But no, there was Chicago Avenue, with Little Sicily and Little Italy, and Spooky Hollow. There would be something there, surely. Disreputable and poor as the district was, people got tired walking or waiting for cars or elevated trains.

He was about to turn back south on Oakley Boulevard, but an arm was raised at the corner. It was a short man in dark clothes and hat. Berwind felt like giving her the gun again, but he knew that this short man was not to be trifled with. It was the same one who had left his cab fifteen minutes earlier.

'Where's your brakes?' he asked calmly as Berwind backed up for him.

'I'll say the breaks are good tonight,' grinned Berwind. After all, perhaps they were. He had had a good night, and got as much from this fare as the whole of an average night's takings.

'Well, brother,' said the small man, leaning back against the cushion, 'I want to go back to that same joint where I started from. On Blue Island Avenue. You know.'

He lit a cigar, and offered Berwind one.

'Thanks, cigarettes are my speed while I'm on duty.'

'Smoke it later, at home,' commanded the other.

Along Oakely Boulevard they pursued a brisk course. At a corner where a party was breaking up, several hands were waved, voices and whistles raised with them. Berwind wished he could get a nice load of thoughtless people into his cab, even if only for a jerk. It would be a relief from the quiet civil man he was carrying.

Hell, morning was coming, and as soon as this trip was done, he was going to check in.

It would be better to ask no questions. Still, they could do nothing to you for asking questions, except not tell you.

'Do you think the Lincoln will be there yet?' Berwind asked cautiously.

'What do you know about the Lincoln?' asked the other loweringly.

'Well, I know there was a Lincoln and a Packard parked outside,' replied Berwind evenly. 'Everybody knows that, I suppose, who came near the place.'

'Everybody means nobody, and don't you forget it,' replied the little dark man significantly. There was no threat in his tone, but a gruesome evenness, which gave the hearer to understand that matters would be as he said.

'Shall I turn over to Western, and come back the same side of the street as before?'

'No, keep right on down Oakley.'

There was a little delay in cutting across the bend of the boulevard for a series of cars were turning it, going north. Three huge limousines they were, glittering in the darkness. The first one had extraordinarily powerful lights, which rested on the yellow cab. Berwind felt a slight jar in the midst of the motor-vibration. Without turning his head he knew that his passenger had hit the floor of the cab.

The first car with its powerful lights, was past, in a burst of speed. The others slowed at once, and Berwind's cap flew from his head. A tornado, a sand-blast, seemed to strike him. He was not conscious of hearing the machine guns, but he would have sworn that there were several, and that hundreds of bullets were striking his cab. In an instant's flash of feeling he was sure that some of the bullets must have struck him, though he could not yet feel the effects of any of them.

As suddenly as though he had been driving at full speed beneath a hose, the storm was over, and the last of the three limousines had tranquilly and swiftly sped away.

Without knowing that he had done so, Berwind had shot his hack into gear and made a block at forty miles an hour before he came to himself long enough to pull up and look into the back of his cab.

The little dark man was still there, on the rubber matting. There was something dark on his face and a dark spot spreading over his shirt front. Under a pale street light it was plain that the face was set in a final grimace. Berwind stopped the cab.

'Now,' he declared to himself, 'the first John Law I can see will be the best friend. It's a mystery to me though, that the motor was not stopped. It felt as though those bullets were raking her from keel to stern.'

Characteristically, he began looking his cab over, from front tires to spare wheel. A real cab pilot would see to his hack first, once certain that his own skin was whole. What if these gangsters did shoot one another up?

Berwind felt a little rubbery in the knees as he made the inspection. There was not a hole in the tires or the hood. If they had been aiming to stop the cab, there would have been holes in the hood about the distributor. There were no perforations in the front part, except beneath the driver's seat.

They knew what they wanted – the man they knew was on the floor in the rear. And they might just as well have gone for the driver too. It was – it was damn generous of them, Berwind thought, his teeth clicking convulsively.

'What's the matter, jockey?' asked a bluecoat bull, tramping leisurely toward him. 'You can't park here. What's your stands for? Haven't you got no stand to go to?'

'Take a look at this,' said Berwind.

'Been shooting your cab full of holes, eh? Can't you boys play without getting rough? Didn't get you, though. What did the other fellow's cab look like?'

'This ain't no cab war,' returned Berwind indignantly. 'Take a look in the back of the cab, I say.'

The policeman opened the door, and the gangster's head fell against him. John Law's face worked a little, and he looked foolish.

'Where did you get this corpse?' he demanded roughly.

'He wasn't a corpse until a couple of minutes ago,' said Berwind impatiently. 'Don't you see any connection between the bullet holes in my duco job and this fellow?'

'You stay here, while I call headquarters. Don't touch him, or you'll be sorry, you –'

'All right,' said Berwind calmly. 'I'll go with you.'

'No, stay here and keep your eye skinned.'

'I sure will.' Berwind sat down on the curb.

The other lumbered off to use a box telephone. In a few minutes he was back.

'Homicide squad is on the way now,' the law grunted. 'How did this come about?'

Berwind had to laugh. 'Why didn't you ask me before you told 'em? ' he asked.

'You better spill the dirt, when the squad comes, that's all I got to say.'

'Then I better not tell a story now and have to change it later.'

A reluctant grin overspread the face of the other.

'I guess you know your onions, kid. You can tell as much as you like. It looks like you steered the guy into this, but then, if he's who I think he is, it don't matter.'

Berwind looked at him, his eyes narrowed.

'That thing in there,' went on the bull, 'looks to me like Lefty Pettiti.'

'What, the guy that's been getting the Scarface mob all burnt up? Why, I thought he had cut in so deep they couldn't get him.'

'That's what he thought. Thought he could croak the Big Baboon himself, I guess.'

'Say,' exclaimed Berwind, then held his peace. Lefty had done that, he suspected.

A long touring car slid to a stop facing his cab at the curb. Three plainclothesmen dismounted, bearing sawed-off shotguns. They were nonchalant at sight of Berwind seated on the curb. One came over to him while the other two looked the cab over.

'Where was you hit?' the dick asked Berwind.

'I wasn't hit, I'm just resting my dogs from pushing the accelerator and the brake all night.'

The others called this dick, and after eyeing Berwind suspiciously up and down, he turned to them.

'It's him, all right,' they told one another. 'He would step in front of it. And one time he had a chance to split with the Big Shot.'

'He had a chance tonight, I think,' said Berwind, joining them. He had concluded that the quickest way out of this predicament if he did not want to be in the coop for a couple of weeks, would be to take the dicks to the restaurant and tell them all he knew.

They all turned and gathered around him, pressing upon him threateningly, eyeing his shoes, leggings, trousers, jacket, and cap.

'Come clean,' they said. 'You better,' they added by way of kindly advice, looking at him as though selecting portions for mastication.

'Yeah. Well, it's a restaurant over here on Blue Island you want to see. I picked this guy up there, and somebody was shot there.'

'Who shot him? This guy?'

'Maybe. I didn't see it. I heard the shot, then this guy comes and grabs my hack.' That, Berwind considered, was putting it neatly enough.

'Come on, then. Bring your cab. You, Lauscher, get on the running-board of the hack. And you – don't start any funny stuff, see,' he adjured Berwind. 'We're coming right along behind.'

It was early dawn as Berwind got his cab under way, and the two cars slowly passed through the gray streets to Blue Island Avenue. A cold foggy exhalation was in the air, which seemed to make more apparent than daylit air the smell of soot and grime.

The frame restaurant with its drab EAT-and DANCE signs looked more commonplace than ever. Surely nothing dramatic ever happened there. One would suppose that the Greek manager would still be sleeping over his cash register.

And so he was. The dicks brought a look of animation to him when they asked what had become of the body of the man shot there.

'Nothing,' he returned. 'They took him away.'

'Who took him away?'

'Fellows he was with. They had a big Lincoln car outside, and they carried him out and put him in it.'

'Was he dead?'

'I think so.'

'Who was he?'

The Greek shrugged, his eyes shifting.

'You'd better come with us, you can talk better at the station.'

The man looked flabbergasted, but not frightened. 'Why, me? I ain't got nothing to do with it,' he muttered.

'Who owns this place?' the captain of detectives asked.

'I do,' said the Greek.

The youngest of the detectives wagged a finger under his nose. 'Now listen. You know better than that. Do you think we come from the sticks to check up on you guys? Scarface de Priest owns this joint. Was it him that was croaked in back here?' They closed in on him.

The Greek nodded.

'And you don't know whether he was dead when they took him away?'

'I think he was,' said the Greek.

They laughed. 'I guess you wouldn't talk if he wasn't. Come on out here to the cab.'

'Say,' said Berwind. 'When do I get away? I got to check in at the North Side garage.'

The youngest of the dicks, to whom he addressed himself, did not reply. The second one turned from the Greek, whom they were escorting, and said, 'You can check in and get some rest at the County Building.'

'Who is this guy?' asked the captain, shoving the Greek's head into the taxi door.

'I dunno. Looks like a guy that was here when the boss got shot.'

'Are you sure of that?'

'Yeah.'

'That lets me out,' repeated Berwind. 'I got to go check in. This guy must have bumped Scarface, then Scarface's bodyguard comes along in three cars and bumps him while I'm driving him. That's all. You got my number, and you can easy find me.'

'That's right. Frank, we don't need this guy now.'

'You can go, as soon as we unload the corpse. But don't leave the city.'

'Where are you going with the corpse? asked Berwind patiently. 'And where do I get my pay for this jerk and the last one?'

'I've called the wagon,' the youngest dick said, emerging from the restaurant. 'They'll be here for the body in a couple of minutes.'

'The three detectives drew aside to question the Greek once more.

There was a drumming and a squeal, and a very brisk but loungingly dressed youth sprang from another taxi which slid to the curb. He seized Berwind by the lapel.

'I'm from the *Tribune*. Are you the driver of the death car?'

'They sprayed my hack,' explained Berwind. The other was already writing in a notebook.

'Who did they get, and how many?' asked the reporter.

'Get it from these guys,' said Berwind. 'I got to go check in.'

'Hold on,' said the other, seizing the tab of his breast pocket. 'You'll tell me the story in your own words, and the *Tribune* will print it under your name, DEATH CAB DRIVER TELLS OWN STORY. Give you a hundred berries. How does that sound?'

'Good,' said Berwind.

'Wait around the corner, then, till I talk to these birds, and then tell me.'

Berwind, however, wasn't moving with the corpse. He sat wearily on the high seat of his cab. For lack of something to do he pulled his metal-covered book from the roof, and began recording his trips. That should have been done before, to afford an alibi. Looking back, he saw that the newspaper man was talking like four to the dicks, and they were saying yes and no when they felt like it. He would soon have the dirt.

In a few minutes the patrol wagon arrived, with uniformed coppers. The body of the gunman was lifted from the back of Berwind's cab and placed in the wagon, and the barred door clanged shut upon it.

The dicks departed in their touring car, taking the Greek with them for questioning. They gave Berwind a settling look as they went away. He would know better than to try any funny stuff, even to skip out. The captain, before leaving, paid the amount marked on the meter. They would search the man's pockets at the morgue, and find plenty.

Berwind and the brisk lad from the paper looked at one another, and the cab driver drew a breath of relief. He was already well-paid for the night, and there was a chance of making a couple of weeks' kale in the few minutes ahead.

When the questions had been answered and the notes made, the reporter said:

'You call around at the *Tribune* a week from Friday. Ask for Skaller. They'll pay for this.'

'One hundred bucks, that right?'

'One hundred it will be, I expect, if the old man will stand for it.'

'Oke. I'll be there for the century.'

All this time the meter of the cab the reporter had arrived in was briskly tick-tocking. Now he entered it, said Tribune Tower, the jockey grinned at Berwind, and they disappeared.

Berwind lost no time in cranking up his tumbril, and getting away. But when he got as far as Racine, which he thought might be a good street to take, if some early working man happened to want a lift to the North side he stopped his cab, got out, and in accordance with his invariable practice, searched the tonneau. You never know whether the passenger might not have left a diamond brooch or a hundred thousand worth of dope there.

He had never yet found either in a cab of his – nothing but an umbrella or a cloak or a book of poetry left by some love-sick girl – but he had not given up hope.

This time he was rewarded. It was just a crumpled bit of paper he found when he lifted the thick perforated rubber matting. Uncurling it, he read:

'Lefty:

I got it straight that Scarface is going to pull some funny stuff tonight at the conference. Better pull it first. He's to kick in or take it. The mob is all set to go, as soon as the job is finished. Blue Island, you know where. The set is staged at Racine.

Zaro.'

What was the meaning of this note, Berwind demanded of the surrounding street. 'Blue Island' obviously indicated the restaurant to which he had been lured by the cravings of the inner man, and which had nearly proved a Siren's Island fatal to his continued existence upon this planet.

Suppose he were to go back there and see who was in charge now that the Greek was gone. If Scarface owned it, it might be his headquarters, and a very dangerous place to investigate.

And what did Racine mean? It might be the Racine Avenue of Chicago in which he stood at that very moment, or he might with less likelihood have meant the town of Racine, Wisconsin.

Berwind did not waste time stopping in order to consider these questions. He mounted his box and cogitated them as he drove. Also he kept an eye peeled for anything that might look like a joint of big-timers on Racine. The trouble with big-time joints was that they did not look like big-time.

The harder he thought the more slowly he drove, until he forgot his aim to deadhead home to the garage and check in. He was beginning to hanker to be in on whatever was happening.

This more than ordinary cruising leisureliness was rewarded. A man and woman stood waiting on the sidewalk. They were in front of a rambling dilapidated old house, set far back from the street, in grounds scattered with neglected shrubs and weeds – an odd place with falling fences, between a new apartment building and a laundry. The man lifted a forefinger.

Berwind automatically slid his cab to a stop, giving the place the once-over at the same time. He felt for some reason that these two had come out of it, and seeing him approach so conveniently, had not bothered to walk on.

The man was dapper in an old-fashioned way, what used to be called a 'dude.' His felt hat was pinched tight, and he wore buttoned shoes. His coat was three inches longer than the style of the present. He carried a suitcase.

The woman, on the other hand, was fairly up-to-date, though plain, in dress. Yet she did not contrast too violently with the appearance of the man. While she paid Berwind and the taxi no more attention than customary in women with escorts, it seemed that she was not accustomed to riding in cabs.

'Let me put that in front beside my seat,' said Berwind.

The man made no answer, but placed the suitcase beside the woman, and climbed in after them.

'Drive out north.'

Well, that was on the way to the garage, at least. Berwind had had it in his mind to decline to take them if the trip had been in another direction. Now he felt that he would not have done so. Though queer loads were not uncommon, he felt somehow that this one would repay the curiosity it aroused.

When they had gone a mile or so, the man spoke again. Up to now silence had been the rule.

'Turn up Milwaukee,' he said.

Berwind grunted. Milwaukee Avenue, aside from being one of the dreariest streets in the city, led northwest, and would lead away from his headquarters. It led, moreover, into an unpopulated region, of waste land, scattered houses and joints, mysterious and lonely spots where if anywhere foul play seemed to be a natural product. What did this pair have on ice?

He began to whistle casually, then turned his head as casually to glance into the tonneau. They might apply a cold-chisel to his head when an opportune spot was reached. You never knew. Perhaps take his cab for a run up the shore of Lake Michigan, jump on a bus to Milwaukee, and then a boat to anywhere.

Of course knocking a cab driver on the head and taking his roll would be only incidental to a larger scheme of operations. But if it was a necessary part of a getaway, then it was too bad for the cab driver.

His glance around told him nothing. The man was rather stiffly upright in the right corner, the woman in the left. They did not attempt to talk. If their trip was to be brief, there would have been nothing remarkable in that. But to be silent throughout a long journey looked a little queer. However, plenty of people did not have much to say in a cab.

One thing his glance had revealed, however: both their gazes – the man's and the woman's – happened to be directed at the suitcase between them. Plainly there was something in their reluctance to allow Berwind to carry it in front with him. And just as plainly there was something in the suitcase.

'Hell, what's gone wrong with my nerves?' Berwind asked himself, as he figured that the something in the suitcase might be anything from a dismembered corpse to a pineapple or an opium cache. 'I might just as well figure it's a bunch of greenbacks that they'll leave for me.'

They were speeding along, crossing diagonally the long streets which ran from one end of Chicago to the other – Ashland, Robey, Western, California, Kedzie. Each one opened up a vista of miles of varying communities along their lengths. The cab sped on. How much farther was it to speed?

They had not yet passed the North Western branch of the Elevated. Perhaps these two would make their getaway by that. They might do worse, Berwind considered.

'Can't you drive a little faster? ' asked the man plaintively.

'Can you fix it with the cops?' asked Berwind, stepping on it.

'Say, I like that crack,' the other snarled suddenly, then abruptly calmed. 'The police would have nothing to say to us, we weren't going more than fifteen miles an hour.'

'All right' Berwind agreed. He gave the cab the gun, and they shot down Racine, the motor drumming thunderously between the steel disk wheels.

'Hold on,' rasped the male passenger, while the woman giggled in a way which made Berwind think all this was foreseen. 'I want you to turn off at Cicero Avenue.'

'Oh. North, I suppose,' said Berwind respectfully.

'Yes, north till I tell you different.'

Well, that meant they would not be heading into Cicero suburb, at any rate.

In a leisurely, businesslike way Berwind piloted the cab into Irving Park Boulevard, and crossed that to turn into Cicero Avenue. They were coming into a scattered section of the city, where vacant lots and ambiguous isolated buildings abounded. Occasionally an apartment house a few stories high, or a warehouse, seemed to emulate dispiritedly the skyscrapers of the far-away Loop.

'Turn here,' said the man suddenly.

Automatically Berwind swerved into a grassy, one-track lane. But as he did so he took the opportunity to look around once more. The man was still on the back seat. If he had sat on one of the small seats, Berwind would have been a little leary. But the road was rough now, and the fellow would have some difficulty in reaching through to slug the driver. He could not spring upon a small seat, because they had to be pulled down deliberately, and on the instant of being released from weight, these seats sprang back against the wall.

As long as the bird perched on the rear seat, Berwind felt fairly safe. If it was a gun, the jolts of the road would make him fire wild.

There was nothing to be done except accept orders. Maybe they were not steering him into an ambush. He had never yet refused to go any place a fare wanted to be taken, and he had voluntarily gone into a good many places he would rather not have gone into, and usually he had come out with a whole skin. Only it would be like his luck, while he had a goof roll of money on him, to lose it. Or perhaps it would be just his luck to make another roll tonight. 'Came the dawn, and the hack driver woke up rich,' he told himself. 'Like hell!'

'What do you think this is, driver, a steeple-chase? Drive a little slower.'

'All right. Sorry. I thought you were in a hurry.'

'Not in that big a hurry, brother,' said the woman.

They were approaching a more desolate tract. An occasional deserted soft-drink and hot-dog booth, and huge illuminated billboards made Berwind think they were getting to something, if it were only a race-track. But the race track was farther north. Dog-racing maybe.

Finally, a new, raw building, freshly-painted clapboards, came into view. Its lower storey was unlighted, apparently, until you saw that the blinds were drawn. A door on the second-storey veranda showed that that was lit up, though the windows were covered. Two cars, a large touring and a limousine, stood in the yard.

'Pull up here for a few minutes, driver,' said the man in silky leashed tones.

Was it a gambling joint, or opium and coke, or a pure and simple speakeasy? Berwind was curious, for somehow he expected something to happen here. Had he known whether the suitcase was light or heavy he might have made a guess. He slid the cab to a stop on the yard of black cindery gravel. Now what?

'You can let your meter run if you like. We won't be long. Then we'll want to go back to the city.'

'Oke. I'll be here.'

The two dismounted, but oddly enough they left the suitcase in the cab. Two pleasant people calling on some friends before setting out on their honeymoon, Berwind thought with a grin. Still he did not bother to demand the amount the meter showed, as he would have done had he thought they might get away on him. But this isolated building was not the city.

He dismounted and stretched his legs about the courtyard. Heavens, there was another orange-and-green cab! He was in luck. Surely the other fellow would be some kind of support, if only what is termed moral.

But further strolling did not reveal the other driver. He must have gone in for a drink. Or perhaps he was in cahoots with this crowd. Berwind was not so buoyant.

The building itself revealed nothing more to his scrutiny. It was most unusually quiet, though he would have thought that those frame walls would have revealed every sound made inside them. He would have poked around to the rear, but he did not want to let his cab out of his sight.

Just as he was about to stroll back to his cab, a groan reached his ears. It came from the rear of the place, that was plain. He would have to go back, now.

At the bottom of a railinged flight of stairs leading from the rear veranda, Berwind found his colleague, minus cap, his leather putteed legs stirring a little. His head seemed to have been bashed in, for its thatch of hair was clotted with blood.

'What you doin' here buddy?' asked Berwind.

'You Yellow?' asked the other without opening his eyes.

'Yeah. Who slugged you?'

'That mob of Scarface's in there,' whimpered the other in a thin piping voice.

'Scarface's mob! Hell, how many mobs has he got?'

'Plenty. Did you run into one?'

'Yeah,' said Berwind again, noncommittally. 'I guess it pays to stay with your hack when you get them invitations!'

'Help me over to my cab, will yuh? If I can get in 'er I c'n drive 'er, don't worry.'

'All right. But give me the low-down. Did they rob you and slug you, or what? Are they making a specialty of cab-drivers tonight? If so, I'll gladly lose my last fare and take it on the lam.'

'I dunno. Give me your mit.'

Berwind got behind him and lifted beneath his armpits. When he had the other on his feet they trundled slowly around the club to the cabs. Berwind opened the door and hoisted him in behind the wheel.

'Want me to crank up for you?'

'Say, you was asking me – about them guys that put the slug on me. I'll hand it to yuh straight.'

His weary tone made Berwind think he had imbibed something within before he had met a black-jack.

'I was driving a couple of fellows out here. Had the jack, they did, and seemed free-and-easy. Well, they let a big Lincoln go when they hailed me. Whether it was theirs or not I don't know. Anyway, they gets outa this Lincoln, and gives me the high sign, and asks to be brought here. I brung them and they wanted me to come inside – '

Berwind was using his eyes and his head while he listened. He saw that this fellow looked a little like himself. Had the bandits made a mistake and, determined to take him for a ride, hailed this fellow. They should have noted the cab number if they were going to do that.

'Got out of a Lincoln, you say. Where?'

'Out the end of Humboldt Park. They didn't know I saw 'em getting out, but I did.'

'Then when they got you out here in the sticks they lay the slug on you, eh?'

'No, they're nice, and friendly, like big shots generally is, and they asks me in to have a little snort to warm me while I wait for 'em. I goes in, of course, and sees the layout. Some swell joint, I'm telling you. You can play everything from seven-up to solitaire. Well, what does they do, but begin razzin me, as though they take me for somebody else. I didn't get it, and I told 'em so. They kinda cooled down, and saw I wasn't the guy they was looking for after all. Then one that was kinda stewed says, Hell, he's seen too much anyhow, and they bend a pipe around my ear before I could lay my dukes on ary a one of 'em. Next thing I know is here I am, and here's you asking me what's the party.'

'Did you hear any names named?' Berwind asked. 'Or was there any talk you could remember?'

'Well, there was some talk of Leftie Louie, and Scarface, and a couple others – Klady, I think, was one name. And they was talking as though this hack man they wanted knew something about the works they didn't want him to split. I guess I acted so dumb they got wise I didn't know a thing about their racket – which I didn't.'

'I guess you struck the same mob I struck, all right.' But Berwind was too cautious to tell what more he knew.

'What ya know? Killers?' whispered the other driver, looking toward the entrance of the place.

'I think we better take it on the lam.'

'All right,' agreed the other woefully. 'I wish I had that drink now that I had before I got hit.' he muttered. 'There's a lot of rough fields and that to drive through. Believe me I keep to good old Chi, after this, where a fellow's safe.'

'I'll crank your car then. Not in gear, is she?' Berwind twisted her tail, and the motor roared. Appalled, he motioned to the other to pipe down – who, instead, shot the cab back from him and turning whirled out of the yard.

Berwind hopped to the head of his own hack, and twirled the crank. At the same instant a group of people appeared at the door of the cabaret, or whatever it was. He was on his seat by the time he saw them, but his impulse to give her the gun and follow his colleague was immediately quenched. He saw guns gleaming, and he did not wait for fire.

The man and woman he had just delivered were there, and two others. Curiously, they were backing out, in silence, and most of them, he saw in a flash, held guns.

Suddenly, inside, the lights went out, and loud reports came.

In the midst of the shouting and firing and hullabaloo, the cab driver sprinted around the rear. He saw out of the corner of his eye as he sped that some of the emerging group had turned to flee to the cars, and thought that, with its motor running, his cab might be commandeered. Nevertheless he felt no call to stand in the line of fire, and he preferred modestly to ensconce himself in the background until the doings should be over.

What was his astonishment when he saw one of the detectives who had found the body of the slain gunman in his cab, standing now at the head of the veranda stairs. Berwind's mind worked fast.

'Give me a rod, quick, and I can clean some of them from the corner. Same mob, ain't it?'

The young detective nodded gleefully, and passed him a gun.

'You stay here and keep everybody out, mind. Better than shooting towards us.' He himself turned away to the interior to join the fray.

'Gee, this is where I get on the right side once,' Berwind thought, tensely watching for any of the gang who might be so misguided as to run around to the back of the building.

There was the sound of a motor howling, and shouts, and more shots. He did not leave his post. Some of the gang was getting away. The police burst out the front door, and another motor shrieked while they made off in pursuit.

'Come out here, Orange,' came a call.

Berwind ran through the building, and found the junior detective rubbing his hands with satisfaction.

'Here's the last of the Louie mob and the Scarface mob,' he said gleefully. 'The boys'll get the guy and the moll that headed off in the bus. And I guess these won't be no trouble. You just hold that gun on them, while I call for the wagon.'

It was a gruesome sight over which Berwind presided, while the detective went to the phone. Here huddled the three strangers of the killer gang he had not seen, though they had got the man in his cab. Their hats were knocked off, and they had fallen apart, one on his face, arms twisted grotesquely, the other backward, with the lapel of his coat swung against his ear. There was a desperate limpness, a horrible abandon about them which burlesqued drunkenness with gruesome effect.

In a moment the detective was back, taking bracelets from his pockets attached them to the wrists of the short fellow, who began to stir.

'Just creased him, worse luck. The others are croaked o.k. You're just in time to see the last of them.'

'I just saw the first of them this evening,' said Berwind. 'It couldn't have been a very large gang.'

A grim look came over the detective's face, and Berwind thought he was about to question him.

'Of course, I don't mean the gang proper. The little fellows will form around another set of leaders. But we got the generals of both of them, and their lieutenants.'

'Then they must have all been in that joint where I went to eat, on Blue Island.'

'No. We got Izzy MacDouth on a perjury rap – income tax, through the Federal fellows. He's the real brains and backbone of the Leftie Louie gang. Then Leftie shot Scarface tonight, and got it later in your cab. And now here's the rest of the big shots, finished for good. We got plenty on this bird,' he added, giving a jerk to the handcuffs on the wrists of the wounded man.

The latter began to groan, helplessly, pathetically, as though he did not know where he was.

'Aw, pardner, give us a break.'

'Give you hell,' said the hard-boiled detective. 'If I heard that crack out of you without the bracelets, I'd turn the gat on you.'

'If I didn't have the bracelets on, you wouldn't have the chance,' snarled the other, suddenly coming to himself. The string of imprecations which followed were not new to Berwind's vocabulary, but the deadly threat in the tones in that scene and time was enough to chill the steadiest pulse.

The detective gave him as good as he sent, when it came to threats, and finally he quieted down to a sullen pretence of indifference.

At last a rumble was heard, which grew into a miniature thunder. Berwind recognized his cab. In the excitement he had not heard it go away. Now he was sure that damage had been done it. The bullet holes earlier in the night were bad enough. The boss would give him hell, not to mention his buddy who drove the cab daytime. Still, she was able to navigate on her own power, he reflected with a grin.

It was the burly captain of detectives who entered the door.

'Well, lads,' he boomed cheerily. 'We cleaned up tonight. Lauscher has got the man and woman in the car, holding them till the wagon calls for them on the way here.' He looked at Berwind benevolently.

'Your cab was here, the saints be praised,' he continued, 'or they would have made a break on us. They busted the timing gear on our car while we were inside, however they did it so quick. I suppose they had an outside man. But that hack of yours! Can she take the rough trails! And the fenders on her! Say, we ran their car into the curb so easy they never knew how it was done. Why, we'd have knocked the pants off them – '

'Is – is she busted up bad – she must be some crocked, ain't she?' Berwind asked.

'Now, never mind that,' said the captain of detectives. 'We'll fix all that with the cab company. Why, you could pay for the repairs yourself, for that matter. Don't you know there's a reward up from the Business Man's Federation of five thousand dollars to any civilian who aids in the capture of any member of either of these gangs? We'll see you cash in on them.'

Berwind almost reeled. His eyes were like saucers. At last he said, 'Taxi pilot wakes up rich is right.'

'What?'

'I guess that's good enough breaks for one night. I'm going to check in.'

INNOCENT MAN

Jack Dolson was driving toward Chicago with the girl who had just become his wife. They felt transformed, yet never more themselves. It was like passing into another country; they had just stepped over the border. It was more like coming into a fortune. Their happiness as they talked and drove kept reminding them of the possession anew. And everything reminded them of their happiness. They were Mr and Mrs Jack Dolson now, shooting along in a sports model which could not look more intimate and dashing.

As they passed towns and villages on the smooth highway, leaving their own village farther and farther behind, the realization became clearer. It was a new world they were riding into, and nearly everything about them was new to match; their luggage, their clothes, even the car seemed new to them.

They had talked about getting married since winter, but Jack wasn't very good at saving, and for a time neither would name the day. It seemed when they did make up their minds to it, it was quite simple, and obstacles evaporated.

It was not necessary to buy a house, or furniture. It was not even necessary to make plans. Jack lost his job, and the insecurity decided him. As for getting another, that was easy. Meanwhile, why put off getting married? They would spend the summer jaunting around, camping with their car, stopping here and there when they got short of cash, while Jack would work the district as a specialty salesman. In the fall he could get some job in the city, sell the car if he had to, and they would take an apartment. They'd get along. Probably he wouldn't have to sell the car.

There had been a little difficulty about this automobile. He wanted one, whether he were getting married or not. But he could not buy a new one outright. He had to keep enough in reserve for the other expenses. And the local agent seemed to be queer. He wanted a larger amount paid down than Jack thought customary.

'Don't you know me?' Jack demanded. 'Did you ever know me to get fired from a job in this town?'

'I don't know, you change pretty often.'

'That don't make any difference, I never got fired. I've lived here all my life, ain't I?'

'Sure you have.'

'Well, then – '

The dealer shook his head. Jack went to the city, and got the model of car he wanted. Of course the monthly payment was quite large. A week afterward he was laid off his job. Three weeks after that was the wedding day. There was no need of telling the dealers in the city these particulars or that he was taking a trip. What difference did it make to them, so long as he made the payments? Grace only knew that the car wasn't fully paid for yet.

Jack enjoyed possession of the car all the more, and the stares of people in their block who knew that he had lost his job. He hoped the local agent observed him driving about town.

Grace's folks had decided that the wedding was to be 'quiet,' since it seemed to have come about so suddenly. There were just a few relatives of hers besides her parents, and his aunt, a widow who had adopted him as a small boy.

Though he got up at five o'clock, the hours seemed to pass with an uproarious speed. Yet there was nothing to do. He had gone over the car the day before, and his aunt had seen to his clothes. He was dumbfounded to find that it was nearly eleven o'clock. He called Grace by telephone, and Grace answered as though she had been posted right beside the receiver. She was ready. Where was he? She was delighted at his thinking of bringing flowers. He joked her: the minister was not there, and nothing much could be done until he and Jack arrived. They lost a minute or two in getting Grace to say over the telephone with people buzzing about her that she loved him.

'Well, good-bye for a couple of minutes Hello! I guess I'll bring the car too, eh?'

'I guess you'd better, unless you want to walk.' Grace had got used to his way of kidding.

Jack got into the car as though he were going for a drive, and his aunt, in black, climbed in after him.

The ceremony was no great ordeal, and everything went smoothly. Somebody told him to put the money he was giving the minister into an envelope, and not just pay him as you pay the grocer. Miss Glamis who used to give Grace music lessons played the wedding march. Grace's old man took her arm, and they came into the front parlour. Jack and the minister were there, waiting. Jack's heart went into his boots, but he reflected that it would soon be over, and it soon was. Except that it was more reading than he had expected, and he had to say 'I will' more times, there was nothing surprising. He was just beginning to get a kick out of it when the whole thing was over.

Of course her mother had to cry, and hardly stopped even when everyone smiled and laughed at the thorough way Jack kissed his bride. Nobody had told him that it was customary, and he had a vague notion that it was the minister who was supposed to kiss her after the ceremony; but he was ready for that kind of emergency.

Everyone burst out talking with congratulations and jokes, and found their way into the dining-room. The table and everything was decorated, and they had a nifty feed, though not heavy, because it was only supposed to be luncheon. Besides, Jack and Grace were in a hurry to get away. They wanted to get away from all this.

Getting away was not so easy. Everyone seemed to be talking at once, and wishing them well, and the music teacher was talking beamingly to Grace's mother and Grace, and her father was shaking hands all round, and finally they got out onto the veranda. Then the minister found a bag of confetti somewhere and began throwing it. So Jack and Grace ran to their car.

Half a dozen fellows he knew were standing at the curb, grinning. Fellows he had played pool with, or baseball. Jack did not know what to do. He had not expected them to hear about the exact time. He wished he could have reached into his car and pulled out a box of fine cigars. But here was where Grace's old man did his stuff. He was the night operator at the depot for twenty years, and he knew a thing or two. He went into the house and out again before anyone knew what was going on, and Jack passed the box around among his buddies. Some were loud and appreciative, and lit up at once. Others were suddenly shy about accepting a cigar. Jack was as kindly as though they had been a bunch of little kids, or as though he had been a god.

Grace was kissing her mother, who had cheered up. The less intimate part of the crowd was drifting away. The minister said:

'I'm like the fellow from Kentucky, I say, "Take her, boy, you're lucky." ' And he threw confetti over the two sitting in the car, again.

Then they drove away. They could hear the noise of tin cans and shouting for a block, and waved their arms back at the people. Others in the street seemed dazed, not recognizing them. In a few minutes they had crossed the railway tracks and were out of town.

It was a marvellous day. June. The world had been made anew. They had had the luck to get married in June, like the people you read about. Whatever happened, they were getting away to a good start. Nothing could have been slicker than the way all the difficulties and formalities had been sledded over, as the roadster was gliding down the smooth state highway. Grace clutched his arm, scarcely trusting herself to speak.

'Wasn't it too marvellous!'

'You tell 'em! It might have been worse, all right.'

'Oh, Jack, I was afraid you would be late, or do something wrong.'

'You know I always have to wait for you to doll up when we have a date.'

'Oh, but this was *different.*'

'I guess it was different. ... Hurray! Denver or bust! Where do we stop tonight?'

'We mustn't go too far today. We're tired, and this is supposed to be a holiday. Oh, I'm so happy.'

Jack made a motion as though to hug her, but another car was meeting them. He said nothing for a while as he drove. The country was beautiful. No other word would suit it. It was just beautiful. Trees along the road would make a fine shade, and then there would be fences and open spaces so that they could see the country, and hills with more trees and different shades of green in the distance. Oats and wheat like a thin green carpet over the level land and the knolls. Then the corn fields, the black soil with corn arching up like little green trees and still leaning away from the last wind storm. The country was swell, and the time. Jack felt like singing: 'What th' hell do we care, what th' hell do we care!' He was as light as a feather. The responsibilities of matrimony gave no sign of overwhelming him. Nothing mattered. He hadn't counted upon that.

They were slipping through the country and the villages faster than they realized, while they were silent or talked. They could not have told whether they met many other cars. Once in a while somebody passed them, without difficulty. Once they passed a truck with a man and woman in its cab enjoying conversation, while empty chicken crates occasionally dropped out at the back of the truck. Jack felt so good he sounded the horn and gestured back with his thumb.

The scenes changed and returned again and again. Most of the farms were well-kept and fine. Now there would be a narrow brick house far back from the road, at the end of a curving lane. Again, a tiny white house trimmed with green, and a huge purple barn looming over its shoulder, and a windmill tower flanking that. Sometimes the fronts of the farms would be carelessly unkempt, while the fields grew fine crops and good cattle, and machinery and tractors filled the barn yard. Others were sleek as city parks, with a trimmed hedge along the front, and evergreens in the lawn. These things struck their attention at long intervals. The country was just a background obligingly picturesque and familiar. They drove on, swept mile after mile of smooth road behind them.

They would see a smoke stack, a grain elevator, and water tower, and they would slow down and pull through another village.

Grace would look at him and pull out a map and identify it.

'Holy smoke! Michigan City already. We must have made time. We must be a hundred and fifty miles from home.'

'Home's where we are, isn't it, dear!'

'Sure is. Where my little girl is, that's home. We can make Chicago easy enough, then we'll be sitting pretty. Some bus!'

'But I thought we decided to stop in some nice quiet town outside. You'll have to drive slowly for miles in the city.'

'Well, anyway, we can make it easy before the hotel clerks are all gone to roost.' Jack grinned.

Grace looked away with a lift of the head.

'All right, dear,' she said sweetly. 'If you think you'd rather keep on. It will give us longer in Chicago.'

'Sure,' returned Jack heartily. 'No law against changing our schedule. We can do exactly as we please for once. Can't we?' His head approached hers. 'If you want to stop off to eat or stay overnight at any of these little burgs, just say the word. We don't want to get too hungry – I mean tired – this trip.'

'Isn't that a cute bungalow?' It was stone and stucco with stone porch pillars.'

The road rippling over hills like a ribbon drew them on through the endless country. Over the next hill they might see – anything. Jack slowed down and put his hand on hers. Then he drew her over toward him. She smiled once more.

'Right in broad daylight!' she mocked.

'We're happy. Aren't we?'

'Of course. We mustn't imagine we're quarrelling when we're not, either.'

The afternoon had not begun to close down before they had signs of the approaching city. Garages and gas-stations became more frequent, and bill-boards, and lunch counters, soft drink stands and barbecues never ceased. Traffic meeting them became thicker.

They passed Gary, in smoke and a trembling sky of daylit flame. The traffic was heavier and evener and faster. There was no other sign of the smoke or the skyscrapers of Chicago. They were driving in a processional entering the great city over the flat plain. On every road there was such a procession, and the city would receive them all, and never know the difference. For a time the road lay alongside a railway, and the trains whistled raucously as they vanished straightaway down the embankment.

'You've never been to Chi, eh?' asked Jack. He knew she had not.

'It's thrilling, isn't it? I can hardly wait after all. We'd better keep on. We can have dinner there.'

'We'll keep along the Lake, I guess. Nicer drive when we get into the city. We can go through Jackson Park that way, and up Michigan Avenue. Right up the main stem.'

It was still broad daylight when they came into the city. Gradually for an hour it had been growing upon them. Long ago they had passed the scattered subdivisions, new bungalows, stakes, cement walks and sewage drains, huge loud billboards. Then waste land, factories, more unopened streets, sidewalks, and drains hidden in weeds. Then the buildings on the highway itself became so thick that they would not tell what lay behind them on either hand. The highway became a street, with sidewalks crossing it. Mingled stores, house, butcher-shops, movie theatres, two and three-storey apartment houses; all drab as though with a sort of monotone of dust collected from the countryside. Yet it was not yet the black grime of the city.

They came to where the double-decked brown city buses turned around, and knew they had reached the city limits. Then they came into Jackson Park. Vistas of green, and vast patterned flower-beds, stone buildings. Mile after mile. The university buildings were like islands of rock moored in the green seas. They went up the Midway and turned North through the labyrinth of Washington Park.

'Oh, I thought Chicago was ugly. It's beautiful.'

The broad coolness of the park was not disturbed by the flash of cars.

'This ain't the half of it. This is Drexel Boulevard we're on, I guess.'

She peered at a sign. 'Yes.'

'We'd better turn off here and get over to Michigan, and we'll know where we are.'

They came on an immensely wide street with parkway, a long plot denying the barrenness of the right and left hand drives. Buildings alternately imposing, tawdry, and insignificant, lined it. Grand Boulevard. The cars drew together to a stop with squeals and hissings and muffled throbs when the red lights sprang out at a corner. Jack turned to the left and pursued the narrow side street.

'Michigan Avenue,' he explained. 'Leads straight downtown. But if you get balled up east of it you may get into a bum section of town.'

The rattling crack of a motorcycle slowed to a rapid asthma beside them.

'Stop!' There was a policeman's badge on the broad dark chest.

They slid to a stop on the grimy pavement. A voice like the baying of a blood-roused hound:

'What in the goddam hell you mean by this stuff? Don't you know enough that you can't make a left-hand turn off that boulevard? Can't you read? CAN'T YOU READ?'

At every word the voice became louder. Jack hastened to reply before something should explode.

'Why, are there signs along there?'

Fury like a storm shaking a twig shook the heavy frame of the officer and his machine. His lean long dark face lengthened as he opened his mouth and from between his tusks his bellows came. He pulled a book from his pocket.

'If I ever catch you again I'll give you a ticket so fast you'll – What's your number?' He roared, writing. 'Now get to hell out of here! If I ever catch you again I'll give you a ticket, see!'

He turned his motorcycle about, and was gone before they had started.

'Did you see any signs about left turns?' Jack asked Grace.

'No,' she laughed. 'He seemed to think there were some.'

'Should have reported him for using such language before a lady,' grunted Jack. 'I bet it would have opened his eyes if he saw me copying *his* number. Them fellows is too smart, anyway.'

'Oh, well, I'm glad he didn't arrest us, anyway. They'd put us in separate jails!' She laughed half hysterically.

'They wouldn't take us to jail. They'd give us a ticket to appear in court to answer the charge on a certain day. Hold up our trip.'

'Well, I'm glad they didn't, anyway.'

'It would have been just one more night, wouldn't it?' he teased her. They both flushed.

Now they turned to the right on Michigan Avenue, and before them stretched fifty blocks in a straight line to the Wrigley Tower and Tribune Tower like thumb and forefinger against the sky. Down the avenue shot the automobiles, four and five abreast on either side of the street, passing one another, jockeying for positions inside or outside, charging across side streets before the lights changed from green to white to red – drawing together in a herd when the lights went red, then off again in a race, slow cars left behind in fifty feet, others howling shrilly in second gear for half a block, then shooting ahead in high, charging forward.

'Soon be in the Loop. They don't care how fast you go as long as you mind the lights.'

To Grace there was something terrible in the impersonal rush of the tide of cars, with people within reaching distance of her on either side, before and behind, the faces white, savage, swarthy, indifferent. Each swoop between changing lights was like a heat in a race. They wanted more.

The gigantic sign of the Century Limited and the Broadway Limited at the Illinois Central depot suddenly assaulted their eyes at the right. An endless stream of yellow taxis was turning across the Avenue into the depot yard and forming a phalanx in ranks abreast before the station.

'Must be expecting somebody else to come in tonight!

It was no time for talking. Jack had been watching the traffic and driving carefully, a little laggingly. Now he turned off to Roosevelt Road, and then after a block north again on Wabash Avenue. They were getting into the Loop. The Elevated trains bellowed over their heads. The street seemed dark as though in a thunderstorm.

A large white restaurant with open front of windows attracted them.

'Let's eat right here and now. Then we can hunt a hotel afterwards. If we don't, time we get settled and all, we'll be starved.'

'Yes, let's,' Grace agreed.

'I don't think I'd better leave the car parked here,' he yelled. A train was clattering past over their heads. 'I'll just stick it in a garage and then come back and eat. There's one I know over here a block or so. We can carry our bags to the hotel.'

'Then will I wait here?'

'You don't mind? It'll save you the walk. I'll take you in the restaurant and get a table.'

'No. I can get a table for us,' said Grace, 'and give an order. It will be all ready when you come back.'

'Atta girl. Order fried oysters for me.' He watched her go into the restaurant; a white-dressed woman meeting her at the door led her back to a table. Then he drove on.

A leisurely huge touring car drew up alongside of him. Four large men. They were squeezing him to the curb.

'Pull in, pull in to the curb,' they yelled. Before he knew what he was doing he had stopped, and they were out and upon him, with pistols and a sawed-off shotgun. He had not noticed the guns before. They were all yelling at once. He was out of his car.

'What's this – '

'Put 'em up! Put up those mits! You son of a – Frisk him, Jake. You're coming with us. Never mind. Come on. We'll take care of the car all right. You get in here.'

'But what's – what's the matter – ?'

'Shut up. Come on, get in here,' growled a fat-necked one towering over him. 'You'll know what it is all right, you sucker.'

He struck Jack on the back of the neck with the edge of his hand as Jack stooped to enter their car.

'Are you police?' Jack asked, finding himself on the seat.

They laughed, insistently.

'Police wouldn't be after you, now, would they?'

'Certainly not!'

'Oh, no!'

The car winged forward.

II

He did not know in what direction he was being taken. As soon as they had knocked him into the car it took a turn, then another; perhaps more turns. He had to keep reminding himself that they were police officers. That became clear in the way the big touring car shouldered traffic aside, and once disregarded the upheld hand of a traffic cop, which thereupon waved them forward.

Nobody said anything. The driver was a big lean man of thirty-five in a yellow raincoat, with yellow hair and felt hat. The fat-necked one sat beside him, a sawed-off shotgun between his knees. In a rack at the back of the front seat stood another sawed-off shotgun. On each side of Jack in the rear seat the other two dicks lounged at ease: on his right, a middle-aged hard, brown-faced tall man with grey in his temples. On the left another of the fat-necked variety, with red jaws and a black derby hat. They did not appear to have their hands on pistols.

'Well, sonny,' remarked the stout one on his left. 'Got you good.'

'Yeh,' said Jack bitterly. 'You got the wrong man. I just got into town a minute or two when you came along. I live in Metropole, Michigan.'

The two in front laughed.

'You should have stayed there.' They chanted in chorus.

'You can call up my people there. I just left today at noon. Ask them all about me.'

'Sure we can,' said the front fat neck, half turning around. 'But we don't have to. We got all the dope on *you* all right. You're in for the works, you are.'

'I want to know what you're arresting me for.'

'They'll tell you at the Bureau. You'll know then all right, my boy,' said the quiet-voiced middle-aged man on his right.

The others did not bother to laugh. Jack's heart sank.

'But I'm innocent. You can't get anything on me. Won't you let me go back to the restaurant and tell my wife? She doesn't know where I am.'

'Not just now,' muttered the man at the wheel.

The lights were glaring, dazzling. The uproar of the city echoed hollowly among the skyscrapers. It was not a busy hour, between afternoon and evening. An occasional roar of the Elevated died away in a bellow like a shout down a rainbarrel. Garish red and gilt of storefronts, and black crowding people, twinkle of electric lights, signs. And he did not recognize a single place.

'Come back and phone my people from the restaurant,' Jack implored the grey-templed one, who seemed to possess sympathy, somewhere. 'I – I just got married today, and I'm on my honeymoon.' He believed it now he had said it.

'Ha!' The man at the wheel shot out a curt laugh and swung the car into an alley. 'Some honeymoon!'

'Some honeymoon you're going to have, kid,' the first fat neck repeated, half turning.

'Come on. I'm innocent, I tell you. I'm innocent. I didn't do a thing. Come back to the restaurant.'

The alley was dark, in spite of an occasional lighted doorway. The long car wallowed sinuously through it.

The two on either side of him did not say a word.

At the end of a hundred yards they drew up in a courtyard. Leisurely and in careful order they got out of the car. Jack hesitated, wildly, but remembered the blow on the back of his neck. The tall gray man strode ahead. Jack felt small between the two stout ones. The long yellow raincoat stayed in the car.

They ascended some stone steps and came into an oak-panelled large room. A uniformed man sat at a desk at the other end.

'What you got there, boys?'

'The big shot,' joked one.

'Car,' returned the other.

'So ye was elopin' with somebody else's car, eh? But you took the wrong street.'

'I was not!' Jack shouted indignantly. 'That's my own car I bought with my own money. I got it – '

The other winked.

'All right, call the people I bought it from if you want to. Call them right here and get it straight. I paid for it – '

'Keep quiet,' said the gray man. 'They gave us the tip on how you paid.'

Jack was silent. The car people had learned that he had left town, and did not know that he intended to pay them at the head office. His pay for the last week was held back through some red tape, and it would have run him close to pay it at once. He had given instructions at home that it was to be sent to him in Chicago, and it had been promised for the day after tomorrow. That would make him a few days late, but the agency should worry, he had thought. They couldn't afford to take back cars from everybody who was a day or two late with their payments, surely.

What was the use of telling this to these beefy-faced functionaries? They had heard many stories.

'Well, the lousy – Of all the – I'll take the car right back to them and get my money. If they couldn't trust me what did they want to sell me the car for? They wanted to sell the thing as bad as I – '

'Cut the noise. We got the dope on your case. Come on.'

Data had been recorded in a ledger, and a card was made out. This colloquy was outside the requirements. Jack stood there, trying to think.

The beefy neck made a move, his face suddenly contorted. Jack jerked his own arm away.

Two hands clenched on each of his arms. He was lifted and hurled forward, thrust with force enough to drive his feet through the floor.

'Be good, you, or you'll talk pretty.'

Through a dark hall which he saw not so plainly as visions of Third Degree, they passed, then down some steps. A door was opened, and he was shoved in. There was a cement floor, a light in the ceiling.

'Heh, Murphy! Here's another one.'

They stayed long enough for the huge young Irishman to look up and receipt his new charge, and were gone. Jack breathed with relief. The Irishman looked like a good fellow, with his olive face and black eyes.

The air stank. There were continual shouts from somewhere beyond the corridor, at the back of this place. The Irishman let out a roar and dashed back, his shirt sleeves swinging.

'Holy Mother!' he bellowed. 'And what in blazes now? What's the matter with you murderin' sons of bitches back there now? I'll come in there and knock your heads together, I will.'

Sporadic yells punctuated the silence.

'Bring you a drink I will not. Do you think this is a hotel?'

'Hey, Murphy! These niggers is trying to – '

'WILL YOU SHUT YOUR BALLY NOISE!' bellowed Murphy in tones to spring the rafters. In the stillness he came back to where Jack was standing. His face was beaming and sweating, and he mopped it with a handkerchief. He was deeply enjoying himself. He wore a dark vest, opened, dark trousers, and a light-coloured shirt turned in at the neck

'Say,' remarked Jack offhandedly. 'Could you let me use your phone? They've got me in here by mistake, and I want to call the people I bought the car from. And I want to call my wife.'

Murphy shook his head as he mopped it, suddenly looking grave and suspicious. He did not reply to the renewed shouts from the cells.

'Give me your watch and your money. Keep the change.' Jack handed them over without thinking.

'Oh, come, Mr Murphy. I just got married today, and my wife will be worrying what's become of me.'

Murphy looked at him. He had sized up many a young fellow before. 'Naw. Keep your change, I said. You might want to buy coffee or cigarettes.' He went and sat down in a senator arm chair behind a counter.

Jack approached him. Murphy looked up.

'Now if you behave yourself I'll leave you out here and not put you in the cell until a couple more of ye comes. So make yourself to home, but don't ye think I'm going to do any phoning for you. You should have chose a better night to get married on.'

Left standing there, suddenly at pause after the action and plunging emotions of the last half hour, Jack Dolson looked about him, hardly seeing anything. He was gripped in nausea. He was sick as he never had been since he had been a small boy. He did not know he felt hopeless or helpless. He wasn't thinking. The nausea rising made him almost indifferent. It was as though he had died; no, not dead; the ignition was not turned off, he had been thrown out of gear. He did not know nor much care what was going to happen. A great wall had toppled upon his hopes and happiness. How could he have believed that he was meant to be married and go on a honeymoon like fortunate people? It seemed that all his life had led up to this in an inevitable way. He could have slumped to the floor without knowing it. Was he standing? He must stand up and look them in the eye and tell them what liars they were.

'Say,' remarked Jack offhandedly, as though he had not spoken before. He told himself the rest. Murphy did not look up. He had to say it aloud. 'Could you let me use your phone? They've got me in here by mistake and I want to let the people I bought the car from know. And I want to call my wife.'

There were no chairs in the place. There was a sort of counter, behind which stood Murphy's chair, with a ledger open upon it. He could sit on the three cement steps inside the door, but the detectives would trample him when they came again, or send the next prisoner plunging down upon his neck. Only the bare cement floor, a dull mahogany colour. The windows were barred, small, and higher than his head. One large electric light bulb blinked down from the ceiling, through a wire cage. It was dazzling when you looked up at it, but upon the room it cast the dull exhalation of a cloudy day, a dreary hazy day of imminent autumn storm. He thought of the June night outside, away from this, the now-dewy country through which he had driven.

The air was choking him.

He was not thinking of Grace. She was just an ache in his heart. Now he began to wonder. What had she done when he did not return? She knew no one he knew to come and bail him out. She wouldn't guess that he had been taken in by the cops. Perhaps she would go to the police, but they would tell her nothing, not until they had finished with him, anyway. He did not know whether she had relatives or friends in the city. If she had perhaps she could find them before the night was over. He pictured her searching through the city hopeless of finding them or her bridegroom. Perhaps being held up in the dark court of some apartment house. She was too good for this cursed world, that was all. He should have known that. Nothing so beautiful as the feeling between them could live. The hideous city, impending, raucously and indifferently intimidating, returned upon him implacable, devouring enemy, intent upon crushing these two. First it would separate them. He would never see Grace again. Without reasoning, he was sure of that. There was nothing to drive that horror out of his mind.

Murphy reappeared, and Jack returned to the commonplace world with his own words, spoken automatically:

'Say, can't you have a heart, Murphy?'

'No I can't have a heart then! What do you think the city pays me for, to get you bozos out when you git in?'

'But there's the phone right there – '

'Here, you come with me.'

He pushed Jack ahead of him down the wide bull-pen, while he drew a key from his pocket. They were passing cells, the doors spaced with white metal gratings, the walls gray. There were no lights in the cells, only the couple of caged ones in the ceiling outside. Back in the gloom of the cells high and low lurked faces, swarthy or pale, ghostlike blotches or grinning masks, peering between the bars. An upstanding fair-haired youth stood in the shadows at one door. A deep voice came out.

'Heh, Murphy, business ain't so much tonight, what's the matter?' His smiling eyes glanced at Jack.

'Niver mind, Red, the night's yet young.' Murphy inadvertently lowered his voice, and unlocked the cell next to Red. The door creaked as he swung it back and looked around for Jack. He seemed to take care not to touch Jack. Then the door clanged shut.

Three men were in the cell before him. They looked at him with indifference for greeting.

The cell was about ten feet long, grimy brick walls to the back. These partition walls were not quite so high as the ceiling, by about four inches. The floor was sticky, hard, dark, and smooth. The furniture consisted of a toilet stool at the back, and a bench of plank along the left side, which made the width, about six feet, seem even less than it was. One of the men was stretched out on this bench, a cap over his face. Another was walking up and down, sedately and slackly, as though carrying a cane. The third was standing idly with his shoulder against the side wall of the cell, one foot crossed over the other.

'Got a cigarette, kid?' asked the latter. He was a man between twenty and forty, with a round swarthy face and a heavy black beard of two-days' growth. His blue clothes were dandruff-strewn. He was wearing no collar or tie. He knew better than to leave them on here. He would want them along with his watch and chain, when he went out. He might have been anything from pushcart man to big-time racketeer. In either case the clothes might have been bought secondhand for the night.

Jack extended to him a cigarette half-drawn from the package.

The man walking passed the other two and stopped facing the door, without speaking. He was middle-sized, well-built, a very fair large-featured longheaded man of about thirty, wearing a soft gray felt hat. When he faced Jack it was plain that his eyes were light gray or blue, floating below white eyebrows, and he did not seem to be looking at anybody or anything. Jack offered him a cigarette too, and put the package in his pocket.

'God, I'm dying for a smoke,' said the plump Secondhand.

The one on the bench stirred and sat up. He was a boy of twenty, swarthy, black-eyed, with a shock of black hair over which he at once pulled the cap, and stood up, stretching himself with mild oaths of boredom.

'Yeah? So'm I. Got a match, Whitey?'

The ash-blonde man waved his cigarette at him. 'Give you the butt.'

Jack pulled out the package again.

'Hell, somebody's come in with cigarettes in the next cell,' said a voice beyond the wall.

The youth puffed complacently, his yellow-swarthy long horse-like cheeks and low wrinkled brow lit up, sooty, by the match.

'What they get you on?'

'They thought I was stealing my own car,' returned Jack.

Secondhand and Whitey were watching him. Sooty bristled up, sticking out his jaw.

'So you don't want to talk to us guys, eh? What ya keeping on ice, huh? Too ritzy for us to associate with, eh? Hell wit' ye.' He turned away to the bench.

'Take it how you like,' remarked Jack equably. 'What did they get you for?'

Sooty was silent. Whitey smiled faintly. 'Good cigarette,' he murmured in a mild, dry voice.

'He's maybe operator in the Daylight Gang, you don't know,' said Secondhand. 'You better treat him with respect, or he'll put you on the spot.'

The youth laughed with a sinister incredulous hee-hee, but furtively eying Jack, who remained indifferent. He became sulky, and said no more.

Jack turned to Whitey.

'Won't they let you use the 'phone here? How do they expect you to get out at all?'

Whitey smiled. 'Will they let you telephone? I guess not. I tried to do so when I came in.' He spoke as though regretfully responsible for this poor management in the hostelry. 'They don't care whether anybody knows you're here or not. They just keep you till you go up.'

'Don't they let you have a lawyer?' It sounded like a fool question.

'If you can get somebody working outside, and get bonded, and get a lawyer, all right. If not, they got you here, and they do their best to get something on you. Then they take you before the judge, and he pronounces sentence. No hurry, even if the jail does get crowded. *Festina lente*, as my old professor used to say, is the motto of the law.'

'You been to college, Whitey?' asked Secondhand. 'Heh?'

A sort of paralysis, then a trembling, seeming to attack Whitey's lips and jaw before he had begun to speak, but when he spoke there was no stammer, his voice came quietly and evenly, the words running smoothly together. It might have been a relic of fright, inhibition, or perhaps dope.

'What did they get you for?'

'They framed me in a store. When they searched me, I didn't have a thing.'

'What's it mean, that Greek you said?' asked Jack.

'Make haste slowly.'

'Yeh,' snorted Sooty. 'That's what I was doing, making slow time with a truck, and a motorcycle mug comes along. He wouldn't have got hep at all only I was going nice and slow.'

The fattish Secondhand smiled cynically. 'You picked the wrong boss, that's all, bimbo. They wouldn't even arrested you.'

'Hell, you're a wise guy, ain't yuh? That's why you're here. My boss has got more jack than you ever see, anyway.'

Secondhand said nothing. Whitey said nothing.

'Out in the South Side?' asked Jack Dolson.

'Yeah, Grand Boulevard.' Somebody snorted.

'That's where I nearly got pinched.'

'Yeah, you nearly did,' sneered Sooty.

Jack was speaking to Whitey. 'I was driving in to town from Michigan, and I made a left-hand turn.'

'Gave you a ticket for that?'

'No, they thought they liked the look of my car, so they nabbed it.'

The others were not curious of details; they shut their mouths and went on smoking. At length Sooty spoke, with something like admiration in his tones.

'Taking it on the lam with the bus, was you?'

'They thought I was. I just bought it a month ago, and the people I bought it from thought I was skipping out without paying.'

'Who squealed on you?' asked Sooty.

It was not such a strange question; but Jack did not know these birds. Yet, he should. In his own town he had known fellows who might have come here, without anybody thinking twice of it, except with amusement. Yet he would not have them or anyone else know that he had been here. It was all somehow portentous and awful. Like a nightmare with worse possibilities at the end of it. Was that because his mind had been running on one track for weeks? Perhaps his honeymoon and his trip with Grace, his arrest and this were all a dream. His aunt would call him, and he would have another day of work before him, with Grace in the evening....

But Grace was not a dream.

He was staring at the darkened cement floor.

Like the others. The caged electric bulb in the ceiling cast a hard light, hard shadows of bars, upon them. Whitey seemed to be leaning his mind upon some fancy, musing a little enjoyably, his gray lips ready to smile with the smile like a deaf person's with which he always began to speak or listen. Long deep wrinkles like white, healed scars furrowed his cheeks in the middle. His face was shallowly pink as though he had shaved recently. Beneath was a prison grayness, lividness. He was a type of convict, with trembling gentle speech, inoffensive air. Hair short below the light felt hat. Perhaps he had not been out long, and would have to go back for another stretch. What was behind those shallow gray-slate, rainpool eyes? That large, well-pointed, a little drooping mouth closed over what?

'Not so much like Harvard, eh?' asked Jack.

Whitey stirred, glancing up. Then he smiled very faintly.

'What rights you got to be hoggin' this bench for all the time?'

Secondhand enquired of Sooty. 'Don't you think nobody else wants to sit down?'

'Git up yourself if you want somebody to sit down.'

'Go sit on the can,' adjured the other. They might have been older and younger brother.

Whitey turned from the door and went to sit on the toilet seat. Jack, suddenly aware of stiffening legs, squeezed on the bench between Secondhand and the feet of Sooty. Both stank.

'Say, Hick, how long you expecting to stay here?' demanded the latter, resting his head on the palms of his hands. 'I been here a week already.'

'Then I'll be here two weeks.'

'Shit,' remarked the other, too indolent to badger such a green punk.

There was silence in the cell, of which they were not conscious, because the air was never quiet. From the cell at each side came jokes, shouts, curses, and laughter. Every little while Murphy came back to bellow at the lot of them.

It was night. The high windows opposite the cells and the ceiling lights became dark, with a glow at the top. If you looked at them long enough, there was a confused radiance penetrating them from the world of Chicago beyond, the wilderness of streets, dirty winds, noise, cars, elevated trains, automobiles, the forests of citizens on the streets and in the shows and joints – celebrants, gun-men, clerks, flappers, hoofers, gangsters, bootleggers, streetwalkers, in all the little nations of every district.

New prisoners were coming in, arrests were being made all over the city. The Force was earning its bread and butter. In ones and twos and Black Maria loads, they were coming. They straggled about the pen, waiting for Murphy to put them into the cells. Old and young, clean and dirty, ragged and spruce. They strayed past the cell doors, leaned against the walls.

Four negroes were briskly stepping it up and down, talking gayly. Three were as gayly dressed.

'Ah wanted to gamble with white folks, but they wouldn't let me take my own bones,' one said, laughing.

Prisoners came from the backs of cells to look out and look on and say a word on the quiet. Red was talking to a child of eighteen with smooth soft cheeks, short stature, thereafter known as Curly.

'What you in for, Bud?'

This kid gulped.

'Oh, God, I been arrested so many times, I don't know what it is now. They won't let me alone. I was just walking up Van Buren Street, by myself, not thinking of anything, when two bulls come along and took me in.'

'Didn't you do nothing?' asked Jack from the next cell.

'Not that I know. They arrest me wherever I go.'

The boy turned and strolled away. There were tear marks down his grimy face.

A hollow-eyed, sharp-nosed man, in black, stooping from the waist, walked past, his hands held behind his back, smoking a cigarette. His eyes were large, luminous, but sharp.

'Got a cigarette, Sport?' called Sooty.

The gaunt man paid no attention. The question was repeated when he passed the cell again. He shook his head without looking up, immensely thoughtful.

'Coke sniffer. Lost his happy dust, that's what's eating him.' Wisely, Secondhand went and sat down on the bench.

Whitey, who had been walking three steps up and three back, head almost erect, as though looking at the horizon, started, and stopped to lean against the wall and look out between the heads of Jack and Sooty.

A little short fellow with a brown-red face and spectacles was strolling about the bullpen, regarding everything with whimsical keenness. He walked with his coat half off, his fists sticking out of the sleeves and locked together behind. His shirt showed at the shoulders and upper arms. A lock of grizzled hair stuck out beneath the side of the cap.

'Going to fight somebody?' called Jack, with misgiving as he spoke.

You might as well get into the spirit of the thing. Here were so many different kinds of fellows. Yet, though it was all right to ask what they were in for, personal remarks were few. They might get sore, and lay for you. But the stocky little man took it in the right way. He peered into the cell and called:

'Well, anyways, they got you a little bit tighter than they got me. I ain't quite behind the bars yet.'

'You'll get there.'

'Don't worry,' came the deep tones of Red in the next cell.

'I'm going to get the ones that got me here,' Shorty remarked. 'Don't you ferget it, when I'm out of here, I get them.'

He looked like a respectable villager, a vegetable gardener, paper-hanger, or something of the sort.

'They'll learn better than to put a fellow in when he's done nothing.'

Thoughtfully the short man felt in his pocket, and pulled out a single cigarette. He walked on when he saw the looks the others cast at it. In a moment he passed the cell as though he had forgotten at which one he had stopped. The short fingers of the broad hand which held the coat sleeve from dropping twitched the ashes from the smoke. The stocky little man peered about him, quite at home, as he strolled.

The others passed and repassed, new ones who had stayed in the front part where Murphy's desk was, and just now discovered that they were allowed to walk back past the cell entrances, peering in with curiosity, fright, enjoyment, recognition. Some were pacing up and down as though they did not know where they were or what they were doing. It was only by a miracle that they remembered the ends of the room, and did not bump into the walls.

Mostly indifferent, they looked at one another only inadvertently. Occasionally there was a group of two or three, exchanging two or three words as they strolled, looking ahead. Now and then an old drunk, fifty or seventy with dark withered skin, deeply bitten with wrinkles, sagging eyes folded beneath young black eyebrows, red-veined cheeks, sidled along. Now and then a brisk dapper man, slickly groomed, with expansive stride. Here was a taxi driver in uniform, the coloured metal band of his cap gleaming. Here was a down-and-outer with greasy buttonless coat, walking on the cuffs of his trousers.

Soon Murphy and a patrolman came back in the bull-pen, and began sorting the contents of the cells. Jack Dolson's cell was turned out, and he and Sooty and Whitey and Secondhand were placed in the next one, to give a cell for the negroes.

Red laughed.

'Welcome to our city. You've been here almost as long as I have, ain't you, Whitey? And I came in Monday.'

'I'm getting tired of it,' said Whitey mildly.

'Great life. They don't give you meals, you can't sleep.'

Red was a fine, upstanding fellow, twenty-two, with a fair skin and a slight glint of golden beard for his three days. His eyes were blue-gray, with flashes of no-colour when he laughed. He was at home as though he had seen all these people before. Yet there was in his laughing acceptance something of the condescension of the oldtimer for the tenderfoot. He had been in this cell longer than anyone else. He stood with head erect beside the door and the light from the ceiling fell through the wire cage and between the iron bars upon his clean-cut features while he talked and laughed.

'Heh, Murphy, don't put any more in here. We got enough. We're going to be crowded if you don't watch out.'

'Aw – you need comp'ny, Red.'

'Well, introduce us, anyway.'

'Ye need none. All of the one kind, yez are.'

Two old leatherneck tramps with gnarled faces and large red noses and a dapper, chubby-faced youth sat on the bench. The newcomers were Jack's cellful and the taxi driver and the coke sniffer, and Curly, the youth who had been tearful over his many arrests.

'Got you with the other fellow, eh?' Red asked the taxi driver. 'Did they have the goods on you?'

Unshaven, tall, of dignified bearing and careful enunciation, the taxi driver looked at him in surprise.

'They've got nothing on me. The other fellow had the stuff, and I happened to be driving him.' The taxi driver shrugged and fished two single bent cigarettes from his pocket and offering one to Red, began to smoke the other, ignoring the others in the cell.

'What was he taking?' asked Whitey.

'Armful of ladies' dresses and coats. I never knew he had them. We was stopped and arguing when the dicks nabbed us. I had rung his fare up, because he wanted to go to Lawrence in the first place. Now he wanted me to take him on to Wilson, so he could get an express to the South Side. But he didn't want me to pull the flag again.'

'Cheap skate, eh? He in the next cell? Fellow in light gray suit?'

'I don't know where he is,' said the taxi driver with some bitterness. 'While we were talking there this carful of dicks comes along with automatic pistols and sawed-off shotguns. I hardly seen them till they gave a yell right on top of us. The fellow was out of the cab, and picking the coats in his arms. Of course they hollered and carried on and wanted to beat him up right there.'

Sooty chuckled amiably. He and the others were listening to the taxi driver's tale.

'Didn't want to beat you up, eh Tunney? They'd had every yellow-jacket on the street on them, eh?'

'What squad was it picked you up? The Paige or the Cadillac?'

'I came in the Paige,' put in Jack. 'It was in the Loop they got me.'

'The Cadillac, but they let me drive my own cab to the station. They took the other fellow in the Cadillac. One of the dicks sat in the back of my cab while we drove along behind, with a gun at my ear. He gave my meter a tap with his knuckles and it stopped. Then when we got to the station he gives it another tap and it started ticking again.'

'That's a dick all over.' Red smiled. 'Show-off.'

'Yeh, he says, "Pull your bill, kid." And when I handed it to him he says, "Charge it." ' The driver joined the general laughter.

'I got the slip yet. It will match the last one printed on my roll in the meter. They don't take that out of my week's pay.'

There was a cackle from the end of the cell from the sallow Coke Sniffer. He was sitting on the stool, grunting a little, his thin form writhing a little, his trousers slid toward his knees.

'Reminds me of a taxi driver I knew myself once,' he remarked, with the smile reserved for telling tales to children. 'He got a cab with a fast meter, and he finally got it so fast it would register fifty cents before he got started. Somebody complained and got him pinched. ... Ugh!'

The others were paying no attention. Curly laughed and told Red:

'Taxis too rich for my blood, these times. They'd save my soles too.'

The taxi driver, however, replied to the Snowbird acrimoniously. 'I guess you forgot. The first thing a cab meter registers is thirty-five cents. Then it jumps to forty-five, and fifty-five, if you travel far enough.'

'You don't have to go the length of Halsted Street either,' said the dapper little fellow on the bench, Bert Tremaine.

The Snowbird shrugged absently, his eyes like pin-points. The others looked curiously at the candid taxi driver, tall, loud-voiced, with a small yellow moustache, the smears of black city dust and the flat-topped cap askew. None of them wanted to have the Snowbird against them, if he should get the leaps, and run amuck before the bulls could fish him out of the cell.

'So you didn't know the fellow had these coats,' said Jack Dolson.

'Never saw him before,' declared the taxi driver. 'Picked him up at the corner of Lawrence and Western, and he had me drive to a little apartment building on Kedzie. Tells me he's had trouble with his wife, and she may try to keep him from getting out with his things. I expected to wait quite a while, but in a minute he's in the cab, slams the door, yelling to give her the gun. I never looked around, and I didn't lose no time getting into high.'

Red chuckled.

'You must have been new to those guys.'

The others became indifferent. Sooty frankly sneered at such greenness. They yawned or twitched while they revolved the tale or rejected it silently as a bunch of lies. But they were taking one another at face value, ready to believe the innocence of anyone else, as they were to tell their own tales. They were brothers here, anyway, on equal footing. Their money and valuables had been taken from them, and they had nothing to fear or hope. They were all in this sweatbox together, and they hated everyone who had had anything to do with their getting there.

Curly groaned.

'Don't I know 'em? They don't frame me any more.' He had an air of swaggering ease, now that he had begun to adjust himself to familiar surroundings. His inquisitive turned-up nose and roving eyes, mischievous mouth, made him seem a child, and he was little more. He wore a dark blue shirt with the collar unbuttoned, and a limp old hat. He might have forgotten that he had wept on his arrest.

In different clothes he might have seemed of the type of Bert Tremaine, the short sporty youth in black pin-striped suit, with chubby face and round eyes. This one was more solid and settled – more unsettled here – a smart salesman of some sort, making fifty a week at twenty-four, and spending it with the expectation of getting a hundred a week at thirty. Pensively with an expression of habitual good-nature that scarcely needs words to demonstrate inherent good-will, he sat there. He was a good mixer, good salesman, the little fellow.

'Got a cigarette?' Sooty asked him.

Bert Tremaine pulled out a yellow paper package, and took one himself. Seeing Whitey's eyes hungrily upon it, he extended it to him. As they were lighting up Secondhand spoke:

'You ain't got one for me?'

'Or me?' It was the rusty-wheel voice of the Snowbird, holding the toilet seat, with his clothes restored to order.

Bert handed the package around to everyone then.

'They won't last long here anyhow,' laughed Red. 'You can buy more in the morning if you've got any change on you.'

'I won't care about buying cigarettes in the morning,' said Bert. 'All I'll ask is to get out.'

'Get out, hell,' laughed Curly. 'We're here for a while.'

'But don't they have to take you before a magistrate or give you some sort of trial?'

'There's a lot of things they're supposed to do, but it doesn't make much difference,' murmured Whitey.

'They can be compelled to give you up, or give you a trial. Either one or the other.'

'Say, is that right?' Sooty and Secondhand were excited. Whitey smiled.

'Sure, that's what is called *Habeus Corpus*,' explained Bert.

'But a writ of *Habeus Corpus* has to be served, same as a warrant,' interposed Whitey. 'And as long as they can keep your friends from knowing where you are, there's nothing can be done.'

'Yeh, they can bulldoze most of them, anyway,' put in Red cynically. 'Most people's scairt to say anything to the police, the dirty lousy kikes and hams. They run in a lot of people that don't do nothing, just to earn their pay, and they let anybody off that's got the jack. That's them.'

There was silence in the cell a minute. They knew that if one began they all would shout out their hatred of the police, abhorrence of their cruelty, loathing of their stupidity. Then the thick-armed dicks would be upon them. God knew what new and infinitely more foolish forms of cruelty they had at their command. Red broke the spell he had made.

'Heh, Murphy,' he yelled. 'We're telling off the police in here. We think you're a lot of lousy scabs that couldn't make a living as second-storey men because you'd have to go easy on your bellies. ... '

'Scabs, is it?' yelled Murphy in tones of jovial infuriation. 'Ye'd better shut up or I'll come back there and I'll knock your heads together, yuh – '

Red turned his face from the bars with a smile.

'You can have lots of fun with him. The other guy, that comes on for daytime, he's a regular crab. Just as soon hit you a clout on the ear with the bracelets as not. You don't have to say a word.'

'Kikes and hams!' shrilled Curly. There was no reply. 'That's the police.' Some of the fellows still wandering about the outer pen grinned sardonically, thinking he had gone off his head.

Sooty was elbowing his way to the bench, alongside Bert Tremaine. Once let him get there, nothing would dislodge him. He wasn't going to have the bones of his legs driven to his shoulders.

The Snowbird turned to Bert.

'What did they tie on you?'

The spruce youth shoved his pearl-gray hat back on his head and began his story.

'It was just an accident they got me.'

There was unanimous silent corroboration. The undoing of all had been the same.

'Accidents better not happen,' laughed somebody.

Bert hesitated a little. 'I mean, I didn't have anything to do with it. Fellow in the next apartment was throwing a party. We had known him quite a while and we used to go in once in a while to see him and his wife. Not think anything of it – to go in and play a few hands of bridge and –

'And fuss around!' simpered Sooty.

'After a while one fellow started a row and claimed somebody had stolen his watch and money. I guess he was stewed anyway. He came late and he'd been drinking before he came. He wanted to clean up on the whole place. Then he thought it was the fellow and his wife who were giving the party that had robbed him, and there was a regular ruction. Don't suppose they'd invited him. We were trying to keep them apart, and first thing, the wagon came. Neighbours must have sent for it, I guess. So here I am. I don't know where they took the other fellows.'

'Did they bring your wife too and the women?'

'No. Only the wife of the fellow that was giving the party, I'll tell 'em they had a time bringing her.'

'Huh. What kind of broad was she? Think she copped the goods?'

'Oh, no, it was just that fellow crazy-drunk. What makes me so mad is being right there around the corner from my own apartment. In ten seconds we could have been away.'

'Lucky they didn't take her too, your wife,' sighed Jack Dolson.

'I don't know what the charge will be.'

'Assault and pocket-picking,' muttered the taxi driver. 'They'll have me for larceny.'

Bert laughed.

'Sure they will,' said the taxi man with cold ferocity. 'I was driving the cab with the fellow in it. Ain't that larceny? If it ain't, the dicks'll beat you up till you tell 'em why it ain't. Sure, I'll get a stretch.'

'POLICE PROTECT JURORS; JUDGE LAUDS VERDICT,' laughed Red.

Bert's expression became sober. 'Maybe it ain't the same when you've got a drag. My wife's folks have a lot of jack.'

'That might make a difference when it comes to trial,' remarked Red with politeness.

There was a shout outside, and Murphy stuck his head between the light and the bars of the door.

'Corcoran! Corcoran here?'

Whitey sifted quietly forward through the herd.

'That's me.'

'Come on out here.' The keys jingled. The door clanged. 'Callin' for ye, somebody is,' he added, closing the door on the toes of Red and the taxi man.

'Didn't think Whitey had any people,' said Red. 'He's been here since yesterday morning. There's no telling.'

Red was still standing at the door, leaning with his back to the wall at times, always erect, as he had been for uncounted hours. The taxi man opposite him leaned his shoulder against the front wall, occasionally turned toward the rear of the cell, then back to the light and the Bull Pen. Sooty had managed to crawl behind the others on the bench and had gone to sleep. Secondhand sat on the edge in front of him, with Bert beside him. The Snowbird still sat in his meagre thin black clothes like an old-fashioned preacher, on the stool at the rear of the cell. It was not a good seat for one of his build, but if he got up he'd have to stand all night. Curly sat at the back of the cell, having the whole width of the bench at Sooty's feet. Jack Dolson was standing at the wall two feet from Red. The two old horse-collars in their thick-grimed pants and vests, squatted along the wall beside him, big knees springing the patches.

They wanted to sleep. So did everyone. But once in a while something would occur to one of them, and a conversation would start, and the others would blink and listen and grunt in their half-slumber.

In a little while Whitey was escorted back and locked in again.

'Who was it?' asked the Coke eagerly.

There was the old convulsive motion of Whitey's lips and cheeks before his calm voice emerged.

'My girl.'

Perhaps it was astonishment which kept everyone from speaking.

'What did she give you?' asked Secondhand. 'Whitey?'

'A buck.'

Again, nobody said anything, though they were calculating the amount of coffee and cigarettes Whitey could buy with his dollar. If he were getting out in the morning, he'd be so glad he'd spend it all. If he stayed longer he'd have to spend it.

'She's going to try to get me out by tomorrow night.'

'I'd give anybody a grand that'd give me a buck,' laughed Red.

The keys jingled. Murphy was at the door again, this time with a hand on the arm of the little guy wearing the overcoat around his back and elbows.

'God, Murphy, full house here,' Red expostulated. 'There's ten, eleven now.'

Murphy rammed the little fellow in. 'Thin wan more won't hurt.'

The two old tramps started to rise as the fellow landed on their knees.

'Don't move, boys, I'll find a place, or my name ain't Enos Standen.'

'Better make it sitting, Enos,' advised Curly.

'Well, that's something I never knew,' said the taxi man. 'That you could put twelve men in one cell.'

'Time we staged a crush-out,' said Curly.

'DETECTIVES DODGE AX BY BIG ROUND-UP OF SUSPECTS,' said Bert Tremaine, speaking in headlines.

Whitey managed to squeeze into a place on the bench. Jack faced him.

'By tonight, you mean. It must be nearly morning now.' Nobody paid any attention. Yet Grace existed. Time existed, while they waited, they waited, they waited. They became everything, as the slow months dragged, as the years impended and fell with muffled force, while heads became gray, faces twitched, and tongues stumbled. While they waited. While they waited. They waited, becoming strange beings.

A dim history of Whitey and all convicts stood in Whitey's quiet ashen face with its lashless eyes that never flickered, watercoloured eyes that seemed intent upon nothingness – lipless mouth, gray shaven skin of the broad face, yellow hair, smoke-blackened felt hat.

Jack was falling into a ghastly waking sleep where he stood. Where had he been that morning? On the road, at home, in Chicago? Grace was somewhere, sick with worrying, searching, walking a room, telephoning friends, the police, home. It would give their married life a black eye all right. Or she was prostrated with grief and bewilderment; the police were taking her and the car to the station. They would hide her and the car. She tried to escape and they shot her. They thought he had stolen the car; he would get five years.

He shook himself roughly against the wall of the cell, his shoulder scraping. Nonsense. It would all come to nothing. Make the most of the strange present. It was more than strange that men could put other men into such a place, shutting them from the sight of the stars and the feel of winds, and furthermore superinduce its horrors, making them actual and believable. To breathe was to take within himself something foul, he felt. No room to turn without touching another body. The ones on the bench were the lucky ones. There was Red beside the door, as he had been and would be for hours. What was the secret behind those bright eyes burning as though their sight penetrated these walls and saw bright sky and bright grass? That face alight with inextinguishable vitality and that deep young voice giving back jovial laughter to the weird sneer of Fate?

Curly stretched himself where he sat, and stood up on the bench, not regarding the slumbering Sooty. He could see over the wall into the next cell, by dint of shoving his small head into the space between the top and the ceiling.

'Holy gee,' he remarked. 'Regular negro convention in there. All niggers,' he went on meditatively, his voice sounding as though it was sinking to the bottom of a well. 'All asleep, too.'

'We ain' asleep,' a Southern voice drawled. 'You needn't think we's all gone to sleep just because we doesn't make so much noise as you folks over theah.'

'What'd he say?' the taxi man asked.

'Said go to hell, they ain't asleep.'

'Ah didn't say nothing of the sort,' the drawl continued conversationally. 'Ah said...'

'Well, go to sleep now, then,' adjured Red, and laughed.

There were grumblings from the next cell and muttered groans as the dark fellows stretched and changed positions. Sooty muttered and tried to turn on his side, whereat the ones sitting on the bench before him quelled him. Curly turned from his inspection of the neighbour cell, spitting farewell. He seemed to be enlivened by the sight of the negroes, and the fact that he addressed Red was the only sign that he might have remembered his tears at his arrest.

'I remember the first time I was arrested. I was just a kid. I was just getting home for Christmas. You know how it is the first time you've been away from home, and then you go back like that. ... I was dragged up in Cleveland, and I took the notion to go out west. I bummed my way out as far as Omaha, and got a job, and now I was coming back for the Christmas holiday. Maybe I would stay at home all winter. I didn't care much what I did. But I had my job to go back to. I wasn't coming home by side-door pullman either, if I did go out that way. I was having the real thing. Gee I felt swell about it. I had a new overcoat and hat, and new suit, everything new. You know how it is.'

They were nearly all listening.

'Yeah, I remember the first job I had and I went home and they couldn't touch me with a ten-foot pole,' Red told him.

'Yeah, the first time,' continued Curly. 'Nothing like it. You never feel so much of a man again.'

They laughed.

'Well, ain't that so? You've got the world right by the tail then; it won't be long till the world knows it, and then you'll be sitting pretty. No sir, you got to hand it to a kid when he comes back home the first time. He'll talk to his dad as though he was his dad's uncle.'

'Great stuff.'

'They get growed up after a while,' came the piping voice of little Enos, beside the two tramps, 'and see how much the world cares.'

'Great stuff is right.' The brown eyes of Curly saw beyond the narrow and shadowy cell with its shadows of bars falling upon the men. His blunt turned-up nose and boyish cheeks, his short mouth, took on an expression of pleasurable recognition. He did not need to mask himself as older men or harder ones would do. He was merely getting away from the ugly cramping present by recalling better times.

'Well, what happened?' asked the taxi man.

Curly shifted his feet upon the bench.

'Oh, nothing. They arrested me here in Chicago on my way through. I got out in time for New Year's, and went on home. But it wasn't the same.

'What, did they pull you off the train?' Jack asked.

'No, I was stopping over a day or two. If I just hadn't done that, it wouldn't have begun. I could kick myself ever since.'

'There always must be a first time,' smiled Whitey.

'Well, that was my first time. You see, I wanted to take a look at Chi, because I had just passed through before. They been arresting me right and left ever since. I might have fought shy of the dicks for years. I can't go outside a roominghouse door without they cop me.'

'Yes, that's the way the breaks go, in streaks,' said the taxi man.

'I wish they would get out of the habit of arresting me,' sniffed the Snowbird gloomily.

'Oh, well!' Curly sang suddenly. 'What the hell do we care, as the college fellows yell!'

'What have they got on you?' one of the two old leathernecks asked the Snowbird softly.

'Oh, me,' the sallow Snowbird swayed his lank body on the stool. 'They got my wife for shoplifting today – that is, yesterday.'

'Got you for the same?' Bert Tremaine asked, with a kind of professional curiosity.

'Oh, yeah.' Wearily. Then he chirped. 'If they don't get you one time they will the next. Don't matter whether you've done anything or not.' There was silence and the Snowbird went on in his own confidential manner.

'A feller never knows how things is going to turn out, does he? You can't plan on nothing, not really, when you come to figure it out. Life is a game of chance. To me it is, anyway,' he added modestly.

Though there was nothing in this saying, they hated him. Someone laughed.

Curly, whistling, started to execute a few steps of Black Bottom where he stood on the bench.

'Heh!' suddenly yelled Sooty at the top of his hoarse, cracked voice. 'Where the hell you think you're dancing? Get down out of there, you – '

'Damn you, quit it,' yelled Secondhand; and Bert lifted his voice and took off his hat to look around.

'Shut up,' adjured Curly moderately, looking down at the first objector. 'Or we'll put you off there and let somebody sleep that can sleep. Eh, Whitey? There's Whitey been here a week and never got a wink of sleep. And Yellow there, too, driving all night.'

'I been driving a big truck,' muttered Sooty, subsiding.

'Must have been *some* rum-runner,' remarked the taxi-man. 'I got some sleep this morning. Just starting the night's work when I picked up the wrong load.'

'Pretty tough.'

'Yeh, if I'd been going crooked I wouldn't have got the pinch. I'd just left my garage about an hour. My third load, pretty good breaks. Then another thing, it was the first day I had my own cab. For the first three or four months they give you old blimps, a different one every day. It's all a fellow can do to keep from being run over.'

'Gets better when you have a cab of your own, don't it?' Bert asked. 'I was riding with one of your fellows just the other night, and he said they make sometimes as much as sixty or seventy dollars a week, tips and all.'

'He was shooting his mouth off. In the winter, when there's more money on the street than any time, he might get as much as fifty dollars, tips and all, for one week, maybe. But that would be the peak. Lots of fellows right now don't get their bonuses, and they been driving a long time.'

'I guess you've lost your job,' said Curly coldly. 'They'll put the skids under you now, all right.'

'Maybe,' said the Taxi-man indifferently. 'The company has its own lawyers to get drivers out of trouble. But they may figure I was operating on my own.'

'You should worry, kid,' said Red.

'Give me a smoke, boys,' said the short ruddy man.

'Well, anyway, I got a kick out of her at the last. We certainly went around those corners, I'm telling you.'

'What's all the doings out in the pen?' asked Snowbird from the rear of the cell.

'Oh, that's a new wagonload just brought in,' said Red. 'They're gamblers. They're swells, big fat pussy guys, smoking cigars and Herbert Tarreytons. Say, they're real. Wait till they come over this way and we'll get some cigarettes. They been having a whale of a time.'

'Holy gee,' said Curly, swinging out from the bench to bring his face to the door. 'One's got a two-quart hat on.'

Snowbird fidgetted at the prospect of cigarettes. Whitey and the taxi man glanced out and went on talking. Bert was sitting with a pearl-gray fedora down on his brows, his chin on his cravat, blinking, amused. The Secondhand wanted to get up too without leaving his seat.

Out in the big room a group of club men and flashily dressed gamblers were standing about talking and joking genially. They had not been frisked with any thoroughness, for a bulge on the hip of one or two showed plainly. They weren't guns. Probably they had given the dicks a nip or two and kept the flasks. Now, when Murphy wasn't looking, one would give another a further gratuitous pony.

'Hey, Jack,' called Curly with an angelic expression, and jerked his head back to summon them. 'Got anything to smoke?'

Sooty bounded from the bench, almost upsetting Bert and Secondhand. Without words, sleepily, briskly, automatically, he squeezed to the door, and stuck his head between Red and Jack. He stuck his long horselike black young face with its shallow slippery eyes into the doorway and called without looking:

'Hey, Buddy, come on over. I ain't had a cigarette for hours.'

A stout, ruddy, smooth-faced forty-year-old came over, feeling in the pocket of his Harris tweed coat for cigarettes, which he stuck through the bars.

'Pass them around.'

'Boy this sure is great.'

'This sure is the berries.'

'We're dying for smokes.'

Everybody was lighting up. At the back of the cell Snowbird was taking the last three cigarettes from the package.

'Well, it's a great life. A night in jail, eh?'

'Expect to get out in the morning, do yuh?' asked Sooty truculently. 'You're gonna get wise.' He would teach this soft fellow something.

'Sure, our solicitors will be around in the morning to bail us out. One fellow over there hasn't anybody to go his bond, so instead of getting a professional bondsman, we're going to club together. Fellow in the stiff hat. Comes from out of town. Well, so long, boys!'

'Here's your cigarette package,' said Red. It had been passed to him. 'I guess they're all gone.'

'Ne' min'.' The gay stout oldster strolled back to his company, with a half-waltzing step, hands clasped beneath his coat which swung like a tail.

'Now he's a sport,' said Red. 'These cheap guys make a fellow sick.'

'Bull, he don't know nuttin' dem guys don't, not really,' Sooty proclaimed with a fresh access of assurance from his sleep. 'In a few days you couldn't pry him from a smoke with a chisel.'

'I wish there was room to stretch yourself,' said Bert, rising. 'Anybody want to sit down?'

Whitey changed places, and Sooty promptly lay down again. Secondhand had never risen since coming in.

'Who's going to sleep now?'

'I'll let you have it till next show-up. Then I'm going to chase you off and sleep myself,' Red boomed in his easily laughing voice. 'I haven't slept since yesterday morning.'

'Well,' spoke up Enos, jammed in like a stove-length in the midst of a carload of posts. 'I wonder who's hugging them now – yous fellows' girls?'

'Hell with them,' said the dapper Bert, with the assurance of a lately married man.

Jack closed his eyes.

'Salvation Army lasses is the only girls you fellows is going to see,' said Red. 'And that's next Sunday morning. They'll come and take up a collection and pray for you.'

'And if you laugh they'll tell you to go to hell,' the taxi man instructed them further.

The tramps, Whitey, Secondhand, most of the others paid no attention. They half nodded as though to hint that sleep was better than talk, even of women. There was a humming from the niggers' cell, then a low powerful voice held in leash:

'What'll I do – when you –
Are far – away –
And I – am blue –
What'll I dooooo?'

Curly began to hum. Protests came from somewhere: 'Shut up.'

'Hold the rumpus.'

'Cut the seranade.'

Red began to hum and then to boom. Pretty soon everybody in the cell was singing and squeaking.

When I'm – alone –
With dreams – of you –
That won't – come true –
What'll I do – what'll I do....
Who'll I te-ell my troubles to – oo?

The voices rose with the pathos of all singing, human voices reaching out to the infinite of beauty never to be expressed in any other form, it might be, in all their various and shifting lives. The songs went on, filling the jail, new ones starting before a fellow could get self-conscious. A few were silent. There were groans as though someone's sleep were being interrupted. The songs went on, reminding the men of times they had heard those same tunes, the words from people they loved now or hated or would have forgotten. The tunes became more languishing and insidious. And the negroes were leading.

I haven't got no Mammy,
No Mammy to rock me to sleep.

'Ah haven't *got* no Mammy,' Curly wailed it, his voice going high above the others. Only now had the Southern accent become plain in his leisurely enunciation.

'I'll tell you fellows,' the taxi man cleared his throat. 'You'll find women at the bottom of all the trouble fellows get into. Most of the fellows are here I'll bet on account of some skirt or other. I don't mean there's any in mine – '

'Of course not. Hell with the broads,' said Curly hastily. 'Let's sing. "I'm sorry I made you cry".'

'No. Cheer up for Christ's sake,' said the taxi man.

They were singing again, and the negroes were in unison. There in the tiny cells they were like lost voyagers in tiny boats on the ocean, surrounded by walls of darkness, in a well of darkness, with flashes and beams from hell, shining through the bars or the ropes which held their little craft below a balloon on a sea of air. Everyone felt changed, as though the adding of this element, music, to the combination, had made a different soul for each. It added to their bitterness or it made them happy. One or two became so sore he shut up, mouth wry as from vinegar. The whole place seemed to ring. Even the gamblers out in the bull-pen looked toward the cells curiously.

'Aw, hell,' said Red. 'What's the use of getting ourselves hoarse? Our singing's not so much.'

'Sure, that goes with me, shut up,' Sooty concurred. 'Singing's a lot of crap.'

'Aw, come on,' said Curly. 'The niggers is getting ahead of us.'

They had struck up 'Deep River,' and the majestic organ tones gave the whites nothing to do but listen. Some of the fellows clapped at the end. But they stopped. 'We'll have the bull down on us,' one of them told the others.

'The air in here is getting no better,' said Bert.

'Hell.' Curly stuck his peak cap over the wall and spat down on the negroes. 'You can't sing.'

'Come on, ye naygurs,' bellowed Murphy, as though just returned with fresh orders from the City Hall. 'Cut it out.'

The negro cell was still. Murphy went away.

'Ah think they're crazy, dem white kids,' murmured a coloured voice.

'Aw, shut up, you dirty black greasy nigger,' shrilled Curly.

Two darkies were drawling softly in the dusk, one telling the other about a Baptist minister he had known in his boyhood.

'We ain' making any noise,' said the other. 'You stop spitting on us in here, or we'll tell the coppers.'

'What's that you saying, you lousy black bugger you?' shrilled Curly.

'I ain' a lousy bugger,' returned the soft voice.

'Aw, shutup, you dirty, lousy big black bugger,' returned Curly enjoyably. The others in his cell were beginning to prick up their ears.

'Can it, kid,' said the taxi driver. 'That's no good.'

Curly paid no attention, but repeated.

'You're a dirty lousy little runt of a black bugger then. I can't see you,' he laughed, 'so if you're not a big bugger, you're a little one.'

'If I ever catch you alone you'll see whether I'm little or not. An' you'll eat yore words whether I'm a – '

'Bummin' black bugger,' chirped Curly.

No reply.

'You got in here for jazzin' your mother,' Curly spat.

'Just wait till I lay hands on you,' came the ominous quiet voice.

Quiet then. Curly's voice rose hysterically.

'Aw, shut up, you dirty mother-jazzing nigger.'

The other negroes were rousing and milling about.

'Who says I'm – '

'Who says anything about *mah* mother? You talk that a way 'bout mah mother and I'll tear yo' clean apart. Yes I will. Come on now, which one was it?' the voice demanded.

'It was the taxi driver,' said another negro voice.

The taxi driver said nothing.

'It was not,' boomed Red.

'Nev mind, I'll find him, the stinkin' rat,' continued the second negro voice.

'Oh, who's scairt of you?' shrilled Curly.

'You better not say that again.' It was the first negro voice.

'Say what, you poor low-life punk? Shit, who's scairt of you?'

No answer.

'Anyway, you're a bunch of half-niggers and mother-jazzers.'

Instantly there was an uproar. The negroes yelled together.

'Git up there somebody and see who it is calling 'at at us. Git up quick!'

Curly turned pale and crouched a little in the corner. He was short and his cap might not be seen above the partition.

'I knows who it is. Don't worry. I knows. Wait till show-up. We'll fix him. It ain't the taxi driver. It's – '

'It's Red.'

It was Red's turn to keep still.

'No, it ain't Red,' said the taxi man authoritatively.

'That's him, that's the taxi fellow,' said a hysterical negro voice. 'That's the one what was callin' we-all names.'

'Shut up, boys,' said Red. 'You won't find out who it was. Your guessing's punk.'

'We'll get him, don't worry.'

'Nobody ain' goin' to call me no – '

'Nobody ain' goin' cast no 'spersions on my – '

Curly began to turn a little green about the mouth, where his grin hung, becoming silly. He kept silent a minute or two, waiting till they would be off guard. There was no sense in being put on the spot for it, he just wanted to razz them. What did the niggers get steamed up over nothing for? Hell. Poor sports. Everybody was, around this flop. He pursed his sensitive mouth as though he was about to cry again.

The niggers were muttering among themselves, and occasionally a loud voice floated up over the cells. They were restraining someone, trying to get him to listen to reason.

'Not likely they have razors,' remarked Jack, with a wink at the taxi man.

'No,' said Red with a glance at Curly. 'They wouldn't get by at the desk.'

'It does look as though little Curly would have to be rap guy for the bunch, though,' said the taxi man.

'Surely they wouldn't have razors in here,' objected Bert. His voice as he spoke resembled Curly's. He could see himself among the negroes, clothes turn to shreds. ...

'You can't tell anything about a nigger,' said Jack wisely.

'I knew a negro once,' began little Enos, who had abandoned his squat.

'No, I knew a shine,' Red laughed. 'They locked him up in solitary, and searched him from top to toe. When he came out he slashed the throat of the lock-up and came within an iota of making a break, only the town whittler was handy with his dukes, and knocked him out. He carried his razor in his hair.'

'Aw, come off,' Curly objected.

'It was a safety razor blade, and he had a tooth-brush handle, hid in the seam of his trousers. The tooth-brush had two little knobs filed on it, to put into the holes of the safety razor blade, you know. Made quite a handy tool, all right. Kind of awkward trying to cut a man's throat with the bare blade. It would twist in your fingers.'

'You better talk about something else,' laughed Jack. He felt one of the party pulling Curly's leg.

'Yeh, I guess so,' grunted the biggest-nosed of the tramps, who had roused and stood up too. Everyone wanted to make a stir, any kind of noise, so that it would seem they had forgotten about the negro episode, and the niggers would not think they were thinking about it, either. It was hard to tell where some things would end.

'It don't make any difference,' said Curly wailfully. 'We're innocent or we wouldn't be here. When you're innocent, you've got to take what's coming. I wouldn't mind taking a rap any time when I've pulled something. But it's the guys that don't do nothing that they git.'

'It's – ah, the law of averages,' said Whitey. 'They let you get by with lots of things, then they'll get you on nothing.'

'That's him. Tha's him all right.' said a negro voice. They had not noticed that the next cell had become quiet again.

'He's ovah on this side, too. I'm going to see him, next time he talks.'

'Then they get you on nothing.'

'Shut up, you blightin' god-dam mother-jazzers!' screamed Curly suddenly. He grinned at the others sickly, as soon as he had yelled. They would see whether he was scared of a bunch of niggers or not.

'Just wait, 'at's all I asks you,' said a high tenor negro voice, slowly. 'You just wait till show-up. I'll fix whoever's saying that, if I got to tear the whole bunch of you apart. You cain't hide. I'll tear you up so your mother wouldn't know you.'

Curly began to go green again, his lips still smiling. But he would not keep still.

'Yeh, they get you on nothing. And that ain't enough, you got to 'ssociate with a lot of damn crazy niggers that want to kill the first white man they see.' He spoke with plaintive indignation.

'Give me a cigarette, somebody, please,' said Whitey. 'You know,' he said, meditatively, 'I'd rather put in six months in stir, or twelve in some good county jail, than a couple of nights like this.'

'Somebody save Whitey's life,' said the taxi man, feeling the unbuttoned pockets of his uniform. Nobody, apparently, had a cigarette.

'Haven't you two got a cigarette?' Curly asked the two old road-pounders.

'We – I have a pipe,' said the smaller of the tramps.

'Boy-friends!' snorted Sooty, who had rolled over on his elbow at mention of cigarettes and peered from between the arms of Bert and Whitey.

Finally from the stool at the end of the cell came the Snowbird's voice.

'I want the first couple or three puffs at it, but you can have it then, Mister.'

From the folds of his black clothes came at length a half-doubled white cigarette. Somebody gave him a match, and he dwelt voluptuously upon his puffs, only four, then he handed the cigarettes to Whitey.

It was quiet in the cell. There was a heavy breathing, and blinking eyes and a high stink. Subdued mutters came from the nigger cell, Curly heard. It sounded as though they were trying to get somebody to cool down. Was some nigger saying, look out for the new guard? Hell with them, the other fellows would stand up for him. He hunched and his knees almost bent and landed on Sooty's head. Most of the men were trying to doze, those sitting on the bench had their arms folded before them to save space, and their heads dropped and jerked toward their wrists; the hats and caps bobbed. Those standing along the wall and wedged serried between these and the bench, stood with heads bent. They could not even doze. There was a constant stirring and jostling, their scuffed shoes bit each other at the edges. Their eyes tried to stare at nothing while they looked into one another's faces – brown, yellow, red, and white in the half-light and the gleams from the caged bulb in the ceiling outside. They looked at each other quietly.

An immense admiration and pity for these men came to Jack Dolson. They were brothers there together.

'Here, have the rest of this cigarette,' said Whitey to him.

'No. Thanks, I been smoking a lot today.'

'Don't you care for it?' The water-coloured eyes became larger.

'Here, I'll take it.' A bony and grimy wrist protruded from between the men on the bench. But Whitey had been too quick to give it, quirtlike with its lash of blue smoke, to the taxi man.

'Aw, gee,' sighed Curly. 'Aw, hell!' He did not say he was tired. Red grinned up at him.

His eyes seemed green as much as blue. He had not moved from his post at the door, could not move now, without disturbing the cell. The screened light and the bars made a network on his head and shoulders, unbowed and lean, and his astonishingly clean white shirt. He wore no coat, but had the shirt sleeves and collar turned in. Belted trousers and yellow low shoes on his slim feet. A thoroughbred look. Perhaps Scandinavian or mixed ancestry. A fellow for pals, girls, a good time, stretches of idleness.

'I'm wondering whether we haven't missed morning, and it's the second morning that's coming now,' said Enos.

'This is some detention camp,' agreed Jack. 'When do they let you out?'

'I wish they'd take us over to the Detective Bureau,' said Red. 'For the ride. I've had my feet prints taken, but they might let me go along and take 'em again to be sure of getting them right.'

'They bring you back here after that?'

'Yeah, soon as they fasten something on you they try you in the court nearest where you pulled the raw one. Then you land in County Jail, if you don't get sentenced right away. They bind you over to Grand Jury, and after you've been in the County Jail five or six months, you get a trial. Isn't that how it works, Whitey?'

'Just about.'

'If you have plenty of jack your lawyers can stretch it out longer yet. But unless you've bumped somebody, the less jack you have the better.'

'Well, I'll take the jack, any time,' said Bert Tremaine.

'But what do they do if they got nothing on you?'

'Try to tie something,' said Curly. 'They figure to bring everybody in, and give 'em records whether they want one or not, as the fellow says.'

'They got to keep raking 'em in,' said the taxi man. 'They got to earn their little old pay envelope. The strong-arm squad isn't much good if it doesn't bring in a few loads once in a while.'

'Yeh, and by the time they get you here a couple of times, you got a record,' the Snowbird said.

'Then the judge gives you the rap.'

'And he doesn't see you again for another two years.'

The biggest of the old horse-collars laughed with a surprising rumble. The smaller one said:

'The oftener the judge sees you the less he likes you.'

'The tireder the judge gets the more retired you git.'

'The less he likes you the more he gives you.'

'Oh, hell,' said Sooty wearily. 'Give me plenty.'

'Won't give me anything,' spoke Bert earnestly. 'I never did anything. They just arrested me with the rest in the house.'

'Found in. You'll get it all right. You'll get plenty, boy.'

'They ain't got nothing on me, either,' Curly moaned. 'But I'm here. I was just walking down the street, that was all.'

'Not fast enough, you wasn't walking fast enough.'

'Never even gave me a ride; ham bull just lands on my shoulder and yanks me in.'

'Can't tell 'em nothing,' said Jack.

'Tell them guys anything – I guess not.'

'That just gives them an excuse to beat you up.'

'Tramp you to jelly that's what they want to do.'

'I tell you one thing. I'd rather be dead. I'd rather be breaking stone the rest of my time. I'd rather be crazy with hop. I'd rather tight the noose in the Big House Dance Hall, or burn. I'd rather be in bug house than be a dick or a cop.'

Low, earnest, ringing tones.

'They're lower than a snake's bottom.'

'All dicks is he-whores.'

'They're stinkers.'

'They're rotten.'

'Write it on the wall: All dicks is sons of bitches.'

'Can't write it there. Can't get at the wall for men.'

'Wait till you get into the pen. You'll have lots of time then.'

'They'll find you out there, and give you the dark cell, solitary and bread and water. Maybe the water cure, or hang you by the thumbs,' said Whitey mildly.

'Tell the judge to write it in the book.'

'Tell the clerk of the court and the court stenographer and the newspaper scribes to write it down and print it in the paper: Dicks is sons of bitches and whoresons.'

'I wouldn't be a bull for all the money in the world.'

Almost tearful earnestness. Oh, for something to do, something more to say, that would convince everyone and everything they meant it. Dicks were beneath all God's creatures. They were from a different planet. They were from hell. They were born of the Devil's grandma. They were fat-necked asses. They were thick carcasses made of owl-dung. Ugh. Dicks. A wave of approaching nausea swept over the cell as they all thought of the vileness of the police.

'Well, they can't make us do the things they do,' Red said philosophically at last.

'All they can do is their worst. If they third degree a man into splitting on himself it don't mean anything. When he gets around to it he'll croak one of them.'

'They get it back when they drive a guy nuts.'

'Damn right. They can only do their worst. The rottener they get the more a guy can stand.'

'They're nuts about putting the fear of God into the guys.'

'Drive a guy bull simple – he's got to shoot every bull he sees – that's how they get that way.'

'Not enough bull simple to put the fear of the Lord into the bulls.'

'I guess,' said Jack, 'when you come right down to it, maybe that's what's the matter with the bulls, they're scairt to death of everybody, and they try to do their worst all the time so nobody will know how scared they are.'

'Skirts and policemen, that's where this life business gets inside your guard,' said the taxi man.

'You said it, Tunney.'

'And money, money too,' said Secondhand. 'There ain't enough of that either.' He looked around amazed when everyone grinned, some aloud.

'No women at all if you get in the tombs.'

A sort of cry or whisper developed in the air. Both. It became so loud that it seemed to be the thought, spoken, and shouted, of every man in the place:

'Show-up!'

Who was shouting it? There was a clanking down the cells. The voices became silent in their buzzing, yet it was heard: Show-up.

'SHOW-UP.'

The word seemed to be coming nearer to their cell. Murphy passed along to the farther cells, opened the nigger cell. 'Little Ambrose is back,' muttered Red. A huge shadow bulked before their bars, and the door opened. 'Come on here, youse stinkers,' Murphy was saluting the negroes. Their faces gleamed in the huddled darkness of their clothes.

Red stepped out as though leaving the lobby of his hotel. Then Jack, the taxi driver, Whitey, suddenly rising from the bench and gliding between the others. Bert, the two tramps, Snowbird. Curly seemed to be trying to get through the crowd without being able to make it until now. He pushed out quietly among the rest, a little wild of eye when he saw the faces of the negroes. Then the little red nose and tortoise shell glasses. Then Secondhand, and Sooty. All out. Twelve.

'All out?' heavily rasped the bull, sticking his front into the door to see that nobody was left.

Instantly there was a buzz among the negroes.

'Whar at's dat guy what done talk ... Whar dat guy?'

'Get on there, niggers,' shouted Murphy behind them.

They were searching the twelve men, trying to pick out the one who had insulted their race. Some were staring at the lank taxi driver, at Sooty, at dapper Bert Tremaine, at Snowbird. They seemed to know Red and Whitey. One man's gaze fastened on Curly. Curly's eyes were active, but he did not let on that he saw anybody. Hands in pockets he strolled among the rest, taking care to be in their midst, toward the end of the big room.

Behind them was Little Ambrose, his shoulders wide as two men, then sloping out to his middle which was thick as four men. His little brown features hugely cased in fat became red as he bellowed.

There was a streaking forward among the niggers. Somehow they were mingled with the others. A squat flat figure, head close to shoulders – it launched forward through the air into their midst.

Each man knew it as the figure reached them. He wasn't looking for them – he was after –

Curly gave a squeal, and leaped three feet up and six away. The razor sliced his ear and the top of his head as he turned and shot away. The nigger was going too. He made a downward slash across Curly's back as they went. But Curly had gone, and Red and the taxi man had the nigger's wrists. Two holding him on either side, then Little Ambrose, blowing his whistle. Murphy was there.

The negroes became quiet as sheep.

The dicks came plunging through the herded cells-ful beyond. The squat nigger was wrenching like a maniac, but as quickly as he freed his wrists they caught his arms again. Someone squealed and let go. He had been nicked by the razor. It was Bert, his pearl-gray hat flying.

Little Ambrose brought the handcuffs ringing down on the negro's head.

Then the dicks fastened another set of bracelets on the nigger's wrists. Blood was streaming over his forehead and his lips. He was suddenly turned to a cast-like adamant. He did not seem to be breathing. The others were puffing as though they had run a mile.

They yanked him with loud oaths. He was soundless. Through the door out along the corridor. Then wild screams were heard. They were giving it to him. He knew now what he was up against. He wouldn't keep still. Scream after scream.

The whites of the other negroes' eyes showed up where they stood huddled. They looked around them to windows and doors. There was no way out.

The men from the other cells looked at them.

Nobody said anything.

Murphy and Little Ambrose were looking at Curly's ear. It was spouting freely and he was laughing.

'Take him away before he gets blood all over the place,' grunted Little Ambrose.

'Here's another man got a slash.' He indicated Bert.

'I guess it's only a slash,' grinned Bert. The slash crossed the sleeve of his pin-stripe suit, and his stiff shirt-cuff had held it except for a short gash about an inch long above the wrist. It was not bleeding, its lips seemed dry already.

'Better take you to the doctor too,' said Murphy.

'Yeh, come on,' said Curly. 'You might get – '

'Shut up, you!' rasped Little Ambrose. 'Hell! Put peroxide on the scratch. Won't catch him bleeding to death.'

'Well, you coming?' said Murphy to Curly, who was holding a dirty handkerchief to his ear.

They went toward the door. Bert seemed forgotten. He looked after them in uncertainty. It was no use following them, he knew. A glance at the hilly Little Ambrose told him that – waiting for a chance to crack somebody on the side of the head. He burrowed into the crowd with his cell-mates. Some of them grinned when they saw his look at the bull and his quick decision.

The negroes were quiet, as though they expected to be forgotten. Little Ambrose wallowed through them to the door, elbowing powerfully right and left.

'Should put a few of you in irons and straitjacket,' he rumbled. 'What in the devil's happened all the ham dicks I don't know,' he muttered to himself. 'Got to open the doors and herd these buggers myself, eh?'

They all followed him into the corridor. Jostling, cursing, grinning at one another unhappily, silent, indifferent, apathetic, unseeing, they came, trudging through with bent heads, as though they feared the roof would be low, or that there would be a low doorway they couldn't see in the dusk. The feet shuffled, the bodies swayed, easing themselves ponderously, deftly, guardedly, recklessly, buoyantly, sleep-walkingly – but slowly. Through the corridor they flooded. The voices of the two or three bulls behind them were like voices of cowherders on the edge of a cattle-drive; no one spoke, yet the air above the shuffling was loud with struggles, smothered hopes, insane resolve, dogged despair, jostling delirium, hysterical courage, numbness, stolidity, sudden oneness with the mob.

Two other dicks stood one at either side of the door entering the show-up room. They didn't do anything but put the fear of the Lord into each one entering. Many a little man ducked or cringed coming through the door and suddenly seeing these two over him. Then they straightened, and some grinned at the fright of themselves and the others, or at this attempt of the dicks to throw a scare into them.

They jostled with their uproarious silent desires, air-ripping stinks, into a yet larger room. One side of it was full already. A row of chests, broad dark coats, shoulders, derby hats, square faces rolly or lined. But the light was not on them. All the dicks in the city, you'd think, there for show-up. Oh, yes, they'd recognize them again, they'd garner them in again in due course. The mills must be filled.

The prisoners gathered into a solid mass in the deep bottom of the room. There was a whisper here and there. A shot of dope was exchanged for a ring. Cigarettes changed hands. But they were mostly very quiet. They knew there was no use of drawing any more. They'd get plenty. They were waiting. They were like a jam of logs, held together and alive with the buoyant element beneath them all.

They were waiting, they were breathing a slightly different air, they were not in the cells now. They could stretch their legs coming and going.

Finally, everybody was inside. The lights were white and strong on the men, shadowy above the detectives. A spotlight shone down upon the middle of the room. There stood the shirt-sleeved Murphy, with his shock of hair, and Little Ambrose with his blue cap stationed himself with a list of names. He began calling them over. It was wonderful that an animal like that could be trained to read.

'Manuel Osperto!' He looked about. Looked up as though Manuel Osperto might produce himself as an apocalyptic vision. 'Isn't Manuel Osperto here? What the hell?' he muttered peevishly, as Murphy started up.

'Come out av ut, before I come and get you.'

Wise looks and cigars of the dicks. They were seeing everything.

'Com – een, I ain't get through. Joost a meenit-a!'

A wiry little large-faced solid Italian with light eyes squeezed and pushed his way out of the crowd from the back. His short muscular arms shoved the bodies away from him vigorously, for he was sure of himself. Nobody could reproach him. Nevertheless a growl or two followed him.

He stood under the light, and Little Ambrose looked him up and down. He shook his shoulders and pulled the lapels of his coat together, blinking a little. The detectives stood looking on with leathery ridged faces.

'Manuel Osperto? Is that right? Heh? No other names?'

'What are you here for?'

At once the little Italian was galvanized. His tongue moved with unratable velocity.

'A man she's come to ma house, she's say she want she should drink did I have some drink, I says maybe we'll see if you not want to drink for nothing, then I can geev you drinka from bat-room, he say I want good wine, I say no have got, he say – '

'What did you do?'

'I did no-thing, me, I tell him, he would not go 'way, I say you go 'way you would wake my child and wife he say shut your goddam mouth, you dirty wop he call me dirty wop-a, I find leetle stillett' to poke him in ribs but he hit me same time and I wake up here.'

'Book you for attempted manslaughter, I guess, Manuel. Where do you come from?'

'Eetaly!' The voice was shrill with surprise.

'Where do you live?' Patiently Murphy asked.

'Maxwell Street.'

'Go on.' A wag of the head. Murphy shoved him roughly to one side. He grinned back joyously at his fellow-captives awaiting the examination. Now he would watch their ordeals.

'Frederick Briscoe. Come on here. Snap out of it.' His deep rasping rumble, the sinister intentness of his bulk robbed his words of all aroma of jocularity. 'Frederick Briscoe and William Orford.'

The long taxi driver squeezed his way to the front. Little Ambrose looked up from the feet to the head almost level with his own. The uniform was shiny from driving, the leather puttees glistened. In his wake a brisk dapper man in blue-gray suit, well-cut hair, slickly shaven, cravetted, came with expansive stride forward.

'Your name Briscoe?'

'Yes.'

'Yes *sir*. You hack drivers got no manners. Frederick Briscoe?'

'Yes – sir.'

'What do you want here?'

'I was driving the man you have here for larceny,' explained the driver carefully, as though he had explained before many times. 'And your men – '

'Oh, yes – Ever been here before?'

'No.'

'And you?'

'No,' said Orford.

'What did you do this time?'

'There was some clothing of my wife's in a neighbouring apartment – '

'And they caught you getting it. You larceny bimbos got to move faster these days. Get on out of here.'

'Jonathan Ayers. Jonathan Ayers.'

The lean Snowbird shuffled forward, his frame bent like a jackknife which might close at any instant. His ridged gray face had become stiffened in a single emotion. He had not slept, nor listened to the others talking, wrangling, joking. He had been intent with a frozen concentration, a burning concentration, on his own one desire. He knew that there was no hope. It would depend a good deal upon what prison he was lodged in whether he would be able to get a single shot. Prisons were not run so that dope-rings flourished now. Prison was to be his portion; he knew it. Nothing but the sound of his own name would have roused him. He shoved his legs forward as though they were sticks.

'Take off your hat.'

'Yes, yes sir.' He was still wearing the mild stone-coloured affair that had attracted the attention of the department store detective because of its very inconspicuousness. His hair was lank and dank, black over the wrinkled yellow forehead.

'What is your name?'

'Jonathan Ayers.'

'Wrong. Guess again.'

'No-n-no sir.'

'You went by the name of Hugh S. Cope eighteen months ago. Come on now.'

'I – don't remember.'

'Well, we remember. We got quite a few of your aliases here. And we're going to get the full bill before we quit. Tell me now. What's your name? Eh?'

No answer. Little Ambrose lifted a hand like a ham.

'Jonathan Ayers. Jonathan Ayers. Jonathan Ayers,' he rattled. 'Isn't that what you call me? You got that on your book. Jonathan Ayers.' The Coke-sniffer's wisp of being shrank.

'Don't worry, we can make you talk. What you here for, this time?'

'They arrested me.'

A crackle of laughter, dying away.

'Yeh, they did, eh? What for, now, did they arrest you?'

'Shoplifting. But I ain't guilty.' He took a step forward.

'Just keep back.' There had been a little change in the position of the hands of the dicks. Jonathan Ayers subsided, fearful. 'Yes, we know all about that. Get on, out of it.'

'Francis Broughton. B. Rough-ton, or Broughton?' There were smiles and knowing jibbs of the derbies and cigars of the dicks. A lean-faced, aquiline negro came from the outskirts.

'So you're one of the murderin' gang, are you? Well, you'll get yours. Who did you murder *before* you got in here?'

'A little – '

'I mean the last time.'

A titter.

'A little girl.'

A hush.

'Oh, you did. Murdered a little girl. You murdered her, eh? Only one?' asked Little Ambrose wittily.

Everyone was watching, listening.

'She was killed. The car I was driving ran over her.'

'Whose car were you driving?'

'My employer's car. I am a private chauffeur.'

'Oh, you was! Well, what did you want to run children down for? Was that your orders?'

'No sir.'

'Don't you know you're going to get life for it?'

'No, sir.'

'Well, you will. Get on.' The heavy arm waved the negro away.

'It was an accident.'

'Say!' roared Little Ambrose. 'Are you going to talk when nobody asks you a question? If you are, we'll take care of you, all right. You better shut up!' He took a step swingingly as though about to launch a kick. The negro turned among the others, facing him.

'Alfred Millais!'

A svelte and elegantly bespatted figure, in a morning coat, impossibly emerged from the throng, and advanced to the lights with an actor's stride.

'Where's your cane?' barked Little Ambrose.

'My stick was retained, with a number of other effects, at the ah – desk.'

'Oh. Why didn't you tell the bounder to let you keep your cane?'

'But it wasn't really worth arguing.' The serene Millais was not permitting himself to be so crudely kidded.

'Yeah? What's the jolt?' Little Ambrose negotiated a sudden change of manner to lowering ferocity.

'The jolt came when I was accused of false pretensions in my art.'

'What art?'

'I was commissioned to paint some portraits, and naturally I received a number of cheques in advance for my work.'

'You still got a line. Go on.'

'It seems there was some misunderstanding about the cheques. Why, I don't know. The banks gave me money on them, and I deposited some of them. Then I gave a cheque to a radio company for a radio in my apartment. The radio man suggested that I go with him to the bank. I was arrested in the bank, and some person standing there told the cops I was a fake. A lie of course, but his testimony was accepted.'

'Did you know this person?'

'Know him? Not I!'

'A portrait painter ought to remember faces. Better stick to your own racket after this and not try no artist stuff.'

'Sir!'

'Move on.'

The figure walked smartly with hips and toes and turned smartly among the examined.

Show-Up went on.

'Rodney R. Brink alias Lefty Carlson. And Carl W. Calliston.'

Two blue suits, dusty, one small man and one large. The smaller came first, briskly but with a sort of furtive side-slip to his step, and a way of holding his head as though his neck hurt.

'Rodney R. Brink, eh? Ever been here before?'

'Yes.' Shy, almost lisping tones out of the corner of the mouth.

'What was that for?'

'Shooting a man. It was self-defence.'

'That's what the court said, eh? Gave you suspended sentence, didn't they?'

'Yes sir.' Almost a smile of gratification came over the gunman's face as he reflected that everyone knew him. He would be a marked man in the cell now.

'And Carl W. Calliston. Hold on. If your name is Rod, his name should be Roscoe shouldn't it?' The dicks snickered quietly. The big pal with swinging shoulders smiled too. 'Roscoe and Rod.'

'What do you want here?'

'Nothing.'

'Well, you're going to get a fair trial. Hold on, what were you arrested for? Don't be in such a hurry.'

'Dey arrested me, dat's all.'

'It must have been because you was with this killer. Move on.'

Show-Up went on. Little Ambrose had disposed of the greater part of his good spirits and wit, accumulation, others would have said, of some years. He did not want even to take the trouble to intimidate the rest. That could be done more handily when he got them back in the cells, with himself in sole charge. If they talked back to him there he would just work on them till he got them in shape to do up in quart jars. He really hated this business of inquisition. When it came to questions and replies, any crook could get away with a lot. Sometimes they even seemed to think they had given him a set-back. The little stinkers! Let him get any one of them alone, and he'd grill them differently, don't you forget it! They didn't fool with little old Ambrose. If the commissioners knew anything they'd put him up a few steps on the Force and his methods could be applied wholesale. He knew some fellows that would be getting out good and quick, if he ever got the power. That gray-haired old Lanigan on the Paige squad who was always trying to give the boys a break – he was one who should go so fast – Might as well have an old woman, that's all. Said he never laid hands on a prisoner, and he hadn't shot one for ten years. If a man was getting away one of the others shot him. Might as well not have him in the squad, a guy like that. Hell, they were getting softer all the time. Things were getting into a rotten mess. There soon would not be prisons enough, they couldn't build them fast enough. And about that time they would be getting so soft about criminals that they wouldn't be sending them to prison at all. Half the population would be deserving a good stiff jolt, and they'd let them all off. That was the way modern notions about crime were going. Women getting into politics, prison investigation, colleges telling people criminals were like other people – all that was raising the devil. The good old simple days when you went out and collared a guy, beat him up, brought him in, gave him Third Degree till he shot the wad, or got him booked *some* way, if you had to frame him, and then packed him away till he got out and did something you could get on him again – those good old days were passed. If things kept on getting worse it wouldn't be safe to give the boys what was coming to them when you felt like it. Hell! But meanwhile, meanwhile, they couldn't very well get at you, they couldn't prove anything on an officer, and boys – he gave them the worth of their money every time. They didn't look sideways at him without getting it back. They rubbed their necks when they saw him, all right. They propped their feet, all right. This whole bunch, now, should be put away in dark cells, solitary, for a week. A week on water and bread would bring a lot of them around. Then bring 'em out and ASK THEM A FEW QUESTIONS.

Show-Up went on. The prisoners said nothing, seemed without curiosity or interest. They were at the same time bored and impatient. Jack Dolson looked about him suffocated with impatience. Perhaps this would clear him and they would let him go. The night was not over yet. Then would begin his hunt for Grace. A nice way to begin a honeymoon. His breast felt hot. Then his indignation was dampened, smothered, in despair. His honeymoon might not begin at all. They only had to frame you. This examination might last all night, leisurely, ponderous, just to bait them. He shifted his feet. His chest hurt him. He understood now why prisoners made dives for nearby windows, never thinking of the rifles of guards. Death was better than this gnawing, burning, this harrowing impatience. Nothing so intense and so enveloping could go by so common a name. It was not impatience but a fever becoming intenser every minute, as he saw there was no hope of surcease. He was glad he was not in the open at that moment, walking with the policemen or under their guns in the automobile. Inevitably he would have run, and been shot down. He wondered why it was that more people were not shot attempting escape. It was not that he was so much thinking of freedom or of Grace. He was just desperate with weariness because nothing seemed to get done. They went about everything as though they had eternity to do it in, counted on taking years to find out whether each man was guilty or not. And then they would not care who was guilty and who was not. Jack's head shook in a shudder, and he shifted his feet once more.

Sooty was beside him, looking at him as totally strange, then said between his bared teeth:

'Some people kin worry a lot about nuttin' at all.'

'Jack Dolson!' The rasping bellow. 'Jack Dolson.'

'Here!' Jack's heart bounded. Little Ambrose stepped forward. It was time someone was getting a clip on the side of the head. They were taking their time as though this was staged for their benefit.

The dicks could see that somebody deserved a clip on the neck. He'd land one for luck.

'Here!' The voice was almost at his elbow. Jack had been pressed into the back corner and came around behind the crowd of prisoners. As he came into the light a perverse flash made him walk meekly as though modest about his innocence. He wasn't going to strut and stride out on the scene brazenly as though pretending innocence, as some men did. He was innocent.

'Don't you know your name, or changed it just when I called you – that it?'

'No, sir.'

'What you mean then, eh?'

'I'm here.'

'Eh?' The stupid bull had been about to tramp on him, but something in the words, or the unchanged grins of the dicks brought him up standing. 'What are you here for, my little sir?' he asked with bitter politeness.

'I was driving my car from Michigan to Chicago – '

'Why didn't you stay there?' Loud laughs from the dicks. 'Youse hicks ought to stay to home.'

Jack was quivering. It seemed that right had departed from the world, that the world had departed, leaving this hell of grinning faces that saw nothing but their own evil.

'A squad arrested me for stealing my car. *My* car.' His sarcasm was futile, nobody believed it, it fell back on his ears like arrows against a stone battlement, and he did not believe himself.

'Well, it ain't yours any more, then, is it?' With jaunty joyousness and cap askew the bull grinned. 'You better pay for your cars before you run away with them.' He was enough for them even with words.

Jack did not answer.

'Well?' They were both mystified. Something should happen, but it wouldn't. 'What are you standing there for ? He ran a fishy eye over his book for the next name.

Jack stepped aside to the legion of the examined. A wink or two and a new kind of grin told him they thought he had got Little Ambrose's goat.

The men stood in an unmoving, unbreathing group, looking on fixedly like animals, hiding the fact that they saw scarcely anything, that they would remember nothing save a few cases, where their interest was stirred by resemblance or personal liking or hatred; or when incongruity, the strangeness of fear, tears, pity, humour, showed themselves. Then they would rouse and look to see.

The crowd increased on the one hand, and decreased on the other, like sand in an hour-glass, like grain running from one elevator to another.

They stood there, patient, as though this were a weeding-out process which would land some of them jobs, as though it were a hunt for someone suitable for a mission. Perhaps the lucky man would be allowed to go to the Pole. But there was nothing important about it. It didn't matter. Crimes, furious activity, escape, stagnation, were all one to them now. They stood there, aware only of bare walls and their own approaching or past turns. They were here and nothing was to be done. They stood.

There wasn't room for the examined between the door and the bright lights where the culprits had to stand. There was a movement among the dicks behind the low wooden gateways. The two who had stood on either side of the entrance now opened the corridor leading to the bull-pen and the cells. Opened the door and rasped:

'Come on here.'

They failed to equal the unique voice and presence of Little Ambrose, but they wore an appearance of satisfaction which all such fellows had. They were on the right side. They were top dog, they were the condemners, not the condemned. They were the priests, and not the sinners. They rubbed their hands inside themselves, while they growled. Nothing could put them at a disadvantage. Except fear, and these were mainly a lot of punks.

III

The men spread out as soon as they reached the bull-pen. They had one idea, to stretch their limbs and ease their aches before they were packed away again. The air was still fouler than in the evening before. The high windows showed gray though the lights were unchanged. Surely it was morning.

The long form of the taxi driver was striding about, cap on the back of his head, log-like leggings cutting arcs against the floor and air. Red strolled hands in pockets. Sooty leaned against the wall smoking a cigarette butt. Whitey, eyes level, shoulders a little hunched, arms unswinging, was walking methodically up and down. Jack wanted to talk to somebody; it should be possible to learn something helpful. He hailed Whitey.

Whitey glanced at him and smiled, continuing his limp walk. As though he did not want to attract attention. Nobody was going around chatting with this one and that one and handing out cigarettes unless he was so green he did not know enough to be afraid of being taken for a stool pigeon.

'What do they do now? They can't keep on putting people in much longer, unless they get a pile-driver to ram the doorways with.'

Whitey smiled grayly. 'They'll take a few wagonloads over to the Bureau to be recorded, and some will go to court, and some to the County Jail for trial.'

'Sweet little system. Served a sentence before?'

The old convulsive movement of jaw and throat, then Whitey's calm voice: 'You take four or five years in the bridewell. It somehow gets inside a man, you know.'

'I should think it would.' Looking at Whitey's dough-coloured face Jack tried for curiosity to feel that endless ocean of hours, the waterdrops of minutes gathering in waves of mornings, afternoons, and evenings. Free! How could a man ever be free who had been so many years behind walls with men who had robbed and killed, where every minute was to serve to remind them they were different from all the world? Every man guessed what slumbered in the other, and feared or matched it. What each man guessed of his own heart the forms of his fellows gave bodily shape. They became Christs or fiends or insane, if they had been men. If they had gone there brutes, they became in the course of years animals with the insane induced cunning of creatures with only one object in life, one goal.

'And just think,' Whitey's soft voice went on. 'If I'd been lucky yesterday, I'd be well-fixed at this time.'

Jack looked at him and shook his head, paused. Whitey walked on.

The loose-jointed stride of the taxi man approached.

'Say, think they'll let us out of here this morning?' Jack spoke as man to man. The other looked at him with the suspicion of a stranger.

'Depends what they've got you booked for.'

'You have to get somebody to go your bond.'

'Don't make any difference. You can't get bond till they lay the charge and you know what you're being bonded for.'

'Yeah, but what can they charge me with? I never stole a car. I bought it and this bunch of hams up and arrest me.'

The taxi man looked at him reflectively. 'Vagrancy, I suppose. Most of the fellows are vagged. It's a round-up, maybe.'

'Well, I got to find out,' said Jack determinedly. 'There must be some foreman or other with a little sense.'

The bull-pen was becoming crowded with prisoners. A drooping lot in the sallow dust-filled air of early morning, the ghost light of the prison. But they were simply a bunch of men. Put them in uniforms and they would be a battalion. Stuffed and in dinner jackets they would be a club. In business sacks and morning coats they would be stock-exchange men. Put them in sets as they were and they would be a movie mob. But they were in a box of stone, and listless on their short promenades as the soldiers of Napoleon on weary stages of the march from Moscow. Jack was convinced as he looked at them that there was no hope for anyone.

The two end cells were being filled, and the negroes had got into theirs. Little Ambrose was looking around as though he knew where every man went. 'Don't you know your cell, you goddam fool?' he was rumbling.

Jack made quick time to the door. Huddled about it and entering were his old cell mates. They knew better than to forget, or to try to get into another crowd. Red had taken possession of the bench and was already asleep. The two tramps, Whitey, Sooty, Secondhand, sat along his flank and at his feet. On the toilet seat sat Snowbird once more. Bert stood beside him at the wall. The taxi driver came in, saw every seat was gone, and squatted beside him. Jack followed suit, his backbone rubbing the wall. The little red-nosed Enos of the horn-rimmed benevolence stood alongside.

'I'm going to sit down in a minute,' he told them. 'I just want to enjoy being taller than you fellows for a little while.'

'Disadvantage being tall, sometimes,' said the taxi man.

'That's right. Curly wasn't very tall, but he shouldn't have stood on the bench and hollered at those niggers. Well, I ain't as tall as him.'

The taxi man shut his mouth and looked at nothing. The spruce gray-flannelled William Orford of show-up was being ushered in by Little Ambrose. Nor did Orford look at his former driver. One thought himself victimized by a crook, and the other thought of a slow rube who might have got them both safe if he had shown any kind of speed.

'What kind of shake-down is this?' he enquired generally. 'Does a man have to pay for the choice seats? And who's that fellow sleeping?'

'A man doesn't,' said the taxi man. 'That's Red.'

Yap, yap, the voice was going from door to door. Little Ambrose would let them know that things were different from Murphy's shift. Little Ambrose was jerking some culprit from the cell to give him a knock or two on the neck and send him plunging head first to the cement floor, whence he was yanked with much shouting and plastering of vile names to his feet and plunged diving back into the midst of his fellows in the cell.

'Knows his oil, whoever he was got it. Don't hear no yelp out of him,' Bert said.

'If they get a man hollering, it encourages them. They soon get him on the run.'

'Hell, not always. I see a guy in San Quentin once. They started to handle him, and he began to call them. You never heard such a line in your life. That guy could talk. Not just cussing.'

'What, did he tell them their pedigree?'

'Before he got through they wondered what they were doing and whether they had any excuse for encumbering the earth. That is, if they had any brains. Of course they beat him up till he hardly had a mouth to talk out of. But he was like Clarence Darrow while he was going.'

'Shut up fellows, he's coming back.'

Silence in the cell beside them at the same instant. There was nothing to match his feeling of power as he trundled forward, his wallowing jaws, his little petulant mouth and his pig eyes glaring ahead. These bodies were his, and if anything had spoiled his supper, if anyone had grinned at the ass on the street car, somebody here would pay.

Ahead of him and into the cell came two dusty blue suits, one small, one large – the one-time killer and his companion.

'Git in here. If there's any funny stuff, you'll go to Bureau on crutches.'

'You too. Hear me?' A bandaged Curly was also shoved inside, grinning.

The smaller of the strange two sucked his finger. His bright mouth smiled and he spoke to the other out of the corner of it. Their smooth olive complexions, straight noses, and intelligent, almost amiable looks somehow made them enigmatic. One thing was sure, they didn't smell so strongly as some of the others, Jack thought.

'We're holding one another up now,' observed the taxi man. 'Safe to fall asleep now if you want to standing up. Can't fall down.'

'Aw, gee,' said Curly. 'I'm going to get my old place.' Carefully he wriggled, and Whitey moved his shoulder, so that Curly could get his feet in the corner of the bench, one each side of Red's sleeping head.

'We'll be out of here in half an hour,' the big newcomer told the other with something like deference.

'Sure. Like hell. You mean half an hour late for breakfast.'

'I tell you we got some little fixer. We won't be here long enough to get hungry. Why, do you think we'd take the rap?'

'A guy don't know just what to think when he gets in here. I'm telling you.'

They were glowering over the Snowbird. They had forced their way through as far as they could, and no one minded, for there was more air at the front.

'Come on, get up. Somebody else wants to use that. You ain't using it anyhow.'

Jonathan Ayers gave one frightened glance up into the big square face and slid from the seat. He couldn't stand, without stepping on someone's toes, or falling against a strange hard body.

'Better slide under the bench,' said Whitey. 'Nothing to disturb you there, you can have a good sleep.'

'Yeh, I can sleep there, all right.' With a yellow grin Snowbird slid underneath the row of feet and lay behind them.

The big fellow sat down quickly before anyone got ahead of him, then fumbled with his trousers.

'Funny somebody else never thought of that long ago,' remarked the taxi man. 'Good place to sleep.'

'Wish I'd thought of it myself,' said Curly with a wink in the direction of the big man on the seat.

There was no room to turn. The squatters along the wall had had to stand up when Orford and Curly and the pair had come. Otherwise their knees would have been used as chairs. Fifteen men in the cell. They did not complain, the benchers nor the burning-footed standers. They were brothers caught in this vile net. Each knew that he had got worse than he deserved, always, and that he did not deserve this, and that his brother did not, either. An immense pity enveloped them. They would have done anything for each other. Fine fellows, every one. But tired.

The night was long. It had been just dusk when Jack Dolson was brought in, and it was midnight and after when the gamblers had come, and that was a long time ago too. Morning could not be very far off, but morning would make no difference of light in this place until late, long after the birds and grasses had been awakened, and the dew gone, and the gardeners were spading in the park among the flowers. Long after the sprinkler trucks had sprayed the pavements and the milkmen had made their rounds. Not until the postmen were bringing mail and common people were going to work and the elevated trains groaned and the motors hissed along the park drives in the sunshine would they know it was morning without seeing any of these things. June morning. Then perhaps for them another day of stifling confinement, or release, sentence for years – new life, new death, or long and cribbed struggle and suspense. Sight for gods and their laughter, how could gods themselves live in that mass and laugh? It was a heightening that was a denial of life. Here they were festering, each man growing to hate himself worse than he hated the others, which made his hate of the others increase and his own self-loathing in turn deepen, in a cumulative wave gathered from smaller waves, joining in a peak. Would it all end in madness?

That was only the thought of a moment. In another they were once more merely a bunch of hapless punks trying to put in a night in the pen.

All was silent in the cell, nothing could be heard from beyond it, save a pig-grunting of sleep in the niggers' cell. Strangely quiet, even in the bull-pen and the corridors beyond. It must be coming morning. The little red-faced Enos had let his head slump forward on his chest, his overcoat still hovering about his shoulders, his eyes closing from time to time. His teeth were grinding. Yes, he would get them, and get them good, for framing him into this.

'He's going to kill 'em for getting him in here,' grinned Jack.

'Yeh.' The others were indifferent, not because they didn't believe the short man, but because it was not important.

There were heavy defying steps that knew where they were going. Little Ambrose himself was coming back to see what made them so quiet. Of course he'd not let them rest a minute before daylight came.

'When he walks, each foot dares the other to come ahead and pass it.'

'Shut up, or they'll dare your rump, them feet.'

'Alfred Millais!' announced Little Ambrose, unlocking the door, and shoving with the weight of his three hundred pounds. It was as though an earthquake had tossed them all.

'Good God! Devils and saints!' But none of them dared speak out the imprecations which the new cell-mate aroused, for fear of being temporarily taken from that company.

The commotion and crush woke Red, sleeping on the bench.

'It's time, all right, for a crush-out. Any kind,' said the taxi man, when Little Ambrose had gone a few minutes.

Red replied as though he had been awake all the time.

'Time for a riot, you mean.' He laughed. 'Riot's no good, though. The fellows that start riots are the old lifers and the guys that haven't guts enough to escape. Not for mine.'

'I wish they'd take us all out in the Maria to get our feets washed and printed,' said Curly.

'Just for the ride,' hummed Enos.

'More perspective there, I hope.' Alfred Millais genially entered the conversation.

'Take us for a ride. I'd just as lief. Remember how Hymee Morrison got taken. They pulled him into a car right in front of his own steel-shuttered house, and got away in a spray of machine-gun from Hymee's right and left bowers. Guess they stabbed him or slugged him before they let him out of the car, then they turned their machine gun on him as he ran across the fields.'

'Did the squad get them?' Jack asked.

'Hahah. It might a *been* the squad, paid by the biggest gang. I guess not, though. Everybody says it was the other gang.'

'I don't catch on with them kind of doings,' said Red. 'I ain't ambitious. What I would like is a tip to a nice little jug to crack. A dark rainy night and no janitor sleeping in the building.'

'Those fellows know they're going to get theirs,' said Bert excitedly. 'They just gamble like anybody else. They handle the gat pretty, and soon they're head of the gang. They make barrels of jack. But that doesn't mean much. They marry some jane and live in a swell twelve-roomed apartment. Good homey husbands, their wives say after they're dead. But it's power they're crazy about. If another gang steps over into their territory, they're out to break it up and go gunning for the leaders.'

He had been reading such things in the Sunday papers, it was plain. The little blue man looked at him from one side like a rooster, and sneered.

'You didn't know,' he said, 'that Dion O'Bannion and Terrible John Torrio, have been doping out a whole city of their own, two miles square, where a guy can go whenever the dicks have to make a raid to hold their jobs.'

'Say, is that right?' asked Jack. 'An underworld city, eh?'

'Hell, kid, where you been?'

'Ambitious is right,' agreed the taxi man, rubbing his leather leggings together. His long-confined legs were becoming itchy. 'That's why they get bumped.'

'I tell you a nice little game,' said Red. 'You go around to these slot machines. After midnight's the best time. There's two or three on every elevated platform. You get off at a station, and you don't go down below at all, because you've paid for your ticket. You're there to wait for another train – express, maybe. Meanwhile you knock these machines up and grab the loot. You want to have a suitcase along for the pennies and jitneys. And to keep your hammer in. Got to wrap that up in rags. Couple of fellows will make quite a bit in one night that way, if you're careful and choose the right El stations.'

'Couldn't make it many nights,' said the biggest of the old tramps.

'Have to be a high-jacker to do it at all,' grunted the biggest of the blue pair, on the toilet seat. 'Big shots in that.'

'Better not try it, boys,' said Curly to the old horsecollars condescendingly.

'You ain't got guts enough to try it yourself, greaseball,' said the big fellow.

Red continued his monologue.

'I took a rap of three years for a car I stole when I was a kid. Now I'm back for more. But when I've put in these three years, me for the straight and narrow path, and I don't mean maybe. You won't catch me riding in any other man's car. I've put in time enough.'

'Well, I'll drive a laundry wagon.'

'I'll give youse guys a tip-off if you've never tried it. The safest way to get a barrel is kidnapping. Just pick the right man that has the jack and the rest is easy.' The biggest of the pair spoke from the corner of his mouth too.

'It may be safer if you don't get caught,' said Bert Tremaine. 'You fellows ought to rehearse jobs like that.'

Bert was trying to think what he would say to his lawyer, and how he'd describe this to the fellows in his office. Jack was wondering whether they would ever start their honeymoon if he stayed there as long as a week. He would feel vile. Whitey told himself he would rather serve a double term, for all its monotony. Except when the time came. It was all in the day. When the world is against you you get yours sometimes. You've got to hold to a mood of acceptance. Take what the world will give you, and go-get what you can get when it won't give you anything. You don't hear any whining. The harder they're hit the less whining you hear.

It was the boobs that howled. Those guys! If you had got a little of your own, the cover charge was payable at sight, any time. If you had done nothing and you got caught, then you *were* getting the dirty end of the stick. No wonder they howled. The only way to get your own was to keep ahead of the game. They'll get you, don't let them get you for nothing. The minute a guy got out of jail he did the biggest job he could think of, and was ready to take another rap. If he didn't have to take it, he was that much ahead. He went on then and did another big job when the time came for it. He was collecting then on the years he had put in and the years he would put in. If he got by with enough he wouldn't kick, would he, at getting life in the end, with a chance of breaking out? If he happened to be simple in one line, like killing for pleasure, then he did kill when the first good chance came, if it was under the noses of fifteen dicks,; and he did no squealing when the rap came. ... The dicks were a breed of jackasses compared to them, to thoroughbred running-horses. Wrong in the head, maybe, but finer, finer. ... Whitey was dozing.

'Hell, I guess sleep's over for tonight,' laughed Red.

'I know what would put me to sleep,' cackled the voice of the Snowbird from beneath the bench, where he was still lying face down – though nobody could see – his face resting on his wrists.

'What, are you down there yet?' Jack laughed, pleased as though recognizing an old acquaintance. They listened a minute then went on talking.

'Hell, you didn't expect *him* to dig himself out, did you?'

'Look here,' said Bert severely. 'If you're not sleeping under there, you should get out and let somebody sleep that can sleep. We can't waste space that way.'

Bert leaned and lurched a little, resting his elbows on his knees. He supposed all this was a dream. The reality might be the days he remembered, and the nights. His office – the apartment. Like a dream they were too, and the reality might be something else to come, the jail, day following on day. He felt that he knew all about that too. He had known these simple youths, these not so harmless prattlers, long ago. They were trying to believe the rest of the world was leagued against them, when it was merely too crowded for them. There was no room for people who did not run in the regular grooves, the dredged channels, the rails with no red switch-lights. If you wanted to be different, all right. You couldn't even get a job again after you started to go crooked. It was all silly, any way you looked at it. Fellows in the regular grooves without knowing why, they were fools and they were wise, far wiser than they could ever know. Far ... far wiser. They didn't know how lucky they were. Far wiser, far. ... Bert's head nodded.

Sooty leaned his long back forward, his head on his hands, elbows propped on his sharp knees. These guys were a lot of slow tramps and farmers. What did they know about big-time rackets like he was mixed in? Why, Andy Tocanni was king of the North-Side gangs, rolling in money always, and he never high-hatted anybody, either. Any of the truck-drivers could walk up to him, tell him he was short of cash, and Andy would peel a layer or two off his roll. Once he took a couple of them out to lunch at the Drake. ... That would be a good place to stick up. ... He ate at the Sheridan Plaza or Edgewater Beach every day – the main dining-room, you bet, too. The tips alone he gave in a week would make any of these cheap punks feel rich for a year. What did they know?

'I wisht I was havin' breakfast at the Onira,' he said moodily.

'There's time yet,' said the taxi man. 'You don't want to have breakfast before about ten, do you?'

'Oh, hell, I'd have to get into some clothes, of course.'

'It must be nice to have a boss that can fix everything.'

'Gee, I bet I'll have a swell time when I get out. Go dancing at the Municipal Pier, and then about one o'clock I'll take the girl friend to the Marigold Gardens.'

'Skoits is no good anyway,' spoke the bigger of the two con men.

'Well, they do a lot of harm,' said Bert judiciously.

'They're all right,' muttered Red. 'Seems like they got to be had. Using hands makes them crazy in the head.'

'They take care of you in the big house, all right,' said the little pal from the corner of his mouth. 'They fix your coffee all right in there. You don't care if you never see a broad.'

'Hell,' said Red. 'Anybody want this place to lie down in? You take it, Yellow,' he said to the taxi driver.

'I take too much room lengthways. Go to it, Whitey.'

Whitey had only to lean back and pull himself into the place, once Red had risen to stand beside Curly on the bench. Then the problem was where to put him. He took more room than Whitey had, and the others grunted. At last he got his old post beside the door.

'Where's the Lawrence Avenue Dude?' he bellowed.

'Still here,' came a shrill response above the hum of the cells. 'I'm going out ahead of you. Cook County Sheik, ain't you, Red?'

'I'm Red from the Red Stir; going back, too.'

'I'm the Sing-Sing Singer,' said Curly. 'Didn't I start the sing-song?'

'Hell, I'm one red-headed guy that stays out of jail after this,' laughed Red.

'Listen,' jeered the voice of the Dude. 'Any old time I come in a jail and don't find you I'll think you've cashed in or I have.'

The rumble of Little Ambrose could be heard from his desk.

'Whataye think this is, an experience colyume in the newspaper?'

'Shut up, fellows,' said Red. The advice was not needed. He went on in a lower tone. 'No, there's no use talking. They haven't built a stir yet a guy couldn't get out of. And there's all kinds of ways, besides climbing the walls. One fellow in Germany bit through a six-inch beam with his teeth. They were worn to stumps. Another fellow took threads from his socks and dipped 'em in glue and sand, and cut the bars. I'm not saying them's my methods, but just the same – if I get it this time.'

'I wouldn't want to bet many dollars on anything said here tonight,' said Jack with an undertone of bitterness.

'Now you're talking, farmer,' said the dapper William Orford. He had been holding an aloof air, his hat at a haughty angle, while his face with yesterday's beard gathered the prison dust in its veil of sweat. 'You won't want to call any of us liars either, I dare say.'

'All men are liars,' said the would-be portrait painter philosophically. 'You don't have to come here to learn that.' Weariness made him lean his elegant frame in its black morning coat against the dank white-washed brick wall. Besides, it saved jostling among these rough fellows. They were never still a moment, always stirring, talking, muttering to one another or to themselves. Like nits in cheese.

Secondhand roused himself to spit and glare about him. He should have spoken up when they were talking about women – broads they called them. It was because of his wife that he was here. She had told him it was all right to go bankrupt, and leave the money in her name. He might have done well enough in his business for a long time yet. That was American notions – letting the women boss things. He'd tell her when he got out. Perhaps she would be afraid and run away if he stayed long. He might get six years or eight or ten. Who could tell? Not even the wise lawyers.

The two worn and sodden tramps breathed stentorously. They had been in stranger places, but they did not feel at home. In the open – there they were in their element. They were old-fashioned bindle-stiffs, and they always got into trouble when they hit the cities. The cops didn't seem to have any use for them any more. They could hardly pass through a town of any size any more without getting jugged. The railway dicks were always on the job, and the brakemen wanted money when you travelled with them. Harmless sort of fellows like them were arrested half the time nowadays. They were too old to change their ways, too gone in the nerves for big-time stuff. About all that was left was losing an eye or a leg and begging on the street. Different from the old days. They could stand it to hit the ties for a stretch then, and there was always a handout whether there was a woodpile or not. Not so tough in those days. ... Sometimes they would be apart for months or years, but they would always meet up at some hoboes' convention or on the road. ... Then they'd stick together for a while. Everything was changing. No room for them ... no room. Everything changing.

And wedged together at the angle of the cell were the two quaintly engaging pals, the blue-suited dusty ones, the mouth-corner-speaking one and the big fellow, bull-headed, flat-shouldered. They could say nothing to each other now, not because there was nothing to say, but because they knew the others would hear. In the first moments after they had entered the cell they had talked as though they had not known the others were there, as though it did not matter what they thought. Now the others were become persons, to be considered more at this moment than anyone they had ever known. Not that they thought this consciously – a lot of hop-heads, tramps, punks, cheap 'vags,' stools maybe. The dicks would trade a one or two-year man to get next a murder. You never knew who was who. You got framed without trying. And stools were everywhere. There was always somebody laying for you. Look at the Cupsom slayer, murdered the day he got into jail by that halfbreed. A sharpened jail soup-spoon in the back did the trick. You might never have seen the guy before.

The question now, the smaller fellow allowed, was, who had framed them this time, and what job was it? They had been stepping high wide and handsome for quite a while, not doing much but throw on the dog; and tonight they had put on old togs and walked down Halsted Street, just ready for anything, and the Cadillac had picked them up. It looked as though their luck had changed. Perhaps the squad had nothing else to do. Or maybe they were hunting for big game, rounding up everybody in the city. That was it. Somebody had bumped a copper, or got half a million from the post-office, and they had to make a showing. Well, everything was clear at their rooms – nothing there except a couple of new suits – not even a key. They had a bank safe-deposit box, but they had the key to that hidden, and as for the password, they wouldn't split that unless they went clean off their tops. They should have a talk, but on the other hand they shouldn't. This was better than being alone in a cell after all. There they would be bound to talk and they would spill something, even if they pretended to be strangers. The dicks would listen all night and get something out of what they didn't say. The dicks were not so dumb. If they wanted to make a case against you, they could, every time. Get them against you and they didn't care for habeus corpus or anything else. They would rearrest you as fast as the writ was served. You never knew where you were. You might take the pinch as a vag, and they would rake up a few things and you'd end up with a fifteen-year sentence. ... Hell, the thought was enough to drive a guy simple and make him knock a few of these stupid heads together....

'No,' Red was speaking reflectively. 'This escaping stuff is not all it ought to be. They give you what for when they catch you. And not many get away for keeps. One guy I heard of found out the grating on the window in the insane hospital was loose, so what does he do but decide to go nuts? Of course when he was examined the croaker said he was sane as anybody. Then things started. They got a system all right, and if a guy ain't nuts when he pretends he is, he generally is when they get through with him. They hung him up by his wrists, with teeth on the inside of the rings. They lashed him, gave him the paddle, soaked in boiling water and dipped in sand. Auger holes in the paddle, you know, to raise the blisters. Then they gave him the water cure.'

'I guess he was crazy, all right,' said Curly.

'Well, the warden wouldn't give up. So one day he went down and gave the guy a red-hot poker for a sword. The guy chattered and grabbed it – both hands, and scorched the flesh off them. Couldn't feed himself for weeks. Still the doctor wouldn't sign. Then they found him eating dirt on the floor of his cell, and gave in. Second night in bug-house, he climbed out.'

'It just shows what a guy can do. The whole works can't hold him if he's got the stuff.' The big pal spoke enthusiastically, beaming at Red as the first person he had seen in the place.

'No use talking, he was the real Kid McCoy.'

'No suite in the bridewell for him.'

'Shut up,' muttered Red. 'Here comes Little Ambrose and his feet.'

'Heavens!' and 'Hell!' In spite of themselves the men could not retain a mutter. Ambrose was bringing another fellow. Not for their cell?

'Get back,' growled the bull to Red and the taxi man. It was the latter who moved, and like a piston the bull's arm shoved into the medley between the row on the bench and the row along the wall a nondescript, typeless individual, twenty or so, grimy-faced, neither dark nor fair, with long heavy freckled nose, small chin, eyes shifty yet intent, narrow forehead, slight stoop. Under his cap he craned and peered frankly for a second, then put on an air of boredom, seeing nothing. Half the others could not see him and did not try.

'Hell,' he complained. 'This is some room and bath in suite, I'll tell 'em.'

The portrait man drew away. William Orford sneered. Others looked at him disapprovingly. They did not want anyone else, if it had been their own brother. They maintained stoical countenances. Jack stared ahead of him. Whitey sat comfortably, his chin in his hands, elbows on spread knees. Bert shifted his hat. The tramps, the con-men, and Sooty drooped drearily, now and then straightening a crick out of their spines. Not listening or seeing. The tramps blinked sometimes, but the con-men never closed an eye. The little one saw everything without flickering an eyelash.

'Seventeen men in the cell now,' announced Bert Tremaine, triumphantly.

'Seventeen, God!' Half of them would not believe it, until they had counted all in sight and the Snowbird beneath the bench.

'Boys!' piped short Enos, by this time bound and trussed by his overcoat. 'Boys, she can't go much farther. Either the walls will have to give way or we'll have to get smaller. Can you tell me any other way out of the problem?'

'They should quit it, putting so many in, would settle it,' said Secondhand.

'We'll have enough to form a "Government Within",' laughed Red.

'Even if you couldn't call it a "Mutual Welfare Association",' said Whitey.

'If someone's bumped a copper,' said the little pal, 'they'll fasten it on all of us, and let us burn. That's their speed. Look at the Olney Bank gang.'

'Sh-sh,' said the dapper William Orford. 'Put adhesive tape on your lips. Pad-luck.'

'Bull-ring lock!'

'Touch wood.'

'Bad luck,' someone murmured.

'Yeh, let 'em try fastening something on me,' said Jack indignantly. 'I got a marriage certificate I got two hundred miles from here yesterday morning. And a licence I got a week ago. Let them laugh that off.'

The others shook their heads, patient at this ingenuousness.

'They can fasten anything on anybody, if they want to.'

'Boys, we're here, and we might as well make the best of it. Maybe the jury wouldn't take the word of every man of us against one bull. But there's one thing sure, they can't make us like they are.'

'I'd rather be a snake in a swamp.'

'Is your broad any good?' demanded William Orford. 'Is she the kind of moll that will do something about springing you?'

Jack was nonplussed.

'She doesn't know anything about such things.'

'My girl is a warbler in a drum – a cabaret. She'll be burnin' up when she finds I've taken the pinch.'

Jack looked curiously at the man, quite conventional as to appearance until he spoke and his face broke into hard grimaces, and a rasping voice. Doubt crept into Jack's mind like smoke into the crevices of a fire-invaded hut. Would anyone escape, could he escape when he had been released, straight in his mind? Wouldn't there be some force compelling him to do something that would bring him back here? That seemed to be the way with the others. But if he did nothing and took nothing, what could there be? He'd be careful, you bet. But things happened. If he ever did get out of this without serving a sentence, another accident might come up, and when he appeared: 'Ever been here before?' old question of the dicks. 'Yes.' – 'Yes, eh? Got a record, have you?' With a record, nothing could save you. They'd fasten something on you every time they pinched you. Wasn't that what he had learned here from the others? Catching people and fastening a rap on them, wasn't that how they got by? made their living?

If you ever show your face again in this town, look out! Don't all the dicks know your map? It didn't matter if you were alone or with an army. They arrest you as quick as they can. He would have to tell Grace what to do when she missed him. She was to get in touch with some lawyer he would pick out, and with every friend they had, and never rest until they had used all the influence they had and got him out, or got bail for him. That was it. But most of all, he and Grace would keep out of this town unless they had to come to it. They'd certainly steer clear of Chi, all right. They certainly would tell the world: 'Clear all the traffic, and let the lights stay green, for we're going to get out, and make time.'

If they ever got each other again and got their car. Boy!

But not likely he would be funny when he got out. If you had stayed long enough you might be forced to things your mind knew you shouldn't do. Sometimes, maybe, you would scarcely know you'd done 'em till afterward. But if he was a little queer in his ways, that would be all. He'd be queer the other way. He would be so honest that people would think he was funny. He didn't care, he'd be funny enough not to get in here again, that was one thing sure.

When he got out!

'God!' invoked one. 'Don't we ever tie the feedbag on in here?'

'It's about time those sandwich boys was bringing the grub and cigarettes around,' said Red, peering out through the bars.

'Service, eh?'

'Boys, I can take care of all the sandwiches they got in their baskets,' said Sooty.

'I guess we all can do pretty well,' said the taxi man. 'This job is just about as hungry a one as mine. Boy, a fellow sure can eat when he shoves a can around the streets all night.'

'Coming now,' sang Red.

'What, are the sandwiches coming now?'

'Just three or four cells down. And Little Ambrose with them.'

A sudden quiet descended on the cell. Each decided how hungry he was, and what the money in his pocket would do toward relieving the state. Their mouths began to water.

There was more bustle in the next cell, toward the front. The two men were outside that door, one with a clothesbasket of sandwiches, the other with a pail and pot of coffee. It seemed as though they never would leave. Listening to the talk was maddening:

'Ain't you got no cigarettes?'

'Sure, kid. No raise in the price, either.'

'Better not be. I didn't come in here to have the price of things raised on me.'

'Here, gi'me. I'm first.'

'Cash customer.'

'Where's the change for that?'

'I got it here, just wait a second,' said the sandwich man hastily.

'Anybody else want more coffee?'

'That what you call coffee?'

'Come on here,' said Red. 'Those fellows got enough. There must be nearly as many in there as here,' he added.

Finally the two actually stood before him and the taxi man. There was a quiet turmoil in the cell, while the men, mouths watering, strove to get a sight of the food – to get within arm's length of it if they could.

Red subsided at once, not saying a word. He even seemed to edge back from the door as though he had no right to be out front now.

The taxi man passed out a quarter and five cents.

'On two,' he said.

'Uh? Two lots?'

'Yes.'

Bert shrugged his shoulders, reflected that the coffee would be all right if it was hot, even with the cream and sugar, and held out fifteen cents.

Curly's hand was through the upper bars, but he had to wait.

When the taxi driver got his he gave a sandwich and one of the cups to Red. Red said:

'Whee, this is good stuff. I run out of change yesterday, and I been going short on feed till I make a banking connection in town.'

'Come on here, snap into it, hand me couple those buns,' snarled Sooty. His hand had been holding forth change over the shoulders of the others.

'I've eaten worse myself,' the taxi man agreed with Red.

Whitey was holding forth the dollar bill his girl had given him.

The Snowbird had crawled out and sat with head and shoulders between knees along the bench. He looked about appealingly, and decided to do without buying. Nobody noticed him.

Curly, standing on the bench, had an advantage over the others, but a responsibility with it. He laid his sandwich on the high bar, dustier than the lower ones, and shoved forth change opposite the faces of the boys for the two pals and later the portrait man. They twisted a cup through to him and he held it while they poured black coffee. No sugar. No milk.

Secondhand was holding back. His mouth was watering, but he had seen the taxi driver give Red a handout. Perhaps somebody would think he had no change either.

Nor did the two apple-cheeked brown tramps make a move to feed themselves.

The men on the other side of the bars were counting their change and getting back their coffee cups. Bert Tremaine who was opposite the tramps looked doubtfully at them.

'Look here, do you fellows want coffee?'

'No. We could stand coffee I guess, but I don't think we got enough change on us,' said one.

'I got a jit,' said the other.

'Give me your nickel,' returned Bert. 'Curly'll get you something. Both want coffee?'

'Better have a sandwich too,' said Enos, pulling forth change.

'I guess everybody feeds.'

'This is where a fellow needs a friend, unless he's going to starve.'

'I ain't had nothing yet,' muttered Snowbird, swaying his long back, closing his eyes. 'Not a thing.'

'Come on, somebody,' commanded Red. 'One more old horsecollar to be fed.

It was William Orford who dug into his flannels.

'Come on, hurry up, can't stand here all day,' said the men. 'Others want to get something too.'

'Tha's right, white man, we's sho hungry in here,' came a melancholy negro voice.

'How many cups in there? Fifteen? We'll get them on the way back.'

'This is what you call a boofay luncheon,' said William Orford.

'There's not much "boeuf" about this tea,' returned the portrait man, who had learned his art during the war in France.

'It's funny they couldn't feed us when they get us here,' complained Jack Dolson.

'Don't be a sorehead,' adjured Curly good-naturedly, and Red added:

'We're not in jail yet. If they get us there they'll have to feed us.'

'Hell, we're eating, anyhow.' Sooty was companionable, now that this was so.

'Yeh, don't forget it.'

They all wolfed their sandwiches and doughnuts down and swallowed the steaming bitter coffee as though neither should be parted a second. Their elbows knocked, and if a morsel fell its possessor hunted it as soon as he had eaten what he held in his hand. They were good-natured; they were together on this thing more than ever. It was like a picnic. They did not need to talk, to make signs to one another of how they felt, nor communicate at all. Satisfaction. At such a moment they were themselves, life became ordinary again, and not so bad. Whatever was to happen would happen. Anyway there would be more meals. They didn't see anyone lying around starved to death. They felt as worthy and well satisfied as though they had worked hard all day and were eating an evening meal at home. Let their worries return upon them when they would; they couldn't faze them now. Nothing could get a fellow's goat while he was tucking a feed into him. Only thing was, it wasn't much of a feed.

'When's them guys coming back with more grub?'

'Aw, the bozos won't be back tonight again, that's one sure thing.'

'Yeh, youze want more to eat, me I didn't have none,' said Second-hand, wagging his head with genial melancholy.

'What, where *are* you, you poor kike?'

'I been here all the time, ain't I?' He was stuck in the far corner of the bench, behind the others.

'Why didn't you holler? One of these rich buggers would pay for a sandwich for you.' demanded Red, with a captain's concern.

'Yeah, you wanta make a play for the rich buggers,' said Sooty, sucking crumbs from his fingers.

'Can't spare you any of mine,' Enos remarked, chucking the last of his sandwich into his mouth.

'You'll go hungry to the stool, at that rate,' chuckled the Coke, making away with his in huge mouthfuls.

'Ha. You forget me, I guess.' Secondhand grinned, quite happy about it. Suddenly he frowned, and reached forward.

'Here, you runt, come across once.'

He was half-behind Snowbird, but the shifty eye of the latter had watched him from the start, and he was ready. There was nothing left; Secondhand held his empty skinny paw, while he munched with full cheeks.

'Here!' laughed Bert. 'Here's a bite of mine left. Catch!'

'Gossake, don't throw it.' But nobody tried to take the half-sandwich from him, and Secondhand was not long getting his mouth full.

'Well, well,' said Snowbird, imitatively generous, with a superior manner. 'Here's a gulp of coffee in the bottom of my cup. You take it. Spit on it and stir the grounds!'

'Hell mit your old coffee.' But he took it.

'Ain't we a brotherly bunch?' sighed Red. 'A little hungrier and we'd eat one another up.'

'When you get in jail,' explained William Orford to Jack, 'you get fed regularly enough, such as they give you.'

'Regular's right.'

'Everything comes regular enough, I guess.'

'If they ain't nothing else they're regular.'

'Reglar gits it.'

'Not regular in their charges, though.'

Gloom settled over the cell. A sickening impatience filled them. Here was morning, and nothing happening. No change, no hope. Morning wasn't even morning any more. It was just a part of night – meant only what night meant, it seemed. They were thinking that after all they had no right to be certain that morning would bring something different. Or any other morning maybe for a good long time. They were up against something, all right. The courage with which they had lasted out the night and the show-up reached its ebb and seemed a mockery now. Laughter, jokes, fellowship, song, consciousness of innocence or of having got the worth of this before – all these things became minor matters, and they could not understand how they had ever built upon them a superiority to their actual plight, the high-hearted go-to-hellness which was the only weapon to overcome prisons. Now they saw all too clearly just what they were up against, and compensations shrank into the background.

Would they get a break? Would the dicks lie in the testimony? Would they book them right away and let them get bail? Would they third-degree them into confessing something the dicks wanted to find out? They would put them – photographs, measurements, feet and thumb prints – into the Rogues' Gallery. Give everybody a record. Would they be left here, or moved from one stinking cell to another over the city so that their people would not find them to get bail? Weeks ... weeks might pass....

But the deep feeling like pity against the dicks which they had shown earlier in the night was gone. They were weary, they would rather be anything in God's earth and sky than creatures that treated men so. They were willing to forget, if they could sleep. But the time for that had passed, though the cell and the whole prison were more quiet than they had been all night.

Where was Grace now, Jack wondered. Hunting him. At the doors of the prison, and they would not tell her he was here. Or they were taking her in, to keep her till he. ... He'd never find her. Little Grace! What, where? Lost. Both lost! Oh, she would come to him, put her arms around him, say: 'It's all crazy, Jack. It never happened. Don't think of it again. It never was.' She would come to him and say, 'Jack I never want to see you again. I'm not going with any fellow that gets arrested and goes to jail.' – 'You must have forgot – we're married. Married!' Oh, the little girl, she would open her sweet eyes at that, she would remember, she would kiss him. All the jails in the world couldn't separate them now. No, she was mad, she would not look at him: a divorce, because he deserted her the marriage night, besides he got into jail. The judge said, 'Aren't you sorry for this poor little woman?' – 'Hell, she wouldn't come to jail with me, I had to go alone.'

'Hell, I'm crazy,' Jack muttered. 'I'm, I been dreaming.'

'Aw, Murphy, one little ... little bhang,' the Snowbird mumbled under the bench.

The old tramps had begun to talk to the portrait man; William Orford to the blue pair; Bert Tremaine and Enos and Secondhand were listening and putting in a word like children. At the front, Curly in his corner at the ceiling had spread out his arms along the top of the wall, to rest his legs. Whitey dozed in the gloom, stretched out on the bench, his hat over his face.

'It's stuffy here,' complained Curly.

'The air would be better under the bench than anywhere else,' said Jack.

'Especially near the back of the cell,' laughed Orford.

'Fellow was in a forest fire up in Michigan told me he stuck close to the ground. Not half so much smoke there.'

'There wouldn't be much difference here,' said Bert. 'It's all so thick you couldn't slice it with a tennis racket.'

'Malaria in the lower ground,' muttered Whitey.

'Kind of small laboratory to work out such an experiment,' Bert said.

'It's big for a lavatory, but as a room, it's a lav,' said Curly.

'How you mean, social laboratory?' Secondhand asked suspiciously.

'He means it's a melting pot,' said Red. 'That's why I've taken off my collar.'

Silence again. No one really had anything to say, unless to tell the inmost fears of their hearts. Jack knew they would not do that. He dozed again. They would not do that. They were a bunch of the boys, in a corner for the moment, taking the count. Nothing to wail or knock the breast about that. His head was nodding again. They were innocent, being men. What did men do on this planet but what lay nearest their hands, what did they try for but what their spirits and bodies hungered for? What else, being men?

The taxi driver was telling his troubles, in a low voice, talking endlessly it seemed. The old cans they gave a new driver. There was not so much as a crank to them. You had to go to the garage early to get the good ones, and half wouldn't have their equipment. The rubber mat in the back would be missing. Somebody would have screwed the button from the accelerator, and you'd have to go to the stock room to get a requisition for a new one, or wear a hole through the sole of your shoe. Or the horn was busted, or you'd get on the street and find you didn't have any brakes to speak of, and you'd have to go slower than ever on that account, so that every other cab on the street cut in ahead and got your pick-ups. ... The others joked him, thinking of their own stories.

Yes, they were innocent, these men, even as they had told with their lies. The comradeship, the encouragement, the little gifts they gave one another – their best. The way they strove to some ideal, the best their senses would let them recognize. The effort to win the approval of the people they had learned to admire. Weren't they all good children? Weren't they, these children, these ruffians, these men, all innocent?

There was a bustle and clanking at the door. The breaths of Little Ambrose. His voice like a sighing fog-horn. What was it now? Who was going out? They stood tense.

'Dolson. Guy here by name Dolson? Come on.' He made a motion to relock the door.

'Hey! Wait. Here I am.' Jack wriggled and tramped. They all fell away. He was out.

'Come on then.'

As they reached the end of the bull-pen, Ambrose spoke.

'Visitor to see you.'

'Who – who is it?'

'Mrs John Dolson, was the name she gave herself.'

Their voices were loud in the bullpen, estranged from the cells.

It was high morning and birds were singing ... sun was shining. ... The grey-haired dick and Grace were in the corridor, both smiling. Little Ambrose unlocked the gate. He had to stay there.

'I should have said good-bye to those fellows,' Jack thought, suddenly, looking back. 'Poor Red. It wasn't his turn.'

Sketches
Corncob Corners and Other Places

HARVEST HOME CHICKEN SUPPER AT BIRDSEYE CENTRE

Wash-day could be quite ignored for one Monday. All morning the telephones kept ringing and each woman on the party line called others.

'Did Mrs Banning say anything to you about bringing tumblers? I've just put my chickens in the oven. I guess they'll have time to cook before they come around for the stuff.'

'Oh, my, I'll have to hurry. I've just finished mixing the dressing for mine. Got the cakes and jellies and everything all ready and in the basket, though.'

But the weather looked bad. If only they didn't get another rain, there'd been so much lately.

Mrs Mears' husband was away with the threshing machine, and wouldn't come till late. So the Banning women called for her at half-past four, with young Herman driving. 'You're going early enough so you can help – the ladies, eh, Herman?' Herman reached around and slammed the door of the car as he drove. He grinned and pored over the road. 'To help Audrey, you mean?' shrilled Julia Banning, beside him. She wore a new grey coat trimmed with a kind of grey fur. 'Don't put your feet in them baskets back there! We don't want no squashy grub.' The girl was in high spirits. 'I wonder how Mrs Corey's going,' her mother remarked, looking into the passing farmyard, where a dozen little white pigs scurried about the door. 'I don't give a darn *how* she's going!' sang out Julia, waving both arms, putting her feet up at the windshield.

The Lombard side-road was terrible. Herman drove slowly for once, but the ruts were so deep and so tortuous that the car shivered heavily as it wriggled along, and Mrs Mears and Mrs Banning in the back seat swayed drunkenly, knocking their hats. 'Now remember we got a new top on this bus, so calm yourself; don't jump through it,' Julia adjured them. Lottie, the youngest child, on her mother's knee, looked from one to another undisturbed. Mrs Mears, holding a coal-oil lamp in one hand and the globe in another, smiled wryly, then gave a light scream; they had leaped out of the rut, and the car clawed at the clay edge of the ditch, muttering fiercely and inclined to turn around.

But soon they were on the county road, and in five minutes Herman had delivered them at the church door. Out jumped Julia, took a dish of salad dressing from the top of Mrs Mears' bushel-basket, and promptly spilled it down the front of her coat. 'Darn!' she said, looking as though she might dash the bowl into the mud.

They carried the baskets into the basement of the church. The opening door greeted them with a smell of coal-oil, fresh lumber, and cooked pumpkin. In the first corner a booth was already set up for the cakes. 'Got anything for here, Julia, heh, got anything for here?' Mrs Wireton, her grey hair already straggly, leaned over the counter. 'Wait a minute; I'm here!' shouted Julia. 'If you ain't got cakes enough – '

Mrs Jameson before the stove in the meat booth – a brown-faced woman with a gold tooth – was watching Julia unpack the chickens. Her stony grey eyes almost bright, she went from one basket to another, peeking into each, then came back and began to help. 'Smashed potatoes! You didn't forget the potatoes, now? Goin' to smash 'em?' She bent and looked up into the girl's eyes, anxious.

'Here, Mrs Steese, you can have the pie booth, then your children won't bother – I mean, you can't wait on the table so well – ' 'All right.' Mrs Steese, a fair woman with a stern smile and hair straight back, promptly set down her baby and lifted two of her children to the bench at the rear. 'Oh, wait –' she cried.

'I've got to introduce the new school-teacher. Here, Miss Alger, come over here, meet these ladies over here in the cake booth. This is the new school teacher, Miss Alger. Now here at the chicken booth, Miss Alger, come and I'll introduce you to these ladies.' ... Finally, the teacher following her, she made the circuit of the basement and came back to the cluster of children on the bench. 'I'll leave you now just to keep an eye on these kids.' She patted on an apron. They clutched the skirt of the girl's new tan suit, and she was thankful that borders were worn. Julia Banning looked her over enquiringly while she took off little Johnnie's coat and wiped Amy's nose. So politely unaware – Herman looked at her with curiosity; he had not been introduced to her; he was helping the men set up the tables. Then there were the benches. 'Think that'll hold?' he grinned, asking Cissie Walkins, an immense girl who went to all the ladies' meetings and took part like an old woman.

Now when the dusk had suddenly come the place seemed full of people; they darkly scurried here and there. A coal-oil stove sputtered in one corner and in another the big wood stove bore steaming pots.

Children played tag or stopped in wonder to realize the variety of food at every hand; or to try the influence of their mother to get a piece. The lamps couldn't be lit for the table until the cloths were laid. But then at last it *was* a sight – two long tables, stretching nearly the length of the church, white, with the knives and forks and spoons strung along the sides. The air became hotter and tenser at every moment. Any time a group of people might come in for supper, or some of those present demand to be served.

'Sugar, sugar!' someone cried. 'We won't have enough sugar. Some takes sugar on their tomatoes.'

'Say, Ed, let's hop in your coup and go down t' the Corners for some sugar,' proposed Julia.

Ed spun on his heel.

'Nothing doing, I got to pour tea.'

Julia looked after at him.

'Mr Mears will be late,' his wife explained with harassed eyes to the minister. 'He's out in the country, and then he's got to call for the Banning men. Maybe we'd better get someone else to be doorkeeper.'

'Doorkeeper? Somebody else? I guess not,' shrilled Mrs Jameson cordially from among her smashed potatoes. 'Why, it wouldn't be a harvest home supper at all without Mr Mears for doorkeeper. Gol! – ' She turned away clapping her hand to her mouth. Mrs Mears did not let on she heard her, and the minister, a short, smooth, pale man, spoke kindly: 'A little while, a little while, Mrs Mears. Our good friend won't fail us.' His hands in pockets bared a broad, black waistcoat as he sauntered to the other side of the room and sat down on a bench, his back to the table.

Before anyone knew how it had come about the tables were filled with squeezing, joking families, their eyes intent on destruction – emptied, and refilled with more families, couples, singles. The lady waitresses strode hither and thither, their face-powder furrowed. An old man's hands went like palsy in his struggles. 'Here,' a woman shouted in his ear kindly. 'That piece is tough. I'll get you a piece of breast.'

Tall youths held teapots high. 'More tea, anybody more tea? More tea, Mr Bell?'

'Pass that light cake up this way, you folks.'

The minister ate near the last, when the whole opposite side of the table was empty, with the two leading laymen of the circuit. Mr Mears was free from the door now – a man who listened anxiously and laughed at everything. Fat Mr Shuman from the other appointment had driven the minister over. They served Mr Shuman so many pieces of chicken with bones that his plate left no room for potatoes and gravy, until he shoved the bones on to his bread and butter plate. Then he couldn't use that for his pie.

'Well, I thought I could eat a lot, but when I look at that pile of bones Shuman has there – ' Mears went off in a slow laughter.

'It looks compromising, Mr Shuman, it looks compromising,' the minister added, smiling.

Mr Shuman held his own: 'Never mind Mr Mears there – I'll bet he'd eat his bones and all. Well, we'll see who eats the most pieces of pie. Did you ever hear the joke about the piece of pie?'

The minister looked politely enquiring across a third cup of tea.

'There's only one thing better than a piece of pie – two pieces.'

His shouts were nearly drowned because Mr Bricker had given all the children horns and rattles from his store. 'They'll remember Bill Bricker as long as they live,' declared T.W. Shuman.

By nine o'clock everyone had been served but the waitresses and portions of their families. 'We're not going to wait for you folks much more,' Julia came down to tell them. 'Go ahead,' they urged her, pieces of cake in one hand, steaming mugs in the other. People for miles around had come for the supper, but Hamish Dobie, the old bachelor, said: 'Threshing tables is bad enough, but when it comes to hoeing in with a mixed bunch like this, in the first place it's hard on the elbows, gives 'em double work, even the kids beside you don't wipe their faces on them, or the rest of them plays tag around the tables.'

Hamish came for the program, at the same time as the people from town who took part in it. The church had a cooler smell of cookery after the basement, for a short time. Asters and dahlias at pulpit and altar, corn and pumpkins in the choir-loft. There was no room for another soul, and benches, three blocks of wood under long planks, had to be brought up from below, hoisted over people's heads for the aisle. Mr Bricker, chairman, leading merchant from the county town, was delighted to see so many present and referred to chickens entering the ministry. After a shrill solo he dispensed with comment, reaching into his pockets took out package after package of candy in slices like gum.

'Now is there anybody didn't get any? Just raise your hands.' And the big man could throw the candy to any corner of the church.

Julia Banning stood on the platform, hemmed, hemmed again, looked to the back seat where Herman sat beside that Melvin girl, laughed in response to the giggling of younger elements, and gave a recitation concerning a race-horse and the race by which it saved its old Kentucky master's fate. There were songs, recitations, readings, quartets, instrumentals, more songs, recitations. One was improvised tuition in the art of courtship demonstrated by an eligible young bachelor teacher in the Sunday school.

'Oh, isn't it awful?' whispered the school-teacher to her friend from town, also on the program.

At a quarter past eleven Mr Bricker ceased his jokes, spoke seriously of the good of getting together, was abetted by the minister, who led in a word of prayer. Then everybody rose and sang 'God Save the King.'

Many, for the most part the men, got out of the church shortly, and stood around the door in the light from it and from their cars, waiting for the women-folk. They were in the basement getting their baskets and dishes, with what remained in them, feeding the members of the program, talking about the cleaning-up there would be to-morrow. When a pile of overcoats on a bench was disturbed howls emerged. Two children had gone to sleep before the program, unwittingly buried. Mrs Banning put her arms akimbo. 'Oh, it's nothing! Just the juvenile band!'

Mr Mears stood on a chair and said, 'The balance of the cooking left over will be for sale.'

'Shut up,' said Julia. 'It's too late – I strike for an eight-hour night.'

'I suppose you won't be honouring us with your company regularly, Miss Alger?'

'No,' said the teacher thoughtfully. 'As long as the weather is good I'll drive back to town every night.'

Nobody remembered the thrill which had run over the church Sunday, yesterday, when even the choir smiled at each other, and the minister had said after a pause: 'There is one other announcement I wish to make. It seems there is to be a chicken supper...!'

CHRISTMAS AT CORNCOB CORNERS

Blue dusk filled the world, flooded the farm, and seeped through the window panes, when young Joseph wakened. Christmas morning. Of course it was early – maybe it was night yet. He had dreamed that his stocking was full of crumpled paper. He would just have to get up, if it were only one o'clock. He lay in agony for an age, which might have been a minute, and then he stirred. Who knew what might be in the stockings, oranges, candy, toys, to say nothing of unimaginable big things that couldn't get into them? Would there? Perhaps he was dreaming again, and would wake up and find it wasn't Christmas at all. But Walter was awake, too, and it kept Joseph going to jump out of bed first.

Hearts in their mouths, they felt their way into the hall, past mother's door, past Allie's door, and it was darker than ever on the stairs. But down in the sitting-room there was a red glow from the stove, and the coals showed dull through the isinglass. Oh, they shivered, with bare feet. Only the wooden clock ticked. It must be night yet, and in the dark they stumbled on the rocker of a chair. But near the stove, that was the place! There hung the stockings, plainly bulging in the glimmer, on the knobs of the family group frame. That would have to take the place of a hearth, mother had said; but it was high. 'Get a chair,' said Joseph. The faces of all those relatives in the picture frame seemed to glow at them in the firelight.

'Wait! Me, too, now!' came a whisper, and Allie stepped from the stairs, all white. They all got chairs and, exploring the stockings, put their toes up to the nickeled stove. They sighed in ecstasy over the presents. 'Just what I wanted. Oh, how could Sandy know?' But every other minute one of the boys would have to jump up and go to the table again to look things over, and come back sucking hard candies. 'Won't I scoot with these skates!'

'But look at my doll!' An hour and a half later their parents found them there, and then the house woke up, with wishes, kisses, laughter, exclamations; and time passed so quickly again that father was in from the chores and they did not need the lamp for breakfast like an ordinary morning, and Allie blew it out while Joseph held his hand above the globe.

After breakfast there were more chores. Allie was lucky; being a girl she could stay in with all the wonderful things which had appeared so suddenly from nowhere, and see mother fix up everything for the Christmas dinner. But Joseph and Walter took some of the candies in the pockets of their sweater coats to suck while they pumped the water.

It was real winter now, not all muddy like it had been right until day before yesterday. A white Christmas, their father called it. 'I'm glad it ain't a green Christmas!' They tugged at the pump handle, and the black sulphur water ran down, away along the trough to the big trough in the barnyard, and the steers came out of the barn and the shed, forty of them, and not one of them knew it was Christmas! And they all sipped the water, and looked about, and breathed frost, and supped more. Soon Father appeared at the stable door and told them that was enough, for now.

It was warmer in the stable, where father was putting straw in the stalls for the horses. 'Do you think Jessie would eat candy?' Walter asked gravely, rubbing his nose with his red mitten. 'You might try.' The little boy walked in beside the road-horse, and, yes, she snorted, and was afraid she would bite the red mitt, but she champed the candy all right. 'Good horsey.'

'Suppose we go and get the mail before we go to the house,' father said, and all three walked down the lane, along the row of pines. The old trees sounded kind of sorry, but the sun was bright, and made fine silver wires of cobweb floating out....

Just in time. There was the mailman, red cheeks between his coat-collar, driving away from the high tin mail-box. They couldn't see him put things in it. 'Merry Christmas! I suppose they've loaded you down to-day,' says father.

'Oh, loaded down, nothing, but I am loaded down with the things people leave in their boxes for me. Thanks for those apples, young man.' The mailman called back as his horse took a trot, and the boys on the bridge waved at him. The water wasn't frozen in the ditch; it was deep, clear brown, and the weeds standing or tipped in it were like little snow-covered trees. 'Come on, boys.'

In the house there were letters, parcels from more people than they could remember. Aunts, uncles, father's mother and father in the

States, mother's people in England. Then just as things got strewn in a fine pile on the table, in came old Mr and Mrs Ogg, that lived on the next farm, and they'd been asked over for Christmas dinner. 'Merry Christmas!' 'Same to you!' They took off their wraps. 'Well, well, well,' said Mr Ogg, and his white moustache moved. He always made the boys think he was pleased and awfully surprised to see them, and patted them on the heads. He had three magnificent red long pencils with rubbers on the ends for them, and a big book of white paper. They made him sharpen the pencils.

Mr Ogg and father sat in the dining-room and talked, and it was funny, because they didn't mention it being Christmas very often, either. In the kitchen Mrs Ogg sat and rocked and talked to mother whether she was in the pantry or not. Once when she was, Joseph whispered to Mrs Ogg, 'I got up at four o'clock this morning to see what was in my stocking!' He drew back and they looked at each other in astonishment. 'My! Did you really?' The old lady was impressed, but forgot right away, and went on talking. So the boys brought all their presents in from the other room to show her. 'And this one's Allie's!' Allie came out of the pantry and saw them, then she ran to the sitting-room and showed her presents herself.

The men passed through the kitchen and went to the barn, but the boys stayed in, and watched mother and Allie sew up the goose, and cracked nuts. 'Goose is good! Goose is good! Goose is good!' With every word Walter hit the table with a fork. 'Mother, make young Walter stop! He's hitting the table!' Then they had an army battle on the floor, until Joseph said, 'I'm hungry' in a surprised way. They waited and waited, and played some more and got hungrier, and then the men came in. 'We thought we'd fix the stock all up. Now we won't have to go near 'em till night.'

'Father, come and see our army! We got a grand army!'

'But, sons, it's dinner time. Wait till afterward.'

And then there was dinner. There was the goose, great and brown. 'He looks like an Indian goose,' said Joseph. And there was dressing, and potatoes, and gravy, and celery, and cranberries and everything – and pudding, but the children were to have jello and whipped cream instead. It was all wonderful, except that once, when nobody was saying anything, Mrs Ogg said, 'Joseph was telling me he got up at four o'clock this morning to see his stocking.'

'Oh!' thought Joseph. 'Women! You can't tell them anything – ' He was going to burst right out, but nobody seemed to notice, and dinner went on the longest time, everybody saying interesting things, until he and Allie and Walter got up from the table and left the rest talking. They danced up and down in the sitting-room, exulting anew. 'Oh, I am so happy, so happy!' It was a kind of song. They looked out of the window at the poor old fields and the snow. There was the oats field, brown with stubble and weeds, and then the smooth wheat-field beyond showed nothing but a curtain of snow streaming over its surface in the wind. But every once in a while the waves would be thin, and there would be sunlight....

It seemed they had only begun to play when mother made them go to bed, to be rested up for the entertainment tonight. And when they woke up and rushed downstairs in the dusk of late afternoon they asked, 'Can we take the sleigh?' Father had it all ready, in case the snow got deep enough, they knew. But he and Mr Ogg were at the barn doing the night chores. Soon they heard the voices of the men, and old Mr Ogg pulled his moustache and raised his eyebrows. 'Well, well, the weesters are up, are they?'

Supper wasn't like any ordinary supper, yet it wasn't so exciting as the sleighride, with the bells, and after that the program in the town hall at Corncob Corners, with something funny they had never seen before. It was called a tableau, and it was like school, only quieter. And there was one piece in which they got up and sang with all the other children, and mother promised them something nice if they stood nice and straight. Coming home they went to sleep before the sleigh came to Mr Ogg's place.

And next week father read out loud in the *Corncob Expositor* a message of thanks from the mailman: 'May the dove of peace always hover over your ridgepoles...' And he smiled, and they thought Christmas was a long way behind. But soon it would be 'New Year's.'

THE DANCE AT CORNCOB CORNERS

'Ladies change to the right hand!'
'All balance partners.'
'Grand right-and-left.'
'Swing partners!'
'Ladies change to the left hand.'
'Next couple to the right.'
'Swing the corner lady, and circle to the right.'

It is the calling-off for those old-time dances without which no truly rural assemblage for this sort of jollification is complete – however thoroughly the young folk may devote their attention to two-steps, turkey-trots, waltzes, or even the Charleston, in between whiles.

Nor do these young folk disdain to take part in the square dances which their elders enjoy so much. In them alone can the whole house as it were be seen on its feet. White-haired men and bearded ones, frowsy mothers of eight (seven present at the dance) and neat farm wives. Bobbed heads, of all colours, even grey; high-heeled pumps, sport-shoes, clodhoppers. Sleek-headed young men whose hands only betray a knowledge of the soil; others ruddy-faced and burly; and an example or two of the perennial ones for whom their clothes are too small everywhere. All mingle gaily, whether the faces be sober or not; all know each other, nod, speak, toss quips and merry by-words back and forth.

'Change partners, ladies to the right!'

'All join hands.'

It is Abe Leathers calling off. Years ago he used to call off every dance of nearly every ball in this end of the county. Now, it is only occasionally that they let him show them how it should be done. His grey moustache moves gravely, and his tenor drawl comes clear and sedate, but beneath his imperturable exterior he is enjoying the whole thing vastly. And when the break-down comes, the orchestra can hardly keep up to him. The only trouble is that there are so few of these 'old-time' dances to be called off through the evening, and he is left sitting at the wall with the old folk. Certainly he can't be expected to learn, or to want to try to learn the funny steps the spring-chickens are all addicted to now-times.

No, he has to look on politely, though disapprovingly, and pass the time with Ed Callister who used to be his rival at 'calling-off' but for years never came to dances after his wife died. He and Ed swap stories the way they used to swap horses: if one gets ahead one time, the other gets ahead next time. And it is the same with Jonas Edwards and Fuller Blott, and Alf McGrew and Dennis Hoyt and the other old fellows.

Ed says: 'You surely had them hoeing it down, all right.'

'Not so bad for an old-timer,' admits Abe modestly, settling back in his chair. 'They don't get up such dances now-times as they used to. "Swing that girl, that pretty little girl, the girl I left behind me!" Remember the time you swung that girl so high her heels knocked two keys off of old Pete's banjo?"

Abe raised a knee and brought his foot down, heavily, slapping himself resoundingly at the same time.

'Say! I guess I do. Rooms them times were so small that the caller to get back into the chimney-corner so the dancers wouldn't run over him when they got milling around. Unless they held it in a barn.'

'Well, sir, no wonder they used to have those fights. Dance wasn't complete without a fight afterward. Then they'd have to have another fight at the next dance to settle that one.'

'What are you Methuselahs telling?' demanded a spruce youth stopping before them.

'Pretty crowded, all right. Used to go on in sets and your tickets was numbered, so you couldn't go on with the other bunch, unless there was enough of them. Might be only a dozen girls or less, and they'd be pretty well tuckered out before the dance was done. But my wife never would dance, and I never would come alone, until she died.'

But most of the men have their wives with them, not to mention their families. In fact a great part of the concourse of people is collected in a fringe, about the edge of the hall, while the older boys and girls, the men and women, dance in the centre in time to what seems, to the onlookers, the uncertain blares of the orchestra.

But the dancers themselves feel differently: 'Nothing the matter with that orchestra,' the boys tell their partners, and 'Keen orchestra, all right!' 'I should say!' The variety of steps is equal to that in dress. Some nimble toes advance, recede, whirl in side-steps, always varying, always swift and light, enjoying evidently a very poem of motion. More advance with regular sliding steps which seldom vary, although it seems as though sparks should appear from the floor or their soles as they conscientiously rasp forward and back, with sideward bendings, joined with lax angularity or clutching desperately as in fear of separation in the mazes of the crowd. And two or three couples, of which one partner is 'just learning,' do not do as well as this. A smothered 'Ouch!' is heard from a girl whose toes have been trampled. Luckily as far as anybody has seen there is no couple on the floor of which both are 'just learning,' probably the combination would detract attention from the other dancers and in general exert a disintegrating effect on the assemblage. But even single learners become scarcer each winter. The children seem to learn almost by second nature, and before you know they are learning at all they are whirling around with the best of them.

One young fellow – though it must be admitted he was a stranger from the city – tried to do the Charleston with Carlotta Bangs, who had seen them dance it herself. But he didn't get very far. He was throwing his feet out in great style and slapping people on the shins, when up steps Peter Arson, the constable, and taps him on the shoulder. Nobody knows what was said, but that was enough. The stranger settled down and danced like the rest.

Listen to the conversation of one young matron in blue with her hand on the shoulder of a boy of ten, her eyes following appreciatively the figure of her husband in the crowd, while she talks out a dance with an old friend.

'The roads were so bad I thought we couldn't get away. The road east of our place was just a sea of mud. I told Ira we couldn't go with the car, and he says, "Oh, well, we'll try the horse and buggy. We'll leave the kids home once." Well, I didn't want to agree to that, and anyway the rigs we saw going along seemed to have all they could do. And our driver is such a little thing you know, and just a colt. So we decided that if we were going to go, the best way was to hitch the heavy team on the jumper and put the whole family on it; so here we are. I said, even if we do live on a back road that's no sign we're going to give in and not go anywhere.'

She laughs, still looking on with enjoyment, humming a bar to the music of the orchestra.

'Now that's what I call real courage,' returns her neighbour, laughingly, also with voice raised to overcome the noise.

'Well, here comes my partner for the next dance. See you again.' She moves away gracefully and effortlessly, her head nodding to some question of her partner.

Before the dance there was supper, scheduled to begin at seven, and actually served from a quarter to eight to nine-thirty. A few at the last tables were inclined to complain a little, but they were given extra-large servings of potato salad and cake and coffee, of which there was plenty left. Anyway as the ladies told each other at the rear of the hall, where things were dished out, what could you expect for fifty cents, and with the evening's dancing and program thrown in to boot? It was more than could get anywhere else for anything like the money. Besides, lots of people got two or three servings, and at first there were pies. Well, it just went to show how some people would never be satisfied, no matter how much they got. But not many heard these rumours, and on the whole everyone was well-pleased, well-filled, and disposed to listen with equanimity to the program.

Several notables were present to address the meeting. The reeve of the township, the village fathers, two ministers, and the local member of parliament, who was the chairman.

All of them, lay or clergy, approved the splendid supper and the fine concourse of people which greeted their sight in the banner township of the banner county of the finest province of the Dominion of Canada. One of the gentlemen commenting on former speeches of his own, deplored his tendency to become humorous. 'One time,' he recorded, 'when I thought I had been particularly witty, I asked my wife, "Did you think I was funny?" "Funny!" she exclaimed, "I thought you were a scream".' This, however, was a somewhat unusual modesty. One man referred to the character of the times in certain cities as 'bibulous.' In them, he explained, there were more Bibles distributed in the hotel bedrooms than in any other cities of the province. The preachers laughed as heartily as anyone at this. Many a solo and duet, recitation and dialogue varied the weight of these speeches, and the chairman himself interpolated no mean number of merry anecdotes and quips.

Benny Slooman, the talented local violinist, played the 'Prisoner's Song' accompanied by a pupil at the piano and another acting as second violin. As an encore he himself, with gravely sweating face, sang the 'Prisoner's Song' while playing the piano. So it was twelve o'clock by the time the program came to an end, people moved about and got limbered up, swung the benches back to the walls, and the dancing began, Benny Slooman and his orchestra being just warmed up to their work now.

There was no nonsense about a gathering like this. When these people had determined upon making a night of it, a night of it they made, whether the children fell asleep in their arms or in various corners on and under benches, or not. Most of the growing children, however, to do them justice, ran about vigorously, and did their best to contribute their full quota to the activities transpiring about them.

And now they are listening in awe to old Abe Leathers calling off once more:

'Ladies change to the right hand ... All balance partners ... Swing partners ... Ladies turn to the right hand ... All join hands!'

And, of course, the orchestra obliges with 'Turkey in the Straw,' 'Arkansas Traveler,' 'Swing that Girl, that Pretty Little Girl, the Girl I Left Behind Me,' and many another old favourite.

Faces become flushed with exercise, pleasure, the close air; and dance after dance goes by until everybody has had enough of his favourite kind, and somebody says if they stay much longer they'll have to have breakfast served.

Not long after this a general breaking-up becomes evident, and at three o'clock most of the people with families are leaving. Then the older people go, and finally the last of the young chattering troop down the stairs into the brightening night.

SOME FOLKS OF OUR VILLAGE

The jazz age of course has reached our town, but most of the young people, the men and women, retain in large part the standards of their mothers and fathers. One such girl, whose name I had better not mention, went into a theatre in the city and demonstrated this fact. She had long been in ill health; with a weak heart, and the family doctor had given her a hypodermic needle with some strychnine and medicated stuff with which to stimulate her heart's action.

This particular afternoon she was feeling rather tired and depressed after a shopping expedition, and betook herself to a matinee of the better sort. It transpired that she sat beside a man who betrayed an interest in her which passed over the bounds of convention. In fact he actually leaned toward her heavily, and otherwise showed her an unwelcome attention which the girl returned in very different kind, though for a long time she ignored it completely.

At length, unable to bear it longer, she thought, 'I'll fix you, Mr Man,' and extricated the hypodermic needle from her effects, aided by the dusk. Along with it she took a black-headed pin of unusual sharpness. Carefully maneuvering her arms, she pushed her hand holding the pin under the other arm and very forcibly into the leaning anatomy of the man next to her. He bounded up with explosive language, and sat down with more of the same. The girl eyed him calmly.

'Now see here, sir,' she said. 'That's no more than you deserve, and your behaviour is not that of a gentleman. Furthermore,' she continued, holding forth the hypodermic needle to his affrighted gaze, 'look what I did it with. You'd better go to a doctor as fast as you can travel.'

The man rose and tore from the theatre.

On a cross-road on my way to school as a boy there stood a hotel. On cold winter days with other boys I used to stop and get warm in the lobby. One morning when it was about zero weather, a little Frenchman came in, his nose blue and his cheeks spotted pale with the cold. He stepped over to the stove, crowded it as closely as he could, and stood there for a quarter of an hour. Then he went over to the bar and ordered a hot whiskey, after which he went back to the stove and stood awhile, shivering a little.

Then he returned to the bar and got another hot whiskey. He did this five times, with intervals of warming between. Then he went to the window and looked out. He turned to the barkeeper, and after getting one more drink he said:

'I guess I go on. I think she's begin to moderate some.'

As in details of history different historians and sources must be consulted before a trustworthy account is to be obtained, if then – so it is necessary to take into consideration two or three versions of the obliquity of Joel Carbank. First take his neighbour, who tells of buying a car-load of barley from Joel, and how when Joel arrived in town with the first wagon-load he refused to deliver even that, because he had learned that barley had advanced half a cent a bushel that morning. Fortunately for the neighbour, Joel had been paid a small advance, which effectually bound the bargain. Then we have the story of the local hog-buyer, who says that he bought fourteen pigs from Joel for a lump sum of money, saw the pigs himself, and gave Joel a memorandum of the fourteen hogs, with the total amount to be paid on delivery. Then, when Joel brought the hogs in to town there were only thirteen of them, for which Joel insisted that he receive the amount agreed upon. The hog-buyer weighed the hogs, got their average weight, subtracted it from the total, and paid him for the thirteen. Joel couldn't get past the paper anyway, and that said, fourteen hogs for so much.

Now we come to Joel's own story. According to Joel, he told the hog-buyer that he had had fourteen hogs, but had butchered one of them or was going to butcher one for his own use. He wanted to sell them for a lump sum, rather than by weight, live or dressed. And the buyer agreed to take them that way, after some bargaining. It was the buyer who wrote the memorandum; after they had agreed upon the amount of the lump sum, and made it fourteen hogs for so much, when he should have known there were only thirteen. Then when he came to have the pigs weighed, the buyer docked him. Altogether, Joel maintained, it was the buyer who was the crooked one.

Our town is not a great distance from the border, and many of the young people go to the United States to work. One of them, Bob Hearst, came home every Saturday night for the week-end. It frequently happened that he carried goods with him for home use, which he was compelled to pass through the customs. One night he got into an argument with the customs officers on the train. It was the midnight train, and he had a pair of new shoes. He was requested to step into the office with them. Bob Hearst had an impressive manner and good lungs.

'Now listen here,' he proclaimed. 'I'm working over the river, and I only go home week-ends. I'm going to bring these shoes back with me Monday morning.'

'You'll have to pay duty on them, then,' returned the customs officer.

'Well, I won't. I'm not buying them to wear over here at all. I'm going right back to the other side.'

'You'll have to pay duty on them. Hurry up.' The customs officer was not inclined to parley longer.

Bob slammed the shoes down upon the desk, and raised his voice anew. 'Look here. I'm leaving these here. I'm not going to pay any duty on them. I'll be back at five o'clock Monday morning, and I want those shoes and I don't mean maybe. You have them here, or there's going to be doings.'

Well, Monday morning came, and Bob Hearst called in at the customs for his shoes, which were duly passed over to him.

Next Saturday night he came home again, and this time he had a pair of shoes for his boy, the little girl, and his wife's mother. The same customs officer came through the train and stopped beside his suitcase. 'What have you got there?' he demanded.

'Shoes!' snarled Hearst. 'And I'm coming back Monday morning at five o'clock.'

'Oh, for Heaven's sake!' returned the customs officer, and passed on.

Anthony Whicher, who owns the planing mill in Lower Warping, told me about Abner Langley. Long as he had kept mill in that part of the country, he had never seen Abner until the latter came into the office one day and asked to be measured. The manager looked at him, a long-faced, slate-eyed fellow, apparently as humorous as a slab of marble. The comparison is apt, because his wishes were connected with obsequies. It was no joke; he reiterated his request. He wanted to be measured for his coffin. Or rather, for the lumber for his coffin. He was going to take the lumber home and build his own coffin. The mill man carefully measured him, and after making an estimate of the lumber required, sawed and planed it for Abner.

This is vouched for as true, but whether Abner Langley still possesses his coffin, or whether he ever made the lumber up into one, is beyond telling. At any rate nobody recalls that he has been buried in it.

It may have been a relative of Abner's, as certainly it was one related in sadistic tendency, who used to come to church, when she came, with a different kind of make-up than the women of to-day are accustomed to employ. Aminto Near's health has always been poor, as everyone knows, for she has told everybody. Of course she is getting on in years now, and in her youth it was fashionable to be ailing and sickly. A girl could not believe that she appeared interesting unless she was wan and peaked and apparently at death's door. The difference between Aminta and the other girls lay in the fact that she did not follow the changing style and become robust and athletic. Even after she was married she was delicate and only ventured out in the worst weather. A rainy

Sunday, or a snowy night, would find her at church or a card party, highly-dressed, and made up with deep black wrinkles beside her mouth and dark circles around her eyes.

As long as his first wife lived Adam Tully was accustomed to coming up from the field at one o'clock in the afternoon and seven or half past seven at night. Then by the time he had got the horses and the other stock fed his wife might have supper or dinner ready. As time went on he gave up complaining and only when they had a new hired man or company would he remember the invariable tardiness. But when after twenty-five years Mrs Tully died, Adam was so accustomed to being late that he did not know what to do when his housekeeper began putting dinner on the table at twelve-thirty and six-thirty, and still lingered in the field till all hours. Lots of the neighbours who had known him all his life no longer blamed his former wife for slowness – she was dead now anyway – but said that Adam had always been that way, and that they were sorry for his new housekeeper: she would have a hard time breaking him in.

It did not take Anthony Whicher long to tell me what he thought about the conditions under which it seems to him that the world is run nowadays.

'In the city,' he told me, 'they do two or three hours work in the forenoon and two or three in the afternoon. If a man was any good he could do two or three more days' work besides his job. I'll just tell you what happened to me once. The big engine, the one that runs the whole mill, broke – water-jacket cracked, and I had to take it to Detroit to get it welded.

'So, I went down bright and early, got over the river on about the first boat, and hunted up the plant. I went through about seventeen different offices, after they began to get opened up, about half-past eight or nine o'clock. Not one of those men or girls in those offices knew who was the proper person to look after what I wanted done. All they did know was that they had nothing to do with it, and they would give me the name and the number of some other office in the building and I'd go and hunt that up.

'I would go into the office. There would be a girl sitting near the door, with telephone receivers clapped over her curls, or just sitting with a pencil or pad in her hand. Anyway, it didn't make any difference, she couldn't see or hear anything for anywhere from forty seconds to a minute and a half. At the end of the stated time she would look up or maybe not look up at all, but anyway she would sing wearily: "He's not i-in!" or "He's in con-ference!" or "See Mr Sapwin." '

'Mr Sapwin would be very cordial. "Oh, yes! Mr Whicher!" he would exclaim. And then he would listen carefully while I told him about what I wanted done. When I had explained it all to him a couple of times in every detail he would rouse and tell me, "Now I tell you what you do Mr Uh. You go to our Mr Eggnogg. He'll fix you up. He's the very man you want. He knows all about it. Yes, he'll fix you up! Good morning!" And Mr Sapwin would feel in his pockets for cigarets.

'Well, then, I'd go to Mr Eggnogg. The girl would tell me that he was out at first, and when I finally reached him by walking right through, he was busy twirling his moustache. When she said he was out, she meant that he was at large. But he got busy and wrote out all I told him on a pad, in shorthand, I guess, or maybe it was Hebrew. But that was all he did do, except tell me to find somebody else. He was terribly sorry he couldn't fix me up himself. But the other fellow would fix me up, all right.

'I didn't seem to be getting anywhere until about the middle of the afternoon, and then I finally found the right fellow, and he told me to go and get the water jacket and take it to the department which was to do the work.

'So I went down to the railway station where I had left the water jacket and found that the express fellows were gone home. I suppose they worked on a six-hour day. I told the fellow that was there a thing or two about that, but he only grinned and told me they wouldn't be open yet when I got back to the plant with it if I could have got it. I guess that was right all right.

'Next morning – I had to stay in the city all night, of course – I got down to the depot and got the piece, and tried to get somebody to take it out for me, but there was nothing but a taxi. Now I want to tell you I was mighty glad when I got it into the plant, and in the right department, and the man in charge said that he could have it fixed by Wednesday.

'But when Wednesday came they didn't have it ready yet. It seemed that their outfit was not big enough to fix the water-jacket, and they were going to send it on to somebody else. "Going to!" I hollered.

"Why didn't you do that right away?" Well, he said they were sending it right over and there would be no difficulty about it this time. Of course, I had to wait around a while to find out how long the next firm were going to keep it. In that case I thought I'd better go over with the thing myself, and I'd know right where I was at. This time it looked as though I had really got to the right place. They said they'd have it ready Friday, and kind of talked as though they knew what they were about. So I went home, though I couldn't run the mill with the main engine broken that way.

'When Friday came I went back to the city bright and early. Got to the plant, asked the head fellow for my water-jacket. He said it was kneading – had the lime and ashes on it, you understand, to make the welding hold. I'd have to come back in the afternoon. Well, that was all right, and I did finally get my piece away. Then I got down to the customs.

'It was the twenty-fourth of May, and the right fellows were away on a holiday and couldn't estimate on it. That was where I flew off the handle. I told the man I was going right on through with that thing that day, if they put me into jail for a hundred and ninety-nine years. It happened that George S–– was there, too, from our town, and he offered to go with me to Walkerville. He knew where the customs fellow lived. So out there we went, and finally got the business done and got away.'

'Quite an experience. Talk about red tape, you certainly got a good sample – '

'But wait,' Anthony Whicher interrupted me. 'That isn't all. When I got the water-jacket home after all this delay, and got the engine and the mill running again, it turned out that he'd just welded a little on the outside, and the thing cracked open in about a week.'

'Pshaw! What did you do then? I daresay you could have made them do it over again and do it right. There's nothing else to be done if one wishes to ensure good workmanship. If people got into their heads that they had to do things thoroughly or they wouldn't get paid for it it would make a lot of difference – '

'Yes. But I was tired of bucking them by that time. I knew I could not do anything to change their system of working a little while in the morning, and coming back the middle of the afternoon and getting ready to go home for the night. It's too late to do anything about that. And the way those girls in the offices would look at me; and Sapwin and Eggnogg they seemed to wonder why I didn't wear snappy clothes like they did. Like to put some of them fellows to work once.'

'Yes, it's not like the old days,' I agreed sincerely, bethinking myself that it was about time that I got on my way. But my old friend had not yet finished his tale.

'What I did finally was send to England for a new part. Then I knew right where I was at. But there was a long wait. I had to hire a traction engine to run the mill while I was waiting for it. Once before that I had to take my lumber down to the mill at the next village, and they let us do our work there.'

'They weren't very good competitors,' I returned.

Anthony laughed. 'That's different than they'd be in the cities. I'll tell you that much. Well, good-day.'

MRS PLETHWICK WAS A CITIZEN

Mrs Plethwick is getting along in years now – she must be, impossible as it seems, really old, but she has continued for a long time to hold the interest of the rising generations as well as she did in the days when the adults of to-day were school children.

This may sound as though she were a famous comedienne or manufacturer of cosmetics, but I am no press agent, and I only put down what I have myself seen and heard – the surface appearance of a mysterious character. When I was a child in the lower school I first knew Mrs Plethwick as the mistress of a quaint house, all gables, with tiny wings of which the windows, narrow and four-paned as they were, seemed to take up the whole width. It was a funny house, with a funny little walk of slats leading from the gravel path of the street, and a funny little fence, low and surmounted with a four-inch scantling laid flatwise.

It was the fence which was the means of wakening me to the unusual qualities of Mrs Plethwick. It seemed that the high-school boys, with their boys' instinct for annoyance, were in the habit of sitting on this scantling in twos and threes at recesses and noon hours, whenever they happened to be passing that way. Of course Mrs Plethwick became vexed, and asked the boys to go away. That made them all the more determined to use the scantling as a seat.

This caused Mrs Plethwick to take drastic measures. She got a quantity of thin, small-headed nails, and drove them into the scantling, thickly enough that there was no room for the boys to sit down. 'She put them in so thick we could almost sit down on them without feeling nothing,' one boy expressed it. And in fact some of the boys would sit down there occasionally after the nails had been driven, but by way of showing the old lady that they were not to be beaten in any such simple manner.

Small villages contain many such individuals as Mrs Plethwick. A rust of the more positive and creative faculties – fully realized – and long neglect may account for the jealous regard they have for what seems to them their rights. They will give neighbour children any amount of flowers, but if one takes a lilac from a bush overhanging the fence, consequences are dire. Approached in the right way they may be all smiles and charm. Yet they may 'sick' the dog or get a shotgun out for persons whom they regard as trespassers. One of the neighbours of Mrs Plethwick could give testimony regarding these generalizations. Mrs Plethwick called upon her duly when she had moved into the house next door. But the neighbour was tardy in returning the call, and no more than courteously distant whenever they caught sight of each other over back yard fences or on the street.

So Mrs Plethwick went into her cellar and exhumed a quantity of old bags and rag carpets. These she hung over the fence dividing the two yards, in such a way that they hung almost wholly on the side of the neighbour. Thus it would appear to anyone who passed around the corner, or glimpsed the fence between the evergreen trees, that the new people possessed an appalling assemblage of junk and rags.

Again, Mrs Plethwick maintained a powerful aversion to cats. She kept canaries, and liked most other birds, and that was the reason for the ferocity she showed when confronted by one of the feline species. 'I'd fix them,' she said, with an exultant high cackle. 'I'd boil them alive.' And there was a vague legend which pictured her in her back yard dipping bound but struggling cats into a steaming wash boiler. When she heard of any boy throwing stones at a bird she would say, 'Oh, if I just had a gun, wouldn't I shoot him!' And again her shrill laughter would ring out.

She became more humanitarian as time went on. Often she would approach a horse tied to a hitching post in front of a store or blacksmith shop. Stealthily she would untie the halter and let the animal go free.

Luckily most of the horses were quiet, long accustomed to wild automobiles and wilder drivers, traction-engines, tilling-machines, tractors, and motorcycles. As a rule, when liberated in this abrupt manner, they walked tranquilly along the street, if their angle of approach to the curb allowed this peregrination. Or if they were parked amid a tangle of other buggies and cars, they might back tentatively against a neighbour, and then abandon the attempt to get away. So that considerable time elapsed before any strong objections were made to this humanitarian impulse of the old lady.

Meantime she continued her other activities. She would suddenly descend upon someone's back or front yard, and wielding rake and hoe and spud for picking up newspapers, would do a thorough job of scavenging and charing. Sometimes she would have a considerable audience, at least a little group of children. 'This yard is not healthy,' she would say. 'Somebody's going to get typhoid, around here. I was thinking especially of you,' she would say to some neighbour child. 'I didn't want you to get typhoid.' The child might laugh, or younger, might shudder at her tone. Occasionally they had been told that Mrs Plethwick was a witch, but even the smallest did not take this too seriously, disarmed by the kindly wrinkled face of the old lady.

Then a thing happened which changed the life of Mrs Plethwick. Her son, the only child, had long since established himself as a doctor in an eastern city. Her husband, a quiet, yellow-moustached little man, now gray, suddenly parted from her. He got meals at the Continental House, and roomed at the home of a nephew.

But Mrs Plethwick became more ardent than ever in her civic activities. At any hour of the night or day she might appear on the streets gathering newspapers, sweeping the asphalt. But it happened that she bought herself a pound of beefsteak at the butcher shop. This strange occurrence was enough to show that she was changing. She had never been inside the butcher shop for years. She did not like the appearance it presented, and ten minutes after buying her meat she had reappeared with a broom and a scrub brush in her hands, and began to clean up the butcher shop.

The butcher, not unnaturally, objected. He did not see the need of this ceremony. He had always been able to take care of his own shop, he guessed, and nobody had laid any complaints, either. He tried to evict Mrs Plethwick with words, and when they failed, tried to push her out by main force and awkwardness. This too proved unavailing, to put it mildly. 'She scratched me,' he told the town clerk, magistrate, and constable rolled in one. These officials proceeded with him to his shop and arrested Mrs Plethwick with all formality.

Next month she was tried and fined, but she would not pay the fine. They could have put her in jail, but technicalities were said to intervene. Still, there was talk of her going to jail. But Mr Plethwick came forward then, and paid the fine. Nobody knows, but he must have plucked up courage and given her a good talking to, though he had never been able to prevail over her before, and secured her promise to behave herself if he paid the fine. At any rate, Mrs Plethwick is seldom in evidence now, and most people have almost forgotten that she lives yet, in the little gabled house tucked behind the much-nailed lawn fence between the hardware store and Banker Hughes.

THE REWARDS OF BLANKENHORN

Nobody had much to say about Elias Blankenhorn. One reason probably was that there was nothing much to be said, either favourably or in a derogatory way. But anyone used to noting such things might have observed that he had the name and the appearance of the makings of a rural old bachelor; that he would naturally develop into one of those 'characters' of whose eccentricities older people tell younger ones and strangers for years.

But to the casual observer for a long time nothing of this would have been expected or foretold. For Elias Blankenhorn was not yet old when the thing happened which made his name a byword in the community and gave him a kind of notoriety which even his indifference saw was far from valuable.

He had always minded his own business as he expressed it, and minded it so well that his neighbours were content to let him continue to do so by flocking by himself. For few men had got into a deal with

Elias and come out at the big end of the horn. Of course he was honest; in those days and among people who had known him all his life it was especial good policy to be honest. Within the law, nobody, even in later years, could accuse him of prosecutable dishonesty; but within that border waited Elias Blankenhorn's cunning, as arbitrary as a leveled pistol.

Of course he was human. It was possible that he really felt the most human of emotions, gratitude. Several boys of the vicinity held views about that, however. His nearest neighbours were the Haskells, and not very near, for Elias' farm amounted to two hundred acres, with an orchard in front and, beyond a patch of melons, fields of grain, hay, and corn. He didn't keep up the fences very well, but he was proud of his crops.

One summer evening two of the Haskell boys came over to tell him that somebody's pigs were in his corn. They even, having nothing much to do, went back to the field with Elias and rounded up the pigs and helped to put them out. As they came back up the lane toward the road, Allan and Carl were not surprised when Elias paused at the gate to the melon patch and after hesitating a moment, made the abrupt declaration:

'Tell you – I'll just give you boys a melon for helping me to-night. I don't like to have pigs in my corn.'

'Especially other people's pigs, eh?' asked Carl, the older of the boys, who knew him well.

Elias Blankenhorn stooped over the vines, moving about until he had selected a melon to offer as his gift.

'Ya-as,' he drawled slyly. 'I don't want to have nobody comin' on me for damages to their hawgs, and I don't want to sue nobody for the corn their hogs eats – 'less I have to. Well, boys, here's your melon.'

Carl extended his hand, and was so surprised that he nearly dropped the melon, but they walked in silence to the house, and then left, Allan calling back his thanks.

When they had gone a few rods down the road in the dusk Carl threw the melon with a thud into the ditch. His brother made a jump forward as if to retrieve it.

'What you want to throw a good melon away for? First I ever knew you didn't like 'em.'

'Good melon, eh?' said Carl disgustedly. 'You take a look at it if you want to. You can have my share. Thank that old skinner!' he added bitterly.

'Why, what's the matter with it? Near as I could see it looked all right, Carl.'

'Rotten,' retorted Carl laconically.

'Rotten!' echoed the younger brother in astonishment. 'Elias must have made a mistake in the dark.'

'Mistake your grandmother! Didn't he feel around and try a dozen of them before he picked out this one for us? Peach of a one, I must say. Don't you say anything, we'll get some better melons than that from Mr Elias, and more'n one, too.'

At home they told their older brother, Ted, who told his friend, a youth known as Newt Galpin and also named the most mischievous and reckless fellow in the community. Among them a plan was arranged.

But Carl's idea of secrecy was abandoned. They told everybody that they were going to raid Elias Blankenhorn's melon patch. It came to the cars of the owner of the said property, and he determined to take measures. He was mightily surprised and more than a trifle annoyed, too, after the way in which he had treated the boys. They should have had more principle than to try to take his melons after he'd been good enough to give them one outright. He wasn't raising melons for fun. Other people had to buy them.

So Elias loaded his gun with fine shot, took an old horseblanket, and went out to the melon patch to sleep, or rather to spend the night. He could hear the boys down the road, talking loudly in the quiet night. Then again he heard them farther back on his own farm. But they couldn't fool him. He wasn't going back there. They wouldn't hurt the grain. He'd stay right by the melons.

The first night he remained awake until morning; and worked in the field next day. The next night the same thing happened, but again the boys didn't come near; and the day after Elias worked as usual. The third night he sat again with his gun beside him and his back to the trunk of an oak tree.

But like the previous nights, all was quiet. After waiting and waiting, staring into the grey darkness, he decided that the boys must have given up their plan, or that they were going about it very quietly. That meant that he had better be more than ever on the alert.

But the night was warm, with soft clouds flocking past the moon, and with only occasionally a quiet breeze. Elias was tired with his two nights of watching, and before he knew it he was asleep with his head bent over to his knees. He woke once and felt for his gun, which was resting across his feet, and listened. But there was no sound.

A little later there were sounds, but Elias did not hear them. They weren't loud, for the boys were careful. They had come down the lane with a democrat and horse, turned them about to face the road behind some bushes, and entered the melon patch.

Quietly they set to work, gathered all the melons their vehicle would contain, picking the largest and firmest ones. The ripe ones they knew by the crispness of the little tendril at the end of the melon.

After that they systematically tore up all the vines, gathered them with thoroughness and piled them into a great heap in the middle of the patch. On this pile they surmounted half a dozen of the most rotten melons they could find. They stood back in a circle and looked at this monument and at each other and snickered, then with warning gestures they dispersed.

Newt Galpin, the daredevil of the party, crept toward Elias Blankenhorn's slumbering figure, while the other boys waited ready at the democrat. Newt softly took the shotgun from where it lay. Afterward he admitted to a little misgiving. 'But if he'd woke up I'd have spoke up and asked to buy some melons.' But his careless bravado did not need that alibi. Elias never stirred, until Newt had reached the rail fence in the lane, jumped over, fired off the gun twice, and left it standing against the fence.

When Elias jumped to his feet the first thing he heard was the rattle of the democrat up the lane. Then when it had reached the road he heard a chorus of whoops from young throats, and shook his fist toward them. He ran a few yards in a dazed way, and then he saw the pile in the middle of the former melon patch.

The democrat went five miles before it stopped in a bush, where the spoils were divided and partly eaten. But all Elias knew or cared to know was that apart from his loss, the boys had accomplished a trick which would serve as a hallmark for him for years: a thorough job.

LAYING A GHOST

'No,' said Joe Parks, 'I've heard several people tell about ghosts and haunts, and such-like, but when it comes right down to believing in them, then I got to smile. I never saw one, you see. When somebody collects a ghost for me, and introduces me to him – or to her – then I'll say they're real, and I'll feel free to tell as many tall yarns about them as the next fellow.'

Anthony Gibard pulled on his pipe thoughtfully, as though deciding something in his mind. Spitting and clearing his throat, he turned to Joe and Lew Everett. He pulled his moustache, not now so walrus-like or Vikingesque as it had been in earlier years.

'You've never seen one. Well, that's different. Can't blame a man who never saw a ghost. He thinks anybody's crazy that has. Of course.' He shook his head thoughtfully, staring at his mitts resting on the warmer atop the kitchen range.

'It's not that I think fellows are lying when they tell about queer things they've seen,' interposed Joe hastily. 'Maybe they seem real to them, but I bet if I was there I'd see through it. Oh, of course, it's true enough for them, if they think so.'

Lew Everett wagged his head in silence.

It was not because he feared that Anthony would disbelieve him that Joe Parks so eagerly disclaimed any disbelief in other people's ghosts. He knew by the signs that since the subject had come up, Anthony Gibard had a story to tell. Anthony's memory reached back to pioneer days in western Ontario, and it embraced also the tales which old men of those days had told him as a boy. He had lived on Pelee Island when that southernmost garden spot had been a waste of swamp and sand, timber and snakes. He had cleared with his own axe more acres of land than either of the young men listening to him would care to cultivate alone. And sometimes he would talk.

He did so now, without prelude.

'This happened down in South Gosfield. You fellows seem to want me to tell you something about haunts, so you can just take this or leave it. I'll put the facts before you, and you can do what you like with them. I was pretty young those days, too, like you fellows. Working out for a farmer down there. Or rather for half the farmers on the concession line, seemed like. People were more neighbourly them days, and they used to have bees to get most of the jobs done. If a man wanted to get his corn husked he held a bee, and the neighbours came, and the womenfolk got a lot of cooking ready, and a good time was had by all. Or if a man got sick and couldn't get his haying done properly, the neighbours would turn and make hay for him. Used to have bees for pretty near everything – buzzing for stove-wood, butchering, and all that sort of thing, not to mention clover hulling, bean-pulling, and all kinds of threshing.

'Well, one time I was at a threshing for one of the neighbours. In the fall it was, kind of late. You know the way a bunch of men will get talking around the supper table, even when they know they've got chores to do when they get home. And the women and girls stand around and join in, glad of a rest, before they clear up and wash the stacks of dishes.

'So we were talking and some young gaffer happened to mention the haunted house. Maybe it was me. You know in those days no community was complete without a haunted house. There was always some house the people couldn't live in because they heard noises or saw sights or felt breezes, or something. Or if there wasn't a house, there would be the graveyard anyway. Well, it was a house this time. Everybody knew what you meant when you talked about the "haunted house."

'A man had been killed there, or at least people thought so. They couldn't prove anything. Let me see, George Calley, that was his name. He was coming home from town one night, the story goes, and he had been around the hotel quite a while. He was pretty drunk, maybe; and there was a railway crossing just near his place. It was just the year after the railway had been first put through. Anyway, the back end of his democrat got hit by the train, and the horses ran away. He was hit, too, but not thrown out. How that could be nobody knows. The horses must have been going pretty fast. Half the top of his head seemed to be taken off, and he was all blood when the team dashed into the barnyard, and he toppled out of the democrat into the well-curb, and his wife found him.

'Anyway, that was the story Mrs Calley told. She moved away not long after he died. The neighbours said the horses had run away and smashed the left hind wheel of the democrat, and he had got home all right, except for being drunk, and that his wife had taken the axe to him, and afterwards thrown him in the well. Then, according to them, she got scairt, and told the neighbours he was in the well.'

'They'd mighty soon investigate anything like that now,' remarked Lew Everett.

'Yes, some funny things used to happen those days, and nothing much ever done about it. Anyway, that was the story of the house, and no matter what people thought about the cause of Calley's death, they knew he had died there in a queer way. There used to be lights appear in the windows in the middle of the night. And one thing sure, that nobody could deny, anybody who took the place, left it mighty soon. Didn't matter whether they bought it or rented it, they was soon mighty glad to get out the quickest way. People kind of began to take it seriously. Even those who never had seen a ghost, and would laugh at them in daytime, put the whip to the horse when they was passing late at night.

'Well, this place where we were making the bee was just the next farm, and I suppose some young gaffer who knew he would have to pass the haunted house going home was pretending to pretend he was afraid.'

'That's kind of complicated!' laughed Joe. 'You mean they really were afraid.'

'Well, more or less. Just wait till I tell you and see if you would have been. There got to be quite a discussion about it right there at the threshing table, and even the girls of the house joined in. The thresher didn't live near there, but several miles away, over in North Essex. There weren't many threshermen in those days. Always knocking around a lot, and seeing more than his neighbours, he kind of thought he was quite a fellow, tough, you understand. What they call a "wise guy" now-times. Well Ruf, he swore by Judas' priest that there was no ghost in that house and never was. Let them bring on their ghosts, he knew what they were, he'd tear the sheets off them every time. They weren't going to give him any hallowe'en stuff.

'So, you know the way people are. Just for argument's sake, some of the fellows broke it to him that there certainly was something wrong there, or these families would not have moved away like they did. Old

Hunter, the man who held the bee, was one of the first. He knew all about it, being so near a neighbour.

' "Why they tell me," he says, "they tell me the last fellow over there never got a wink of sleep for six weeks. Every night there would be thumpings on the veranda enough to shake the house. And then they'd begin up in the attic. And there would be hoots and screeches to make your blood run cold. It's all right to say there ain't no such thing, but when people pick up and move out with lock, stock, and barrel, you got to admit there's something into it." '

'No, no, Ruf he wouldn't have it that way. It was all a lot of foolishness, only he used a stronger word. "I'll have to buy that place myself," he says, "and we'll see whether it's true or no."

'The girls chimed in here. They were big strapping girls, used to doing a man's work in the field many's the time, and they had been listening to the men talk for quite a while and not saying much. Now they tells Ruf the thresherman:

' "You don't need to buy the place, Ruf. Why don't you just go there and stay all night some time? Then you'll find out for sure."

'There was some chaffering back and forth, and Ruf pounded his fist on the table. "By jingoes, I will," says he. "I'll go right to-night, since I'm here. I'll bet any man here that I go there, and that there ain't no ghost."

'They were mostly good church-people, and didn't believe in betting, whether they had a weakness for ghosts or not. But Ruf was sitting beside me, and he says to me, "I s'pose you want to come along." And I, being a reckless sort of gawk in those days – I was big for my age but just in my teens – I said, "You bet I would go."

'After supper, the rest of the neighbours went home, and Ruf put the smoke screen over the stack of his traction engine, and bedded it down for the night, and I hung around and waited for him. I had told my boss I wasn't going home with him that night, and he didn't seem to mind having all the chores alone. Curious to find out what would happen, I guess.

'About nine o'clock, when it was good and dark, and a nippy cold October wind blowing, we walked over to the place George Calley had got killed in. The gate posts had rotted out, and the lane was getting grass in already, and the lawn was a mass of tall weeds. It was a story and a half frame house, sort of a bluish colour. The buildings behind the house were grey and looked ready to fall.

'We crept up the lane, and across the lawn, and Ruf stamped on the veranda. "Come on, ghosts," he says, "if you're not ghosts now, I'll make you ghosts."

'The door was locked, so we hoisted a window and crawled in. It was the front parlour we landed in, quite a small room, but it certainly echoed loud if you made the least bit of noise. I lit the lantern I had brought. After a bit Ruf says, "Let's go and take a look at all the rooms. Start here." There was a sort of cubby-hole in the room, the under-stairs part, with a door to it. We opened it, and looked in. Nothing there. Then we went out in the hall, and looked upstairs, but thought we'd better do the downstairs first. We did the sitting room and another room, and the kitchen, and the pantry. It was kind of dark, having no window, but we thought we could see all round it. But Ruf drew the lantern along the floor and seen there was a sort of trap-door.

'There didn't seem to be any basement to the place, so we were curious. He pried the door up with his jack-knife, and we held the lantern down the hole. It was all black. "Nothing down there," says Ruf. He lay on his stomach and held the lantern down as far as he could. "I'll go down just for fun." I could see the place was no bigger than a cistern, and was likely a sort of pit to keep apples and potatoes in. So he takes hold of the sides of the hole, and lowers himself down it. His head was just beneath the floor.

'The minute he got down there, there came such a howl and shriek and tramping as you never heard. It seemed to be above us, upstairs, maybe in the attic. Anyway, Ruf was out of that hole so quick you'd think dynamite had been put under him.

' "What was that?" he gabbles, "what was that?"

' "Nothing much," I says, my teeth chattering. "It was away up in the attic."

'We weren't long getting out of there, and I was going past the stair to the parlour. If the doors hadn't been locked I'd have mighty soon got out of them. But Ruf stormed and said we would go up to the attic. But he got cooled down enough that he thought we'd better search the upstairs bedrooms first. When we went into the second one, there was a sharp crack. It came just like lightning. I nearly jumped backward to the hall, before I realized it came from downstairs.

'Well, we looked through all the downstairs rooms again, and just as we came to the pantry again there was another clatter and the most soulless and chilling wail from upstairs. You'd thought we'd be getting used to it, but this time Ruf jumped about six inches himself. Then he swore, and gave a yell.

' "We'll get you!" he hollers. "Man or devil, we know you're here, and we're gonto get you."

'So upstairs again we were going, when halfway up, Ruf told me to keep the lantern down there, and he would go up and root him out. If he came down, I'd have the lantern, and I could see him. It was getting moonlight, so Ruf could see his way around in some of the rooms and the hall. He tramps up them hollow stairs, and I waits, my knees knocking together. Pretty soon he gives a yell, no words, just a yell, and I wondered what's happened. Then he gives a jump, and begins running around overhead, I could hear him clattering around. "I'll catch you!" he hollers. He stumbled and ran and raised a tremendous racket, and from the sound he went up the attic stairs.

'That was when my hair began to stand up. For when he went up the stairs, I heard other footsteps. They were lighter than Ruf's, and went ahead. If all the brains hadn't been scairt out of me I would have remembered that ghosts aren't supposed to make a noise, but I waited in agony, until the steps came bounding lightly down. Ruf hollered:

' "Look out, he's coming. Look out!"

'I put the lantern down and braced myself for the worst, when there was a terrible hoot right behind me. I nearly dropped, but I must have turned and I saw a white thing, scuttling into the pantry. Then before I turned another white shape was coming down the bottom stairs, Ruf hot after it.

' "Stop it!" he yells. I held out my arms at the foot, not knowing what I was doing, and it dashed right through, knocked me over. Ruf yanked me up and we stood there. When we could hear our breathing, we heard other breathing out in the pantry. "Well," panted Ruf, "they're alive, anyway. Pick up your lantern and come on."

'There was a dash and a scuttling just as we came to the pantry, but we had them trapped. There was no door nor window to the place, and they didn't have time to raise the trap-door. Ruf made one dash, and puts his long arms around the two shapes in the corner and hung on like grim death. They began to struggle the same way, but he held, and I come and held the arms of one of them.'

'And what, what were they like?' asked Joe and Lew in one breath.

'They was the two girls from the next farm,' said old Anthony Gibard.

'Well, well, well. I can't believe that somehow. What would they be wanting? Did they scare the other people too?'

'Of course. Their old man wanted the farm, and the best way to get it cheap was to scare everybody offn it.'

HEART OF IRONWOOD TEA

The three men seated at the table on the country club verandah lingered for many minutes over their tea. They were of middle age or beyond, and they were disposed to take a brief assumption of indolence philosophically. Two of them had done eighteen holes that afternoon, and the other, the youngest, nine. This should have refreshed their brains, as golf was intended to do. But instead it seemed, particularly after the meal, to have wearied their bodies and inclined their thoughts to lazy reminiscence. Both business and golf were momentarily neglected. They were speculating on the virtues of faith healing.

Clark Holme had just been telling about the way in which his wife's mother, in England, was able to take warts from the hands of people in Canada, on being told of them. He didn't believe in it, he said, but there it was; he had known it to happen, for a fact.

The others did not believe in it either. They were polite enough not to be emphatic, and their mood of relaxation made the otherwise hardened businessmen inclined to be lenient. Finally John Lantern – 'Gaunt John,' the others called him, usually in his absence – spoke up in his quiet voice. He was a lean man of perhaps sixty-odd, dressed in clothes of quality, though inconspicuously and carelessly.

'You fellows,' he began, 'Don't see much in these manifestations because they've never come within your own personal experience. As something to read about, and to doubt, along with a great deal else that you read – Oh yes. But then you're younger than I am.' (This mention of his age was John Lantern's only affectation, for he was keener than many younger men.) 'and neither of you was reared in a pioneer settlement of western Ontario.

'Things were a good deal different then. I don't need to waste your time telling you about isolation and the denseness of the bush, and that sort of thing. To come to the point, we don't have the ague now as people used to in those days. I mean young people and grown-ups, otherwise healthy. I was sixteen when this thing occurred, or rather this series of incidents, and I had the ague. Badly, too. It seemed that no home-made remedy would cure it, and there were no doctors nearer than twenty-five miles, at Chatham. Or nothing but heart of ironwood tea. It was an Indian woman who told my people about that.

'I'd a good deal rather she had kept the information to herself, for the cure was worse than the disease. It seems the recipe consisted in cutting down an ironwood tree, and there were lots of them then, wherever they have all gone now. You cut it up, split a block of it down to the heart, and this centre of the tree was boiled in water. The concoction which resulted was given the name of tea, for some reason or other which puzzled me greatly at the time. For the stuff was so noxious that I – well I thought I'd really die. Bitter! Holy hickory! or rather, unholy ironwood. Of course children don't like medicine, and I was only a child then. My parents, like most pioneer parents, had authority in full biblical measure, though I was fifteen or sixteen years old and thought myself a man. In fact, I used to take a man's part in every kind of work that came along, making ties, splitting rails, spiles, cradling in harvest time, anything.

'But at any rate the heart of ironwood tea did cure me of the ague. One day when I was convalescing it happened that there was nobody else in the shanty. I'd been wanting to get outdoors for several days, so they had taken my clothes away. But I did manage to find some of my father's; including a huge long pair of home-spun trousers. So I took my axe and set forth into the bush.

'I set to work systematically, and I cut down every ironwood tree I could find. Never a one that I saw did I leave standing, for about a mile on every side of the house. Finally on my way back home I came on one I'd missed, a slim, tall ironwood tree in the middle of a clump of maples and buttonwood. Of course I chopped it down, too, finishing off a good day for a boy who had just been sick. The wood was hard, but in those days we had good axes. A chopping was held as sacred. I remember when I was smaller, if my father's axe was not in use, we youngsters were forbidden absolutely to go near it.

'Well, when I got this tree chopped off, I tossed my axe aside and made a jump to get away. I saw that the trunk was going to fall straight down, because the limbs of the other trees around it were holding it on all sides. But I saw it too late, and the whole tree just slipped down a foot over the stump I had chopped, and rested on the ground. Or it would have rested on the ground if my father's trouser-leg had not interfered. It was lucky that the trunk didn't drop on to my foot, but it caught the bottom of the trousers, which were as big, for me at least, as those the young fellows wear nowadays.

'Well, there I was, caught. I had thrown my axe away and I couldn't chop off the stump. What was I to do.'

'Get out of the trousers,' said Clark Holme, relighting his cigar.

'That's what I did. I got the axe and came back and cut off the point of the trunk. I climbed into my clothes again and went back to the house, and told nobody about it.' Lantern was silent, while he rummaged for a match.

Burgess, the youngest of the three, he who because of business had done only nine holes of golf, had been listening with a smile which seemed rather sceptical. He began cautiously:

'Your point is, that you didn't like the ironwood tea and yet, it cured you largely because of its effect on your imagination?'

'Not at all,' replied Lantern equably, after a leisurely instant. 'No imagination about that stuff. If people had the ague now I'd recommend ironwood tea, if it were obtainable. It certainly was effective for the time, and perhaps it wasn't so noxious to take as I thought then. At any rate I would find it more reasonable to have faith in it than in what finally did cure me for good.'

'Oh, you weren't finished with your story,' muttered Burgess. Holme, the Englishman who had told of his mother-in-law's sorcerous powers, smiled, and waited.

'No. Nothing much happened until a year later. Then I began to have the ague again. I saw the old witch of an Indian woman, and she told me once more, take heart of ironwood tea. I told her right away she'd never get me to take any more of that stuff. I'd cut down all the ironwood trees within a mile of the place, and she could just make up her mind I would have nothing more to do with it; and not to tell my parents to get any of it either.

'Well, the old girl seemed to take that to heart pretty well, and she told me that if I really wanted to get done with the ague for good, and never be bothered with it again, to get a piece of rope and tie three knots in it and tie the rope around the trunk of an elm tree. And I went and – . Yes, you fellows can smile, but that's what I did.'

'Hm!' Burgess cleared his throat. 'And it really cured you. At any rate you never had to employ that remedy again.'

'Never had the ague again to this day. Of course like you I don't believe in it. But that's just what happened.' He looked keenly at Burgess, almost questioningly. Or at least that was the way in which the younger man seemed to take it, for instead of expressing incredulity he looked from Holme to Lantern, and clearing his throat hesitantly he began to speak. And the first words he said were:

'That reminds me of a case which happened to come under my own observation.'

A ROW OF HORSE STALLS

'Old Belle's in her second childhood.'

'How's that?' I looked at the long-haired black mare lazily blinking in the morning sunlight. Her back was sunken with years, her lip hung, but her eyes were alert as ever, and showed no white. Her limbs too were hard and firm as ever – a well-preserved old lady, sometimes even overcome with the high spirits of youth, as I knew from experience in trying to get her into the barn after letting her out to pasture. She led me a merry chase, until in the stable she slipped out the door into the barnyard, thence into the barn; and finally in the stable she entered every other stall but the right one.

'Can't you see? She's smacking her lips yet. I was here in the yard milking and set down the big twelve-quart milking pail right full, and milking another cow. Old Belle comes along and drinks the whole thing up. Yes sir, every drop.'

'Well, that's a joke. That's new to me. I never heard of a horse drinking milk. She certainly is in her second childhood.'

'Thought she was a colt again. Well, I guess it'll do her good.'

'As long as it doesn't put more of the Old Nick into her than she has now, it'll be all right.' I realized that the farmer's leniency was due to admiration for the trick with which the mare had demonstrated her cleverness. He had raised her and her mother before her, from pioneer stock which was among the first to come into Essex County.

'Her mother was cunning as her, but not so mean. She was wild though. Boys, she was wild! Hauling logs, them times when we used to be working in the bush, I tell you a man had to keep his wits about him and his eyes open with old Belle. I called her Belle, too, and this one after her; and this one's youngest colt, out in the pasture is Belle the third. But she was good to pull. I mind one time when I had a mate for her just about like her, same build, kind of chunky and yet quick and keen, same weight, same colour, kind of smoky brown-black. He was a good horse too, not so flighty as her. Well, we had another team there and trying to roll up a big log on the sleigh. They couldn't do it.

'They'd just see-saw, this other team, though I lay it a good deal to the driver, and finally one rests its head over its mate's neck.'

'That's a good sign, when you want them to pull.'

'Yes, they're just about ready to give up then. Well, this team did give up, and so I says I'd roll it up with mine. That was a mighty big log, I'm telling you. I says to the boys, you block her if she stops part way up the skids. But she never stopped when she began to roll up. Old Belle and Barney took hold of that chain, and snaked her up on that sleigh so nice and easy – ' The farmer shook his head reminiscently.

'Just what breed of horse are they?' I asked quizzically.

'They're not pure-bred, never was I guess from the time my father first got them. They were French-Canadian with a little English thoroughbred. That first team of my father's was famous in the whole county. He used to take them to the county fair, and generally they got first place, singly or as a team. And when he died I drove them myself, young as I was. I tell you I was proud driving that team around the race course in a democrat. I wouldn't have called the queen my grandmother at that moment. Well, after a while mother sold the farm and the team was sold for five hundred dollars. That was some price for farm horses in those days, and at a sale. And I got one of the colts, that was Old Belle the first, and I called this one Belle the second. Now she's old too, and I've sold some of her colts, and some of them are over in the pasture, and I'm breaking one in. Been mixing shire in the line, and that makes a heavier horse, good for farm work, and not so flighty.'

'I should think you'd have to break Belle herself in, oftener than the colts.' It was a natural comment, for that very week we had gone to the bush lot for some poles with which to mend the fence over the river. We drove Belle and a younger horse back through the bush, and colts and other members of the family circled around the wagon in gleeful gallop, as though rejoicing that they did not have to pull the wagon at so sedate a pace. When we came to a slim, spiring ash, we stopped, and taking the axe I began to chop, the farmer standing nearby. The other horses were still near, chasing each other through the brush and paths. When the echoing strokes of the axe stopped there was a pause, then the slim tree fell, without much noise.

But it was noise enough for Belle and her comrade. Belle made the first jump, like lightning, and seemed to be two leaps ahead of the heavier horse, so that they began to go in a circle. I ran on the instant, and caught the line of the big horse, but that did not faze old Belle. Still, I might have stopped them before they really got speed up, had not a tree interposed between me and the horse, and they had gone a few yards before I got the line again and finally brought them to a standstill just as they collided with another tree. It came right between the two horses, and their whole impact came on the neckyoke, so that a hame-strap and a martingale was broken.

'It's her back that ought to be broken,' the farmer fumed. 'But that's the way she always has been. When you'd go to catch her when she was young, she'd run right over you. Didn't matter if you had a stick in your hand. She'd right past you, or knock you down. And run away if you turned your back. Never could trust her farther than you could throw her by the tail. So of late years, when she's getting tamed down some, I don't have a great deal of sympathy for her, but work her just the same as the rest.'

'I think she needs some breaking in yet!' We both laughed, but I have been wondering whether the laugh was not on Belle's side.

In those early days horses perhaps possessed more individuality. At any rate they were treated more roughly, and in many cases reacted with vigour. The dispositions of horses of late years have been better, probably as much because they have been treated better as because of the fact that the breeds have been improving. But in pioneer times men had a harder time, were harder themselves, and treated their livestock accordingly.

There is a story of old Dolph Byrne, a cattle dealer of the early days, a man tight in a bargain as he was uncouth in his ways. He bought a horse with the reputation for being 'bad-headed' with which to drive out in the country for cattle. He used to tell of the first time he hitched Nance in the buggy. His roaring voice boomed:

'She kicked her foot through the dash-board, and I made her go for about a mile!'

No doubt with word and deed he encouraged Nance as she traversed the mile on three legs, and a record was made. Then when they got home Dolph unharnessed her carefully, save for the bridle which he clutched with one hand, while with the other he seized half a rail – and the dance began. When they were both thoroughly weary, and Nance had had a sound beating without having been able to reach the able-bodied Dolph, he turned her into the stable. She went into the wrong stall, and Dolph clubbed her in every square yard of the stable until she had gone into the stall which belonged to her. Then Dolph conciliated her by way of showing her where she was safe.

Still, Nance must have been of the same cast-iron temper as Dolph Byrne, for he was never able to break her of kicking unseasonably, or of running away whenever he would leave her to drive his cattle a few yards, if he happened to be alone. So he sold her.

Al Wrongley, the new master, was more crafty. He was going to cure Nance without the expenditure of a lot of elbow-grease. He got a bushel of corncobs, and one rainy day went into the loft above her stall. All day he dropped corncobs on the mare beneath. But at the end of the day she kicked as high as ever, every time one struck her. Al had to give up, too.

But horses may have different motives for kicking, as human beings have for the various antics through which they go. A mill man in the village once kept a horse for which he had no use in particular, except when he hitched him in the buggy to go down country roads collecting unpaid bills. All day this horse, Cliff by name, would turn about on the shavings of his narrow box stall, listening to the rumble and feeling the vibration of the mill, until once more he would be taken out for a drive in the country.

Finally the mill man decided to get a car, and left the horse with his brother-in-law, who was to get whatever work he could out of him in return for his board. The farmer turned Cliff into the barnyard, and then there was a surprise. Cliff was shod for the road, and he began to kick the other horses. 'Why, he was a tartar,' the farmer would say afterward, 'he'd have killed them, wicked.' Cliff would even run after the others to corner them, and kick desperately. They were all strangers to him, and therefore seemed dangerous. But after a while, when he had become acquainted with the other horses, he never kicked, and was very peaceable. It was cowardice which made him so pugnacious.

On the other hand horses in those days sometimes showed a devotion to their masters and a fortitude under over-driving or hard drives in bad weather, which would seem strange to the youths who pilot gasoline buggies on their errands of business or pleasure. In those days good drivers were many, and rivalry in the matters of speed and fine turn-outs was keen. Every fall fair had a class for the best lady driver, horse, and equipment to be considered. The young men would loan their rigs to a sister or the girl they were 'keeping company with' to engage in this tourney. And to see those fine, graceful animals trot off down the track, to turn and wheel across it (without a squeal of the wheel against the buggy-box) was something no one was likely to forget. One of the prize-winning horses was called Sadie, and Sadie's sole purpose for existence was to take driving the young lady who drove her at the fair, with the permission of a proud owner-suitor.

The little standard-bred mare was very intelligent, and the lines could be left hanging over the dashboard for convenient lengths of time, while Sadie trotted on sedately as though they had never been released. To reach the girl's home a side road had to be used, leading to another main road. There was no difference in the length of these side roads, and usually, beyond temporary conditions of the road, it made no difference which one was taken. But Sadie had her own ideas about this, and coming to a side road she would pause, look down it, and if its looks did not suit her, go on to the next one.

Not only could Sadie be trusted to keep the road and avoid any sort of accident, whether the driver were asleep or awake, but she actually liked roading. The minute her master began to clean her and put the harness on, she became impatient. And, left standing before the buggy-shed she would wait until the man had pulled out the buggy, and then, while he held up the shafts, would trot up and turn beneath them with a flourish, and back between them to be hitched.

The whims and impulses of these warm-blooded light horses are generally more entertaining than the more phlegmatic draughters. If trained properly and not abused, they often develop a charming individuality. Such was Lily, scion of a distinguished family of race-horses, who nevertheless was never trained for the track, but used for a buggy horse. Such common tricks were hers as eating oats from the hand, with much play of large eyes finely set in a beautiful small head, shaking hands, and allowing herself to be caught by the forelock in the field or pasture – unless the would-be catcher happened to be someone whom she did not like.

With all patience she submitted to the drudgery of field work, dragging heavy implements at a snail's pace all day; always up on the bit, and doing her full share of the pulling, and sometimes more, unless the load happened to be too heavy. Once she was hitched with a heavy draught mare, Lide, to haul wheat from the field over soft lanes. For the job the double-tree was set over, giving her an advantage. Coming into the barn was a hill, and on this slope Lily always dug her toes in heroically, and managed to hold her share of the huge load, her head nodding coquettish pride in being able to do so, as though she were pulling a full half. Perhaps she did not know, or perhaps she did know and was still proud.

For a time Lily's mate was another light blood mare, Dinah. A dark brown, lean mare with the most expressive ears ever seen, Dinah was one of those rarities, a completely individualized horse. I have never seen another like her, nor am I especially anxious to see one. Yet in a way there was an admirable side to her character.

Perhaps her early history explained some of her less agreeable traits. She was a difficult colt to break, and her owner, an old bachelor, was determined that the breaking be literal and thorough. He worked her hard in the field all day, and let his brothers or himself take her for fifteen and twenty-mile drives at night. The temper of her own with which she had been born was not improved, and though she was not actually vicious, in the way of biting or unprovoked kicking, she was mean, in as many small ways as circumstances permitted, and could always be counted upon to give the maximum of trouble and inconvenience.

Her most persistent vice was kicking whenever the line or any part of the harness caught her tail, which was frequently, as she switched continually, at flies or imaginary flies, when she wished to annoy the man who was working around her, hitching her up, or say pitching hay. She caught the line once when hitched to a hay-rack, and began to kick in her remorseless way. The boy who was driving started back, and just in time, for her shod heels shivered a board of the rack just opposite his head. Again when the ladies of the family drove Dinah to church, she drew up before the building in state, and then, before the waiting worshippers, she caught the line and began to kick straight up in the air. The ladies never knew how they got out of that buggy, but they did, unharmed, and probably as expeditiously as ever before or since.

Again, with Lily as head team on a ponderous road-scraper, the long line leading over the heads of the first team to the scraper became entangled. Dinah's rear quarters flashed into the air again and again, and this tightened the line to Lily's bit. So Lily, too, began to rear, but from the other end. There the two of them were, Lily with head aloft, and Dinah with flashing heels equally high.

She was tough as seven-year-old lightning, as the saying goes, yet lurked behind the other horses in the field, and always had to be hitched in the shortest link of the tugs in order to make her do anything like her share. Yet she was more willing in the buggy, and tireless. She had a dash of thoroughbred blood and hence was not particularly distinguished as a trotter or pacer – not unusually fast. So one Saturday night coming from town, a midsummer night when dust half hid the lamp-posts at the end of the long King street, the race she put up was quite unexpected.

A local man with a track-trained pacer drew up alongside and passed. Dinah's driver let him go for a half a mile or so, and then drew out and in turn passed him, by dint of making Dinah run. When Dinah ran alongside a trotting or pacing horse it reminded one of Mark Twain's comparison: the other horse was the gravel train, and Dinah was the telegraphic message being despatched over the wire alongside. Another mile or so must have passed in this way, then the man with the pacer drew up alongside again. But again Dinah began to run. 'He thinks he can get the old girl tired out,' remarked the driver; and certainly the average horse is not good for a very great distance of hard running. Again and again the pacer drew up alongside, only to find Dinah unwearied in her dust-stirring propensities.

It followed that the occupation which suited her best of all, the activity in which she really found herself was horse-back riding. Here was where that dash of thoroughbred blood came in. She liked to race automobiles. They were not so fast then as now, and usually she picked a second-hand or unwary one.

Dinah would be gallopping briskly toward home, when she would hear a car coming. Then the sound of her hoof-beats increased like a first patter of raindrops into a downpour. One marvelled that her speed could increase so incredibly and quickly. For acceleration she had most cars beaten. And when the automobile drew up with her, her abandoned gallop quickened still more. Of course she could not hold abreast for more than an instant or two if the driver of the automobile cared to 'open it up.' But once up a gravel road over a little hill after a rain she passed an antique car obviously rattling its best. That was her hour of triumph.

Perhaps if she is allowed another incarnation as certain religions would provide her, she may be a Sappho or a Sarah Bernhardt. Or if a horse again, she may more luckily not be required to drag heavy harrows about the scenery at a snail's pace, but may be asked to do nothing but run – race cars which are geared so as to be just passible. It is a hereafter which she would approve.

I said above that in a way her character was admirable. That should perhaps be modified. Not as a horse, but more in the way a human temperament is to be admired, does her fineness become apparent. Nothing sufficed to break her spirit, and she was as unquenchably determined to submit to nothing as she was freshly able to enjoy herself in activity which she did like, after the galling years of almost her whole lifetime.

A tousled long-haired ragamuffin, an apache of the herd is the cross-bred colt. He is nameless, and doesn't care, and nobody else will care until he is ready to be hitched to the roller, and expected to obey gee and haw! Being the only young colt, he has learned to get his own way among the larger horses by sheer unmitigated fierceness of expression or perhaps being youngest, he is a privileged character, and is allowed to take liberties with the others on that account.

Running loose all winter, first in pasture and then in the partially enclosed bottom of an old barn which gave upon a large yard, the colt became long-haired and mishapen. Twice a day a man came to the bush farm and threw great heaps of hay on the ground at distances great enough that if horses eating at separate piles could turn back to back they could kick while they dined. The colt does not kick. He lays his ears back and turns a wicked-looking head in the direction of any piece of horseflesh who presumes to look at the morsel of hay or the cob of corn upon which he has elected to dine. 'Lay his ears back' is inexact, for they seem to be never in any other posture than an expressive equine scowl.

The only time he was known not to have the ears back was when the hired boy, tired of his regularly pawing the water-pail and spilling it, swung a blow to his muzzle. The colt wheeled and stood for a while, his ears pricked forward apparently considering some engrossing idea – the first contact with man, perhaps. But more likely he was merely astonished, didn't know what to think, and forgot to look fierce.

I dare say that few people have thought much, or with great urgency, about the monotony of the life of the average horse on the average farm. The farmer himself probably would think that with a valet (namely, himself) to care for its every need, if not to its every whim, as in the case of the race horse, that its lot, including hours of labour only about two-thirds as long as his own, is nothing to make speeches about.

Yet the most isolated western homesteader leads a career of hectic adventure and rich variety compared with that of his horses. Even the light horses are seldom used in the buggy, and the others never go to town but for a load of merchandise, or to take crops thither, or to get shod. Many work barefoot, and never leave the farm for years at a time, save to neighbours' threshings. If ever they become as experimentally speculative as they are contemplative, if ever a whiff of human restlessness touches them – well, the rest may be left to your imagination. There might be a conspiracy and some fine morning every man who approached a horse might be neatly despatched.

These sobering considerations are merely prelude to the brief tale of Sam, one of those horses to whom nothing happened. What could? He was mere horse, and except for long furrows, pasture romps and rollings, an occasional runaway in which he was only accessory, to vary his faithful service, he knew nothing. But one night when all the farm lay in the stillness of midsummer moonlight, the huge Percheron stallion broke out of his box-stall, and conveniently picked on Sam. His clamping teeth closed on the old horse's neck, and he never left go, notwithstanding Sam's scream of agony, until the farmer appeared on the scene. Sam always carried the scar.

On the other hand there are horses which have led lives of almost bewildering variety, like some race horses and others which would manage to make things interesting wherever they happened to be. Such was Mack, of dubious ancestry and unhallowed memory.

One of his early masters clubbed him over the ears and made him a little crazy, or at least added to the uncertainties of his temperamental disposition. Thereafter he used his bony-jawed head as a club and to enter his stall with the purpose of putting a halter or bridle on him was like entering the radius of a flail. Particularly when his ears or the region of his neck immediately back of them was touched, he released a violent thump toward his would-be driver's head. When he was brought up from work he showed an aristocratic disinclination to drink with the bridle on, and as it was as strenuous an undertaking to get his bridle off as on, and there was a chance of his running away, he sometimes missed watering.

An eccentric lack of decorum also marked his behaviour at work. He would nip his mate, if it happened to be Lily, until she became frantic; and even Dinah could not always haughtily ignore him. Perhaps he considered it a jocund teasing. And thrusting out his chin to nip the neckyoke or the other horse, always he wore the same yellow-toothed grin, a Roosevelt-Wilson-Fairbanks smile.

When the driver chirped at Mack he needed to be wary, for Mack's chin would thrust out violently enough either to jerk the lines from the driver's hands or to pull him off his balance. At the same time, however, he made a full plunge forward, which tended to effect an equilibrium by throwing the driver backward. He scarcely ever trotted, no matter what his mate did, but becoming excited took up a choppy gallop, and his back, the shape of an upturned skiff, seemed to rock on waves of dusty air.

'Circus oss,' the English hired man called him, for he was all over in a minute, and absolutely incalculable in intention and antic. Once in flytime in the lane at the water trough he staged a pretty fracas. By this time he had been tamed or rather gentled by good treatment enough that he could be bridled in the open, providing there was a halter on his head to which to hold while the operation was going on. So Mack never missed a drink now. This noon the English hired man and another were hitching up Mack and Dinah after watering them. Just as the bridle drew over Mack's head and his line had been snapped to the bridle of Dinah, he struck at an annoying fly with his great splay foot. Perhaps he struck the full-blooded green buzzer – or perhaps he missed it. At any rate his hoof caught in one of the under straps of the harness, and he began to twirl rapidly on three legs, brushing the men aside in his rapid revolutions and jerking Dinah violently.

It seemed that there was nothing to be done. The men stood off and watched the ballet. 'He doesn't want to let Dinah catch that line once,' yelled one, 'or she'll sure kick herself loose, and him, too.' Mack wrapped himself up pretty well and the line to Dinah's bit broke, yet somehow Dinah clamped upon a piece, and began to kick. Luckily she was not shod, and her blows did not strike Mack, when they struck him at all, in the legs, the most dangerous place. They seemed merely to tickle his ribs, or at most to bruise his quarters. Finally Dinah was free, and did her kicking in solitary splendour. But poor Mack had become so entangled that he finally sank to the ground, his head drawn to his hocks, like a sleeping lamb – except that his snorts of terror and exhaustion would have blown a small lamb away.

Maud and Jess were two colts as pretty as the township could show. They had grown up together, been broken together, and were given the same feed and care. These resulted in their being each fifteen hundred pounds of smooth-coated, round-bodied, even-dispositioned horseflesh. Good pullers and never lazy, but well cared for, they were the pride of their owner. The latter, however, decided to retire from farming, and was forced to sell them for trucking in the city, since for that purpose they commanded the highest price.

It was equivalent to being sold down river to the carefully matured, almost pampered country horses. In the city they dragged heavy loads about the sweltering and clamorous streets, and received such offhand care as the teamster of the time gave. Saturday night a great wad of hay was rolled into their mangers and the front of the stalls, which had to last until Monday morning. They escaped the fate of lymphangytis which usually attends such feeding, but they did not stand the daily and year-long impact of the city pavements so well. Corns, burnings, poor shoeing, made them old in two years.

It happened that at the end of this time their first owner became bored with his retirement and bought another farm, a small one. He approached the man who had bought his team, who was able to trace it, and in due course he rebought Maud and Jess and took them to his little farm.

Here once more they knew good care, easy work occasionally, and pasture romps again, long browsings and long dozes in the shade of elms. The other horses at first tried to bully or tease the strangers, but they kept their solid well-matched forms together and bothered none; and presently their own colts had crowded out those others.

HITCHING BERTHA TO THE SLEIGH

It had snowed heavily the night before and, save the chores, there was nothing for the Galpin boys to do. To be sure, on a well and variously stocked farm, that means more than a little. So it was not until Angus and Tad, the younger ones and Tom, aged fourteen, had milked the cows, fed and watered the horses, cows and fattening steers, given chop and swill to the pigs, brought down fresh straw from the barn above, started the gasoline engine pumping a fresh supply of water, put hay down from the mow for dinner, carried corn-stalks out into the barnyard for the steers to nibble, and done a few other minor jobs, that the big idea came.

The big idea concerned Bertha. And it concerned their father, since he might not have approved of it and since it was well not to risk anything by asking his permission, particularly as he was going to town that morning in the cutter. So they were unusually attentive in getting his road-horse cleaned, harnessed, and hitched to the cutter, and in putting halter, blanket, and buffalo-robe beneath the seat. Finally, about half past ten o'clock, they saw him off with more enthusiasm than they cared to show.

Then they returned to the comparative warmth of the barn to consider their plans for Bertha.

'Do you think maybe she might get snow-blind perhaps,' ventured Tad, 'if we took her out on a day like this? She's never been outside the barn yet except to get weighed sometimes, and she's nearly six months old.'

'Aw!' exclaimed Angus conclusively. 'She don't know what snow-blind is. What does a calf want with getting snow-blind? Only explorers get snow-blind. You never read – '

Tom, their elder, was leaning over the iron enclosure, trying absent-mindedly to pat the animal on the head.

'Well, well, Bertha,' he said with a grin. 'Well, well, Bertha.'

In the dim stable the calf seemed to be black, though there was a tinge of red. She stood stolidly regarding the boys for a minute, meanwhile off-handedly licking her nose.

Then, without warning, her solid thick form began to cavort about the enclosure in the deep straw, with much twisting and bucking, the while her damp muzzle gleamed and the whites of her eyes showed occasionally. The straw rustled and flew in the air as high as the manger. Bertha seemed to stop her dance only for lack of a partner.

'See, she knows what you're talking about,' said Tad, seriously. 'Do you think maybe we'd ought to have took her out when Paw was home?'

'Naw,' said Tom briefly. 'He wouldn't help.'

'Maybe,' Angus considered, 'we might have told him before he went. Bertha might run away and – '

'Might catch up with him on the road and pass, eh?' They all laughed, but rather uneasily.

The boys and calf regarded each other with unfeigned interest.

'I tell you what,' proposed Angus, who was the middle in age, and accustomed to mediate with a course of compromise. 'Let's just tie a rope on her halter and take her out to get weighed this time, same as we generally always do. Then if she's quiet we can go ahead. We'll get the sleigh and things all ready.'

But this plan was promptly and effectively vetoed. 'You're scairt. Aw, yer scairt!' It was Tad, the youngest, who hopped about in sudden ecstasy similar to that of the calf whittling one forefinger at them, 'Sha-ame, yer scairt!'

The others did not say anything. But they felt somehow that Tad counted on being the youngest, and on getting out of the risky part of hitching up the five hundred pound calf.

'Scairt, am I! I'll scairt you!' Angus leaped at him and the two rolled in a pile of hay put down for dinner, and were rapidly buried in a whirling storm of it. Tom paid no attention but looked at the calf, which still maintained interest in him, and grinned.

'Well, well, Bertha. Come on and be nice calfums!' He held out his mittened hand and then drew back as Bertha proceeded to lick at it with a rough tongue.

He turned away to the horse stable adjoining, when the other two emerged from the hay, puffing and still pulling and jostling each other.

'You've gone and got hayseed down my neck,' muttered Tad darkly, glaring at his brother.

'Aw, you're a hayseed anyhow!' With a sweeping movement from behind Angus pulled Tad's 'toboggan' cap over his eyes.

But before another round could start Tom called from the stable. 'Come on here, shake a wicked limb!' He was whistling casually as he sorted straps and bits of harness. 'If we're going to hitch up that calf we better be getting at it, unless we're all scairt like youse two are. Go and get the sleigh, and all the loose binder-twine you can find from the straw-stack.'

In half an hour the boys had assembled and fastened together two pieces of line to serve as tugs, connected them with each side of the front of the handsleigh, two pieces of clothesline to serve as lines, and numberless pieces of bindertwine to fasten these together at strategic places.

'What do you want with lines for though?' Angus demanded. 'You don't drive calves with a bit in the mouth. You drive them with a yoke.'

'Say, that's right! Only we don't know how to make a yoke.'

'Fasten the lines on 'er horns.'

'Bertha ain't got no horns,' shrilled Tad. 'She's just a young cow.'

'She had! I felt 'em last time we weighed her.'

'She ain't!'

'She has!'

'You'll soon see when she bunts you. Come on now, we'll hitch up.' The sleigh was drawn up formally outside the stable door, with the tugs attached to it. The problem which remained was that of connecting Bertha with them. Carrying ropes, string, and straps, they proceeded to her enclosure.

'Now you hold these,' proceeded Tom, officially, 'and I'll go in and tie the rope to her halter, and then this strap around her neck for a collar to tie the tugs to, and – '

'Yes, you'll talk about it, but let's see you do it,' they jeered.

With offended dignity the older boy turned away, unlatched the iron-grated door, and entered the box-stall. 'You better come in too, so she can't run all over and get away.' Crouching, he softly put one foot before the other, extending one hand with a strap. 'Well, well, Bertha,' he murmured soothingly.

Bertha woofed and bucked to one side, but in a moment, probably not wishing to forego an outing, she subsided and allowed them to tie everything they had to her, only occasionally lifting her head abruptly to chuck them under the chins. They all held to the straps and ropes as Tom led her out through the alleyway into the horse-stable and out the door. They had a moment of anxiety behind the horse stalls, because Maud, the old mare, was cross and might haul off and kick if Bertha got away and began gambolling.

But finally they got the calf hitched to the sleigh. Tom, with the wisdom of his years, was wondering who would ride, when both together the others yelled, 'I borrow to drive and ride on the sleigh!'

'All right,' he agreed, 'I'll hold the halter till you get going. Then I'll let you drive without me.'

Each begged to drive alone, but he persuaded them to allow each other on board. And not too soon. The excitement had been telling on Bertha, and she was rearing to go. When they did go, they had not traveled two yards when Bertha, who almost appeared to hold a preconceived idea on the subject, lowered her head and took up a pace which Tom, running alongside, did not find it expedient to match. He threw the rope to the boys and watched the equipage rapidly vanish down the road. One reason for this turn of events was that they had underestimated Bertha's length of limbs. The tugs not being long enough, at every jump she hit her heels on the sled.

'Say, they're hitting the high spots.' Tom remembered at the moment that Bertha was being reared as a baby beef, and that this episode, however exhilarating to all concerned, would not add much fat to her ribs. But now nothing was to be done.

He stood and watched boys, sled, and calf strike a snowdrift and vanish in swirls of snow. Then it could be seen that the boys had fallen off, while the calf, still faithfully followed by the sleigh, leaped into the ditch and scrambled along its bottom.

Why couldn't those two have held on? Now he'd have to catch her.

But as Tom ran excitement filled him, and he yelled, 'Well, well, Bertha! Go it!'

TRYING TO PLEASE THE LADIES

The smoke rising from the tin pipe which surmounted the little building was the liveliest thing in the village that muddy autumn afternoon. The building itself was covered with tin, of a conformation to suggest cement blocks or possible stone masonry; but it had not yet rusted enough for that. With an anxious glance at the four-panel large window taking up one-half of the front, a boy of eleven stepped to the door and entered.

Three men sprawled on chairs in the barbership, one reading part of the day's already battered paper, the other contributing to the amenities of the barber and his assistant, a new young man whom they called Percy and laughed at because he claimed that he had attended a barber college.

'Just in time, m'boy,' said one of the men.

The boy smiled and was silent.

'Just in time for a wait,' grinned another. 'I tell you, that's just how it happened. I wouldn't have believed it if I hadn't of seen it myself. But that girl can dance, she can. He says to me, Ambrose says, "Carlotta can dance with a cup of water on her head, balancing." "Well, tell you what I'll do," I says, "I'll bet you!" Off he goes, hunts Carlotta up, and they get a cup from the banquet dishes. Teedle-ump-de-dee. Off she goes, dances with the cup on her head, nice as you please.' The man twiddled his fingers at arm's length.

'Bet it was empty,' said the barber. Percy looked at him as though in shocked alarm.

'Naw – I guess not, anyway what's the difference – '

'Bet you lost your bet, that's what I bet!'

'No, sir, I wasn't bettin', I tell you. That's where he overreached himself. Got in such a hurry he wouldn't listen, when I was tryin' to give him money. If he only knowed it – haw, haw!' The ruddy-faced youngish man in a tight misted blue coat and baggy trousers twisted his chair out from the wall, leaning with his feet doubled back on each side and drummed on the rungs with heavy fingers. The boy seemed almost afraid to listen to the talk of the men. He sat near the door and gazed steadily at the glass billow of the show case at the window, in which as well as cigars and plug tobacco there were chocolate bars and gum.

Gradually the patrons of the place were served, and as each one departed and the afternoon passed it seemed unlikely that more would appear before the evening rush. Finally only the boy remained and the two barbers. In silence the proprietor sat down on one of the chairs along the wall and began reading the paper as his customers had done.

Red haired Percy turned on his heel beside his chair, flourished his hand, slapped one oxford on the floor, and said, 'Next!' Then he secured a cloth-covered board from behind the mirror and placed it across the arms of the chair. The boy hesitatingly ascended and perched on the board. Percy dragged a white sheet over him and began to cut his hair.

'Say,' he finally addressed his employer's reflection in the mirror. 'Do you believe all that fellow said about Carlotta Dunning dancing with the cup of tea on her head? Seems kind of fishy to me.'

'Can't never tell about Tob's stories,' mumbled the barber without looking up from the paper.

'I know she's a nice girl – or I mean – I never been introduced, but – but that's a little too much to swallow.'

The barber grunted.

'She done it at home,' the boy said suddenly from beneath the white swathing, and promptly looked as though he had not opened his mouth.

'What's that?' gasped Percy, nervously, his scissors tweaking the boy's hair. 'Oh, you saw her, too, eh. How's that, you weren't invited to the dance, were you?'

'No,' said the boy glumly.

'Never mind, neither was I,' the youth giggled. 'How do you know, then?'

'Well, I guess I should ought to know, when she's my sister.'

'Oh!'

The young fellow was more flustered than ever – combed swiftly, brandished his scissors like lightning, and clipped a spot a couple of inches above the boy's ear to the skin. The latter wriggled and held his peace. Nobody said anything. The little gas stove became louder and louder, and the silence seemed as heavy as the air, weighted with tobacco smoke, various 'tonics' and the relic emanations of much-worn heavy clothing. Percy worked faster and faster.

Finally the barber laid down his paper, rose, stretched himself and sighed.

'Guess I'll slip into Punch's place a couple minutes. If the shop fills up you holler.' He went out, shaking the building with his steps and the closing of the door.

'So you're Carlotta's brother, are you?' said Percy with jovial superiority, rumpling the boy's head, sprinkling green liquid on it until it was soaked, and massaging it until the boy's reflection seemed to quiver and he was wagged almost off his high board and had to recover his place. Then he combed it nicely, plastered it down with a brush, and, drawing the sheet away, said casually:

'Say, I wonder if you'd mind just saying something to your sister about what we said here. Tell her I'd – tell her Percy Gardiner would like to meet her and said she's the prettiest girl he ever seen.'

Fishing in a pocket, the boy extended a quarter and a ten cent piece.

'Keep the change,' said Percy, winking at him. 'What about it? That all right with you?'

'All right, I'll tell her,' murmured the boy doubtfully, but replacing the money without delay.

Half an hour later he reappeared in the barber shop, red-faced as though from running. The barber was returning behind him with a patron, and Percy had another in the chair.

'Say,' said the boy, directly addressing the red-haired youth, 'my sister says to tell you you're no gentleman to talk about her in a barber-shop and – '

Percy, after one start of panic surprise, begged him to keep still, comb to lips, with an ingratiating smile and shake of the head, motioning him to the door. Only to meet the stare of the boss coming in, with the other man looking over his shoulder.

'And if it wasn't you that said it,' the boy went on, in a high, clear recitation, 'you'd ought to of put those big bums out. She wouldn't speak to you for a hundred dollars. And another thing she says to tell you, you cut my hair so's I can't go to church, she says she won't be seen with me in such a hair-cut at a sheep-shearing, and she says to tell you you're nothing but a big bum.' Turning in a businesslike way, the boy marched out.

His face becoming redder and redder as he listened, the youth reached excitedly for a powder can and began sprinkling talcum on the half-trimmed head of the farmer in the chair. Then seeing what he had done he fled to the back room, took a drink, jangling the dipper against the pail, and when the laughter had died down came out again. The farmer raised himself and looked his tormentor accusingly in the eye, then sank back again with a sigh. Though the boy had gone, the barber and the other customer were far from silent.

NO GUMPTION

Archie Buzzard was about twenty years old, and more popular with himself than with his mother. Not that Mrs Buzzard was lacking in normal affection for her son, but it did not come so much to the surface when the latter insisted in forgetting that he had a mother to keep and a farm to run, and instead ran after the Nolan girl or others.

Mrs Buzzard tried to give the impression that she had nothing personally against the Nolan girl. Yet the sight of that red-auburn head, that vivid complexion from which the freckles were not yet removed, those white hands, invariably put her out of humour, and made her think that any other girl would be preferable – that is, less dangerous – for Archie to be playing around with. She told herself that she did not mind Archie going out once in a while, but when it came to a dance two and sometimes three times a week, that meant that Archie was forgetting all about the fact that he had responsibilities to the land, and forgetting the seriousness of life, of which Mrs Buzzard was thoroughly convinced.

Archie himself did not see the cause for worrying in this way. The farm was a good farm, one hundred acres of arable land, and had been pretty well paid for when his father died three years ago. His mother and he had worked hard, raised good crops, paid the taxes and interest and a considerable of the principal. Once in a while they had hired a man, but mostly Archie was able to get the work done with a three-horse team. Mrs Buzzard had always fed large flocks of chickens and turkeys, and now she went into ducks and guinea-fowl, and made such a good garden, that it alone almost kept the house in the summer, including what vegetables and berries were sold, and gave them canned preserves for the winter. A few times Mrs Buzzard actually went into the field and drove the mower or binder and she was always about the barns seeing that the pigs and calves got the extra attention which brought extra profits.

In fact she got into the way of thinking that Archie would do nothing properly unless she were there to oversee the matter. And Archie, who was only seventeen when these preoccupations had been devolved upon him, had seemed to accept this point of view before he got in with the fast bunch at the village. But lately he was paying no attention to the objurgations, sermons, and reprimands of his mother. He wouldn't argue with her, or raise any dissent to her general propositions anent the good policy of raising much crops and converting the same into many hundredweight of bacon hogs and baby-beef cattle, and the necessity of doing this with a thoroughness only possible to young men who remained at home of an evening and retired for the labours of another day sufficiently early to rise at five o'clock in the morning.

But the fact that Archie agreed to everything his mother said, verbally, did not cause him to stop his regular trips to the village, or to the Nolan farm and thence with that girl to the dance at the Beach. He must have learned to dance without lessons, for his attendance at a dance, reported by a conscientious neighbour, was the first inkling his mother had that he had ever thought of such frivolities. There was the matter of a new suit as well, though Archie already had a good blue one which he had worn very little in the last two years.

The fact that Archie got his own way quietly without undue disagreement, and still carried on the farm work with no appearance of deterioration in the general well being of the place, should have warned Mrs Buzzard that she was bound eventually to be overruled. In fact it did so warn her, and she began to scold and to nag. She made certain he was up in the morning every bit as early as before, and when he showed a disposition to take a nap under the trees at noon after the horses had been given their grain, she routed him out and told him to bag up a load of chop to take to the mill, or to get the two colts harnessed for work in the afternoon, so they wouldn't be getting wild, after the trouble it had been to break them in.

But soon Archie began to demur. He would grunt when she started to sermonize, and though he neglected nothing from intention, he would often forget to oil the machinery, or leave the gates open and have to run after stock which had escaped.

He was thinking of the Nolan girl. The less his mother thought of her the more Archie did. Her blue mischievous eyes haunted him, and scarcely a noon hour was complete without a conversation with her over the 'phone. Once or twice she went to the length of calling him herself, and his mother had to summon him from the barn with disgust in her tones. The very voice of the girl, to her simpering and affected, made her angry. And she listened to her son's replies and his awkward badinage with set lips while she cleared the table or washed the dishes. 'You've got no gumption,' she said. 'You're a softie, that's what you are. What do you always want to be running around for?'

Finally before the summer was done it came to a show-down, or appeared to do so. It was three o'clock in the morning, and his mother met him at the door. She convicted him of leaving the cow in the alfalfa field after nightfall in a heavy dew. Though he stayed up the rest of the night, the cow died, and Mrs Buzzard's case was strengthened immensely. She took advantage of the fact.

He was not to see the Nolan girl until the harvest was over. Nor was he to call her by telephone. Though he agreed only under duress, he did agree.

But all this did not convince Archie that he was wrong; only that it was good policy to avoid the company he had been keeping. He really believed that, and considered that his mother was right in her conviction that more money could be made at farming by the avoidance of social festivities. He started to work again next morning with the firm conviction to forget Allie.

The resolve, however, had begun to weaken a little at the end of the first week. He approached his mother with the proposal that he call the

Nolan girl to apprise her of the fact that he would not squire her at the week dance, the Friday night one, which he had not missed for months, however seldom he might see her in the intervals. Mrs Buzzard did not want to agree to this, but she could present no valid objection. She did not give the boy any definite answer.

So Archie put off calling until night, and after supper, while his mother went out to work in the garden, he planned that he would talk with Allie. He did not want anyone to hear what he had to say. It would be difficult, and yet he had to tell her, he felt. And he had to hear her voice once more. He was only twenty, and he wanted to be sensible, but he had not been happy during the past week.

But when supper time came his mother saw his glance toward the 'phone and told him:

'Did you know they've changed the central for the people over on the Sixth? To get them now we've got to call the central at Bradford, and that means we've got to pay fifteen cents every time. Maybe you'd better not call.'

Archie said nothing, but he was struck with surprise. After supper, when his mother had gone out into the still, bright evening, he looked at the 'phone a long time, thinking. It would cost as much to call her up and cancel the date – and cancel everything, he reminded himself, as it would cost in gasoline to go over and see her. The more frequently he revolved this fact, the more convinced he became that he should not put his mother to this expense. It would come in the monthly bill, and she would talk. And the bill would be more than the normal rate, because he could not say everything in three minutes. Perhaps it would save a good deal to drive over. Besides, she had insisted on his not calling.

So in a very few minutes he was dressed in his best and trotting toward the garage. He could do the chores when he got home. The thing now, he felt, was to avoid discussion. And if there were discussion, it would be a warm, possibly a fatal one. He must see Allie.

He did. He came, he saw, and was conquered anew. But coming home after the dance, he told Allie that his mother thought he had better not see her any more.

'Why?' asked Allie, with astonishment, pursing her lips, fair eyebrows rising toward her auburn hair.

'She thinks I don't look after the farm so well then when I'm out so much.'

Allie in the moonlight appeared thoughtful. 'It seems as if we ought to get married.'

'Why – ! Could we?' Archie looked at her in astonishment before his arms tightened around her. She did not reply. 'Of course we could,' he answered himself firmly.

And within a few months, that is what happened.

'Perhaps you'll settle down and have some gumption,' remarked his mother, grim, but not unpleasant.

A BOY'S GIRL

Perhaps it was because Henrietta Grey had no brothers when she was a little girl, or perhaps it was because she had only one sister, Lila, much older, that she played mostly with boys. The neighbour boys, of course, were not at first too anxious to allow an intrusion of the fair sex. But Henrietta skipped so vigorously, played tag and hide-and-seek so fleetly and cunningly, and even won so many marbles away from them, that the boys soon took her presence among them as a matter of course.

In fact her membership of the gang went so far that she was not only in good standing, with no need for a defensive attitude to maintain it, but Henrietta had more to say than anyone else when it came to the matter of allowing new boys to enter or expelling an old one in her bad graces for the term of perhaps two days. Henrietta held sway with an absolutism to be envied of other rulers, when she chose, and perhaps the reason that she was able to rule was that she seldom chose to do so.

There was no kindergarten in the village, and Henrietta was not thrown among members of her own sex at an early age, to induce class consciousness. In the years which kindergarten would have occupied, and after, it was no unusual sight, her appearance in the midst of admiring boys, swinging on some gate which overhung the gravel paths which served as sidewalks in the village, teetering, playing croquet – a vivid little figure, with black flying hair, brown eyes, merry red lips never still. She possessed apparently unbounded energy, and led the boys in almost any game they had a mind to choose. Yet she did not become exactly hoydenish; she was not a tomboy, quite. School, which she began at the age of half-past six, or the influence of her mother, may have made the difference.

It was a difference which made it possible for her to take large part in such activities as I have mentioned, and yet on Sundays and state occasions to be as prim and fluffy as the blue ribbons on her hat and the braids of her hair. Though the eyes of this second Henrietta Grey sparkled in their old dark way, they were unconscious seemingly of the other Henrietta, and in fact might have been scandalized at her. Unless, like the other little girls seated so primly on either side of her, they were envious of that free creature.

School, of course, made a difference. She could not very well escape from the other girls, and openly join the great herd of wild boys who for fifteen minutes morning and afternoon recess, not to mention at noon hour and before and after school, made the roomy yard a cheerful bedlam of wiry young humanity. And whether she knew it or not the standards of more 'proper' girls were being imposed upon her, not to mention those of a series of girl teachers, very conscientious and intent upon imparting refinement.

Still, in the periodic epidemic of note-sending, Henrietta was sure to get notes from half the boys in the room, to reply to all of them either calligraphically or by open nods, smiles, or if the missive had been too teasing, by protrusions of the tongue. She was perfectly shameless, or so it appeared to the teacher, and caused the whole network of subterranean crime to be unearthed and exposed. But when any such epidemic of mischief broke out anew, Henrietta Grey would be in the forefront again.

And when the stage had been reached at which boys offered to carry some girl's schoolbooks home for her, Henrietta had more bids of the sort than she knew what to do with. For she was inclined to be impartial with her favours, and the boys knew that each had a chance. Once, at the end of the spring term when Easter holidays were beginning, she studiously decided to take most of her books home, so that she might do what her elders were incessantly urging her to do, catch up with her studies. As she unpacked book after book from her desk her neighbours gaped with astonishment, and Hughie Morgan, who was accustomed to carry her books more frequently than the others, whispered across the aisle a word that was his undoing:

'I want some help for that job.'

Henrietta said nothing, but her mischievous black eyes turned to Johnnie Loring, in the next seat beyond. When she was leaving he came forward, as well as Hughie, and Henrietta openly asked two or three other boys, 'Aren't you going to help me carry all these books home? They're heavy as lead.' The other girls pretended shocked amusement.

The upshot was that though she could have had a boy to carry each book she had a procession of half a dozen, who gathered about her gate, and later the porch. Finally someone proposed that they all repair to the ice-cream parlour and confectionery, on King Street – provided the party should 'go dutch.' Johnny Loring, however, managed to achieve the honour of paying for Henrietta's chocolate sundae.

'She's certainly a boy's girl all right,' said the baker and confectioner's wife, watching the troop going away, with various tinglings of the harness bell which hung against the top of the door. 'Likes to keep with the boys.

'A real dead-game sport. The boys don't put up no kick about being with her, either. She can swim, row a boat, play baseball or tennis better than any girl in high school. Better than most of the boys, I don't doubt.'

The better half became dubious. 'That's all right. That's the kind of a girl that takes with the boys. But she'll be growing up one of these times. Then that flip kind get to be regular flirts, but I notice they don't very often get married.'

'Don't you worry. Henrietta's all right.'

If Henrietta's mother had heard this colloquy, and fancied it typical of the reaction of the village, she would have worried, more than she did. Mrs Grey was a rather precise woman, who tried to inculcate some of the qualities she had acquired. But her husband's people had been of that flyaway sort, and Mr Grey encouraged his daughter in anything she seemed bent on doing. To his view it seemed that she could do nothing wrong. Henrietta was getting to be a big girl now. It was time she was acting more like a young lady. She should sing in the choir. Perhaps that would help make her realize the importance of being prim.

As leader of the choir Mrs Grey's task in getting Henrietta into it was simple compared with her undertaking as a mother to see that Henrietta attended the practicings and the services themselves, with a minimum of unnecessary gaiety. Nothing, however, could tame her spirits, and on the most solemn occasions something would strike her as funny – say the sight of Deacon Rising nodding his head toward his wife's shoulder, until one nod jerked him awake – or was it a pin-prick? – and Henrietta would have to retrieve a hymn-book from the rack in front of her to hold before her only partially smothered merriment.

Perhaps her attendance in the choir had a good effect on Hughie Morgan and Johnnie Loring, for they came to church more regularly. Hughie by this time had gone into his father's business of tinsmithing and plumbing, in so far as the village had need at that time for plumbers. He flew about the country on a fiery red motorcycle which seemed to have little regard for the state of the traffic or the seasonal conditions of the roads.

Behind Hughie on the demoniac motorcycle rode Henrietta Grey.

This was something her mother did not know about for the first few times. But she might as well never have known, for all the practical avail the knowledge was. The girl would have left home for a walk in the evening, or on some trifling errand to the General Store and Postoffice, and she would be gone for a long time, or so it seemed to her mother. Then there would be a raucous artillery sound and Hughie would breeze around the corner at an angle of forty-five degrees, with Hen clinging on behind, hair, scarf, and skirts flying, eyes dancing.

'It's a funny thing to me,' Mrs Grey would say with weighty sarcasm, 'that you've got so little to do that you have to go gallivanting that way. And I thought you were going to the store.'

'I was,' Henrietta would return with bland patience. 'But Hughie happened along with his motorcycle. Say, Mom, they've got a new name for it now. Go-devil.'

Mrs Grey frowned. 'A noise – a noise-demon would be more fitting. But it's strange that you never hear it until it's coming back, then you can hear it for miles, and everybody in the village sees – But when you're going away nobody can hear a sound.'

Henrietta turned away hastily. 'It is strange,' she admitted.

Her merriment did not escape her mother. 'Henrietta! Listen to me! This has got to stop. I can't have you going on this way and becoming the talk of the town.'

'Why pick on poor Hugh, just because he hasn't a sedan, when the other boys take me driving, too? If I knew anyone with a mule and a racing cart I'd go with him, maybe. Don't you think I would be becoming to a mule and a cart and – '

Her mother did not smile. 'You may not find so much to laugh about – if this kind of thing goes on.'

But in the house her father was smiling, hedged behind his newspaper and his moustache. 'What have you been doing to your mother's feelings now?' he asked, scarcely listening to the explanation.

Henrietta, if her mother had known it, was already the talk of the town, of that part of the town which gathers in the drug-store, the barber-shop, the steps of the New Continental Hotel. Her frequent goings and comings on the fiery motorcycle were noted and commented upon variously. The fact that the other young people seemed to pay no attention, and many of the youths of the place took her out whenever the opportunity came, made no difference. In the eyes of back-yard line-fence gossip and elderly scandal-mongering, Henrietta's unstaid past was against her.

Came the occasion of the wiener-roast at the lake, one June night. All the young people of the village who paired were going down to Lake Erie, five miles away, roast marshmallows and frankfurters, with such accompanying jollities as they could contrive extemporaneously. Johnnie Loring had secured Henrietta's promise to go with him in his coupe. He counted a good deal on this, for it had been some time since he had gone out with Henrietta.

Perhaps it was accidental that Henrietta should have been ready to go at least half an hour before the time appointed, which was at least an hour before proceedings actually began. And it may have been accidental that Hughie Morgan should happen along on his subduedly put-putting steed.

'You look like a damsel in distress,' he proclaimed, pausing and leaning on the handlebars. He was groomed carefully, and his reddish hair mostly restrained by a hat.

'I am,' she confessed, with unwonted sobriety.'Why don't you rescue me?'

'Let's go.' He held the motorcycle firmly.

They were about five minutes reaching the lake, and found that no others of their party had arrived. It was moonlight, as the organizers had planned, but it was also windy. Lake Erie was a broad, endless waste of agitation. Creamy and shadowed rollers near shore, dark cloud-shadows and silver lines to the horizon. And over all the water before them, the land behind, the wind, endless, insistent. The small trees beside them were like fountains in the wind and the strong moonlight, endlessly swaying, tossing thier grey green under the June moon.

'I don't feel like a wienie-roast,' murmured Henrietta, quite close.

'Neither do I. Let's go somewhere else.' They looked once more at the scene before them, and again bestrode the motorcycle.

Johnnie and the rest of the party did not waste much speculation on their whereabouts, but when they had not reappeared by the following night, talk became open. The evening after that the two raucous cylinders were heard again, and the red steed held a course to the Grey porch.

'Where have you been?' gasped Mrs Grey, when her feelings would permit her. She looked accusingly at Hughie, who stood statuesque beside his machine. It was he who spoke.

'We've been to London.'

'And gone two days – '

'Oh, we've been other places. You see, it was our honeymoon.'

Mrs Grey seemed about to collapse, when her husband came out of the house.

'Congratulations,' he boomed. But his voice was softer as he held his daughter in his arms.

THE FURNACE CAUSES WARMTH

It is strange that some people whom one would otherwise expect to show considerable sense sometimes appear to have lost every atom of the brains with which they are endowed. That appears to be the case with my wife. If I seem to be expressing myself strongly, I can only ask a patient hearing, and it will become manifest that I am one of those husbands whose long-suffering patience makes the reading of the funny papers so tragic a thing for me.

I always feel sorry for poor Al, and for that downtrodden Mr Jiggs, but it appears to me that they represent a vast proportion of our citizenry who are too high-minded to speak out when they are misunderstood and abused by their wives. Well, I am going to change all that. I am going to speak out this once anyway, and if nothing happens I may speak out again.

You might think that if a woman had the discrimination to sort me out from her male acquaintances and marry me, that she would continue to develop these intellectual attainments after marriage. Not so Lavinia. She seems sadly changed in the last few years.

We had been living in an apartment, but this winter we decided a house would suit our needs better. Every man's house, they say, is his castle. He can do what he likes there, and no one shall say him nay. This is especially the case when he is right and knows he is right and the other person is wrong and – But I am getting ahead of my story. As I was saying, I used to think that that was the case. I still think it should be. But it seems sometimes that it is not the case. There is certain domestic routine where it doesn't make any difference how right you are, you might as well be wrong.

Take the furnace, for example. Or leave it alone, would be wiser, but I can't expect you to understand that until you have seen what I am driving at.

The furnace is a useful unobtrusive sort of creature, if left alone, and allowed to do its work in peace. That is the trouble. If it blew up and ascended through the roof pushing the chimney with it, whenever it was maltreated, or got temperamental on the general principles of the automobile and the radio and electric light sockets and your favourite golf stick when you want to make a good drive with it, people might treat it with more consideration. But since it is meek and uncomplaining, they have no scruples about abusing its trusting nature.

It is chiefly women who do this. Ask any man if you doubt it.

'Now the furnace is all fixed for the day,' I told my wife, and bade her good-by. I expected to work with the tranquil assurance that everything was going well at home and that Lavinia was as free of care, at least as far as warmth was concerned, as I was in my office. In fact I was satisfied, that first day. But what did I find when I got home at night?

I admit that Lavinia was clever. She welcomed me as usual, and not even the most astute detective would have discerned the deception which she was practising. I said:

'Well, how did you and that furnace get along? Forgot all about it, I'll bet. That's better than your old apartments. And when you do want a little more heat you don't hunt up any old janitor, you go down to the bin and take out the odd shovelful. While if there's too much heat, you shut her down and save coal-bills.'

I hear my readers snicker. Doubtless they have spouted the same sort of optimistic tosh. But I was to learn better. Lavinia said:

'That's just what I was thinking. The house didn't seem to be getting warm, so this morning after you went to the office I went down and opened the dampers. You wouldn't believe how much difference it made. Long before noon it was almost too warm. Of course I shut the bottom door and the dampers then, and the house has been perfectly comfortable ever since. I didn't even need to look at the furnace again. Who would have thought it could be so simple?'

I looked at Lavinia, and I opened my mouth to say something, then I thought better of it and went down cellar to see what had been going on. There was a sort of deadly quiet in the atmosphere of the furnace room. Any householder will know what I mean. With frozen calm and a sort of numbness about the heart, I opened the furnace door.

It might have been a cave I was looking into. When my sight became accustomed to the darkness, I perceived that deep, deep down there were certain red veins or seams in the bed of chalky gray white and yellow with which that furnace was filled. I left the door open and went upstairs to Lavinia.

She was sitting at the window turning over the pages of the woman's style magazine I had remembered to bring her. I sat down and lit my pipe, crossed my legs, and prepared to devote to this matter my full rated horsepower of intellectual voltage, if you understand me.

'It was nice of you to remember to get my magazine,' she said, looking up. 'We're going to have scalloped potatoes for dinner.' She rose to go to the kitchen, probably remembering that I hated scalloped potatoes. I raised my hand, and having got my pipe drawing well, I asked her:

'Lavinia,' I said. 'Lavinia, don't you know anything about furnaces?'

'Why, what do you mean?' she asked as if it were innocently.

'Don't you know that if you open the dampers and let it go, the coal all goes up the chimney and you're wasting it?'

She looked relieved. 'Don't be silly,' she said. 'Isn't it warm enough here?'

I remained calm. 'It is warm enough here,' I conceded. 'But how long is it going to stay warm?'

She shrugged her shoulders in the ignorant annoying way women sometimes have.

'No.' I was still adopting a quiet and reasonable, almost soothing tone. 'I am merely facing the facts, and I want you to face them, too.'

'Well, it goes without saying that you want me to face the facts, whether you do or not. Perhaps some time you'll tell me what you think the facts are so that I can face them.' If you can beat a woman at dodging an issue and obscuring the main trend of the argument at stake, let me know, somebody. They never hold to the same line of reasoning for two minutes in succession. They'll do anything to sidetrack you when they see you're really beginning to talk cold turkey.

'Well,' I repeated, rather insistently. I was beginning to become a bit impatient. 'You really want to face the facts, do you? If you had wanted to face the facts you might have opened the furnace door and looked in. And if you still want to face them you might come down with me now and face 'em.'

'Oh, it's the furnace you're talking about, is it?' There was a lack of tenderness in her tone in this reference. She would like to blame everything on the poor furnace.

'No, it's you I'm talking about, not the furnace. The furnace I have every reason to believe is all right.' It was time to really get down to cases, I saw.

'Oh, I see what you mean,' Lavinia laughed. 'The furnace is all right as long as you are taking care of it. When I open and close the dampers or touch it in any way, it's not. I see.' She turned to go into the kitchen. 'Isn't that just like a man? Oh, I see!' she sang.

I got up and followed her.

'Please, Lavinia, try and act as though you had the minimum of common sense endowed a sparrow, and listen – '

'A sparrow knows enough to keep warm,' Lavinia returned calmly, taking a dish from the oven.

'For two cents I'd let you get warm the best way you could. Do you know what has happened? The furnace is out.'

The news did not appear to faze Lavinia. 'What of it? I dare say furnaces go out sometimes.'

'When people go meddling with them when they don't know the door from the flue. You opened the dampers when I was gone, didn't you?'

'Of course I did. I looked in, and it all looked black, as though the fire was going out. When I went and looked again at noon, the fire was all nice and red. So I shut the dampers.'

'Didn't I tell you I had left the furnace in good shape, and that you wouldn't need to look at it all day?'

'Yes, but it was going out.'

'It has gone out now, because you burnt the coal up too fast. Now I've got to go down and dig out all those cinders, and get kindling split up and a lot of wood and start the whole thing up again. Just because you couldn't keep your hands off the dampers.' I was beginning to get a trifle impatient.

'I'm sorry,' Lavinia said. 'Anyway, the house is nice and warm.'

I did not say anything more, or at least nothing that Lavinia could hear, while I shoveled out the cinders and started the fire again. But I vowed a vow that thereafter the business of taking care of the furnace should be left to me entirely.

Lavinia at length came to understand this, and for a time all went well. I shook the fire down first thing in the morning, shoveled in more coal, opened the dampers, and closed them again just before I went down to the office. And at night the dampers would be still closed.

Then the weather became colder. Lavinia complained that it was cold in the mornings. So as a concession I would leave the dampers slightly opened and tell her that she might close them half an hour after I had gone. But some nights when I came home the fire was low and I could shake out a whole panful of cinders. We had several talks about this, but the same thing kept happening. Then one night the furnace was out again.

'Look here, Lavinia,' I said. 'The furnace is out.'

'Is it? I'm sorry.' She had become so accustomed to our discussions of the furnace problem that she did not even appear interested at this news.

'You don't seem to care a – a darn,' I told her bitterly.

'I'm not going to freeze, just because you go away and leave the dampers closed. I'd rather keep the house warm.'

I threw up my hands and went down to the furnace. When I came up again I fear I lost my temper. I told her that thereafter she was not to touch the furnace on any account. Lavinia said:

'We won't talk about it any more.'

But trust a woman to have the last word. When we have guests and the other ladies begin to talk about their husbands, Lavinia will sweetly say:

'My husband has the funniest ideas about furnaces. He regards them as sort of jewel-cases. You put the coal in for safe keeping and you leave it there all day and expect it to be just the same as it was when you put it in.'

The other ladies laugh pleasantly, and I wink at the men. Now you know what my wink means, and can sympathize. Some time I shall tell you more.

I BUY A DOG–ALMOST

The two little boys stood at the window, staring in with perfect absorption. I was waiting for a street car and forgot them, and turning in a few moments saw that they were still gazing into the window. Occasionally they would look at each other and laugh, gesturing on the pane with mittened little hands. I strolled over.

Three tiny puppies, a West Highland terrier, an Irish terrier, and a Scotch carn were wrestling within a wicker cage, a roofless kennel. Usually one was underneath, another making the most of his advantage, and the third would watch at a distance a second, and then make an important lunge forward to grab an ear or a foreleg. They were having a great time among the rustling strips of paper which formed the carpet of their house.

'Gee, ain't they fighters, though!'

'That white one when he gets bigger wouldn't I like to have him! He'd lick all the dogs in the block!'

The other boy shoved his mitts on, and shook his head. 'No, he wouldn't, not if I had that other little fellow – that's an Irish terrier. They can fight – I bet.'

'Oh, boy!' They sighed, simultaneously. Apparently it was a hopeless prospect.

Forgetting my car I opened the door and entered the dog shop. The floor was covered with sawdust, and a drove of tiny puppies, much of a size but variegated in colour, was swarming about, under tables and counters and the raised cages, and then out into the middle of the floor. At the other end of the room the proprietor, as I judged by the fact that although he wore a hat he was without an overcoat, was talking to a large man, a thick woman, and a young girl. He was holding a tiny Boston bull terrier in his hands, an elderly man with grizzled hair.

'Ah, him was so seepy him wonders what it's all about. But him knows a whole lot for how little him is! Aren't they just cute?' he turned to the onlookers. 'And I just love to talk baby talk to them. ... Yes, I think you're wonderful, that's what I do.'

'I don't want a toy dog,' said the lady decisively.

'Oh, let me hold it!' exclaimed the girl, stretching out her hands.

The old man gave her the quiet little creature, and came toward me, where I was watching the antics of a couple of third-grown Airedales. This augmented my indecision. I was trying to think of someone to whom I could give a puppy – since apparently puppies were the only sort of dogs sold, and since I could not house a dog myself.

'Was there any particular kind of dog you wanted?' he asked deferentially.

But this was just a formality, for he turned back to his more prospective customers when I said, 'I'm just trying to choose.'

The young girl was evidently pleading with her parents for the possession of a little black crinkly-faced Pomeranian.

The bell on the door jingled, and a brisk young man entered. From his pearl grey spats to his black derby he exhaled purpose. The proprietor, sensing business, turned.

'Have you a wire-haired terrier for sale?'

'Why,' drawled the old man, 'we have, but not here. Out at our kennels in the country we can get you one. We have West Highland, and Irish and Scotch Carn terriers...'

'No, no. Why insist if you haven't a wire-haired? Nothing else will do.'

'Wire-haired terrier is the breed the Prince of Wales keeps, is it not?'

'Why, I understand the prince recently bought such a dog. But he probably has others. Now we have everything. You might like a Pom. There are the black, and the chocolate biscuit Pomeranians. Just yesterday an American came in. I'll tell you who he was. He lived in Kentucky. He owns the Tòno-System Drug Compound. Come in, looked at a chocolate biscuit. "How much for that puppy?" he asks me. "You can have that puppy," says I, "for òne hundred dollars." I didn't know him, you understand, from Adam's off ox. "That puppy's daddy," I says, "took a sweepstakes at the Kennel Show." "No use trying to beat you down any, then," the Yankee says, and he pulls out his wallet and hands me the hundred dollar bill. Meant business though I can't say that if I was buying a dog – '

I had been inspecting a show case filled with dog collars, dog biscuit, and dog blankets and muzzles. On the wall hung slender leather lines with hand-holds at the ends. But I could see that the young gentleman was somewhat less assured than he had been upon the time of his entrance. In fact he seemed perturbed. I was perturbed myself.

'And what – how much – that is, how do you value your wire-haired terriers?'

'Was um dettin' hundry?' the proprietor enquired, picking up a wrinkled-faced Boston bull. His own white moustache curled sympathetically. 'Yes, indeed, um wants um's supper. Why, forty-five to a hundred dollars, for a genuine wire-hair. Would you like me to call up the kennels, and bring one out? They could have one here for you to-morrow morning. You could come in then and look at it.'

'Well, that would be very convenient – but no, dash it, I can't come in to-morrow morning, as luck would have it. I just thought that I'd like to see one the same kind as the prince has, and if I happened to take a fancy to him I'd buy it. Some other time. Good afternoon.'

The man, woman, and girl were still discussing pros and cons in regard to the purchase of the puppy to which the girl clung, but our elderly friend apparently did not wish to hasten their decision. He turned to me, as though the wire-haired young man had never been there.

'See. He's got the double twist in his tail. Feel it.' The little flexible spike twisted toward me. 'Real Boston bull, I want to be telling you. Daddy champion of Canada, and dam first in her class. Got to amputate that tail though. Yes,' he held the tiny wrinkled brown face with its blue eyes and turned-back ears to his own. 'Got to take off 'at tail. Used to bite 'em off, but somehow I could never be so callous as that.'

'Still, if it heals better – ' I ventured.

'Yes, but I'm a funny fellow, in some ways, anyway. Now I'm seventy-two years old. You wouldn't think it, if I'd shaved this morning. I get up every morning at five o'clock. People generally are inclined to sleep too much, it seems to me. And when I'm going along the street and I feel like running or skipping I ups and run or skip. Always been that way. Kind of careless.'

'Well, as long as you don't get careless enough to skip in front of an automobile or locomotive, your carelessness will amuse others and do you no harm – I mean it will amuse – '

'But I'm serious, too, you know. I write sermons. Great fellow for writing. I'll show you one of the sermons I've written. I've got a two-bushel bag of poems, too. But wait till I've sold these people their dog.'

A man had entered from a back room and was feeding the puppies. There was a receding wave of yelps. The kennel immediately before him heard him and smelt the food, and gave cry, until the food was before them, then they subsided to silent but diligent mastication, and the next cageful took up the cry.

'Here,' said the old man to the dog hostler. 'Take him out and cut off his tail, then when he has his supper he'll forget it.' The man obediently took the puppy into the back room.

'Well, have you decided you can't go home without that puppy, lady?' he addressed the trio.

'My wife thinks we don't need a dog,' returned the man. His daughter looked at him pleadingly.

'You think he's too little and it would be inconvenient to train him, I suppose. As a matter of fact they're better that way. The younger you get them after they're weaned the better. Oh, wonderfully intelligent, one of these puppies. And where there are young people – have you any younger children? Nobody can tell how much children value animals, and how much they need them. In the country the little folks have the animals always about them, the dog, the cats, the old pet horses, the ducks and chickens – they have a whole world the city child knows nothing about. City children have nothing; and they're just starving for a pet. I've seen boys stand at the window there and look in at the puppies for half an hour. Grown-up men, too. People need them, they need the company of animals. Now I dare say if you took this little dog home and raised him he'd get to be one of the family, and you'd get so fond of him you'd wonder how you ever could have got along without him.'

'They make nice pets,' agreed the man, hesitantly, looking at his wife. 'Well, what about it?'

The daughter turned to her mother also, but the final colloquy was not made public, for a shrill yelping came from the back room, swift, rhythmic, and piercing. Gradually it became slower and softer and the man emerged and placed the puppy in a cage with the others, where he began to eat his supper.

'It's the iodine hurts him, not getting it cut off,' he told me in an undertone. He reached for his steaming pan of food which stood on a table strewn with loaves of bread from which half the paper wrappings had been torn.

'What do you feed them?'

'This is dog biscuit and hamburger steak. Of course, they like it warm. Good diet for growing.'

'Now, if there's anything, anything at all you want to ask me about, you just call me up. You'd better call me up in the morning anyway and tell me how he's getting along,' the old gentleman was saying.

'Thank you, we'll do that,' said the lady. Her husband was unfolding a roll of bills. The girl had skipped to the door holding the puppy high, and thence to their car outside.

'Yes, sir, there's something funny about dogs,' declared my friend when they had gone. 'Just to show you. I went down to the dog pound at the city hall. I go once in a while in hopes of finding something worth while, though most of the lost and strayed dogs that get in there are mongrels. The ones that are not disposed of by sale are put out of the road, of course. Well, sir, there was a dog there, fine looking collie but of no especial breeding, and he took a fancy to me. He would come to the front and look at me, and put his paw out. I didn't want the dog, and I didn't pay any attention to him. But he came up again when I was going out. Well, I walked a few blocks and then I had to go back. I didn't want the dog, had no use for him, you understand. I had hardly looked at him. Yet I had to go back and buy him. He knew if he didn't get out of there he'd be a dead dog. And he certainly – '

'He must have put his appeal across.'

'Yes, sir, and the deal turned out all right. I sold him right away for more than I gave for him, and now he's got a good home, and well contented.'

This was interesting, but time was flying and I feared that I might be called upon to read the sermon or poems of which my host had told me.

'I was thinking of buying a dog myself this afternoon,' I said. 'You've got a fine stock here. But tell me, what would you charge to board a good dog for a couple of weeks?'

'Why, about five or six dollars, depending upon the size of the dog. A couple of weeks you say?'

'No, it would hardly do,' I returned musingly. 'You see, this is the way of it. I was thinking of buying a pet dog for my aunt, who is a maiden lady of mature years. At first I was undecided about the breed. An Alsatian police dog might please her, because she has gone to the movies and seen Strongheart, and then again an Airedale, or a nice bit of a Blackmask Pekinese. But I happened to remember that my aunt is going away to visit some relatives in Montreal for a couple of weeks. Now the old lady is not exactly stingy, and she would appreciate having a nice dog, but if she had to pay for his board for the duration of her visit, she might not appreciate the gift, and she might even make derogatory remarks about my good sense in making her the present of a dog at such a time. Accordingly it appears inevitable that I should postpone my purchase.'

The old man took it well.

'In other words, you're a journalist. Drop in in a couple of weeks anyway and we'll have another talk. Perhaps your aunt will have another idea.'

Criticism

CANADIAN LETTER

Northwood, Ontario, May

In the field this morning the sun was warm, and when I came back to pick up my hat the mice had nibbled the leather band of the old Borsalino; but they had not found the apples in my coat pockets. The corn land is ready, the green of oats is almost as deep as that of the winter wheat; dandelions have usurped the pastures, and the trees of the bush are all clothed. The Clydesdales behind whom I ride on the disc harrow put their feet down with deft pasterns, shaking the long white hair, and left them slowly. ... But now at twilight, in the soft air, light exhaled by green, the grey rain transfixed pear blossoms before my window, which have drifted on the grey clods. The pear tree, undivested, stands gracious, unaware.

The Dominion of Canada! It is hard to be skeptical, not to think that there are infinite spiritual possibilities in a land as huge and undeveloped as this, open to the variety and potency of influences which bear upon it, heritage of the racial amalgam already emergent. Canada might look, except for these stipulations so familiar to Americans, somehow as America appears to Europe. Even now one dare not report the 'dumb Russia' Carlyle saw eighty years ago. But first the influences.

In part they are banal enough. Briefly there is the 'democratic' standardization which makes for fewer and fewer individuals. We are a part, of course, of the thing happening from the Rio Grande north, and trying to happen elsewhere, and it is possible to think that 'Canadian' cannot be anything more, ever, than 'Middle West' or 'Virginian' or 'New England.' The same clothes, movies, news, automobiles, grafts, liquors, success complex, clubs. But, there is more. Our cities are small and far apart, they only accent the real life of the land. The girls wear cloche bonnets over bobbed hair, roll their own, but more are healthy-looking than pretty; a little clay always adheres to the heel of our tanned youth's dancing pump, a little chaff has got into his cigarette-holder. There is, before and after all, the land, and room for anything. Nobody can forget that.

Why not a Canadian literature? ... It might be supposed that all Canada hears the question, since it is always possible to start enlivening discussion in newspapers, when some professor assures the ladies that we have not yet produced a Keats, and the columnists and editorial writers join full cry with citations of dozens, yes dozens of fine poets, real poets, Canadians, whatever the leaden-domed devotee of exotic and fossil letters may say. Rotarians and branches of the Canadian Club (in whatever superinduced and palliative comatose frame) have hearkened to optimism or objurgation concerning the hypothetical national literature – as like as not from the lips of the local author, whose stirring epic 'The Skunk-Trapper's Daughter' is selling so nicely, or whose cantata 'The Emerald Bluebird' was given with such success by local talent in the Opera House. There are animate and vocal denials that Canada may not yet rival and surpass the older, effete nations of the world in every way. ... That is, we have writings which may be read endurably if one has become embroiled by saying that they are or are not all that they should be, or – these cases are fewer – if one is constrained by profession to the reading.

It was not until our adoption of *Maria Chapdelaine* on its appearance in English, *circa* 1921, that these guesses, warnings, hopes, deprecations, and plaints began to be heard generally, and now the *Canadian Bookman* lends an impartial ear to tens of these voices – which is a good augury, specially as one or two will bethink themselves like Edwin Ford Piper's bad man: 'It seemed like there was too much talk,/ So the doin's they begin' – and turn to create some new poems or sound prose. But there has been for a generation or two (as long as there has been any) only one reading public in Canada, which preferred Dickens to Thackeray or *vice versa*, admired Shakespeare and Milton whenever they were mentioned, and found our pioneers in poetry such as Lampman and Campbell good, because they 'got their inspiration from Nature' like Wordsworth; professionals and bourgeois who were very advanced when reading 'the Russians' Tolstoy and Turgenev. In those days the emerging bard of the back concessions nearly always appeared in the local paper with a stale catalogue of nature, in the *Canadian Magazine*, and presently was bound in a book, to become one of 'our Canadian poets' sacred from any response save eleemosynary platform quotation. And of course to a large portion of this public anyone who wrote a novel or a history of his native township and got it bound in red cloth was a 'great author.'

The fascination of what's easy has held us. And this is likely to become more oppressive as time goes on; for now increasingly we have the popular American magazines everywhere to vitiate any possibility of taste; and our too-few book-stores are piled with Zane Grey and

Hutchinson. Contempt for the printed word is bound to result on the part of the very people of whom the artist, whether of completely Tolstoyan conviction or not and against his will or not, inevitably hopes the most in a new country. And we have the necessary host of semi-specialized journals, farm papers, religious weeklies, women's magazines, without standards. The fascination of what's easy, 'because of the dollars' bluntly. As soon as our writers attain a technic of sufficient dexterity that they can manoeuver material to such advantage, the American editor is upon them. So we have produced numbers of American best sellers. There may be little hazard in saying that none of these had the divine fire in him; but it is nonsense to pretend that some were not capable of better things. A man may not take to writing because he wants money (he would be a fool, and otherwise unedifying) but once caught, he is bound to concern himself with enough money to enable him to keep coals beneath his resolve to go on writing. He can do that in Canada partly through one or two prototypical Satevpos and Woman's Companions, by showing that golf-love-business and country club values are as seductive north of the Great Lakes as south of them, patting Canada on the back for being like the States; or, emigrating, his chances are better with more popular magazines, describing a Canada of snow, half-bred revenge, and beaded-lashed wood-nymphs – a Canada the demand for which has subtly corrupted nearly all efforts at expression.

Even for conservative work there is no market here, only the 'standard' organs of the United States, since they pay better than the English ones. The *Canadian Forum*, perhaps the most important and intelligent magazine we have, calls itself 'A Journal of Literature and Politics,' cogently except that literature is rather consistently omitted. Confidence, as well as judgment, is what readers and editors in Canada need, that there may be a few to know a sound piece of writing before it has been praised in the *London Mercury* or the New York *Evening Post*. Lift themselves by their bootlaces? ... Yet there is one thing which is practicable, and which might make all the difference in our prospects until and after we have a larger body of enlightened book buyers. A magazine devoted to creative work should be established, perhaps only a few pages every month, yet chosen for vital quality, and which should give a voice to what is actually being lived among us. And I will be ready to bet that the tones will not be too like those from other fields.

One comes near forgetting in our engrossing possibilities that such realistic expression does not weigh so vastly according to purely literary values. Gun-playing West and North or chimes-auraëd cathedral towns may be absurd; but it is not so necessary that art should portray a reality which we can identify without going farther than the window or the mirror, as that it should embody a life of its own. What our country of almost ten millions *should* do and provide as audience and background is nugatory speculation. Yet, inevitably, abundantly, it should be hopeful. Always there is the possiblity that somewhere in the life of the real Canada is some creator, for whom these matters are not much, to build a different *Buddenbrooks* or *Growth of the Soil*, with whom perchance some American press shall make us acquainted. When he arrives, Canada shall have reached her spiritual majority.

Meanwhile good work comes out of Canada, as it were inadvertently. A few individuals here and there will insist on expressing themselves in forms of personally shaped art. On them the conditions I have described impinge according to their own individuality. We have room for all schools, space to be free of all schools. If this space is largely a matter of the indifference of our population, our refuge is the discerning audience of the other English-speaking countries. To this our writers must appeal, and it is generally safe to say that the best are those who have met with critical approval outside Canada. I am not thinking of the case of the popular writer like E. Barrington and Arthur Stringer (they happen to be our best of that class) who wins popularity with American magazines and then can boost his prices to imitative Canadian magazines. Even such as he is usually recognized first elsewhere. Poets like Wilson MacDonald and E.J. Pratt with their best laurels thus not only because of editorial ignorance here, which in any case is amended eventually, but because of the small total audience of the few vital magazines, only a much smaller portion, however great potentially, belongs to Canada. Wilson MacDonald is planning a collection, *Out of the Wilderness*, of his later poems, many of which possess an austere and wild earthy magic not found elsewhere. E.J. Pratt, also a native son, if from Newfoundland, has just brought forth as a book *The Witches' Brew*, a poem concerned with a sea-cat, and divers other monsters of the deep, with the shades of many immortals, through a hilarious night. The chief and exceedingly rare fault is that it is just about half long enough. It appeared first, I understand, in the *London Mercury*.

As for prose writers, we have Mazo de la Roche, whose first novel, *Possession*, was probably the best-effected piece of the sort which has been done in Canada; I have not seen her latest, *Delight*. F.P. Grove, in *Settlers of the Marsh*, has done work perhaps crude and needlessly 'powerful' in the Scandinavian mode, but honest and vital. William Arthur Deacon of *Saturday Night* is our most lively man of ideas in literary journalism. The scholars, like Edward Sapir, author of *Language* and Pelham Edgar of *Henry James, Man and Author*, do not concern themselves extensively with Canadian letters. And there is Merrill Denison, realistic dramatist, author of the collection *The Unheroic North*, which contains the only long Canadian play of excellence, *Marsh Hay*. From these people much can be hoped, and from others emergent with whom it may be left to magazines like *This Quarter*, *Poetry*, and the *Criterion* to make us acquainted from time to time; and also from the improved work of writers like Katherine Hale and Pierre Coalfleet who have already found a public. Not least from Martha Ostenso, regarded as a Canadian hero, whose *Wild Geese* while lacking in originality, shows incalculable promise. While the worst cannot be said of prize contests, this selection from first novels for film and magazine use, though it may not have been the best, was fortunate. It is a pleasure to see work so good receive so much publicity.

Nothing at all can longer be expected from the older writers, naturally. Their contributions were made at a time when any impulse in a backwater would have been valued. Bliss Carman must read his lyrics from coast to coast. Tom MacInnes in the careless exuberance of his gift poured out a multitude of verses; after a brief stay here he has returned to the Orient, continuing a sojourn of many years. Leacock's humour is of course generally acceptable, in Sunday papers or not. Duncan Campbell Scott in 1921 gave us *Beauty and Life* with sincere and adult thought and unfertile artistry. And Charles G.D. Roberts, author of the best forty books of prose and verse by a single Canadian, recently published a brochure, first in the series, 'Canadian Poetry Chapbooks' which the Ryerson Press is inaugurating. The brochure was called *The Sweet o' the Year*, and contained lines like 'The upland hills are green again,/ The river runs serene again' with perhaps seventeen other 'eens I've never thank heaven seen again. *The Sweet o' the Year* was limited to five hundred copies, and I understand that to the puzzlement of all concerned it did not sell at all. Many of us Canadians do not yet realize that poetry must have, or rather has a connection with life, but we seem to be learning to be frank about what we do not like. This is the most hopeful note on which to close. Perhaps if Arthur Stringer were to put forward now, instead of in 1914, his *Open Water*, which contained more poetry than any previous Canadian volume, as well as a thoughtful consideration of free verse, its reception would be more real, and he would not turn so wholeheartedly as he did to writing mystery stories.

A POET IN ARMS FOR POETRY

A slender wiry-built figure of medium height, a man of whom you can well believe that he is fond of tennis and skating, and that he was never beaten at the hundred-yard dash, with a face lean and almost ascetic, yet young, with well-coloured cheeks and dark piercing eyes and the elfin look of a seer and roamer in the wilderness, a necromancer and a rebel, one who 'has trod on fairy grass,' and eloquent, lean, and lightning-like hands – such a person has been astonishing and fascinating American audiences. It is the Canadian poet, Wilson MacDonald, reading his poems in the gripping way in which no one else can read them.

In Canada too he has held audiences spell-bound, and his reputation among those who knew poetry has always been of the highest. Yet we in Canada have been nearer to him, and perhaps have seen more of the man than of the poet – the man whose personality, his astounding feats of legerdemain, his outspoken interviews in the newspapers, have almost become legendary.

Wilson MacDonald believes in Canada, but first of all in a part of her future which can be built by the hands of poets alone. And when he witnesses the way in which poets too often are treated during their lifetime, he is ready to fight.

'No poet,' he says, 'should endure hardship after the age of thirty-five. At that age he should be given a handsome salary for life. There is no reason why it shouldn't and couldn't be done. Think what the world would have been without poets. And even the direct financial returns would make it possible. Do you know that ten million dollars have been made from Burns' poems since his death? And two hundred and fifty millions have been made from the work of dead poets. The interest on such an amount is ample to provide for the poets of today. But on the contrary they have nothing but difficulty in making a living, and this always in the years when they are struggling hardest for recognition of their work.

'It is not that I believe that poets should have an easy time and soft berths. The simple life is imperative for a prophetic artist. Not always for art; because all manner of men, all sorts of worldings, have produced works of art. But not works of original vision, such as you find in Tolstoi or Whitman or Romain Rolland.

'You see,' he continued, 'inspiration is a matter of getting in tune with the infinite. No one can achieve that; he can hardly be made to think unless he has endured unhappiness and arrived at a unified conception of life as a whole. For that reason a poet should suffer; or rather he has suffered. He won't be a poet unless he has. And to add privation and financial trouble to it is like adding patina to the bells of Saint Mary's.'

He made these remarks in the sitting room of his home in a well-known apartment hotel, where the brightness of a fire in the electric grate was added to a quiet warmth of welcome. In this room, from his desk at the bay window, Wilson MacDonald can look over the tops of trees which hide the residence streets, to the tall buildings of downtown Toronto, and a glimpse, widened in winter, of the Lake.

And yet how near is that black tide that swirls
At Yonge and Queen, from dawn to midnight stars:
  The frowning men, and gaudy, painted girls
  Who lean their joys upon a broken reed
And burn their souls to drive their flaming cars.

Where had one expected to find him living? In the woods, perhaps, listening for those secrets of Nature he has endeavoured so faithfully to transmute? He does spend a portion of each year in the Georgian Bay country. But the poet's concern after all is with mankind, and it is fitting that he should be mingling with the crowd while yet an aloof, sympathetic, and disinterested spectator of the Canadian scene – a dreamer and a man of action, pondering the wonders of the human heart.

Yet Wilson MacDonald's life has known trouble, while poetry has always been an integral part of it. Old residents of Norfolk County say that at the age of three he declared that he was going to be a poet. He carried a Moody and Watts *Hymnal* with him everywhere, and his favourite author in this book was 'Anon.'

Wilson MacDonald's father was a brilliant orator and a lover of the woods and of poetry. His mother was a splendid musician and a cultured woman. Had his parents lived beyond his boyhood undoubtedly that early predilection for poetry would have been given the utmost encouragement. But at an early age the future poet was bereaved of his mother and sent to school.

His memories of Port Dover Public School are the most pleasant of all connected with his education. His teachers were finely sympathetic, and he was popular among his schoolmates. Moreover his scholastic record is one which can scarcely be matched. He led his classes monthly and yearly in all examinations, regularly for six years, and at the examinations for entrance to high school won the highest marks in the province.

'Then,' he continued, 'I was sent to Woodstock College. My first error was to skip the first year, and begin work with the second. Any other period might have been skipped more feasibly, because in that year the study of language was started. But I passed all the examinations. Frankly, I hated Woodstock College. I was a mere youngster of twelve, and there were only six other students enrolled who were under the age of eighteen. I received very little encouragement and only two of my teachers showed the slightest sympathy with my aspirations.

Probably these unhappy childhood experiences laid the foundations for the humanitarian feeling, the passion for fair play, and the intense hatred of intolerance which permeates his whole work. This poet does not believe that any nation can be legislated into Heaven, and he is against all prohibitions and censorships. Nothing of good can be accomplished, he feels, by telling people what they are not to do. In the same way he is strongly opposed to capital punishment. A man has committed murder; then society, in the deputized form of a few individuals, takes upon itself to pose as his judge and to murder him. This results inevitably in the execution of innocent persons. If only one innocent person were executed in fifty years, Mr MacDonald holds, capital punishment would be stigmatized as a blot upon the human race, which brutalizes every person involved. It is in matters such as these, solely against intolerance, that Wilson MacDonald loses his own tolerance.

After graduation from Woodstock College, he enjoyed greatly the continuation of his studies at McMaster University. Boys who have become his lifelong friends were met there, and his teachers, such as Dr Theodore H. Rand and Professor McClay were a source of inspiration to him. It was at about this time that his first poems appeared, in the Toronto *Globe* and the Boston *Transcript*.

Followed seven years of writing advertisements in the United States, very repugnant to the poet in him. 'As long as I had a dollar in my pocket,' he recalled, 'I declined such tasks. Still it was work which produced a livelihood, and I have made as much as $150 in one day in Pittsburgh. But I was compelled to give it up, or have my genius destroyed. Even then, it took five years of hard writing to wean me from the commercial influence. That is why some of my earlier poetry is so inferior to my later. But for fifteen years now I haven't allowed a commercial touch to come near my pen.' A record, by the way, which few writers, and fewer poets, can match.

Since the return to poesy, he has travelled the length and bredth of Canada – the coast of Labrador, the Maritime Provinces, Quebec, the Hudson Bay country, the prairies north and south, British Columbia, its interior and coast, and Vancouver Island – so that he knows Canada as no other Canadian writer knows it. One is to take literally his 'Adventurer's Song':

I have tried the strength of the surf where the last sun leaves the world;
I have walked Ontario's lilac lanes, in the late May's wistful weather.
I have breasted winds off Labrador where the whole sea-strength is hurled;
I have bound, high in the Selkirks, blue and gold flowers together.
I have roamed in lands where blue lakes gleam like the fallen tears of gods;
I have trailed in the cold Saskatchewan to the undiscovered places.
I have heard the gorse on Beacon Hill breaking their golden pods;
I have watched the blue St Lawrence leave the grim Laurentian bases.
I come sun-tanned from a great marauding of wind and wave and tree;
And the copper hue of a savage face peers upward through my singing.

All that I love is in my song: the tang of the great West Sea
And the Loon's laugh and the gull's shriek and the pale star's
swinging.

We talked of the origin of his poems in his first book, *The Song of the Prairie Land*, and in *Out of the Wilderness*, which is selling so widely in three editions here and in the United States. The fine 'Song to the Valiant,' which first appeared in the *London Mercury*, had its inspiration in a walk over Mount Royal in a terrific rain storm, a wild two hours' experience which resulted in the ecstacy of the lines. Perhaps the most inspired long poem came after awakening from a dream. It is called *The Miracle Songs of Jesus*, and was printed separately as a tiny book. 'Exit,' a well-nigh perfect elegy, was written under the stress of the death in her teens of a very dear friend. 'Ghost Hornpipes' was written on a train, and originated partly in the idea that the higher the sea-gull flies, the lower its shadow dips into the water. 'The Berry-Pickers,' perhaps his most exquisite lyric, was written upon a boat *en route* to a summer resort in Georgian Bay. And 'November,' a long ode to that month, was composed on a dreary day, in the wish to sing the unsung things. 'For a hundred poems about June,' Mr MacDonald remarked, 'there is scarcely one about November.'

But the bright afternoon had been passing more quickly than I realized, until Mr MacDonald proposed that I remain and take supper with him. 'If you don't mind doing without meat. It won't take long. I'm accustomed to preparing my own meals.'

While the meal was being prepared I opened the door of the living-room and stepped out upon the little stone porch with its extensive view; the city lay outspread in a drifting haze brightened in spots where the rays of the setting sun reached roofs or windows. And the tonic coolness of the air made the glow of the hearth doubly appreciated when I came in. Picking up Wilson MacDonald's new book, a beautifully bound copy of the American edition just off the press, I read 'The Song of the New Communities,' and that inspired a question, with which I pursued my host to the kitchen.

In this spotless large room he was going about the preparation of the meal in a workmanlike manner, and the result proved highly satisfactory. It included a salad for which Mr MacDonald is famous, and nuts after the dessert. One gathered that he never eats meat. My question which arose from reading 'The Song of the New Communities' concerned his attitude to the city of his residence; for I knew that as well as being a citizen of the world, as every poet is in the best sense, that he was an ardent patriot and a far-seeing citizen, never hesitating to voice candidly his criticism of any course which seemed unworthy.

'Toronto,' he remarked, 'has failed to make the most of her opportunities. There is the matter of that great park in the East end which might have been purchased some years ago for $10,000, and later for $100,000, but which would now cost $2,000,000. The buildings in Toronto are often haphazard and poor. Bloor Street should be made into one of the noblest of thoroughfares. And then the opportunity given by the Lake is being neglected. There is no reason why the railway could not be run underground, and a fine boulevard and parkway built over it. Instead of that there is the meretricious dazzle of Sunnyside and its bright lights. Such an amusement park should be inland. Even Chicago, with its fame for ugliness has a magnificent system of parks along the many miles of its lake-front. And the last great tragedy for Toronto would be to put a bridge over to the Island, refting seclusion from it – its most beautiful possession.'

Back in the living-room, with a cigarette – Mr MacDonald, by the way, is the only writer I know who does not smoke – hearing the poet read some of his poems was a rare pleasure, one which the thousands of his many audiences would have valued. His reading has a haunting melodic rhythm, a magnetic sadness if there be such a thing, quite in keeping with the content of many of the poems, and which rises to a vigour of prophetic denunciation in the humanitarian poems such as 'Volga,' 'Nineteen Twenty-Six,' and the 'Song of the Rebel' which inveighs against the 'civilized disorder' of the modern city.

But, first and last, poetry is his life. 'The origin of poetry?' he thoughtfully repeated my question. 'The desire for rhythm is the origin of poetry. Man first approached it in the dance. Then music evolved as a higher form. Desire for the expression of a philosophy then took place, and coupled with rhythm made the high art of poetry. Naturally, as children of a Creator, the spirit of creation is in us. This desire for creation enters the origin of poetry, which is the most spiritual creation. Poetry is the utmost flowering of the human spirit.'

THE CANADIAN SHORT STORY

What, approximately, is the matter with the Canadian short story? The question is not in itself encouraging, though a search for answers to it may reveal potentialities as well as pitfalls. But the fact of the short story arriving at the stage of being considered at all as a division of our literature, is more or less significant. For I daresay that most people have pretty well passed it by until lately, left it unregarded in the magazines, except as a pleasant, more or less innocuous way of passing a quarter or half an hour. Nothing was the matter with it, so far as it went, they might have said. Now the publishers' lists show a number of books of stories by Canadian writers, of a quality above the average of the rest of our fiction, and a moment seems to have come for reflecting on this genre as displayed predominantly.

The most obvious defect of our magazine fiction is Americanization. Good stories are constantly being written in the United States, and many of the magazines print one now and then (a periodical with, I think, the second largest circulation, prints, or used to print, numbers of them); but it is only too clear that the short story there is pre-eminently a commercial article, except in a very few magazines of small circulation. I do not mean that English popular magazines are better, for it is doubtful whether they are as good. But their influence has not been so strong, because the chances of their printing the work of Canadian writers has been less and the money reward smaller.

The criterion of the American magazine is 'What the Public Wants,' and literature being as it is a matter of individuality, the public is not likely to want what a new writer has in him to give – at least until its taste for him has been cultivated. What does the new writer, positively original or not, do about this, usually? He studies what the magazines have made the public believe it wants and, the instinct of self-preservation being strong, seeing in this course his only salvation, oftener than not attempts emulation. Naturally he is scarcely ever successful. Too frequently he has nothing to record and no knowledge instinctive or aetiological of literature to aid him in attempting to record it. And when he has both or either of these, and produces or shows ability to produce good work, he is looked upon by the more wideawake editors as promising, though his contributions may not fit into the requisitions of 'our readers' – as we have trained them. At this point the young writer is sure if he has escaped so far, to be canvassed by the correspondence schools giving courses in short story writing, and to consider their merits, which are practical if not so numerous as their publicity may insist.

The correspondence school has its finger on the markets, knows what is acceptable and what is not. And it has the short story reduced to a formula so regular that at the end of the course anyone with the minimum of acumen can turn out a story to conform in this way. And if the student transcends the minimum, has observed the life through which he has passed, and absorbed the current expedient notions which take the place of a philosophy of life in popular fiction, and indeed largely in daily life itself, he is prepared for his task and, granted industry and a knack with words, he will be a successful writer of short stories.

Now this does not seem the best way to form good writers. Doubtless they can and possibly they have been formed in this way, if we give a certain latitude to the word 'good.' It may even be that writers have or could go through this and become great – by shedding the induced fetishes. But innately the method seems better calculated to spoil good short story writers.

To be one of these, first of all, one must have known life. But we all have known that, and it is a matter of individuality and training whether we can present it in objectified pictures. Individuality it is that counts; it is his view of the world which the artist seeks to impart as Henry James has said. But if individuality is a prerequisite, so is training. (Commonplaces, these, surprisingly too often ignored.) And literary training, by which I mean study of the masters, is precisely what the beginner usually lacks. But he will not begin by imitating nobody, as teachers sometimes advise; even if he be a genius he cannot do that. He has been impressed, let us say, by some aspects or ironies of life. But he cannot record them independently, without reference to other writings. Indeed, it is his reading of other writers which as likely as not has brought him to a consciousness of life and helped to shape it within him – which at least has caused him to desire to impart himself. In his struggles to express what he has seen and dreamed, therefore, he will adopt the methods of writers whom he admires and wishes to emulate.

So this is the fault of the popular magazine and the correspondence school: the beginning writer has let himself accept them at their face value (he does want cash and applause), even before he has taken the second step necessary for success with them, of accepting life itself at its face value; and even if he tries to imagine honestly he is handicapped by a fortuitous rather than an inevitable technique.

Now technique is not merely an exterior matter; or even if it be that it is as the bark of a tree is exterior – and essential. Your subject will be changed, added to, weakened, heightened, or diminished, by a change of method. And it is just in the mould-like effect of 'plot' as understood which tends to make the short story a dead art form. It has become possible to know after the second paragraph of the plot story how it will end – unless the writer is a disciple of O. Henry, in which case one can count on the opposite to his expectations. One correspondence school, I understand, selects Maupassant's 'La Parure' as a model in structure; another, a Canadian course which I have read, seems to hold up Charles A. Van Loan as a foremost exponent.

On the results of the conditions of the past scarcely more than a word is necessary here. To me they appear ominous enough; for I have never yet seen a good story by a Canadian author in a Canadian magazine. I do not doubt at all that there have been such. The point is that the run of stories in Canadian magazines has been such that I have not had the patience to read enough of them to discover good ones, and I claim to be fairly omnivorous about such reading. It is not my purpose to affront popular editorships, as one youthful writer must have wished to do by saying that so far as practical evidence of the knowledge was visible they did not know a short story from a bill of lading; nor yet the conductors of correspondence schools. With them it is a matter of business, and they dare not be fooled there. What I wish to attempt is to give a word of advice from an experience not yet too frequently revised by time, to a few beginning writers of promise who, I feel sure, must exist and who may chance on these words.

What then is such an aspirant to do? First, consider his position. He does not want to turn out the sort of writing which the sensationally popular and would-be popular journals are sure to publish, much and naturally as he would like a large audience. But if he is determined to illustrate a new point of view he is to remind himself that there are not more than half a dozen literary magazines, all of small circulation and (except the endowed ones), giving small pay, into which he can hope that his work will fit. So that unless he too is endowed he can not hope to make a living from his art, or even see many examples of it published, for a number of years. Of course, when his name is made he can count on the 'standard' magazines. These strike a balance, being also refuges for some of the popular writers in their less melting and less heroic moods. Book publication too may come with an established trade-mark. To all this he must reconcile himself, the sooner the better, if he really means to attempt craftsmanship in the short story. It means a curtailment in the practice of his art, for it will not pay to try to write in any manner, as little in that of the most recent cult as of the Sunday supplement – though either may teach him things about his own method. Neither is it wise to do other work as near in method as the novel unless he is genuinely drawn to it. But if he can write novels, I think that the present hospitality to new talent will save him from the necessity of doing anything but his best, of appealing for popularity. That is, if he cannot make money from other literary work which really commands his doing, he will have to content himself with looking forward to the pre-eminent rewards of consciously well-achieved effort and the approbation of small audiences, chiefly of other writers.

And next – if he still adheres to his determination – read the masterpieces of literature, and not of one literature or one age of literature. Only in this way will he come at a sense of life as it has been in the souls of the spokesmen of mankind. He must read them as one concerned by life, primarily, before they will help him as literature. But incidentally he will gain a knowledge of his instrument, of the weight and texture of language. This sounds discouraging and perhaps pedantic in our day, but there is still no philtre of achievement. Of course he will not read all the masterpieces! I know from experience that, however fortunately situated for doing so, he will not, and cannot, and if he is really a writer he will be impelled to attempt a contribution of his own before he reaches this goal. But before he begins let him study the best short stories of which he can obtain cognizance. All the kinds; not merely one school. Only thus may he have background enough to free himself of the influence of the magazine story, which, if his has been a normally uncloistered life, he has always had with him.

And not alone the magazine story. By reading many of the masters of the form he can escape from the disadvantages of a single technique and, if he is gifted, he can strive, though probably he will not succeed, to combine disparate virtues in his view of existence to make a new form of his own. For it is not too much technique which ails the popular story, it is not too little, of too arbitrary a kind. The fact is forgotten that Maupassant, to whom journalism as well as this kind of writing shall always owe a debt, did not always care to live up to his vocation as a plot model. There are such stories as 'Clair de Lune' in, I think, the 'Boule de Suif' volume, in which the structure is so blended with the atmosphere and feeling that the 'planned' element, the brick upon brick method which makes Maupassant a model for the correspondence schools, is altogether absent at the first reading. It is usually this way in any finished story. The great art is that which is concealed. So in calling for more technique rather than less, one should be careful to counsel the emulation of no one writer, be he various as Tchehov himself. Schnitzler and O. Henry will not be of equal value for any two writers, yet both should be studied.

But, as a young London critic has written, public agitation in favor of technique will accomplish little. The standard must be within. Every good writer takes care for the methods which shall further his purpose. If his purpose is high it is the same. Let him learn some of the elements of his art from a correspondence school if he elects; the important thing is to learn them and to hold to an interest in matters beyond the elements. But he cannot learn to be a good story writer there nor, unless he gets a great deal of fun out of them, from such preparatory occupations as I may have made only to seem laborious. His study at best will help him articulate; and, if his eye be true and his emotions universal and directed, he will be one of the artists for which Canada has awaited to heighten the consciousness of portions of her life. And it may be that a time will come at which he can find a publisher awaiting him in his own country.

INTRODUCTION TO 'CANADIAN SHORT STORIES'*

At the outset of a new era there is opportunity to look back upon the old; and in nothing have we more clearly passed an epoch than in the short story, here in Canada. Literature as a whole is changing, new fields are being broken, new crops are being raised in them, and the changes apparent in other countries show counterparts in our development.

* Reprinted by permission of the Macmillan Company of Canada Ltd.

The short story has shared in the disadvantages of other types of literature and of culture as a whole in Canada. It is vain to say that it might have sprung from the soil as a new variant of the traditional form. There has been no national Burbank to create a Canadian subspecies of the short story as there was to breed Marquis wheat. It emerged, as the short story in the United States did, in a spirited emulation at best, or a shallow imitativeness at worst, of foreign models. This was natural in the case, unless we had managed without a literature for a few hundred years until we evolved a national consciousness of our own. But the pioneers did what was possible, in raising the old crops on new fields. Literature in the United States is only lately emerging from the imitative stage, and there are signs that it is doing the same thing here.

Obviously it has been harder for us to attain to anything like originality. Conventions have held sway with the compulsion of a tradition of romantic externals – they have been maintained as hardened patterns in a commercial exploitation of a last frontier. Some of these conventions are almost as remote from the life of Canada as the Latin-inscribed scrolls of monks and scholars were from the life of mediaeval Europe. The result is that much of our writing has seemed mechanical, and the literary flowering whereby it may be seen that the roots of a nation's life are sound has often had the aroma of wax and paper.

These are generalizations made from the facts. It is with the more or less successful exceptions that we are dealing in this book. Here are difficulties enough in the way of high expression in any country and in any age. What is wanted is a few talents strong enough to overcome all such things. Criticism *à thèse*, sociological criticism particularly, when applied to literature, may be more than usually futile, human wisdom being finite in its application. But it is not unreasonable to assume that Canadian literature might have been different if Canada's status and condition among nations had been different. We had a new country but old peoples; wealth collectively and in the future, but individual poverty; a store of tradition and a prevalent illiteracy – and so much to be done that we had little time to study how we should do it.

Assuredly it was a momentous work, this making of a nation on the material side. And since we were necessarily consecrated to the task, we were bound to feel, whether we knew it and admitted it or not, inferior to those nations which had done their building, or which possessed developed resources and more fully utilized wealth. Only by being self-contained and true to our individuality could we have attained to an indigenous literature. How could we be so? It took a more than usually vigorous talent to achieve any sort of adequate expression, in face of the difficulties. Not many very successfully attempted it, but of some of these men it is not unfair to claim that in happier circumstances they might have been great.

The general materialism had imposed a false aesthetics, on this continent. A permissible view of the history of literature shows the singer as being at first merely one of his tribe, singing unconsciously its grief or triumph in times of stress; later the poet had assumed his office, and as the bard, delegated to sing by whatever powers there were; still later the poet became himself, and wrote only of what concerned himself and his inmost soul. The poets achieved this evolution earlier than other workers in literature, because it became patent that unless the poet and his subject were one, neither amounted to anything. But prose writers have been consciously striving to revert to the tribal era, with their appeals to mob feeling and vulgar interests. Hence the barren nature of much of the multitudinous flotsam of periodical literature and best-sellers. The tendency has been upheld curiously, if only indirectly, by the classical theory of objectivity. In an absolute sense there is no objectivity. When Flaubert is bringing some undeniable picture to your recognition, he is doing it only to impose upon you some emotion which is part of his plan and the outgrowth of his own emotion. What is known as realism is only a means to an end, the end being a personal projection of the world. In passing beyond realism, even while they employ it, the significant writers of our time are achieving a portion of evolution. But most tale-spinners did not even achieve realism, and were willing to forego their possibilities in the interest of material rewards bestowed as a result of such a course in other countries.

Possibly it was a necessity for something more than material rewards which pulled our most gifted men away from their country, and perhaps Canada would be prepared to grant that something – appreciation, mainly – now when they return full of years and honours. But if it was not money which took him away, it was acceptance of materialistic standards which proved the ruination of the writer entering competitive conditions in England and the United States. Not content with an escape from poverty, which has been the lot of the singer since David plucked his harp before Saul, he has insisted upon his deserts, and tried to vie with the luxury of the Sauls of this day himself – a course fatal to his self-respect and his sense of a calling. It is a 'standard of living' to which many writers feel called more imperatively than to their professed art. Something of the guild spirit might be helpful. It has been said that the English writers of the nineties embodied this in a sort; they did not have wives, homes, lands, or motor cars, but they had an inalienable sense of professional integrity, and they brought into being works of real merit, if of a minor order: and from the Rhymers' Club came William Butler Yeats. The little 'Group of the Sixties' here partook in a degree of this advantage in their early poetry. But for the most part our men had to begin in a non-conducting sort of atmosphere, a sort of vacuum of poor acoustic properties, whence they passed to one where they were deafened by the noise of the mob. Our loss in the case of a writer of such endowment as Arthur Stringer's is perhaps proportionately greater than that sustained by American literature when Jack London became a victim of American criteria of success.

In this general state of affairs the short story has had to take its chance. But it has come out better than most other forms of literature, for a variety of reasons. (Because of brevity, most obviously and plausibly. Many people, given the right opportunity and circumstance, might produce a meritorious lyric or brief tale.). We have had no national drama because, more than fiction, drama is a communal art, and there has not been a body of people interested enough, moved enough, by Canadian life to appreciate its 'counterfeit presentment' on the stage. We could not even have poetic drama which signified much, because that, and its writers, must be rooted in the soil. Shakespeare might write of Rome or Denmark, but his imagination was England, and the people responded. For similar reasons the novel has been forbidden to us. Not enough people had the courage and tolerance of life to face its implications in the large, or enough love to endure seeing it carried to its aesthetic and emotional heightening and logical ends in sustained art. Isolated exceptions like *Maria Chapdelaine*, where the creator was cut off from any influence between himself and his subject, but was supported in his own power by the strength derived from an old and powerful, but still fresh and vital tradition of art, prove this contention.

The fact that the short story has fared as well or perhaps better than other forms in Canada is, however, largely owing to the nature of its appeal, which is elemental. People like to listen to an interesting tale, whatever its canon. And if the coincidence occurs that a vigorous, strongly coloured, even adventurous life is available to the tale-teller, his appeal is immediate and direct. So we find that these early fragmentary delineations could have a measure of truth and vitality impossible to the novel, which followed the course and destiny of years in a way inoffensive to a hopeful people. Within the limits of entertainment there was little need for glossing details.

Yet in typical Northern stories there is no actual acceptance of life and hence, paradoxically, a frequently disinterested gusto and ease in evoking it. The Wilds are grim, yes, the Barrens may claim your life; bad men and wild animals abound. But yet there is youth, health, virtue, above all, luck. These talismans forbid tragedy, and if there is death, it is only a possible death, and that too is a matter of luck. Such an attitude precludes a tragic philosophy, and makes of life a game: it is a survival perhaps of biological necessity in Northern peoples. In older civilizations, where life has been easier for many generations, there is an acceptance of fate as necessity inhering in character, which results in a different conception of art. Hence it is that the work of Sir Gilbert Parker is at its best when it is avowedly Canadian, though his talented and imperialistic globetrotting has taken him into many lands. His warmblooded, courageous tales and his theatrically urbane hero, Pierre, have had a definite part in forming a Canadian tradition. Sheer imaginative gusto and magnanimity can impart to materials of any sort a real value, while a cheap commercialism will lower them to a species of wish-fulfillment to which any high view of life, partaking of tragedy or of comedy, is impossible.

In the literature of older lands, animals were regarded as domestic servants, even as comrades, or simply as quarry. It remained for Canadian writers to visualize wild beasts as individuals, motivated by sense appeals and reasoning intelligence; and the result has been not a new form, but a hybrid of subject matter. The freshened point of view made possible by the use of animals (or household furniture, if you will) as characters was in the main neglected, and reactions were shown in fixed patterns dictated by sentiment or moral prejudice. And this when the freedom should have permitted a naturalistic acceptance and a poetry of the real, or a phantastic humorous or satirical expression. A genuine sense of continuity, a few finely objective stories, notably the early ones of Charles G.D. Roberts, the innovator of this type, were followed by many, many tales containing more or less valuable information in natural history, and no value as art.

A most significant circumstance in the development of the Canadian short story has been the dearth of editors to encourage and discover writers of value. A patient reading of our magazines will reveal a plain delinquency, more especially in recent years than in the days when writers of any kind were scarce enough, and the best ones were less easily evaded. But of our better writers of the last generation, practically all have been obliged to adjust their contributions to foreign markets, and having won fame in other countries, were complaisantly recognized at home. Meanwhile magazines were being run with the avowed intention of discovering native talent; instead of which they were encouraging, in the main, third-rate imitators of third-rate foreign models. Still, times are changing, and if we do not get the two or three editors of genius whom we need, conditions will improve anyway. If editors refuse to lead the public, the public quite possibly will lead the editors, for the grade of even some of the most popular foreign weeklies and women's journals is good enough to force a kind of improvement by their competition. Many thousands of Canadians are learning to see their own daily life, and to demand its presentment with a degree of realism. This may result, opportunely, in the upbuilding of great popular magazines, and finally an appreciative and representative audience may stand ready to welcome the best that our most gifted writers can create. The long neglect of such a writer as Will E. Ingersoll, almost the only one to depict our farming millions, may then be impossible.

But we shall not need to wait for such a development before we shall have able interpreters. Our best writers in the past accomplished what they did against the stream of the populace in other countries, and within something like a backwater of indifference in their own. But there has been a sudden growth of consciousness. It is, paradoxically, just when the rest of world literature is suffering a reversion to aristocratic standards that such writers as Merrill Denison and Morley Callaghan can appear. We can't lift ourselves by our bootlaces, and not until other nations have done so do we arrive at the stage where it is recognized that each creative book is not to be read by every person who can read – which was the case as recently as the time of Dickens. Whatever the gifts of the new men may prove to be, they should have less trouble than their forerunners in making them effective.

Obstacles detrimental to a truly indigenous literature have made more salient, however, the actual achievement of our writers. There is such a thing as a Canadian spirit, and perhaps in no other department of literature is it so vivid and indubitable. Stephen Leacock and Marjorie Pickthall, who were born in England, show it. Albert Hickman's 'Canadian Nights,' in spite of limitations and derivations, could have been written by a Canadian only; nor could his irrepressibly wrestling and idealistic young drunkards of good family have been the same in another country. There are the inspired phantasies of Norman Duncan; and there is that story of E.W. Thomson, in which a lumberman of property discovers a former employee stealing provisions after having rejected unsatisfactory wages. The lumberman takes him back, making him a loan of what he needs for his family, and heartens him with words – a story which in an American or English magazine, or in one of ours now, would seem completely and viciously sentimental, and which was simply a true vision of pioneer virtue and that neighbourliness necessary in a new country. And a perfect flowering of art is embodied in one volume, *In the Village of Viger*, by Duncan Campbell Scott. It is work which has had an unobtrusive influence; but it stands out after thirty years as the most satisfyingly individual contribution to the Canadian short story.

DUNCAN CAMPBELL SCOTT

The newly published volume of the collected *Poems of Duncan Campbell Scott* presents an opportunity to estimate the character and tendency of his work as a whole. Though Scott has shown for something like thirty years an accomplishment distinguished in our poetry, it is somewhat surprising to find how little of his earlier work has been discarded in this book and how all of it gains by the careful arrangement found here, which gives the effect of a unity through variety unusual in such collections. The book is as readable as most novels.

This impression is owing to notable balance of qualities, a unity of perception and mood, an intellectual clarity seldom absent and seldom permitted to dull pure feeling. There is less of the preacher and propagandist than in almost any other poet of comparable power of thought, and there is a clearer singing than would have seemed possible to detached afterthought. His muse is one to –

Out of the lives we lived only those things choose
That left no thirst, no ardors, and no stings,
Out of the life to come the dreams that chime
Consistent with imaginary time.

Though everything has been experienced, and in so far as the soul is infinite found wanting, there is no mockery here, no bitterness, and but little regret, only an unfailing reflective enjoyment – 'For beauty is stored in some exquisite fashion' – which finds best of life's store,

The power to reassemble
Memories of passion and endeavor
That made Life throb and tremble
But are no more.

This is a mood of detachment which made for clear vision and sure rendering even in the poet's early work. *The Magic House*, printed in 1893, *Labor and the Angel*, in 1898, *New World Lyrics and Ballads*, in 1905, and *Spring on Mattagami*, 1906, show a more typical or constant Scott than *Lundy's Lane and Other Poems*, 1916.

The latter volume is, comparatively speaking at least, a failure, with surprisingly ill-considered inclusions. The title poem has an easy, too easy, and powerful swing, like a burlesque of the newspaper war-ballad. Genuine feeling in the circumstances only spoils it. 'Height of Land' avoids a mincing measure, but it presents swamps and wilds in a way which does not allow the reader to forget that it is a cultivated and critical intelligence which views these expanses. Rather commonplace thoughts upon the nature of things may be found in 'Meditation at Perugia,' and there are even such lines as –

Give, Poet, give!
Thus only shalt thou live.
Give! for 'tis thy joyous doom
To charm, to comfort, to illume.

Altogether it is a book whose moments of insight, not to say inspiration, are rare, save for an occasional lyric like the perfect 'The Closed Door' and the lines introducing 'A Mystery Play,' which are hard, clear, and objective.

Yet there is a measure always, which, save for the last quotation, would make one believe Scott incapable of really bad verse. The

'Fragment of an Ode to Canada' begins with stale afflatus like the copy for a special advertisement to be illustrated in full colour, but reality and happy description creep into it. Again and again the reader is astonished by an alchemy which transmutes that old bane of the poets, the set subject, into something of authentic and personal feeling. The 'Lines in Memory of Edmund Morris' subtly blend reminiscence and description and include these:

Tears are the crushed essence of this world,
The wine of life, and he who treads the press
Is lofty with imperious disregard
Of the burst grapes, the red tears, and the murk.
But nay! that is a thought of the old poets,
Who sullied life with the passional bitterness
Of their world-weary hearts.

They are a plain recognition of the futility of reliance upon impulse without reservation. Naturally, it can find no place in passionate love lyrics, except as a curious acrid flavor; but it is introduced into a part of 'Variations upon an Eighteenth Century Theme:

Youth is a blossom yellow at the edge,
All full of honeyed pleasantness,
If you leave it, it will wither in the hedge,
If you pluck it, it will wither none the less;
Then pluck it – that were better after all,
But pluck it with a sort of wistfulness,
Yea, pluck it if you must, and let it fall
Regretfully, with a last touch of tenderness,
Before the color and the honey all
Are flown away
And you are holding but a withered tress
Of passion and of loveliness.
Now let it fall –
Yet hold it – hold it – 'tis thy youth!
Nay, let it fall – fall – fall –
Caress it ere it fall,
Then let it fall and die.

This is one of a series of poems, a unit in itself rather than a portion of a longer poem. The pieces are varied in manner and quality, and the unity running through them is rather tenuous. The influence of the art of music is shown here, as notably in 'Adagio' and 'Senza Fine,' but not especially fruitfully: these are not more moving than others.

They are found in the little volume, *Beauty and Life*, published in 1922, which is one of the most even and finest in our literature and is now included, spread throughout the collected poems. Several of the lyrics are well-nigh matchless in their way, and there is in the 'Ode for the Keats Centenary' a contribution hardly to be surpassed in English literature. Here is a sustained conception which never falters from beauty and relevance – and of how many 'odes' can that be said? Though it flows into magnificent lyric interludes, the indispensable generalities are always based on reality; particularizing the case of their subject, Keats:

Truth, 'tis a doubtful art
To make Hope sweeten
Time as it flows;
For no man knows
Until the very last,
Whether it be a sovereign herb that he has eaten,
Or his own heart.

And 'The Flight,' a dramatic scene, contains admirable dialogue in the form of poetry – civilized, whimsical, restrained, with a delicate emphasis on fancy and emotion. In such poems as these the rationalizing faculty of the poet has a legitimate artistic place; and in how many others there are lines, passages, in which thought and poetry melt into one, in tranquil, reflective feeling. It is not surprising that some show a tendency to keep on writing, letting whimsy follow fancy, and phrase be added to thought, until the poem might well be endless. Such are the fine 'Reverie' and 'The Fragment of a Letter' containing this:

'Tis winged impromptu and the occasion strange
That gives to beauty its full power and range.
The bird was nature; and his casual giving,
Us to ourselves – for what we gain from living,
When we possess our souls or seem to own,
Is not the peak of knowledge, but the tone
Of feeling; is not the problem solved, but just
The hope of solving opened out and thrust

A little further into the spirit air;
But whether there be demonstration there
We know not; no more than the growing vines
When they commission their young eager bines
To find amid the void a clinging-spit
Know whether it be really there or not.

The subject matter upon which these faculties of restraint and fancy are exercised is varied. There are the nature pieces, without which no book of Canadian poetry is complete; but here they do not smack so much as usual of the catalogue. There are poems about Indians and their life, which are based upon long knowledge and observation and yet avoid anything approaching photographic realism. Of such are 'The Forsaken' and 'Powassan's Drum,' 'The Onondaga Madonna,' 'The Mission of the Trees,' and 'The Half-Breed Girl,' whose mingled ancestral impulses are described:

Her heart is shaken with longing
    For the strange still years,
For what she knows and knows not,
    For the wells of ancient tears.

A voice calls from the rapids,
    Deep, careless, and free,
A voice that is larger than her life
    Or than her death shall be.

She covers her face with her blanket,
    Her fierce soul hates her breath,
As it cried with a sudden passion
    For life or death.

And there are numerous childpoems of delicate and sure perception. Charmingly turned, well-nigh flawless lyrics abound, and their choice will be a matter of the taste of the reader. 'The Wood Peewee,' 'Sailor's Sweetheart,' 'Life and a Soul,' 'Ecstasy,' 'The Ghost's Story,' 'Bells,' 'The Enigma,' 'The Mower,' 'Spring Night,' the 'Thirteen Songs,' notably 'Sorrow is come like a swallow to nest,' and the three 'June Lyrics.' These have a delicacy of expression, a strength of feeling, and an inevitable natural flow, freshness, and spontaneity which makes them ever to be valued.

Ballads like 'The Piper of Arll,' such stories as that of Dominique de Gourgues and his revenge for the Spanish atrocities perpetrated upon the Huguenot settlement planted on the coast of Florida, Indian tales like 'The Mission of the Trees,' folk superstition like 'Catnip Jack,' are vivid and inspiriting and form a link between the other poetry of Duncan Campbell Scott and his prose stories, *In the Village of Viger*, now out of print, and *The Witching of Elspie*, a volume of fiction published three years ago. These stories, mainly historical, show a knowledge of the north country and a faithfulness to the knowledge, which the novels of this locale, not to mention the movies, have not yet attained. They are honest and sure-footed works, in pleasing style, but they do not show the combination of qualities which makes this writer's poetry unique.

Much of such work, prose and verse, might have been written anywhere in the English-speaking world, by a man cultured, urbane, of keen observation and delicate imagination. But there is enough that could have been conceived only in Canada by a son of Canada to give the work an indigenous value independent of the fact that on purely literary bases it ranks among the highest which has been produced here.

Similarly with comparatively youthful matters of technique which have become accepted as traditional: pain and passion and longing, lonely love and longed-for death, snowflakes and rose leaves, high desire and laughter and tears, flutters of hope and falser fancies thronging – perhaps he had gone as far as may be by invoking these things by name and reasoning about them, rather than invoking them, more poignantly, in memorable picture, song, or story. Yet he has done that too, many times, in poems which are almost completely objective, or which even convey themselves solely by inference. Such is 'The Lovers':

The robins round the lilac tree
    Were fluttering in the rain –
Before we knew – the cloud had fled,
    The sky was fair again.

Before we knew – the young sweet moon
    With rose was drifted o'er,
The dusk had drowsed the stream and lit
    The lights along the shore.

The stars were faint – before we knew
 The night was on the lawn:
Before we knew – a shadow stirred
 It must have been the dawn.

There is variety enough within a charm which is always actual to make this volume interesting to all lovers of poetry and qualities which make it a contribution, important and permanent as human reckonings go, to Canadian literature.

LETTER TO MISS FRANKFURTH*

Northwood, RR 2, Ontario
May 10, 1925

Dear Miss Frankfurth:*
'I am at my house in the country, and it rains,' writes Sherwood Anderson. Same here. Twilight. In my little office (of which because it is new and has a floor of bird's-eye maple, I am conscious) I watch the grey rain transfix the pear-blossoms drifted on the grey clods; the pear tree itself graciously unaware, and the green everywhere, distant and near exhales a light of its own.

Yes, I like it here, and think that we have a good farm, with modern buildings, as farms go, and I hope that we will not have to move another year. I have been putting hand to the plow, with result of one small poem and no addition to my small enough store of general amiability.

Make my letters critical, so that you may learn from them! Alas, I'm not an edifying person, and Goethe meant well: that men hear only what they are capable of feeling. Willa Cather – this is not from the sublime to the insignificant – says that about the only way one person can help another is by in some measure understanding them; and I feel that I owe you a great deal.

You have admirably vindicated your reaction to Stephens' work. My difference perhaps lies in looking at it more as a writer than as a

* The identity of Miss Frankfurth has not been established.

human being. 'The Call of the Hills' for example, I see as a big subject spoiled by banality of vision and language. I read of 'folded leaves, /The fingers of a tree' and I wonder why he could not have found a less stale metaphor, or, better, evoked the tree or its leaves without figure of speech at all. You see Stephens' work as a whole: I recall only a somewhat snippy review I wrote of it in *Can Bookman* couple of years ago. (It has been highly praised elsewhere.) Details of craftsmanship scamped or awry spoil any piece of writing for me, and it is only after the mind assents to the technical mastery that the emotion is allowed to reach me. (That is, in poems; in a novel, one is sometimes carried away: a mediocre talent suffices to make a book live, providing the writer is really moved, and this explains the success of the Ethel Dells. When the intellect assents to this real emotion and to the structure, we have genuine literature – or even when it doesn't assent, providing the author has an imagination powerful enough to create a world of his own which makes everything credible, ex. Dickens.) Some of the free-versers and likewise the jinglers lay themselves open equally: 'A powerful governing intelligence; the ability to select and reject; to determine the congruity of material; to accept or modify the image which, upon representation, turns out to be harmonious or inadequate; the feeling for unity and the recognition of it when achieved – these are the constituents of the process of transformation, and the qualities which distinguish the true artist from the naïve rhapsodist who merely *expresses* himself.'

You see that I do not discuss the ideas behind these poems. Perhaps it is a defect in my education which makes me see them, in cases as such as this, as irrelevant. It does not matter greatly that Thomas Hardy sees God as a great Ironist and men as fools and wittols who laugh when they should surge to the Exits; what matters is that *something* has been effective in showing him life and life he passes on to us: things all men know, that life is slow and yet brief, beauty far-off and yet tormenting. Shakespeare tells us that there is a glory in the human heart which can make the world luminous and glorious. Very well, there are many truths in the world, and it is only apparently that they contradict each other. The question for the artist is, will they bring imagination to white heat, so that he can use his art to shape its forms – not theirs.

Yes, 'Nocturne of Remembered Spring' is fine. I have wondered why Conrad Aiken is not of the first table, instead of being at the head of the second – in critical estimation. Perhaps he is. A poem of his in

March Dial, 1921 has meant so much to me ever since that I am tempted to copy its entirety for you. Also there is a sonnet of Edna St Vincent Millay's which seems very fine – sonorous, and of austere and gorgeous imagery.

While at Blenheim I did the ninth writing of my little story, and looking at it again I wonder whether I've got it right yet. ... Last stanza of 'Lids,' 'But the colt was too heavy' she could run away from the body, her grief, anything. ... I am told that I should 'go out more,' even for more 'material' – when I have more now than I know how to devise a technique to render! In Chicago I found two books – with sufficient detail, I think – and at least two short stories. ... Marjorie and I have laid out a tennis court, and she is quite good, though like most girls has a tendency to dance daintily on the toes and strike at the ball a second after it has passed. ... Such organizations as you speak are indeed painful subjects to thinking people, especially when they have some definite object. The cultural clubs of the states are bad enough, and yet the remuneration which does come to literature once it has been recognized comes mostly, I fear, from those hundred of thousands. I'll bet they buy Conrad, and where's the woman who appreciates Conrad? I've seen only one I thought sincere, and she is so odd that she may turn out a writer when she grows up!

It is fortunate I have not many correspondents so appreciative and discursive as you, or I know where my time would go. Until next time,

With best wishes,

P.S. Your reading program interests me. I've always wanted to go into Ancient History. I've kept a list of books to read if I ever got near a large library (and had leisure) if it would help I might sort out a list of general subjects you could try on Coatar(?) Library. Or are you going on with A. History?

THE POETIC FRUITION OF IRELAND

Ireland has now reached a period in her literary expression, coincident with her changes in polity. One of her eminent critics, Mr John Eglinton, has suggested that she is discovering the time of political subordination to England, which freed her energies for creative outlets, to have been an epoch after all of unwitting happiness. More than an element of truth may be discovered in this, from the humanistic view. In Ireland's life as a nation it is to be hoped that the future, with its mutations, holds her most fortunate period. But if we speak, as now, of the poet, it is always to the past that he looks for happiness; and though he cannot be segregated from the life about him, he may be content to accept the early disclaimer of Yeats:

We have no art to set the statesman right;
We have done enough of meddling – who can please
A young girl in the indolence of her youth,
Or an old man upon a winter's night?

Nevertheless there is the political obligation, and Mr Yeats himself is a senator, whether or not he spoke as such in mentioning the necessity for a newer 'idealism of labor and thought.' And again, in his latest comment, 'The Need for Audacity of Thought,' he says 'To some extent Ireland but shows in an acute form the European problem, and must seek a remedy where the best minds of Europe seek it – in audacity of speculation and creation. We must consider anew the foundations of existence, bringing to the discussion – diplomacies and prudencies put away – all relevant thought.'

So that, clearly, the time is well fitted for summing up the achievements of the past, and for such an anthology as that of Mr Lennox Robinson, well-named, 'A Golden Treasury of Irish Verse.' In the foreword, 'I have collected here what seem to me to be some of our most beautiful Irish poems,' he says, 'I have chosen many poems which were originally written in Gaelic and which have been translated by poets into beautiful English, and unlike many other Irish anthologies I have included no poem merely because its patriotic sentiments have made it popular.' And those who know the wealth of Irish verse will know that this means that the collection is really, as the publishers claim, made 'for lovers of fine poetry and for them alone.'

The arrangement is not chronological nor by defined sections. Instead there is a progression or cycle of thought and mood linking poem to poem throughout the book. This cycle makes clear a unity of intent and of desire which is truly phenomenal. To be sure, excepting the translations from the Gaelic, little of value was written in English before the beginning of the nineteenth century. And it may be the necessity of a compromise – perhaps now triumphant but no less than before constrained – in the use of an alien language – that makes the similarity of tone or rather of rhythm, so conspicuous. At any rate the spirit of such older poets as William Allingham, Emily Brontë, George Darley, Aubrey De Vere, Sir John Ferguson, Mangan, Thomas Parnell, is quite as evidently linked to that of the younger living poets, Padraic Colum, Herbert Trench, H. Stuart, Francis Ledgwidge, E.R. Dodds, Joseph Campbell, as to the predecessors of these latter, the older men of our own day, Yeats, Synge, Stephens, and 'A.E.'

And this unity is of a quite special kind. All of these writers celebrate the same valour and love, death and regret, which is found in great poetry everywhere; and they do this in a fitting manner. They seem all at some moment to have had the office of major poet thrust upon them. They have upheld it for the most part with austerity but scarcely with ease. Through all these poems runs a chord of unwillingness which might have been borrowed with the language, and this is indigenous, part of heritage. 'Who art thou, starry ghost?' questions Herbert Trench,

Who art thou, starry ghost,
  That ridest on the air
At the head of all the host,
  And art so burning-eyed
  For all thy strengthlessness?
    World, I am no less
Than She whom thou has awaited;
  She, who remade Poland out of nothingness
    And hath created
Ireland, out of breath of pride
  In the reed-bed of despair.

There is more in such utterances as these than a gesture of temporary disillusion, hardened into a convention. A great and sad love weighs upon the least poet of these many, and some of its greatness is loaned him. It is for Ireland. 'Lament,' 'dirge,' and 'adieu' are favorite words. There is much singing of exile, and a perversity of renunciation:

I wish that all music were mute
And I to all beauty were blind.

One translation from the Gaelic runs:

I do not know of anything under the sky
That is friendly to or favorable to the Gael,
But only the sea that our need brings us to,
Or the wind that blows to the harbor,
The ship that is bearing us away from Ireland;
And there is reason that these are reconciled with us,
For we increase the sea with our tears,
And the wandering wind with our sighs.

Perversity is a harsh and hasty word, yet many an Englishman must have felt that the quality typified the Irish genius (along with exaggeration) even in the famous humor, of which there is little here. And this even in the most moving utterances:

My grief is on the sea,
  How the waves of it roll!
For they heave between me
  And the love of my soul.

Or, more gentle,

She bid me take life easy, as the grass grows on the weirs;
But I was young and foolish, and now am full of tears.

The words of some other Irish bard, writing elsewhere, come to mind:

For the great Gaels of Ireland
Are the men that God made mad,
And all their wars were merry
And all their songs are sad.

But this is an attempt at defining – not vilifying – as summarily and clearly if roughly, as the present limitations allow, what would need years of thought and inspiration to define – a national spirit. The poems themselves do it much better, with a combination of individual traits, and without the dangers of generalization which is bound to enter into the most conscientious criticism.

For it is Ireland itself in the spirit which we have in this book. Aside from the qualities mentioned there is a heroic and pure loveliness emanated, hardly to be surpassed elsewhere – centred, it may be, in 'The Song of Wandering Aengus.' Who that heard him in Toronto can forget Yeats' rendering, a manner precisely harmonious:

I went into the hazel wood,
  Because a fire was in my head,
And cut and peeled a hazel wand,
  And hooked a berry to a thread;
And when white moths were on the wing,
  And moth-like stars were flickering out,
I dropped the berry in a stream
  And caught a little silver trout.

When I had laid it on the floor,
  I went to blow the fire a-flame,
But something rustled on the floor,
  And some one called me by my name:
It had become a glimmering girl,
  With apple-blossom in her hair,
Who called me by my name and ran
  And faded through the brightening air.

Though I am old with wandering,
  Through hollow lands and hilly lands,
I will find out where she has gone,
  And kiss her lips and take her hands;
And walk among long dappled grass,
  And pluck till time and times are done,
The silver apples of the moon,
  The golden apples of the sun.

It is an other-world beauty, that echoes with the past and unforgotten dreams of youth. These poets are men enchanted, 'who have trod on fairy grass.' An elfin wildness is found in the lines of James Stephens, in those of 'A.E.,' whose bright words are like bright leaves falling. One of the selections is called The Outcast:

Sometimes when alone
  At the dark close of day,
Men meet an outlawed majesty
  And hurry away.

They come to the lighted house;
  They talk to their dear;

They crucify the mystery
  With words of good cheer.

When love and life are over,
  And flight's at an end,
On the outcast majesty
  They lean as a friend.

There are many bits of landscape from the Irish countryside, like this of Katherine Tynan:

Out upon the sand-dunes thrive the coarse long grasses,
  Herons standing knee-deep in the brackish pool,
Overhead the sunset fire and flame amasses,
  And the moon to eastward rises pale and cool:
Rose and green about her silver-grey and pearly,
  Chequered with the black rooks flying home to bed.

And 'The Sheep,' by Seumus O'Sullivan:

Slowly they pass
In the grey of the evening
Over the wet road,
A flock of sheep.
Slowly they wend
In the grey of the gloaming,
Over the wet road
That winds through the town.
Slowly they pass,
And gleaming whitely
Vanish away
In the grey of the evening...

Yet there is no plethora of description, nor of the conventional adjuncts of witches, leprechaun, haunted castles, swans, bog mist, and so forth, which imitators of the Irish tradition employ. Rather do most of these poems speak in a language universal and common to men everywhere. Herbert Trench speaks for his fellow-craftsmen in the lyric cry:

Come let us make love deathless, thou and I,
  Seeing that our footing on the earth is brief –

Seeing that her multitudes sweep out to die
  Mocking at all that passes their belief.

Quotations from even so richly beautiful a volume must come to an end, and since the hope of Ireland's continuing to express the spirit within her lies with the poets to come, it may be closed by words of the youngest poet represented here. Mr Stuart's poem is called 'The Fountain':

The fountain falls from laughing mouth of stone
In crescent laughter thru' the scented gloom
And from the corner of the curvèd lip
The drops like petals gather, fall, and slip,
From carven leaf to leaf. I am alone
By the slim, white, unwitherable plume
The water flaunts against a deathless sky.
And I, who found in mutability
A little music and a little laughter,
See there before me Beauty's strange hereafter;
The immortal ghost, too gay, too sad, to die.

Possibly an English collection such as this, over as many years, would show as many names, and poetry as fine; but not, I venture, to so high a level of quality in the slightest verses. And if a name is wanted to compare with the greatest, let us give that of William Butler Yeats. Moreover to him, more than to any other save possibly 'A.E.,' is to be credited the great force of the renaissance of these late years. Yet how much is not owed by all living writers to the select taste of the Irish reading public, which permits the artist to unfold his individual gift, yet upholds him from the menace or blandishment of the mob, and from surface eccentricity! This is a book demonstrably valuable to Canada.

A GREAT POET OF TO-DAY

Edwin Arlington Robinson

Probably the most impressive thing about the work of Edwin Arlington Robinson, as revealed in retrospective survey permitted by a collected edition, is the number of characters which he, in poems mostly brief and lyrical or monologuing, and without recourse to poetic or prose drama or to fiction, has created. The word is used advisedly. The characters of a poet generally are puppets invented as illustrative of the generalization which he for the nonce must formulate in his poem. Robinson's characters are real as those of the great creators have been, and as memorable. In this matter of unforgettable *personae* he surely rivals Balzac and Dickens, if the comparative volume of the work and the relative nature of it is considered.

These characters too are of the universal stuff of human nature, but while their individualities unfold freely, they are seen as it were through a medium – the style, the personality, the method or what you will. So that as one knows a canvas of the masters of painting and can say at once: That is a Rubens, this is a Picasso, likewise one can usually say after quotation of ten lines: That is Robinson. Yet this medium is not intrusive; actually one of the reasons that it is so easily identified is that it is clear and apparently casual, fitting the matter as well-made garments fit a form. It is a sinuous idiom, which allows the freest expression to the foibles and intricacies of character.

Who can forget for example, John Gorham, or the man Flammonde,

> With firm address and foreign air,
> With news of nations in his talk,
> And something royal in his walk,

who reconciled enemies, encouraged talent, made life, in short, different where he lived. Or the totally effaced yet ever-memorable mother in 'The Gift of God' who idealized her son, though

> Perchance a canvass of the town
>   Would find him far from flags and shouts,
> And leave him only the renown
>   Of many smiles and many doubts.

Then, after the realism of such traits, the poem ends as it should – in a way which brings perfection near:

> She crowns him with her gratefulness,
>   And says again that life is good;
> And should the gift of God be less
>   In him than in her motherhood,

His fame, though vague, will not be small
  As upward through her dream he fares,
Half clouded by a crimson fall
  Of roses thrown on marble stairs.

Or less than most, who will forget that amazing 'Ben Johnson Entertains a Man From Stratford,' in which the creator of *Volpone* with a monologue paints a surpassing picture of Shakespeare, of himself, and of the times, in matchlessly sinuous blank verse. For example, this expression of the Bard in the doldrums, unbosoming himself to his friend:

It's all a world where bugs and emperors
Go singularly back to the same dust,
Each in his time; and the old ordered stars
That sang together, Ben, will sing the same
Old stave to-morrow.

'The Unforgiven' is a marvellously documented psychology of marriage, from one who has been a bachelor all his life. As an example of his perfectly natural, almost casual manipulation of the sonnet form, take 'Another Dark Lady.'

Think not, because I wonder where you fled,
That I would lift a pin to see you there;
You may, for me, be prowling anywhere,
So long as you show not your little head:
No dark and evil story of the dead
Would leave you less pernicious or less fair –
Not even Lilith with her famous hair;
And Lilith was the devil, I have read.

I cannot hate you, for I loved you then.
The woods were golden then. There was a road
Through beeches; and I said their smooth feet showed
Like yours. Truth must have heard me from afar,
For I shall never have to learn again
That yours are cloven as no beeches' are.

And there is Bewick, the dejected bankrupt who haunts the offices of his former business associates and borrows pittances from them wherewith to live. Or 'The Man Against the Sky,' title poem of perhaps

Robinson's most mature volume, who may have been a prophet of an art 'immovable to old idolatries.'

He may have been a player without a part,
Annoyed that even the sun should have the skies
For such a flaming way to advertise;
He may have been a painter sick at heart
With Nature's toiling for a new surprise;
He may have been a cynic, who now, for all
Of anything divine that his effete
Negation may have tasted,
Saw truth in his own image, rather small,
Forbore to fever the ephemeral,
Found any barren height a good retreat
From any swarming street,
And in the sun saw power superbly wasted;
And when the primitive old-fashioned stars
Came out to shine again on joys and wars
More primitive, and all arrayed for doom,
He may have proved the world a sorry thing
In his imagining,
And life a lighted highway to the tomb.

Again, John Evereldown, with his senile imaginings, and the ironic fate of the lonely artist of 'Her Eyes,' who after renouncing life, turns, and limns,

A perilous face – and an angel's too...
And he wonders yet what her love could be
To punish him after that strife so grim.

And there is 'Richard Cory,' a matchless character-sketch and ballad comprised in sixteen lines, which may be once more quoted:

Whenever Richard Cory went down town,
    We people on the pavement looked at him:
He was a gentleman from sole to crown,
    Clean favored, and imperially slim.

And he was always quietly arrayed,
    And he was always human when he talked,

But still he fluttered pulses when he said,
  'Good morning,' and he glittered when he walked.

And he was rich – yes, richer than a king –
  And admirably schooled in every grace:
In fine, we thought that he was everything
  To make us wish that we were in his place.

So on we worked, and waited for the light,
  And went without the meat, and cursed the bread;
And Richard Cory, one calm summer night,
  Went home and put a bullet through his head.

One does not forget Richard Cory, companion of the inscrutable Flammonde, nor Reuben Bright, the butcher, who after prolonged and meticulous obsequies of his wife 'Tore down the slaughter house.' Or 'Aaron Stark,'

Glad for the murmur of his hard renown,
Year after year he shambled through the town,
A loveless exile moving with a staff;
And oftentimes there crept into his ears
A sound of alien pity, touched with tears –
And then (and then only) did Aaron laugh.

While 'Fleming Helphenstine,' concerning an urbane pair suddenly awakened to each others' eyes, and the 'Song at Shannon's,' in which two part silently, neither knowing what the other has heard, finely realize the incommunicability of life.

Bonaparte, Merlin, John Brown, Ben Jonson, Lancelot, and so forth, speak more plausibly than perhaps through any other poet, yet on the other hand we have 'Three Taverns,' a soliloquy of Paul, which seems utterly a failure. Hamilton and Burr converse as they may have thought and written, to an effect of most convincing eloquence, with many a shrewd cut of irony, as 'You smile as if your spirit lived at ease with error.' Bonaparte remarks 'that great kings look very small when they are put to bed.' Captain Craig, however, in the long poem of that name, is more like a character in a book, say a play of Ibsen, and it is perhaps opportune to quote only one shrewd observation of his:

But as the bitterness that loads your tears
Makes Dead Sea swimming easy, so the gloom

The penance, and the woeful pride you keep
Makes bitterness your buoyance of the world.

In 'Merlin,' longer than any of Tennyson's *Idylls*, a colloquial diction seems at first sight almost irreverent, at least recalling the classical poet, as for instance:

I know the worm, and his worm's name is Mordred,
Albeit the streets are not yet saying so.

The dialogue, and perhaps the whole poem, is better than Tennyson in psychological detail, and in the total effect. In much dialogue we are given what Vivien and Merlin might have thought or felt, but saving a superhuman articulateness for those times, never said.

Fine as the longer poems are, such as 'Avon's Harvest,' 'The Man Who Died Twice,' and so forth, it must be confessed that to this reader at least they do not produce a commensurate effect with the brief and unforgettable ballads such as 'The Mill,' in the volume entitled *The Three Taverns*, and the masterly sonnets everywhere. They do, however, show Robinson to be the Conrad of the narrative poem. Browning had been its Henry James, if the anachronism may be pardoned, and brought to it psychology and character interplay; but Robinson came at once to subtilize this method and to add to it color and human richness. To me the most wholly successful long poem is 'Isaac and Archibald,' included in the early volume, *Captain Craig*, published in 1902. It is a shrewd and characteristic *genre* picture of two old farm men, seen by a child on a hot summer afternoon. It was a journey Isaac and the boy made to see what Archibald had done with his oats.

...It was high time
Those oats were cut, said Isaac; and he feared
That Archibald – well, he could never feel
Quite sure of Archibald.

And the good old man invited – that is, permitted – the boy to go along. In this visit of an afternoon is disclosed the characters of these two old men, of the life and *milieu* in which they have lived, seen through the mellowed vision of one who had been that boy. It deserves a place among the world's masterpieces of this sort, not far from Wordsworth's 'Michael,' if comparisons must be made. And add to it the brief counterpart in character, 'Mr Flood's Party,' warm and human picture as American literature can show, and without a false word. With these two alone Robinson could claim the highest consideration as an artist and a man.

While properly one may be averse from pinning the autobiographical tag to any notably fine work, perhaps it is safe to assume that Edwin Arlington Robinson was that boy who knew Isaac and Archibald and their thrifty farms. At any rate he has known New England life since his boyhood, and assimilated much more than the local culture, to create in a manner edifying to readers anywhere. There are aspects of America forgotten or barely indicated in his work. Perhaps in not tuning his lay to piping days and spots, he retains something more truly universal. Fortunately, though his poems on the surface at least take the intellect into account as much as the heart, he was recognized early by Theodore Roosevelt and others, and was enabled to continue his career with a minimum of hampering. Not long ago his fiftieth birthday was the occasion of national rejoicing and tribute. In 1922 his *Collected Poems* won the Pulitzer Prize. Moreover, he continues to write, in surprising quality.

I have tried with examples to indicate the distinction of Robinson among poets. In what has been called an age of numbskull lyrics he shows the intellectual power of a philosopher, curbed from mellifluent generalities with a knowledge of and integrity to human idiosyncrasy matched by the better novelists. It is an equipment which few poets can boast or co-ordinate with the singing gift successfully. He is chary of 'description' in the old sense, though he is capable of marvellous atmospheric effects, simple or complex, as

A dreary, cold, unwholesome day.
        Racked overhead –
As if the world were turning the wrong way,
        And the sun dead.

But he claims also that:

        Towers of sound
And flowers of sense are but a waste of heaven
Where there is none to know them from the rocks
And sand-grass of his own monotony
That makes earth less than earth.

Occasionally there is a poem like 'The Wilderness,' or 'The Klondike,' but usually Robinson recalls with the Greeks that the stuff of poetry is the eternal heart of man. Occasionally there are ballads or villanelles which some one else might have done as well or in the like manner, but in the main it must be said that this poet's individuality has been sufficient to proclaim itself through the medium and the materials which have been used many times before, in the creation of a personal art which critics agree, more than in regard to that of any other living poet, that it is the finest which America possesses.

A SHROPSHIRE LAD

It seems that there are types of humankind always awaiting creation or embodiment in art. Beyond their local circle and habitation they are not to be known otherwise. We should not have become acquainted with Bazaroff sixty years ago, or with the myriads of Mr Pecksniffs, Mr Macawbers, etc. of Dickens, had not the writers seen and understood them well enough to recreate them for future generations and other countries. While the nature of man does not change, from earliest time, conversely it is unlimited in character-mutation. And for the artist, the poet, the task is only to mine this gold.

How else should the world be known to itself? Misapprehension is plentiful, and travellers' tales of, for instance, the coldness and phlegm of Englishmen might have obscured traits as real as those recorded, had not Shakespeare and Dickens blown off steam for the whole race. And it is the same with one more type, portrayed distinctively by A.E. Housman thirty years ago, in *A Shropshire Lad.* Doubtless for centuries there had subsisted this soil-loving, life-loving, inarticulate but artlessly downright yeoman, the backbone of English armies and, in later stages, for all his rootedness in England, particularly rural England, the basis of such large things as colonization and world exploration. But never before had this character been lifted to appreciable reality, in poetry universal and comprehensible, it appears to me, to any age and any temperament capable of understanding in this medium.

This does not mean everybody. The disadvantages are obvious. *A Shropshire Lad* is 'pure poetry,' and as such most simple, of a classic clarity which recalls the fact that it is the masters of poetry, Goethe notably, who are read first in the study of languages such as German. Moreover the Lad himself is very naïve. Though the implications are solid enough for philosophic speculation, it is a combination one would think not very sympathetic to the 'disreputable psychologism' which Thomas Mann finds in this age. Yet poetry has recovered sooner from this malady than some of the other arts, having had its measles in Browning a little earlier.

Nothing could be farther from Browning than Housman. The virtuoso role-assumer might never have lived, for any discoverable stigma in Housman's poems. What would the yea-saying protagonist of all's-wellness say to this; a counterpart as it is of the gregarious hilarity of youth shown in the pieces on the rural fair:

There pass the careless people
    That call their souls their own;
Here by the road I loiter,
    How idle and alone.

Ah, past the plunge of plummet,
    In seas I cannot sound,
My heart and soul and senses,
    World without end, are drowned.

His folly has not fellow
    Beneath the blue of day
That gives to man or woman
    His heart and soul away.

There flowers no balm to sain him
    From east of earth to west
That's lost for everlasting
    The heart out of his breast.

Here by the labouring highway
    With empty hands I stroll:
Sea-deep, till doomsday morning,
    Lie lost my heart and soul.

There is a curious quality in these verses nowhere else to be found. It is the stoicism of youth, health and English spirits in the midst of old English land, associations of immemorial custom, buildings, trees, songs; and with that the sadness of youth, its certainty so newly and irrevocably learned, of the inevitability of love and death. The two chords, in fact, have seldom been so plangently struck from the symbolic lyre. And always with an overtone as of some more fateful emotion of futility combined with a zest for living which is unquenchable.

In this view *sub specie aeternitas* all quirks of destiny become possible, nay, seemly and becoming, not a matter of indifference yet all apparently equal components of life.

Leave your home behind, lad,
And reach your friends your hand,

the recruit is adjured and,

Come you home a hero,
Or come not home at all,
The lads you leave will mind you
Till Ludlow tower shall fall.

And there remains to 'make the foes of English / Be sorry you were born.' Again, in a grimly casual ballad two brothers converse of the brother one of them has just murdered:

My mother thinks us long away;
'Tis time the field were mown.
She had two sons at rising day,
Tonight she'll be alone.

Such feeling has been the lot of youth becoming entangled with a world he does not understand, from time immemorial, but scarcely before was it so exquisitely and inevitably expressed. But recognition of such matters does not hinder real enjoyment. Spring brings a lightening, and in 'March' he sees 'Brutes in field and brutes in pen / Leap that the world goes round again.' While,

Twice a week the winter through
Here stood I to keep the goal:
Football then was fighting sorrow
For the young man's soul.

Now in Maytime to the wicket
Out I march with bat and pad.

See the son of grief at cricket
  Trying to be glad.

Try I will; no harm in trying:
  Wonder 'tis how little mirth
Keeps the bones of man from lying
  On the bed of earth.

'To An Athlete Dying Young' tells of two carryings, shoulder high, one in triumph, and again the same man, newly 'townsman of a stiller town.' County fairs, soldiers marching, wranglings with friends, ploughing, the Welsh Marches with their historic memories, Lent lilies, are seen through fresh eyes. Wenlock wood reminds him in historic wise of man's ancient trouble:

On Wenlock Edge the wood's in trouble;
  His forest fleece the Wreckin heaves;
The gale, it plies the saplings double,
  And thick on Severn snow the leaves.

'Twould blow like this through hold and hanger
  When Uricon the city stood:
'Tis the old wind in the old anger,
  But then it threshed another wood.

Then, 'twas before my time, the Roman
  At yonder heaving hill would stare:
The blood that warms an English yeoman,
  The thoughts that hurt him, they were there.

There, like the wind through the woods in riot,
  Through him the gale of youth blew high;
The tree of man was never quiet;
  Then, 'twas the Roman, now 'tis I.

The gale, it plies the saplings double,
  It blows so hard, 'twill soon be gone:
Today the Roman and his trouble
  Are ashes under Uricon.

Led by the symbolic Merry Guide, with his 'gay regards of promise and sure unslackened stride,'

Buoyed on the heaven-heard whisper
    Of dancing leaflets whirled
From all the woods that Autumn
    Bereaves in all the world,

the Lad takes to the Open Road, and in London he misses the help of Nature when he is sad, the solace of the accompanying 'beautiful and death-struck year,' the while he sees

In many an eye that measures me
The mortal sickness of a mind
Too unhappy to be kind.

And with Spring again comes the ever-recurring nostalgia of the country, expressed with perfect naturalness of tone, lamenting yet not plaintive before the inevitable changes of life:

'Tis time, I think by Wenlock town
    The golden broom should blow;
The hawthorn sprinkled up and down
    Should charge the land with snow.

Spring will not wait the loiterer's time
    Who keeps so long away;
So others wear the broom and climb
    The hedgerows heaped with May.

Oh tarnish late on Wenlock Edge,
    Gold that I never see;
Lie long, high snowdrifts in the hedge
    That will not shower on me.

The reaction from this ubiquitous melancholy, beside him wherever he goes, is found in a momentary expression of a sort of emotional nihilism:

Think no more, lad; laugh, be jolly:
    Why should men make haste to die?
Empty heads and tongues a-talking
Make the rough road easy walking,
And the feather pate of folly
    Bears the falling sky.

Oh, 'tis jesting, dancing, drinking
  Spins the heavy world around.
If young hearts were not so clever,
Oh, they would be young forever:
Think no more; 'tis only thinking
  Lays lads under ground.

And the day of battle finds the same fatalism,

...Since the man that runs away
Lives to die another day,
And cowards' funerals, when they come
Are not wept so well at home.

But throughout this harping, not to abuse the word, on two or three strings, there are notes of relieving humour, and finally there is a long piece giving perspective to what has gone before, in which a friend of the poet is made to expostulate with him:

Terence; this is stupid stuff:
You eat your victuals fast enough;
There can't be much amiss, 'tis clear,
To see the rate you drink your beer.

But the verse he makes 'would give a chap the belly-ache.'

The cow, the old cow, she is dead;
It sleeps well, the horned head;
We poor lads, 'tis our turn now
To hear such tunes as killed the cow.

The poet replying admits that there are brisker pipes than poetry, 'And malt does more than Milton can / To justify God's ways to man...'

Look within the pewter pot
To see the world as the world's not.

Moreover it jibes with the life he sees:

And while the sun and moon endure
Luck's a chance, but trouble's sure....

And he concludes with a parable of a king who reigned in the East, where kings were poisoned with frequency and impunity, and this one became so used to it that he remained uninjured.

They put arsenic in his meat
And stared aghast to watch him eat;
They poured strychnine in his cup
And shook to see him drink it up;
They shook, they stared as white's their shirt:
Them it was their poison hurt.
– I tell the tale I heard told.
Mithridates, he died old.

It is hard to explain the popularity of this little volume, in view of the hard philosophy which might be assumed to balance its music. At any rate it went into edition after edition, in the United States as well as England. No volume of comparable quality, it seems safe to say, has had a like reception, and it is still sold in popular editions, vital in its charm and force as it was thirty years ago. This is undoubtedly owing to the universal character of the Lad and his plaints and rejoicings, the vital qualities of his zest and despairs. But additionally there was the contrast with the reigning artificial *Yellow Book* school of the nineties, then in the ascendancy with Wilde, Yeats, Symons, LeGallienne as high-priests. Alfred Austin had succeeded Tennyson, and altogether it must have seemed to readers not familiar with older writers that poetry was not very much of this world.

Then Housman arrived on this flower-plot scene with his lad made of the stuff of eternal human clay, with the high spirits, the wistfulness, the flesh and blood, dreams and passions known to the English scene for centuries and crying out for portrayal. The scene itself, moreover, was not neglected. Here were bits of description always pertinent to mood and always expressive to the English eye. Here, in fine, was life, and the public which loved poetry was not long in discovering it, as well as many others who had never thought to find it in the medium of verses.

The freshness of vision which characterized this volume never passed away: there were no further volumes to disappoint readers or to beguile them into further hope for still better things, or a return of the old magic. The poet's fate seemed to be that of his athlete dying young, whom he enviously apostrophized:

Now you will not swell the rout
Of lads that wore their honours out,
Runners whom renown outran
And the name died before the man.

Mr Housman devoted himself to scholastic pursuits for thirty years, of a sort calculated to drown the spontaneous outbursts of song which had characterized earlier years. Truly the spirit of man is capable of all things; and only more remarkable than this conversion is the return of the poet to his Parnassian pastures after more than a score of years, which resulted in the recent publication of *Last Poems.* The title, as the author insists, is literal, and we shall hear no more.

It is a return with a difference. The lad is the same, yet changed as all things and persons change, and since all change is obnoxious it cannot be expected that this book should be more satisfactory than other sequels. Something has been lost: only roughly can it be expressed as youth, spontaneity. And something has been added; the trick of the mind shows through. The scholasticism which so long had surrounded the author has been restrained rigorously, but one may guess that while still himself – he could not, indeed, always be rereading his own book – he has conned many times such masters as Burns and Heine, and Uhland.

There is no imitation. Still the Lad sings lustily, and in many cases because he must. But now he knows that he must, and why, and with determination he pursues his ends. This is not to say that there are not occasionally poems as successful as those of the first volume. Many are more nearly perfect, but this very faultlessness is faulty, to the fault-finding at least. Compare for instance the symbolic account of the crucification [sic] in the first book, and the already famous and much-quoted 'Eight O'Clock' of the *Last Poems.*

He stood, and heard the steeple
    Sprinkle the quarters on the morning town.
One, two, three, four, to market-place and people
    It tossed them down.

Strapped, noosed, nighing his hour,
    He stood and counted them and cursed his luck;
And then the clock collected in the tower
    Its strength, and struck.

Here we have a perfection of the means and the substance of poetry which is seldom equalled, and a remorselessness of logic elsewhere which the first book hardly equalled, yet – perhaps it is too carping to say so – the tone does not carry, not so clearly and lightheartedly.

The subjects of the first volume, Jubilee bonfires, village sports of running, cricket, football; rustic murder, the London and Northwestern Railway through the eyes of a countryman, the Shropshire Light Infantry, ploughs, lovers on stiles; the ringing of church bells; the suicide ('The dead are more in muster / At Hughley than the quick') the moonlit road which leads to and from home, are not greatly changed in the *Last Poems*. The same part taken in Nature, the same sense of futile bravery, songs of human soldiers, musings in taverns which embody a philosophy of acceptance:

My lad, no pair of kings our mothers bore;
Our only portion is the estate of man:
We want the moon, but we shall get no more.

And if there is less of love in terms of longing and present blissful uncertainty, the pang is greater of the inevitable, if only anticipated, parting, and the chords struck more plangent. The lines are impeccable and yet sometimes lacking in vigour and savour. Simplicity becomes *simplesse*. They seem just an echo, and as long as we value poetry for its rarity it must be confessed that this book does not add to the reputation of thirty years ago. It is more or less of a complement, but had it been one of half a dozen it must have been less, and it is doubtful whether the original *Shropshire Lad* should survive in its present esteem.

Nevertheless on the basis of these two handfuls of lyrics, Housman has been granted place among the eminent poets of our time and, contingently the great of any time in literature. Certainly his absence from the ranks of capable British poets of the era would make an irretrievable gap, and any of his successors would not have been quite what they are, had he not worked and lived with his Lad, and translated his moods into the universal music of the race to which he belonged.

KATHERINE MANSFIELD

What appears most to have struck the critics who first saluted the work of Miss Katherine Mansfield was its resemblance to that of Chekhov. There soon was a unanimous cry; and now to dismiss her stories so is a postprandial commonplace, though not more defining of the stories themselves than of the speakers' inertness.

Undoubtedly there is usually a basis for these things, outside of preconcertation; and here it is quite as sound as it is obvious. But such generalizations do little to characterize a writer's talent. The influence of Chekhov is becoming evident to greater and less degrees and varying ways, in the most diverse places; and truly, since he is to the short story what Shakespeare is to the poetic drama, the form can never be quite the same again. But in Katherine Mansfield the influence of Chekhov is more than anything else an accidental matter, existing because as a conscious artist she would not forego the advantages of that improved and revolutionizing technique.

By this I mean that the resemblance between Chekhov and one of the two or three writers in that *genre* of our time to approach him, is due to something more than imitation, something more profound than the assumption through long discipleship of the master's outlook. It lies in a realization which her work exhibits of the principle which Goethe enunciated: 'All that happens is a symbol and, by representing itself perfectly, it reveals the significance of all else.' Goethe did not create a form of the short story to illustrate this principle. But Chekhov modulated one which did, perfectly. And for Katherine Mansfield and others who succeed Chekhov, their task has been immeasurably simplified. Without transilient experiment in the arts, as in the sciences, advance is not possible; and this is the contribution of our age to the short story.

This does not mean – in fact it is the whole point of the relation of Miss Mansfield's genius to the great Russian that it does not – that the spirit of Chekhov's individual crisis will invade our best writers henceforth; and still less that his technique will be literally adopted. The individuality of the artist as much as ever will be necessarily his own; but in the short story in proportion as he realizes the possibilities of this principle will his work be modified, coloured by a new spirit.

In Katherine Mansfield (it is perhaps a secret of the concatenation which spells her genius) this new spirit complemented her own. For she was by nature a poet, a lyric poet. And for a lyric poet, in a subtilized way, the principle of Goethe mentioned above, of the universality of the particular when impeccably limned, has always been self-evident.

'I wish, when one writes about things one didn't dramatize them so,' she writes in her journal; and this is more than an index to a struggle toward the subjectivism of her contemporaries. It is the poet struggling with the objective world necessary to the short story writer.

But that objective world meant something different to her than to most artists. For even more than most she continued after growing up to live in childhood. At the times of greatest inspiration, such as the time of her happy marriage, and of the palling tragedy of her brother's death in the war, it was to her childhood experiences, surely consciously, that she turned. And indeed all her work is tinged with something of a childhood radiance. a spirit which finds every detail of the exterior world important, and yet whose observation of these details exists only as a background to be lighted prismatically by mood.

So much is this the case that her world which she created in three short volumes (the last two scarcely added to it) might be taken as the vision of a child seeing every detail and thrust back again and again to surface observation by the enigmatic character of the things it sees. It is a strange world of watches that hate you, stars that say, 'Let's throw something,' palms like 'immense untidy birds' or like 'spiders,' of tiny owls perched and calling, 'More pork; more pork,' of lanterns 'burning softly as if for themselves.'

Yet, as with children, these things do not stay in the mind, they melt, shift into a mood, unforeseeable, poignant, lyric, or suddenly weary. We do not remember these details, however sharply present they may have been at their moment. Yet as by a child they seem to be recorded for love of themselves. One might almost prefigure a naïve faith that somehow these minutiae should matter, should index ineffable inward things, so that when she sees that they do not, she is impelled to the impassioned query which sounds through all her pages, and which may prevent them from quite limning those imponderables she sought.

We see this in an effect of which she may or may not have been conscious, the relation of her London to her New Zealand stories. Her long early residence in the latter place, to say nothing of this sensitiveness to externals might have led one to prophesy surely an emphasis upon scene; yet, for all the vividness of which each story is an example we are given little feeling of 'local colour' in the usual sense. Her people are indigenous anywhere in the best way – as the people of the great creators have been made, to be sure with a less obvious artifice.

They are, however, very much creatures of our most-present age. It was that perhaps, the pressure of the time, which forced the exterior world upon her attention, so that she did not become a poet in the traditional manner. It did more. Hers was too true a soul to become one of those of whom someone says, 'Civilization has driven them mad, and they simply must cry out.' But it did hurt her, and made her heart more tender and her acceptance of futility the more complete, the while questioning was not to be smothered. In how many stories is it not implicit – this question –

'The wind had dropped, and the sun burned more fiercely than ever. Outside the two swing doors there is a thick mass of children like flies at the mouth of a sweet-jar.

'And up, up the hill come the people, with ticklers and golliwogs, and roses and feathers. Up, up they thrust into the light and heat, shouting, laughing, squealing, as though they were being pushed up by something far below, and by the sun far ahead of them – drawn up into the full bright dazzling radiance to ... what?'

The accent is usually her own, but the query has come to be that of our period, and to the traditionally-minded it must seem more tiresome than prototypical Wertherism became. In this author it may be heard again and again, and often as the chief note of the story, as it is in 'The Canary,' which may be compared with Sherwood Anderson's 'I Want to Know Why' and 'I'm a Fool.' The realization comes a little too patly, as though the narrator knew she existed just to say those words, to remind herself of 'something sad in life. It is hard to say what it is. I don't mean the sorrow that we all know, like illness and poverty and death. No, it is something different. It is there, deep down, deep down, part of one, like one's breathing. However hard I work and tire myself I have only to stop to know it is there, waiting. I often wonder if everybody feels the same.'

And 'The Life of Ma Parker' it seems to me should have been a masterpiece, save for the last obvious sentence of the last paragraph:

'There was a wind like ice. People went flitting by, very fast; the men walked like scissors; the women trod like cats. And nobody knew – Nobody cared.'

This, taken from its context as here looks almost as sentimental as the pity lavished on such subjects as that of *Trilby* in novels of the last century. In fact it is more than coincidental that other writers, and to a degree more explicit, show the spirit of our day as still quite incurably *fin de siècle.* It is as if the age took on an added hopelessness on discovering no improvement in itself with the numerical addition to the calendar twenty-five years ago, and determined to be more aggravatedly *fin de siècle* than the nineties.

To turn from enticing conjecture, it is certain that Katherine Mansfield's characters exist to express an attitude to life – 'hideous, revolting, simply revolting.' 'Life is dreadful,' Matilda murmurs (in 'The Wind Blows'), her cheek against her music teacher's tweed shoulder. 'But she does not feel it's dreadful at all. He says something about "waiting" and "marking time" and "that rare thing, a woman," but she does not hear. It is so comfortable ... for ever...

'Suddenly the door opens, and in pops Marie Swainson, hours before her time.'

Now this irruption into the mood is more than one more application of the common knowledge (since Flaubert) that inward experience is considerably a matter of such irruptions. It illustrates the curious brooding of Katherine Mansfield on the unpleasant. For the first girl was merely 'the-girl-before-her,' but this one is particularized by name. If this seem but a niggling and sharp application of her own kind of vision, the premise is upheld also in the following extract from her journal.

'Oct. 1921. I wonder why it should be so difficult to be humble. I do not think I am a good writer; I realize my faults better than anyone else could realize them. I know exactly when I fail. And yet, when I have finished a story and before I have begun another, I catch myself *preening* my feathers. It is disheartening. There seems to be some bad old pride in my heart; a root of it that puts out a thick shoot on the slightest provocation. ... This interferes very much with work. One can't be calm, clear, good, as one must be, while it goes on. I look at the mountains, I try to pray – and I think of something *clever.* It's a kind of excitement within one which shouldn't be there. Calm yourself. Clear yourself. And anything that I write in this mood will be no good; it will be full of *sediment.* If I were well, I would go off by myself somewhere and sit under a tree. One must learn, one must practice to *forget* oneself. I can't tell the truth about Aunt Anne unless I am free to enter her life without self-consciousness. Oh, God! I am divided still, I am bad, I fill in my personal life. I lapse into impatience, temper, vanity, and so I fail as thy priest. Perhaps poetry will help.

'I have just thoroughly cleaned and attended to my fountain pen. If after this it leaks, then it is *no* gentleman!'

One asks, does this and the extract below define a new phase which according to J. Middleton Murry was to come into her work, or is it merely a part of the process necessary before that new cycle? From an unfinished story in 'The Dove's Nest':

'As you have gathered, the Christian names of Mr and Mrs Williams were Gwendolen and Gerald. How well they went together! They sounded married. Gwendolen-Gerald. Gwendolen wrote them, bracketed, on bits of blotting paper, on the backs of old envelopes, on the Stores' catalogue. They looked married.

'Gerald, when they were on their honeymoon, had made an awfully good joke about them. He had said one morning, "I say, had it ever struck you that both our names begin with *G?* Gwendolen-Gerald. You're a *G*," and he had pointed his razor at her – he was shaving – "and I'm a *G*. Two *G*s. Gee-Gee. See?"

'Oh, Gwendolen saw immediately. It was really most witty. Quite brilliant! And so – sweet and unexpected of him to have thought of it. Gee-Gee. Oh, *very* good! She wished she could have told it to people. She had an idea that some people thought Gerald had not a very strong sense of humour. All the more precious for that reason, however.

' "My dear, did you think of it at this moment? I mean – did you just make it up on the spot?"

'Gerald, rubbing the lather with a finger, nodded. "Flashed into my mind while I was soaping my face," he said seriously. "It's a queer thing" – and he dipped the razor into the pot of hot water. – "I've noticed it before. Shaving gives me ideas." It did indeed, thought Gwendolen...'

This is perhaps the nearest to a hint that she could have despised her people. And still there is in her very choice of 'subjects' if not in her treatment of them – neurotics, children, enchained old maids, timid newly wedded pairs, mostly a sense of how though these people may be contemned, she only pities them. In one story, 'The Stranger,' she balances her two recurring types, in the kind, brutally unimaginative husband and the conscious, 'nice' wife, so dispassionately and perfectly, that one finds his intense dislike transferred to the story itself.

This should not be to say that Katherine Mansfield was preoccupied disproportionately with unpleasant things. To do so would be as great an inaccuracy as it could in the case of any of her younger contemporaries. Though sensitive to nearly everything, it was beauty which remained to obsess her; beauty came from the pain-filled alembic. In what other way could she have made into a poem that terrible amusing story, perhaps her masterpiece, 'The Daughters of the Late Colonel'? And, to descend to details, one remembers such things as the description of tired rich Mr Neaves' house as he comes to it. 'And somehow, it seemed to old Mr Neaves that the house and the flowers, and even the fresh marks on the drive were saying, "There is young life here. There are girls –" ' And that bright morning in the breakfast room of the Burnell family in 'At the Bay," with the sea sounding and the sun shining through open windows and the perfectly neat grandmother cutting bread for the waiting father at the table, and the three exquisite blue-clad little girls sedulously carrying the dishes of porridge to the table. It is like a clear, airy water-colour.

Of the application of her almost consciously naïve child-view to her work in general, I have already spoken. Her delight in children as shown in the stories explicitly devoted to them, particularly 'Prelude,' 'At the Bay,' and 'Sun and Moon' led to some of the most beautiful formulizations of this expanse of life which art can show. These stories, the first two of which concern the same family, and which have been spoken of by Rebecca West as portions of one novel, may not be quoted to advantage. But in 'A Married Man's Story' is one of the most complete suggestive adumbrations of a phase of childhood I have ever seen; which at the moment seems to render the first half of *David Copperfield* supererogatory; and here it is given in little more than a page:

'Do you remember your childhood? I am always coming across these marvellous accounts by writers who declare that they remember "everything." I certainly don't. The dark stretches, the blanks, are much bigger than the bright glimpses. I seem to have spent most of my time like a plant in a cupboard. Now and again when the sun shone, a careless hand thrust me out on the window-sill, and a careless hand whipped me in again – and that was all. But what happened in the darkness – I wonder? Did one grow? pale stem ... timid leaves ... white reluctant bud. No wonder I was hated at school. Even the masters shrunk from me. I somehow knew that my soft hesitating voice disgusted them. I knew, too, how they turned away from my shocked, staring eyes. I was small and thin, and I smelled of the shop; my nickname was Gregory Powder. School was a tin building, stuck on the raw hillside. There were dark red streaks like blood in the oozing clay banks of the playground. I hide in the dark passage, where the coats hang, and am discovered there by one of the masters. "What are you doing there in the dark?" His terrible voice kills me; I die before his eyes. I am standing in a ring of thrust-out heads; some are grinning, some look greedy, some are spitting. And it is always cold. Big crushed-up clouds press across the sky; the rusty water in the school tank is frozen; the bells sound numb. One day they put a dead bird in my overcoat pocket. I found it just when I reached home. Oh, what a strange flutter there was at my heart, when I drew out that terribly soft, cold little body, with the legs thin as pins and the claws wrung. I sat on the back door step in the yard and put the bird in my cap. The feathers round the neck looked wet, and there was a tiny tuft just above the closed eyes that stood up, too. How tightly the beak was shut! I could not see the mark where it was divided. I stretched out one wing and touched the soft, secret down underneath; I tried to make the claws curl round my little finger. But I didn't feel sorry for it – no! I wondered. The smoke from our kitchen chimney poured downwards, and flakes of soot floated – soft, light in the air. Through a big crack in the cement yard a poor looking plant with dull, reddish flowers had pushed its way. I looked at the dead bird again. ... And that is the first time I remember singing – rather ... listening to a silent voice inside a little cage that was me.'

The last sentence typifies a common tendency in this and other modern work, to a sort of symbolic imagism. And one still fails to see that it is an improvement on Chekhov's somehow mysteriously putting the object or fact before us without symbols of any sort. – And then, figures are unplentiful enough that they are (soon wearisomely) repeated in this and the other writer.

And of course the whole quotation illustrates her attitude as I have all along been trying to define it; and in doing so adumbrates the reason that she did not try the novel. It was not because her experience did not provide her with material enough. Notwithstanding the exact rightness which will give permanence to the work which she left, it is doubtful whether her experience up to the time of her death should have offered themes for any real addition to the number of her written short stories; but she certainly did not lack material for a novel or novels. Nor, I think, was her poetic approach the reason for her not attempting more sustained work. The reason was, surely, a knowledge that in being sincere every mood would necessarily play *obbligato* to her pervading weary questioning, the negative conviction that life had passed everybody by. In the words of the artist in 'Daphne': 'It seemed to me suddenly so preposterous that two people should be as happy as we were and not be happier.'

There, perhaps, is the clue to her genius.

FREDERICK PHILIP GROVE

A Canadian of Canadians

In the development of America one of the most curious of phenomena is the fervour – the completely and practically manifested patriotism, of adoptive citizens. We are speaking here of what may be called the genuine article, not of the self-complacency of the immigrant who has made his pile in this country, genuine as it may be and worthy as he may be. And one of the most outstanding cases of this, one that could not be more genuine, is that of Frederick Philip Grove, who was born and 'educated' for the most part, in Europe, and who is now and has been for a score of years or more, a Canadian of Canadians.

In contradistinction to the many able and well-equipped men who have come from Europe to play a part in this country, Mr Grove's whole bent, his utmost energies, appear to have been directed to making himself a Canadian, making others Canadians, all to the glory of Canada with whose possibilities he became enamoured. Thus he stands out even among the artists and writers upon whom the spiritual leadership of the country depends; and his books, aside from purely literary considerations, have an immediate value and interest which can scarcely be estimated justly.

As to the books themselves, they number five: *Over Prairie Trails* (1922); *The Turn of the Year* (1923); *Settlers of the Marsh*, a novel (1925); *A Search for America* (1927); *Our Daily Bread*, a novel (1928). To get some idea of what manner of man Grove is, we should consider first *A Search for America*, as it deals with the early life of its author, and in particular and most exhaustively with his Americanization. His family was a Swedish-Scottish one, of wealth, and he was given every advantage of luxury and of training. The youth responded to this culture with an ambition to 'master nothing less than all human knowledge.' Thus though his energies were scattered, and he became something of a man about town – a somewhat Faustian one, it is to be presumed – he was not idle. He says of this period:

> My work lacked simply that measure of co-ordination which might have made it useful for the purpose of earning a living when the necessity arose. I mastered, for instance, five modern languages, wrote an occasional tract in tolerable Latin, and read Homer and Plato with great fluency before I was twenty-two. I dabbled in Mathematics and in Science, and even attended courses in Medicine. Theology and Jurisprudence were about the only two fields of human endeavour which I shunned altogether.

At the age of twenty-four, when he was reaching a position to gratify his ambitions, his family suddenly lost its wealth. For some time he endeavoured to continue his studies together with his habits of a young man about town (he knew some of the greatest artists and writers of Paris rather as a patron than as a student), but the two roles would not be combined, and he decided to emigrate to America. Thus we find him landing at Montreal, a slim youth of over six feet in height, with the Scandinavian fairness, with the diffidence of the stranger and the courteous bearing of one accustomed to dealing with his inferiors – and with almost no money. Obviously, an interesting time awaits him.

It is in Toronto that his search for work is rewarded finally with a position as busboy in a restaurant, from which he is promoted to waiter. As soon as he had risen to the height of this profession he was induced, partly by the mendacity of a fellow-waiter, to go to New York. The episode of the waitership is described at length, and the difference in manners of European and American indicated (here everybody, even the friendly ones, seemed bent on 'rubbing it in'); also the difference in *mores:* his fellow waiters were not above graft. He perceives, to his own alarm, a great truth regarding the relation of the immigrant to crime:

> Hunger, despair, and helpless loneliness are strange prompters. I had begun to think less harshly of him who sins against society. ... The path of the immigrant is sown with temptation: temptation of a spiritual kind – he is tempted to charge all his troubles to some incomprehensible vice in the very constitution of the new country or the new society into which he came. His need and distress may

> become extreme. If he sins, the society against which he sins is foreign to him, just as truly as he is foreign to it. What he sees of American morals is often, too often, not what shows them at their best.

A steady sense of values is needed by the average immigrant to maintain his integrity in the face of such conditions as are found in Canada, not to mention the cities of the United States, where the causes of foreign delinquency require such study.

In New York Mr Grove became a book-agent, selling cheap 'sets.' But he was not a successful canvasser, because his conscience forbade his closing a sale when he felt that the prospective customer could not afford to buy the books. This difficulty was overcome when he began selling sets at fifteen hundred dollars and up to moneyed men; but after varied adventures alone and in sales team throughout the country, he discovers that this is nothing less than a swindle: the cheap sets have been merely rebound to sell at the exorbitant figures.

The section which follows is called 'The Depths,' and in it we find Mr Grove hoboing about the southern states and the ranches of the Mississippi River. He was quite destitute, except for the things the river brought him: one day a large tea kettle, the next a pumpkin, corn, a well preserved ham which in his state of ill-health made him ill. Few people does he meet in his wanderings now. One hermit keeps him a day or two to get over his illness, and says no word until Grove mentions that it is about time for him to be moving. Then he says: 'I reckon.'

Finally his health breaks, but providentially he falls into the hands of a country doctor who calls in specialists and at length puts him on his feet with a job. But there follow more wanderings, riding on the rods of trains, work as a harvest hand, before he settles and finds his niche. It is a story which is not only typical of America, but in a sense universal.

None the less the book is not wholly successful. With a wonderful mass of material, and with the greatest sincerity and impartiality, there is shown a lack of artistic power which is all the more strange and almost impossible at first to define. One comes to the conclusion that the author depends, as nearly all the autobiographers in history have done, upon the fact that his story is true, and does not devote enough pains to making it seem true. Thus many a tawdry romance of an underworld the authors have never seen will appear truer than Grove's story, in its rendering. Possibly the very wealth of the material, the wealth of erudition of the author, has made simple directness and concreteness more difficult. The language is often abstract and the characters not fully visualized. But on the whole, lacking this artistic perfection which is the rarest thing in biography, the book is a notable one.

A Search for America occupies in Grove's experience only the first two or three years which he spent on this continent. He finally took up the profession of teaching in Manitoba, to which he has been devoted more or less ever since, for a score of years. A more valuable person for the Canadianization of foreign-born children would be hard to find. All the time he was writing, and in 1922 his first book was published, *Over Prairie Trails.* The present reviewer finds this the most satisfactory book which Mr Grove has given us. It is not a novel, nor is it even meant to form a connected narrative. Yet it has an epic zest and largeness which is the rarest of qualities. It is the story of winter drives over the prairie which Grove made every weekend from the place where he taught school to the town where his wife and his little girl lived, and where the former also taught. The drives were some thirty miles each way, and the trail was for the most part difficult and almost impassible with snow. Two horses pulled the cutter, Peter and Dan; they deserve a place with Black Beauty and all the horses pictured in fiction. But Mr Grove's whimsical naturalism in picturing these horses is surpassed by his comprehensiveness, his grasp of the whole sweep and of the smallest of minutiae of the prairie. In this respect he is truly unrivalled. There is no mood of the weather, no weed or flower or grass which escapes him. He is convinced that the kingdom of heaven lies all around us and his book is 'like a botany book on fire,' as Professor Phelps says in his introduction to the volume which followed it, *The Turn of the Year.* There is of course the eloquence of the devotee of 'Nature,' but it is based upon the naturalism of the observer, the man of erudition to whom everything is interesting. And underlying these things are the human values: will he succeed in making this heroic drive to meet his wife and child? Often in the account of these very real blizzards, with their shifting trails, their desolation, the prairie horses chasing ahead of his team, loth to get off the trail and sink in the deep snow, the cold, the silence, while 'stripped of all accidentals, the universe swings on its way,' the anxiety – often it looks as though the destination will not be reached. And once, on the last trip of the book, he does stop at a farmhouse halfway, to continue in the morning. *Over Prairie Trails* is a superb evocation of the prairie winter, sketched in appropriately huge strokes.

The Turn of the Year is not so successful. Its material is more various, consisting of essays and sketches of western life with emphasis on natural phenomena; but it is lacking in the unity and force which characterized the first book. It does remind one, however, of what a beautiful novel Mr Grove could write with characters suited to the atmosphere he can paint so well, and with the place made into one of the characters.

It is surprising in that case to find Mr Grove's novels on the whole so unsatisfactory. *Settlers of the Marsh* is powerfully conceived, the honesty and forthright intentions of the author are apparent, yet the book as a whole misses that finality of effect which it should have. In some instances it is downright awkward and childish, as when every few pages we are shown the depravity of the 'fallen woman' the hero has married by the fact that she plasters her face with powder. One cannot help conclude that the novel is a strange harness to Mr Grove's talent. He has to leave so many things unsaid, and forego the advantage of so many branches of his varied learning, that the finished novel must seem a very fragmentary thing.

The same things hold true to a lesser degree of *Our Daily Bread*, Mr Grove's latest novel, just published. The conventions of novel-writing have taken so much of his attention that the novel itself seems to have been less fully conceived than, one feels sure, it was. We have here the prairie farmer, the pioneer, and his fate. His own seed turn aside from what has been his great purpose. ...

With this theme, as fine as any presented to the novelist, Mr Grove has not been wholly successful. He writes faithfully, he knows what he is writing about, one feels that he knows the characters from birth. But the combination of the whole fails to glow. *Our Daily Bread* is a book which deserves and will get a wide reading, and while it is not that prairie novel which we expect Mr Grove will give us, his work as a whole is a definite contribution to Canadian tradition.

THE POETICAL WORKS OF WILFRED CAMPBELL

It is an impressive-looking book, this volume of the *Poetical Works of Wilfred Campbell*, quiet, dignified, and solid; it suggests that we are going to be able in a few years to have a shelf of our own 'standard poets' which in format at least, including the involuntary influence of format on the literary mind, need not avoid comparison with our shelves of English and American classics. The shelves should be separate, however, for though Campbell is a classic he is a Canadian classic, and not to be associated without disservice to himself and to us with those of our neighbours.

This is not to say that attempts should not be made to relate his art with generally accepted canons. Such an attempt I mean to make, in the opinion that only in this way can we chance to apprise ourselves of the relative value of our writers. But there is for us an absolute value in a poet such as Campbell, which shall continue to be, even when and if it is transmuted into one chiefly historical. Students of comparative literature may be reminded that the early chapters of histories of literature contain the names of writers which we need not stop to identify with the work behind them. The worth of the latter to any but the curious in other countries is negligible, and yet the historian and indeed the nation in general may well look back in gratitude and pride to their work, finding in it early clear expressions of national phases, which later if not more gifted writers in more auspicious times were to make universally valuable. Rabelais is precious to any reader anywhere (any to whom he *is* precious, that is; the reader's nationality makes no difference); but Antoine de la Sale is valuable only to students of that age of his country.

So I think it may eventuate with the reputation of Wilfred Campbell. A diffidence is appropriate in us who are not yet posterity, but it is safe to express a comparative certainty that he will always be a Canadian classic. Possibly save for students he will not be for export, but among us his value will be stable until the remote time at which his country has changed fundamentally from its past self. Then he will be looked back to by the historiographer and the scholar as one of the earliest builders. And the anthologist of the future, that arbitrator whose eye poets try to catch and to placate, will surely include a poem or two of his – possibly 'Wood Lyric' or the equally famous 'Earth,' or 'August' or 'The Journey.' But my personal surmise would have me name for survival

The Earth Spirit

Down these golden uplands I
Move with sunny wind and sky,
Where the ghosts of waters are,
To the gates of dusk and star.

And I know that as I go,
She whose bosom is the snow
Of the birch and aspen tree,
Dreams these sunny dreams with me.

She whose glance and gleam of hair
Are the ruddy spinning rare
Of the gold glint of the sun
In the wood when day is done;

She whose inner speech is heard
In the hush of wind and bird,
And whose soul is as a star
Cradled where the hill-lakes are.

II

I have quoted those stanzas in that place as an example of the choice achievement of this poet, which, with my high opinion of it, I would not appear to underrate in any effort to indicate my impression of – not to evaluate – the nature of his art and the personality with which it is imbued. Possibly to many staunch readers it will seem that it is a little hasty and anticipatory to reduce this full volume to a page or two in the anthologies of a century hence. But if we will examine Campbell's work in its entirety we shall find that much of it is already obviously dated and, so far as intrinsic vitality is concerned, best forgotten.

The course of his life patently lent a considerable influence to his work. Most decisive was the fact of his being born a clergyman's son, which gave him the advantage of an early contact with the culture of his father's generation and, as well, decided to a degree the subjects of his writing. At first he was preoccupied almost entirely, as he was to be always pre-eminently, by exterior nature. So his father's periodical change of residence chanced to serve him. He had been born at Berlin (Kitchener now) and the rolling and not unpicturesque but tilled and settled country there could not have satisfied his feeling for primitive and rather obvious beauty, as it was fed at Wiarton, in the Lake District, on an arm of Georgian Bay, before Colpoy Bay, with small lakes in the seven miles between the town and the rugged headlands of Huron.

In the first volume, *Lake Lyrics*, 1889, he attempts to picture these scenes. Without, save perhaps in the exquisite pastel, 'Indian Summer' and 'Canadian Folksong,' reaching the level of his best work, his average here is not below the average of his work as a whole. These poems were more than setting-up exercises for later more arduous labours. They would possibly not have been, if Campbell had continued his development in the measure of their promise. When we compare the early work of the great English poets with that of their prime, it is evident that much has been foreshadowed which the first readers could not have precisely expected. But *Lake Lyrics* gives us the essence of Campbell's poetic gift, in as clear expressions on occasion as it was ever to have. His love for nature generally was not to become greatly deeper, nor the expression of it much more felicitous, though the modicum of observed detail was to be augmented in study. His love of humanity generally, on the other hand, is, it is true, merely indicated, and so is his reluctance to bother with human character in particular, in an exception proving the rule, 'Dan'l and Mat,' an obvious failure. And there is 'Lazarus,' a good conception which inspired treatment might have raised to distinction. One can say that he knows Campbell's work on appraising the best of his first book.

But, it is true, this first volume does not give us Campbell's mystic feeling and his sense of the grotesque and the arabesque – to borrow from the original title of Poe's tales – which afterward so frequently lured his pen. There is power in 'The Dread Voyage' and in 'The Last Ride.' This poem is indeed fine, as may be seen in such lines as

Who are the mimes of the air
That wept on the woe of our flight,

That chanted a bitter despair
To the dark haunted heart of the night?

or

And the hoarse great tongues of the tide,
As it beat on the black of that place.

And its fineness might have reached the pitch of absolute beauty had its intensity in the poet's mind passed over into the restraint and swiftness (partly due to chariness with figures) which marks Coleridge's 'Rime of the Ancient Mariner.' Again there is 'Sir Lancelot,' one of the best, if we allow its conventional point of view and its obscuring metaphors, while 'Unabsolved, a Dramatic Monologue' shows an unsuspected tendency to go on writing without saying much. But of the flower of this type of work (on the side of the more human preoccupation) is to be found 'The Mother,' while on the side of phantasy 'The Dreamers' excels, a sombre vision beautiful and enigmatic as its title. It is unfortunately too long for quotation, but this is the first stanza:

They lingered on the middle heights
    Betwixt the brown earth and the heaven;
They whispered, 'We are not the night's,
    But pallid children of the even.'

While in what may be called the staple nature poem, there are such fine things as 'An August Reverie,' 'In Spring Fields,' 'In a June Night,' 'On a Summer Shore' – in which a definite personal feeling quickens description – and the fine sonnet, 'On the Shore.'

In such title as these and as 'Winter,' 'Dusk,' 'Autumn,' 'The Rideau River,' 'How One Winter Came to the Lake Region,' we gain a hint of the nature of the source of the fount of Campbell's inspiration. He is drawn to express himself on set subjects, to write 'occasional poems' almost preponderantly. In the preface to 'Collected Poems,' published in 1905, he cites Goethe as an exemplar in simplicity of language and subject matter, and if the influence of that master is not too obvious, it was not entirely lost; particularly in this matter of the occasional poem. Goethe wrote innumerable verses of this type; but Campbell appears not to have seen that there are varieties of occasional poems, too. There is the poem whose subject has welled up in the poet's heart, as much parcel of him as tears are of his natural constitution. And there is the poem which is found outside of the poet, chiefly its ornamentation, and, of course, inevitably the choice itself being his part in it. I mean that Campbell looked at minutiae and generalities of nature, and decided that this or that would do for the subject of a poem, instead of simply saying what was in his heart, as is the way of the great poets, and using nature as setting and atmosphere. 'For all good poetry,' to quote Wordsworth's 'Observations,' is 'the spontaneous overflow of powerful feelings.'

It is only this capacity for deep feeling which warrants a poet's allowing factitious and exterior phenomena to come into his work. It does not seem of course to make much difference what subject Thomas Hardy takes for a lyric, but the truth is that the subject is already within him, so that he merely allows this or that external circumstance to annotate it. Poets may make men witty, as according to the Baconian tag, but the consummation results from something a little different from wit in the poet himself. A sublimation, since neither word is appropriate; but occasional poems are usually *prima facie* exhibitions of wit, Campbell's always such. One of the worst examples which could be cited is 'Stella Flammarium: An Ode to Halley's Comet,' even to its title. It tempts to perverse quotation, to show how bad a poem of Campbell's could be, but the reader may verify my impression on page 285 of the present edition. There is the jejuneness of 'Sebastien Cabot' and the celebratory poems generally. (It is pedantic maybe, writing of a day of 'poetic license,' to interject the plaint that 'splendour' is not a verb, as used here.) And in 'Out of Pompeii' there is with the usual simplicity, ineptitude, and banality. Even the best poems, as 'Wind' and the fine realization of 'The Soul's House' suffer a little from this method, playing with an idea, embroidering it usually, though less in these cases, by the unrestrained use of metaphor. 'Earth' is justly famed, and in it there is more than usual excuse for bringing in Egypt, Greece, etc., and surrounding the subject with associations which may or may not otherwise add to its beauty. But when one comes to such a noble and profoundly emotional piece as 'The Bereavement of the Fields,' the elegy to Lampman, one may well cease cavilling and let those lines roll through the spirit, reminding oneself that it is not the occasional poem with which one finds fault, but the too frequently uninspired use of it. It all comes back to Wordsworth, defining the distinction of his own work: 'That the feeling therein developed gives importance to the action and situation, and not the action and situation to the feeling.'

III

In this matter of the occasional poem I have forsaken the orderly treatment of Campbell's successive books in the search for examples to be found throughout his work. A concern with his relation to his time, with the disadvantages and ameliorations of the Victorian age, brings us back. As *Lake Lyrics* merely hinted at the mystical Campbell, who spoke out more clearly, as clearly as is possible to mystics, in *The Dread Voyage and Other Poems,* so this latter volume scarcely hints at the existence of a celebrant civic and didactic Campbell, who was to attain his fullness, qualitatively, in the *Beyond the Hills of Dream* volume and, thereafter quantitatively as well, through *Collected Poems, Sagas of Vaster Britain,* and *Posthumous Poems.*

Undoubtedly the Victorian age influenced Wilfred Campbell strongly, beyond reminiscences mellow and frequent – frequently banal too, it may be added – to the point of occasional brief plagiarisms: 'life's unresting sea' (Holmes in his verse is as much a Victorian as any who lived within the Empire), 'far-flung,' 'splendid world' and much stereotyped metaphor, clichés, 'Mid all the world's loud fray,' and so forth. 'Bygone murmurs are in my ears,' he says; but they are in the ears of all writers, and the few who eschew them wholly will never be either popular or classics. No, it is mainly not a matter of plagiarism in which the Victorians influenced him adversely, but his choice of them as the chief treasure-store of his material. He could not of course escape the onus of his age, but had he cared as greatly for say the Elizabethans, more permanent work would have eventuated; there would have been an improvement even if he had turned a sympathetic ear to the *Yellow Book* school in London which in the time of his youth was engaged in a negation of Victorianism in its chiefest haunt. But sympathies of course go by favour rather than by logic. Campbell was constituted as he was. Yet, impermanent as its more blatant exemplars have proved, the current London school would have brought to him a balance which he sorely needed.

As it is, he is scarcely within the tradition, but too obviously following it. He is a Victorian after the time. He should have used that age as a springboard from which to dive to new seas. Or, if the figure is extreme, he should have entwined threads of the Victorian fabric through a woof of his own pattern. It is a matter of associations. One need not quite accept the dictum of the French Dadaists of our own day that aesthetics exemplify the power of a stronger mind over a weaker (where then would be the many cases such as Goethe's admiration, even emulation, of *The Vicar of Wakefield?*) But undoubtedly suggestion has much to do with literary art. As certain words awake certain responses and emotions remaining the same demand the same stimuli, it is not only inevitable that good literature should owe to tradition, but reminiscence of earlier work has been recognized as a legitimate effect, even when it passes to plagiarism of those great plagiarists we name the classics. So that when we find a poet wanting, it may be because he has not seemed to borrow incidently through his predecessors, water from the great well of life. This, as shown in the case of Whitman, is not a fortunate matter for the poet, though it may eventuate as such for his fame. Though, otherwise, it may be that he has not gone to the well of life at all, but only dipped his cup into the pails of other men. And essentially it cannot be glossed that this is the case of Campbell.

He was widely read, and his technique displays the influence of no single predecessor, which was all to the good. The same applies equally to his thought and subject matter. But the gain in his case is less, for if he did not look at things wholly in the light, say, of Shelley's vision, he did not look at them either through eyes of his own. It was no case of imitation, but simply that he reacted to the conventional stimuli in the conventional way, supplying a norm of Victorian opinion and taste in verse.

His best nature poetry is saved from this composite influence in so far as he had a more or less fresh field of phenomena to witness, in the landscape of Canada. But when he came to write of individuals, events and tendencies of the age, we see traces of the fallacy which our generation, having swept it aside, regards as pathetic. He accepted with humble but not unpleased responsibility the conception of the poet as a 'prophet.' Browning and Morris were prophets, why should Canada not require one? One of his recent reviewers remarked that he felt the need of filling the gap left by the death of Tennyson; and certainly his 'Victoria,' 'Sebastien Cabot,' 'Commemoration Ode,' and his civic celebrations without exception give evidence of the responsibility.

In this kind of writing the most comprehensive emotion is necessary. But despite the civilizing of ages, and the subjection for ages to a communal life, the spirit of man has continued to put its most beautiful expression into personally felt emotions, lyric cries wrung from the individual soul, or conceptions of uniquely living characters, as in Shakespeare and Hardy. Whitman almost alone succeeded in imparting a genuine emotion for his brothers generally; and how often even he is unsuccessful and half-convincing! It may be called the self-centered imagination of man as a race, but the feeling for humanity as a whole is never so clear and strong as for individuals; and even when it is conspicuous it may be referred to personal issues.

Since this is man's constitution, the communal feeling had best be very deftly manipulated to appear authentic (appearing is necessary to being in literature), much less to live as poetry, even when the writer is plainly sincere, as Campbell was. It is only his obvious belief in his preoccupation which makes possible the reading of this type of his work. Tennyson had a touch in these matters equalled by few. He was the laureate *par excellence.* And since even Tennyson's political obsessions have come to seem a little fatuous, Campbell is at a great disadvantage through choosing so directly to emulate him.

It is not necessary to quote these now official-sounding verses, in which the tendency became stronger and stronger to pat Man on the head for his 'Eternal possibility ... to rise to nobler futures, loftier peaks of golden sunrise visions, climbing on to those vast vistas of the ideal man.' The many examples speak in a single tone. In some of his better pieces it is as insistent as elsewhere. 'An August Reverie' ends with (for a poet) an anomalous glorification of Thought, while 'In a June Night' with its fine apostrophe to Beauty makes her practically useful, as lifting 'the heart of man to higher planes of strength and greatness.' It is scarcely fair possibly to recall stanzas written in a hectic time, such as this, unrivalled as it is in our author's output. It is from 'Our Dead':

We are either on God's side or evil's,
    We are either perjured or true –
And that, which we set out to do in the first place,
    That must we do.

But in truth, for all his acceptance of it, Wilfred Campbell inveighed against his time with a frequency the casual reader might overlook. That was probably just, since though he glorified it he suffered from its pressure. In a different age, which is to say a different place – since mid-Victorianism reigned in Canadian cities of his youth and maturity and in the New England he inhabited as a clergyman for three years –

he might have realized a different self. 'The spirit and not the form make earth's literature,' he wrote, but had the spirit he sought to embody and evoke been an original one it might have led him to fresher modes of utterance. In 'The Lyre Degenerate' we find his expressing an obtuse vision. 'The literature of the soul of nature as found in the great poets is inspiring; but the decadent worship of beast, gnat, and straddle-bug in the animal story and the artificial nature-verse of to-day is degrading. It is time that men of thought and spirit regenerate the world of America from its present materialistic slough with its consequent superficial cult of neo-paganism.' And he sings:

Vanished the golden Homer,
  Vanished the great god Pan,
Vanished the mighty mind of Greece,
  The ancient visions of man.

Gone are the mighty moderns,
  Hands that swept the keys,
That ran the splendid gamut of dream
  Of life's deep harmonies.

Dead are the lofty dreamers,
  The true and the wise of earth,
Who stirred the spirits of yearning men
  And gave new impulse birth.

It is not necessary to defend the animal story and the artificial nature-verse, beyond which apparently he could not see, nor to name names, such as Hudson's, to value the preciousness of man's late realization of continuity, and all that it has meant in the shaping spirit of the arts. The lament for the unapproachable past is perennial, and it is not surprising that Campbell indulged in it. But it is a little surprising that he should with such reposeful confidence let it appear in the light of day. It was the accepted standards of his time which made him take the prophet's role for the reverse of its actuality.

IV

In this half-unwilling adjustment I am persuaded that we find the essence of Wilfred Campbell's gift. His ideals were high, and all his surroundings and the influence of the literature then looked upon as the last word in human genius, urged him to a millenial outlook. He sought the realization of his ideals and moral concepts vicariously, in song, not satisfied, as the great poets usually have been, to accept, even embrace, life itself, maintaining a fine integrity, to let its 'uplift' derive from its own essence.

It is true that he appealed in 'The Heart of Song' for immediacy of inspiration:

How can we strike the lyre of life,
And sound the future's battle-strife
  Unless our hearts be vibrant too?

And this is scarcely contradicted by 'The Betrayed Singer,' the plaint of a singer who came 'through the world, the world of grim to-day,' and which ends,

How long, O life, this mighty ill,
  This reign of hate? How long
Permit to dree their evil weird
  Earth's murderers of Song?

But such poems are only more nearly explicit than his work in general. Some strange vision or insight had made him see life and humanity as essentially prosaic, and accordingly he sought in metaphor, natural phenomena, and 'big' subjects a compensation. He only half remembered the

dreams the gods
Do send to kill the common ways of earth,
And make all else but drear and dull and bleak.
(Lancelot)

Remembered wholly, the dreams would have shaped a great gift. Remembered as they were, they are responsible for the faculty which we find in him. Unforgotten but unshaped in memory, they served merely to blind him to the beauty of common life, so that he took refuge, now in natural minutiae, now in blatant generalities of moral and social and political import. Yet this unblamable disability would not keep him from making fine poems of such conceits as that of 'The Dryad,' effecting a fusion of fancifulness and good honest fancy. The yearning of maladjustment and aversion from life is shown in 'The Higher Kinship,' which I quote in full:

Life is too grim with anxious eating care
  To cherish what is best. Our souls are scarred

By daily agonies, and our conscience marred
By petty tyrannies that waste and wear.
Why is this human fate so hard to bear?
Could we but live with hill-lakes silver-starred,
Or where the eternal silence leaneth toward
The awful front of nature, waste and bare,
Then might we, brothers to the lofty thought
And inward self-communion of her dream,
Into that closer kin with love be brought
Where mighty hills and woods and waters, wan,
Moon-paved at midnight, or godlike at dawn,
Hold all earth's aspirations in their gleam.

This aversion it was, I think, which, unconscious as it must have been, led him to seem to avoid individuality. Few volumes of the bulk of this one have so little of psychological idiosyncrasy, even so little broadly personal. It seems that the only individuals who interested him were those from whom he would wring a sermonized poem. And this brings us to the root of the matter. He had himself no new point of view, in which to relate individuals and experience. 'There is no complex where the spirit rules,' he wrote, and taking the psychoanalytical meaning of 'complex,' we find an application in his reluctance to concern himself with the personal and immediate. It must have seemed petty to him, and he would have contemned the modern novelist and his concerns deriving from James and Flaubert.

V

Until now we have been attempting to consider definitely our author's outlook and the basis of his art; a task in which it is easy to become too exact, for nothing is more certain than that no poet has embodied the ideal in his respect, even if any critic has conceived it. The ideal changes each decade and at any time its protagonists are apt to apply their conceptions of it too stringently to its embodiments of a generation earlier. But only by checking up the debit side of the ledger can we arrive at a just estimate.

Campbell's conception of his art may have been all wrong, and his art itself somewhat appliqué, but that could not manacle his sincerity. The sonnet just quoted may be cited. Nor could it keep him from occasional achievements which on all counts must be regarded as very fine. The initial *Lake Lyrics* contains a piece, 'Old Voices,' perhaps most clearly characteristic – if that is not an anomalous term – of his more personal effort. It is not great poetry, being somewhat Longfellow, but honest, adequate. Later he was to do better, as in 'Return No More,' in which the apparent rococo touch serves only to show how consummate it is:

> Return no more, O splendid sun,
> Sweet days come back no more:
> Bring back no more the budding hours,
> The springtime to my door.
>
> The calling bird, the waking brook
> Make mock upon mine ear:
> For she who loved them with me then
> Went out with yesteryear.
>
> Fold, fold the year for aye in snows,
> Howl, Winter, by my door:
> For she, my rose, my bloom of life,
> Is snow for evermore.

And there is the fine realization of 'The Journey':

> The wind of the day blows downward
> From the moor and the far lone height;
> And sinks to rest on the brooding breast
> Of the hushed and mothering night.
>
> The river sweeps from the mountain
> To find its peace in the sea;
> But O, my heart, thou must yearn on
> To all eternity.
>
> Restless, unsatisfied, longing,
> Evermore doomed to roam;
> For thou has gone on a journey long
> To those hills of the soul's far home.

'The Soul's House,' on the adjacent theme, should be read with this. Campbell's search for simplicity of language in these best pieces is well justified, but if it saved him from the meretricious purple patch, it also meant that he is rememberable by fewer fine single lines than almost any other of our poets. There are a few: 'Standing apart, with sad, incurious gaze,' 'Only the winds of unremembering blow,' 'And all the night was music-stirred,' 'One by one the lonely stars came out,' and 'Over the meres the wintry moon looked down,' 'While far, blue, fading hills in mists elude my sight.' This latter is from 'Autumn,' a couple of stanzas of which I must quote, for they catch a mood, and with a delicate precision which is rare:

How often, in the still, rich frosted days,
　Down the slow hours of some tranced afternoon,
Have my feet wandered in a mad sweet maze,
　Hunting the wind, that, like some haunting tune,
　Peopled with memories all the great, gold swoon
Of rustling woodlands, streams and leafy ways,
　Ever eluding, fluting, sweet, before
　Fading to rest at last in gold-green leafy core.

Far out beside some great, hill-cradled stream,
　Winding along in sinuous blue for miles,
By tented elms, in fields that sleep and dream,
　Warm marsh-lands where the warm sun slopes and smiles,
　Where through the haze the harsh grasshopper files
His rasping note, the pallid asters gleam,
　And golden-rod flames in the smoky light,
　While far, blue, fading hills in mist elude my sight.

It is in full consciousness of the risk involved that I venture to name what are for me Campbell's three best poems. 'The Earth-Spirit' which I quoted at the beginning of this article should share that distinction with 'The Mystery' and the first of the two 'Night' sonnets – 'The Mystery' perhaps as much as anything because it is so divorced from superimposed values, and evokes so well the pure spirit of poetry for which its author so frequently tried:

When autumn's silence tranced the skies,
　And all life held its breath,
Unto Rosanna's lips and eyes
　Came the white moth of death –

That moth whose wings are feathered light,
　From out oblivion's deep,

With magic pinions, petalled white,
   Of folded sleep on sleep –

And fluttered dim and vague and grey,
   Above her lips and brow:
And other beauties gild life's day
   With other glories now.

From earth's hushed pallor of the morn,
   And love's dim trance of night
From out the realms of sleep, reborn,
   Fell on her soft and white,

With those pale dreams of old which tame
   The tide of the heart's wild will:
And all that mask of love became
   A mystery white and still.

Night

I hear the drip, drip of the rain to-night
Outside my window, and the querulous wind,
That moans so piteous, like a feeble mind,
Crooning its sorrow in the gusty light.
I hark to voices of the dark's affright –
A.nature-sadness man hath not divined –
And dream strange woes unknown to humankind –
The anguish of the universal blight.

O Night, wild, troubled brother, Thou and I
Are one in sympathy of conscious pain.
I read life's anguish in thy strife of rain
And weird wind-voices. In thine hours that fly,
On raven wings, I dream the years that fall,
The dull, blind years that surely silence all.

In defining a poet's limitations one should not be blind to what he was within them. We find Campbell unable always to find a subject within himself, and compelled to take one from exterior nature and decorate it as best he might; or turning to careless journalization of the grand manner in pseudo-laureate attempts, in both falling sometimes into ineptitude and banality, and failing through both, as Wordsworth did not, to realize a particular interest in his kind, even one which like Wordsworth's should be

> not verily
> For their own sakes, but for the fields and hills
> Where was their occupation and abode.

But there remains a residuum of soundness, honesty, and beauty which, though its best examples may be comparatively few, have earned him a sure place in Canadian literature.

THE POETRY OF ARCHIBALD LAMPMAN

Though a new and perhaps final volume of the selected poems of Archibald Lampman has recently appeared, his work is of the sort which does not depend upon seasonal notice. More, perhaps, than that of any other Canadian poet, it is objective; and his vignettes of the outward Canadian scene will always have a present value, if an historic one. Indeed Lampman wrote of natural circumstance with such care in observation, such faithfulness of tone and almost submissiveness of mood, that his readers might be excused for forgetting or scarcely perceiving the definite relation he bore to the life and the thought of his time in general. We see in the admirable introduction by his friend and fellow-poet, Duncan Campbell Scott, that his life was not without storm and stress, and yet for the majority of poetry-lovers his name evokes clear and tranquil pictures of the Canadian countryside.

Long furrows, steaming horses in the sun, a stump shorn of surrounding grass, quaint crows filling the forest with din, pines – 'tall slim priests of storm' – snowbirds like tossing spray, piping frogs, the nearness of spring sounds, beardlike rows of icicles below cabin eaves, the eternal little speedwell in the grass, the vesper-sparrow's song, the roar of rapids in the dark, the path of the moon across water, the wild raspberry, blueberry, juniper, spikenard, trees and their shadows, the lift of hills, the peace of lakes, drive of rivers, 'the wind, the world-old rhapsodist,' and again the cherry cheeks of lumberjacks and teamsters, the squeaking runners of sleighs bearing logs and cordwood!

Of these matters, with the undertone or obbligato of his own moods, Archibald Lampman formed his poems. It was Canada, reproduced in a spirit sensitive and open to new impressions, rendered with unassuming artistic certainty. So clearly was this the case that recognition was not long in coming, and the best of incentives, the regard of his fellow-workers. 'Lampman never worked in loneliness or without appreciation,' writes Dr Scott. 'He might feel that his soul was parched by routine, but he never felt that other desolating consciousness that no one heeded or comprehended him.' Yet perhaps this lack of tension between the poet and his environment was the element which kept him from development in the measure of those possibilities which became plain in him toward the end of his life. We are not concerned with failure here, but with the question why Lampman, with his elements of greatness and his artistic discipline, did not, even in his thirty-eight years, became a great poet.

He was born in 1861, of six national blood-strains, French, Dutch, German, Swiss, Scottish, and English, at Morpeth, Kent County, Ontario. The combination of racial tendencies, Celtic temperament, and Saxon endurance, which had produced in his family adventurous and sedentary types – Loyalist stock – made Lampman what he was, and gave him an unusual balance of qualities. His father was a clergyman of the Church of England, so that he early experienced the life of a number of small communities. These changes, however, did not seem to stimulate the proclivities of a connoisseur so much in human character as in the outer forms of nature. The study and the field seem to have occupied his days. His father, moreover, with a fondness for what was called *belles lettres*, adhered to the critical faiths of the eighteenth century. The Augustan age of English literature had produced Dryden and Pope as its poetical prototypes, and there had been Addison and Fielding; it was an age civilized, life-loving, more brutal, and more formal than others before and since. Though the young poet in effect rebelled against such tenets and repudiated such heroes, he was affected by them, even as he turned to the more transcendental Shelley and Keats and Wordsworth. If he seemed to lean too heavily upon these latter, it may be recalled that the generations moved more slowly then, and that the distance of Kent County from England counted for more. Moreover, literature is always considerably a matter of fashion, and young poets in such places still write from Tennyson and Arnold, proportionately no more remote from their own experiences. Hence the peculiar fusion of qualities in Lampman's muse – since the form of poetry was primarily a function of taste. Though he lived in the later part of the Victorian age, he was not primarily a Victorian.

Lampman entered Trinity College, Toronto, in 1879, and graduated in 1882. It is plain that the state of Canadian culture at this time was peculiar. The feeling of isolation, of the impossibility of emulating classical achievement, and the consequent delight and triumph in any attempt to break what seemed to amount to a spell, may be described by himself. He is referring to the first volume of poetry published by Charles G.D. Roberts:

> One May evening somebody lent me *Orion and Other Poems*, then recently published. Like most of the young fellows about me, I had been under the depressing conviction that we were situated hopelessly on the outskirts of civilization, where no art and no literature could be, and that it was useless to expect that anything great could be done by any of our companions, still more useless to expect that we could do it ourselves. I sat up most of the night reading and re-reading *Orion* in a state of the wildest excitement, and when I went to bed I could not sleep. It seemed to me a wonderful thing that such work could be done by a Canadian, by a young man, one of ourselves. It was like a voice from some new paradise of art, calling us to be up and doing.

Perhaps had there not been a group of writers at this time, Scott, Roberts, Carman, E.W. Thomson, W.W. Campbell, and Lampman, the work of none of these men individually should have had the definite qualities which it possessed. This country was legitimately a province of England, as culturally the United States was; and the normal response of a writer to his environment was that of a more or less thoroughly transplanted Englishman. It is obvious, moreover, that the audience to which he is addressing himself exerts a pressure of influence upon the artist, and that his work is really an adjustment made so that he can be understood, even when it is essentially self-expression. Hence came the peculiarities of much of the literary work of Lampman's time. To have accepted Canadian experience and written of Canada in terms of nothing else would have been, if not impossible, at least immediately fruitless and unrewarded. Life had not been going on long enough in Canada for many people to have a vivid sense of it; and if they read, they hoped to see something after the approved models of Europe. Later, of course, came the cult of Canada as a scene of conventional romantic adventure. This was fostered by the public of other countries, and still reverberates here. In Lampman's time readers were so few that they could scarcely be reached at all save through the daily newspapers, but had to be approached by means of English and imitative American publications. The group to which he belonged maintained a balance between enthusiasm for their native land and emulation of the accepted masters of English literature.

At best, accordingly, the poet in Canada did well to keep his eye on the object, Canadian landscape, more rarely Canadian character and situations; the eye of one taught by all-too-few favourite English masters. Sometimes such a one did not even keep his eye accurately upon the object, and too often he lapsed into a weak-kneed banality of line and a dependence upon the quality of recognition in his reader. 'That is good verse, it reminds me of Shelley.' It is not to be supposed that a poet of Lampman's gifts would now begin a sonnet, 'Beautiful are thy hills, Wayagamack,' or celebrate April in such strophes, fine in their way, as

Pale season, watcher in unvexed suspense,
Still priestess of the patient middle day,
Betwixt wild March's humoured petulance
And the warm wooing of green kirtled May,
Maid month of sunny peace and sober gray,
Weaver of flowers in sunward glades that ring
With murmur of libation to the spring;

As memory of pain, all past, is peace,
And joy, dream-tasted, hath the deepest cheer,
So art thou sweetest of all months that lease
The twelve short spaces of the flying year.
The bloomless days are dead, and frozen fear
No more for many moons shall vex the earth,
Dreaming of summer and fruit-laden mirth.

To write in this way now would be equivalent to building one of those rambling, barrack-like houses once common to New England and our eastern landscapes, with fancy scrollings on the gables and the verandas. Such passing fads detract from basic and enduring qualities, in poetry truth of thought, integrity of feeling, and tempered expression, by which any structure outlasts the needs of one or two generations of men.

In Lampman's work we see a manifestation of the cult of nature, as it had become traditional since Rousseau and Goethe's *Werther* and Wordsworth; unabashed, despite a few dissenting voices, like Carlyle's bellow in *Characteristics.* Nature was not merely an inspiration to veracity and a high view of man – who is after all man's only subject – but an entity separate and outside of man and his manufactured concerns. Yet she was, contradictorily, a presiding goddess to whom he attributed his own qualities and even moods. Nature was calm and aloof, or tempestuous and moody with or in contrast with man; while, as a matter of fact, she is nothing of the sort, but simply nature. Man, according to such a criterion, was to turn to nature, not because he was so much man that he was kin to all creation, but because he was tired, sick with being man, and desirous of rest and a forgetting within a serene impersonality, a soothing power to which he could moreover assign his own tempers, 'or wailful or divine.'

Beyond this cult of nature for nature's sake, which has been the bane of gifts not vigorous enough to deal with experienced reality as a whole, Lampman was evolving. His acceptance of convention was mostly formal and tentative. He had a deep trust in reality, when others tended to fly to abstractions and idealizations. So it is a thing to be remarked that no poet has made clearer and more definite pictures, which are objective in the sense of meaning much the same to every reader, and at the same time has induced feeling, reported a fusion of the preconceived mood of nature and that of the poet. The famous 'Heat' is an example of this, and among many others a stanza of 'In October':

Here will I sit upon this naked stone,
  Draw my coat closer with my numbed hands,
And hear the ferns sigh, and the wet woods moan,
  And send my heart out to the ashen lands;
And I will ask myself what golden madness,
  What balmed breaths of dreamland spicery,
What visions of soft laughter and light sadness
  Were sweet last month to me.

And poems like 'In November,' with plain statement and occasional prosaic lines, often crystallize in a felicitous naming of the poet's mood:

A nameless and unnatural cheer,
A pleasure secret and austere.

There was a passion for exactitude in description and in the use of words which gives Lampman's work unusual definiteness and outline. He had a real feeling for the exterior world. Nor is the human figure always forgotten, though met as seldom as in the walk through forests and fields on a winter's day:

Across a waste and solitary rise
    A ploughman urges his dull team,
A stooped gray figure with prone brow
    That plunges bending to the plough
With strong, uneven steps. The stream
    Rings and re-echoes with his furious cries.

Such glimpses as these, brief as they are, show that Lampman was not writing from imagination of bucolic swains in the pages of other poets, but from his own quite definite observation. Most felicitous, for example, is the last stanza of 'By an Autumn Stream,' which evokes a feeling familiar to anyone who has experienced autumn in the open:

All things that be
Seem plunged into silence, distraught,
By some stern, some necessitous thought:
It wraps and enthralls
Marsh, meadows and forest; and falls
Also on me.

After graduation from Trinity College, Lampman took to teaching in a high school, but finding the profession uncongenial, entered the Civil Service in Ottawa, in the Post Office Department, in 1883. This post he occupied until his death in 1899. It is curious that one of our earliest poets, and one dedicated to the aspects of newness, should for his virtues be sentenced to sedentary routine. This influence of such a life upon one given to the joys of the fields and the study was bound to make itself felt in the course of years. There is little feeling of frustration or maladjustment apparent in Lampman's poetry, and yet it existed in his life. He intended to remain with the Civil Service until 1899, the year in which he died, and then he intended if possible to be superannuated and, retiring to the country, to devote himself to poetry. The amount of annual income necessary for this course was still less at that time than it is now, but the thing was not to be compassed, Lampman failed in health, and in brief it may be said that Canada allowed her poet to die. In 1895 he wrote:

> I am getting well weary of things. I was so far gone in hypochondria on Saturday last that I had not the spirit to go to my office at all. I went straggling up the Gatineau Road, and spent the whole day and most of the next under the blue sky and the eager sun; and then I began to perceive that there were actually trees and grass and beautifully loitering clouds in the tender fields of heaven; I got to see at last that it was really June, and that perhaps I was alive after all.

By the following year he had reached a philosophy of desperation, no longer caring about his fortunes, having 'given up for good and all the notion of writing anything large or important.' It was necessary for every man to ascertain his capabilities and his relation to the world, and adjust himself accordingly. 'All our troubles in reality proceed from nothing but vanity, if we track them to their source. We form an ideal of ourselves, and claim what seems to be due to that ideal. The ideal of myself is entitled to love and approbation does not appear, and I fret and abuse the constitution of things. To the ideal of myself money and power and practical success are no doubt due, but they do not come, and again I abuse the constitution of things.'

This is playing the devil's advocate with a bitter vengeance. To any reasoning intelligence it is plain that Lampman was within his rights in abusing the constitution of things. Seeing how this country lavished and continues to lavish prosperity upon men whose services, not always to call them such, could more easily be dispensed with, and seeing that it is because of a few men like Lampman that civilizations are remembered, it appears unfair that he could not have been rewarded with the right to live.

But if the opportunity of fulfilling his gift and the nature with which he was endowed was denied him, there were compensations, and there was growth of a kind. While the routine monotony of his day's work went on, and its lack of event acted as a pall to the quick spirit of poetry, it was chiefly the lack of leisure which prevented Lampman from doing his best work. Perhaps his sense of life was heightened by the very circumstances which made expression of it so difficult. Dr Scott in the introduction says finely: 'The life of poetry is in the imagination; there lies the ground of true adventure, and though the poet's imagination may be starved and parched by the lack of variety in life, he persists nevertheless to make poetry out of its dust and ashes, out of its lets and hindrances, and even greatest poetry out of the small frets and sorrows that he shares with all mankind.' As time went on, Lampman's writing, which had concerned itself with endeared natural objects, widened to include the major human emotions, and there even appeared a sense of character, if not of psychological subtlety. While it is unlikely that he would ever have rivalled Browning, he probably would have developed this side of his nature as time went on. It would be interesting to know, for example, whether 'The Cup of Life' and 'Personality' were not written in the order in which I quote them:

One after one the high emotions fade:
Time's wheeling measure empties and refills
Year after year; we seek no more the hills
That lured our youth divine and unafraid,
But swarming on some common highway, made
Beaten and smooth, plod onward with blind feet,
And only where the crowded crossways meet
We halt and question, anxious and dismayed.
Yet can we not escape it; some we know
Have angered and grown mad, some scornfully laughed:
Yet surely to each lip – to mine, to thine –
Comes with strange scent and pallid poisonous glow
The cup of Life, that dull Circean draught,
That taints us all, and turns the half to swine.

This explicit doubt and misgiving before life becomes a more quiet sense of its mystery in 'Personality':

O differing human heart,
Why is it that I tremble when thine eyes,
Thy human eyes and beautiful human speech,
Draw me, and stir within my soul
That subtle ineradicable longing

For tender comradeship?
It is because I cannot all at once,
Through the half-lights and phantom-haunted mists
That separate and enshroud us life from life,
Discern the nearness or the strangeness of thy paths,
Nor plumb thy depths.
I am like one that comes alone at night
To a strange stream, and by an unknown ford
Stands, and for a moment yearns and shrinks,
Being ignorant of the water, though so quiet it is,
So softly murmurous,
So silvered by the familiar moon.

Such realization came but seldom, almost as infrequently as his use of free verse, so that such a fine evocation of the interwoven strands of fate as we find in 'The Railway Station' is scarcely representative, but the more to be valued:

The darkness brings no quiet here, the light,
No waking: ever on my blinded brain
The flare of lights, the rush, and cry, and strain,
The engine's scream, the hiss and thunder smite;
I see the hurrying crowds, the clasp, the flight,
Faces that touch, eyes that are dim with pain:
I see the hoarse wheels turn, and the great train
Move labouring out into the bourneless night.
So many souls within its deep recesses,
So many bright, so many mournful eyes:
Mine eyes that watch grow fixed with dreams and guesses;
What threads of life, what hidden histories,
What sweet or passionate dreams and dark distresses,
What unknown thoughts, what various agonies!

But it is usually to escape from such matters, and the too-exigent pressure, that Lampman turns to nature, walking in field and wood:

Ah! I was weary of the drifting hours,
  The echoing city towers,
The blind gray streets, the jingle of the throng,
  Weary of hope that, like a shape of stone,

Sat near at hand without a smile or moan,
And weary most of song.

So it came about that, instead of a pure delight in external nature, which had informed the substance of June with its tranquil and lovely lines, 'Heat' and 'Morning on the Lievre,' flawless in their way with a few slight perfect words, we find him talking of 'doubt and care, the ghostly masters of this world'; and when he would escape, he is burdened with a 'soul shaped to its accustomed load of silly cares and microscopic dreams.' There are signs that for Lampman nearly every city was 'The City of the End of Things,' where 'Flit figures that with clanking hands obey a hideous routine. / And from their iron lips is blown a dreadful and monotonous cry' – a terrific vision of the end of a mechanistic era. This poem, because of its enigmatic and nightmare quality, is more impressive than more explicit plaints like 'The City':

Canst thou not rest, O city,
That liest so wide and fair?
Shall never an hour bring pity,
Nor end be found for care?

In 'Chaucer' he mourns for the passing of hearty and oblivious days, and sees that now 'too well we see the drop of life lost in eternity.' He finds the hunger of Xenophanes still preying on the hearts of men who probe 'the same implacable mysteries,' who toil and 'bear the same unquenchable hope, the same despair.'

Yet this very attitude, which might be construed as a puritanic doubt of life which largely made life what it was at that period, developed into a higher and larger conviction, which is only now beginning to reach the minds of the generality of men. It can best be expressed by Lampman himself:

> This conception is the child of science, reinforced by the poetry that is inherent in the facts of the universe and all existence. Thus reinforced, the conception is a religious one. It is independent of the ancient creeds, for it does not trust for its effects to any system of post mortem rewards and punishments. It is different from the old Stoic virtue of the philosophers, which at bottom was merely prudence, a utilitarian quality. This modern conception is not a materialistic one, although at first it may seem so; it is, as I have said,

poetic and intrinsically religious. It comes to those whom the new knowledge has made acquainted with the vast facts and secrets of life, arming them with a breadth and majesty of vision which withers away from the soul the greeds and lusts and meannesses of the old, narrow and ignorant humanity. The small ambitions and petty passions of this world seem infinitesimal indeed to him who once enters into the new conception and lives, as it were, in the very presence of eternity. As yet this new spiritual force acts only upon the few, for it is a modern thing, but its growth is sure. Spreading downward, with the steady extension and dissemination of culture, from mass to mass, it may in the end work its way into the mental character and spiritual habit of all mankind. Then indeed the world will become less and less a hospital, and the old cankerous maladies gradually decline and disappear.

In the same gradual way, one feels, this conception of life would have permeated the conscious mind and the spirit of Archibald Lampman, and taken the outward form of more poetry to measure with the finest which he left; and perhaps work finer, even in the most adverse circumstances, than any which he was privileged to do. There was a balance of qualities in his gift rarely to be found in a poet; and while this conception would have taken its part in all that he wrote, he would not have forgotten that poetry is to make things real – those of the imagination, and of the tangible world: 'simple, sensuous and passionate' were the words with which Milton described poetry. He would not have become bogged in moral preoccupations as Wordsworth was, nor on the other hand would he have found the be-all and end-all in the senses, as Swinburne did. His art was controlled, and conscious. Dr Scott tells us how he first wrote the last two lines of 'Winter Uplands':

Though the heart plays us false and life be bare,
The truth of Beauty haunts us everywhere.

This creditable but quite extraneous sentiment was changed to the objective completion of the present version.

In truth it must be admitted that there was little of lyric excess and abandon, little of any kind of excess, in Lampman's muse. He delighted in June days and January mornings, but it was a mild delight. The note of zest is struck infrequently, as in 'In the Wilds,' where 'The savage vigour of the forest creeps into our veins, and laughs upon our lips,' and the measures of 'April in the Hills':

I feel the tumult of new birth;
I waken with the wakening earth;
I match the bluebird in her mirth;
  And wild with wind and sun,
A treasurer of immortal days,
I roam the glorious world with praise,
The hillsides and the woodland ways,
  Till earth and I are one.

This is contradistinct from inspired description such as we find in 'The Piano':

Low brooding cadences that dream and cry,
Life's stress and passion echoing straight and clear;
Wild flights of notes that clamour and beat high
Into the storm and battle, or drop sheer;
Strange majesties of sound beyond all words
Ringing on clouds and thunderous heights sublime;
Sad detonance of golden tones and chords
That tremble with the secret of all time....

Typical is the poem 'In May,' where the poet, overborne by grief the night before, and aware that his lot may be the same tomorrow, finds distraction and an 'hour of blessedness' by entering into the manifold life of birds, sowers, rivers, roads, and trees. He prays to Earth, 'the mother who was long before our day' for 'Some little of thy light and majesty.' And in her voices he finds that

To him who hears them, grief beyond control,
Or joy inscrutable without a name
Wakes in his heart thoughts bedded there, impearled,
Before the birth and making of the world.

Lampman's feeling was deep and genuine, his sight unusually clear, and what from any point of view could be called lapses are rare. He found in the wind a brother and in the voice of frogs the voice of 'earth our mother.' He moaned, 'O Life! O Life!. ... And the very word seemed sad,' until he heard a veery, when 'the very word seemed sweet.' His goal was

song,
Whose substance should be Nature's song, clear and strong,
Bound in a casket of majestic rhyme.

And on the other hand such ruling moderation seldom became actually austere. 'Sapphics' gives such an embodiment to an oft-repeated conception of the relation of nature and human destiny, as far as could be wished from jingling banality:

Clothed in splendour, beautifully sad and silent,
Comes the autumn over the woods and highlands,
Golden, rose-red, full of divine rememberance,
Full of foreboding.

Soon the maples, soon will the glowing birches,
Stripped of all that summer and love had dowered them,
Dream, sad-limbed, beholding their pomp and treasure
Ruthlessly scattered:

Yet they quail not: Winter with wind and iron
Comes and finds them silent and uncomplaining,
Finds them tameless, beautiful still and gracious,
Gravely enduring.

Me too changes, bitter and full of evil,
Dream by dream have plundered and left me naked,
Gray with sorrow. Even the days before me
Fade into twilight.

Mute and barren. Yet will I keep my spirit
Clear and valiant, brother to these my noble
Elms and maples, utterly grave and fearless,
Grandly ungrieving.

Brief the span is, counting the years of mortals,
Strange and sad; it passes, and then the bright earth,
Careless mother, gleaming with gold and azure,
Lovely with blossom –

Shining with anemones, mixed with roses,
Daisies mild-eyed, grasses and honeyed clover –
You and me, and all of us, met and equal,
Softly shall cover.

Sometimes it is possible to judge the position of a writer, or that he would prefer to occupy, and his judgment of his own capabilities, by his ideal among the masters who have gone before. In the case of Lampman we find that his prevailing temperate quality and his search for the happy medium led him to find a poet on the highest plane in Matthew Arnold, rather than others of his age who embodied desperate qualities in a more extreme manner. 'The whole range of life, time and eternity, the mysteries and beauties of existence and its deepest spiritual problems are continually present to his mind. In his genius is that rare combination of philosophy and the poetic impulse in the highest degree which has given us our few solitary poets.' Yet this ideal of nobility does not close Lampman's eyes to reality, and we find him painting this deeply shaded caricature of 'The Poets':

Half god, half brute, within the self-same shell,
Changers with every hour from dawn till even,
Who dream with angels in the gate of heaven,
And skirt with curious eyes the brinks of hell,
Children of Pan, whom some, the few, love well,
But most draw back, and know not what to say,
Poor shining angels, whom the hoofs betray,
Whose pinions frighten with their goatish smell.
Half brutish, half divine, but all of earth,
Half-way 'twixt hell and heaven, near to man,
The whole world's tangle gathered in one span,
Full of this human torture and this mirth:
Life with its hope and error, toil and bliss,
Earth-born, earth-reared, ye know it as it is.

This brings us logically to the subject of Lampman's sonnets. The qualities which he most admired when expressed in brief compass find their best form in the sonnet, while the discipline of the form was one which, sympathetic to him, he did not allow to become too rigid. In the remainder of his work metrical experiments are few, and we seldom find him seeking a variant in poetic expression to suit his own needs. Accordingly it is not surprising to find that the sonnets, of which there are more than a hundred, when taken as a unit, constitute the most impressive portion of Lampman's work. This strictest and most exigent of poetic forms awkward in the hands of any save the most expert, and unsatisfying frequently with them, he made into an expressive medium of his own. Crisp, apparently bare sentences build a firm structure, a clear picture, a moment of emotional realization. Like most simplicity, it is deceptive; the reader's attention is seldom strained more than by reading a newspaper paragraph. While as for the vague, irrelevant sublimity which is usually drawn from the sonneteer by the demands of rhyme in the way that evidence is drawn from a witness by a cross-questioning lawyer, it is in Lampman generally absent. In pictorial quality these sonnets remind one of clear water-colours, and the even excellence of picture in like number and quality seldom has been equalled. They form in their sort a body of work which will not suffer by any legitimate comparison. It is no small merit, if a negative one, that of few other poets in any age can it be said that they wrote so few meretricious lines.

Not to quote one of these sonnets is impossible; and it is almost as difficult, if one has known Lampman's work for long, to apply purely critical judgment. Therefore 'Evening' may be taken, not as representing the best, but an old personal predilection:

From upland slopes I see the cows file by,
Lowing, great-chested, down the homeward trail,
By dusking fields and meadows shining pale
With moon-tipped dandelions. Flickering high,
A peevish night-hawk in the western sky
Beats up into the lucent solitudes,
Or drops with griding wing. The stilly woods
Grow dark and deep, and gloom mysteriously,
Cool night wings creep, and whisper in mine ear,
The homely cricket gossips at my feet,
From far-off pools and wastes of reed I hear,
Clear and soft-piped, the chanting frogs break sweet
In full Pandean chorus. One by one
Shine out the stars, and the great night comes on.

And 'Late November'; though many of the sonnets were not professedly landscapes:

The hills and leafless forests slowly yield
To the thick-driving snow. A little while
And night shall darken down. In shouting file
The woodmen's carts go by me homeward wheeled,

Past the thin fading stubbles, half concealed,
Now golden-gray, sowed softly through with snow,
Where the last ploughman follows still his row,
Turning black furrows through the whitening field.
Far off the village lamps begin to gleam,
Fast drives the snow, and no man comes this way;
The hills grow wintry white, and bleak winds moan
About the naked uplands. I alone
Am neither sad, nor shelterless, nor gray,
Wrapped round with thought, content to watch and dream.

Lampman may be figured as in his poem, one listening in the darkness, stirred by all the currents of life in a wind, and its changelessness in a moon. The forces of life, the primary emotions, were present to him; and if individual character and interactions of temperament were a trifle misty, that was perhaps the defect of his merits, the price of his poetic qualities. There are signs, too, that give the measure of a growth which his years were not to fulfill before he died. But he passed 'with creative eye' over the country which the farmer and the lumberman and the railway-builder had possessed, and reaped another, more enduring harvest. What he left as heritage will long mean 'Canada' in the minds of his countrymen, as surely as her fields and lakes were Canada to him.

LITERATURE OF CANADA

Poetry and Prose in Reprint
Douglas Lochhead, General Editor

1 *Collected Poems*, Isabella Valancy Crawford
Introduction by James Reaney

2 *The St Lawrence and the Saguenay and Other Poems, & Hesperus and Other Poems and Lyrics*, Charles Sangster
Introduction by Gordon Johnston

3 *Our Intellectual Strength and Weakness*, John George Bourinot
'English-Canadian Literature,' Thomas Guthrie Marquis
'French-Canadian Literature,' Camille Roy
Introduction by Clara Thomas

4 *Selections from Canadian Poets*, Edward Hartley Dewart
Introduction by Douglas Lochhead

5 *Poems and Essays*, Joseph Howe
Introduction by Malcolm G. Parks

6 *Rockbound: A Novel*, Frank Parker Day
Introduction by Allan Bevan

7 *The Homesteaders*, Robert J.C. Stead
Introduction by Susan Wood Glicksohn

8 *The Measure of the Rule*, Robert Barr
Introduction by Louis K. MacKendrick

9 *Selected Poetry and Critical Prose*, Charles G.D. Roberts
Edited with an introduction and notes by W.J. Keith

10 *Old Man Savarin Stories: Tales of Canada and Canadians*
E.W. Thomson
Introduction by Linda Sheshko

11 *Dreamland and Other Poems & Tecumseh: A Drama*, Charles Mair
Introduction by Norman Shrive

12 *The Poems of Archibald Lampman (including At the Long Sault)*
Archibald Lampman
Introduction by Margaret Coulby Whitridge

13 *The Poetical Works of Alexander McLachlan*, Alexander McLachlan
Introduction by E. Margaret Fulton

14 *Angéline de Montbrun*, Laure Conan
Translated and introduced by Yves Brunelle

15 *The White Savannahs*, W.E. Collin
Introduction by Germaine Warkentin

16 *The Search for English-Canadian Literature: An Anthology of Critical Articles from the Nineteenth and Early Twentieth Centuries*
Edited and introduced by Carl Ballstadt

17 *The First Day of Spring: Stories and Other Prose*, Raymond Knister
Selected and introduced by Peter Stevens